MAGISTER LUDI

Something like chess but far more intricate, the game of Magister Ludi known as the Glass Bead Game is thought in its purest form, a synthesis through which philosophy, art, music and scientific law are appreciated simultaneously. The scholar-players are isolated within Castalia, an autonomous elite institution devoted wholly to the mind and the imagination . . .

"Part romance, part philosophical tract, part utopian fantasy. Its theme is one that preoccupied Hesse earlier: the conflict between, and the need to synthesize, thought and action, intellect and the flesh . . . A fascinating novel, well translated at last."

—Book-of-the-Month Club News

MAGISTER LUDI
(The Glass Bead Game)

HERMANN HESSE

TRANSLATED FROM THE GERMAN
DAS GLASPERLENSPIEL
by Richard and Clara Winston

with a Foreword by
Theodore Ziolkowski

BANTAM BOOKS
TORONTO • NEW YORK • LONDON • SYDNEY • AUCKLAND

MAGISTER LUDI

recently published as THE GLASS BEAD GAME

*A Bantam Book / published by arrangement with
Holt, Rinehart and Winston, Inc.*

PRINTING HISTORY

*Originally published in German under the title of
Das Glasperlenspiel, Copyright 1943 by
Fretz & Wasmuth Verlag AG Zürich*

Holt edition published October 1969

Bantam edition / October 1970

2nd printing . . . October 1970	9th printing . . . . . June 1976
3rd printing . . . January 1972	10th printing . . . . March 1978
4th printing . . September 1972	11th printing . . . . March 1980
5th printing . . December 1972	12th printing . . February 1980
6th printing . . December 1973	13th printing . . . . . June 1982
7th printing . . . . . . April 1974	14th printing . December 1983
8th printing . . . January 1976	15th printing . . . . . June 1986

*Bantam Books are published by Bantam Books, Inc. Its trade-
mark, consisting of the words "Bantam Books" and the portrayal of a rooster, is Registered in U.S. Patent and Trademark
Office and in other countries. Marca Registrada. Bantam
Books, Inc., 666 Fifth Avenue, New York, New York 10103.*

PRINTED IN THE UNITED STATES OF AMERICA

KR   24 23 22 21 20 19 18   17 16 15

FOREWORD BY
THEODORE ZIOLKOWSKI

THE GLASS BEAD GAME, Hermann Hesse's last major work, appeared in Switzerland in 1943. When Thomas Mann, then living in California, received the two volumes of that first edition, he was dumbfounded by the conspicuous parallels between Hesse's "Tentative Sketch of the Life of Magister Ludi Joseph Knecht" and the novel that he himself was writing, *Doctor Faustus* (1947). For all their differences in mood, style and theme, both works employ a similar fiction: a pleasant though somewhat pompous narrator recounts, with a sympathy matched only by his pedantry, the life of a man whom he loves and admires. Since in each case the narrator is incapable of fully comprehending the problematic genius of his biographical subject, an ironic tension is produced between the limited perspective of the narrator and the fuller vision that he unwittingly conveys to the reader. Both authors were obsessed, in addition, with the self-destructive course of modern civilization, and this concern pervades both novels. But Mann's view is more immediate. His narrator, Serenus Zeitblom, can see and hear the exploding bombs of World War Two as he writes, and the spectacular career of the composer Adrian Leverkühn parallels with ominous precision the history of Germany from the declining Empire through the

shortlived brilliance of the Weimar Republic to the raging madness of National Socialism. In Hesse's novel, in
contrast, that same period is described with the detachment of a narrator looking back at the "Age of the Feuilleton" from a vantage point in the distant future. Unlike
Mann's Leverkühn, Hesse's Joseph Knecht succeeds in
analyzing the dangers of an excessive aestheticism and
acts to avert the catastrophe of intellectual irresponsi-
bility. In both novels, finally, the authors slyly weave
their experience of our culture into a pastiche of hidden
quotations and characters *à clef*.

Thomas Mann, immediately sensing that the serious
theme of Hesse's novel was enclosed within "a cunning
artistic joke," recognized the source of its humor in "the
parody of biography and the grave scholarly attitude."
But people won't dare to laugh, he wrote Hesse. "And
you will be secretly annoyed at their dead-earnest respect." Hesse was pleased that his friend had put a
finger on the comic aspect of the novel, but Mann's pre-
diction was correct. In the quarter-century since its pub-
lication, *The Glass Bead Game* has enjoyed the adulation
customarily awarded to literary "classics." Indeed,
largely on its merits Hesse received in 1946 the Nobel
Prize for which Mann, among others, had repeatedly
nominated him. Hesse's *opus magnum* was one of the
first works by a distinguished emigré to be published in
Germany after the war, and it has been regularly re-
printed there since 1946. The book was dutifully translated into English, Swedish, French, Spanish, Italian,
and other languages. But the novel, whose title has supplied us with one of those imagistically suggestive catchwords for our age, like "the Waste Land" or "the Magic
Mountain," has suffered the fate of many classics—it is
less frequently read than cited, more often studied than
appreciated. In Germany many readers, blandly ignoring
the implicit criticism in the novel, tended to see in
Hesse's cultural province nothing but a welcome utopian
escape from the harsh postwar realities. More discerning
European critics have usually been so preoccupied with
the fashionably grave implications that they have neither
laughed at its humor nor smiled at its ironies.

In part these one-sided readings are understandable,

for the humor is often hidden in private jokes of the
sort to which Hesse became increasingly partial in his
later years. The games begin on the title-page, for the
motto attributed to "Albertus Secundus" is actually fictitious. Hesse wrote the motto himself and had it translated into Latin by two former schoolmates, who are
cited in Latin abbreviation as the editors: Franz Schall
("noise" or *Clangor*) and Feinhals ("slender neck" or
Collo fino). The book is full of this "onomastic comedy"
that appealed to Thomas Mann, also a master of the
art. Thus Carlo Ferromonte is an italianized form of the
name of the author's nephew, Karl Isenberg, who assisted Hesse with the music history that is interwoven with
the history of the Glass Bead Game. The "inventor" of
the Game, Bastian Perrot of Calw, gets his name from
Heinrich Perrot, the owner of a machine shop where
Hesse once worked for a year after he dropped out of
school. The figure of Thomas von der Trave is a detailed
and easily recognizable portrait of Thomas Mann, who
was born in the town of Lübeck on the river Trave. In
the person of Fritz Tegularius, Hesse has given us his interpretation of the brilliant but unbalanced character of
Friedrich Nietzsche. And Tegularius' spiritual opponent
in the novel, Father Jacobus, borrows some of his words
and most of his ideas from Nietzsche's antagonist, the
historian Jakob Burckhardt. The reader who fails to
catch these sometimes obscure references is not only missing much of the fun of the book, he is also unaware of its
implications in the realm of cultural history and criticism.

The reception of *The Glass Bead Game* in this country has been affected by other factors as well. The
book has been available since 1949 under the misleading
title *Magister Ludi*. But if it failed to make an impact,
this was due equally to the translation by Mervyn Savill,
which fails to bring out its irony, and to the fluctuations
of Hesse's reputation in the United States. Although
Hesse's stature was recognized in Europe (where he was
praised by such admirers as Thomas Mann, André Gide,
and T.S. Eliot) for some thirty years before he received
the Nobel Prize, *Time* magazine noted in 1949 that his
works were still virtually unknown here. His eightieth
birthday, widely celebrated abroad, passed unnoticed

in the United States in 1957. And when Hesse died in
1962, a New York *Times* obituary stated that he was
"largely unapproachable" for American readers. This
neglect is due in part to the introspective, lyrical quality
of his novels, which depart radically from the more
realistic tradition that dominated American fiction between the world wars. But another circumstance is probably more important in accounting for the lack of interest
in his works for a good fifteen years after he received the
Nobel Prize. Hesse's novels fictionalize the admonitions
of an outsider who urges us to question accepted values,
to rebel against the system, to challenge conventional
"reality" in the light of higher ideals. For almost two
decades after World War Two our society was characterized largely by the button-down-collar mentality of
a silent generation whose goal it was to become a part of
the establishment and to reap its benefits as rapidly as
possible. Such ages have little use for critics of the system and prophets of the ideal.

But times have changed, and Hesse has suddenly become—to use a current shibboleth—relevant. But rele-
vance resides in the mind of the perceiver, and the under-
thirty generation that has embraced Hesse in the sixties
as an underground classic is better known for its rebelliousness than for its sense of irony. As a result, the Hesse
cult in the United States has revolved primarily around
such painfully humorless works as *Demian* and *Siddhartha*, in which readers have discovered an anticipation of their infatuation with Eastern mysticism, pacifism,
the search for personal values, and revolt against the
establishment. Those who have gone on to *Steppenwolf*
have greeted it as a psychedelic orgy of sex, drugs, and
jazz, but have conveniently overlooked the ironic attitude through which those superficial effects are put
back into perspective by the author. It was partly as a
reaction against such self-indulgent interpretations,
which he encountered as much as forty years ago, that
Hesse undertook *The Glass Bead Game*.

What is the "Glass Bead Game"? In the idyllic poem
"Hours in the Garden" (1936), which he wrote during
the composition of his novel, Hesse speaks of "a game
of thoughts called the Glass Bead Game" that he

practiced while burning leaves in his garden. As the ashes filter down through the grate, he says, "I hear music and see men of the past and future. I see wise men and poets and scholars and artists harmoniously building the hundred-gated cathedral of Mind." These lines depict as personal experience that intellectual pastime that Hesse, in his novel, was to define as "the *unio mystica* of all separate members of the *Universitas Litterarum*" and that he bodied out symbolically in the form of an elaborate Game performed according to the strictest rules and with supreme virtuosity by the mandarins of his spiritual province. This is really all that we need to know. The Glass Bead Game is an act of mental synthesis through which the spiritual values of all ages are perceived as simultaneously present and vitally alive. It was with full artistic consciousness that Hesse described the Game in such a way as to make it seem vividly real within the novel and yet to defy any specific imitation in reality. The humorless readers who complained to Hesse that they had invented the Game before he put it into his novel—Hesse actually received letters asserting this!— completely missed the point. For the Game is of course purely a symbol of the human imagination and emphatically not a patentable "Monopoly" of the mind.

The Game, in turn, is the focal point and *raison d'être* of an entire province of the spirit called Castalia (from the Parnassian spring sacred to the Muses) and located in an unspecified future. (Hesse has indicated that he thought of his narrator as writing around the beginning of the twenty-fifth century.) But again Hesse makes it clear that he is not predicting a specific utopia but, rather, trying to represent the model of a reality that has actually existed from time to time in such orders as the Platonic academies or yoga schools. It is "a spiritual culture worth living in and serving," he explained to one correspondent. Castalia, in other words, represents any human institution devoted wholly and exclusively to affairs of the mind and imagination. As such, the spiritual province of the novel constitutes the goal of a search upon which Hesse had been embarked for many years. But this last novel is at the same time the document of an intense personal crisis, for it depicts not only the fulfillment of a long sought ideal, but also its ultimate rejection.

Hesse's literary career parallels the development of modern literature from a *fin de siècle* aestheticism through expressionism to a contemporary sense of human commitment. Born in the Black Forest town of Calw in 1877, Hesse in his youth reflected the neo-romanticism then prevalent among many writers of his generation in England, France, and Germany. The misty yearnings of his earliest stories and poems display the frank escapism of a young man who is not at all at home in the bourgeois reality of Wilhelmine Germany and who projects his dreams into a romantic kingdom that he locates, according to the title of one work, "An Hour beyond Midnight." But the success of his first major novel, *Peter Camenzind* (1904), reconciled the young writer, at least temporarily, with a world that was prepared to bestow upon him the material rewards of literary fame. From aestheticism he shifted to the melancholy realism that marked his next poems and stories as well as the novels *Under the Wheel* (1906), *Gertrude* (1910), and *Rosshalde* (1914). Putting aside his romantic longings, he assumed the role of a settled family man who advocated in his fictions a bittersweet doctrine of renunciation and compromise.

But the war brought a radical change. Hesse, who had been living in Switzerland since 1912, found that his outspoken pacifism alienated many of his former friends and readers, who succumbed to the wave of martial exhilaration sweeping over Europe in August of 1914. Meanwhile, family and marital difficulties shattered the illusion of a happy life that he had carefully sought to preserve for some ten years. A lengthy psychoanalytic treatment at the hands of a disciple of Jung in 1916 and 1917 completed his disillusionment with his present state and the process of psychic re-evaluation. Hesse came to the conclusion that he had been living a lie and denying the authentic impulses of his own being. In 1919 he moved to the village of Montagnola, near Lugano in southern Switzerland, where he lived in relative seclusion until his death in 1962. Here he wrote most of the major works for which he has subsequently become famous and in which he sought to discover a more mature ideal of the spirit to replace that "reality" with which he had become disenchanted.

In several essays that he wrote around 1920—most notably in pieces on Nietzsche and Dostoevsky—Hesse argued that men must seek a new morality that, transcending the conventional dichotomy of good and evil, will embrace all extremes of life in one unified vision. A later essay, "A Bit of Theology" (1932), outlines the three-stage progression toward this goal. The child, he says, is born into a state of unity with all being. It is only when the child is taught about good and evil that he advances to a second level of individuation characterized by despair and alienation; for he has been made aware of laws and moral codes, but feels incapable of adhering to the arbitrary standards established by conventional religious or moral systems since they exclude so much of what seems perfectly natural. A few men— like the hero of *Siddhartha* or those whom Hesse calls "the Immortals" in *Steppenwolf*—manage to attain a third level of awareness where they are once again capable of accepting all being. But most men are condemned to live on the second level, sustained only by a sense of humor through which they neutralize oppressive reality and by an act of the imagination through which they share from time to time in the kingdom of the Immortals, the realm of spirit.

Hesse's novels trace this struggle in the lives of heroes set against backgrounds from different ages of civilization. In each case the triadic rhythm of development is the same; only the historical circumstances differ. In *Demian* (1919) the milieu is that of the student generation of the turbulent years immediately preceding World War I. The hero of *Siddhartha* (1922) progresses through the three stages in the classical India of Buddha. *Steppenwolf* (1927) ironically depicts the dilemma of a European intellectual confronted with the tawdry pop culture of the twenties, while the dual protagonists of *Narcissus and Goldmund* (1930) act out their individuation in the waning of the Middle Ages. In the thinly veiled symbolic autobiography of *The Journey to the East* (1932), finally, the hero joins a League of Journeyers to the East in a timeless present set sometime after "the Great War." Each novel postulates the possibility of a spiritual kingdom toward which the hero strives, whether he reaches it or not.

Castalia is clearly another attempt, this time projected into the future, to represent this same ideal: a symbolic realm where all spiritual values are kept alive and present, specifically through the practice of the Glass Bead Game. In this sense, then, the novel was originally envisaged as yet another variation in Hesse's continuing search for a spiritual dimension of life, for it depicts a future society in which the realm of Culture is set apart to pursue its goals in splendid isolation, unsullied by the "reality" that Hesse had grown to distrust.

The Glass Bead Game was a continuation and intensification in another sense as well. Hesse was aware of the fact that his earlier novels had employed the same basic pattern of individual development against different historical backgrounds. He now decided to incorporate this structural tendency into a single new novel. The idea that came to him, he wrote to a friend in 1945, was "reincarnation as a mode of expression for stability in the midst of flux." Long before he began writing, he remarks, he had in mind "an individual but supratemporal life . . . a man who experiences in a series of rebirths the grand epochs in the history of mankind." The novel, in other words, was to consist of a number of parallel lives, ranging through time, presumably, from the prehistoric past to the remote future. But the emphasis was to be distributed evenly among the parts. "The book is going to contain several biographies of the same man, who lives on earth at different times—or at least thinks that he had such existences," he wrote to his sister in 1934. Around this time Hesse wrote and published separately three such biographies: one about a prehistoric rainmaker; one set in the Golden Age of India; and a third depicting an episode from the patristic period of the early Christian church. (A fourth life, set among the Pietists of eighteenth-century Swabia, occupied Hesse for almost a year, but was never published during his lifetime.)

As we now read the novel in its final form, of course,

the arrangement of the parts is different. The biography of Joseph Knecht, which was to have been but the last in a long series of parallel lives, has grown to comprise the twelve central chapters of the book. The history of the Glass Bead Game and the organization of the cultural province are sketched in a lengthy introduction, and the three parallel lives, along with some poems, are added in an appendix as school exercises of young Knecht. Why this shift in plan, which seems to have taken place in the mid-thirties after parts of the book had already been written and published? At first it was simply a matter of expediency. Hesse found that he could best render "the inner reality of Castalia" through the figure of a dominating central figure. "And so Knecht stepped into the center of the narrative." In fact, in the first three chapters of his biography we get a far clearer idea of the Castalian ideal at its finest than in the narrator's more abstract introduction.

But Joseph Knecht ends by defecting from Castalia, a conclusion that was far from Hesse's mind when he first dreamed of this new version of the spiritual kingdom and when he wrote the first of the lives. At least two factors contributed to change Hesse's attitude toward the ideal which he had been striving to portray in so many works for almost twenty years. First, the sheer reality of contemporary events—the disintegration of the Weimar Republic, the rise of Hitler, the horrors of Nazism—opened Hesse's eyes to the failure of the intellectuals and convinced him of the futility of any spiritual realm divorced wholly from contemporary social reality. His ideal had to give way, he wrote, "under the pressures of the moment." This is the meaning that emerges clearly from young Knecht's debates with that emissary from the outside world, Plinio Designori, who argues that a life consecrated exclusively to the mind is not only unfruitful, but also dangerous. Fritz Tegularius, the brilliant scholar who is totally unfit for any position of responsibility in the order, is the living example of the excesses of an aestheticism cultivated in isolation from reality. Secondly, Hesse's growing uneasiness regarding an absolute spiritual kingdom was substantiated by his study of Burckhardt's writings. It is Burckhardt, in the person of Father Jacobus, who convinces Knecht-Hesse that even the most perfect spiritual institution, in the eyes of history, is a relative organism. In order to survive it must adapt itself to the social exigencies of the times. The central chapters of the biography, therefore, recapitulate in fictional form Hesse's own shift from his original belief in a haughty Nietzschean elitism to a more compassionate social consciousness shaped by Burckhardt's historicism. The ideological tensions between Knecht, Plinio, and Father Jacobus reflect on the level of character the areas of Culture, State, and Church, whose complex interrelationships Burckhardt investigated in his *Observations on World History* (a course of lectures delivered in 1870–1871 and posthumously published in 1905).

Seen in this light and put into the contemporary idiom, Knecht's life represents typologically the radicalization of the intellectual, who moves from the *vita contemplativa* not to the opposite extreme of the *vita activa*, but to an intermediate position of responsible action controlled by dispassionate reflection. It is essential to understand that Knecht's defection from Castalia, far from implying any repudiation of the spiritual ideal, simply calls for a new consciousness of the social responsibility of the intellectual. Knecht remains true to his name, which means "servant." Now his service takes on a fuller meaning. By quitting Castalia, Knecht fulfills two functions. He serves Castalia by warning it, through his example, to forsake its posture of arrogant and self-indulgent autonomy, which can lead ultimately only to its destruction. And he makes a commitment by putting spirit and intellect at the service of the world outside in the person of his pupil, the youth Tito. Knecht's death has been variously interpreted, and certainly that final scene has symbolic overtones that expand its dimensions. But Hesse made its basic meaning quite clear in a letter of 1947. "He leaves behind a Tito for whom this sacrificial death of a man vastly superior to him will remain forever an admonition and an example." The spiritual ideal, once attained, has now been put back into the service of life.

The Glass Bead Game, then, is indispensable for a complete understanding of Hesse's thought. It is possible to read *Siddhartha* as a self-centered pursuit of nirvana, but Joseph Knecht gives up his life out of a sense of commitment to a fellow human being. It is possible to see in *Steppenwolf* a heady glorification of hip or even hippie culture, but Joseph Knecht shows that the only true culture is that which responds to the social requirements of the times. *The Glass Bead Game,* finally, makes it clear that Hesse advocates thoughtful commitment over self-indulgent solipsism, responsible action over mindless revolt. For Joseph Knecht is no impetuous radical thrusting non-negotiable demands upon the institution and demanding amnesty from the consequences of his deeds. He attains through disciplined achievement the highest status in the Order and commits himself to action only after thoughtfully assessing its implications for Castalia and the consequences for himself. Above all —for the novel is not a philosophical tract or a political pamphlet, but a work of art—Hesse suggests that revolt need not be irrational and violent, that indeed it is more effective when it is rational and ironic. This is the value of the temporal distance, the double perspective vouchsafed by the fiction. In the Introduction, looking back at our own civilization from the vantage point of the future, we see it in all its glaring self-contradictions. At the same time, we look ahead to the Castalia of the future, where the problems of our age are displayed in a realistic abstraction that permits us to consider them rationally and dispassionately. Castalia has more than a little in common with the intellectual and cultural institutions of the sixties, to the extent that they have become autonomous empires cut off from the social needs of mankind and cultivating their own Glass Bead Games in glorious isolation. And Knecht's conviction that a State ruled without the tempering influence of Culture is doomed to brutishness reflects a prevalent contemporary concern: our computerized society has become so bureaucratically impersonal that it is no longer guided sufficiently by forces that are in the highest sense humane. The longer we consider Hesse's novel, the more clearly we realize that it is not a telescope focused on an imaginary future, but a mirror reflecting with disturbing sharpness a paradigm of present reality.

All of these considerations justify a new translation of Hesse's late masterpiece. Our society has caught up with his vision. And Richard and Clara Winston have produced a translation that is eminently usable for this age. I do not mean merely that their translation is "correct" in avoiding the many mistakes of the earlier English version. More important: they have succeeded in catching the sense and style of the book. They realize that with this last novel Hesse shifted his focus from the individual to the institution; hence they have not made the mistake of calling it *Magister Ludi,* which would suggest that it is simply another German *Bildungsroman,* a pretty fiction of personal development unrelated to the more general concerns of society. Instead, they have reinstated the title that Hesse gave to the original (*Das Glasperlenspiel*), which sums up in a word the glory and tragedy of culture in our time. By capturing the monkish tone of the narrator, who repeats himself with clerical pedantry, the translation opens up the irony of the work. For the Castalian self-obsession from which Knecht defects is nowhere more evident than in the smug complacency of the narrator in the Introduction and opening chapters. Ironically, as he learns to appreciate the meaning of Knecht's life by writing his biography, the narrator assumes a more humane and, in the finest sense, "spiritual" tone, thus vindicating Knecht's action.

Perhaps even the worst translation could not conceal the "message" of Hesse's novel. But only a subtle, sensitive one can render what Thomas Mann called "the parody of biography and the grave scholarly attitude." It is easy, too easy, to be sober and grave. That is in fact the most serious shortcoming of Hesse's most ardent admirers at present. This new translation of *The Glass Bead Game* offers the American reader the opportunity, as Thomas Mann suggested, to dare to laugh. If parody alone can adequately render the reality of our times, only irony offers us the freedom and detachment that are the essential condition of responsible analysis and action. This is the final aesthetic meaning of *The Glass Bead Game.*

May 1969   THEODORE ZIOLKOWSKI

THE GLASS BEAD GAME

*A tentative sketch of the life of
Magister Ludi Joseph Knecht
together with
Knecht's posthumous writings
edited by*

HERMANN HESSE

dedicated to
the Journeyers
to the East

CONTENTS

THE
GLASS BEAD
GAME:
A GENERAL
INTRODUCTION TO
ITS HISTORY
FOR THE
LAYMAN

... Non entia enim licet quodammodo levibusque ho-minibus facilius atque incuriosius verbis reddere quam entia, veruntamen pio diligentique rerum scriptori plane aliter res se habet: nihil tantum repugnat ne verbis illus-tretur, at nihil adeo necesse est ante hominum oculos proponere ut certas quasdam res, quas esse neque demonstrari neque probari potest, quae contra eo ipso, quod pii diligentesque viri illas quasi ut entia tractant, enti nascendique facultati paululum appropinquant.

ALBERTUS SECUNDUS
tract. de cristall. spirit.
ed. Clangor et Collof. lib. I, cap. 28.

In Joseph Knecht's holograph translation:

... For although in a certain sense and for light-minded persons non-existent things can be more easily and ir-responsibly represented in words than existing things, for the serious and conscientious historian it is just the reverse. Nothing is harder, yet nothing is more necessary, than to speak of certain things whose existence is neither demonstrable nor probable. The very fact that serious and conscientious men treat them as existing things brings them a step closer to existence and to the possibility of being born.

It is our intention to preserve in these pages what scant biographical material we have been able to collect concerning Joseph Knecht, or Ludi Magister Josephus III, as he is called in the Archives of the Glass Bead Game. We are not unaware that this endeavor runs, or seems to run, somewhat counter to the prevailing laws and usages of our intellectual life. For, after all, obliteration of individuality, the maximum integration of the individual into the hierarchy of the educators and scholars, has ever been one of our ruling principles. And in the course of our long tradition this principle has been observed with such thoroughness that today it is exceedingly difficult, and in many cases completely impossible, to obtain biographical and psychological information on various persons who have served the hierarchy in exemplary fashion. In very many cases it is no longer even possible to determine their original names. The hierarchic organization cherishes the ideal of anonymity, and comes very close to the realization of that ideal. This fact remains one of the abiding characteristics of intellectual life in our Province.

If we have nevertheless persisted in our endeavor to determine some of the facts about the life of Ludi Magister Josephus III, and at least to sketch the outlines of his character, we believe we have done so not out of any cult of personality, nor out of disobedience to the customs, but on the contrary solely in the service of truth and scholarship. It is an old idea that the more pointedly and logically we formulate a thesis, the more irresistibly it cries out for its antithesis. We uphold and venerate the idea that underlies the anonymity of our authorities and our intellectual life. But a glance at the early history of that life of the mind we now lead, namely, a glance at the development of the Glass Bead Game, shows us irrefutably that every phase of its development, every extension, every change, every essential segment of its history, whether it be seen as progressive or conservative, bears the plain imprint of the person who introduced the change. He was not necessarily its sole or actual author, but he was the instrument of transformation and perfection.

Certainly, what nowadays we understand by personality is something quite different from what the biographers and historians of earlier times meant by it. For them, and especially for the writers of those days who had a distinct taste for biography, the essence of a personality seems to have been deviance, abnormality, uniqueness, in fact all too often the pathological. We moderns, on the other hand, do not even speak of major personalities until we encounter men who have gone beyond all original and idiosyncratic qualities to achieve the greatest possible integration into the generality, the greatest possible service to the suprapersonal. If we look closely into the matter we shall see that the ancients had already perceived this ideal. The figure of the Sage or Perfect One among the ancient Chinese, for example, or the ideal of Socratic ethics, can scarcely be distinguished from our present ideal; and many a great organization, such as the Roman Church in the eras of its greatest power, has recognized similar principles. Indeed, many of its greatest figures, such as St. Thomas Aquinas, appear to us—like early Greek sculptures—more the classical representatives of types than individuals.

Nevertheless, in the period before the reformation of the intellectual life, a reformation which began in the twentieth century and of which we are the heirs, that authentic ancient ideal had patently come near to being entirely lost. We are astonished when the biographies of those times rather garrulously relate how many brothers and sisters the hero had, or what psychological scars and blotches were left behind from his casting off the skins of childhood and puberty, from the struggle for position and the search for love. We moderns are not interested in a hero's pathology or family history, nor in his drives, his digestion, and how he sleeps. Not even his intellectual background—the influence upon his development of his favorite studies, favorite reading, and so on—is particularly important to us. For us, a man is a hero and deserves special interest only if his nature and his education have rendered him able to let his individuality be almost perfectly absorbed in its hierarchic function without at the same time forfeiting the vigorous, fresh, admirable impetus which make for the savor and worth of the individual. And if conflicts arise between the individual and the hierarchy, we regard these very conflicts as a touchstone for the stature of a personality. We do not approve of the rebel who is driven by his desires and passions to infringements upon law and order; we find all the more worthy of our reverence the memory of those who tragically sacrificed themselves for the greater whole.

These latter are the heroes, and in the case of these truly exemplary men, interest in the individual, in the name, face, and gesture, seems to us permissible and natural. For we do not regard even the perfect hierarchy, the most harmonious organization, as a machine put together out of lifeless units that count for nothing in themselves, but as a living body, formed of parts and animated by organs which possess their own nature and freedom. Every one of them shares in the miracle of life. In this sense, then, we have endeavored to obtain information on the life of Joseph Knecht, Master of the Glass Bead Game, and especially to collect everything written by himself. We have, moreover, obtained several manuscripts we consider worth reading.

What we have to say about Knecht's personality and life is surely familiar in whole or in part to a good many members of the Order, especially the Glass Bead Game players, and for this reason among others our book is not addressed to this circle alone, but is intended to appeal more widely to sympathetic readers.

For the narrower circle, our book would need neither introduction nor commentary. But since we also wish our hero's life and writings to be studied outside the Order, we are confronted with the somewhat difficult task of prefacing our book with a brief popular introduction, for that less-prepared reader, into the meaning and history of the Glass Bead Game. We stress that this introduction is intended only for popular consumption and makes no claim whatsoever to clarifying the questions being discussed within the Order itself on the problems and history of the Game. The time for an objective account of that subject is still far in the future.

Let no one, therefore, expect from us a complete history and theory of the Glass Bead Game. Even authors of higher rank and competence than ourself would not be capable of providing that at the present time. That task must remain reserved to later ages, if the sources and the intellectual prerequisites for the task have not previously been lost. Still less is our essay intended as a textbook of the Glass Bead Game; indeed, no such thing will ever be written. The only way to learn the rules of this Game of games is to take the usual prescribed course, which requires many years; and none of the initiates could ever possibly have any interest in making these rules easier to learn.

These rules, the sign language and grammar of the Game, constitute a kind of highly developed secret language drawing upon several sciences and arts, but especially mathematics and music (and/or musicology), and capable of expressing and establishing interrelationships between the content and conclusions of nearly all scholarly disciplines. The Glass Bead Game is thus a mode of playing with the total contents and values of our culture; it plays with them as, say, in the great age of the arts a painter might have played with the colors on his palette. All the insights, noble thoughts, and works of art that the human race has produced in its creative eras, all that subsequent periods of scholarly study have reduced to concepts and converted into intellectual property—on all this immense body of intellectual values the Glass Bead Game player plays like the organist on an organ. And this organ has attained an almost unimaginable perfection; its manuals and pedals range over the entire intellectual cosmos; its stops are almost beyond number. Theoretically this instrument is capable of reproducing in the Game the entire intellectual content of the universe. These manuals, pedals, and stops are now fixed. Changes in their number and order, and attempts at perfecting them, are actually no longer feasible except in theory. Any enrichment of the language of the Game by addition of new contents is subject to the strictest conceivable control by the directorate of the Game. On the other hand, within this fixed structure, or to abide by our image, within the complicated mechanism of this giant organ, a whole universe of possibilities and combinations is available to the individual player. For even two out of a thousand stringently played games to resemble each other more than superficially is hardly possible. Even if it should so happen that two players by chance were to choose precisely the same small assortment of themes for the content of their Game, these two Games could present an entirely different appearance and run an entirely different course, depending on the qualities of mind, character, mood, and virtuosity of the players.

How far back the historian wishes to place the origins and antecedents of the Glass Bead Game is, ultimately, a matter of his personal choice. For like every great idea it has no real beginning; rather, it has always been, at least the idea of it. We find it foreshadowed, as a dim anticipation and hope, in a good many earlier ages. There are hints of it in Pythagoras, for example, and then among Hellenistic Gnostic circles in the late period of classical civilization. We find it equally among the ancient Chinese, then again at the several pinnacles of Arabic-Moorish culture; and the path of its prehistory leads on through Scholasticism and Humanism to the academies of mathematicians of the seventeenth and eighteenth centuries and on to the Romantic philosophies and the runes of Novalis's hallucinatory visions. This same eternal idea, which for us has been embodied in the Glass Bead Game, has underlain every movement of Mind toward the ideal goal of a *universitas litterarum*, every Platonic academy, every league of an intellectual elite, every *rapprochement* between the exact and the more liberal disciplines, every effort toward reconciliation between science and art or science and religion. Men like Abelard, Leibniz, and Hegel unquestionably were familiar with the dream of capturing the universe of the intellect in concentric systems, and pairing the living beauty of thought and art with the magical expressiveness of the exact sciences. In that age in which music and mathematics almost simultaneously attained classical heights, approaches and cross-fertilizations between the two disciplines occurred frequently. And two centuries earlier we find in Nicholas of Cues sentences of the same tenor, such as this: "The mind adapts itself to potentiality in order to measure everything in the mode of potentiality, and to absolute necessity in order to measure everything in the mode of unity and simplicity as God does, and to the necessity of nexus in order to measure everything with respect to its peculiar nature; finally, it adapts itself to determinate potentiality in order to measure everything with respect to its existence. But furthermore the mind also measures symbolically, by comparison, as when it employs numerals and geometric figures and equates other things with them."

Incidentally, this is not the only one of Nicholas's ideas that almost seems to suggest our Glass Bead Game, or corresponds to and springs from a similar branch of the imagination as the play of thought which occurs in the Game. Many similar echoes can be found in his writings. His pleasure in mathematics also, and his delight and skill in using constructions and axioms of Euclidean geometry as similes to clarify theological and philosophical concepts, likewise appear to be very close to the mentality of the Game. At times even his peculiar Latin (abounding in words of his own coinage, whose meaning, however, was perfectly plain to any Latin scholar) calls to mind the improvisatory agility of the Game's language.

As the epigraph of our treatise may already have suggested, Albertus Secundus deserves an equal place among the ancestors of the Glass Bead Game. And we suspect, although we cannot prove this by citations, that the idea of the Game also dominated the minds of those learned musicians of the sixteenth, seventeenth, and eighteenth centuries who based their musical compositions on mathematical speculations. Here and there in the ancient litera-

tures we encounter legends of wise and mysterious games
that were conceived and played by scholars, monks, or
the courtiers of cultured princes. These might take the
form of chess games in which the pieces and squares had
secret meanings in addition to their usual functions. And
of course everyone has heard those fables and legends
from the formative years of all civilizations which ascribe
to music powers far greater than those of any mere art:
the capacity to control men and nations. These accounts
make of music a kind of secret regent, or a lawbook
for men and their governments. From the most ancient
days of China to the myths of the Greeks we find the
concept of an ideal, heavenly life for men under the
hegemony of music. The Glass Bead Game is intimately
bound up with this cult of music ("in eternal transmuta-
tions the secret power of song greets us here below,"
says Novalis).

Although we thus recognize the idea of the Game as
eternally present, and therefore existent in vague stirrings
long before it became a reality, its realization in the form
we know it nevertheless has its specific history. We shall
now attempt to give a brief account of the most important stages in that history.

The beginnings of the intellectual movement whose
fruits are, among many others, the establishment of the
Order and the Glass Bead Game itself, may be traced
back to a period which Plinius Ziegenhalss, the historian
of literature, designated as the Age of the Feuilleton, by
which name it has been known ever since. Such tags are
pretty, but dangerous; they constantly tempt us to a
biased view of the era in question. And as a matter of
fact the Age of the Feuilleton was by no means un-
cultured; it was not even intellectually impoverished. But
if we may believe Ziegenhalss, that age appears to have
had only the dimmest notion of what to do with culture.
Or rather, it did not know how to assign culture its proper place within the economy of life and the nation. To
be frank, we really are very poorly informed about that
era, even though it is the soil out of which almost everything that distinguishes our cultural life today has grown.
It was, according to Ziegenhalss, an era emphatically

"bourgeois" and given to an almost untrammeled individualism. If in order to suggest the atmosphere we cite some of its features from Ziegenhalss' description, we may at least do so with the confidence that these features have not been invented, badly drawn, or grossly exaggerated. For the great scholar has documented them from a vast number of literary and other sources. We take our cue from this scholar, who so far has been the sole serious investigator of the Feuilletonistic Age. As we read, we should remember that it is easy and foolish to sneer at the mistakes or barbarities of remote ages.

Since the end of the Middle Ages, intellectual life in Europe seems to have evolved along two major lines. The first of these was the liberation of thought and belief from the sway of all authority. In practice this meant the struggle of Reason, which at last felt it had come of age and won its independence, against the domination of the Roman Church. The second trend, on the other hand, was the covert but passionate search for a means to confer legitimacy on this freedom, for a new and sufficient authority arising out of Reason itself. We can probably generalize and say that Mind has by and large won this often strangely contradictory battle for two aims basically at odds with each other.

Has the gain been worth the countless victims? Has our present structure of the life of the mind been sufficiently developed, and is it likely to endure long enough, to justify as worthwhile sacrifices all the sufferings, convulsions, and abnormalities: the trials of heretics, the burnings at stake, the many "geniuses" who ended in madness or suicide? For us, it is not permissible to ask these questions. History is as it has happened. Whether it was good, whether it would have been better not to have happened, whether we will or will not acknowledge that it has had "meaning"—all this is irrelevant. Thus those struggles for the "freedom" of the human intellect likewise "happened," and subsequently, in the course of the aforementioned Age of the Feuilleton, men came to enjoy an incredible degree of intellectual freedom, more than they could stand. For while they had overthrown the tutelage of the Church completely, and that of the State partially, they had not succeeded in formulating an authentic law they could respect, a genuinely new authority and legitimacy. Ziegenhalss recounts some truly astonishing examples of the intellect's debasement, venality, and self-betrayal during that period.

We must confess that we cannot provide an unequivocal definition of those products from which the age takes its name, the feuilletons. They seem to have formed an uncommonly popular section of the daily newspapers, were produced by the millions, and were a major source of mental pabulum for the reader in want of culture. They reported on, or rather "chatted" about, a thousand-and-one items of knowledge. It would seem, moreover, that the cleverer among the writers of them poked fun at their own work. Ziegenhalss, at any rate, contends that many such pieces are so incomprehensible that they can only be viewed as self-persiflage on the part of the authors. Quite possibly these manufactured articles do indeed contain a quantity of irony and self-mockery which cannot be understood until the key is found again. The producers of these trivia were in some cases attached to the staffs of the newspapers; in other cases they were free-lance scriveners. Frequently they enjoyed the high-sounding title of "writer," but a great many of them seem to have belonged to the scholar class. Quite a few were celebrated university professors.

Among the favorite subjects of such essays were anecdotes taken from the lives or correspondence of famous men and women. They bore such titles as "Friedrich Nietzsche and Women's Fashions of 1870," or "The Composer Rossini's Favorite Dishes," or "The Role of the Lapdog in the Lives of Great Courtesans," and so on. Another popular type of article was the historical background piece on what was currently being talked about among the well-to-do, such as "The Dream of Creating Gold Through the Centuries," or "Physico-chemical Experiments in Influencing the Weather," and hundreds of similar subjects. When we look at the titles that Ziegenhalss cites, we feel surprise that there should have been people who devoured such chitchat for their daily reading; but what astonishes us far more is that authors of repute and of decent education should have helped to "service" this gigantic consumption of empty whimsies. Significantly, "service" was the expression used; it was also the word denoting the relationship of man to the machine at that time.

In some periods interviews with well-known personalities on current problems were particularly popular. Ziegenhalss devotes a separate chapter to these. Noted chemists or piano virtuosos would be queried about politics, for example, or popular actors, dancers, gymnasts, aviators, or even poets would be drawn out on the benefits and drawbacks of being a bachelor, or on the presumptive causes of financial crises, and so on. All that mattered in these pieces was to link a well-known name with a subject of current topical interest. The reader may consult Ziegenhalss for some truly startling examples; he gives hundreds.

As we have said, no doubt a goodly dash of irony was mixed in with all this busy productivity; it may even have been a demonic irony, the irony of desperation—it is very hard indeed for us to put ourselves in the place of those people so that we can truly understand them. But the great majority, who seem to have been strikingly fond of reading, must have accepted all these grotesque things with credulous earnestness. If a famous painting changed owners, if a precious manuscript was sold at auction, if an old palace burned down, if the bearer of an aristocratic name was involved in a scandal, the readers of many thousands of feature articles at once learned the facts. What is more, on that same day or by the next day at the latest they received an additional dose of anecdotal, historical, psychological, erotic, and other stuff on the catchword of the moment. A torrent of zealous scribbling poured out over every ephemeral incident, and in quality, assortment, and phraseology all this material bore the mark of mass goods rapidly and irresponsibly turned out.

Incidentally, there appear to have been certain games which were regular concomitants of the feature article. The readers themselves took the active role in these games, which put to use some of their glut of information fodder. A long disquisition by Ziegenhalss on the curious subject of "Crossword Puzzles" describes the phenomenon. Thousands upon thousands of persons, the majority of whom did heavy work and led a hard life, spent their leisure hours sitting over squares and crosses made of letters of the alphabet, filling in the gaps according to certain rules. But let us be wary of seeing only the absurd or insane aspect of this, and let us abstain from ridiculing it. For these people with their childish puzzle games and their cultural feature articles were by no means innocuous children or playful Phæacians. Rather, they dwelt anxiously among political, economic, and moral ferments and earthquakes, waged a number of frightful wars and civil wars, and their little cultural games were not just charming, meaningless childishness. These games sprang from their deep need to close their eyes and flee from unsolved problems and anxious forebodings of doom into an imaginary world as innocuous as possible. They assiduously learned to drive automobiles, to play difficult card games and lose themselves in crossword puzzles—for they faced death, fear, pain, and hunger almost without defenses, could no longer accept the consolations of the churches, and could obtain no useful advice from Reason. These people who read so many articles and listened to so many lectures did not take the time and trouble to strengthen themselves against fear, to combat the dread of death within themselves; they moved spasmodically on through life and had no belief in a tomorrow.

For there was also a good deal of lecturing, and we must briefly discuss this somewhat more dignified variant of the feature article. Both specialists and intellectual privateers supplied the middle-class citizens of the age (who were still deeply attached to the notion of culture, although it had long since been robbed of its former meaning) with large numbers of lectures. Such talks were not only in the nature of festival orations for special occasions; there was a frantic trade in them, and they were given in almost incomprehensible quantities. In those days the citizen of a medium-sized town or his wife could at least once a week (in big cities pretty much every night) attend lectures offering theoretical instruction on some subject or other: on works of art, poets, scholars, researchers, world tours. The members of the audience at these lectures remained purely passive, and although some relationship between audience and content, some previous knowledge, preparation, and receptivity were tacitly assumed in most cases nothing of the sort was present. There were entertaining, impassioned, or witty lectures on Goethe, say, in which he would be depicted descending from a post chaise wearing a blue frock-coat to seduce some Strassburg or Wetzlar girl; or on Arabic culture; in all of them a number of fashionable phrases were shaken up like dice in a cup and everyone was delighted if he dimly recognized one or two catchwords. People heard lectures on writers whose works they had never read and never meant to, sometimes accompanied by pictures projected on a screen. At these lectures, as in the feature articles in the newspapers, they struggled through a deluge of isolated cultural facts and fragments of knowledge robbed of all meaning. To put it briefly, they were already on the verge of that dreadful devaluation of the Word which produced, at first in secret and within the narrowest circles, that ascetically heroic countermovement which soon afterward began to flow visibly and powerfully, and ushered in the new self-discipline and dignity of the human intellect.

It must be granted that many aspects of the intellectual life of that era showed energy and grandeur. We moderns explain its concomitant uncertainty and falseness as a symptom of the horror which seized men when at the end of an era of apparent victory and success they found themselves suddenly confronting a void: great material scarcity, a period of political and military crises, and an accelerating distrust of the intellect itself, of its own virtue and dignity and even of its own existence. Yet that very period, filled though it was with premonitions of doom, was marked by some very fine intellectual achievements, including the beginnings of a science of music of which we are the grateful heirs.

But although it is easy to fit any given segment of the past neatly and intelligibly into the patterns of world history, contemporaries are never able to see their own place in the patterns. Consequently, even as intellectual ambitions and achievements declined rapidly during that period, intellectuals in particular were stricken by terrible doubts and a sense of despair. They had just fully realized (a discovery that had been in the air, here and there, from the time of Nietzsche on) that the youth and the creative period of our culture was over, that old age and twilight had set in. Suddenly everyone felt this and many bluntly expressed this view; it was used to explain many of the alarming signs of the time: the dreary mechanization of life, the profound debasement of morality, the decline of faith among nations, the inauthenticity of art. The "music of decline" had sounded, as in that wonderful Chinese fable; like a thrumming bass on the organ its reverberations faded slowly out over decades; its throbbing could be heard in the corruption of the schools, periodicals, and universities, in melancholia and insanity among those artists and critics who could still be taken seriously; it raged as untrammeled and amateurish overproduction in all the arts. Various attitudes could be taken toward this enemy who had breached the walls and could no longer be exorcised. Some of the best tacitly acknowledged and stoically endured the bitter truth. Some attempted to deny its existence, and thanks to the shoddy thinking of some of the literary prophets of cultural doom, found a good many weak points in their thesis. Moreover, those who took exception to the aforementioned prophets could be sure of a hearing and influence among the bourgeoisie. For the allegation that the culture he had only yesterday been proud to possess was no longer alive, that the education and art he revered could no longer be regarded as genuine education and genuine art, seemed to the bourgeois as brazen and intolerable as the sudden inflations of currency and the revolutions which threatened his accumulated capital.

Another possible immunization against the general mood of doom was cynicism. People went dancing and dismissed all anxiety about the future as old-fashioned folly; people composed heady articles about the approaching end of art, science, and language. In that feuilleton world they had constructed of paper, people postulated the total capitulation of Mind, the bankruptcy of ideas, and pretended to be looking on with cynical calm or bacchantic rapture as not only art, culture, morality, and honesty, but also Europe and "the world" proceeded to their doom. Among the good there prevailed

a quietly resigned gloom, among the wicked a malicious
pessimism. The fact was that a breakdown of outmoded
forms, and a degree of reshuffling both of the world and
its morality by means of politics and war, had to take
place before the culture itself became capable of real
self-analysis and a new organization.

Yet during the decades of transition this culture had
not slumbered. Rather, during the very period of its decay and seeming capitulation by the artists, professors,
and feature writers, it entered into a phase of intense
alertness and self-examination. The medium of this
change lay in the consciences of a few individuals. Even
during the heyday of the feuilleton there were everywhere individuals and small groups who had resolved
to remain faithful to true culture and to devote all their
energies to preserving for the future a core of good tradition, discipline, method, and intellectual rigor. We are
today ignorant of many details, but in general the process
of self-examination, reflection, and conscious resistance
to decline seems to have centered mostly in two groups.
The cultural conscience of scholars found refuge in the
investigations and didactic methods of the history of
music, for this discipline was just reaching its height at
that time, and even in the midst of the feuilleton world
two famous seminaries fostered an exemplary methodology, characterized by care and thoroughness. Moreover,
as if destiny wished to smile comfortingly upon this tiny,
brave cohort, at this saddest of times there took place
that glorious miracle which was in itself pure chance,
but which gave the effect of a divine corroboration: the
rediscovery of eleven manuscripts of Johann Sebastian
Bach, which had been in the keeping of his son Friede-
mann.

A second focus of resistance to degeneration was the
League of Journeyers to the East. The brethren of that
League cultivated a spiritual rather than an intellectual
discipline. They fostered piety and reverence, and to
them we owe important elements in our present form of
cultural life and of the Glass Bead Game, in particular
the contemplative elements. The Journeyers also contributed to new insights into the nature of our culture and
the possibilities of its continuance, not so much by ana-

lytical and scholarly work as by their capacity, based on ancient secret exercises, for mystic identification with remote ages and cultural conditions. Among them, for example, were itinerant instrumentalists and minstrels who were said to have the ability to perform the music of earlier epochs with perfect ancient purity. Thus they could play and sing a piece of music from 1600 or 1650 exactly as if all the subsequent modes, refinements, and virtuoso achievements were still unknown. This was an astonishing feat in a period in which the mania for dynamics and *gradazione* dominated all music-making, when the music itself was almost forgotten in discussions of the conductor's execution and "conception." When an orchestra of the Journeyers first publicly performed a suite from the time before Handel completely without *crescendi* and *diminuendi*, with the naïveté and chasteness of another age and world, some among the audience are said to have been totally uncomprehending, but others listened with fresh attention and had the impression that they were hearing music for the first time in their lives. In the League's concert hall between Bremgarten and Morbio, one member built a Bach organ as perfectly as Johann Sebastian Bach would have had it built had he had the means and opportunity. Obeying a principle even then current in the League, the organ builder concealed his name, calling himself Silbermann after his eighteenth-century predecessor.

In discussing these matters we have approached the sources from which our modern concept of culture sprang. One of the chief of these was the most recent of the scholarly disciplines, the history of music and the aesthetics of music. Another was the great advance in mathematics that soon followed. To these was added a sprinkling of the wisdom of the Journeyers to the East and, closely related to the new conception and interpretation of music, that courageous new attitude, compounded of serenity and resignation, toward the aging of cultures. It would be pointless to say much about these matters here, since they are familiar to everyone. The most important consequence of this new attitude, or rather this new subordination to the cultural process, was that men largely ceased to produce works of art.

Moreover, intellectuals gradually withdrew from the bustle of the world. Finally, and no less important—indeed, the climax of the whole development—there arose the Glass Bead Game.

The growing profundity of musical science, which can already be observed soon after 1900 when feuilletonism was still at its height, naturally exerted enormous influence upon the beginnings of the Game. We, the heirs of musicology, believe we know more about the music of the great creative centuries, especially the seventeenth and eighteenth, and in a certain sense even understand it better than all previous epochs, including that of classical music itself. As descendants, of course, our relation to classical music differs totally from that of our predecessors in the creative ages. Our intellectualized veneration for true music, all too frequently tainted by melancholic resignation, is a far cry from the charming, simplehearted delight in music-making of those days. We tend to envy those happier times whenever our pleasure in their music makes us forget the conditions and tribulations amid which it was begotten. Almost the entire twentieth century considered philosophy, or else literature, to be the great lasting achievement of that cultural era which lies between the end of the Middle Ages and modern times. We, however, have for generations given the palm to mathematics and music. Ever since we have renounced—on the whole, at any rate—trying to vie creatively with those generations, ever since we have also forsworn the worship of harmony in music-making, and of that purely sensuous cult of dynamics—a cult that dominated musical practices for a good two centuries after the time of Beethoven and early Romanticism—ever since then we have been able to understand, more purely and more correctly, the general image of that culture whose heirs we are. Or so we believe in our uncreative, retrospective, but reverent fashion! We no longer have any of the exuberant fecundity of those days. For us it is almost incomprehensible that musical style in the fifteenth and sixteenth centuries could be preserved for so long a time in unalloyed purity. How could it be, we ask, that among the vast quantities of music written at that time we fail to find a trace of anything bad? How could the eighteenth century, the time of incipient degeneration, still send hurtling into the skies a fireworks display of styles, fashions, and schools, blazing briefly but with such self-assurance? Nevertheless, we believe that we have uncovered the secret of what we now call classical music, that we have understood the spirit, the virtue, and the piety of those generations, and have taken all that as our model. Nowadays, for example, we do not think much of the theology and the ecclesiastical culture of the eighteenth century, or the philosophy of the Enlightenment; but we consider the cantatas, passions, and preludes of Bach the ultimate quintessence of Christian culture.

Incidentally, there exists an ancient and honorable exemplar for the attitude of our own culture toward music, a model to which the players of the Glass Bead Game look back with great veneration. We recall that in the legendary China of the Old Kings, music was accorded a dominant place in state and court. It was held that if music throve, all was well with culture and morality and with the kingdom itself. The music masters were required to be the strictest guardians of the original purity of the "venerable keys." If music decayed, that was taken as a sure sign of the downfall of the regime and the state. The poets told horrific fables about the forbidden, diabolic, heaven-offending keys, such as the Tsing Shang key, and Tsing Tse, the "music of decline"; no sooner were these wicked notes struck in the Royal Palace than the sky darkened, the walls trembled and collapsed, and kingdom and sovereign went to their doom. We might quote many other sayings by the ancient writers, but we shall cite here only a few passages from the chapter on music in Lü Bu We's *Spring and Autumn*:

"The origins of music lie far back in the past. Music arises from Measure and is rooted in the great Oneness. The great Oneness begets the two poles; the two poles beget the power of Darkness and of Light.

"When the world is at peace, when all things are tranquil and all men obey their superiors in all their courses, then music can be perfected. When desires and passions do not turn into wrongful paths, music can be perfected. Perfect music has its cause. It arises from equilibrium.

Equilibrium arises from righteousness, and righteousness arises from the meaning of the cosmos. Therefore one can speak about music only with a man who has perceived the meaning of the cosmos.

"Music is founded on the harmony between heaven and earth, on the concord of obscurity and brightness.

"Decaying states and men ripe for doom do not, of course, lack music either, but their music is not serene. Therefore, the more tempestuous the music, the more doleful are the people, the more imperiled the country, the more the sovereign declines. In this way the essence of music is lost.

"What all sacred sovereigns have loved in music was its serenity. The tyrants Giae and Jou Sin made tempestuous music. They thought loud sounds beautiful and massed effects interesting. They strove for new and rare tonal effects, for notes which no ear had ever heard hitherto. They sought to surpass each other, and overstepped all bounds.

"The cause of the degeneration of the Chu state was its invention of magic music. Such music is indeed tempestuous enough, but in truth it has departed from the essence of music. Because it has departed from the essence of real music, this music is not serene. If music is not serene, the people grumble and life is deranged. All this arises from mistaking the nature of music and seeking only tempestuous tonal effects.

"Therefore the music of a well-ordered age is calm and cheerful, and so is its government. The music of a restive age is excited and fierce, and its government is perverted. The music of a decaying state is sentimental and sad, and its government is imperiled."

The words of this Chinese writer point fairly distinctly to the origins and to the real although almost forgotten meaning of all music. For in prehistoric times music, like the dance and every other artistic endeavor, was a branch of magic, one of the old and legitimate instruments of wonder-working. Beginning with rhythm (clapping of hands, tramping, beating of sticks and primitive drums), it was a powerful, tried-and-true device for putting large numbers of people "in tune" with one another, engendering the same mood, co-ordinating the pace of their breathing and heartbeats, encouraging them to invoke and conjure up the eternal powers, to dance, to compete, to make war, to worship. And music has retained this original, pure, primordially powerful character, its magic, far longer than the other arts. We need only recall the many testimonies of historians and poets to the power of music, from the Greeks to Goethe in his *Novelle*. In practice, marches and the dance have never lost their importance. . . . But let us return to our subject.

We shall now give a brief summary of the beginnings of the Glass Bead Game. It appears to have arisen simultaneously in Germany and in England. In both countries, moreover, it was originally a kind of exercise employed by those small groups of musicologists and musicians who worked and studied in the new seminaries of musical theory. If we compare the original state of the Game with its subsequent developments and its present form, it is much like comparing a musical score of the period before 1500, with its primitive notes and absence of bar lines, with an eighteenth-century score, let alone with one from the nineteenth with its confusing excess of symbols for dynamics, tempi, phrasing, and so on, which often made the printing of such scores a complex technical problem.

The Game was at first nothing more than a witty method for developing memory and ingenuity among students and musicians. And as we have said, it was played both in England and Germany before it was "invented" here in the Musical Academy of Cologne, and was given the name it bears to this day, after so many generations, although it has long ceased to have anything to do with glass beads.

The inventor, Bastian Perrot of Calw, a rather eccentric but clever, sociable, and humane musicologist, used glass beads instead of letters, numerals, notes, or other graphic symbols. Perrot, who incidentally has also bequeathed to us a treatise on the *Apogee and Decline of Counterpoint*, found that the pupils at the Cologne Seminary had a rather elaborate game they used to play. One would call out, in the standardized abbreviations of their science, motifs or initial bars of classical compositions, whereupon the other had to respond with the continuation of the piece, or better still with a higher or lower voice, a contrasting theme, and so forth. It was an exercise in memory and improvisation quite similar to the sort of thing probably in vogue among ardent pupils of counterpoint in the days of Schütz, Pachelbel, and Bach—although it would then not have been done in theoretical formulas, but in practice on the cembalo, lute, or flute, or with the voice.

Bastian Perrot in all probability was a member of the Journeyers to the East. He was partial to handicrafts and had himself built several pianos and clavichords in the ancient style. Legend has it that he was adept at playing the violin in the old way, forgotten since 1800, with a high-arched bow and hand-regulated tension of the bow hairs. Given these interests, it was perhaps only natural that he should have constructed a frame, modeled on a child's abacus, a frame with several dozen wires on which could be strung glass beads of various sizes, shapes, and colors. The wires corresponded to the lines of the musical staff, the beads to the time-values of the notes, and so on. In this way he could represent with beads musical quotations or invented themes, could alter, transpose, and develop them, change them and set them in counterpoint to one another. In technical terms this was a mere plaything, but the pupils liked it; it was imitated and became fashionable in England too. For a time the game of musical exercises was played in this charmingly primitive manner. And as is so often the case, an enduring and significant institution received its name from a passing and incidental circumstance. For what later evolved out of that students' sport and Perrot's bead-strung wires bears to this day the name by which it became popularly known, the Glass Bead Game.

A bare two or three decades later the Game seems to have lost some of its popularity among students of music, but instead was taken over by mathematicians. For a long while, indeed, a characteristic feature in the Game's history was that it was constantly preferred, used, and further elaborated by whatever branch of learning happened to be experiencing a period of high development or a renaissance. The mathematicians brought the

Game to a high degree of flexibility and capacity for sublimation, so that it began to acquire something approaching a consciousness of itself and its possibilities. This process paralleled the general evolution of cultural consciousness, which had survived the great crisis and had, as Plinius Ziegenhalss puts it, "with modest pride accepted the fate of belonging to a culture past its prime, as was the case with the culture of late antiquity: Hellenistic culture in the Alexandrian Age."

So much for Ziegenhalss. We shall now attempt to sketch the further steps in the history of the Glass Bead Game. Having passed from the musical to the mathematical seminaries (a change which took place in France and England somewhat sooner than in Germany), the Game was so far developed that it was capable of expressing mathematical processes by special symbols and abbreviations. The players, mutually elaborating these processes, threw these abstract formulas at one another, displaying the sequences and possibilities of their science. This mathematical and astronomical game of formulas required great attentiveness, keenness, and concentration. Among mathematicians, even in those days, the reputation of being a good Glass Bead Game player meant a great deal; it was equivalent to being a very good mathematician.

At various times the Game was taken up and imitated by nearly all the scientific and scholarly disciplines, that is, adapted to the special fields. There is documented evidence for its application to the fields of classical philology and logic. The analytical study of musical values had led to the reduction of musical events to physical and mathematical formulas. Soon afterward philology borrowed this method and began to measure linguistic configurations as physics measures processes in nature. The visual arts soon followed suit, architecture having already led the way in establishing the links between visual art and mathematics. Thereafter more and more new relations, analogies, and correspondences were discovered among the abstract formulas obtained in this way. Each discipline which seized upon the Game created its own language of formulas, abbreviations, and possible combinations. Everywhere, the elite intellectual youth developed a passion for these Games, with their dialogues and progressions of formulas. The Game was not mere practice and mere recreation; it became a form of concentrated self-awareness for intellectuals. Mathematicians in particular played it with a virtuosity and formal strictness at once athletic and ascetic. It afforded them a pleasure which somewhat compensated for their renunciation of worldly pleasures and ambitions. For by then such renunciation had already become a regular thing for intellectuals. The Glass Bead Game contributed largely to the complete defeat of feuilletonism and to that newly awakened delight in strict mental exercises to which we owe the origin of a new, monastically austere intellectual discipline.

The world had changed. The life of the mind in the Age of the Feuilleton might be compared to a degenerate plant which was squandering its strength in excessive vegetative growth, and the subsequent corrections to pruning the plant back to the roots. The young people who now proposed to devote themselves to intellectual studies no longer took the term to mean attending a university and taking a nibble of this or that from the dainties offered by celebrated and loquacious professors who without authority offered them the crumbs of what had once been higher education. Now they had to study just as stringently and methodically as the engineers and technicians of the past, if not more so. They had a steep path to climb, had to purify and strengthen their minds by dint of mathematics and scholastic exercises in Aristotelian philosophy. Moreover, they had to learn to renounce all those benefits which previous generations of scholars had considered worth striving for: rapid and easy money-making, celebrity and public honors, the homage of the newspapers, marriages with daughters of bankers and industrialists, a pampered and luxurious style of life. The writers with heavy sales, Nobel Prizes, and lovely country houses, the celebrated physicians with decorations and liveried servants, the professors with wealthy wives and brilliant salons, the chemists with posts on boards of directors, the philosophers with feuilleton factories who delivered charming lectures in overcrowded halls, for which they were re-

warded with thunderous applause and floral tributes—
all such public figures disappeared and have not come
back to this day. Even so, no doubt, there were still
plenty of talented young people for whom such personages
were envied models. But the paths to honors, riches,
fame, and luxury now no longer led through lecture
halls, academies, and doctoral theses. The deeply debased intellectual professions were bankrupt in the
world's eyes. But in compensation they had regained a
fanatical and penitential devotion to art and thought.
Those talented persons whose desires tended more toward glory or comfortable living had to turn their backs
on the intellectual life, which had become so austere,
and seek out occupations which still provided opportunities for comfort and money-making.

It would lead us too far afield to attempt to describe
in detail how the world of Mind, after its purification,
won a place for itself in the State. Experience soon
showed that a few generations of lax and unscrupulous
intellectual discipline had also sufficed to inflict serious
harm on practical life. Competence and responsibility
had grown increasingly rare in all the higher professions, including even those concerned with technology.
To remedy this, supervision of the things of the mind
among the people and in government came to be consigned more and more to the "intellectuals" in the best
sense of the word. This was particularly the case with
the entire educational system; and indeed the situation
is little changed to this day. In almost all the countries
of Europe today the schools that are not still administered by the Roman Church are in the hands of those
anonymous Orders which fill their ranks from the elite
among the intellectuals. Although public opinion occasionally decries the strictness and the reputed arrogance
of this caste, and although individuals have occasionally
revolted against it, this leadership stands unshaken. Its
integrity, its renunciation of all benefits and advantages
other than intellectual ones, maintains and protects it.
But it is also supported by what has long since become
common knowledge, or at least a universal sense, that
the continuance of civilization depends on this strict
schooling. People know, or dimly feel, that if thinking

is not kept pure and keen, and if respect for the world of
the mind is no longer operative, ships and automobiles
will soon cease to run right, the engineer's slide rule
and the computations of banks and stock exchanges will
forfeit validity and authority, and chaos will ensue. It
took long enough in all conscience for realization to come
that the externals of civilization—technology, industry,
commerce, and so on—also require a common basis of
intellectual honesty and morality.

To return now to the Glass Bead Game: what it
lacked in those days was the capacity for universality,
for rising above all the disciplines. The astronomers,
the classicists, the scholastics, the music students all
played their Games according to their ingenious rules,
but the Game had a special language and set of rules
for every discipline and subdiscipline. It required half
a century before the first step was taken toward spanning
these gulfs. The reason for this slowness was undoubtedly
more moral than formal and technical. The means for
building the spans could even then have been found,
but along with the newly regenerated intellectual life
went a puritanical shrinking from "foolish digressions,"
from intermingling of disciplines and categories. There
was also a profound and justified fear of relapse into the
sin of superficiality and feuilletonism.

It was the achievement of one individual which
brought the Glass Bead Game almost in one leap to an
awareness of its potentialities, and thus to the verge of
its capacity for universal elaboration. And once again
this advance was connected with music. A Swiss musicologist with a passion for mathematics gave a new twist
to the Game, and thereby opened the way for its supreme
development. This great man's name in civil life can
no longer be ascertained; by his time the cult of personality in intellectual fields had already been dispensed
with. He lives on in history as Lusor (or also, Joculator)
Basiliensis. Although his invention, like all inventions,
was the product of his own personal merit and grace, it
in no way sprang solely from personal needs and ambitions, but was impelled by a more powerful motive.
There was a passionate craving among all the intellectuals of his age for a means to express their new con-

cepts. They longed for philosophy, for synthesis. The erstwhile happiness of pure withdrawal each into his own discipline was now felt to be inadequate. Here and there a scholar broke through the barriers of his specialty and tried to advance into the terrain of universality. Some dreamed of a new alphabet, a new language of symbols through which they could formulate and exchange their new intellectual experiences.

Testimony to the strength of this impulse may be found in the essay "Chinese Warning Cry," by a Parisian scholar of those years. The author, mocked by many in his day as a sort of Don Quixote (incidentally, he was a distinguished scholar in the field of Chinese philology), pointed out the dangers facing culture, in spite of its present honorable condition, if it neglected to develop an international language of symbols. Such a language, like the ancient Chinese script, should be able to express the most complex matters graphically, without excluding individual imagination and inventiveness, in such a way as to be understandable to all the scholars of the world. It was at this point that Joculator Basiliensis applied himself to the problem. He invented for the Glass Bead Game the principles of a new language, a language of symbols and formulas, in which mathematics and music played an equal part, so that it became possible to combine astronomical and musical formulas, to reduce mathematics and music to a common denominator, as it were. Although what he did was by no means conclusive, this unknown man from Basel certainly laid the foundations for all that came later in the history of our beloved Game.

The Glass Bead Game, formerly the specialized entertainment of mathematicians in one era, philologists or musicians in another era, now more and more cast its spell upon all true intellectuals. Many an old university, many a lodge, and especially the age-old League of Journeyers to the East, turned to it. Some of the Catholic Orders likewise scented a new intellectual atmosphere and yielded to its lure. At some Benedictine abbeys the monks devoted themselves to the Game so intensely that even in those early days the question was hotly debated—it was subsequently to crop up again now and then—whether this game ought to be tolerated, supported, or forbidden by Church and Curia.

After Joculator Basiliensis' grand accomplishment, the Game rapidly evolved into what it is today: the quintessence of intellectuality and art, the sublime cult, the *unio mystica* of all separate members of the *Universitas Litterarum*. In our lives it has partially taken over the role of art, partially that of speculative philosophy. Indeed, in the days of Plinius Ziegenhalss, for instance, it was often called by a different name, one common in the literature of the Feuilletonistic Age. That name, which for many a prophetic spirit in those days embodied a visionary ideal, was: Magic Theater.

For all that the Glass Bead Game had grown infinitely in technique and range since its beginnings, for all the intellectual demands it made upon its players, and for all that it had become a sublime art and science, in the days of Joculator Basiliensis it still was lacking in an essential element. Up to that time every game had been a serial arrangement, an ordering, grouping, and confronting of concentrated concepts from many fields of thought and aesthetics, a rapid recollection of eternal values and forms, a brief, virtuoso flight through the realms of the mind. Only after some time did there enter into the Game, from the intellectual stock of the educational system and especially from the habits and customs of the Journeyers to the East, the idea of contemplation.

This new element arose out of an observed evil. Mnemonists, people with freakish memories and no other virtues, were capable of playing dazzling games, dismaying and confusing the other participants by their rapid muster of countless ideas. In the course of time such displays of virtuosity fell more and more under a strict ban, and contemplation became a highly important component of the Game. Ultimately, for the audiences at each Game it became the main thing. This was the necessary turning toward the religious spirit. What had formerly mattered was following the sequences of ideas and the whole intellectual mosaic of a Game with rapid attentiveness, practiced memory, and full understanding. But there now arose the demand for a deeper and more spiritual approach. After each symbol conjured up by the director of a Game, each player was required to perform silent, formal meditation on the content, origin, and meaning of this symbol, to call to mind intensively and organically its full purport. The members of the Order and of the Game associations brought the technique and practice of contemplation with them from their elite schools, where the art of contemplation and meditation was nurtured with the greatest care. In this way the hieroglyphs of the Game were kept from degenerating into mere empty signs.

Hitherto, by the way, the Glass Bead Game, in spite of its popularity among scholars, had remained a purely private form of exercise. It could be played alone, by pairs, or by many, although unusually brilliant, well-composed, and successful Games were sometimes written down and circulated from city to city and country to country for admiration or criticism. Now, however, the Game slowly began to be enriched by a new function, for it became a public ceremonial. To this day everyone is free to play the Game privately, and young people are especially fond of doing so. But nowadays virtually everyone associates the Glass Bead Game with ceremonial public Games. They take place under the leadership of a few superior Masters who are directly subordinate to the Ludi Magister, or Master of the Game, of their country, with invited guests listening raptly, and a wider audience all over the world following with closest attention. Some of these Games last for days and weeks, and while such a Game is being celebrated all the players and guests—obeying precepts which even govern the length of time they are allowed to sleep—live an ascetic and selfless life of absolute absorption, comparable to the strictly regulated penitence required of the participants in one of St. Ignatius Loyola's exercises.

There is scarcely any more we need add. Under the shifting hegemony of now this, now that science or art, the Game of games had developed into a kind of universal language through which the players could express values and set these in relation to one another.

Throughout its history the Game was closely allied with music, and usually proceeded according to musical or mathematical rules. One theme, two themes, or three themes were stated, elaborated, varied, and underwent a development quite similar to that of the theme in a Bach fugue or a concerto movement. A Game, for example, might start from a given astronomical configuration, or from the actual theme of a Bach fugue, or from a sentence out of Leibniz or the Upanishads, and from this theme, depending on the intentions and talents of the player, it could either further explore and elaborate the initial motif or else enrich its expressiveness by allusions to kindred concepts. Beginners learned how to establish parallels, by means of the Game's symbols, between a piece of classical music and the formula for some law of nature. Experts and Masters of the Game freely wove the initial theme into unlimited combinations. For a long time one school of players favored the technique of stating side by side, developing in counterpoint, and finally harmoniously combining two hostile themes or ideas, such as law and freedom, individual and community. In such a Game the goal was to develop both themes or theses with complete equality and impartiality, to evolve out of thesis and antithesis the purest possible synthesis. In general, aside from certain brilliant exceptions, Games with discordant, negative, or skeptical conclusions were unpopular and at times actually forbidden. This followed directly from the meaning the Game had acquired at its height for the players. It represented an elite, symbolic form of seeking for perfection, a sublime alchemy, an approach to that Mind which beyond all images and multiplicities is one within itself—in other words, to God. Pious thinkers of earlier times had represented the life of creatures, say, as a mode of motion toward God, and had considered that the variety of the phenomenal world reached perfection and ultimate cognition only in the divine Unity. Similarly, the symbols and formulas of the Glass Bead Game combined structurally, musically, and philosophically within the framework of a universal language, were nourished by all the sciences and arts, and strove in play to achieve perfection, pure being, the fullness of reality. Thus, "realizing" was a favorite expression among the players. They considered their Games a path from Becoming to Being, from potentiality to reality. We would like to remind the reader once again of the sentences quoted above from Nicholas of Cues.

Incidentally, the terminology of Christian theology, or at any rate that part of it which seemed to have become a part of the general cultural heritage, was naturally absorbed into the symbolic language of the Game. Thus one of the principles of the Creed, a passage from the Bible, a phrase from one of the Church Fathers, or from the Latin text of the Mass could be expressed and taken into the Game just as easily and aptly as an axiom of geometry or a melody of Mozart. We would scarcely be exaggerating if we ventured to say that for the small circle of genuine Glass Bead Game players the Game was virtually equivalent to worship, although it deliberately eschewed developing any theology of its own.

In struggling for their continued existence in the midst of soulless world powers, both the Glass Bead Game players and the Roman Church had become too dependent upon each other for either to permit a decisive confrontation between them, although that danger was always present, since the intellectual honesty and the authentic impulse to reach incisive, unequivocal formulations drove the partisans of both toward a parting of the ways. That parting, however, never took place. Rome vacillated between a benevolent and a hostile attitude toward the Game, for a good many of the most talented persons in the Roman congregations, and in the ranks of the high and the highest clergy, were players. And the Game itself, ever since public matches and a Ludi Magister had been instituted, enjoyed the protection of the Order and of the education ministries, both of which always behaved with the greatest possible courtesy and chivalry toward Rome. Pope Pius XV, who as a cardinal had been an excellent and ardent Glass Bead Game player, as pontiff followed the example of all his predecessors in bidding the Game farewell forever; but he went a step further and actually attempted to put the Game on trial. It was a near thing; had he carried out his intention,

Catholics would have been forbidden to play the Game. But the pope died before matters came to that point, and a widely read biography of this rather important man has represented his attitude toward the Glass Bead Game as one of deep passion which in his pontifical office he could vent only in the form of hostility.

The Game had been played freely by individuals and cliques, and for a long time amiably promoted by the ministries of education, before it acquired the status of a public institution. It was first organized as such in France and England; other countries followed fairly rapidly. In each country a Game Commission and a supreme head of the Game, bearing the title of Ludi Magister, were established. Official matches, played under the personal direction of the Magister, were exalted into cultural festivals. Like all high functionaries in cultural life, the Magister of course remained anonymous. Aside from a few intimates, no one knew his name. Official and international communications media, such as radio and so on, were made available only for the great official matches over which the Ludi Magister personally presided. Among the duties of the Magister, in addition to conducting the public Games, was supervision of the players and the schools of the Game. Above all, however, the Magister had to keep strict watch over the further elaboration of the Game. The World Commission of the Magisters of all countries alone decided on the acceptance of new symbols and formulas into the existing stock of the Game (which scarcely ever occurs nowadays), on modifications of the rules, on the desirability of including new fields within the purview of the Game. If the Game is regarded as a kind of world language for thoughtful men, the Games Commissions of the various countries under the leadership of their Magisters form as a whole the Academy which guards the vocabulary, the development, and the purity of this language. Each country's Commission possesses its Archive of the Game, that is, the register of all hitherto examined and accepted symbols and decipherments, whose number long ago by far exceeded the number of the ancient Chinese ideographs.

In general, a passing grade in the final examination

in one of the academies, especially one of the elite
schools, is considered sufficient qualification for a Glass
Bead Game player; but in the past and to this day
superior competence in one of the principal fields of
scholarship or in music is tacitly assumed. To rise
some day to membership in one of the Games Commissions, or even to Ludi Magister, is the dream of almost every fifteen-year-old in the elite schools. But by
the time these youth have become doctoral candidates,
only a tiny percentage still seriously cling to their ambition to serve the Glass Bead Game and take an active
part in its further development. On the other hand, all
these lovers of the Game diligently study the lore of the
Game and practice meditation. At the "great" Games
they form that innermost ring of reverent and devoted
participants which gives the public matches their ceremonial character and keeps them from devolving into
mere aesthetic displays. To these real players and devotees, the Ludi Magister is a prince or high priest, almost a deity.

But for every independent player, and especially for
the Magister, the Glass Bead Game is primarily a form
of music-making, somewhat in the sense of those words
that Joseph Knecht once spoke concerning the nature of
classical music:

"We consider classical music to be the epitome and
quintessence of our culture, because it is that culture's
clearest, most significant gesture and expression. In this
music we possess the heritage of classical antiquity and
Christianity, a spirit of serenely cheerful and brave piety,
a superbly chivalric morality. For in the final analysis
every important cultural gesture comes down to a
morality, a model for human behavior concentrated into
a gesture. As we know, between 1500 and 1800 a wide
variety of music was made; styles and means of expression were extremely variegated; but the spirit, or rather
the morality, was everywhere the same. The human
attitude of which classical music is the expression is always the same; it is always based on the same kind of
insight into life and strives for the same kind of victory
over blind chance. Classical music as gesture signifies
knowledge of the tragedy of the human condition,

affirmation of human destiny, courage, cheerful serenity. The grace of a minuet by Handel or Couperin, the sensuality sublimated into delicate gesture to be found in many Italian composers or in Mozart, the tranquil, composed readiness for death in Bach—always there may be heard in these works a defiance, a death-defying intrepidity, a gallantry, and a note of superhuman laughter, of immortal gay serenity. Let that same note also sound in our Glass Bead Games, and in our whole lives, acts, and sufferings."

These words were noted down by one of Knecht's pupils. With them we bring to an end our consideration of the Glass Bead Game.

THE
LIFE
OF
MAGISTER
LUDI
JOSEPH
KNECHT

ONE

THE CALL

No KNOWLEDGE HAS come down to us of Joseph Knecht's origins. Like many other pupils of the elite schools, he either lost his parents early in childhood, or the Board of Educators removed him from unfavorable home conditions and took charge of him. In any case, he was spared the conflict between elite school and home which complicates the youth of many other boys of his type, makes entry into the Order more difficult, and in some cases transforms highly gifted young people into problem personalities.

Knecht was one of those fortunates who seem born for Castalia, for the Order, and for service in the Board of Educators. Although he was not spared the perplexities of the life of the mind, it was given to him to experience without personal bitterness the tragedy inherent in every life consecrated to thought. Indeed, it is probably not so much this tragedy in itself that has tempted us to delve so deeply into the personality of Joseph Knecht; rather, it was the tranquil, cheerful, not to say radiant manner in which he brought his destiny and his talents to fruition. Like every man of importance he had his *daimonion* and his *amor fati;* but in him *amor fati* mani-

fests itself to us free of somberness and fanaticism.
Granted, there is always much that is hidden, and we
must not forget that the writing of history—however dryly
it is done and however sincere the desire for objectivity—
remains literature. History's third dimension is always
fiction.

Thus, to select some examples of greatness, we have
no idea whether Johann Sebastian Bach or Wolfgang
Amadeus Mozart actually lived in a cheerful or a despon-
dent manner. Mozart moves us with that peculiarly touching and endearing grace of early blossoming and fading;
Bach stands for the edifying and comforting submission
to God's paternal plan of which suffering and dying form
a part. But we do not really read these qualities from
their biographies and from such facts about their private
lives as have come down to us; we read them solely from
their works, from their music. Furthermore, although we
know Bach's biography and deduce his personality from
his music, we involuntarily include his posthumous destiny in the picture. We conceive him as living with the
knowledge, which causes him a silent smile, that all his
work would be forgotten after his death, that his manuscripts would be treated as so much waste paper, that
one of his sons instead of himself would be considered
"the great Bach," and harvest the success he himself
merited, and that after his work had been rediscovered
it would be plunged into the misunderstandings and barbarities of the Age of the Feuilleton, and so on. Similarly, we tend to ascribe to Mozart, while still alive and
flourishing, and producing his soundest work, some
knowledge of his security in the hands of death, some
premonition of the kindness with which death would
embrace him. Where a body of work exists, the historian
cannot help himself; he must sum it up, along with the
life of the creator of that work, as two inseparable halves
of a living unity. So we do with Mozart or with Bach;
so we also do with Knecht, although he belongs to our
essentially uncreative era and has not left behind any
body of work of the same nature as those masters.

In attempting to trace the course of Knecht's life we
are also attempting to interpret it, and although as historians we must deeply regret the scantiness of authenti-

cated information on the last period of his life, we were
nevertheless encouraged to undertake the task precisely
because this last part of Knecht's life has become a
legend. We have taken over this legend and adhere to its
spirit, whether or not it is merely a pious fiction. Just
as we know nothing about Knecht's birth and origins,
we know nothing about his death. But we have not the
slightest reason for assuming that this death could have
been a matter of pure chance. We regard his life, insofar
as it is known, as built up in a clear succession of stages;
and if in our speculations about its end we gladly accept
the legend and faithfully report it, we do so because
what the legend tells us about the last stage of his life
seems to correspond fully with the previous stages. We go
so far as to admit that the manner in which his life drifts
gently off into legend appears to us organic and right,
just as it imposes no strain on our credulity to believe
in the continued existence of a constellation that has vanished below the horizon. Within the world in which we
live—and by we I mean the author of this present work
and the reader—Joseph Knecht reached the summit and
achieved the maximum. As Magister Ludi he became the
leader and prototype of all those who strive toward and
cultivate the things of the mind. He administered and
increased the cultural heritage that had been handed
down to him, for he was high priest of a temple that
is sacred to each and every one of us. But he did more
than attain the realm of a Master, did more than fill the
office at the very summit of our hierarchy. He moved
on beyond it; he grew out of it into a dimension whose
nature we can only reverently guess at. And for that very
reason it seems to us perfectly appropriate, and in keeping with his life, that his biography should also have surpassed the usual dimensions and at the end passed on
into legend. We accept the miracle of this fact and rejoice
in it without any inclination to pry into it interpretively.
But insofar as Knecht's life is historical—and it is that
up to one specific day—we intend to treat it as such. It
has been our endeavor, therefore, to transmit the tradition
exactly as it has been revealed to us by our researches.

Concerning his childhood before he entered the elite
schools, we know only a single incident. It is, however,

one of symbolic importance, for it signifies the first great call of the realm of Mind to him, the voice of his vocation. And it is characteristic that this first call came not from science or scholarship, but from music. We owe this fragment of biography, as we do almost all the recollections of Knecht's personal life, to the jottings of a pupil of the Glass Bead Game, a loyal admirer who kept a record of many of the remarks and stories of his great teacher.

Knecht must have been twelve or thirteen years old at the time. For quite a while he had been a scholarship pupil in the Latin school of Berolfingen, a small town on the fringes of the Zaberwald. Probably Berolfingen was also his birthplace. His teachers at the school, and especially his music teacher, had already recommended him two or three times to the highest Board for admission into the elite schools. But Knecht knew nothing about this and had as yet had no encounters with the elite or with any of the masters of the highest Board of Educators. His music teacher, from whom he was learning violin and the lute, told him that the Music Master would shortly be coming to Berolfingen to inspect music instruction at the school. Therefore Joseph must practice like a good boy and not embarrass his teacher.

The news stirred the boy deeply, for of course he knew quite well who the Music Master was. He was not to be compared with the school inspectors who visited twice a year, coming from somewhere in the higher reaches of the Board of Educators. The Music Master was one of the twelve demigods, one of the twelve supreme heads of this most respected of Boards. In all musical affairs he was the supreme authority for the entire country. To think that the Music Master himself, the Magister Musicae in person, would be coming to Berolfingen! There was only one person in the world whom Joseph might have regarded as still more legendary and mysterious: the Master of the Glass Bead Game.

Joseph was filled in advance with an enormous and timorous reverence for the impending visitor. He imagined the Music Master variously as a king, as one of the Twelve Apostles, or as one of the legendary great artists of classical times, a Michael Praetorius or a Claudio Monteverdi, a J. J. Froberger or Johann Sebastian Bach.

And he looked forward with a joy as deep as his terror to the appearance of this mighty star. That one of the demigods and archangels, one of the mysterious and almighty regents of the world of thought, was to appear in the flesh here in town and in the Latin school; that he was going to see him, and that the Master might possibly speak to him, examine him, reprimand or praise him, was a kind of miracle and rare prodigy in the skies. Moreover, as the teachers assured him, this was to be the first time in decades that a Magister Musicae in person would be visiting the town and the little Latin school. The boy pictured the forthcoming event in a great variety of ways. Above all he imagined a great public festival and a reception such as he had once experienced when a new mayor had taken office, with brass bands and streets strung with banners; there might even be fireworks. Knecht's schoolmates also had such fantasies and hopes. His happy excitement was subdued only by the thought that he himself might come too close to this great man, and that his playing and his answers might be so bad that he would end up unbearably disgraced. But this anxiety was sweet as well as tormenting. Secretly, without admitting it to himself, he did not think the whole eagerly anticipated festival with its flags and fireworks nearly so fine, so entrancing, important, and miraculously delightful as the very possibility that he, little Joseph Knecht, would be seeing this man at close quarters, that in fact the Master was paying this visit to Berolfingen just a little on his, Joseph's, account—for he was after all coming to examine the state of musical instruction, and the music teacher obviously thought it possible that the Master would examine him as well.

But perhaps it would not come to that—alas, it probably would not. After all, it was hardly possible. The Master would have better things to do than to listen to a small boy's violin playing. He would probably want to see and hear only the older, more advanced pupils.

Such were the boy's thoughts as he awaited the day. And the day, when it came, began with a disappointment. No music blared in the streets, no flags and garlands hung from the houses. As on every other day, Joseph had to gather up his books and notebooks and go to the ordinary classes. And even in the classroom there was not the slightest sign of decoration or festivity. Everything was ordinary and normal. Class began; the teacher wore his everyday smock; he made no speeches, did not so much as mention the great guest of honor.

But during the second or third hour the guest came nevertheless. There was a knock at the door; the school janitor came in and informed the teacher that Joseph Knecht was to present himself to the music teacher in fifteen minutes. And he had better make sure that his hair was decently combed and his hands and fingernails clean.

Knecht turned pale with fright. He stumbled from the classroom, ran to the dormitory, put down his books, washed and combed his hair. Trembling, he took his violin case and his book of exercises. With a lump in his throat, he made his way to the music rooms in the annex. An excited schoolmate met him on the stairs, pointed to a practice room, and told him: "You're supposed to wait here till they call you."

The wait was short, but seemed to him an eternity. No one called him, but a man entered the room. A very old man, it seemed to him at first, not very tall, white-haired, with a fine, clear face and penetrating, light-blue eyes. The gaze of those eyes might have been frightening, but they were serenely cheerful as well as penetrating, neither laughing nor smiling, but filled with a calm, quietly radiant cheerfulness. He shook hands with the boy, nodded, and sat down with deliberation on the stool in front of the old practice piano. "You are Joseph Knecht?" he said. "Your teacher seems content with you. I think he is fond of you. Come, let's make a little music together."

Knecht had already taken out his violin. The old man struck the A, and the boy tuned. Then he looked inquiringly, anxiously, at the Music Master.

"What would you like to play?" the Master asked.

The boy could not say a word. He was filled to the brim with awe of the old man. Never had he seen a person like this. Hesitantly, he picked up his exercise book and held it out to the Master.

"No," the Master said, "I want you to play from

memory, and not an exercise but something easy that you know by heart. Perhaps a song you like."

Knecht was confused, and so enchanted by this face and those eyes that he could not answer. He was deeply ashamed of his confusion, but unable to speak. The Master did not insist. With one finger, he struck the first notes of a melody, and looked questioningly at the boy. Joseph nodded and at once played the melody with pleasure. It was one of the old songs which were often sung in school.

"Once more," the Master said.

Knecht repeated the melody, and the old man now played a second voice to go with it. Now the old song rang through the small practice room in two parts.

"Once more."

Knecht played, and the Master played the second part, and a third part also. Now the beautiful old song rang through the room in three parts.

"Once more." And the Master played three voices along with the melody.

"A lovely song," the Master said softly. "Play it again, in the alto this time."

The Master gave him the first note, and Knecht played, the Master accompanying with the other three voices. Again and again the Master said, "Once more," and each time he sounded merrier. Knecht played the melody in the tenor, each time accompanied by two or three parts. They played the song many times, and with every repetition the song was involuntarily enriched with embellishments and variations. The bare little room resounded festively in the cheerful light of the forenoon.

After a while the old man stopped. "Is that enough?" he asked. Knecht shook his head and began again. The Master chimed in gaily with his three voices, and the four parts drew their thin, lucid lines, spoke to one another, mutually supported, crossed, and wove around one another in delightful windings and figurations. The boy and the old man ceased to think of anything else; they surrendered themselves to the lovely, congenial lines and figurations they formed as their parts crisscrossed. Caught in the network their music was creating, they swayed gently along with it, obeying an unseen conductor. Finally, when the melody had come to an end once more, the Master turned his head and asked: "Did you like that, Joseph?"

Gratefully, his face glowing, Knecht looked at him. He was radiant, but still speechless.

"Do you happen to know what a fugue is?" the Master now asked.

Knecht looked dubious. He had already heard fugues, but had not yet studied them in class.

"Very well," the Master said, "then I'll show you. You'll grasp it quicker if we make a fugue ourselves. Now then, the first thing we need for a fugue is a theme, and we don't have to look far for the theme. We'll take it from our song."

He played a brief phrase, a fragment of the song's melody. It sounded strange, cut out in that way, without head or tail. He played the theme once more, and this time he went on to the first entrance; the second entrance changed the interval of a fifth to a fourth; the third repeated the first an octave higher, as did the fourth with the second. The exposition concluded with a cadence in the key of the dominant. The second working-out modulated more freely to other keys; the third, tending toward the subdominant, ended with a cadence on the tonic.

The boy looked at the player's clever white fingers, saw the course of the development faintly mirrored in his concentrated expression, while his eyes remained quiet under half-closed lids. Joseph's heart swelled with veneration, with love for the Master. His ear drank in the fugue; it seemed to him that he was hearing music for the first time in his life. Behind the music being created in his presence he sensed the world of Mind, the joy-giving harmony of law and freedom, of service and rule. He surrendered himself, and vowed to serve that world and this Master. In those few minutes he saw himself and his life, saw the whole cosmos guided, ordered, and interpreted by the spirit of music. And when the playing had come to an end, he saw this magician and king for whom he felt so intense a reverence pause for a little while longer, slightly bowed over the keys, with half-closed eyes, his face softly glowing from within.

Joseph did not know whether he ought to rejoice at the
bliss of this moment, or weep because it was over.

The old man slowly raised himself from the piano stool,
fixed those cheerful blue eyes piercingly and at the same
time with unimaginable friendliness upon him, and said:
"Making music together is the best way for two people
to become friends. There is none easier. That is a fine
thing. I hope you and I shall remain friends. Perhaps
you too will learn how to make fugues, Joseph."

He shook hands with Joseph and took his leave. But in
the doorway he turned once more and gave Joseph a
parting greeting, with a look and a ceremonious little inclination of his head.

Many years later Knecht told his pupil that when he
stepped out of the building, he found the town and the
world far more transformed and enchanted than if there
had been flags, garlands, and streamers, or displays of
fireworks. He had experienced his vocation, which may
surely be spoken of as a sacrament. The ideal world,
which hitherto his young soul had known only by hearsay and in wild dreams, had suddenly taken on visible
lineaments for him. Its gates had opened invitingly. This
world, he now saw, did not exist only in some vague,
remote past or future; it was here and was active; it
glowed, sent messengers, apostles, ambassadors, men like
this old Magister (who by the way was not nearly so old
as he then seemed to Joseph). And through this venerable messenger an admonition and a call had come from
that world even to him, the insignificant Latin school
pupil.

Such was the meaning of the experience for him. It took
weeks before he actually realized, and was convinced,
that the magical events of that sacramental hour corresponded to a precise event in the real world, that the
summons was not just a sense of happiness and admonition in his own soul and his own conscience, but a show
of favor and an exhortation from the earthly powers. For
in the long run it could not be concealed that the Music
Master's visit had been neither a matter of chance nor a
real inspection of the school. Rather, Knecht's name had
stood for some time on the lists of pupils who seemed
deserving of education in the elite school. At any rate,

on the basis of his teachers' reports he had been so recommended to the Board of Educators. The boy had been recommended for good character and as a Latinist, but the highest praise had come from his music teacher. Therefore the Music Master had chosen to stop off for a few hours in Berolfingen, in the course of an official mission, in order to see this pupil. In his examination he was not so much interested in Joseph's Latin or his fingering (in these matters he relied on the teachers' reports, which he nevertheless spent an hour going over) as whether the boy had it in him by nature to become a musician in the higher sense of the word, whether he had the capacity for enthusiasm, subordination, reverence, worshipful service. As a rule, and for very good reasons, the teachers in the public schools were anything but liberal in their recommendations of pupils for the "elite." Nevertheless, now and then someone would be pushed out of more or less unsavory motives. Quite often, too, from sheer lack of insight a teacher would stubbornly recommend some pet pupil who had few virtues aside from diligence, ambition, and a certain shrewdness in his conduct toward the teachers. The Music Master particularly disliked this kind of boy. He could tell at once whether a pupil was aware that his future career was at stake, and woe to the boy who approached him too adroitly, too cannily, too cleverly, let alone one who tried to flatter him. In a good many cases such candidates were rejected without even an examination.

Knecht, on the other hand, had delighted the old Music Master. He had liked him very much. As he continued his journey he recalled the boy with pleasure. He had made no notes and entered no marks for him in his notebook, but he took with him the memory of the unspoiled, modest boy, and upon his return he inscribed his name in his own hand on the list of pupils who had been examined personally by a member of the Board of Educators and been found worthy of admission.

Joseph had occasionally heard talk in school about this list, and in a great variety of tones. The pupils called it "the golden book," but sometimes they disrespectfully referred to it as the "climbers' catalogue." Whenever a teacher mentioned the list—if only to remind a pupil that

a lout like him could never hope to win a place on it—
there would be a note of solemnity, of respect, and also
of self-importance in his voice. But if the pupils mentioned the catalogue, they usually spoke in a jeering tone
and with somewhat exaggerated indifference. Once Joseph
had heard a schoolmate say: "Go on, what do I care
about that stupid climbers' catalogue. You won't see a
regular feller's name on it, that's one sure thing. The
teachers keep it for all the worst grinds and creeps."

A curious period followed Joseph's wonderful experience
with the Music Master. He still did not know that he now
belonged to the *electi*, to the *flos juventutis*, as the elite
pupils were called in the Order. At first it did not enter
his mind that there might be practical consequences and
tangible effects of the episode upon his general destiny
or his daily life. While for his teachers he was already
marked by distinction and on the verge of departure, he
himself was conscious of his call almost entirely as a
process within himself. Even so, it made a clear dividing
line in his life. Although the hour with the sorcerer (as
he often thought of the Music Master) had only brought
to fruition, or brought closer, something he had already
sensed in his own heart, that hour nevertheless clearly
separated the past from the present and the future—just
as an awakened dreamer, even if he wakes up in the
same surroundings that he has seen in his dream, cannot
really doubt that he is now awake. There are many types
and kinds of vocation, but the core of the experience is
always the same: the soul is awakened by it, transformed
or exalted, so that instead of dreams and presentiments
from within a summons comes from without. A portion
of reality presents itself and makes its claim.

In this case the portion of reality had been the Music
Master. This remote, venerated demigod, this archangel
from the highest spheres of heaven, had appeared in the
flesh. Joseph had seen his omniscient blue eyes. He had sat
on the stool at the practice piano, had made music with
Joseph, made music wonderfully; almost without words
he had shown him what music really was, had blessed
him, and vanished.

For the present Joseph was incapable of reflecting on
possible practical consequences, on all that might flow

out of this event, for he was much too preoccupied with
the immediate reverberations of it within himself. Like
a young plant hitherto quietly and intermittently developing which suddenly begins to breathe harder and to
grow, as though in a miraculous hour it has become
aware of the law which shapes it and begins to strive
toward the fulfillment of its being, the boy, touched by
the magician's hand, began rapidly and eagerly to gather
and tauten his energies. He felt changed, growing; he
felt new tensions and new harmonies between himself
and the world. There were times, now, in music, Latin,
and mathematics, when he could master tasks that were
still far beyond his age and the scope of his schoolmates.
Sometimes he felt capable of any achievements. At other
times he might forget everything and daydream with a
new softness and surrender, listen to the wind or the rain,
gaze into the chalice of a flower or the moving waters
of the river, understanding nothing, divining everything,
lost in sympathy, curiosity, the craving to comprehend,
carried away from his own self toward another, toward
the world, toward the mystery and sacrament, the at
once painful and lovely disporting of the world of appearances.

Thus, beginning from within and growing toward the
meeting and confirmation of self and world, the vocation
of Joseph Knecht developed in perfect purity. He passed
through all its stages, tasted all its joys and anxieties.
Unhampered by sudden revelations and indiscretions,
the sublime process moved to its conclusion. His was the
typical evolution of every noble mind; working and growing harmoniously and at the same tempo, the inner self
and the outer world approached each other. At the end
of these developments the boy became aware of his
situation and of the fate that awaited him. He realized
that his teachers were treating him like a colleague, even
like a guest of honor whose departure is expected at any
moment, and that his schoolmates were half admiring or
envying him, half avoiding or even distrusting him. Some
of his enemies now openly mocked and hated him, and
he found himself more and more separated from and deserted by former friends. But by then the same process
of separation and isolation had been completed within

himself. His own feelings had taught him to regard the teachers more and more as associates rather than superiors; his former friends had become temporary companions of the road, now left behind. He no longer felt that he was among equals in his school and his town. He was no longer in the right place. Everything he had known had become permeated by a hidden death, a solvent of unreality, a sense of belonging to the past. It had all become a makeshift, like worn-out clothing that no longer fitted. And as the end of his stay at the Latin school approached, this slow outgrowing of a beloved and harmonious home town, this shedding of a way of life no longer right for him, this living on the verge of departure—interspersed though the mood of parting was by moments of supreme rejoicing and radiant self-assurance—became a terrible torment to him, an almost intolerable pressure and suffering. For everything was slipping from him without his being sure that it was not really himself who was abandoning everything. He could not say whether he should not be blaming himself for this perishing and estrangement of his dear and accustomed world. Perhaps he had killed it by ambition, by arrogance, by pride, by disloyalty and lack of love. Among the pangs inherent in a genuine vocation, these are the bitterest. One who has received the call takes, in accepting it, not only a gift and a commandment, but also something akin to guilt. Similarly, the soldier who is snatched from the ranks of his comrades and raised to the status of officer is the worthier of promotion, the more he pays for it with a feeling of guilty conscience toward his comrades.

Joseph Knecht, however, had the good fortune to go through this evolution undisturbed and in utter innocence. When at last the faculty informed him of his distinction and his impending admission to the elite schools, he was for the moment completely surprised, although a moment later this novelty seemed to him something he had long known and been expecting. Yet only now did he recall that for weeks the word *electus,* or "elite boy," had now and again been sneeringly called out behind his back. He had heard it, but only half heard, and had never imagined it as anything but a taunt. He had taken it to mean not that his schoolmates were actually calling him an *electus*, but that they were jeering: "You're so stuck up you think you're an *electus*." Occasionally he had suffered from the gulf that had opened between himself and his schoolmates, but in fact he would never have considered himself an *electus*. He had become conscious of the call not as a rise in rank, but only as an inward admonition and encouragement. And yet—in spite of everything, had he not known it all along, divined it, felt it again and again? Now it had come; his raptures were confirmed, made legitimate; his suffering had had meaning; the clothing he had worn, by now unbearably old and too tight, could be discarded at last. A new suit was waiting for him.

With his admission into the elite, Knecht's life was transferred to a different plane. The first and decisive step in his development had been taken. It is by no means the rule for all elite pupils that official admission to the elite coincides with the inner experience of vocation. That is a matter of grace, or to put it in banal terms, sheer good fortune. The young man to whom it does happen starts out with an advantage, just as it is an advantage to be endowed with felicitous qualities of body and soul. Almost all elite pupils regard their election as a piece of great good fortune, a distinction they are proud of, and a great many of them have previously felt an ardent longing for that distinction. But for most of the elect the transition from the ordinary schools of their home towns to the schools of Castalia comes harder than they had imagined, and entails a good many unexpected disappointments. Especially for pupils who were happy and loved in their homes, the change represents a very difficult parting and renunciation. The result is a rather considerable number of transfers back home, especially during the first two elite years. The reason for these is not a lack of talent and industry, but the inability of the pupils to adapt to boarding-school life and to the idea of more and more severing their ties to family and home until ultimately they would cease to know and to respect any allegiance other than to the Order.

On the other hand, there were occasionally pupils for

whom admission to the elite schools meant above all freedom from home or an oppressive school, from an oversevere father, say, or a disagreeable teacher. These youngsters breathed easier for a while, but they had expected such vast and impossible changes in their whole life that disillusionment soon followed.

The real climbers and model pupils, the young pedants, could also not always hold their own in Castalia. Not that they would have been unable to cope with their studies. But in the elite, studies and marks were not the only criterion. There were other pedagogical and artistic goals which sometimes proved too much for such pupils. Nevertheless, within the system of four great elite schools with their numerous subdivisions and branch institutions there was room for a great variety of talents, and an aspiring mathematician or a student of languages and literatures, if he really had the makings of a scholar, would not be misprized for a lack of musical or philosophical talent. Even in Castalia, in fact, there were at times very strong tendencies toward cultivation of the pure, sober disciplines, and the advocates of such tendencies not only denigrated the "visionaries," that is, the devotees of music and the other arts, but even sometimes went so far as to forswear and ban, within their own circle, everything artistic, and especially the Glass Bead Game.

Since all that is known to us of Knecht's life took place in Castalia, in that most tranquil and serene region of our mountainous country, which in the old days used to be called, in the poet Goethe's phrase, "the pedagogical province," we shall at the risk of boring the reader with matters long familiar once more briefly sketch the character of famous Castalia and the structure of her schools. These schools, for brevity known as the elite schools, constitute a wise and flexible system by means of which the administration (a Council of Studies consisting of twenty councillors, ten representing the Board of Educators and ten representing the Order) draws candidates from among the most gifted pupils in the various sections and schools of the country, in order to supply new generations for the Order and for all the important offices in the secondary school system and the universities. The

multitude of ordinary schools, gymnasia, and other schools
in the country, whether technical or humanistic in
character, are for more than ninety per cent of our students preparatory schools for the professions. They ter-
minate with an entrance examination for the university.
At the university there is a specific course of study for
each subject. Such is the standard curriculum for our students, as everyone knows. These schools make reasonably strict demands and do their best to exclude the un-
talented.

But alongside or above these schools we have the system of elite schools, to which only the pupils of extraordinary gifts and character are admitted. Entrance to
them is not controlled by examinations. Instead, the elite
pupils are chosen by their teachers, according to their
judgment, and are recommended to the Castalian authorities. One day a teacher suggests to a child of eleven
or twelve that if he wished he could perhaps enter one
of the Castalian schools next semester. Does he feel
attracted by the idea; does he feel any vocation for it?
The boy is given time to think it over. If he then agrees,
and if the unqualified consent of both parents is obtained,
one of the elite schools admits him on probation. The
directors and the highest-level teachers of these elite
schools (by no means the faculties of the universities)
form the Board of Educators, which has charge of all
education and all intellectual organizations in the country. Once a boy becomes an elite pupil (and assuming
he does not fail any of the courses, in which case he
is sent back to the ordinary schools) he no longer has
to prepare for a profession or some specialty that will
subsequently become his livelihood. Rather, the Order
and the hierarchy of academics are recruited from among
the elite pupils, everyone from the grammar school
teachers to the highest officers, the twelve Directors of
Studies, also called Masters, and the Ludi Magister, the
director of the Glass Bead Game.

As a rule, the last courses in the elite schools are completed between the ages of twenty-two and twenty-five.
The graduate is then admitted to the Order. Thereafter,
all educational and research institutions of the Order and
of the Board of Educators are available to the former elite

pupils, all the libraries, archives, laboratories, and so on, together with a large staff of teachers if they desire further study, and all the facilities of the Glass Bead Game. A degree of specialization begins even during the school years. In the upper ranges of the elite schools those who show special aptitudes for languages, philosophy, mathematics, or whatever are shifted to the curriculum which provides the best nourishment for their talents. Most of these pupils end up as subject teachers in the public schools and universities. They remain, even though they have left Castalia, members of the Order for life. That is to say, they stand at an austere remove from the "normals" (those who were not educated in the elite schools) and can never—unless they resign the Order—become professional men, such as doctors, lawyers, engineers, and so on. They are subject for life to the rules of the Order, which include poverty and bachelorhood. The common people call them in a half-derisive, half-respectful tone "the mandarins."

Thus the bulk of former elite pupils find their ultimate destiny as schoolmasters. The tiny remainder, the top flight of the Castalian schools, can devote themselves to free study for as long as they please. A contemplative, diligent intellectual life is reserved for them. Many a highly gifted person who for one reason or another, perhaps some physical defect or quirk of character, is not suited to become a teacher or to hold a responsible post in the superior or inferior Boards of Educators, may go on studying, researching, or collecting throughout his life as a pensioner of the authorities. His contribution to society then consists mostly of works of pure scholarship. Some are placed as advisers to dictionary committees, archives, libraries, and so on; others pursue scholarship as art for art's sake. A good many of them have devoted their lives to highly abstruse and sometimes peculiar subjects, such as Lodovicus Crudelis who toiled for thirty years translating all extant ancient Egyptian texts into both Greek and Sanscrit, or the somewhat peculiar Chattus Calvensis II who has bequeathed to us four immense folio volumes on *The Pronunciation of Latin in the Universities of Southern Italy toward the End of the Twelfth Century*. This work was intended as Part One of a *History of the*

Pronunciation of Latin from the Twelfth to the Sixteenth Centuries. But in spite of its one thousand manuscript pages, it has remained a fragment, for no one has carried on the work.

It is understandable that there has been a good deal of joking about purely learned works of this type. Their actual value for the future of scholarship and for the people as a whole cannot be demonstrated. Nevertheless, scholarship, as was true for art in the olden days, must indeed have far-flung grazing grounds, and in pursuit of a subject which interests no one but himself a scholar can accumulate knowledge which provides colleagues with information as valuable as that stored in a dictionary or an archive.

As far as possible, scholarly works such as the above-mentioned were printed. The real scholars were left in almost total freedom to ply their studies and their Games, and no one objected that a good many of their works seemed to bring no immediate benefits to the people or the community and, inevitably, seemed to nonscholars merely luxurious frivolities. A good many of these scholars have been smiled at for the nature of their studies, but none has ever been reproved, let alone had his privileges withdrawn. Nor were they merely tolerated; they enjoyed the respect of the populace, in spite of being the butts of many jokes. This respect was founded on the sacrifice with which all members of the scholarly community paid for their intellectual privileges. They had many amenities; they had a modest allotment of food, clothing, and shelter; they had splendid libraries, collections, and laboratories at their disposal. But in return they renounced lush living, marriage, and family. As a monastic community they were excluded from competition in the world. They owned no property, received no titles and honors, and in material things had to content themselves with a very simple life. If one wanted to expend the years of his life deciphering a single ancient inscription, he was free to do so, and would even be helped. But if he desired good living, rich clothing, money, or titles, he found these things inexorably barred. Those for whom such gratifications were important usually returned to "the world" quite young; they be-

came paid teachers or tutors or journalists; they married
or in other ways sought out a life to suit their tastes.

When the time came for Joseph Knecht to leave
Berolfingen, it was his music teacher who accompanied
him to the railroad station. Saying good-by to this teacher
was painful, and his heart also swelled a little with a
feeling of loneliness and uncertainty after the train
started and the whitewashed stepped gable of the old
castle tower dropped out of sight and did not reappear.
Many another pupil has set out on this first journey with
far more turbulent feelings, frightened and in tears. Joseph
had inwardly already transferred his allegiance; he withstood the journey well. And he did not have far to go.
He had been assigned to the Eschholz school. There
had been pictures of this school hanging in his principal's
office. Eschholz was the largest and the newest complex
of schools in Castalia. The buildings were all modern.
There was no town in the vicinity, only a village-like
small settlement set among woods. Beyond the settlement
the school spread out, wide, level, and cheerful, the
buildings enclosing a large open quadrangle. In the center
of the quadrangle, arranged like the five on a die, five
enormous, stately trees raised their dark cones to the
sky. The huge rectangle was partly in lawn, partly in
gravel, its expanse broken only by two large swimming
pools, fed by running water. Wide, shallow steps led
down to the pools. At the entrance to this sunny plaza
stood the schoolhouse, the only tall building in the complex. There were two wings, each flanked by a five-
columned portico. All the rest of the buildings enclosing
the quadrangle were very low, flat, and unadorned,
divided into perfectly equal sections, each of which led
out into the plaza through an arcade and down a low
flight of steps. Pots of flowers stood in the openings of
most of the arcades.
In keeping with Castalian custom, Joseph was not received by a school attendant and taken to a principal or
a committee of teachers. Instead, a schoolmate met him,
a tall, good-looking boy in clothes of blue linen, a few
years older than Joseph. He shook hands, saying, "My
name is Oscar; I'm the senior boy in Hellas House,

where you will be living. I've been assigned to welcome you and show you around. You're not expected to attend classes until tomorrow, so we have plenty of time to look around. You'll get the hang of things soon enough. And until you have become adjusted, please consider me your friend and mentor, and your protector as well, in case some of the fellows bother you. There are always some who think they have to haze the new boys a little. But it won't be bad, take it from me. I'll show you Hellas House first, so you'll see where you're going to live."

Thus, in the traditional fashion, Oscar greeted the newcomer; the housemaster had appointed him Joseph's mentor, and he in fact made an effort to play his part well. It is, after all, a part the seniors usually find congenial, and if a fifteen-year-old takes the trouble to charm a thirteen-year-old by employing a tone of affable comradeship with a touch of patronage, he will almost always succeed. During Joseph's first few days his mentor treated him like a guest whom a courteous host pampers in the hope that he will, should he happen to depart the next day, take away with him a good impression of host and house.

Joseph was shown to a room which he would be sharing with two other boys. He was served rusks and a cup of fruit juice. He was shown the whole of Hellas House, one of the dormitories of the large quadrangle; he was shown where to hang his towel in the steam bath, and in which corner he was allowed to keep potted plants, if he wanted them. Before evening fell he was also taken to the launderer at the washhouse, where a blue linen suit was selected and fitted for him.

From the very first Joseph felt at ease in the place. He gaily fell in with Oscar's tone and showed only the slightest trace of bashfulness, although he naturally regarded this older boy, who had obviously been at home in Castalia for a long time, as something of a demigod. He even enjoyed the bits of showing-off, as when Oscar would weave a complicated Greek quotation into his talk only to recall politely that the new boy of course couldn't understand, naturally not, how could he be expected to!

In any case, life at a boarding school was nothing new
to Joseph. He fitted in without difficulty. For that matter,
no important events of his years at Eschholz have been
recorded. The terrible fire in the schoolhouse must have
happened after his time. Portions of his scholastic
record have been traced; they show that he occasionally
had the highest marks in music and Latin, and somewhat above average in mathematics and Greek. Now
and then there are entries about him in the "House
Book," such as *ingenium valde capax, studia non an-
gusta, mores probantur* or *ingenium felix et profec-
tuum avidissimum, moribus placet officiosis*." What
punishments he received at Eschholz can no longer be
determined; the disciplinary register was lost in the fire,
along with so much else. There is the testimony of a
fellow pupil that during the four years at Eschholz
Knecht was punished only once (by being excluded
from the weekly outing), and that his demerit had consisted in obstinately refusing to name a schoolmate who
had done something against the rules. The anecdote
sounds plausible. Knecht undoubtedly was always a
good comrade and never servile toward his superiors.
Nevertheless, it seems highly unlikely that this was
actually his sole punishment in four years.

Since our data on Knecht's early period in the elite
school are so sparse, we cite a passage from one of his
later lectures on the Glass Bead Game. Knecht's own
manuscripts of these lectures for beginners are not
available, it should be noted; he delivered them ex-
temporaneously, and a pupil took them down in shorthand. At one point Knecht speaks about analogies and
associations in the Glass Bead Game, and in regard to the
latter distinguishes between "legitimate," universally
comprehensible associations and those that are "private"
or subjective. He remarks: "To give you an example of
private associations that do not forfeit their private value
although they have no place in the Glass Bead Game, I
shall tell you of one such association that goes back to
my own schooldays. I was about fourteen years old, and
it was the season when spring is already in the air, Feb-
ruary or March. One afternoon a schoolmate invited
me to go out with him to cut a few elder switches. He

wanted to use them as pipes for a model water mill. We set out, and it must have been an unusually beautiful day in the world or in my own mind, for it has remained in my memory, and vouchsafed me a little experience. The ground was wet, but free of snow; strong green shoots were already breaking through on the edge of streams. Buds and the first opening catkins were already lending a tinge of color to the bare bushes, and the air was full of scent, a scent imbued with life and with contradictions. There were smells of damp soil, decaying leaves, and young growth; any moment one expected to smell the first violets although there were none yet.

"We came to the elder bushes. They had tiny buds, but no leaves, and as I cut off a twig, a powerful, bitter-sweet scent wafted toward me. It seemed to gather and multiply all the other smells of spring within itself. I was completely stunned by it; I smelled my knife, smelled my hand, smelled the elder twig. It was the sap that gave off so insistent and irresistible a fragrance. We did not talk about it, but my friend also thoughtfully smelled for a long time. The fragrance meant something to him also.

"Well now, every experience has its element of magic. In this case the onset of spring, which had enthralled me as I walked over the wet, squishing meadows and smelled the soil and the buds, had now been concentrated into a sensual symbol by the *fortissimo* of that elder shrub's fragrance. Possibly I would never have forgotten this scent even if the experience had remained isolated. Rather, every future encounter with that smell deep into my old age would in all probability have revived the memory of that first time I had consciously experienced the fragrance. But now a second element entered in. At that time I had found an old volume of music at my piano teacher's. It was a volume of songs by Franz Schubert, and it exerted a strong attraction upon me. I had leafed through it one time when I had a rather long wait for the teacher, and had asked to borrow it for a few days. In my leisure hours I gave myself up to the ecstasy of discovery. Up to that time I had not known Schubert at all, and I was totally captivated by him. And now, on the day of that walk to the elderberry bush or the day after, I discovered Schubert's spring song, *"Die linden Lüfte sind erwacht,"* and the first chords of the piano accompaniment assailed me like something already familiar. Those chords had exactly the same fragrance as the sap of the young elder, just as bittersweet, just as strong and compressed, just as full of the forthcoming spring. From that time on the association of earliest spring, fragrance of elder, Schubert chords has been fixed and absolutely valid, for me. As soon as the first chord is struck I immediately smell the tartness of the sap, and both together mean to me: spring is on the way.

"This private association of mine is a precious possession I would not willingly give up. But the fact that two sensual experiences leap up every time I think, 'spring is coming'—that fact is my own personal affair. It can be communicated, certainly, as I have communicated it to you just now. But it cannot be transmitted. I can make you understand my association, but I cannot so affect a single one of you that my private association will become a valid symbol for you in your turn, a mechanism which infallibly reacts on call and always follows the same course."

One of Knecht's fellow pupils, who later rose to the rank of First Archivist of the Glass Bead Game, maintained that Knecht on the whole had been a merry boy, though without a trace of boisterousness. When playing music he would sometimes have a wonderfully rapt, blissful expression. He was rarely seen in an excited or passionate mood, except at the rhythmic ball game, which he loved. But there were times when this friendly, healthy boy attracted attention, and gave rise to mockery or anxiety. This happened when pupils were dismissed, a fairly frequent occurrence in the lower classes of the elite schools. The first time a classmate was missing from classes and games, did not return next day, and word went around that he was not sick but dismissed, had already departed and would not be returning, Knecht was more than subdued. For days on end he seemed to be distraught.

Years later he himself commented on this matter: "Every time a pupil was sent back from Eschholz and left us, I felt as if someone had died. If I had been asked

the reason for my sorrow, I would have said that I felt
pity for the poor fellow who had spoiled his future by
frivolity and laziness, and that there was also an element
of anxiety in my feeling, fear that this might possibly happen to me some day. Only after I had experienced the
same thing many times, and basically no longer believed
that the same fate could overtake me as well, did I begin
to see somewhat more deeply into the matter. I then
no longer felt the expulsion of an *electus* merely as a
misfortune and punishment. I came to realize that the
dismissed boys in a good many cases were quite glad to
be returning home. I felt that it was no longer solely a
matter of judgment and punishment, but that the 'world'
out there, from which we *electi* had all come once upon
a time, had not abruptly ceased to exist as it had seemed
to me. Rather, for a good many among us it remained a
great and attractive reality which tempted and ultimately
recalled these boys. And perhaps it was that not only for
individuals, but for all of us; perhaps it was by no means
only the weaker and inferior souls upon whom the remote world exerted so strong an attraction. Possibly the
apparent relapse they had suffered was not a fall and a
cause for suffering, but a leap forward and a positive
act. Perhaps we who were so good about remaining in
Eschholz were in fact the weaklings and the cowards."

As we shall see, these thoughts were to return to him,
and very forcefully.

Every encounter with the Music Master was a great
joy to him. The Master came to Eschholz once every two
or three months at least to supervise the music classes.
He also frequently stayed a few days as the guest of one
of the teachers who was a close friend. Once he personally conducted the final rehearsals for the performance
of a vesper by Monteverdi. But above all he kept an eye
on the more talented of the music pupils, and Knecht
was among the honored recipients of his paternal friendship. Every so often he would sit at the piano with
Joseph in one of the practice rooms and go through the
works of his favorite composers with him, or else play
over a classical example from one of the old handbooks
on the theory of composition. "To construct a canon with
the Music Master, or to hear him develop a badly con-

structed one to its absurd logical conclusion, frequently had about it a solemnity, or I might also say, a gaiety, like nothing else in the world. Sometimes one could scarcely contain one's tears, and sometimes one could not stop laughing. One emerged from a private music lesson with him as from a bath or a massage."

Knecht's schooldays at Eschholz at last drew to a close. Along with a dozen or so other pupils of his level he was to be transferred to a school on the next stage or level. The principal delivered the usual speech to these candidates, describing once again the significance and the rules of the Castalian schools and more or less sketching for the graduates, in the name of the Order, the path they would be traveling, at the end of which they would be qualified to enter the Order themselves. This solemn address was part of the program for a day of ceremonies and festivities during which teachers and fellow pupils alike treat the graduates like guests. On such days there are always carefully prepared performances—this time it was a great seventeenth-century cantata—and the Music Master had come in order to hear it.

After the principal's address, while everyone was on the way to the bravely bedecked dining hall, Knecht approached the Master with a question. "The principal," he said, "told us how things are outside of Castalia, in the ordinary schools and colleges. He said that the students at the universities study for the 'free' professions. If I understood him rightly, these are professions we do not even have here in Castalia. What is the meaning of that? Why are just those professions called 'free'? And why should we Castalians be excluded from them?"

The Magister Musicae drew the young man aside and stood with him under one of the giant trees. An almost sly smile puckered the skin around his eyes into little wrinkles as he replied: "Your name is Knecht,* my friend, and perhaps for that reason the word 'free' is so alluring for you. But do not take it too seriously in this case. When the non-Castalians speak of the free professions, the word may sound very serious and even inspiring. But when we use it, we intend it ironically. Freedom

---

* Serf, servant.

exists in those professions only to the extent that the student chooses the profession himself. That produces an appearance of freedom, although in most cases the choice is made less by the student than by his family, and many a father would sooner bite off his tongue than really allow his son free choice. But perhaps that is a slander; let us drop this objection. Let us say that the freedom exists, but it is limited to the one unique act of choosing the profession. Afterward all freedom is over. When he begins his studies at the university, the doctor, lawyer, or engineer is forced into an extremely rigid curriculum which ends with a series of examinations. If he passes them, he receives his license and can thereafter pursue his profession in seeming freedom. But in doing so he becomes the slave of base powers; he is dependent on success, on money, on his ambition, his hunger for fame, on whether or not people like him. He must submit to elections, must earn money, must take part in the ruthless competition of castes, families, political parties, newspapers. In return he has the freedom to become successful and well-to-do, and to be hated by the unsuccessful, or vice versa. For the elite pupil and later member of the Order, everything is the other way around. He does not 'choose' any profession. He does not imagine that he is a better judge of his own talents than are his teachers. He accepts the place and the function within the hierarchy that his superiors choose for him—if, that is, the matter is not reversed and the qualities, gifts, and faults of the pupil compel the teachers to send him to one place or another. In the midst of this seeming unfreedom every *electus* enjoys the greatest imaginable freedom after his early courses. Whereas the man in the 'free' professions must submit to a narrow and rigid course of studies with rigid examinations in order to train for his future career, the *electus*, as soon as he begins studying independently, enjoys so much freedom that there are many who all their lives choose the most abstruse and frequently almost foolish studies, and may continue without hindrance as long as their conduct does not degenerate. The natural teacher is employed as teacher, the natural educator as educator, the natural translator as translator; each, as if of his own accord, finds his way to the place in which he can serve, and in serving be free. Moreover, for the rest of his life he is saved from that 'freedom' of career which means such terrible slavery. He knows nothing of the struggle for money, fame, rank; he recognizes no parties, no dichotomy between the individual and the office, between what is private and what is public; he feels no dependence upon success. Now do you see, my son, that when we speak of the free professions, the word 'free' is meant rather humorously."

Knecht's departure from Eschholz marked the end of an era in his life. If hitherto he had lived a happy childhood, in a willing subordination and harmony almost without problems, there now began a period of struggle, development, and complex difficulties. He was about seventeen years old when he was informed of his impending transfer. A number of his classmates received the same announcement, and for a short while there was no more important question among the elect, and none more discussed, than the place to which each of them would be transplanted. In keeping with tradition, they were told only a few days before their departure, and between the graduation ceremony and departure there were several days of vacation.

During this vacation something splendid happened to Knecht. The Music Master proposed he take a walking trip and visit him, spending a few days as his guest. That was a great and rare honor. Early one morning Knecht set out with a fellow graduate—for he was still considered an Eschholz pupil, and at this level boys were not allowed to travel alone. They tramped toward the forest and the mountains, and when after three hours of steady climbing through shady woods they reached a treeless summit, they saw far below them, already small and easy to grasp as a whole, their Eschholz, recognizable even at this distance by the dark mass of the five giant trees, the quadrangle with its segments of lawn and sparkling pools, the tall schoolhouse, the service buildings, the village, the famous grove of ash trees from which the school took its name. The two youths stood still, looking down. A good many of us cherish the memory of this lovely view; it was then not very different from the way it looks today, for the buildings were rebuilt after the great fire, and three of the five tall trees survived the blaze. They saw their school lying below them, their home for many years, to which they would soon be bidding good-by, and both of them felt their hearts contract at the sight.

"I think I've never before really seen how beautiful it is," Joseph's companion said. "But I suppose it's because I'm seeing it for the first time as something I must leave and say farewell to."

"That's exactly it," Knecht said. "You're right, I feel the same way. But even though we are going away, we won't after all be leaving Eschholz. Only the ones who have gone away forever have really left it, like Otto, for instance, who could make up such funny bits of Latin doggerel, or Charlemagne, who could swim so long under water, and the others. They really said farewell and broke away. It's a long time since I've thought about them, but now they come back to me. Laugh at me if you like, but in spite of everything there's something impressive to me about those apostates, just as there is a grandeur about the fallen angel Lucifer. Perhaps they did the wrong thing, or rather, undoubtedly they did the wrong thing, but all the same they did something, accomplished something; they ventured a leap, and that took courage. We others have been hardworking and patient and reasonable, but we haven't done anything, we haven't taken any leaps."

"I don't know," his companion said. "Many of them neither did anything nor ventured anything; they simply fooled around until they were dismissed. But maybe I don't quite understand you. What do you mean about leaping?"

"I mean being able to take a plunge, to take things seriously, to—well, that's just it, to leap. I wouldn't want to leap back to my former home and my former life; it doesn't attract me and I've almost forgotten it. But I do wish that if ever the time comes and it proves to be necessary, that I too will be able to free myself and leap, only not backward into something inferior, but forward and into something higher."

"Well, that is what we are headed for. Eschholz was

one step; the next will be higher, and finally the Order awaits us."

"Yes, but that isn't what I meant. Let's move on, *amice*; walking is so great, it will cheer me up again. We've really given ourselves a case of the dumps."

This mood and those words, which his classmate recorded, already sound the note which prevailed during the stormy period of Knecht's adolescence.

The hikers tramped for two days before they reached the Music Master's current home, Monteport, high in the mountains, where the Master lived in the former monastery, giving a course for conductors. Knecht's classmate was lodged in the guest house, while Knecht himself was assigned a small cell in the Magister's apartment. He had barely unpacked his knapsack and washed when his host came in. The venerable man shook hands with the boy, sat down with a small sigh, and for a few minutes closed his eyes, as was his habit when he was very tired. Then, looking up with a friendly smile, he said: "Forgive me; I am not a very good host. You have just come from a long hike and must be tired, and to tell the truth so am I—my day is somewhat overcrowded— but if you are not yet ready for bed, I should like to have an hour with you in my study. You will be staying here two days, and tomorrow both you and your classmate will be dining with me, but unfortunately my time is so limited, and we must somehow manage to save the few hours I need for you. So shall we begin right away?"

He led Knecht into a large vaulted cell empty of furniture but for an old piano and two chairs. They sat down in the chairs.

"You will soon be entering another stage," the Master said. "There you will learn all sorts of new things, some of them very pleasant. Probably you'll also begin dabbling in the Glass Bead Game before long. All that is very fine and important, but one thing is more important than anything else: you are going to learn meditation there. Supposedly all the students learn it, but one can't go checking up on them. I want you to learn it properly and well, just as well as music; then everything else will follow of its own accord. Therefore I'd like to give you the first two or three lessons myself; that was the purpose of my invitation. So today and tomorrow and the day after tomorrow let us try to meditate for an hour each day, and moreover on music. You will be given a glass of milk now, so that hunger and thirst do not disturb you; supper will be brought to us later."

He rapped on the door, and a glass of milk was brought in.

"Drink slowly, slowly," he admonished. "Take your time, and do not speak."

Knecht drank his cool milk very slowly. Opposite him, the dear man sat with his eyes closed again. His face looked very old, but friendly; it was full of peace, and he was smiling to himself, as though he had stepped down into his own thoughts like a tired man into a footbath. Tranquility streamed from him. Knecht felt it, and himself grew calmer.

Now the Magister turned on his chair and placed his hands on the piano. He played a theme, and carried it forward with variations; it seemed to be a piece by some Italian master. He instructed his guest to imagine the progress of the music as a dance, a continuous series of balancing exercises, a succession of smaller or larger steps from the middle of an axis of symmetry, and to focus his mind entirely on the figure which these steps formed. He played the bars once more, silently reflected on them, played them again, then sat quite still, hands on his knees, eyes half closed, without the slightest movement, repeating and contemplating the music within himself. His pupil, too, listened within himself, saw fragments of lines of notes before him, saw something moving, something stepping, dancing, and hovering, and tried to perceive and read the movement as if it were the curves in the line of a bird's flight. The pattern grew confused and he lost it; he had to begin over again; for a moment his concentration left him and he was in a void. He looked around and saw the Master's still, abstracted face floating palely in the twilight, found his way back again to that mental space he had drifted out of. He heard the music sounding in it again, saw it striding along, saw it inscribing the line of its movement, and followed in his mind the dancing feet of the invisible dancers. . . .

It seemed to him that a long time had passed before he glided out of that space once more, again became aware of the chair he sat on, the mat-covered stone floor, the dimmer dusk outside the windows. He felt someone regarding him, looked up and into the eyes of the Music Master, who was attentively studying him. The Master gave him an almost imperceptible nod, with one finger played *pianissimo* the last variation of the Italian piece, and stood up.

"Stay on," he said. "I shall be back. Try once again to track down the music; pay attention to the figure. But don't force yourself; it's only a game. If you should fall asleep over it, there's no harm."

He left; there was still a task awaiting him, left over from the overcrowded day. It was no easy and pleasant task, none that he would have wished for. One of the students in the conducting course was a gifted but vain and overbearing person. The Music Master would have to speak to him now, curbing his bad habits, showing him his faults, all this with an even balance of solicitude and superiority, love and authority. He sighed. What a pity that no arrangements were ever final, that recognized errors were never eliminated for good, that again and again the selfsame failings had to be combated, the selfsame weeds plucked out. Talent without character, virtuosity without values, had dominated musical life in the Age of the Feuilleton, had been extirpated during the musical Renaissance—and here was that same spirit again, making vigorous growth.

When he returned from his errand to have supper with Joseph, he found the boy sitting still, but contented and no longer tired in the least. "It was beautiful," Joseph said dreamily. "While it was going on, the music vanished completely; it changed."

"Let it reverberate inside you," the Master said, leading him into a small chamber where a table was set with bread and fruit. They ate, and the Master invited him to sit in on the conducting course for a while in the morning. Just before showing his guest to his cell and retiring for the night, he said: "During your meditation you saw something; the music appeared to you as a figure. If you feel so minded, try to copy it down."

In the guest cell Knecht found pencils and paper on the table, and before he went to bed he tried to draw the figure which the music had assumed for him. He drew a line, and moving diagonally off from the line at rhythmic intervals short tributary lines. It looked something like the arrangement of leaves on the twig of a tree. What he had produced did not satisfy him, but he felt impelled to try it again and yet again. At last he playfully curved the line into a circle from which the tributary lines radiated, like flowers in a garland. Then he went to bed and fell asleep quickly. He dreamed that he was once again on that height above the woods, where he had rested with his classmate, and saw dear Eschholz spread out below him. And as he looked down, the quadrangle of the school building contracted into an oval and then spread out to a circle, a garland, and the garland began turning slowly; it turned with increasing speed, until at last it was whirling madly and burst, flying apart into twinkling stars.

He had forgotten this dream by the time he awoke. But later, during a morning walk, the Master asked him whether he had dreamt, and it seemed to him that he must have had an unpleasant experience in his dreams. He thought, recovered the dream, told it, and was astonished at how innocuous it sounded. The Master listened closely.

"Should we be mindful of dreams?" Joseph asked. "Can we interpret them?"

The Master looked into his eyes and said tersely: "We should be mindful of everything, for we can interpret everything."

After they had walked on a bit, he asked paternally: "Which school would you most like to enter?"

Joseph flushed. He murmured quickly: "Waldzell, I think!"

The Master nodded. "I thought so. Of course you know the old saying: '*Gignit autem artificiosam*' . . ."

Still blushing, Joseph completed the saying familiar to every student: "*Gignit autem artificiosam lusorum gentem Cella Silvestris*": "But Waldzell breeds the skillful Glass Bead Game players."

The old man gave him a warm look. "Probably that is

your path, Joseph. As you well know, there are some who
do not think well of the Glass Bead Game. They say it
is a substitute for the arts, and that the players are mere
popularizers; that they can no longer be regarded as
truly devoted to the things of the mind, but are merely
artistic dilettantes given to improvisation and feckless
fancy. You will see how much or how little truth there is
in that. Perhaps you yourself have notions about the Glass
Bead Game, expecting more of it than it will give you, or
perhaps the reverse. There is no doubt that the Game has
its dangers. For that very reason we love it; only the
weak are sent out on paths without perils. But never forget what I have told you so often: our mission is to
recognize contraries for what they are: first of all as
contraries, but then as opposite poles of a unity. Such
is the nature of the Glass Bead Game. The artistically
inclined delight in the Game because it provides opportunities for improvisation and fantasy. The strict
scholars and scientists despise it—and so do some musicians also—because, they say, it lacks that degree of
strictness which their specialties can achieve. Well and
good, you will encounter these antinomies, and in time
you will discover that they are subjective, not objective
—that, for example, a fancy-free artist avoids pure mathematics or logic not because he understands them and
could say something about them if he wished, but because he instinctively inclines toward other things. Such
instinctive and violent inclinations and disinclinations
are signs by which you can recognize the pettier souls. In
great souls and superior minds, these passions are not
found. Each of us is merely one human being, merely an
experiment, a way station. But each of us should be on
the way toward perfection, should be striving to reach
the center, not the periphery. Remember this: one can
be a strict logician or grammarian, and at the same time
full of imagination and music. One can be a musician or
Glass Bead Game player and at the same time wholly
devoted to rule and order. The kind of person we want
to develop, the kind of person we aim to become, would
at any time be able to exchange his discipline or art for
any other. He would infuse the Glass Bead Game with
crystalline logic, and grammar with creative imagination.

That is how we ought to be. We should be so constituted that we can at any time be placed in a different position without offering resistance or losing our heads."

"I think I understand," Joseph said. "But are not those who have such strong preferences and aversions simply more passionate natures, others just more sober and temperate?"

"That seems to be true and yet it is not," the Master replied, laughing. "To be capable of everything and do justice to everything, one certainly does not need less spiritual force and élan and warmth, but more. What you call passion is not spiritual force, but friction between the soul and the outside world. Where passion dominates, that does not signify the presence of greater desire and ambition, but rather the misdirection of these qualities toward an isolated and false goal, with a consequent tension and sultriness in the atmosphere. Those who direct the maximum force of their desires toward the center, toward true being, toward perfection, seem quieter than the passionate souls because the flame of their fervor cannot always be seen. In argument, for example, they will not shout and wave their arms. But I assure you, they are nevertheless burning with subdued fires."

"Oh, if only it were possible to find understanding," Joseph exclaimed. "If only there were a dogma to believe in. Everything is contradictory, everything tangential; there are no certainties anywhere. Everything can be interpreted one way and then again interpreted in the opposite sense. The whole of world history can be explained as development and progress and can also be seen as nothing but decadence and meaninglessness. Isn't there any truth? Is there no real and valid doctrine?"

The Master had never heard him speak so fervently. He walked on in silence for a little, then said: "There is truth, my boy. But the doctrine you desire, absolute, perfect dogma that alone provides wisdom, does not exist. Nor should you long for a perfect doctrine, my friend. Rather, you should long for the perfection of yourself. The deity is within *you*, not in ideas and books. Truth is lived, not taught. Be prepared for conflicts, Joseph Knecht—I can see they have already begun."

During those few days Joseph for the first time saw his beloved Magister in his everyday life and work, and he felt intense admiration, although only a small part of what the Music Master accomplished every day came into view. But most of all the Master won his heart by taking such an interest in him, by having invited him, and by managing to spare hours for him despite his being often so overworked and overtired. Nor was it only the lessons. If this introduction to meditation made so deep and lasting an impression upon him, it did so, as he later learned to appreciate, not because the Master's technique was so especially subtle and unique, but only because of the Master's personality and example. His later teachers, who instructed him in meditation during the following year, gave him more guidance, more precise lessons; they controlled results more closely, asked more questions, managed to do more correcting. The Music Master, confident of his power over this young man, did very little teaching and talking. Mostly, he merely set themes and showed the way by example. Knecht observed the way the Master often looked so old and worn out, but after sinking into himself with half-closed eyes he would once again manage to look so tranquil, vigorous, cheerful, and friendly. To Joseph this renewal was a persuasive demonstration of the right way to the true springs, the way from restiveness to peace. Whatever the Master had to say about this matter was casually imparted to Knecht on brief walks or at meals.

We know also that at this time the Magister gave Knecht some first hints and suggestions about the Glass Bead Game, but none of his actual words have been preserved. Joseph was also struck by the fact that the Master took some trouble with Joseph's companion, so that the boy would not feel he was only a hanger-on. The old man seemed to think of everything.

The brief stay in Monteport, the three lessons in meditation, attendance at the course for conductors, the few talks with the Master, meant a great deal to Joseph Knecht. There was no question but that the Master had found the most effective time for interposing briefly in Knecht's life. The chief purpose of his invitation, as he had said, had been to commend meditation to Joseph;

but this invitation had been no less important in itself, as a distinction and a token that he was well thought of, that his superiors expected something of him. It was the second stage of vocation. He had been granted some insight into the inner spheres. If one of the twelve Masters summoned a pupil at his level to come so close, that was not just an act of personal benevolence. What a Master did was always more than personal.

Before they left, each of the boys received a small gift: the scores of two Bach choral preludes for Joseph, a handsome pocket edition of Horace for his friend. The Master, as he was bidding good-by to Joseph, said to him: "In a few days you will learn which school you have been assigned to. I come to the higher schools less frequently than to Eschholz, but I am sure we shall see each other there too, if I keep in good health. If you care to, you might write me a letter once a year, especially about the course of your musical studies. Criticism of your teachers is not prohibited, but I am not so concerned about that. A great many things await you; I hope you will meet the challenges. Our Castalia is not supposed to be merely an elite; it ought above all to be a hierarchy, a structure in which every brick derives its meaning only from its place in the whole. There is no path leading out of this whole, and one who climbs higher and is assigned to greater and greater tasks does not acquire more freedom, only more and more responsibilities. Till we meet again, young friend. It was a pleasure to me to have you here."

The two boys tramped back, and both were gayer and more talkative than they had been on the way to Monteport. The few days in different air and amid different sights, the contact with a different sphere of life, had relaxed them, made them freer from Eschholz and the mood of parting there. It had also made them doubly eager for change and the future. At many a resting place in the forest, or above one of the precipitous gorges in the vicinity of Monteport, they took their wooden flutes from their pockets and played duets, mostly folksongs. By the time they had once again reached that peak above Eschholz, with its prospect of the institution and its trees, the conversation they had had there seemed to both of them far away in the past. All things had taken on a new aspect. They did not say a word about it; they felt a little ashamed of what they had felt and said so short a while ago, which already had become outmoded and insubstantial.

In Eschholz they had to wait only until the following day to learn their destinations. Knecht had been assigned to Waldzell.

TWO

WALDZELL

"BUT WALDZELL BREEDS the skillful Glass Bead Game players," runs the old saying about this famous school. Among the Castalian schools of the second and third levels, it was the one most devoted to the arts. That is to say, whereas at other schools a particular branch of scholarship was distinctly dominant, such as classical philology in Keuperheim, Aristotelian and Scholastic philosophy in Porta, mathematics in Planvaste, Waldzell traditionally cultivated a tendency toward universality and toward an alliance between scholarship and the arts. The highest symbol of these tendencies was the Glass Bead Game. Even here, as at all the other schools, the Game was by no means taught officially and as a compulsory subject. But Waldzell students devoted their private studies almost exclusively to it. Then again, the town of Waldzell was after all the seat of the official Glass Bead Game and its institutions. The famous Game Hall for the ceremonial games was located here, as was the enormous Game Archives, with its officialdom and its libraries. Here, too, was the residence of the Ludi Magister. And although these institutions existed altogether independently and the school was in no way attached to them, the spirit of the

institutions permeated the school. Something of the hallowed atmosphere of the great public Games spread over
the whole area. The town itself was very proud of being
the home not only of a school, but of the Game also.
The townspeople called the students "scholars" and referred to those who attended the Game School as "lusers"
—a corruption of *lusores*.

The Waldzell school was, incidentally, the smallest of
the Castalian schools. The number of students rarely exceeded sixty, and undoubtedly this circumstance also
helped to lend it an air of uniqueness and aristocracy, of
special distinction, for here was the very elite of the elite.
Moreover, during the past several decades this venerable
school had produced many Masters and the majority of
Glass Bead Game players. Not that Waldzell's brilliant
reputation was entirely uncontested. Some thought that
the Waldzellers were priggish aesthetes and pampered
princes, useless for anything but the Glass Bead Game.
At times there would be a vogue among the schools for
making sardonic comments on the Waldzell students;
but the very harshness of the jokes and criticisms proves
that jealousy and envy underlay them. All in all, the
transfer to Waldzell in itself implied a certain distinction. Joseph Knecht, too, realized that, and although he
was not ambitious in the vulgar sense of the word, he
accepted the distinction with a measure of joyous pride.

Along with several schoolmates, he arrived in Waldzell on foot. Full of high expectations and ready for whatever might come, he walked through the southern gate
and was instantly enchanted by the dark-brown aspect
of the town and the great bulk of the former Cistercian
monastery in which the school had been established. Even
before he had been given his new uniform, immediately
after the reception snack in the porter's lodge, he set out
alone to explore his new home. He found the footpath
that ran along the remains of the ancient town wall above
the river, stood on the arched bridge and listened to the
roaring of the millrace, walked past the graveyard and
down the lane of linden trees. He saw and recognized,
beyond the tall hedges, the Vicus Lusorum, the adjacent
little settlement of the Glass Bead Game players. Here
were the Festival Hall, the Archives, the classrooms, the

houses for guests and teachers. He saw coming from one
of these houses a man in the dress of the Glass Bead
Game players, and decided that this must be one of the
fabulous *lusores*, possibly the Magister Ludi in person.
The spell of this atmosphere exerted a tremendous force
upon him. Everything here seemed old, venerable, sanctified, rich with tradition; here one was quite a bit closer
to the Center than in Eschholz. And as he returned from
the Glass Bead Game district, he began to feel other
spells, possibly less venerable, but no less exciting. They
came from the town itself, this sample of the profane
world with its business and commerce, its dogs and children, its smells of stores and handicrafts, its bearded
citizens and fat wives behind the shop doors, the children
playing and clamoring, the girls throwing mocking looks.
Many things reminded him of remote worlds he had once
known, of Berolfingen. He had thought all that entirely
forgotten. Now deep layers in his soul responded to all
this, to the scenes, the sounds, the smells. A world less
tranquil than that of Eschholz, but richer and more
colorful, seemed to be awaiting him here.

As a matter of fact, the school at first turned out to be
the exact continuation of his previous school, although
with the addition of several new subjects. Nothing was
really new there except the meditation exercises; and after
all the Music Master had already given him a foretaste
of these. He accepted meditation willingly enough, but
without regarding it as more than a pleasant, relaxing
game. Only somewhat later—as we shall see in due time
—would he have a living experience of its true value.

The headmaster of Waldzell, Otto Zbinden, was an
unusual, somewhat eccentric man who inspired a certain amount of fear. He was nearing sixty at the time
Knecht entered. A good many of the entries we have
examined concerning Joseph Knecht are set down in his
handsome and impetuous handwriting. But at the beginning the young man's curiosity was captured far less by
the teachers than by his fellow students. With two of
these in particular Knecht struck up a lively relationship, for which there is ample documentation. The first
of these was Carlo Ferromonte, a boy his own age to
whom he became attached during his very first months

at Waldzell. (Ferromonte later rose to the second-highest rank on the Board, as deputy to the Music Master; we are indebted to him for, among other things, a *History of Styles in Sixteenth-Century Lute Music.*) The other boys called him "Rice Eater" and prized him for his aptitude at sports. His friendship with Joseph began with talks about music and led to joint studying and practicing which continued for several years; we are informed about this partly by Knecht's rare but copious letters to the Music Master. In the first of these letters Knecht calls Ferromonte a "specialist and connoisseur in music rich in ornamentation, embellishments, trills, etc." The boys played Couperin, Purcell, and other masters of the period around 1700. In one of the letters Knecht gives a detailed account of these practice sessions and this music "in which many of the pieces have some embellishment over almost every note." He continues: "After one has played nothing but turns, shakes, and mordents for a few hours, one's fingers feel as if they are charged with electricity."

In fact he made great progress in music. By his second or third year at Waldzell he was reading and playing the notations, clefs, abbreviations, and figured basses of all centuries and styles with tolerable fluency. He had made himself at home in the realm of Western music, as much of it as has been preserved for us, in that special way that proceeds from practical craftsmanship and is not above taking utmost heed of a piece of music's sensuous and technical aspects as a means for penetrating the spirit. His intense concern with the sensuous quality of music, his efforts to understand the spirit of various musical styles from the physical nature of the sounds, the sensations in the ear, deterred him for a remarkably long time from devoting himself to the elementary course in the Glass Bead Game. In one of his lectures in subsequent years he remarked: "One who knows music only from the extracts which the Glass Bead Game distills from it may well be a good Glass Bead Game player, but he is far from being a musician, and presumably he is no historian either. Music does not consist only in those purely intellectual oscillations and figurations which we have abstracted from it. All through the ages its pleasure has primarily consisted in its sensuous character, in the outpouring of breath, in the beating of time, in the colorations, frictions, and stimuli which arise from the blending of voices in the concord of instruments. Certainly the spirit is the main thing, and certainly the invention of new instruments and the alteration of old ones, the introduction of new keys and new rules or new taboos regarding construction and harmony are always mere gestures and superficialities, even as the costumes and fashions of nations are superficialities. But one must have apprehended and tasted these superficial and sensuous distinctions with the senses to be able to interpret from them the nature of eras and styles. We make music with our hands and fingers, with our mouths and lungs, not with our brains alone, and someone who can read notes but has no command of any instrument should not join in the dialogue of music. Thus, too, the history of music is hardly to be understood solely in terms of an abstract history of styles. For example, the periods of decadence in music would remain totally incomprehensible if we failed to recognize in each one of them the preponderance of the sensuous and quantitative elements over the 'spiritual element.' "

For a time it appeared as if Knecht had decided to become nothing but a musician. In favor of music he neglected all the optional subjects, including the introductory course in the Glass Bead Game, to such an extent that toward the end of the first semester the headmaster called him to an accounting. Knecht refused to be intimidated; he stubbornly insisted on his rights. It is said that he told the headmaster: "If I fail in any official subject, you could rightly reprimand me. On the other hand I have the right to devote three quarters or even four quarters of my free time to music. I stand on the statutes of the school." Headmaster Zbinden was sensible enough not to insist, but he naturally remembered this student and is said to have treated him with cold severity for a long time.

This peculiar period in Knecht's student days lasted for more than a year, probably for about a year and a half. He received normal but not brilliant marks and—to judge by the incident with the headmaster—his behavior

was marked by a rather defiant withdrawal, no note-
worthy friendships, but in compensation this extraordinary passion for music-making. He abstained from almost
all private studies, including the Glass Bead Game. Several of these traits are undoubtedly signs of puberty;
during this period he probably encountered the other
sex only by chance, and mistrustfully; presumably he was
quite shy—like so many Eschholz pupils if they do not
happen to have sisters at home. He read a great deal,
especially the German philosophers: Leibniz, Kant, and
the Romantics, among whom Hegel exerted by far the
strongest attraction upon him.

We must now give some account of that other fellow
student who played a significant part in Knecht's life at
Waldzell: the hospitant Plinio Designori. Hospitants
were boys who went through the elite schools as guests,
that is, without the intention of remaining permanently
in the Pedagogic Province and entering the Order. Such
hospitants turned up every so often, although they were
quite rare, for the Board of Educators was naturally averse
to the idea of educating students who intended to return
home and into the world after they finished their studies
at the elite schools. However, the country had several old
patrician families who had performed notable services for
Castalia at the time of its foundation and in which the
custom still prevailed (it has not entirely died out to this
day) of having one of the sons educated as a guest in the
elite schools. It had become an established prerogative
for those few families, although of course the boys in
question had to be gifted enough to meet the standards of
the schools.

These hospitants, although in every respect subject to
the same rules as all elite students, formed an exceptional
group within the student body if only because they did
not grow increasingly estranged from their native soil
and their families with each passing year. On the contrary, they spent all the holidays at home and always
remained guests and strangers among their fellow students, since they preserved the habits and ways of thinking of their place of origin. Home, a worldly career, a
profession and marriage awaited them. Only on very rare
occasions did it happen that such a guest student, capti-

vated by the spirit of the Province, would obtain the consent of his family and after all remain in Castalia and enter the Order. On the other hand, in the history of our country there have been several statesmen who were guest students in their youth, and now and then, when public opinion for one reason or another had turned against the elite schools and the Order, these statesmen came stoutly to the defense of both.

Plinio Designori, then, was one such hospitant whom Joseph Knecht—slightly his junior—encountered in Waldzell. He was a talented young man, particularly brilliant in talk and debate, fiery and somewhat restive in temperament. His presence often troubled Headmaster Zbinden, for although he was a good student and gave no cause for reprimands, he made no effort to forget his exceptional position as a hospitant and to fall into line as inconspicuously as possible. On the contrary, he frankly and belligerently professed a non-Castalian, worldly point of view.

Inevitably, a special relationship sprang up between these two students. Both were extremely gifted and both had a vocation; these qualities made them brothers, although in everything else they were opposites. It would have required a teacher of unusual insight and skill to extract the quintessence from the problem that thus arose and to employ the rules of dialectics to derive synthesis from the antitheses. Headmaster Zbinden did not lack the talent or will; he was not one of those teachers who find geniuses an embarrassment. But for this particular case he lacked the important prerequisite: the trust of both students. Plinio, who enjoyed the role of outsider and revolutionary, remained permanently on his guard in his dealings with the headmaster; and unfortunately the headmaster had clashed with Joseph Knecht over that question of his private studies, so that Knecht, too, would not have turned to Zbinden for advice.

Fortunately, there was the Music Master. Knecht did turn to him with a request for help and advice, and the wise old musician took the matter seriously and directed the course of the game with masterly skill, as we shall see. In the hands of this Master the greatest danger and temptation in young Knecht's life was converted into an honorable task, and the young man proved able to cope with it. The psychological history of the friendship-and-enmity between Joseph and Plinio—a sonata movement on two themes, or a dialectical interplay between two minds—went somewhat as follows.

At first, of course, it was Designori who attracted his opponent. He was the elder; he was a handsome, fiery, and well-spoken young man; and above all he was one of those "from outside," a non-Castalian, a boy from the world, a person with father and mother, uncles, aunts, brothers, and sisters, one for whom Castalia with all its rules, traditions, and ideals represented only a stage along the road, a limited sojourn. For this *rara avis* Castalia was not the world; for him Waldzell was a school like any other; for him the "return to the world" was no disgrace and punishment; the future awaiting him was not the Order but career, marriage, politics, in short that "real life" which every Castalian secretly longed to know more about. For the "world" was the same thing for a Castalian that it had long ago been for the penitents and monks: something inferior and forbidden, no doubt, but nonetheless mysterious, tempting, fascinating. And Plinio truly made no secret of his attachment to the world; he was not in the least ashamed of it. On the contrary, he was proud of it. With a zeal still half boyish and histrionic, but also half consciously propagandistic, he stressed his own differentness. He seized every pretext for setting his secular views and standards against those of Castalia, and contending that his own were better, juster, more natural, more human. In these arguments he bandied about words like "nature" and "common sense," to the discredit of the overrefined, unworldly spirit of the school. He made use of slogans and hyperbole, but had the good taste and tact not to descend to crude provocations, but more or less to give the methods of disputation customary in Waldzell their due. He wanted to defend the "world" and the unreflective life against the "arrogant scholastic intellectuality" of Castalia, but he also wanted to prove that he could do so with his opponents' weapons. He did not want to be thought the dull-witted brute blindly trampling around in the flower garden of culture.

Now and again Joseph Knecht had stood, a silent but attentive listener, on the edges of small groups of students whose center was Designori. Plinio usually did most of the talking. With curiosity, astonishment, and alarm Joseph had heard Plinio excoriating all authority, everything that was held sacred in Castalia. He heard everything questioned, everything he believed in exposed as dubious or ridiculous. Joseph soon noted that many in the audience did not take these speeches seriously; some, it was clear, listened only for the fun of it, as people listen to a barker at a fair. Frequently, too, he heard some of the boys answer Plinio's charges sarcastically or seriously. Still there were always several schoolmates gathered around this boy Plinio; he was always the center of attention, and whether or not there happened to be an opponent in the group, he always exerted an attraction so strong that it was akin to seduction.

Joseph himself was as much stirred as those others who gathered around the lively orator and listened to his tirades with astonishment or laughter. In spite of the trepidation and even fear that he felt during such speeches, Joseph was aware of their sinister attraction for him. He was drawn to them not just because they were amusing. On the contrary, they seemed to concern him directly and seriously. Not that he would inwardly have agreed with the audacious orator, but there were doubts whose very existence or possibility you had only to know about and you instantly began to suffer them. At the beginning it was not any serious suffering; it was merely a matter of being slightly disturbed, uneasy—a feeling compounded of powerful urge and guilty conscience.

The time had to come, and it came, when Designori noticed that among his listeners was one to whom his words meant more than rousing entertainment and the fun of argument: a fair-haired boy who looked handsome and finely wrought, but rather shy, and who blushed and gave terse, embarrassed replies when Plinio said a friendly word to him. Evidently this boy had been trailing after him for some time, Plinio thought, and decided to reward him with a friendly gesture and win him over completely by inviting him to his room that afternoon. To Plinio's surprise the boy held off, would not linger to talk with him, and declined the invitation. Provoked, the older boy began courting the reticent Joseph. Possibly he did so at first only out of vanity, but later he went about it in all seriousness, for he sensed an antagonist who would be perhaps a future friend, perhaps the opposite. Again and again he saw Joseph hanging around near him, and noted the intensity with which Joseph listened, but the shy boy would always retreat as soon as he tried to approach him.

There were reasons behind this conduct. Joseph had long since come to feel that this other boy would mean something important to him, perhaps something fine, an enlargement of his horizon, insight or illumination, perhaps also temptation and danger. Whatever it was, this was a test he had to pass. He had told his friend Ferromonte about the first stirrings of skepticism and restlessness that Plinio's talks had aroused in him, but his friend had paid little attention; he dismissed Plinio as a conceited and self-important fellow not worth listening to, and promptly buried himself in his music again. Instinct warned Joseph that the headmaster was the proper authority to whom to bring his doubts and queries; but since that little clash he no longer had a cordial and candid relationship with Zbinden. He was afraid the headmaster might regard his coming to him with this question as a kind of talebearing.

In this dilemma, which grew increasingly painful because of Plinio's efforts to strike up a friendship, he turned to his patron and guardian angel, the Music Master, and wrote him a very long letter which has been preserved. In part, it read:

"I am not yet certain whether Plinio hopes to win me over to his way of thinking, or whether he merely wants someone to discuss these matters with. I hope it is the latter, for to convert me to his views would mean leading me into disloyalty and destroying my life, which after all is rooted in Castalia. I have no parents and friends on the outside to whom I could return if I should ever really desire to. But even if Plinio's sacrilegious speeches are not aimed at conversion and influencing, they leave me at a loss. For to be perfectly frank with you, dear Master, there is something in Plinio's point of view that

I cannot gainsay; he appeals to a voice within me which sometimes strongly seconds what he says. Presumably it is the voice of nature, and it runs utterly counter to my education and the outlook customary among us. When Plinio calls our teachers and Masters a priestly caste and us a pack of spoon-fed eunuchs, he is of course using coarse and exaggerated language, but there may well be some truth to what he says, for otherwise I would hardly be so upset by it. Plinio can say the most startling and discouraging things. For example, he contends that the Glass Bead Game is a retrogression to the Age of the Feuilleton, sheer irresponsible playing around with an alphabet into which we have broken down the languages of the different arts and sciences. It's nothing but associations and toying with analogies, he says. Or again he declares that our resigned sterility proves the worthlessness of our whole culture and our intellectual attitudes. We analyze the laws and techniques of all the styles and periods of music, he points out, but produce no new music ourselves. We read and exposit Pindar or Goethe and are ashamed to create verse ourselves. Those are accusations I cannot laugh at. And they are not the worst; they are not the ones that wound me most. It is bad enough when he says, for example, that we Castalians lead the life of artifically reared songbirds, do not earn our bread ourselves, never face necessity and the struggle for existence, neither know or wish to know anything about that portion of humanity whose labor and poverty provide the base for our lives of luxury."

The letter concluded: "Perhaps I have abused your friendliness and kindness, *Reverendissime*, and I am prepared to be reproved. Scold me, impose penances on me—I shall be grateful for them. But I am in dire need of advice. I can sustain the present situation for a little while longer. But I cannot shape it into any real and fruitful development, for I am too weak and inexperienced. Moreover, and perhaps this is the worst of all, I cannot confide in our headmaster unless you explicitly command me to do so. That is why I have troubled you with this affair, which is becoming a source of great distress to me."

It would be of the greatest value to us if we also possessed the Master's reply to this cry for help in black and white. But the reply was given orally. Shortly after Knecht wrote, the Magister Musicae himself arrived in Waldzell to direct an examination in music, and during the days he spent there he devoted considerable time to his young friend. We know of this from Knecht's later recollections. The Music Master did not make things easy for him. He began by looking closely into Knecht's grades and into the matter of his private studies as well. The latter, he decided, were much too one-sided; in this regard the headmaster had been right, and he insisted that Knecht admit as much to the headmaster. He gave precise directives for Knecht's conduct toward Designori, and did not leave until this question, too, had been discussed with Headmaster Zbinden. The outcome was twofold: that remarkable joust between Designori and Knecht, which none who looked on would ever forget; and an entirely new relationship between Knecht and the headmaster. Not that this relationship ever partook of the affection and mystery that linked Knecht to the Music Master, but at least it was lucid and relaxed.

The course that had been traced for Knecht determined the shape of his life for some time. He had been given leave to accept Designori's friendship, to expose himself to his influence and his attacks without intervention or supervision by his teachers. But his mentor specifically charged him to defend Castalia against the critic, and to raise the clash of views to the highest level. That meant, among other things, that Joseph had to make an intensive study of the fundamentals of the prevailing system in Castalia and in the Order, and to recall them to mind again and again. The debates between the two friendly opponents soon became famous, and drew large audiences. Designori's aggressive and ironic tone became subtler, his formulations stricter and more responsible, his criticism more objective. Hitherto Plinio had been the winner in this contest; coming from the "world," he possessed its experience, its methods, its means of attack, and some of its ruthlessness as well. From conversations with adults at home he knew all the indictments the world could muster against Castalia. But now Knecht's replies forced him to realize that although he knew the world quite well, better than any Castalian, he did not by any means know Castalia and its spirit as well as those who were at home here, for whom Castalia had become both native soil and destiny. He was forced to realize, and ultimately to admit, that he was a guest here, not a native; that the outside world had no exclusive claim on self-evident principles and truths arrived at through centuries of experience. Here too, in the Pedagogic Province, there was a tradition, what might even be called a "nature," with which he was only imperfectly acquainted and which was now being upheld by its spokesman, Joseph Knecht.

Knecht, for his part, in order to cope with his part as apologist, was obliged to put a great deal of study, meditation, and self-discipline into clarifying and deepening his understanding of what he was required to defend. In rhetoric Designori remained his superior; his worldly training and cleverness supported his natural fire and ambition. Even when he was being defeated on a point, he managed to think of the audience and contrive a facesaving or witty line of retreat. Knecht, on the other hand, when his opponent had driven him into a corner, was apt to say: "I shall have to think about that for a while, Plinio. Wait a few days; I'll come back to that point."

The relationship had thus been given a dignified form. In fact, for the participants and the listeners the dispute had already become an indispensable element in the school life of Waldzell. But the pressure and the conflict had scarcely grown any easier for Knecht. Because of the high degree of confidence and responsibility that had been placed upon him, he mastered his assignment, and it is proof of the strength and soundness of his nature that he carried it out without any visible damage. But privately, he suffered a great deal. If he felt friendship for Plinio, he felt it not only for an engaging and clever, cosmopolitan and articulate schoolmate, but also for that alien world which his friend and opponent represented, with which he was becoming acquainted, however dimly, in Plinio's personality, words, and gestures: that so-called "real" world in which there were loving mothers and children, hungry people and poorhouses, newspapers and election campaigns; that primitive and at the same time subtle world to which Plinio returned at every vacation in order to visit his parents, brothers, and sisters, to pay court to girls, to attend union meetings, or stay as a guest at elegant clubs, while Joseph remained in Castalia, went tramping or swimming, practiced Froberger's subtle and different fugues, or read Hegel.

Joseph had no doubt that he belonged in Castalia and was rightly leading a Castalian life, a life without family, without a variety of legendary amusements, a life without newspapers and also without poverty and hunger—though for all that Plinio hammered away at the drones' existence of the elite students, he too had so far never gone hungry or earned his own bread. No, Plinio's world was not better and sounder. But it was there, it existed, and as Joseph knew from history it had always been and had always been similar to what it now was. Many nations had never known any other pattern, had no elite schools and Pedagogic Province, no Order, Masters, and Glass Bead Game. The great majority of all human beings on the globe lived a life different from that of Castalia, simpler, more primitive, more dangerous, more disorderly, less sheltered. And this primitive world was innate in every man; everyone felt something of it in his own heart, had some curiosity about it, some nostalgia for it, some sympathy with it. The true task was to be fair to it, to keep a place for it in one's own heart, but still not relapse into it. For alongside it and superior to it was the second world, that of Castalia, the world of Mind—artificial, more orderly, more secure, but still in need of constant supervision and study. To serve the hierarchy, but without doing an injustice to that other world, let alone despising it, and also without eying it with vague desire or nostalgia—that must be the right course. For did not the small world of Castalia serve the great world, provide it with teachers, books, methods, act as guardian for the purity of its intellectual functions and its morality? Castalia remained the training ground and refuge for that small band of men whose lives were to be consecrated to Mind and to truth. Then why were these two worlds apparently unable to live in fraternal harmony, parallel and intertwined; why could an individual not cherish and unite both within himself?

One of the rare visits from the Music Master came upon a day when Joseph, exhausted by his task, was having a hard time preserving his balance. The Master diagnosed his state from a few of the boy's allusions; he read it even more plainly in Joseph's strained appearance, his restive looks, his somewhat nervous movements. He asked a few probing questions, was met by moroseness and uncommunicativeness, and gave up that approach. Seriously concerned, he took the boy to one of the practice rooms under the pretext of telling him about a minor musicological discovery. He had Joseph bring in and tune a clavichord, and involved him in a long tutoring session on the origin of sonata form until the young man somewhat forgot his anxieties, yielded, and listened, relaxed and grateful, to the Master's words and playing. Patiently, the Music Master took what time was needed to put Joseph into a receptive state. And when he had succeeded, when his lecture was over and he had concluded by playing one of the Gabrieli sonatas, he stood up, began slowly pacing the little room, and told a story.

"Many years ago I was once much preoccupied with this sonata. That was during the period of my free studies, before I was called to teaching and later to the post of Music Master. At the time I was ambitious to work out a history of the sonata from a new point of view; but then for a while I stopped making any progress at all. I began more and more to doubt whether all these musical and historical researches had any value whatsoever, whether they were really any more than vacuous play for idle people, a scanty aesthetic substitute for living a real life. In short, I had to pass through one of those crises in which all studies, all intellectual efforts, everything that we mean by the life of the mind, appear dubious and devalued and in which we tend to envy every peasant at the plow and every pair of lovers at evening, or every bird singing in a tree and every cicada chirping in the summer grass, because they seem to us to be living such natural, fulfilled, and happy lives. We know nothing of their troubles, of course, of the elements of harshness, danger, and suffering in their lot. In brief, I had pretty well lost my equilibrium. It was far from a pleasant state; in fact it was very hard to bear. I thought up the wildest schemes for escaping and gaining my freedom. For example, I imagined myself going out into the world as an itinerant musician and playing dances for wedding parties. If some recruiting officer from afar had appeared, as in old tales, and coaxed me to don a uniform and follow any company of soldiers into any war, I would have gone along. And so things went from bad to worse, as so often happens to people in such moods. I so thoroughly lost my grip on myself that I could no longer deal with my trouble alone, and had to seek help."

He paused for a moment and chuckled softly under his breath. Then he continued: "Naturally I had a studies adviser, as the rules require, and of course it would have been sensible and right as well as my duty to ask him for advice. But the fact is, Joseph, that precisely when we run into difficulties and stray from our path and are most in need of correction, precisely then we feel the greatest disinclination to return to the normal way and seek out the normal form of correction. My adviser had been dissatisfied with my last quarterly report; he had offered serious objections to it; but I had thought myself on the way to new discoveries and had rather resented his objections. In brief, I did not like the idea of going to him; I did not want to eat humble pie and admit that he had been right. Nor did I want to confide in my friends. But there was an eccentric in the vicinity whom I knew only by sight and hearsay, a Sanscrit scholar who went by the nickname of 'the Yogi.' One day, when my state of mind had grown sufficiently unbearable, I paid a call on this man, whose solitariness and oddity I had both smiled at and secretly admired. I went to his cell intending to talk with him, but found him in meditation; he had adopted the ritual Hindu posture and could not be reached at all. With a faint smile on his face, he hovered, as it were, in total aloofness. I could do nothing but stand at the door and wait until he returned from his absorption. This took a very long time, an hour or two hours, and at last I grew tired and slid to the floor. There I sat, leaning against the wall, continuing to wait. At the end I saw the man slowly awaken; he moved his head slightly, stretched his shoulders, slowly uncrossed his legs, and as he was about to stand up his gaze fell upon me.

" 'What do you want?' he asked.

"I stood up and said, without thinking and without really knowing what I was saying: 'It's the sonatas of Andrea Gabrieli.'

"He stood up at this point, seated me in his lone chair, and perched himself on the edge of the table. 'Gabrieli?' he said. 'What has he done to you with his sonatas?'

"I began to tell him what had been happening to me, and to confess the predicament I was in. He asked me about my background with an exactness that seemed to me pedantic. He wanted to know about my studies of Gabrieli and the sonata, at what hour I rose in the morning, how long I read, how much I practiced, when were my mealtimes and when I went to bed. I had confided in him, in fact imposed myself on him, so that I had to put up with his questions, but they made me ashamed; they probed more and more mercilessly into details, and forced me to an analysis of my whole intellectual and moral life during the past weeks and months.

"Then the Yogi suddenly fell silent, and when I looked puzzled he shrugged and said: 'Don't you see yourself where the fault lies?' But I could not see it. At this point he recapitulated with astonishing exactness everything he had learned from me by his questioning. He went back to the first signs of fatigue, repugnance, and intellectual constipation, and showed me that this could have happened only to someone who had submerged himself disproportionately in his studies and that it was high time for me to recover my self-control, and to regain my energy with outside help. Since I had taken the liberty of discontinuing my regular meditation exercises, he pointed out, I should at least have realized what was wrong as soon as the first evil consequences appeared, and should have resumed meditation. He was perfectly right. I had omitted meditating for quite a while on the grounds that I had no time, was too distracted or out of spirits, or too busy and excited with my studies. Moreover, as time went on I had completely lost all awareness of my continuous sin of omission. Even now, when I was desperate and had almost run aground, it had taken an outsider to remind me of it. As a matter of fact, I was to have the greatest difficulty snapping out of this state of neglect. I had to return to the training routines and beginners' exercises in meditation in order gradually to relearn the art of composing myself and sinking into contemplation."

With a small sigh the Magister ceased pacing the room. "That is what happened to me, and to this day I am still a little ashamed to talk about it. But the fact is, Joseph, that the more we demand of ourselves, or the more our task at any given time demands of us, the more dependent we are on meditation as a wellspring of energy, as the ever-renewing concord of mind and soul. And—I could if I wished give you quite a few more examples of this—the more intensively a task requires our energies, arousing and exalting us at one time, tiring and depressing us at another, the more easily we may come to neglect this wellspring, just as when we are carried away by some intellectual work we easily forget to attend to the body. The really great men in the history of the world have all either known how to meditate or have unconsciously found their way to the place to which meditation leads us. Even the most vigorous and gifted among the others all failed and were defeated in the end because their task or their ambitious dream seized hold of them, made them into persons so possessed that they lost the capacity for liberating themselves from present things, and attaining perspective. Well, you know all this; it's taught during the first exercises, of course. But it is inexorably true. How inexorably true it is, one realizes only after having gone astray."

This story had just enough effect upon Joseph for him to apprehend the risk he himself was running, so that he turned to his meditation exercises with renewed seriousness. What really impressed him was the fact that the Master had for the first time revealed to him something of his personal life, of his youth and early studies. For the first time Joseph fully realized that even a demigod, even a Master, had once been young and capable of erring. He felt gratitude, too, for the confidence the revered Master had placed in him by making this confession. It was possible for one to go astray, to flag, to make mistakes, to break rules, and still to deal with all such difficulties, to find one's way back, and in the end even to become a Master. Joseph overcame the crisis.

During the two or three years at Waldzell during which the friendship between Plinio and Joseph continued, the school watched the spectacle of these combative friends like a drama in which everyone had at least some small part, from the headmaster to the youngest freshman. The two worlds, the two principles, had become embodied in Knecht and Designori; each stimulated the other; every disputation became a solemn and symbolic contest which concerned everyone at the school. From every contact with his native soil on the holiday visits home Plinio would bring back new energy; and from every withdrawal for reflection, from every new book, every meditation exercise, every meeting with the Magister Musicae Joseph also derived new energy, made himself better fitted to be the representative and advocate of Castalia. As a child he had experienced his first vocation. Now he experienced the second. These years shaped and forged him into the perfect Castalian.

He had also some time ago completed his elementary lessons in the Glass Bead Game and even then, during holidays and under the eye of a Games Director, had begun sketching out his own Glass Bead Games. In this activity he now discovered one of the most abundant sources of joy and relaxation. Not since he had insatiably practiced harpsichord and piano pieces with Carlo Ferromonte had anything done him so much good, so refreshed, strengthened, reassured, and delighted him as did these first advances into the starry firmament of the Glass Bead Game.

During these same years young Joseph Knecht wrote those poems which have been preserved in Ferromonte's copy. It is quite possible that there were originally more of them than have come down to us, and it may be assumed that the poems, the earliest of which dates back to a time before Knecht's introduction to the Glass Bead

Game, helped him to carry out his role and to withstand the many tests of those critical years. Here and there in these poems, some skillfully wrought and some hastily scribbled, every reader will discover traces of the profound upheaval and crisis through which Knecht was then passing under the influence of Plinio. A good many of the lines sound a note of profound disturbance, of fundamental doubts about himself and the meaning of his life—until, in the poem entitled "The Glass Bead Game" he seems to have attained belief and surrender. Incidentally, a measure of concession to Plinio's world, an element of rebellion against certain unwritten laws of Castalia, is contained in the mere fact that he wrote these poems and even on occasion showed them to several schoolmates. For while Castalia has in general renounced the production of works of art (even musical production is known and tolerated there only in the form of stylistically rigid composition exercises), writing poetry was regarded as the most impossible, ridiculous, and prohibited of conceivable acts. Thus these poems were anything but a game, anything but an idle calligraphic amusement; it took high pressure to start this flow of productivity, and a certain defiant courage was required to admit to the writing of these verses.

It should also be mentioned that Plinio Designori likewise underwent considerable change and development under the influence of his antagonist. This was reflected in more than the refinement of his methods of argument. During the comradely rivalry of those school years Plinio saw his opponent steadily rising and maturing into an exemplary Castalian. The figure of his friend more and more vigorously and vividly embodied for him the spirit of the Province. Just as he himself had infected Joseph with some of the atmospheric turbulence of his own world, he for his part inhaled the Castalian air and succumbed to its charm and power. In his last year at the school, after a two-hour disputation on the ideals and perils of monasticism, fought out in the presence of the highest Glass Bead Game class, Plinio took Joseph out for a walk and made a confession to him. We quote it from a letter of Ferromonte's:

"Of course I've known for a long time, Joseph, that

you are not the credulous Glass Bead Game player and
Castalian saint whose part you have been playing so
splendidly. Each of us stands at an exposed spot in this
battle, and each of us probably knows that what he is
fighting against rightfully exists and has its undeniable
value. You yourself take the side of intensive cultivation
of the mind, I the side of natural life. In our contest you
have learned to track down the dangers of the natural
life and have made them your target. Your function has
been to point out how natural, naive living without
discipline of the mind is bound to become a mire into
which men sink, reverting to bestiality. And I for my
part must remind you again and again how risky,
dangerous, and ultimately sterile is a life based purely
upon mind. Good, each defends what he believes to be
primary, you mind and I nature. But don't take offense—
it sometimes seems to me that you actually and naively
consider me an enemy of your Castalian principles, a
fellow who fundamentally regards your studies, exercises, and games as mere tomfoolery, even though he
briefly joins in them for one reason or another. How
wrong you would be if you really believed that, my
friend. I'll confess to you that I am infatuated with your
hierarchy, that it often enthralls me like happiness itself.
I'll confess to you that some months ago, when I was at
home with my parents for a while, I had it out with my
father and won his permission for me to remain a Castalian and enter the Order if this should be my desire and
decision at the end of my schooldays. I was happy when
he at last gave his consent. As it happens, I shall not
make use of his permission; I've recently realized that.
Not that I've lost my taste for it, not at all. But I more
and more see that for me to remain among you would
mean escaping. It would be a fine, a noble escape perhaps,
but still an escape. I shall return and become a man of
the outside world, but one who continues grateful to your
Castalia, who will go on practicing a good many of your
exercises, and will come every year to join in the celebration of the great Glass Bead Game."

Knecht informed his friend Ferromonte of Plinio's
confession with deep emotion. And Ferromonte himself
added, in the letter we have just cited: "To me, as a

musician, this confession of Plinio, to whom I had not always been entirely fair, was like a musical experience. The contrast of world and Mind, or of Plinio and Joseph, had before my eyes been transfigured from the conflict of two irreconcilable principles into a double concerto."

When Plinio had come to the end of his four-year course and was about to return home, he brought the headmaster a letter from his father inviting Joseph Knecht to spend the coming vacation with him. This was an unusual proposal. Leaves for journeys and stays outside the Pedagogic Province did exist, chiefly for purposes of study. They were not so very rare, but were exceptional and generally granted only to older and more seasoned researchers, never to younger students still at school. But since the invitation had come from so highly esteemed a family and personage, Headmaster Zbinden did not presume to reject it on his own, but presented it to a committee of the Board of Educators. The reply was a laconic refusal. The friends had to say good-by to each other.

"We'll try the invitation again sometime," Plinio said. "Sooner or later it will work out. You must someday see my home and meet my family, and realize that we are not just commercial-minded scum. I shall miss you very much. And make sure, Joseph, that you rise quickly in this complicated Castalia of yours. Of course you're highly suited to become a member of the hierarchy, but in my opinion more at the top than the bottom of the heap —in spite of your name. I prophesy a great future for you; one of these days you'll be a Magister and be counted among the illustrious."

Joseph gave him a sad look.

"Go ahead and make fun of me," he said, struggling with the emotion of parting. "I am not so ambitious as you, and if I should ever attain to some office, you will long since have become president or mayor, university professor or deputy. Think kindly of us, Plinio, and of Castalia; don't become entirely estranged from us. After all, there have to be a few people in the outside world who know more about Castalia than the jokes they make about us out there."

They shook hands, and Plinio departed.

For his last year in Waldzell, Joseph remained out of the limelight. His exposed and strenuous function as a more or less public personality had suddenly come to an end. Castalia no longer needed a defender. Joseph devoted his free time during that year chiefly to the Glass Bead Game, which enthralled him more and more. A notebook of jottings from that period, dealing with the meaning and theory of the Game, begins with the sentence: "The whole of both physical and mental life is a dynamic phenomenon, of which the Glass Bead Game basically comprehends only the aesthetic side, and does so predominantly as an image of rhythmic processes."

THREE

YEARS OF FREEDOM

JOSEPH KNECHT WAS about twenty-four years old at this
time. With graduation from Waldzell, his school days
were over, and there now began his years of free study.
With the exception of his uneventful boyhood in Eschholz, these were probably the most serene and happy
years of his life. There is, after all, always something
wonderful and touchingly beautiful about a young man,
for the first time released from the bonds of schooling,
making his first ventures toward the infinite horizons of the
mind. At this point he has not yet seen any of his illusions
dissipated, or doubted either his own capacity for endless dedication or the boundlessness of the world of
thought.

Especially for young men with gifts like those of
Joseph Knecht, who have not been driven by a single
talent to concentrate on a specialty, but whose nature
rather aims at integration, synthesis, and universality, this
springtide of free study is often a period of intense happiness and very nearly of intoxication. Were it not preceded by the discipline of the elite schools, by the
psychic hygiene of meditation exercises and the lenient
supervision of the Board of Educators, this freedom

would even be dangerous for such natures and might prove a nemesis to many, as it used to be to innumerable highly gifted young men in the ages before our present educational pattern was set, in the pre-Castalian centuries. The universities in those days literally swarmed with young Faustian spirits who embarked with all sails set upon the high seas of learning and academic freedom, and ran aground on all the shoals of untrammeled dilettantism. Faust himself, after all, was the prototype of brilliant amateurishness and its consequent tragedy.

In Castalia, as it happens, the intellectual freedom of the student is infinitely greater than it ever was at the universities of earlier ages, since the available materials and opportunities for study are far ampler. Moreover, studies in Castalia are in no way restricted or colored by material considerations, by ambition, timidity, straitened circumstances of the parents, prospects for livelihood and career, and so on. In the academies, seminars, libraries, archives, and laboratories of the Pedagogic Province every student is completely equal, no matter what his origins and prospects. The hierarchy grades the student solely by his qualities of mind and character. On the other hand most of the freedoms, temptations, and dangers to which so many talented youths succumb at the secular universities simply do not exist in Castalia. Not that there is a dearth of danger, passion, and bedazzlement there—how could these elements ever be completely absent from human life? But at least certain opportunities for going off the rails, for disappointment and disaster, have been eliminated. There is no danger of the Castalian student's becoming a drinker. Nor can he waste the years of his youth in tomfoolery, or the empty braggadocio of secret societies, as did some generations of students in olden times. Nor is he apt to make the discovery someday that his degree was a mistake, that there are gaps in his preparatory education which can never be filled. The Castalian order of things protects him against such blunders.

The danger of wasting himself on women or on losing himself in sports is also minimal. As far as women are concerned, the Castalian student is not subject to the temptations and dangers of marriage, nor is he oppressed by the prudery of a good many past eras which imposed continence on students or else made them turn to more or less venal and sluttish women. Since there is no marriage for the Castalians, love is not governed by a morality directed toward marriage. Since the Castalian has no money and virtually no property, he also cannot purchase love. It is customary in the Province for the daughters of the citizenry not to marry early, and in the years before marriage they look upon students and scholars as particularly desirable lovers. The young men, for their part, are not interested in birth and fortune, are prone to grant at least equal importance to mental and emotional capacities, are usually endowed with imagination and humor and, since they have no money, must make their repayment by giving more of themselves than others would. In Castalia the sweetheart of a student does not ask herself: will he marry me? She knows he will not. Actually, there have been occasions when he did; every so often an elite student would return to the world by way of marriage, giving up Castalia and membership in the Order. But these few, rare cases of apostasy in the history of the schools and of the Order amount to little more than a curiosity.

After graduation from the preparatory schools the elite student truly enjoys a remarkable degree of freedom and self-determination in choosing among the fields of knowledge and research. Unless a student's own talents and interests dictate natural bounds from the start, the only limit on this freedom is his obligation to present a plan of study for each semester. The authorities oversee the execution of this plan in only the mildest way. For young men of versatile talents and interests—and Knecht was one of these—the scope thus allowed him is wonderfully enticing and a source of continual delight. The authorities permit such students, if they do not drift into sheer idleness, almost paradisiacal freedom. The student may dabble in all sorts of fields, combine the widest variety of subjects, fall in love with six or eight disciplines simultaneously, or confine himself to a narrower selection from the beginning. Aside from observing the general rules of morality that apply to the whole Province and the Order, nothing is asked of him except presentation once a year of the record of the lectures he has attended, the books he has read, and the research he has undertaken at the various institutes. His performance comes in for closer check only when he attends technical courses and seminars, including courses in the Glass Bead Game and at the Conservatory of Music. Here every student has to take the official examinations and write the papers or do the work required by the head of the seminar, as is only natural. But no one forces him to take such courses. For semesters or for years he may, if he pleases, merely make use of the libraries and listen to lectures. Students who take a long while before deciding upon a single field of knowledge thereby delay their admission into the Order, but the authorities show great patience in allowing and even encouraging their explorations of all possible disciplines and types of study. Aside from good moral conduct, nothing is required of them except the composition of a "Life" every year.

It is to this old and much-mocked custom that we owe the three "Lives" by Knecht written during his years of free study. These were, then, not a purely voluntary and unofficial, not to say secret and more or less illicit kind of literary activity, such as his poems written at Waldzell had been, but a normal and official assignment. Far back in the earliest days of the Pedagogic Province the custom had arisen of requiring the younger students, those who had not yet been admitted to the Order, to compose from time to time a special kind of essay or stylistic exercise which was called a "Life." It was to be a fictitious autobiography set in any period of the past the writer chose. The student's assignment was to transpose himself back to the surroundings, culture, and intellectual climate of any earlier era and to imagine himself living a suitable life in that period. Depending on the times and the fashion, imperial Rome, seventeenth-century France, or fifteenth-century Italy might be the period most favored, or Periclean Athens or Austria in the time of Mozart. Among language specialists it had become the custom to compose their imaginary biographies in the language of the country and the style of the period in which they were best versed. Thus there had been highly ingenious Lives

written in the style of the Papal Curia at Rome around
the year 1200, in monastic Latin, in the Italian of the
"Cento Novelle Antiche," in the French of Montaigne,
and the baroque German of Martin Opitz.

A remnant of the ancient Asian doctrine of reincarnation and the transmigration of souls survived in this
playful, highly flexible form. All teachers and students
were familiar with the concept that their present existence might have been preceded by others, in other
bodies, at other times, under other conditions. To be sure
they did not believe this in any strict sense; there was
no element of dogma in the idea. Rather, it was an
exercise, a game for the imaginative faculties, to conceive of oneself in different conditions and surroundings.
In writing such Lives students made a stab at a cautious
penetration of past cultures, times, and countries, just
as they did in many seminars on stylistics, and in the
Glass Bead Game as well. They learned to regard their
own persons as masks, as the transitory garb of an entele-
chy. The custom of writing such Lives had its charm,
and a good many solid benefits as well, or it probably
would not have endured for so long.

Incidentally, there was a rather considerable number
of students who not only more or less believed in the
idea of reincarnation, but also in the truth of their own
fictional Lives. Thus the majority of these imaginary pre-
existences were not merely stylistic exercises and historical studies, but also creations of wishful thinking and
exalted self-portraits. The authors cast themselves as the
characters they longed to become. They portrayed their
dream and their ideal. Furthermore, from the pedagogic
point of view the Lives were not a bad idea at all. They
provided a legitimate channel for the creative urge of
youth. Although serious, creative literary work had been
frowned on for generations, and replaced partly by scholarship, partly by the Glass Bead Game, youth's artistic
impulse had not been crushed. In these Lives, which
were often elaborated into small novels, it found a permissible means of expression. What is more, while writing these Lives some of the authors took their first steps
into the land of self-knowledge.

Incidentally, the students frequently used their Lives

for critical and revolutionary outbursts on the contemporary world and on Castalia. The teachers usually regarded such sallies with understanding benevolence. In addition, these Lives were extremely revealing to the teachers during those periods in which the students enjoyed maximum freedom and were subject to no close supervision. The compositions often provided astonishingly clear insight into the intellectual and moral state of the authors.

Three such Lives written by Joseph Knecht have been preserved. We intend to reproduce their full text, and regard them as possibly the most valuable part of our book. There is much room for conjecture as to whether he wrote only these three Lives, or whether there might have been others which have been lost. All we know definitely is that after Knecht handed in his third, "Indian" Life, the Secretariat of the Board of Educators suggested that if he wrote any additional Lives he ought to set them in an era historically closer to the present and more richly documented, and that he should pay more attention to historical detail. We know from anecdotes and letters that he thereupon actually engaged in preliminary research for a Life set in the eighteenth century. He cast himself as a Swabian pastor who subsequently turned from the service of the Church to music, who had been a disciple of Johann Albrecht Bengel, a friend of Oetinger, and for a while a guest of Zinzendorf's congregation of Moravian Brethren. We know that he was reading and taking notes on a quantity of old and often out-of-the-way books on church organization, Pietism, and Zinzendorf, as well as on the liturgy and church music of the period. We know also that he was fascinated with Oetinger, the charismatic prelate, and that he felt genuine love and veneration for Magister Bengel; he went to some pains to have a photograph made of Bengel's portrait and for a while had the picture standing on his desk. He also honestly tried to write an account of Zinzendorf, who both intrigued and repelled him. But in the end he dropped this project, content with what he had learned from it. He declared that he had lost the capacity for making a Life out of these materials through having studied the subject from too many angles and accumulated too many details. In view of this statement, we may justifiably regard the three Lives he did complete rather as the creations of a poetic spirit than the works of a scholar. In saying this we do not think we are doing them any injustice.

In addition to the freedom of the student at last permitted to range at will in self-chosen studies, Knecht now enjoyed a different kind of freedom and relaxation. He had not, after all, been merely a student like all the others; he had not only submitted to the strict training, the exacting schedules, the careful supervision and scrutiny of the teachers, in a word to all the rigor of elite schooling. For along with all that, because of his relationship to Plinio he had borne the far greater strain of a responsibility which had in part spurred him to the utmost of his potentialities, in part drawn heavily on his energies. In assuming the role of public advocate of Castalia he had taken on a responsibility that was really too much for his years and his strength. He had run grave risks, and succeeded only by applying excessive will power and talent. In fact, without the Music Master's powerful assistance from afar, he would not have been able to carry his assignment to its conclusion.

At the end of those unusual years at Waldzell we find him, a young man of twenty-four, mature beyond his age and somewhat overstrained, but amazingly bearing no visible traces of damage. But the degree to which his whole nature had been taxed and brought to the verge of exhaustion is apparent, although there is no direct documentation for it, from the way he employed the first few years of that freedom he had at last attained, and for which he had no doubt deeply yearned. Having stood in so conspicuous a position during his last years at school, he immediately and completely withdrew from the public eye. Indeed, when we seek the traces of his life at that time, we have the impression that if he could he would have made himself invisible. No surroundings and no society seemed undemanding enough for him, no mode of living private enough. For example, he replied curtly and reluctantly to several long and tempestuous letters from Designori, then ceased to answer altogether. The famous student Knecht vanished and could no longer be located; but in Waldzell his fame continued to flower, and in time became almost a legend.

At the beginning of his years of free study he avoided Waldzell for the reasons given. This meant that for the time being he eschewed the graduate and postgraduate courses in the Glass Bead Game. But although to the superficial observer Knecht was ostentatiously neglecting the Game, we know that on the contrary the entire seemingly wayward and disconnected, and certainly altogether unusual course of his studies had been influenced by the Glass Bead Game and led back to it and to the service of the Game. We mean to discuss this somewhat at length, for this trait was characteristic. Joseph Knecht employed his freedom for study in the strangest and most idiosyncratic fashion, one that revealed an astonishing youthful genius. During his years at Waldzell he had, as was usual, taken the official introduction to the Glass Bead Game and the review course as well. During his last school year and among his friends he already had the reputation of being an excellent player. But then he was gripped with such a passion for this Game of games that after completing another course and while still in school he had been admitted to a course for players of the second stage, which was a very rare distinction indeed.

Some years later he told his friend and later assistant, Fritz Tegularius (who had at school taken the review course along with him) of an experience which not only decided his destiny as a Glass Bead Game player, but also greatly influenced the course of his studies. The letter is extant; the passage runs: "Let me remind you of the time the two of us, assigned to the same group, were so eagerly working on our first sketches for Glass Bead Games. Do you recall a certain day and a certain game? Our group leader had given us various suggestions and proposed all sorts of themes for us to choose from. We had just arrived at the delicate transition from astronomy, mathematics, and physics to the sciences of language and history, and the leader was a virtuoso in the art of setting traps for eager beginners like us and luring us on to the thin ice of impermissible abstractions and analogies. He would slip into our hands tempting baubles taken from etymology and comparative linguistics, and enjoyed seeing us grab them and come to grief. We counted Greek quantities until we were worn out, only to feel the rug pulled out from under us when he suddenly confronted us with the possibility, in fact the necessity, of accentual instead of a quantitative scansion, and so on. In formal terms he did his job brilliantly, and quite properly, although I did not like the spirit of it. He showed us false trails and lured us into faulty conjectures, partly with the good intention of familiarizing us with the perils, but also a little in order to laugh at us for being such stupid boys and to instil a heavy dose of skepticism into those of us who were most enthusiastic about the Game. And yet as things turned out it happened under his instruction and in the course of one of his complicated trick experiments—we were timidly and awkwardly trying to sketch a halfway decent Game problem—that I was all at once seized by the meaning and the greatness of our Game, and was shaken by it to the core of my being. We were picking apart a problem in linguistic history and, as it were, examining close up the peak period of glory in the history of a language; in minutes we had traced the path which had taken it several centuries. And I was powerfully gripped by the vision of transitoriness: the way before our eyes such a complex, ancient, venerable organism, slowly built up over many generations, reaches its highest point, which already contains the germ of decay, and the whole intelligently articulated structure begins to droop, to degenerate, to totter toward its doom. And at the same time the thought abruptly shot through me, with a joyful, startled amazement, that despite the decay and death of that language it had not been lost, that its youth, maturity, and downfall were preserved in our memory, in our knowledge of it and its history, and would survive and could at any time be reconstructed in the symbols and formulas of scholarship as well as in the recondite formulations of the Glass Bead Game. I suddenly realized that in the language, or at any rate in the spirit of the Glass Bead Game, everything actually was all-meaningful, that every symbol and combination of symbols led not hither and yon, not to single examples, experiments, and proofs, but into the center, the mystery and innermost heart of the world, into primal knowledge. Every transition from major to minor in a sonata, every transformation of a myth or a religious cult, every classical or artistic formulation was, I realized in that flashing moment, if seen with a truly meditative mind, nothing but a direct route into the interior of the cosmic mystery, where in the alternation between inhaling and exhaling, between heaven and earth, between Yin and Yang, holiness is forever being created.

"Of course by that time I had attended many a well-constructed and well-executed Game. Listening, I had often been exalted and overjoyed by the insights such Games afforded; but up to that time I had repeatedly been inclined to doubt the real value and importance of the Game. After all, every neatly solved problem in mathematics could provide intellectual pleasure; every good piece of music could exalt and expand the soul toward universality when heard, and even more when played; and every reverent meditation could soothe the heart and tune it to harmony with the universe. But perhaps for that very reason, my doubts whispered, the Glass Bead Game was merely a formal art, a clever skill, a witty combination, so that it would be better not to play this Game, but to occupy oneself with uncontaminated mathematics and good music.

"But now for the first time I had heard the inner voice of the Game itself, its meaning. It had reached me and penetrated me, and since that moment I have believed that our royal game is truly a *lingua sacra*, a sacred and divine language. You will remember, for you remarked on it yourself at the time, that a change had taken place within me, a summons had come to me. I can compare it only to that unforgettable call which once lifted my heart and transformed my life when as a boy I was tested by the Magister Musicae and summoned to Castalia. You noticed it; I felt that at the time, although you said not a word about it. Let us say no more about it today. But now I have something to ask you, and in order to explain my request I must tell you something that no one else knows or is to know: that my seemingly disorganized studies at the present time are not the result of

whim, but of a definite underlying plan. You will recall,
at least in general outline, the Glass Bead Game exercise
we constructed at that time, as pupils in the Third Course,
and with the leader's assistance—in the course of which
I heard that voice and experienced my vocation as a
lusor. That game began with a rhythmic analysis of a
fugal theme and in the center of it was a sentence attributed to Confucius. Now I am studying that entire
game from beginning to end. That is, I am working
through each of its phrases, translating it from the language of the Game back into its original language, into
mathematics, ornament, Chinese, Greek, and so on. At
least this once in my life I intend to restudy and reconstruct systematically the entire content of a Glass Bead
Game. I have already finished the first part, and it has
taken me two years. Of course it is going to cost me
quite a few years more. But since we are granted our
famous freedom of study in Castalia, this is how I mean
to use it. I am familiar with the objections to such a
procedure. Most of our teachers would say: We have devoted several centuries to inventing and elaborating the
Glass Bead Game as a universal language and method
for expressing all intellectual concepts and all artistic
values and reducing them to a common denominator.
Now you come along and want to check over everything
to see if it is correct. That will take you a lifetime, and
you will regret it.

"Well, I shall not take a lifetime and I hope I won't
regret it. And now for my request. Since at present you
are working in the Game Archives and I for special reasons prefer to keep away from Waldzell for a good while
longer, I hope you will answer quite a barrage of questions for me every so often. That is, I shall be asking you
to send me from the Archives the unabbreviated forms
of the official clefs and symbols for all sorts of themes.
I am counting on you, and counting on your asking reciprocal favors as soon as there is anything I can do for
you."

Perhaps this is the place to cite that other passage
from Knecht's letters which also deals with the Glass
Bead Game, although the letter in question, addressed
to the Music Master, was written at least a year or two

later. "I imagine," Knecht wrote to his patron, "that one can be an excellent Glass Bead Game player, even a virtuoso, and perhaps even a thoroughly competent Magister Ludi, without having any inkling of the real mystery of the Game and its ultimate meaning. It might even be that one who does guess or know the truth might prove a greater danger to the Game, were he to become a specialist in the Game, or a Game leader. For the dark interior, the esoterics of the Game, points down into the One and All, into those depths where the eternal Atman eternally breathes in and out, sufficient unto itself. One who had experienced the ultimate meaning of the Game within himself would by that fact no longer be a player; he would no longer dwell in the world of multiplicity and would no longer be able to delight in invention, construction, and combination, since he would know altogether different joys and raptures. Because I think I have come close to the meaning of the Glass Bead Game, it will be better for me and for others if I do not make the Game my profession, but instead shift to music."

The Music Master, who usually confined his correspondence to a minimum, was evidently troubled by these remarks and replied with a rather lengthy piece of friendly admonition: "It is good that you yourself do not require a master of the Game to be an 'esoteric' in your sense of the word, for I hope you wrote that without irony. A Game Master or teacher who was primarily concerned with being close enough to the 'innermost meaning' would be a very bad teacher. To be candid, I myself, for example, have never in my life said a word to my pupils about the 'meaning' of music; if there is one, it does not need my explanations. On the other I have always made a great point of having my pupils count their eighths and sixteenths nicely. Whatever you become, teacher, scholar, or musician, have respect for the 'meaning,' but do not imagine that it can be taught. Once upon a time the philosophers of history ruined half of world history with their efforts to teach such 'meaning'; they inaugurated the Age of the Feuilleton and are partly to blame for quantities of spilled blood. If I were introducing pupils to Homer or Greek tragedy,

say, I would also not try to tell them that the poetry is
one of the manifestations of the divine, but would endeavor to make the poetry accessible to them by imparting a precise knowledge of its linguistic and metrical strategies. The task of the teacher and scholar is to
study means, cultivate tradition, and preserve the purity
of methods, not to deal in incommunicable experiences
which are reserved to the elect—who often enough pay a
high price for this privilege."

There is no other mention of the Glass Bead Game
and its "esoteric" aspect in all the rest of Knecht's correspondence of that period. Indeed, he does not seem
to have written many letters, or else some of them have
been lost. At any rate, the largest and best-preserved
correspondence, that with Ferromonte, deals almost
entirely with problems of music and musical stylistic
analysis.

Thus there was a special meaning and resolution behind the peculiar zigzag course of Knecht's studies,
which consisted in nothing less than the circumstantial
retracing and prolonged analysis of a single Game pattern. In order to assimilate the contents of this one pattern, which the schoolboys had composed as an exercise
within a few days, and which could be read off in a quarter hour in the language of the Glass Bead Game, he spent
year after year sitting in lecture halls and libraries, studying Froberger and Alessandro Scarlatti, fugues and
sonata form, reviewing mathematics, learning Chinese,
working through a system of tonal figuration and the
Feustelian theory of the correspondence between the
scale of colors and the musical keys.

We may ask why he had chosen this toilsome, eccentric, and above all lonely path, for his ultimate goal (outside of Castalia, people would say: his choice of profession) was undoubtedly the Glass Bead Game. He might
freely have entered one of the institutes of the Vicus
Lusorum, the settlement of Glass Bead Game players in
Waldzell, as a guest scholar. In that case all the special
studies connected with the Game would have been made
easier for him. Advice and information on all questions
of detail would have been available to him at any time,
and in addition he could have pursued his studies among

other scholars in the same field, young men with the same devotion to the Game, instead of struggling alone in a state that often amounted to voluntary banishment. Be that as it may, he went his own way. We suspect that he avoided Waldzell partly to expunge as far as possible from his own mind and the minds of others the memory of his role as a student there, partly so that he would not stumble into a similar role among the community of Glass Bead Game players. For he probably bore away the feeling from those early days that he was predestined to become a leader and spokesman, and he did all that he could to outwit the obtrusiveness of fate. He sensed in advance the weight of responsibility; he could already feel it toward his fellow students from Waldzell, who went on adulating him even though he withdrew from them. And he felt it especially toward Tegularius, who would go through fire and water for him—this he knew instinctively.

Therefore he sought seclusion and contemplation, while his destiny tried to propel him forward into the public realm. It is in these terms that we imagine his state of mind at the time. But there was another important factor that deterred him from taking the usual courses at the higher Glass Bead Game academies and made an outsider of him. That was an inexorable urge toward research arising from his former doubts about the Glass Bead Game. To be sure, he had once tasted the experience that the Game could be played in a supreme and sacred sense; but he had also seen that the majority of players and students of the Game, and even some of the leaders and teachers, by no means shared that lofty and sacramental feeling for the Game. They did not regard the Game language as a *lingua sacra*, but more as an ingenious kind of stenography. They practiced the Game as an interesting or amusing specialty, an intellectual sport or an arena for ambition. In fact, as his letter to the Music Master shows, he already sensed that the search for ultimate meaning does not necessarily determine the quality of the player, that its superficial aspects were also essential to the Game, that it comprised technique, science, and social institution. In short, he had doubts and divided feelings; the Game was a vital ques-

tion for him, had become the chief problem of his life,
and he was by no means disposed to let well-meaning
spiritual guides ease his struggles or benignly smiling
teachers dismiss them as trivial.

Naturally he could have made any one of the tens of
thousands of recorded Glass Bead Games and the millions of possible games the basis of his studies. He knew
this and therefore proceeded from that chance Game
plan that he and his schoolmates had composed in an
elementary course. It was the game in which he had for
the first time grasped the meaning of all Glass Bead
Games and experienced his vocation as a player. During
those years he kept with him at all times an outline of that
Game, noted down in the usual shorthand. In the symbols, ciphers, signatures, and abbreviations of the Game
language an astronomical formula, the principles of form
underlying an old sonata, an utterance of Confucius,
and so on, were written down. A reader who chanced
to be ignorant of the Glass Bead Game might imagine
such a Game pattern as rather similar to the pattern of a
chess game, except that the significances of the pieces
and the potentialities of their relationships to one another
and their effect upon one another multiplied manyfold
and an actual content must be ascribed to each piece,
each constellation, each chess move, of which this move,
configuration, and so on is the symbol.

Knecht's studies went beyond the task of acquainting
himself in the utmost detail with the contents, principles,
books, and systems contained in the Game plan, and
retracting as he went a way back through various cultures, sciences, languages, arts, and centuries. He had also
set himself the task that none of his teachers even
recognized, of employing these objects to check in detail
the systems and possibilities of expression in the art of
the Glass Bead Game.

To anticipate his results: here and there he found a
gap, an inadequacy, but on the whole our Glass Bead
Game withstood his stringent reassessment. Otherwise he
would not have returned to it at the end of his work.

If we were writing a study in cultural history, a good
many of the places and scenes of Knecht's student days
would certainly merit description. As far as possible he

preferred places where he could work alone, or with only a very few others, and to some of these places he retained a lifelong grateful attachment. He frequently stayed in Monteport, sometimes as the Music Master's guest, sometimes as a participant in a musicological seminar. Twice we find him in Hirsland, the headquarters of the Order, as a participant in the "Great Exercise," the twelve-day period of fasting and meditation. He used later to tell his intimates with special affection about the "Bamboo Grove," the lovely hermitage which was the scene of his *I Ching* studies. There he learned and experienced things of crucial importance. There, too, guided by a wonderful premonition or Providence, he found unique surroundings and an extraordinary person: the founder and inmate of the Chinese hermitage, who was called Elder Brother. We think it proper to describe at greater length this most remarkable episode in his years of free study.

Knecht had begun his studies of the Chinese language and classics in the famous Far Eastern College which for generations had been affiliated to St. Urban's, the academic complex devoted to classical philology. There he had made rapid progress in reading and writing and also struck up friendships with several of the Chinese working there, and had learned a number of the odes of the *Shih Ching* by heart. In the second year of his stay he turned to a more and more intense study of the *I Ching*, the Book of Changes. The Chinese provided him with all sorts of information, but no introductory course; there was no teacher available in the college, and after Knecht had repeatedly petitioned them for an instructor for a thorough study of the *I Ching*, he was told about Elder Brother and his hermitage.

It had become apparent to Knecht that his interest in the Book of Changes was leading him into a field which the teachers at the college preferred to keep at a distance, and he therefore grew more cautious in his inquiries. Now, as he made efforts to obtain further information about this legendary Elder Brother, it became obvious to him that the hermit enjoyed a measure of respect, and indeed a degree of fame, but more as an eccentric loner than as a scholar. Knecht sensed that he

would have to help himself; he finished a paper he had
begun for a seminar as quickly as possible, and took his
leave. On foot, he made his way to the region in which
the mysterious man, perhaps a sage and Master, perhaps a fool, had long ago established his Bamboo Grove.

He had gathered a few bits of information about the
hermit. Some twenty-five years before, the man had
been the most promising student in the Chinese Department. He seemed to have been born for these studies,
outdid his best teachers, both Chinese by birth and
Westerners, in the technique of brush writing and the
deciphering of ancient texts, but became somewhat
notorious for the zeal with which he also tried to make
himself into a Chinese in outward matters also. Thus he
obstinately refused to address his superiors, from the instructor of a seminar to the Masters, by their titles, as
all other students did. Instead, he called them "My
Elder Brother," until at last this appellation became attached to himself as a nickname. He devoted special
attention to the oracular game of the *I Ching*, and developed a masterly skill at practicing it with the traditional
yarrow stalks. Along with the ancient commentaries on
the Book of Changes, his favorite book was the philosophical work of Chuang Tzu. Evidently the rationalistic,
somewhat antimystical, and declaredly Confucian spirit
of the Chinese Department of the college, as Knecht
encountered it, had already been prevalent at that time,
for one day Elder Brother left the Institute, which would
gladly have kept him as a teacher, and set out on a walking tour, armed with brush, Chinese ink saucer, and two
or three books. He made his way to the southern part of
the country, turning up here and there to visit for a while
with brethren of the Order. He looked for and finally
found the suitable spot for the hermitage he planned,
stubbornly bombarded both the secular authorities and
the Order with written and oral petitions until they
granted him the right to settle there and cultivate the
area. Ever since, he had been living in an idyllic retreat
strictly governed by ancient Chinese principles. Some
referred to him with amusement as a crank, others venerated him as a kind of saint. But apparently he was content with himself and at peace with the world, devoting

his days to meditation and the copying of ancient scrolls whenever he was not occupied with his Bamboo Grove, which sheltered from the north wind a carefully laid out Chinese miniature garden.

Joseph Knecht, then, tramped toward this hermitage, making frequent stops to rest, delighting in the landscape that lay smiling beneath him as soon as he had climbed through the mountain passes, stretching southward in a blue haze, with sunlit terraced vineyards, brown stone walls alive with lizards, stately chestnut groves, a piquant mingling of southland and high mountain country. It was late afternoon when he reached the Bamboo Grove. He entered and looked with astonishment upon a Chinese pavilion set in the midst of a curious garden, with a splashing fountain fed by a wooden pipe. The overflow ran along a gravel bed into a masonry basin, in whose crevices all sorts of green plants flourished. A few goldfish swam around in the still, crystalline water. Fragile and peaceful, the feathery crowns of the bamboos swayed on their strong, slender shafts. The sward was punctuated by stone slabs carved with inscriptions in the classical style.

A frail man dressed in tan linen, glasses over blue eyes that bore a tentative look, straightened up from a flower bed over which he had been bending and slowly approached the visitor. His manner was not unfriendly, but it had that somewhat awkward shyness rather common among solitaries and recluses. He looked inquiringly at Knecht and waited for what he had to say. With some embarrassment Knecht spoke the Chinese words he had already formulated: "The young disciple takes the liberty of paying his respects to Elder Brother."

"The well-bred guest is welcome," Elder Brother said. "May a young colleague always be welcome to a bowl of tea and a little agreeable conversation; and a bed for the night may be found for him, if this is desired."

Knecht kowtowed, expressed his thanks, and was led into the pavilion and served tea. Then he was shown the garden, the carved slabs, the pond, the goldfish, and was even told the age of the fish. Until suppertime they sat under the swaying bamboos exchanging courtesies, verses from odes, and sayings from the classical writers.

They looked at the flowers and took pleasure in the fading pinks of sunset along the mountain ranges. Then they re-entered the house. Elder Brother served bread and fruit, cooked an excellent pancake for each of them on a tiny stove, and after they had eaten he asked in German the purpose of his visit, and in German Knecht explained why he had come and what he desired, which was to stay as long as Elder Brother permitted him, and to become his disciple.

"We shall discuss that tomorrow," the hermit said, and showed his guest to a bed.

Next morning Knecht sat down by the goldfish pool and gazed into the cool small world of darkness and light and magically shimmering colors, where the bodies of the golden fish glided in the dark greenish blueness and inky blackness. Now and then, just when the entire world seemed enchanted, asleep forever in a dreamy spell, the fish would dart with a supple and yet alarming movement, like flashes of crystal and gold, through the somnolent darkness. He looked down, becoming more and more absorbed, daydreaming rather than meditating, and was not conscious when Elder Brother stepped softly out of the house, paused, and stood for a long time watching his bemused guest. When Knecht at last shook off his abstraction and stood up, he was no longer there, but his voice soon called from inside an invitation to tea. They greeted each other briefly, drank tea, and sat listening in the matutinal stillness to the sound of the small jet of water from the fountain, a melody of eternity. Then the hermit stood up, busied himself here and there about the irregularly shaped room, now and then glancing, blinking rapidly, at Knecht. Suddenly he asked: "Are you ready to don your shoes and continue your journeying?"

Knecht hesitated. Then he said: "If it must be so, I am ready."

"And if it should chance that you stay here a little while, are you ready to be obedient and to keep as still as a goldfish?"

Again Knecht said he was ready.

"It is well," Elder Brother said. "Now I shall lay the stalks and consult the oracle."

While Knecht sat and looked on with an awe equal to his curiosity, keeping "as still as a goldfish," Elder Brother fetched from a wooden beaker, which was rather a kind of quiver, a handful of sticks. These were the yarrow stalks. He counted them out carefully, returned one part of the bundle to the vessel, laid a stalk aside, divided the rest into two equal bundles, kept one in his left hand, and with the sensitive fingertips of his right hand took tiny little clusters from the pack in his left. He counted these and laid them aside until only a few stalks remained. These he held between two fingers of his left hand. After thus reducing one bundle by ritual counting to a few stalks, he followed the same procedure with the other bundle. He laid the counted stalks to one side, then went through both bundles again, one after the other, counting, clamping small remnants of bundles between two fingers. His fingers performed all this with economical motions and quiet agility; it looked like an occult game of skill governed by strict rules, practiced thousands of times and brought to a high degree of virtuoso dexterity. After he had gone through the same process several times, three small bundles remained. From the number of stalks in them he read an ideograph which he drew with a tapering brush on a small piece of paper. Now the whole complicated procedure began anew; the sticks were divided again into two equal bundles, counted, laid aside, thrust between fingers, until in the end again three tiny bundles remained which resulted in a second ideograph. Moved about like dancers, making very soft, dry clicks, the stalks came together, changed places, formed bundles, were separated, were counted anew; they shifted positions rhythmically, with a ghostly sureness. At the end of each process an ideograph was written, until finally the positive and negative symbols stood in six lines one above the other. The stalks were gathered up and carefully replaced in their container. The sage sat crosslegged on the floor of reed matting, for a long time silently examining the result of the augury on the sheet of paper.

"It is the sign Mong," he said. "This sign bears the name: youthful folly. Above the mountain, below the water; above Gen, below Kan. At the foot of the fountain the spring bubbles forth, the symbol of youth. The verdict reads:

> Youthful folly wins success.
> I do not seek the young fool,
> The young fool seeks me.
> At the first oracle I give knowledge.
> If he asks again, it is importunity.
> If he importunes, I give no knowledge.
> Perseverance is beneficial."

Knecht had been holding his breath from sheer suspense. In the ensuing silence he involuntarily gave a deep sigh of relief. He did not dare to ask. But he thought he had understood: the young fool had turned up; he would be permitted to stay. Even while he was still enthralled by the sublime marionettes' dance of fingers and sticks, which he had watched for so long and which looked so persuasively meaningful, the result took hold of him. The oracle had spoken; it had decided in his favor.

We would not have described this episode in such detail if Knecht himself had not so frequently related it to his friends with a certain relish. Now we shall return to our scholarly account.

Knecht remained at the Bamboo Grove for months and learned to manipulate the yarrow stalks almost as well as his teacher. The latter spent an hour a day with him, practicing counting the sticks, imparting the grammar and symbolism of the oracular language, and drilling him in writing and memorizing the sixty-four signs. He read to Knecht from ancient commentaries, and every so often, on particularly good days, told him a story by Chuang Tzu. For the rest, the disciple learned to tend the garden, wash the brushes, and prepare the Chinese ink. He also learned to make soup and tea, gather brushwood, observe the weather, and handle the Chinese calendar. But his rare attempts to introduce the Glass Bead Game and music into their sparing conversations yielded no results whatsoever; they seemed to fall upon deaf ears, or else were turned aside with a forbearing smile or a proverb such as, "Dense clouds, no rain," or, "Nobility is without flaw." But when Knecht had a small clavichord sent from Monteport and spent an hour a day playing, Elder Brother made no objection. Once Knecht confessed to his teacher that he wished to learn enough to be able to incorporate the system of the *I Ching* into the Glass Bead Game. Elder Brother laughed. "Go ahead and try," he exclaimed. "You'll see how it turns out. Anyone can create a pretty little bamboo garden in the world. But I doubt that the gardener would succeed in incorporating the world in his bamboo grove."

But enough of this. We shall mention only the one further fact that some years later, when Knecht was already a highly respected personage in Waldzell and invited Elder Brother to give a course there, he received no answer.

Afterward Joseph Knecht described the months he lived in the Bamboo Grove as an unusually happy time. He also frequently referred to it as the "beginning of my awakening"—and in fact from that period on the image of "awakening" turns up more and more often in his remarks, with a meaning similar to although not quite the same as that he had formerly attributed to the image of vocation. It could be assumed that the "awakening" signified knowledge of himself and of the place he occupied within the Castalian and the general human order of things; but it seems to us that the accent increasingly shifts toward self-knowledge in the sense that from the "beginning of his awakening" Knecht came closer and closer to a sense of his special, unique position and destiny, while at the same time the concepts and categories of the traditional hierarchy of the world and of the special Castalian hierarchy became for him more and more relative matters.

His Chinese studies were far from concluded during his stay in the Bamboo Grove. They continued, and Knecht made particular efforts to acquire a knowledge of ancient Chinese music. Everywhere in the older Chinese writers he encountered praise of music as one of the primal sources of all order, morality, beauty, and health. This broad, ethical view of music was familiar to him from of old, for the Music Master could be regarded as the very embodiment of it.

Without ever forsaking the fundamental plan of his studies, which as we have seen he outlined in his letter to Fritz Tegularius, he pushed forward energetically on a broad front wherever he scented an element of essential value to himself, that is to say, wherever the path of "awakening," on which he had already set out, seemed to lead him. One of the positive results of his period of apprenticeship with Elder Brother was that he overcame his resistance against returning to Waldzell. Henceforth he participated in one of the advanced courses there every year, and without quite realizing how it had happened he became a personage regarded with interest and esteem in the Vicus Lusorum. He belonged to that central and most sensitive organ of the entire Game organization, that anonymous group of players of proven worth in whose hands lay the destinies of the Game at any given time, or at least the type of play that happened to be in fashion.

Officials of the Game institutes belonged to but did not dominate this group, which usually met in several remote, quiet rooms of the Game Archives. There the members beguiled their time with critical studies of the Game, championing the inclusion of new subject areas, or arguing for their exclusion, debating for or against certain constantly shifting tastes in regard to the form, the procedures, the sporting aspects of the Glass Bead Game. Everyone who had made a place for himself in this group was a virtuoso of the Game; each knew to a hair the talents and peculiarities of all the others. The atmosphere was like that in the corridors of a government ministry or an aristocratic club where the rulers and those who will take over their responsibilities in the near future meet and get to know one another. A muted, polished tone prevailed in this group. Its members were ambitious without showing it, keen-eyed and critical to excess. Many in Castalia, and some in the rest of the country outside the Province, regarded this elite as the ultimate flower of Castalian tradition, the cream of an exclusive intellectual aristocracy, and a good many youths dreamed for years of some day belonging to it themselves. To others, however, this elect circle of candidates for the higher reaches in the hierarchy of the Glass

Bead Game seemed odious and debased, a clique of haughty idlers, brilliant but spoiled geniuses who lacked all feeling for life and reality, an arrogant and fundamentally parasitic company of dandies and climbers who had made a silly game, a sterile self-indulgence of the mind, their vocation and the content of their life.

Knecht was untouched by either of these attitudes. It did not matter to him whether he figured in student gossip as some sort of phenomenon or as a parvenu and climber. What was important to him were his studies, all of which now centered around the Game. Another preoccupation was, perhaps, that one question of whether the Game really was the supreme achievement of Castalia and worth devoting one's life to. For even as he was familiarizing himself with the ever more recondite mysteries of the Game's laws and potentialities, even as he became more and more at home in the labyrinths of the Archives and the complex inner world of the Game's symbolism, his doubts had by no means been silenced. He had already learned by experience that faith and doubt belong together, that they govern each other like inhaling and exhaling, and that his very advances in all aspects of the Game's mirocosm naturally sharpened his eyes to all the dubiousness of the Game. For a little while, perhaps, the idyll in the Bamboo Grove had reassured him, or perhaps one might say confused him. The example of Elder Brother had shown him that there were ways of escaping from this dubiousness. It was possible, for example, as that recluse had done, to turn oneself into a Chinese, shut oneself off behind a garden hedge, and live in a self-sufficient and beautiful kind of perfection. One might also become a Pythagorean or a monk and scholastic—but these were still escapes, renunciations of universality possible and permissible only to a few. They involved renunciation of the present and the future in favor of something perfect enough, but past. Knecht had sensed in good time that this type of escape was not the way for him. But what then was the way for him? Aside from his great talent for music and for the Glass Bead Game, he was aware of still other forces within himself, a certain inner independence, a self-reliance which by no means barred him or hampered him from serving, but demanded of him that he serve only the highest master. And this strength, this independence, this self-reliance, was not just a trait in his character, it was not just inturned and effective only upon himself; it also affected the outside world.

As early as his years at school, and especially during the period of his contest with Plinio Designori, Joseph Knecht had often noticed that many schoolmates his own age, but even more the younger boys, liked him, sought his friendship, and moreover tended to let him dominate them. They asked him for advice, put themselves under his influence. Ever since, this experience had been repeated frequently. It had its pleasant and flattering side; it satisfied ambition and strengthened self-confidence. But it also had another, a dark and terrifying side. For there was something bad and unpalatable about the attitude one took toward these schoolmates so eager for advice, guidance, and an example, about the impulse to despise them for their lack of self-reliance and dignity, and about the occasional secret temptation to make them (at least in thought) into obedient slaves. Moreover, during the time with Plinio he had had a taste of the responsibility, strain, and psychological burden which is the price paid for every brilliant and publicly representative position. He knew also that the Music Master sometimes felt weighed down by his own position. It was lovely, and tempting, to exert power over men and to shine before others, but power also had its perditions and perils. History, after all, consisted of an unbroken succession of rulers, leaders, bosses, and commanders who with extremely rare exceptions had all begun well and ended badly. All of them, at least so they said, had striven for power for the sake of the good; afterward they had become obsessed and numbed by power and loved it for its own sake.

What he must do was to sanctify and make wholesome the power Nature had bestowed on him by placing it in the service of the hierarchy. This was something he had always taken for granted. But where was his rightful place, where would his energies be put to best use and bear fruit? The capacity to attract and more or less to influence others, especially those younger than himself, would of course have been useful to an army officer or a politician; but in Castalia there was no place for such occupations. Here these qualities were useful only to the teacher and educator, but Knecht felt hardly drawn to such work. If it had been a question of his own desires alone, he would have preferred the life of the independent scholar to all others—or else that of a Glass Bead Game player. And in reaching this conclusion he once more faced the old, tormenting question: was this game really the highest, really the sovereign in the realm of the intellect? Was it not, in spite of everything and everyone, in the end merely a game after all? Did it really merit full devotion, lifelong service? Generations ago this famous Game had begun as a kind of substitute for art, and for many it was gradually developing into a kind of religion, allowing highly trained intellects to indulge in contemplation, edification, and devotional exercises.

Obviously, the old conflict between aesthetics and ethics was going on in Knecht. The question never fully expressed but likewise never entirely suppressed, was the very one that had now and then erupted, dark and threatening, from beneath the surface of the schoolboy poems he had written in Waldzell. That question was addressed not just to the Glass Bead Game, but to Castalia as a whole.

There was a period when this whole complex of problems troubled him so deeply that he was always dreaming of debates with Designori. And one day, as he was strolling across one of the spacious courtyards of the Waldzell Players' Village, he heard someone behind him calling his name. The voice sounded very familiar, although he did not recognize it at once. When he turned around he saw a tall young man with a trim beard rushing tempestuously toward him. It was Plinio, and with a surge of affection and warm memories, Joseph greeted him heartily. They arranged to meet that evening. Plinio, who had long ago finished his studies at the universities in the outside world and was already a government official, had come to Waldzell on holiday for a short guest course in the Glass Bead Game, as he had in fact done once before, several years earlier.

The evening they spent together, however, proved an embarrassment to both friends. Plinio was here as a guest student, a tolerated dilettante from outside; although he was pursuing his course with great eagerness, it was nevertheless a course for outsiders and amateurs. The distance between them was too great; he was facing a professional, an initiate whose very delicacy and polite interest in his friend's enthusiasm for the Glass Bead Game inevitably made him feel that he was not a colleague but a child playfully dabbling on the outer edges of a science which the other understood to its very core. Knecht tried to turn the conversation away from the Game by asking Plinio about his official functions and his life on the outside. And now Joseph was the laggard and the child who asked innocent questions and was tactfully tutored. Plinio had gone into law, was seeking political influence, and was about to become engaged to the daughter of a party leader. He spoke a language that Joseph only half understood; many recurrent expressions sounded empty to him, or seemed to have no content. At any rate he realized that Plinio counted for something in his world, knew his way about in it, and had ambitious aims. But the two worlds, which ten years ago both youths had each touched with tentative curiosity and a measure of sympathy, had by now grown irreconcilably apart.

Joseph could appreciate the fact that this man of the world and politician had retained a certain attachment to Castalia. This was, after all, the second time he was sacrificing a holiday to the Glass Bead Game. But in the end, Joseph thought, it was pretty much the same as if he were one day to pay a visit to Plinio's district and attend a few sessions of the court as a curious guest, and have Plinio show him through a few factories or welfare institutions. Both were disappointed. Knecht found his former friend coarse and superficial. Designori, for his part, found his former schoolmate distinctly haughty in his exclusive esotericism and intellectuality; he seemed to Plinio to have become a "pure intellect" altogether absorbed by himself and his sport.

Both made an effort, however, and Designori had all sorts of tales to tell, about his studies and examinations, about journeys to England and to the south, political meetings, parliament. At one point, moreover, he said something that sounded like a threat or a warning. "You will see," he said. "Soon there will be times of unrest, perhaps wars, in which case your whole existence in Castalia might well come under attack."

Joseph did not take this too seriously. He merely asked: "And what about you, Plinio? In that case would you be for or against Castalia?"

"Oh that," Plinio said with a forced smile. "It's not likely that I'd be asked my opinion. But of course I favor the undisturbed continuance of Castalia; otherwise I wouldn't be here, you know. Still and all, although your material requirements are so modest, Castalia costs the country quite a little sum every year."

"Yes," Joseph said, laughing, "it amounts, I am told, to about a tenth of what our country used to spend annually for armaments during the Century of Wars."

They met several more times, and the closer the end of Plinio's course approached, the more assiduous they became in courtesies toward each other. But it was a relief to both when the two or three weeks were over and Plinio departed.

The Magister Ludi at that time was Thomas von der Trave, a famous, widely traveled, and cosmopolitan man, gracious and obliging toward everyone who approached him, but severe to the point of fanaticism in guarding the Game against contamination. He was a great worker, something unsuspected by those who knew him only in his public role, dressed in his festive robes to conduct the great Games, or receiving delegations from abroad. He was said to be a cool, even icy rationalist, whose relationship to the arts was one of mere distant civility. Among the young and ardent amateurs of the Glass Bead Game, rather deprecatory opinions of him could be heard at times—misjudgments, for if he was not an enthusiast and in the great public games tended to avoid touching on grand and exciting themes, the brilliant construction and unequalled form of his games proved to the *cognoscenti* his total grasp of the subtlest problems of the Game's world.

One day the Magister Ludi sent for Joseph Knecht. He

received him in his home, in everyday clothes, and asked whether he would care to come for half an hour every day at this same time for the next few days. Knecht, who had never before had any private dealings with the Master, was somewhat astonished.

For the present, the Master showed him a bulky memorandum, a proposal he had received from an organist—one of the innumerable proposals which the directorate of the Game regularly had to examine. Usually these were suggestions for the admission of new material to the Archives. One man, for example, had made a meticulous study of the history of the madrigal and discovered in the development of the style a curve that he had expressed both musically and mathematically, so that it could be included in the vocabulary of the Game. Another had examined the rhythmic structure of Julius Caesar's Latin and discovered the most striking congruences with the results of well-known studies of the intervals in Byzantine hymns. Or again some fanatic had once more unearthed some new cabala hidden in the musical notation of the fifteenth century. Then there were the tempestuous letters from abstruse experimenters who could arrive at the most astounding conclusions from, say, a comparison of the horoscopes of Goethe and Spinoza; such letters often included pretty and seemingly enlightening geometric drawings in several colors.

Knecht attacked the manuscript with eagerness. He himself, after all, had often pondered such proposals, although he had never submitted any. Every active Glass Bead Game player naturally dreams of a constant expansion of the fields of the Game until they include the entire universe. Or rather, he constantly performs such expansions in his imagination and his private Games, and cherishes the secret desire for the ones which seem to prove their viability to be crowned by official acceptance. The true and ultimate finesse in the private Games of advanced players consists, of course, in their developing such mastery over the expressive, nomenclatural, and formative factors of the Game that they can inject individual and original ideas into any given Game played with objective historical materials. A distinguished bota-

nist once whimsically expressed the idea in an aphorism:
"The Glass Bead Game should admit of everything,
even that a single plant should chat in Latin with Lin-
naeus."

Knecht, then, helped the Magister analyze the suggestion. The half-hour passed swiftly. He came punctually
the next day, and so for two weeks came daily for a
half-hour session with the Magister Ludi. During the
first few days it struck him that the Master was asking
him to work carefully and critically through altogether
inferior memoranda, whose uselessness was evident at
first glance. He wondered that the Master had time for
this sort of thing, and gradually became aware that the
purpose was not just to lighten the Master's work load.
Rather, this assignment, although necessary in itself,
was giving the Master a chance to subject him, the
young adept, to an extremely courteous but stringent
examination. What was taking place was rather similar
to the appearance of the Music Master in his boyhood; he
suddenly became aware of it now by the behavior of his
associates, who treated him more shyly, reservedly, and
sometimes with ironic respect. Something was in the
wind; he sensed it; but now it was far less a source of
joy than it had been then.

After the last of these sessions the Magister Ludi said
in his rather high, courteous voice and in that carefully
enunciated speech of his, but without the slightest solemnity: "Very well; you need not come tomorrow. Our
business is completed for the moment. But I shall soon
be having to trouble you again. Many thanks for your
collaboration; it has been valuable to me. Incidentally, in
my opinion you ought to apply for your admission to
the Order now. There will be no difficulties; I have
already informed the heads of the Order." As he rose
he added: "One word more, just by the way. Probably
you too sometimes incline, as most good Glass Bead Game
players do in their youth, to use our Game as a kind of
instrument for philosophizing. My words alone will not
cure you of that, but nevertheless I shall say them: Philosophizing should be done only with legitimate tools,
those of philosophy. Our Game is neither philosophy nor
religion; it is a discipline of its own, in character most

akin to art. It is an art *sui generis*. One makes greater
strides if one holds to that view from the first than if one
reaches it only after a hundred failures. The philosopher
Kant—he is little known today, but he was a formidable
thinker—once said that theological philosophizing was
'a magic lantern of chimeras.' We should not make our
Glass Bead Game into that."

Joseph was surprised. His excitement was so great that
he almost failed to hear the last cautionary remarks. It
had flashed through his mind that this meant the end of
his freedom, the completion of his period of study, admission to the Order, and his imminent enrollment in
the ranks of the hierarchy. He expressed his thanks with
a low bow, and went promptly to the secretariat of the
Order in Waldzell, where sure enough he found himself
already inscribed on the list of new nominees to the
Order. Like all students at his level, he knew the rules
of the Order fairly well, and remembered that the ceremony of admission could be performed by every member of the Order who held an official post in the higher
ranks. He therefore requested that this be done by the
Music Master, obtained a pass and a short furlough, and
next day set out for Monteport, where his patron and
friend was staying. He found the venerable old Master
ailing, but was welcomed with rejoicing.

"You have come just in time," the old man said. "Soon
I would no longer be empowered to receive you into the
Order as a younger brother. I am about to resign my
office; my release has already been granted."

The ceremony itself was simple. On the following day
the Music Master invited two brothers of the Order to
be present as witnesses, as prescribed by the statutes.
Previously, he had given Knecht a paragraph from the
rules as the subject of a meditation exercise. It was the
familiar passage: "If the high Authority appoints you to
an office, know this: every step upward on the ladder of
offices is not a step into freedom but into bondage. The
higher the office, the tighter the bondage. The greater
the power of the office, the stricter the service. The
stronger the personality, the less self-will."

The group then assembled in the Magister's music
cell, the same in which Knecht had long ago been in-

troduced to the art of meditation. The Master called upon the novice, in honor of the initiation, to play a chorale prelude by Bach. Then one of the witnesses read aloud the abbreviated version of the rules of the Order, and the Music Master himself asked the ritual questions and received his young friend's oath. He accorded Joseph another hour; they sat in the garden and the Master advised him on how to identify himself with the rules and live by them. "It is good," he said, "that at the moment I am departing you are stepping into the breach; it is as if I had a son who will stand in my stead." And when he saw Joseph's sad look he added: "Come now, don't be downcast. I'm not. I am very tired and looking forward to the leisure I mean to enjoy, and which you will share with me frequently, I hope. And next time we meet, use the familiar pronoun of address to me. I could not offer that as long as I held office." He dismissed him with that winning smile which Joseph had now known for twenty years.

Knecht returned quickly to Waldzell, for he had been given only three days leave. He was barely back when the Magister Ludi sent for him, greeted him affably as one colleague to another, and congratulated him on his admission to the Order. "All that is now lacking to make us completely colleagues and associates," he continued, "is your assignment to a definite place in our organization."

Joseph was somewhat taken aback. So this would be the end of his freedom.

"Oh," he said timidly, "I hope I can prove useful in some modest spot somewhere. But to be candid with you, I had been hoping I would be able to continue studying freely for a while longer."

The Magister looked straight into his eyes with a faintly ironic smile. "You say 'a while,' but how long is that?"

Knecht gave an embarrassed laugh. "I really don't know."

"So I thought," the Master said. "You are still speaking the language of students and thinking in student terms, Joseph Knecht. That is quite all right now, but soon it will no longer be all right, for we need you. Besides, you

know that later on, even in the highest offices of our
Order, you can obtain leaves for purposes of study, if you
can persuade the authorities of the value of these studies.
My predecessor and teacher, for example, while he was
still Magister Ludi and an old man, requested and received
a full year's furlough for studies in the London Archives.
But he received his furlough not for 'a while,' but for a
specific number of months, weeks, and days. Henceforth
you will have to count on that. And now I have a proposal
to make to you. We need a reliable man who is as yet
unknown outside our circle for a special mission."

The assignment was the following. The Benedictine
monastery of Mariafels, one of the oldest centers of
learning in the country, which maintained friendly relations with Castalia and in particular had favored the
Glass Bead Game for decades, had asked him to send a
young teacher for a prolonged stay, to give introductory
courses in the Game and also to stimulate the few advanced players in the monastery. The Magister's choice
had fallen upon Joseph Knecht. That was why he had
been so discreetly tested; that was why his entry into the
Order had been accelerated.

FOUR

TWO ORDERS

IN A GOOD many respects Joseph Knecht's situation was once again similar to that in his Latin school days after the Music Master's visit. Joseph himself would scarcely have imagined that the appointment to Mariafels represented a special distinction and a large first step on the ladder of the hierarchy, but he was after all a good deal wiser about such matters nowadays and could plainly read the significance of his summons in the attitude and conduct of his fellow students. Of course he had belonged for some time to the innermost circle within the elite of the Glass Bead Game players, but now the unusual assignment marked him to all and sundry as a young man whom the superiors had their eye on and whom they intended to employ. His associates and ambitious fellow players did not exactly withdraw or become unfriendly—the members of this highly aristocratic group were far too well-mannered for that—but an aloofness nevertheless arose. Yesterday's friend might well be tomorrow's superior, and this circle registered and expressed such gradations and differentiations by the most delicate shades of behavior.

One exception was Fritz Tegularius, whom we may

well call, next to Ferromonte, Joseph Knecht's closest
friend throughout his life. Tegularius, destined by his
gifts for the highest achievements but severely hampered
by certain deficiencies of health, balance, and self-confidence, was the same age as Knecht at the time of
Knecht's admission to the Order—that is, about thirty-
four—and had first met him some ten years earlier in a
Glass Bead Game course. At the time Knecht had sensed
how strong an attraction he exerted upon this quiet
and rather melancholy youth. With that psychological
instinct which he possessed even then, although without
precisely knowing it, he likewise grasped the essence
of this love on the part of Tegularius. It was friendship
ready for unconditional devotion, a respect capable of the
utmost subordination. It was imbued with an almost
religious fervor, but overshadowed and held in bounds
by an aristocratic reserve and a foreboding of inner
tragedy. In the beginning, still shaken and oversensitive,
not to say suspicious, as a result of the Designori episode,
Knecht had held Tegularius at a distance by consistent
sternness, although he too felt drawn to this interesting
and unusual schoolfellow. For a characterization of Tegularius we may use a page from Knecht's confidential
memoranda which, years later, he regularly drew up for
the exclusive use of the highest authorities. It reads:

"Tegularius. Personal friend of the writer. Recipient of
several honors at school in Keuperheim. Good classical
philologist, strong interest in philosophy, worked on Leibniz, Bolzano, subsequently Plato. The most brilliant and
gifted Glass Bead Game player I know. He would be
predestined for Magister Ludi were it not that his character, together with his frail health, make him completely unsuited for that position. T. should never be
appointed to an outstanding, representative, or organiza-
tional position; that would be a misfortune for him and
for the office. His deficiency takes physical form in states
of low vitality, periods of insomnia and nervous aches,
psychologically in spells of melancholy, a hunger for solitude, fear of duties and responsibilities, and probably
also in thoughts of suicide. Dangerous though his situation is, by the aid of meditation and great self-discipline
he keeps himself going so courageously that most of his

acquaintances have no idea of how severely he suffers and are aware only of his great shyness and taciturnity. But although T. unfortunately is not fitted for higher posts, he is nevertheless a jewel in the Vicus Lusorum, an altogether irreplaceable treasure. He has mastered the technique of our game like a great musician his instrument; he instinctively finds the most delicate nuances, and is also an exceptional instructor. In the advanced and highest review courses—for my part he would be wasted in the lower ones—I could scarcely manage without him any longer. The way he analyzes the specimen Games of boys without ever discouraging them, the way he detects their tricks, infallibly recognizes and exposes everything imitative or purely decorative, the way he finds the sources of error in a Game that has started well but then gone astray, and lays these errors bare like flawlessly prepared anatomical specimens—is altogether unique. It is this sharp and incorruptible talent for analysis and correction that assures him the respect of students and colleagues, which otherwise might have been jeopardized by his unstable demeanor and shyness.

"I should like to cite an example to illustrate T.'s brilliance as a Glass Bead Game player. During the early days of my friendship with him, when both of us were already finding little more to learn by way of technique in our courses, he once—it was a moment of unusual trust—allowed me to look at several games he had composed. I saw at a glance that they were brilliantly devised and somehow novel and original in style, asked to borrow the sketches for study, and discovered that these Game compositions were true literary productions, so amazing and singular that I feel I should speak of them here. These Games were little dramas, in structure almost pure monologues, reflecting the imperiled but brilliant life of the author's mind like a perfect self-portrait. The various themes and groups of themes on which the Games were based, and their sequences and confrontations, were brilliantly conceived, dialectically orchestrated and counterpoised. But beyond that, the synthesis and harmonization of the opposing voices was not carried to the ultimate conclusion in the usual classical manner; rather, this harmonization underwent a whole series of refrac-

tions, of splintering into overtones, and paused each
time, as if wearied and despairing, just on the point of
dissolution, finally fading out in questioning and doubt.
As a result, those Games possessed a stirring chromat-
ics, of a kind never before ventured, as far as I know.
Moreover, the Games as a whole expressed a tragic
doubt and renunciation; they became figurative statements of the dubiousness of all intellectual endeavor.
At the same time, in their intellectual structure as well
as in their calligraphic technique and perfection, they
were so extraordinarily beautiful that they brought tears
to one's eyes. Each of these Games moved with such
gravity and sincerity toward solution, only at the last so
nobly to forgo the attempt at solution, that it was like a
perfect elegy upon the transitoriness inherent in all beautiful things and the ultimate dubiety immanent in all
soaring flights of the intellect.

"Item: I would recommend Tegularius, if he should
outlive me or my term in office, as an extremely fine,
precious, but imperiled treasure. He should be granted
maximum freedom; he should be consulted on all important questions concerning the Game. But students
should never be placed in his sole guidance."

In the course of the years this remarkable man had
become Knecht's true friend. He admired Knecht's capacity for leadership as well as his mind, and showed a touching devotion toward him. In fact, much of what we
know about Knecht has been handed down by Tegularius.
In the innermost circle of younger Glass Bead Game
players he was perhaps the only one who did not envy
his friend for the important assignment he had received,
and the only one for whom Knecht's absence for an indefinite time meant an almost unbearable anguish and
sense of loss.

Joseph himself rejoiced in the new state of affairs as
soon as he recovered from the shock of suddenly being
shorn of his beloved freedom. He felt eagerness to travel,
pleasure in activity, and curiosity about the alien world
to which he was being sent. Incidentally, he was not
allowed to depart for Mariafels without preparation; first
he was assigned to the "Police" for three weeks. That
was the students' name for the small department within

the Board of Educators which might be called its Political
Department or even its Foreign Ministry, were these
not somewhat grandiose names for so small an affair.
There he received instruction in the rules of conduct for
brothers of the Order during their stays in the outside
world. Dubois, the head of this office, personally devoted
an hour to him nearly every day. This conscientious
man seemed worried that an altogether untried young
man without the faintest knowledge of the world should
be sent to such a foreign post. He made no attempt to
conceal his disapproval of the Magister Ludi's decision,
and took extra pains to inform this new member of the
Order on the facts of life in the outside world and the
means for effectively combatting its perils. His sincere
paternal solicitude fortunately was matched by Joseph's
willingness to be instructed. The result was that during
those hours of introduction into the rules of intercourse
with the world, the teacher conceived a real affection
for Joseph Knecht, and finally felt able to dismiss him reassured and fully confident that the young man would
be able to carry out his mission successfully. Dubois even
tried, more out of personal good will than the demands
of politics, to give Joseph a kind of additional assignment on his own behalf. As one of Castalia's few "politicians," Dubois was one of that tiny group of officials
whose thoughts and studies were largely devoted to sus-
taining the legal and economic continuance of Castalia,
to regulating its relationship to the outside world and the
problems that arose from its dependence on the world.
The great majority of Castalians, the officials no less
than the scholars and students, lived in their Pedagogic
Province and their Order as if these constituted a stable,
eternal, inevitable world. They knew, of course, that it
had not always existed, that it had come into being
slowly and amid bitter struggles in times of cruel distress; they knew it had originated at the end of the
Age of Wars out of a double source: the heroically ascetic
efforts of scholars, artists, and thinkers who had come
to their senses, and the profound craving of the exhausted, bled, and betrayed peoples for order, normal-
ity, reason, lawfulness, and moderation. Castalians knew
this, and understood the function of all the Orders and

Pedagogic Provinces throughout the world: to abstain
from government and competition and instead to assure
stability for the spiritual foundations of moderation and
law everywhere. But that the present order of things
was not to be taken for granted, that it presupposed a certain harmony between the world and the guardians of
culture, that this harmony could always be disrupted,
and that world history taken as a whole by no means
furthered what was desirable, rational, and beautiful in
the life of man, but at best only occasionally tolerated
it as an exception—all this they did not realize. Except
for those few political thinkers like Dubois, almost all
Castalians were unaware of the secret complex of problems underlying the existence of Castalia. Once Knecht
won the confidence of Dubois, he was given a glimpse of
the political foundations of Castalia. At first the subject
struck him as rather repellent and uninteresting—which,
indeed, was the reaction of most members of the Order.
But then he recalled Plinio Designori's remark about possible dangers to Castalia. Along with that recollection
there flooded back into his mind the whole bitter aftertaste of his youthful debates with Plinio, seemingly long
since settled and forgotten. Now these suddenly seemed
to him of the highest importance and, moreover, a stage
on the road to his "awakening."

At the end of their last talk Dubois said to him: "I
think I can let you go now. You are to adhere strictly
to the assignment his honor the Magister Ludi has given
you, and no less strictly to the rules of conduct we have
taught you here. It was a pleasure to me to be able to
help you. You will see that the three weeks we have kept
you were not time lost. And if you should ever want to
recompense me for my contribution to your education,
I can suggest a way. You will be entering a Benedictine
abbey, and if you stay there a while and commend yourself to the Fathers, you will probably hear political conversations and sense political currents among the venerable Fathers and their guests. If you would occasionally
inform me about such matters, I would be grateful.
Please understand me aright: you are certainly not to regard yourself as a kind of spy or in any way misuse con-
fidences. You are not to pass along anything that goes

against your conscience. I guarantee that we will use any information we may receive only in the interest of our Order and Castalia. We are not real politicians and have no power at all, but we too are dependent on the world, which either needs or tolerates us. Circumstances may arise in which we might profit by knowing that a statesman is making a retreat in a monastery, or that the Pope is said to be ill, or that new candidates have been added to the list of future cardinals. We are not dependent on your information—we have quite a variety of sources—but one little source more can do no harm. Go now, you need not say yes or no to this matter. For the present all that is needed is for you to comport yourself well in your official assignment and do us honor among the spiritual Fathers. Bon voyage."

In the *Book of Changes*, which Knecht consulted by means of the yarrow stalk ritual before he set out, he counted out the hexagram Lü, which signifies "The Wanderer," and the augury: "Success through smallness. Persistence is good fortune to the wanderer." He found a six for the second place, which yielded the interpretation:

> The wanderer comes to the inn.
> He has his possessions with him.
> He receives the persistent attentions of a young servant.

Knecht's leave-taking went off cheerfully, except that his last talk with Tegularius proved to be a hard test of both their characters. Fritz controlled himself by extreme effort and appeared absolutely frozen in the coolness he forced himself to display. For him, the best he had was departing with his friend. Knecht's nature did not permit so passionate and above all so exclusive an attachment to a friend. If need be, he could get along without one and could direct his affections easily toward new objects and people. This parting was not a painful loss for him; but he knew his friend well enough to know what a shock and trial it meant for him, and he was concerned. He had given much thought to the nature of this friendship, and had once spoken about it with the Music Master. To a certain extent he had learned to objectify his own experience and feelings, and to regard them critically. In so doing he had become aware that it was not really, or at any rate not only, his friend's great talent that attracted him to Tegularius. Rather, it was the association of this talent with such serious defects, such great fragility. And he realized that the single-mindedness of the love Tegularius offered him had not only its beautiful aspect, but also a dangerous attraction, for it tempted him to display his power over one weaker in strength though not in love. Therefore in this relationship he had made restraint and self-discipline his duty to the last. Fond though he was of Tegularius, the friendship would not have acquired so deep a meaning for him if it had not taught him something about the dominion he had over others weaker and less secure than himself. He learned that this power to influence others was part and parcel of the educator's gift, and that it concealed dangers and imposed responsibility. Tegularius, after all, was only one of many. In the eyes of quite a few others Knecht read silent courtship.

At the same time, during the past year he had become far more conscious of the highly charged atmosphere in which he lived in the Glass Bead Game village. For there he was part of an officially nonexistent but very sharply defined circle, or class, the finest elite among the candidates and tutors of the Glass Bead Game. Now and then one or another of that group would be called upon to serve in an auxiliary capacity under the Magister or Archivist, or to help teach one of the Game courses; but they were never assigned to the lower or middle level of officialdom or the teaching corps. They provided the reserve for filling vacancies in leading posts. They knew one another thoroughly; they had almost no illusions about talents, characters, and achievements. And precisely because among these initiates and aspirants for the highest dignities each one was pre-eminent, each of the very first rank in performance, knowledge, and academic record—precisely for that reason those traits and nuances of character which predestined a candidate for leadership and success inevitably counted for a great deal and were closely observed. A dash more or less of graciousness, of suasion with younger men or with the authorities, of amiability, was of great importance in this group and could give

its possessor a definitive edge over his rivals. Fritz Tegularius plainly belonged to this circle merely as an outsider; he was tolerated as a guest but kept at the periphery because he had no gift for rule. Just as plainly
Knecht belonged to the innermost circle. What appealed
to the young and made them his admirers was his
wholesome vigor and still youthful charm which appeared to be resistant to passions, incorruptible and
then again boyishly irresponsible—a kind of innocence,
that is. And what commended him to his superiors was
the reverse side of this innocence: his freedom from
ambition and craving for success.

Of late, the effects of his personality had begun to
dawn upon the young man. He became aware of his attraction for those below him, and gradually, belatedly,
of how he affected those above him. And when he
looked back from his new standpoint of awareness to
his boyhood, he found both lines running through his
life and shaping it. Classmates and younger boys had
always courted him; superiors had taken benevolent note
of him. There had been exceptions, such as Headmaster
Zbinden; but on the other hand he had been recipient
of such distinctions as the patronage of the Music Master,
and latterly of Dubois and the Magister Ludi. It was all
perfectly plain, in spite of which Knecht had never been
willing to see it and accept it in its entirety. Obviously
his fate was to enter the elite everywhere, to find admiring friends and highly placed patrons. It happened
of its own accord, without his trying. Obviously he
would not be allowed to settle down in the shadows at
the base of the hierarchy; he must move steadily toward
its apex, approach the bright light at the top. He would
not be a subordinate or an independent scholar; he
would be a master. That he grasped this later than others
in a similar position gave him that indescribable extra
magic, that note of innocence.

But why was it that he realized it so late, and so reluctantly? Because he had not sought it at all, and did
not want it. He had no need to dominate, took no pleasure in commanding; he desired the contemplative far
more than the active life, and would have been content
to spend many years more, if not his whole life, as an

obscure student, an inquiring and reverent pilgrim
through the sanctuaries of the past, the cathedrals of
music, the gardens and forests of mythology, languages
and ideas. Now that he saw himself being pushed inexorably into the *vita activa* he was more than ever
aware of the tensions of the aspirations, the rivalries,
the ambitions among those around him. He felt his innocence threatened and no longer tenable. Now, he
realized, he must desire and affirm the position that was
being thrust upon him; otherwise he would be haunted by
a feeling of imprisonment and nostalgia for the freedom
of the past ten years. And since he was not as yet altogether ready for that affirmation, he felt his temporary departure from Waldzell and the Province, his journey out
into the world, as a great relief and release.

The monastery of Mariafels, through the many centuries of its existence, had shared in the making and the
suffering of the history of the West. It had experienced
periods of flowering and decline, had passed through rebirths and new nadirs, and had been at various times and
in assorted fields famous and brilliant. Once a center of
Scholastic learning and the art of disputation, still possessing an enormous library of medieval theology, it had
risen to new glory after periods of slackness and sluggishness. It then became famous for its music, its much-
praised choir, and the Masses and oratorios composed and
performed by the Fathers. From those days it still retained a fine musical tradition, half a dozen nut-brown
chests full of music manuscripts, and the finest organ in
the country. Then the monastery had entered a political
era, which had likewise left behind a tradition and a certain skill. In times of war and barbarization Mariafels had
several times become a little island of rationality where
the better minds among the opposed parties cautiously
sought each other out and groped their way toward
reconciliation. And once—that was the last high point
in its history—Mariafels had been the birthplace of a peace
treaty which for a while met the longings of the exhausted
nations. Afterward, when a new age began and Castalia
was founded, the monastery took an attitude of wait-
and-see, was in fact rather hostile, presumably on instruc-

tions from Rome. A request from the Board of Educators
to grant hospitality to a scholar who wished to work for
a time in the monastery's Scholastic library was politely
turned down, as was an invitation to send a representative to a conference of musicologists. Intercourse between Castalia and the monastery had first begun in the
time of Abbot Pius, who in his latter years became keenly
interested in the Glass Bead Game. Ever since then a
friendly though not very lively relationship had developed. Books were exchanged, reciprocal hospitality
granted. Knecht's patron, the Music Master, had spent a
few weeks in Mariafels during his younger years, copying
music manuscripts and playing the famous organ.
Knecht knew of this, and rejoiced at the prospect of
staying in a place of which his venerated Master had
occasionally spoken with pleasure.

The respect and politeness with which he was received went so far beyond his expectations that he felt
rather embarrassed. This was, after all, the first time that
Castalia had offered the monastery a Glass Bead Game
player of high distinction for an indefinite period. Joseph
had learned from Dubois that he was not to regard himself as an individual, especially during the early period of
his stay, but solely as the representative of Castalia, and
that he was to accept and respond both to courtesies and
possible aloofness solely as an ambassador. That attitude
helped him through his initial constraint.

He likewise soon overcame the feelings of strangeness,
anxiety, and mild excitability which troubled his first few
nights and kept him from sleeping. And since Abbot
Gervasius displayed a good-natured and merry benevolence toward him, he quickly came to feel at ease in
his new environment. The freshness and vigor of the
landscape delighted him. The monastery was situated in
rough, mountainous country, full of abrupt cliffs and pockets of rich pasture where handsome cattle grazed. He
savored with deep pleasure the massiveness and size of
the ancient buildings, in which the history of many centuries could be read. He enjoyed the beauty and simple
comfort of his apartment, two rooms on the top floor of
the guest wing. For recreation he went on exploratory
walks through the fine little city-state with its two

churches, cloisters, archives, library, Abbot's apartment, and courtyards, with its extensive barns filled with thrifty livestock, its gurgling fountains, gigantic vaulted wine and fruit cellars, its two refectories, the famous chapter house, the well-tended gardens and the workshops of the lay brothers: cooper, cobbler, tailor, smith, and so on, all forming a small village around the largest courtyard. He was granted entry to the library; the organist showed him the great organ and allowed him to play on it; and he was strongly attracted to the chests in which an impressive number of unpublished and to some extent quite unknown music manuscripts of earlier ages awaited study.

The monks did not seem to be terribly impatient for him to begin his official functions. Not only days but weeks passed before anyone seriously brought up the real purpose of his presence there. From his first day, it was true, some of the Fathers, and the Abbot himself in particular, had been eager to chat with Joseph about the Glass Bead Game. But no one said anything about instruction or any other systematic work with the Game. In other respects, too, Knecht felt that the manners, style of life, and general tone of intercourse among the monks was couched in a tempo hitherto unknown to him. There was a kind of venerable slowness, a leisurely and benign patience in which all these Fathers seemed to share, including those whose temperaments seemed rather more active. It was the spirit of their Order, the millennial pace of an age-old, privileged community whose orderly existence had survived hundreds of vicissitudes. They all shared it, as every bee shares the fate of its hive, sleeps its sleep, suffers its sufferings, trembles with its trembling. This Benedictine temper seemed at first glance less intellectual, less supple and acute, less active than the style of life in Castalia, but on the other hand calmer, less malleable, older, more resistant to tribulation. The spirit and mentality of this place had long ago achieved a harmony with nature.

With curiosity and intense interest, and with great admiration as well, Knecht submitted to the mood of life in this monastery, which at a time before Castalia existed had been almost the same as it was now, and even then fifteen hundred years old, and which was so congenial to the contemplative side of his nature. He was an honored guest, honored far beyond his expectations and deserts; but he felt distinctly that these courtesies were a matter of form and custom and not specially addressed to him as a person, nor to the spirit of Castalia or of the Glass Bead Game. Rather, the Benedictines were displaying the majestic politeness of an ancient power to a younger one. He had been only partly prepared for this implicit superiority, and after a while, for all that his life in Mariafels was proving so agreeable, he began to feel so insecure that he asked his authorities for more precise instructions on how to conduct himself. The Magister Ludi in person wrote him a few lines: "Don't worry about taking all the time you need for your study of the life there. Profit by your days, learn, try to make yourself well liked and useful, insofar as you find your hosts receptive, but do not obtrude yourself, and never seem more impatient, never seem to be under more pressure than they. Even if they should go on treating you for an entire year as if each day were your first as a guest in their house, enter calmly into the spirit of it and behave as if two or even ten years more do not matter to you. Take it as a test in the practice of patience. Meditate carefully. If time hangs heavy on your hands, set aside a few hours every day, no more than four, for some regular work, study, or the copying of manuscripts, say. But avoid giving the impression of diligence; be at the disposal of everyone who wishes to chat with you."

Knecht followed this advice, and soon began feeling more relaxed. Hitherto he had been thinking too much of his assignment to act as instructor to amateur Glass Bead Game players—the ostensible reason for his mission here—whereas the Fathers of the monastery were treating him rather as the envoy of a friendly power who must be kept in good humor. And when at last Abbot Gervasius recollected the assignment, and brought him together with several of the monks who had already had an introduction to the art of the Glass Bead Game and hoped he would give them a more advanced course, it turned out to his astonishment and his intense disap-

pointment that the noble Game was cultivated in a most
superficial and amateurish way at this hospitable place.
He would evidently have to content himself with a very
modest level of knowledge of the Game. Slowly, though,
he came to realize that he had not really been sent here
for the sake of lifting the standards of the Glass Bead
Game in the monastery. The assignment of coaching the
few Fathers moderately devoted to the Game and equip-
ping them with a modest degree of skill was easy, much
too easy. Any other adept at the Game, even if he were
still far from belonging to the elite, would have been
equal to the task. Instruction, then, could not be the real
purpose of his mission. He began to realize that he had
probably been sent here less to teach than to learn.

However, just as he thought he had grasped this, his
authority in the monastery, and consequently his self-
assurance, was unexpectedly reinforced. This came in
the nick of time, for in spite of all the charms of being a
guest there, he had already at times begun to feel his
stay as something like a punitive transfer. One day, however, in a conversation with the Abbot he inadvertently
made some allusion to the Chinese *I Ching*. The Abbot
showed marked interest, asked a few questions, and
could not disguise his delight when he found his guest
so unexpectedly versed in Chinese and the *Book of
Changes*. The Abbot, too, was fond of the *I Ching*. He
knew no Chinese, and his knowledge of the book of
oracles and other Chinese mysteries was limited—in all
their scholarly interests the present inmates of the monastery seemed content with a harmless smattering. Nevertheless, this intelligent man, who was so much more
experienced and worldly-wise than his guest, obviously
had a real feeling for the spirit of ancient Chinese attitudes toward politics and life. A conversation of unusual
liveliness ensued. For the first time real warmth was
injected into the prevailing tone of remote courtesy between host and guest. The consequence was that Knecht
was asked to give the Abbot instruction in the *I Ching*
twice a week.

While his relationship to his host, the Abbot, thus increased in liveliness and meaning, while his friendly fel-
lowship with the organist throve and the small ecclesiasti-

cal state in which he lived gradually became familiar
territory to him, the promise of the oracle he had consulted before leaving Castalia also neared fulfillment.
As the wanderer who carried his possessions with him,
he had been promised not only the shelter of an inn
but also "the persistent attentions of a young servant."
The wanderer felt justified in taking the consummation of
this promise as a good sign, a sign that he in truth had
"his possessions with him." In other words, far away
from the schools, teachers, friends, patrons, and helpers,
far from the nourishing and salutary home atmosphere
of Castalia, he carried within himself the spirit and the
energies of the Province, and with their aid he was moving toward an active and useful life.

The foretold "young servant," as it turned out, appeared in the shape of a seminary pupil named Anton.
Although this young man subsequently played no part
in Joseph Knecht's life, in Joseph's peculiarly divided
mood during his sojourn in the monastery the boy seemed
a harbinger of new and greater things. Anton was a close-
mouthed youngster, but temperamental and talented looking, and almost ready for admission into the community
of monks. Joseph's path often crossed his, whereas he
scarcely knew any of the other seminary pupils, who
were confined in a wing by themselves, where guests
were not admitted. In fact it was obvious that they were
being kept from contact with him. Seminary pupils were
not permitted to participate in the Game course.

Anton worked as a helper in the library several times
a week. Here it was that Knecht met him, and occasionally had a few words with him. As time went on,
it became evident to Knecht that this young man with
the intense eyes under heavy black brows was devoted
to him with that enthusiasm and readiness to serve so
typical of the boyish adoration he had encountered so
often by now. Although every time it happened he felt
a desire to fend it off, he had long ago come to recognize
it as a vital element in the life of the Castalian Order.
But in the monastery he decided to be doubly withdrawn; he felt it would be a violation of hospitality to
exert any sway over this boy who was still subject to the
discipline of religious education. Moreover, he was well

aware that strict chastity was the commandment here, and this, it seemed to him, could make a boyish infatuation even more dangerous. In any case, he must avoid any chance of giving offense, and he governed himself accordingly.

In the library, the one place where he habitually met Anton, he also made the acquaintance of a man he had at first almost failed to notice, so modest was his appearance. In time, however, he was to know him very well indeed, and to love him for the rest of his life with the kind of grateful reverence he felt, otherwise, only toward the now retired Music Master. The man was Father Jacobus, perhaps the most eminent historian of the Benedictine Order. He was at that time about sixty, a spare, elderly man with a sparrow hawk's head on a long, sinewy neck. Seen from the front, his face had something dull and lifeless about it, since he was chary of gazing outward; but his profile, with the boldly curved line of the forehead, the deep furrow above the sharp bridge of his hooked nose, and the rather short but attractively shaped chin, suggested a definite and original personality.

This quiet old man—who, incidentally, on closer acquaintance could be extremely vivacious—had a table of his own in a small room off the main hall of the library. Though the monastery possessed such priceless books, he seemed to be the only really serious working scholar in the place. It was, by the way, the novice Anton who by chance called Joseph Knecht's attention to Father Jacobus. Knecht had noticed that the room in which the scholar had his table was regarded almost as a private domain. The few users of the library entered it only if they had to, and then moved softly and respectfully on tiptoe, although the Father bent over his books did not appear to be easily disturbed. Knecht, of course, quickly imitated this circumspection, and thereby remained at a remove from the industrious old man.

One day, however, when Anton had brought Father Jacobus some books, Knecht noticed how the young man lingered a moment at the open door of the study, looking back at the scholar already absorbed in his work again. There was adoration in Anton's face, an expression of

admiration and reverence mingled with those emotions of
affectionate consideration and helpfulness that well-bred
youth sometimes manifests toward the paltriness and
fragility of age. Knecht's first reaction was delight; the
sight was pleasing in itself, as well as evidence that Anton could so look up to older men without any trace
of physical feeling. A rather sarcastic thought followed
immediately, a thought Joseph felt almost ashamed of:
how poor the state of scholarship must be in this institution that the only seriously active scholar in the
place was stared at as if he were a fabulous beast. Nevertheless, Anton's look of reverent admiration for the old
man opened Knecht's eyes. He became aware of the
learned Father's existence. He himself took to throwing
a glance now and then at the man, discovered his Roman
profile, and gradually found out one thing and another
about Father Jacobus which seemed to suggest a most
extraordinary mind and character. Knecht had already
learned that he was a historian and regarded as the
foremost authority on the history of the Benedictine
Order.

One day the Father spoke to him. His manner of
speech had none of the broad, deliberately benevolent,
deliberately good-natured, somewhat avuncular tone
which seemed to be the style of the monastery. Speaking
in a low and almost timorous voice, but placing his
stresses with a wonderful precision, he invited Joseph
to visit him in his room after vespers. "You will find in
me," he said, "neither a specialist on the history of Castalia nor a Glass Bead Game player. But since, as it now
seems, our two so different Orders are forming ever-
closer ties of friendship, I should not wish to exclude
myself, and would be happy to take personal advantage
now and then of your presence among us."

He spoke with utter seriousness, but his low voice and
shrewd old face conferred upon his all-too-polite phrases
that wonderful note of equivocation, ranging through the
whole compass from earnestness to irony, from deference
to faint mockery, from passionate engagement to playfulness, such as may be sensed when two holy men or
two princes of the Church greet each other with endless
bows in a game of mutual courtesies and trial of patience.

This blending of superiority and mockery, of wisdom and obstinate ceremonial, was deeply familiar to Joseph Knecht from his studies of Chinese language and life. He found it marvelously refreshing, and realized that it was some time since he had last heard this tone—which, among others, the Glass Bead Game Master Thomas commanded with consummate skill. With gratitude and pleasure, Joseph accepted the invitation.

That evening he called at the Father's rather isolated apartment at the end of a quiet side-wing of the monastery. As he stood in the corridor, wondering which door to knock at, he heard piano music, to his considerable surprise. It was a sonata by Purcell, played unpretentiously and without virtuosity, but cleanly and in impeccable tempo. The pure music sounded through the door; its heartfelt gaiety and sweet triads reminded him of the days in Waldzell when he had practiced pieces of this sort on various instruments with his friend Ferromonte. He waited, listening with deep enjoyment, for the end of the sonata. In the still, twilit corridor it sounded so lonely and unworldly, and so brave and innocent also, both childlike and superior, as all good music must in the midst of the unredeemed muteness of the world.

He knocked at the door. Father Jacobus called, "Come in," and received him with his unassuming dignity. Two candles were still burning by the small piano. "Yes," Father Jacobus said in answer to Knecht's question, "I play for a half-hour or even an hour every night. I usually call a halt to my day's work when darkness falls and would rather not read or write during the hours before sleep."

They talked about music, about Purcell, Handel, the ancient musical tradition among the Benedictines—of all the Catholic Orders the one most devoted to the arts. Knecht expressed a desire to know something of the history of the Order. The conversation grew lively and touched on a hundred questions. The old monk's historical knowledge seemed to be truly astounding, but he frankly admitted that the history of Castalia, of the Castalian idea and Order, had not interested him. He had scarcely studied it, he said, and did not conceal his critical attitude toward this Castalia whose "Order" he regarded as an imitation of the Christian models, and fundamentally a blasphemous imitation since the Castalian Order had no religion, no God, and no Church as its basis. Knecht listened respectfully, but pointed out that other than Benedictine and Roman Catholic views of religion, God and the Church were possible, and moreover had existed, and that it would not do to deny the purity of their intentions nor their profound influence on the life of the mind.

"Quite so," Jacobus said. "No doubt you are thinking of the Protestants, among others. They were unable to preserve religion and the Church, but at times they displayed a great deal of courage and produced some exemplary men. I spent some years studying the various attempts at reconciliation among the hostile Christian denominations and churches, especially those of the period around 1700, when we find such people as the philosopher and mathematician Leibniz and that eccentric Count Zinsendorf endeavoring to reunite the inimical brothers. Altogether, the eighteenth century, hasty and shallow though it often seems in its judgments, has such a rich and many-faceted intellectual history. The Protestants of that period strike me as particularly interesting. There was one man I discovered, a philologist, teacher, and educator of great stature—a Swabian Pietist, by the way—whose moral influence can be clearly traced for two hundred years after his death. But that is another subject. Let us return to the question of the legitimacy and historical mission of real Orders. . . ."

"Oh no," Joseph Knecht broke in. "Please say more about this teacher you have just mentioned. I almost think I can guess who he is."

"Guess."

"I thought at first of Francke of Halle, but since you say he was a Swabian I can think of none other than Johann Albrecht Bengel."

Jacobus laughed. An expression of pleasure transfigured his face. "You surprise me, my friend," he exclaimed. "It was indeed Bengel I had in mind. How do you happen to know of him? Or is it normal in your astonishing Province that people know such abstruse

and forgotten things and names? I would vouch that if
you were to ask all the Fathers, teachers, and pupils in
our monastery, and those of the last few generations as
well, not one would know this name."

"In Castalia, too, few would know it, perhaps no one
besides myself and two of my friends. I once engaged in
studies of eighteenth-century Pietism for private reasons,
and as it happened I was much impressed by several
Swabian theologians—chief among them Bengel. At the
time he seemed to me the ideal teacher and guide for
youth. I was so taken with the man that I even had a
photo made of his portrait in an old book, and kept it
above my desk."

Father Jacobus continued to chuckle. "Our meeting is
certainly taking place under unusual auspices," he said.
"It is remarkable enough that you and I should both
have come upon this forgotten man in the course of our
studies. Perhaps it is even more remarkable that this
Swabian Protestant should have been able to influence
both a Benedictine monk and a Castalian Glass Bead
Game player. Incidentally, I imagine that your Glass
Bead Game is an art requiring a great deal of imagination, and wonder that so stringently sober a man as
Bengel should have attracted you."

Knecht, too, chuckled with amusement. "Well," he
said, "if you recall that Bengel devoted years of study
to the Revelation of St. John, and what sort of system
he devised for interpreting its prophecies, you will have
to admit that our friend could be the very opposite of
sober."

"That is true," Father Jacobus admitted gaily. "And
how do you explain such contradictions?"

"If you will permit me a joke, I would say that what
Bengel lacked, and unconsciously longed for, was the
Glass Bead Game. You see, I consider him among the
secret forerunners and ancestors of our Game."

Cautiously, once again entirely in earnest, Jacobus
countered: "It strikes me as rather bold to annex Bengel,
of all people, for your pedigree. How do you justify it?"

"It was only a joke, but a joke that can be defended.
While he was still quite young, before he became engrossed in his great work on the Bible, Bengel once

told friends of a cherished plan of his. He hoped, he said, to arrange and sum up all the knowledge of his time, symmetrically and synoptically, around a central idea. That is precisely what the Glass Bead Game does."

"After all, the whole eighteenth century toyed with the encyclopedic idea," Father Jacobus protested.

"So it did," Joseph agreed. "But what Bengel meant was not just a juxtaposition of the fields of knowledge and research, but an interrelationship, an organic denominator. And that is one of the basic ideas of the Glass Bead Game. In fact, I would go further in my claims: if Bengel had possessed a system similar to that offered by our Game, he probably would have been spared all the misguided effort involved in his calculation of the prophetic numbers and his annunciation of the Antichrist and the Millennial Kingdom. Bengel did not quite find what he longed for: the way to channel all his various talents toward a single goal. Instead, his mathematical gifts in association with his philological bent produced that weird blend of pedantry and wild imagination, the 'order of the ages,' which occupied him for so many years."

"It is fortunate you are not a historian," Jacobus commented. "You tend to let your own imagination run away with you. But I understand what you mean. I am myself a pedant only in my own discipline."

It was a fruitful conversation, out of which sprang mutual understanding and a kind of friendship. It seemed to the Benedictine scholar more than coincidence, or at least a very special kind of coincidence, that the two of them—each operating within his own, Benedictine or Castalian, limitations—should have discovered this poor instructor at a Württemberg monastery, this man at once fine-strung and rock-hard, at once visionary and practical. Father Jacobus concluded that there must be something linking the two of them for the same unspectacular magnet to affect them both so powerfully. And from that evening on, which had begun with the Purcell sonata, that link actually existed. Jacobus enjoyed the exchange of views with so well trained yet still so supple a young mind; this was a pleasure he did not often have. And Knecht found his association with the historian, and the

education Jacobus provided, a new stage on the path of
awakening—that path which he nowadays identified as
his life. To put the matter succinctly: from Father Jacobus he learned history. He learned the laws and contradictions of historical studies and historiography. And beyond
that, in the following years he learned to see the present
and his own life as historical realities.

Their talks often grew into regular disputations, with
formal attacks and rebuttals. In the beginning it was
Father Jacobus who proved to be the more aggressive
of the pair. The more deeply he came to know his young
friend's mind, the more he regretted that so promising a young man should have grown up without
the discipline of a religious education, rather in
the pseudo-discipline of an intellectual and aesthetic
system of thought. Whenever he found something
objectionable in Knecht's way of thinking, he blamed
it on that "modern" Castalian spirit with its ab-
struseness and its fondness for frivolous abstractions. And whenever Knecht surprised him by wholesome
views and remarks akin to his own thought, he exulted
because his young friend's sound nature had so well
withstood the damage of Castalian education. Joseph
took this criticism of Castalia very calmly, repelling the
attacks only when the old scholar seemed to him to have
gone too far in his passion. But among the good Father's
belittling remarks about Castalia were some whose partial
truth Joseph had to admit, and on one point he changed
his mind completely during his stay in Mariafels. This
had to do with the relationship of Castalian thought to
world history, any sense of which, Father Jacobus said,
was totally lacking in Castalia. "You mathematicians
and Glass Bead Game players," he would say, "have
distilled a kind of world history to suit your own tastes.
It consists of nothing but the history of ideas and of art.
Your history is bloodless and lacking in reality. You know
all about the decay of Latin syntax in the second or third
centuries and don't know a thing about Alexander or
Caesar or Jesus Christ. You treat world history as a mathematician does mathematics, in which nothing but laws
and formulas exist, no reality, no good and evil, no time,

no yesterday, no tomorrow, nothing but an eternal, shallow mathematical present."

"But how is anyone to study history without attempting to bring order into it?" Knecht asked.

"Of course one should bring order into history," Jacobus thundered. "Every science is, among other things, a method of ordering, simplifying, making the indigestible digestible for the mind. We think we have recognized a few laws in history and try to apply them to our investigations of historical truth. Suppose an anatomist is dissecting a body. He does not confront wholly surprising discoveries. Rather, he finds beneath the epidermis a congeries of organs, muscles, tendons, and bones which generally conform to a pattern he has brought to his work. But if the anatomist sees nothing but his pattern, and ignores the unique, individual reality of his object, then he is a Castalian, a Glass Bead Game player; he is using mathematics on the least appropriate object. I have no quarrel with the student of history who brings to his work a touchingly childish, innocent faith in the power of our minds and our methods to order reality; but first and foremost he must respect the incomprehensible truth, reality, and uniqueness of events. Studying history, my friend, is no joke and no irresponsible game. To study history one must know in advance that one is attempting something fundamentally impossible, yet necessary and highly important. To study history means submitting to chaos and nevertheless retaining faith in order and meaning. It is a very serious task, young man, and possibly a tragic one."

Among the remarks of Father Jacobus which Knecht at the time quoted in letters to his friends, here is one more characteristic outburst:

"Great men are to youth like the raisins in the cake of world history. They are also part of its actual substance, of course, and it is not so simple and easy as might be thought to distinguish the really great men from the pseudo-greats. Among the latter, it is the historical moment itself, and their ability to foresee its coming and seize it, that gives them the semblance of greatness. Quite a few historians and biographers, to say nothing of journalists, consider this ability to divine and seize

upon a historical moment—in other words, temporary
success—as in itself a mark of greatness. The corporal
who becomes a dictator overnight, or the courtesan
who for a while controls the good or ill humor of a ruler
of the world, are favorite figures of such historians. And
idealistically minded youths, on the other hand, most
love the tragic failures, the martyrs, those who came on
the scene a moment too soon or too late. For me, since I
am after all chiefly a historian of our Benedictine Order,
the most attractive and amazing aspects of history, and
the most deserving of study, are not individuals and not
coups, triumphs, or downfalls; rather I love and am insatiably curious about such phenomena as our congregation. For it is one of those long-lived organizations whose
purpose is to gather, educate, and reshape men's minds
and souls, to make a nobility of them, not by eugenics,
not by blood, but by the spirit—a nobility as capable of
serving as of ruling. In Greek history I was fascinated
not by the galaxy of heroes and not by the obtrusive
shouting in the Agora, but by efforts such as those of the
Pythagorean brotherhood or the Platonic Academy. In
Chinese history no other feature is so striking as the
longevity of the Confucian system. And in our own Occidental history the Christian Church and the Orders
which serve it as part of its structure, seem to me historical elements of the foremost importance. The fact that
an adventurer contrives to conquer or found a kingdom
which lasts twenty, fifty, or even a hundred years, or
that a well-meaning idealist on a royal or imperial throne
once in a while brings greater honesty into politics, or
attempts to carry some visionary cultural project to fruition; that under high pressure a nation or other community has been capable of incredible feats of achievement
and suffering—all that interests me far less than the ever-
recurrent efforts to establish such organizations as our
Order, and that some of these efforts have endured for
a thousand or two thousand years. I shall say nothing
of holy Church itself; for us believers it is beyond discussion. But that communities such as the Benedictines,
the Dominicans, later the Jesuits and others, have survived for centuries and, despite their ups and downs,
the assaults upon them, and the adaptations they have

made, retain their face and their voice, their gesture, their individual soul—this is, for me, the most remarkable and meritorious phenomenon in history."

Knecht even admired Father Jacobus's spells of angry unfairness. At the time, however, he had no notion of who Father Jacobus really was. He regarded him solely as a profound and brilliant scholar and was unaware that here was someone who was consciously participating in world history, and helping to shape it as the leading statesman of his Order. As an expert in contemporary politics as well as political history, Father Jacobus was constantly being approached from many sides for information, advice, and mediation. For some two years, up to the time of his first vacation, Knecht continued to think of Father Jacobus solely as a scholar, knowing no more of the man's life, activity, reputation, and influence than the monk cared to reveal. The learned Father knew how to keep his counsel, even in friendship; and his brothers in the monastery were also far abler at concealment than Joseph would have imagined.

After some two years Knecht had adapted to the life in the monastery as perfectly as any guest and outsider could. From time to time he had helped the organist modestly continue the thin thread of an ancient and great tradition in the monastery's small chorus of motet singers. He had made several finds in the monastic musical archives and had sent to Waldzell, and especially to Monteport, several copies of old works. He had trained a small beginners' class of Glass Bead Game players, among whom the most zealous pupil was young Anton. He had taught Abbot Gervasius no Chinese, but had at least imparted the technique of manipulating the yarrow sticks and an improved method of meditating on the aphorisms in the Book of Oracles. The Abbot had grown accustomed to him, and had long since stopped trying to coax his guest into taking an occasional glass of wine. The semiannual reports sent by the Abbot to the Glass Bead Game Master, in reply to official inquiries as to the usefulness of Joseph Knecht, were full of praise. In Castalia, the lesson plans and marks in Knecht's Game course were scrutinized even more closely than these reports; the middling level of instruction was recognized,

but the Castalian authorities were satisfied with the way
the teacher had adapted to this level and, in general, to
the customs and the spirit of the monastery. They were
even more pleased, and truly surprised—although they
kept this to themselves—by his frequent and friendly association with the famous Father Jacobus.

This association had borne all sorts of fruits, and perhaps we may be permitted to say a word about these even
at the cost of anticipating our story somewhat; or at any
rate about the fruit which Knecht most prized. It ripened
slowly, slowly, grew as tentatively and warily as the
seeds of high mountain trees that have been planted
down in the lush lowlands: these seeds, consigned to
rich soil and a kindly climate, carry in themselves as
their legacy the restraint and mistrust with which their
forebears grew; the slow tempo of growth belongs among
their hereditary traits. Thus the prudent old man, accustomed to keep close watch over all possible influences
upon him, permitted the element of Castalian spirit
brought to him by his young friend and antipodal colleague to strike root only reluctantly and inch by inch.
Gradually, however, it sprouted; and of all the good
things that Knecht experienced in his years at the monastery, this was the best and most precious of all to him:
this scanty, hesitant growth of trust and openness from
seemingly hopeless beginnings on the part of the experienced older man, this slowly germinating and even
more slowly admitted sympathy for his younger admirer
as a person and, beyond that, for the specifically Castalian elements in his personality. Step by step the younger
man, seemingly little more than pupil, listener, and
learner, led Father Jacobus—who initially had used the
words "Castalian" and Glass Bead Game player only
with ironic emphasis, and often as outright invective—
toward a tolerant and ultimately respectful acceptance
of this other mentality, this other Order, this other attempt to create an aristocracy of the spirit. Father Jacobus ceased to carp at the youth of the Order, though
with its little more than two centuries the Benedictines
were the elder by some fifteen hundred years. He ceased
to regard the Glass Bead Game as mere aesthetic dandy-

ism; and he ceased to rule out the prospect of friendship and alliance between two Orders so ill matched in age.

Joseph regarded this partial conquest of Father Jacobus as a personal cause for rejoicing. He remained unaware that the authorities considered it the utmost of his accomplishments on his mission to Mariafels. Now and again he wondered in vain what was the real reason for his assignment to the monastery. Though initially it had seemed to be a promotion and distinction envied by his competitors, could it not signify a form of inglorious premature retirement, a relegation to a dead end? But then one could learn something everywhere, so why not here too? On the other hand, from the Castalian point of view this monastery, Father Jacobus alone excepted, was certainly no garden of learning or model of scholarship. He wondered, too, whether his isolation among nothing but unexacting dilettantes was not already affecting his prowess in the Glass Bead Game. He could not quite tell whether he was losing ground. For all his uncertainty, however, he was helped by his lack of ambition as well as his already quite advanced *amor fati*. On the whole his life as a guest and unimportant teacher in this cosy old monastic world was more to his liking than his last months at Waldzell as one of a circle of ambitious men. If fate wished to leave him forever in this small colonial post, he would certainly try to change some aspects of his life here—for example, contrive to bring one of his friends here or at least ask for a longish leave in Castalia every year—but for the rest he would be content.

The reader of this biographical sketch may possibly be waiting for an account of another side of Knecht's experience in the monastery, namely the religious side. But we can venture only some tentative hints. It is certainly likely that Knecht had some deeply felt encounter with religion, with Christianity as daily practiced in the monastery. In fact from some of his later remarks and attitudes it is quite clear that he did. But whether and to what extent he became a Christian is a question we must leave unanswered; these realms are closed to our researches. In addition to the respect for religions generally cultivated in Castalia, Knecht had a kind of

inner reverence which we would scarcely be wrong to
call pious. Moreover, he had already been well instructed
in the schools on the classical forms of Christian doctrine,
especially in connection with his studies of church music.
Above all he was well acquainted with the sacramental
meaning and ritual of the Mass.

With a good deal of astonishment as well as reverence,
he had found among the Benedictines a living religion
which he had hitherto known only theoretically and historically. He attended many services, and after he had
familiarized himself with some of the writings of Father
Jacobus, and taken to heart some of their talks, he became fully aware of how phenomenal this Christianity
was—a religion that through the centuries had so many
times become unmodern and outmoded, antiquated and
rigid, but had repeatedly recalled the sources of its being
and thereby renewed itself, once again leaving behind
those aspects which in their time had been modern and
victorious. He did not seriously resist the idea, presented
to him every so often in those talks, that perhaps Castalian culture was merely a secularized and transitory off-
shoot of Christian culture in its Occidental form, which
would some day be reabsorbed by its parent. Even if
that were so, he once remarked to Father Jacobus, his,
Joseph Knecht's, own place lay within the Castalian
and not the Benedictine system; he had to serve the
former, not the latter, and prove himself within it. His
task was to work for the system of which he was a member, without asking whether it could claim perpetual
existence, or even a long span of life. He could only regard conversion as a rather undignified form of escape,
he said. In similar fashion Johann Albrecht Bengel,
whom they both venerated, had in his time served a
small and transitory sect without neglecting his duties to
the Eternal. Piety, which is to say faithful service and
loyalty up to the point of sacrificing one's life, was part
and parcel of every creed and every stage of individual
development; such service and loyalty were the only
valid measure of devoutness.

Knecht had been staying with the Benedictine Fathers
for some two years when a visitor appeared at the monastery who was kept apart from him with great care. Even

a casual introduction was avoided. His curiosity roused
by these procedures, he observed the stranger for the
few days of his visit and indulged in all sorts of speculations. He became convinced that the stranger's religious
habit was a disguise. The unknown held long conferences
behind closed doors with the Abbot and Father Jacobus,
and was always receiving and sending urgent messages.
Knecht, who by now had at least heard rumors about
the political connections and traditions of the monastery,
guessed that the guest must be a high-ranking statesman on a secret mission, or a sovereign traveling in-
cognito. As he reflected on the matter, he recalled several
guests of the past few months whose visits, in hindsight,
seemed to him equally mysterious or significant. Now he
remembered the chief of the Castalian "police," his
friendly mentor Dubois, and the request that he keep an
eye on such events in the monastery. And although he
still felt neither the urge nor the vocation for making
such reports, his conscience troubled him for having not
written to the kindly man for so long a time. No doubt
Dubois was disappointed in him. So he wrote him a long
letter, tried to explain his silence, and in order to give
some substance to his letter said a few words about his
association with Father Jacobus. He had no idea how
carefully and by how many important persons his letter
would be read back in Castalia.

FIVE

THE MISSION

KNECHT'S FIRST STAY at the monastery lasted two years. At this time he was in his thirty-seventh year. One morning, some two months after his long letter to Dubois, he was called into the Abbot's office. He expected the affable Abbot would want to chat a bit about Chinese, and made his appearance promptly. Gervasius came forward to meet him, a letter in hand.

"I have been honored with a commission for you, my esteemed friend," he said gaily in his amiably patronizing manner, and promptly dropped into the ironically teasing tone that had developed as an expression of the still unclarified amity between the religious and the Castalian Orders—the tone that was actually a creation of Father Jacobus. "Incidentally, my respects to your Magister Ludi. What letters he writes! The honorable gentleman has written to me in Latin, Heaven knows why. When you Castalians do something, one never knows whether you intend a courtesy or mockery, an honor or a rap on the knuckles. At any rate, the venerable *dominus* has written to me in the kind of Latin that no one in our whole Order could manage at this time, except possibly Father Jacobus. It's a Latin that might have come directly out of

the school of Cicero, but laced with a carefully measured
dash of Church Latin—and of course it's again impossible
to tell whether that is intended naively as bait for us
padres, or meant ironically, or simply springs from an
irresistible impulse to playact, stylize, and embellish. At
any rate, his honor writes that your esteemed authorities
wish to see and embrace you once again, and also to
determine to what extent your long stay among semi-
barbarians like us has had a morally and stylistically
corrupting effect upon you. In brief, if I have correctly
interpreted the lengthy epistle, a leave has been granted
you, and I have been requested to send my guest home
to Waldzell for an indefinite term, but not forever; on the
contrary, the authorities contemplate your returning by
and by, if that seems agreeable to us. I must beg your
pardon; I am scarcely capable of appreciating all the
subtleties of the letter. Nor do I imagine that Magister
Thomas expected me to. I have been asked to transmit
to you this notice; and now go and consider whether
and when you wish to depart. We shall miss you, my
friend, and if you should stay away too long we shall
not fail to demand your return."

In the envelope the Abbot had given him Knecht
found a terse notice from the Board informing him that
a leave had been granted him both as a vacation and for
consultation with his superiors, and that he was expected in Waldzell in the near future. He need not see
the current Game course for beginners through to the
end unless the Abbot specifically asked him to. The
former Music Master sent his regards. As he read that
line, Joseph started and grew pensive. How had the
writer of the letter, the Magister Ludi, been asked to
pass on this greeting, which in any case did not really fit
the official tone of the letter? There must have been a
conference of the entire Board, to which the former
Music Master had been invited. Very well, the meetings
and decisions of the Board of Educators did not concern him, but the tone of these greetings struck him as
strange. The message sounded curiously as if it were directed to an equal. It did not matter what question had
been discussed at the conference; the regards proved
that the highest authorities had also talked about Joseph

Knecht on that occasion. Was something new in the offing? Was he to be recalled? And would this be a promotion or a setback? But the letter spoke only of a leave. To be sure he was eager for this leave; he would have gladly left the next day. But at least he must say good-by to his pupils and leave instruction for them. Anton would be very saddened by his departure. And he also owed a farewell visit to some of the Fathers.

At this point he thought of Jacobus, and to his mild astonishment he felt a slight ache, an emotion which told him that his heart was more attached to Mariafels than he had realized. Here he lacked many of the things which he was used to, and which were dear to him; and in the course of the two years, distance and deprivation had made Castalia even more beautiful in his imagination. But at this moment he saw clearly that what Father Jacobus meant to him was irreplaceable, and that he would miss it in Castalia. At the same time he realized more clearly than ever how much he had learned in the monastery. Because of his experiences here, he looked forward with rejoicing and confidence to the journey to Waldzell, to reunions, to the Glass Bead Game, and his holiday. But his happiness would have been far less were it not for the prospect of returning.

Coming to an abrupt resolution, he called on Father Jacobus. He told him of his recall, and of his surprise to find underneath his pleasure at going home and seeing friends a joyful anticipation of returning. This joy, he said respectfully, was chiefly connected with Father Jacobus himself. Therefore he had summoned up his courage and was venturing to ask a great favor: when he returned, would Father Jacobus be his mentor, if only for an hour or two a week?

Father Jacobus gave a deprecating laugh, and once more came forth with elegantly sardonic compliments: a simple monk could only gape in mute admiration and shake his head in wonder at the surpassing range of Castalian culture. But Joseph could gather that the refusal was not meant seriously, and as they shook hands in parting Father Jacobus said amiably that he could rest easy about his request, he would gladly do what he could

for him, and he bade Joseph good-by with heartfelt
warmth.

Gladly, he set out for his vacation at home, already
sure in his heart that his period in the monastery had
not been profitless. At departure he felt like a boy, but
he soon realized that he was no boy and no longer a
youth either. He realized that by the feelings of embarrassment and inner resistance that flooded him as
soon as he tried, by a gesture, a shout, some childish
act, to give vent to the mood of release and of schoolboy
happiness at vacation time. No doubt about it, the
things that once had been natural and a relief, a jubilant
cry to the birds in a tree, a marching song chanted
aloud, swinging along the road in a light, rhythmical
dance-step—these would not do any more. They would
have come out stiff and forced, would have been foolish
and childish. He felt that he was a man, young in feelings and youthful in strength, but no longer used to surrendering to the mood of the moment, no longer free,
instead kept on his mettle, tied down and duty-bound—
by what? By an official post? By the task of representing
his country and his Order to the monks? No, rather it
was the Order itself, the hierarchy. As he engaged in
this sudden self-analysis, he realized that he had incom-
prehensibly grown into the hierarchy, become part of
its structure. His constraint came from the responsibility,
from belonging to the higher collectivity. This it was that
made many young men old and many old men appear
young, that held you, supported you, and at the same
time deprived you of your freedom like the stake to
which a sapling is tied. This it was that took away your
innocence even while it demanded ever more limpid
purity.

In Monteport he paid his respects to the former Music
Master, who in his younger years had himself once been
a guest at Mariafels and studied Benedictine music
there. He plied Joseph with many questions about the
place. Joseph found the old man somewhat more subdued and withdrawn, but stronger and gayer in appearance than he had been at their last meeting. The
fatigue had departed from his face; it was not that he
had grown younger since resigning his office, but he

definitely looked handsomer and more spiritualized.
Knecht was struck by the fact that though he inquired
about the organ, the chests of music manuscripts, and
the choral singing in Mariafels, and even wanted to hear
whether the tree in the cloister garden was still standing,
he seemed to have no curiosity about Knecht's work
there, the Glass Bead Game course, or the purpose of
his present leave. Before he continued his journey, however, the old man gave him a valuable hint. "I have
heard," he said with seeming jocularity, "that you have
become something of a diplomat. Not really a very nice
occupation, but it seems our people are satisfied with
you. Interpret that as you like. But if it doesn't happen
to be your ambition to stay in this occupation forever,
then be on your guard, Joseph. I think they want to cap-
ture you for it. Defend yourself; you have the right to.
. . . No, ask me no questions; I shall not say a word more.
You will see."

In spite of this warning, which he carried with him
like a thorn in his flesh, Joseph felt something like rapture on returning to Waldzell. It was as if Waldzell
were not only home and the most beautiful place in the
world, but as if it had become even lovelier and more
interesting in the meanwhile; or else he was returning
with fresh and keener eyes. And this applied not only
to the gates, towers, trees, and river, to the courtyards and
halls and familiar faces. During this furlough he felt a
heightened receptivity to the spirit of Waldzell, to the
Order and the Glass Bead Game. It was the grateful
understanding of the homecoming traveler now grown
matured and wiser. "I feel," he said to his friend Tegularius at the end of an enthusiastic eulogy on Waldzell
and Castalia, "I feel as if I spent all my years here asleep,
happy enough, to be sure, but unconscious. Now I feel
awake and see everything sharply and clearly, indubitable reality. To think that two years abroad can so
sharpen one's vision."

He enjoyed his vacation as if it were a prolonged
festival. His greatest pleasure came from the games and
discussions with his fellow members of the elite at the
Vicus Lusorum, from seeing friends again, and from the
genius loci of Waldzell. This soaring sense of happiness

did not reach its peak, however, until after his first audience with the Glass Bead Game Master; up to then his joy had been mingled with trepidation.

The Magister Ludi asked fewer questions than Knecht had anticipated. He scarcely mentioned the Game course for beginners and Joseph's studies in the music archives. On the other hand, he could not hear enough about Father Jacobus, referred back to him again and again, and was interested in every morsel Joseph could tell him about this man. From the Magister's great friendliness Joseph concluded that they were satisfied with him and his mission among the Benedictines, very satisfied indeed. His conclusion was confirmed by the conduct of Monsieur Dubois, to whom he was promptly sent by Magister Thomas. "You've done a splendid job," Dubois said. With a low laugh, he added: "My instinct was certainly at fault when I advised against your being sent to the monastery. Your winning over the great Father Jacobus in addition to the Abbot, and making him more favorable toward Castalia, is a great deal—more than anyone dared to hope for."

Two days later Magister Thomas invited Joseph, together with Dubois and the current head of the Waldzell elite school, Zbinden's successor, to dinner. During the conversation hour after dinner the new Music Master unexpectedly turned up, as did the Archivist of the Order —two more members of the Supreme Board. One of them took Joseph along to the guest house for a lengthy talk. This invitation for the first time moved Knecht publicly into the most intimate circle of candidates for high office, and set up between himself and the average member of the Game elite a barrier which Knecht, now keenly alert to such matters, at once felt acutely.

For the present he was given a vacation of four weeks and the customary official's pass to the guest houses of the Province. Although no duties were assigned to him, and he was not even asked to report, it was evident that he was under observation by his superiors. For when he went on a few visits and outings, once to Keuperheim, once to Hirsland, and once to the College of Far Eastern Studies, invitations from the high officials in these places were immediately forthcoming. Within those few weeks

he actually became acquainted with the entire Board of
the Order and with the majority of the Masters and directors of studies. Had it not been for these highly official invitations and encounters, these outings would
have betokened a return to the freedom of his years of
study. He began to cut back on the visits, chiefly out of
consideration for Tegularius, who was painfully sensitive
to these infringements on their time together, but also
for the sake of the Glass Bead Game. For he was very
eager to participate in the newest exercises and to test
himself on the latest problems. For this, Tegularius
proved to be of invaluable assistance to him.

His other close friend, Ferromonte, had joined the
staff of the new Music Master, and Joseph was able to
see him only twice during this period. He found him
hard-working and happy in his work, engrossed in a
major musicological task involving the persistence of
Greek music in the dances and folksongs of the Balkan
countries. Enthusiastically, Ferromonte told his friend
about his latest discoveries. He had been exploring the
era at the end of the eighteenth century, when baroque
music was beginning to decline and was taking in new
materials from Slavic folk music.

However, Knecht spent the greater part of these holidays in Waldzell occupied with the Glass Bead Game.
With Fritz Tegularius he went over the notes Fritz had
taken on a private seminar the Magister had given for
advanced players during the past two semesters. After
his two years of deprivation Knecht again plunged with
all his energy into the noble world of the Game, whose
magic seemed to him as inseparable from his life and as
indispensable to it as music.

The last days of his vacation arrived before the Magister Ludi came around to mentioning Joseph's mission
in Mariafels, and his next task for the immediate future.
He chatted casually at first, but soon changed to a more
earnest and insistent tone as he told Joseph about a plan
conceived by the Board which the majority of the Masters, as well as Monsieur Dubois, considered highly important: the plan to establish a permanent Castalian representative at the Holy See. The historic moment had
come, Master Thomas explained in his engaging, urbane

manner, or at any rate was drawing near, for bridging the ancient gulf between Rome and the Order. In future dangers, they would undoubtedly have common enemies, would share a common fate, and hence were natural allies. In the long run the present state of affairs was untenable and, properly speaking, undignified. It would not do for the two powers, whose historic task in the world was to preserve and foster the things of the spirit and the cause of peace, to go on existing side by side almost as strangers to each other. The Roman Church had survived the shocks of the last great epoch of wars, had lived through the crises despite severe losses, and had emerged renewed and purified, whereas the secular centers of the arts and sciences had gone under in the general decline of culture. It was out of their ruins that the Order and the Castalian ideal had arisen. For that very reason, and because of its venerable age, it was right and proper to grant the Church precedence. She was the older, more distinguished power, her worth tested in more and greater storms. For the present, the problem was to awaken the Roman Catholics to greater awareness of the kinship between the two powers, and their dependence upon each other in all future crises.

(At this point Knecht thought: "Oh, so they want to send me to Rome, possibly forever." Mindful of the former Music Master's warning, he inwardly put himself in a posture of defense.)

An important step forward, Master Thomas continued, had already been taken as a result of Knecht's mission in Mariafels. In itself this mission had been only a polite gesture, imposing no obligations and undertaken without ulterior motives at the invitation of the others. Otherwise, of course, the Board would not have sent a politically innocent Glass Bead Game player, but some younger official from Dubois's department. But as it turned out this experiment, this innocuous mission, had had astonishing results. A leading mind of contemporary Catholicism, Father Jacobus, had been made acquainted with the spirit of Castalia and had come to take a favorable view of that spirit, which he had hitherto flatly rejected. The authorities were grateful to Joseph Knecht for the part he had played. Here lay the significance of his mission. The fur-

ther course of Knecht's work must be regarded in the light
of it, since all future efforts at *rapprochement* would be
built upon this success. He had been granted a vacation—
which could be somewhat extended if he wished—and
most of the members of the higher authorities had met
and talked with him. His superiors had expressed their
confidence in Knecht and had now charged the Magister
Ludi to send him on a special assignment and with
broader powers back to Mariafels, where he was, happily,
sure of a friendly reception.

He paused as if to allow time for a question, but Joseph
only signified by a courteous gesture of submission that
he was all attention and was awaiting his orders.

"The assignment I have for you now," the Magister
went on, "is the following. We are planning, sooner or
later, to establish a permanent embassy of our Order at
the Vatican, if possible on a reciprocal basis. As the
younger group, we are ready to adopt a highly deferential
though of course not servile attitude toward Rome; we
are quite willing to accept second place and allow Rome
the first. Perhaps—I am no more sure of it than Dubois
—the Pope would accept our offer straightaway. But we
cannot risk a rebuff. As it happens, there is a man within
our reach whose voice has the greatest influence in Rome:
Father Jacobus. And your assignment is to return to the
Benedictine monastery, live there as you have already
done, engage in studies, give an inconsequential course
in the Glass Bead Game, and devote all your attention
and care to slowly winning Father Jacobus over to our
side and seeing to it that he promises to support our plans
in Rome. In other words, this time the goal of your mission is precisely defined. It does not matter much how
long you take to achieve it; we imagine that it will require at least a year, but it might also be two or several
years. You are by now acquainted with the Benedictine
tempo and have learned to adjust to it. Under no circumstances must we give the impression of being impatient or overeager; the affair must ripen of its own accord, right? I hope you agree to this assignment, and that
you will frankly express any objections you may have.
You may have a few days to think it over if you like."

Knecht, for whom the assignment was not such a surprise, thanks to some recent conversations, replied that he had no need to think it over. He obediently accepted, but added: "You know, sir, that missions of this kind are most successful when the emissary has no inner resistances and inhibitions to overcome. I have no reluctance about accepting; I understand the importance of the task and hope I can do justice to it. But I do feel a certain anxiety about my future. Be so kind, Magister, to hear me admit my entirely personal, egotistic concern. I am a Glass Bead Game player. As you know, due to my mission among the Benedictines I have omitted my studies of the Game for two full years. I have learned nothing new and have neglected my art. Now at least another year and probably more will be added. I should not like to fall still further behind during this time. Therefore I would like to be allowed frequent brief leaves to visit Waldzell and continual radio contact with the lectures and special exercises of your seminar for advanced players."

"But of course," the Master said. There was already a note of dismissal in his tone, but Knecht raised his voice and spoke of his other anxiety: that if his mission in Mariafels succeeded he might be sent to Rome or employed otherwise for diplomatic work. "Any such prospect," he concluded, "would have a depressing effect upon me and hamper my efforts at the monastery. For I would not at all like to be permanently consigned to the diplomatic service."

The Magister frowned and raised his finger chidingly. "You speak of being consigned. Really, the word is ill chosen. No one here ever thought of it as a consigning, but rather as a distinction, a promotion. I am not authorized to give you any information or make any promises in regard to the way we shall be employing you in the future. But by a stretch of the imagination I can understand your doubts, and probably I shall be able to help you if your fears really prove to be justified. And now listen to me: you have a certain gift for making yourself agreeable and well liked. An enemy might almost call you a charmer. Presumably this gift of yours prompted the Board to make this second assignment to the monastery. But do not use your gift too freely, Joseph, and set no immoderate value on your achievements. If you succeed with Father

Jacobus, that will be the proper moment for you to address a personal request to the Board. Today it seems to me premature. Let me know when you are ready to leave."

Joseph received these words in silence, laying more weight on the benevolence behind them than the patent reprimand. Soon thereafter he returned to Mariafels.

There he found the security of a precisely defined task a great benefaction. Moreover, this task was important and honorable, and in one respect it coincided with his own deepest desires: to come as close as possible to Father Jacobus and to win his full friendship. At the monastery he was evidently taken seriously as an envoy now, and was thought to have been raised in rank. The conduct of the dignitaries of the abbey, especially Abbot Gervasius himself, made that plain to him. They were as friendly as ever, but a discernible degree more respectful than before. They no longer treated Joseph as a young guest of no standing, toward whom they showed civility for the sake of his origins and out of benevolence toward him personally. He was now received as a high-ranking Castalian official, given the deference due to an ambassador plenipotentiary. No longer blind in these matters, Joseph drew his own conclusions.

Nevertheless, he could discover no change in Father Jacobus's attitude toward him. The old scholar greeted him with friendliness and pleasure. Without waiting to be asked or reminded, he himself brought up the matter of their working together. Joseph was deeply touched. He rearranged his schedule; his daily routine was now very different from what it had been before his vacation. This time the Glass Bead Game course no longer formed the center of his work and duties. He gave up his studies in the music archives and his friendly collaboration with the organist. Now his chief concern was the instruction he received from Father Jacobus: lessons in several branches of historical science. The monk introduced his special pupil to the background and early history of the Benedictine Order and to the sources for the early Middle Ages. He set aside a special hour in which they would read together one of the old chroniclers in the original. Father Jacobus was not displeased when Knecht pleaded to have young Anton participate in the lessons; but he had little difficulty persuading Joseph that even the best-intentioned third party could prove a serious hindrance to this kind of intensely private instruction. In consequence, Anton, who knew nothing of Knecht's efforts on his behalf, was invited to take part only in the readings of the chronicler, and was overjoyed. Undoubtedly these lessons constituted a distinction for the young monk, concerning whose life we have no further information. They must have been a supreme pleasure and stimulus, for he was being allowed to share in the work and intellectual exchange of two of the purest and most original minds of his age. Share, however, is perhaps an exaggeration; for the most part the young recruit merely listened.

Joseph repaid Father Jacobus by giving him an introduction to the history and structure of Castalia and the main ideas underlying the Glass Bead Game. This instruction followed immediately after his own lessons in epigraphy and source work, the pupil becoming the teacher and the honored teacher an attentive listener and often a captious critic and questioner. For a long while the reverend Father continued to hold the whole Castalian mentality in distrust. Because he saw no real religious attitude in it, he doubted its capacity to rear the kind of human being he could take seriously, despite the fact that Knecht himself represented so fine a product of Castalian education. Even long after he had undergone a kind of conversion, insofar as that was possible, through Knecht's teaching and example, and was prepared to recommend the *rapprochement* of Castalia to Rome, this distrust never entirely died. Knecht's notes are full of striking examples of it, jotted down at the moment. We shall quote from one of them:

Father Jacobus: "You are great scholars and aesthetes, you Castalians. You measure the weight of the vowels in an old poem and relate the resulting formula to that of a planet's orbit. That is delightful, but it is a game. And indeed your supreme mystery and symbol, the Glass Bead Game, is also a game. I grant that you try to exalt this pretty game into something akin to a sacrament, or at least to a device for edification. But sacraments do not spring from such endeavors. The game remains a game."

Joseph: "You mean, reverend Father, that we lack the foundation of theology?"

Father Jacobus: "Come now, of theology we will not speak. You are much too far from that. You could at least do with a few simpler foundations, with a science of man, for example, a real doctrine and real knowledge about the human race. You do not know man, do not understand him in his bestiality and as the image of God. All you know is the Castalian, a special product, a caste, a rare experiment in breeding."

For Knecht, of course, it was an extraordinary piece of good fortune that these hours of instruction and discourse provided him with the widest field and the most favorable opportunities to carry out his assignment of gaining Father Jacobus's approval of Castalia and convincing him of the value of an alliance. The situation in fact was so favorable to his purposes that he soon began to feel twinges of conscience. He came to think it shameful and unworthy when they sat together, or strolled back and forth in the cloisters, that the reverend man should be so trustfully sacrificing his time, when he was all the while the object of secret political designs. Knecht could not have accepted this situation in silence for long, and he was already considering just how to make his disclosure when, to his surprise, the old man anticipated him.

"My dear friend," he said to him with seeming off-handedness one day, "we have really found our way to a most pleasant and, I would hope, also a fruitful kind of exchange. The two activities that have been my favorites throughout my life, learning and teaching, have fused into a fine new combination during our joint working sessions, and for me that has come at just the right time, for I am beginning to age and cannot imagine any better cure and refreshment than our lessons. As far as I am concerned, therefore, I am the one who gains from our exchange. On the other hand, I am not so sure, my friend, that you and particularly those whose envoy you are and whom you serve will have profited from the business as much as they may hope. I should like to avert any future disappointment and would be sorry to have any unclear relationship arise between us. Therefore permit an old hand a question. I have of course had occasion to think about the reason for your sojourn in our little abbey, pleasant as it is for me. Until recently, that is up to the time of your vacation, it seemed to me that the purpose of your presence among us was not completely clear even to yourself. Was my observation correct?"

"It was."

"Good. Since your return from that vacation, this has changed. You are no longer puzzling or anxious about the reason for your presence here. You know why you are here. Am I right?—Good, then I have not guessed wrong. Presumably I am also not guessing wrong in my notion of the reason. You have a diplomatic assignment, and it concerns neither our monastery nor our Abbot, but me. As you see, not very much is left of your secret. To clarify the situation completely, I shall take the final step and ask you to inform me fully about the rest of it. What is your assignment?"

Knecht had sprung to his feet and stood facing Father Jacobus, surprised, embarrassed, feeling something close to dismay. "You are right," he cried, "but at the same time that you relieve me of a burden, you also shame me by speaking first. I have long been considering how I could manage to give our relationship the clarity you have established so rapidly. The one saving thing is that my request for instruction and our agreement fell in the period before my vacation. Otherwise it truly would have seemed as if the whole thing had been diplomacy on my part, and our studies merely a pretext."

The old man spoke with friendly reassurance: "I merely wanted to help both of us move forward a step. There is no need for you to aver the purity of your motives. If I have anticipated you and helped speed the coming of something that also seems desirable to you, all is well."

After Knecht had told him the nature of his assignment, he commented: "Your superiors in Castalia are not exactly brilliant diplomats, but they are not so bad either, and they know a good thing when they see it. I shall give all the consideration to your mission, and my decision will depend partly on how well you can explain your Castalian constitution and ideals, and make them seem plausible to me. Let us give ourselves all the time we need for that." Seeing that Knecht still looked somewhat crestfallen, he gave a brittle laugh and said: "If you like, you can also regard my proceeding thus as a kind of lesson. We are two diplomats, and diplomats' intercourse is always a combat, no matter how friendly a form it may take. In our struggle, as it happens, I was momentarily at a disadvantage; I had lost the initiative. You knew more than I. Now the balance has been restored. The chess move was successful; therefore it was the right one."

Knecht thought it important to win Father Jacobus's approval for the Castalian authorities' project; but it seemed to him far more important to learn as much as possible from him, and for his own part to serve this learned and powerful man as a reliable guide to the Castalian world. A good many of Knecht's friends and later disciples envied him as remarkable men are always envied, not only for their greatness of soul and energy, but also for their seeming luck, their seeming preferment by destiny. The lesser man sees in the greater as much as he can see, and Joseph Knecht's career cannot help striking every observer as unusually brilliant, rapid, and seemingly effortless. Certainly we are tempted to say of that period in his life: he was lucky. Nor would we wish to try to explain this "luck" rationalistically or moralistically, either as the causal result of external circumstances or as a kind of reward for special virtue. Luck has nothing to do with rationality or morality; by its nature it has about it a quality akin to magic, belonging to a primitive, more youthful stage of mankind's history. The lucky innocent, showered with gifts by the fairies, pampered by the gods, is not the object of rational study, and hence not a fit subject for biographical analysis; he is a symbol who always stands outside the personal and the historical realms. Nevertheless, there are outstanding men with whose lives "luck" is intimately bound up, even though that luck may consist merely in the fact that they and the task proper to their talents actually intersect on the plane of history and biography, that they are born neither too soon nor too late. Knecht seems to have been one of these. Thus his life, at least for a considerable part of his way, gives the impression that everything desirable simply fell into his lap. We do not wish to deny or to gloss over this aspect of his life. Moreover, we could explain it rationally only by a biographical method which is not ours, neither desired nor permitted in Castalia; that is, we would have to enter into an almost unlimited discussion of the most personal, most private matters, of health and sickness, the oscillations and curves in his vitality and self-confidence. We are quite sure that any such biographical approach—which is out of the question for us—would reveal a perfect balance between Knecht's "luck" and his suffering, but nevertheless would falsify our portrayal of his person and his life.

But enough digression. We were saying that many of those who knew Knecht, or had only heard of him, envied him. Probably few things in his life seemed to lesser folk so enviable as his relationship to the old Benedictine Father, for he was at one and the same time pupil and teacher, taker and giver, conquered and conqueror, friend and collaborator. Moreover, none of Knecht's conquests since his successful courting of Elder Brother in the Bamboo Grove had given him such happiness. No other had made him feel so intensely honored and abashed, rewarded and stimulated. Of his later favorite pupils, almost all have testified to how frequently, gladly, and joyfully he would refer to Father Jacobus. Knecht learned from the Benedictine something he could scarcely have learned in the Castalia of those days. He acquired an overview of the methods of historical knowledge and the tools of historical research, and had his first practice in applying them. But far beyond that, he experienced history not as an intellectual discipline, but as reality, as life; and in keeping with that, the transformation and elevation of his own personal life into history. This was something he could not have learned from a mere scholar. Father Jacobus was not only far more than a scholar, a seer, and a sage; he was also a mover and shaper. He had used the position in which fate had placed him not just to warm himself at the cozy fires of a contemplative existence; he had allowed the winds of the world to blow through his scholar's den and admitted the perils and forebodings of the age into his heart. He had taken action, had shared the blame and the responsibility for the events of his time; he had not contented himself with

surveying, arranging, and interpreting the happenings of
the distant past. And he had not dealt only with ideas, but
with the refractoriness of matter and the obstinacy of
men. Together with his associate and antagonist, a recently deceased Jesuit, he was regarded as the real archi-
tect of the diplomatic and moral power and the impressive
political prestige that the Roman Church had regained after ages of meekly borne ineffectuality and in-
significance.

Although teacher and pupil scarcely ever discussed
current politics (the Benedictine's practice in holding
his counsel as well as the younger man's reluctance to be
drawn into such issues combined to prevent that), Father
Jacobus's political position and activities so permeated
his mind that all his opinions, all of his glances into the
thicket of the world's squabbles were those of the practical statesman. Not that he was an ambitious or an intrigu-
ing politician. He was no regent and leader, no climber
either, but a councilor and arbitrator, a man whose conduct was tempered by sagacity, whose efforts were re-
strained by a profound insight into the inadequacies and
difficulties of human nature, but whose fame, experience,
knowledge of men and conditions, as well as his personal
integrity and altruism, had enabled him to gain significant power.

Knecht had known nothing of all this when he came to
Mariafels. He had even been ignorant of Father Jacobus's
name. The majority of the inhabitants of Castalia lived
in a state of political innocence and naïveté such as had
been quite common among the professors of earlier ages;
they had no political rights and duties, scarcely ever saw
a newspaper. Such was the habit of the average Castalian,
such his attitude. Repugnance for current events, politics,
newspapers, was even greater among the Glass Bead
Game players who liked to think of themselves as the
real elite, the cream of the Province, and went to some
lengths not to let anything cloud the rarefied atmosphere
of their scholarly and artistic existences. As we have
seen, at the time of his first appearance at the monastery,
Knecht had come not as a diplomatic envoy but solely
as a teacher of the Glass Bead Game, and had no political
knowledge aside from what Monsieur Dubois had man-

aged to instil in a few weeks. He was by comparison much more knowing now, but he had by no means surrendered the Waldzeller's distaste for engaging in current politics. Although his association with Father Jacobus had awakened him politically and taught him a good deal, this had not happened because Knecht was drawn to this realm. It just happened, as an inevitable though incidental consequence.

In order to add to his equipment and the better to fulfill his honorable task of lecturing *de rebus castaliensibus* to his pupil, Father Jacobus, Knecht had brought with him from Waldzell literature on the constitution and history of the Province, on the system of the elite schools, and on the evolution of the Glass Bead Game. Some of these books had served him twenty years before during his struggle with Plinio Designori—and he had not looked at them since. Others, meant specially for the officials of Castalia, had been barred to him as a student. Now he read them for the first time. The result was that at the very time his areas of study were so notably expanding, he was also forced once again to contemplate, understand, and reinforce his own intellectual and historical base. In his efforts to present the nature of the Order and of the Castalian system to Father Jacobus with maximum simplicity and clarity, he inevitably stumbled over the weakest point in his own and all Castalian education. He found that he himself had only a pale and rigidly schematic notion of the historical conditions which had led to the foundation of the Order and everything that followed from it. His picture of the conditions which had furthered the growth of the new system lacked all vividness and orderliness. Since Father Jacobus was anything but a passive pupil, the result was an intensified collaboration, an extremely animated exchange of views. While Joseph tried to present the history of his Castalian Order, Jacobus helped him to see many aspects of this history in the proper light for the first time, and to discern its roots in the general history of nations. Because of the Benedictine's temperament, these discussions often turned into passionate disputes, and as we shall see they continued to bear fruit years later and remained a vital influence down to the end of Knecht's life. On the other hand, the close attention Father Jacobus had given Knecht's exposition, and the thoroughness with which he came to know and appreciate Castalia, was evidenced by his subsequent conduct. Due to the work of these two men, there arose between Rome and Castalia a benevolent neutrality and occasional scholarly exchange which now and then developed into actual co-operation and alliance and ultimately produced the concord which continues to this day. In time Father Jacobus asked to be introduced to the theory of the Glass Bead Game—which he had originally pooh-poohed—for he sensed that here lay the secret of the Order and what might be called its faith or religion. Once he had consented to penetrate into this world he had hitherto known only from hearsay, and for which he had felt little liking, he resolutely proceeded in his shrewd and energetic way straight toward its center. And although he did not become a Glass Bead Game player—he was in any case far too old for that—the devotees of the Game and the Order outside the borders of Castalia had hardly a friend as earnest and as influential as the great Benedictine.

Now and then, after a session of joint work, Father Jacobus would indicate that he would be at home to Joseph that evening. After the strenuous lessons and the tense discussions, those were peaceful hours. Joseph frequently brought his clavichord along, or a violin, and the old man would sit down at the piano in the gentle light of a candle whose sweet fragrance of wax filled the small room like the music of Corelli, Scarlatti, Telemann, or Bach which they played alternately or together. The old man's bedtime came early, while Knecht, refreshed by these brief musical vespers, would continue his studies into the night, to the limits his self-discipline permitted.

Aside from his lessons with Father Jacobus, his perfunctory course in the Game, and an occasional Chinese colloquium with Abbot Gervasius, we also find Knecht engaged at this time in an elaborate task. He was taking part in the annual competition of the Waldzell elite, from which he had abstained in the past two years. The competition involved working out sketches for Games based on three or four prescribed main themes. Stress was placed on new, bold, and original associations of themes, impeccable logic, and beautiful calligraphy. Moreover, this was the sole occasion when competitors were permitted to overstep the bounds of the canon. That is, they could employ new symbols not yet admitted to the official code and vocabulary of hieroglyphs. This made the competition—which in any case was the most exciting annual event in Waldzell except for the great public ceremonial games—a contest among the most promising advocates of new Game symbols, and the very highest distinction for a winner in this competition consisted in the recognition of his proposed additions to the grammar and vocabulary of the Game and their acceptance into the Game Archives and the Game language. This was a very rare distinction indeed; usually the winner had to be content only with the ceremonial performance of his Game as the best candidate's Game of the year. Once, some twenty-five years ago, the great Thomas von der Trave, the present Magister Ludi, had been awarded this honor with his new abbreviations for the alchemical significance of the signs of the zodiac—later, too, Magister Thomas made large contributions to the study and classification of alchemy as a highly meaningful secret language.

For his entry Knecht chose not to draw on any new Game symbols such as virtually every candidate had in readiness. He also refrained from using his Game as an avowal of attachment to the psychological method of Game construction, although that would have been closer to his inclinations. Instead, he built up a Game modern and personal enough in its structure and themes, but of transparently clear, classical composition and strictly symmetrical development in the vein of the old masters. Perhaps distance from Waldzell and the Game Archives forced him to take this line; perhaps his historical studies made too great demands on his time and strength; but it may also be that he was more or less consciously guided by the desire to shape his Game so that it would correspond as closely as possible to the taste of his teacher and friend, Father Jacobus. We do not know.

We have used the phrase "psychological method of Game construction," and perhaps some of our readers will not immediately understand it. In Knecht's day it was a slogan bandied about a good deal. No doubt all periods have seen currents, vogues, struggles, and differing views and approaches among the initiates of the Glass Bead Game. At that time two opposing concepts of the Game called forth controversy and discussion. The foremost players distinguished two principal types of Game, the formal and the psychological. We know that Knecht, like Tegularius—although the latter kept out of the arguments—belonged to the champions of the latter type. Knecht, however, instead of speaking of the "psychological" mode of play usually preferred the word "pedagogical."

In the formal Game the player sought to compose out of the objective content of every game, out of the mathematical, linguistic, musical, and other elements, as dense, coherent, and formally perfect a unity and harmony as possible. In the psychological Game, on the other hand, the object was to create unity and harmony, cosmic roundedness and perfection, not so much in the choice, arrangement, interweaving, association, and contrast of the contents as in the meditation which followed every stage of the Game. All the stress was placed on this meditation. Such a psychological—or to use Knecht's word, pedagogical—Game did not display perfection to the outward eye. Rather, it guided the player, by means of its succession of precisely prescribed meditations, toward experiencing perfection and divinity. "The Game as I conceive it," Knecht once wrote to the former Music Master, "encompasses the player after the completion of meditation as the surface of a sphere encompasses its center, and leaves him with the feeling that he has extracted from the universe of accident and confusion a totally symmetrical and harmonious cosmos, and absorbed it into himself."

Knecht's entry, then, was a formally rather than a psychologically constructed Game. Possibly he wanted to prove to his superiors, and to himself as well, that in spite of his elementary course and diplomatic mission in Mariafels, he had lost none of his deftness, elegance, and virtuosity and had not suffered from lack of practice. If so, he succeeded in proving it. Since the final elaboration and clean copy of his Game outline could only be completed in the Waldzell Archives, he entrusted this task to

his friend Tegularius, who was himself participating in
the competition. Joseph was able to hand his drafts to
his friend personally, and to discuss them with him, as
well as to go over Tegularius's own outline; for Fritz
was finally able to come to the monastery for three days.
Magister Thomas had at last authorized the visit, after
Knecht had made two previous requests in vain.

Eager as Tegularius had been to come, and for all the
curiosity he, as an insular Castalian, had about life in the
monastery, he felt extremely uncomfortable there. Sensitive as he was, he nearly fell ill amid all the alien impressions and among these friendly but simple, healthy, and
somewhat rough-hewn people, not one of whom would
have had the slightest understanding for his thoughts,
cares, and problems. "You live here as if you were on
another planet," he said to his friend, "and I don't see
how you have been able to stand it for three years. I certainly admire you for that. To be sure, your Fathers are
polite enough toward me, but I feel rejected and repelled
by everything here. Nothing meets me halfway, nothing
is natural and easy, nothing can be assimilated without
resistance and pain. If I had to live here for two weeks, I
would feel as if I were in hell."

Knecht had a difficult time with him. Moreover, it
was disconcerting to witness, for the first time as an onlooker, how alien the two Orders, the two worlds were to
one another. He felt, too, that his oversensitive friend
with his air of anxious helplessness was not making a
good impression among the monks. Nevertheless, they re-
vised their respective Game plans for the competition
thoroughly, each critically examining the other's work.
When, after an hour of this Knecht went over to Father
Jacobus in the other wing, or to a meal, he had the feeling that he was being suddenly transported from his native
country to an entirely different land, with a different soil
and air, different climate, and different stars.

After Fritz had departed, Joseph drew out Father Jacobus on his impressions. "I hope," Jacobus said, "that the
majority of Castalians are more like you than your friend.
You have shown us an inexperienced, overbred, weakly,
and nevertheless, I am afraid, arrogant kind of person. I
shall go on taking you as more representative; otherwise

I should certainly be unjust to your kind. For this unfortunate, sensitive, overintelligent, fidgety person could spoil one's respect for your whole Province."

"Well," Knecht replied, "I imagine that in the course of the centuries you noble Benedictines have now and then had sickly, physically feeble, but for that very reason mentally sound and able men, such as my friend. I suppose it was imprudent of me to have invited him here, where everyone has a sharp eye for his weaknesses but no sense of his great virtues. He has done me a great kindness by coming." And he explained to Father Jacobus about his joining in the competition. The Benedictine was pleased with Knecht for defending his friend. "Well answered," he said with a friendly laugh. "But it strikes me that all of your friends are difficult to get along with."

He enjoyed Knecht's bewilderment and astonished expression for a moment, then added casually: "This time I am referring to someone outside Castalia. Have you heard anything new about your friend Plinio Designori?"

Joseph's astonishment increased; stunned, he asked for an explanation.

It seemed that Designori had written a political polemic professing violently anticlerical views, and incidentally strongly attacking Father Jacobus. Through friends in the Catholic press, Jacobus had obtained information on Designori, and in this way had learned of Plinio's schooldays in Castalia and his relationship to Knecht.

Joseph asked to borrow Plinio's article; and after he had read it he and Father Jacobus had their first discussion of current politics. A few more, but only a few, followed. "It was strange and almost alarming," Joseph wrote to Ferromonte, "for me to see the figure of our Plinio—and by-the-by my own—suddenly standing on the stage of the world's politics. This was something I had never imagined." As it turned out, Father Jacobus spoke of Plinio's polemic in rather appreciative terms. At any rate, he showed no sign of having taken offense. He praised Designori's style, commenting that his training in the elite school showed up clearly; in the run of everyday politics, one had to settle for a far lower level of intelligence, he said.

About this time Ferromonte sent Knecht a copy of the

first part of his subsequently famous work entitled *The Reception and Absorption of Slavic Folk Music by German Art Music from Joseph Haydn on*. In Knecht's letter of acknowledgment we find, among other things: "You have drawn a cogent conclusion from your studies, which I was privileged to share for a while. The two chapters dealing with Schubert, and especially with the quartets, are among the soundest examples of modern musicology that I have read. Think of me sometimes; I am very far from any such harvest as you have reaped. Although I have reason to be content with my life here—for my mission in Mariafels appears to be meeting with some success—I do occasionally feel that being so far from the Province and the Waldzell circle to which I belong is distinctly oppressive. I am learning a tremendous amount here, but adding neither to my certainties nor my professional skills, only to my problems. I must grant, though, a widening of horizon. However, I now feel much easier about the insecurity, strangeness, despondency, distraitness, self-doubt, and other ills that frequently assailed me during my first two years here. Tegularius was here recently—for only three days, but much as he had looked forward to seeing me and curious though he was about Mariafels, by the second day he could scarcely bear it any longer, so depressed and out of place did he feel. Since a monastery is after all a rather sheltered, peaceful world, and favorable enough to things of the spirit, in no way like a jail, a barracks, or a factory, I conclude from my experience that people from our dear Province are a good deal more pampered and oversensitive than we realize."

At about the date of this letter to Carlo, Knecht persuaded Father Jacobus to address a brief letter to the directorate of the Castalian Order acquiescing in the proposed diplomatic step. To this Jacobus added the request that they would permit "the Glass Bead Game player Joseph Knecht, who is universally popular here" and who was kindly giving him a private course *de rebus castaliensibus*, to remain for a while longer. The Castalian authorities were, of course, glad to oblige. Joseph, who had been thinking that he was still very far from any such "harvest," received a commendation, signed by the

directorate and by Monsieur Dubois, congratulating him
on the success of his mission. But what struck him as
most important about this honorific document and what
gave him the greatest pleasure (he reported it in well-
nigh triumphant tones in a note to Fritz) was a short
sentence to the effect that the Order had been informed
by the Magister Ludi of his desire to return to the Vicus
Lusorum, and was disposed to grant this request after
completion of his present assignment. Joseph also read
this passage aloud to Father Jacobus and now confessed
how greatly he had feared possible permanent banishment from Castalia and being sent to Rome. Laughing,
Father Jacobus commented: "Yes, my friend, there is
something about Orders; one prefers living in their
bosom rather than out on the periphery, let alone in
exile. You've touched the soiled fringes of politics here,
but now go right ahead and forget it, for you are not a
politician. But do not break your troth with history, even
though it may remain forever a secondary subject and a
hobby for you. For you had the makings of a historian.
And now let us profit by our time together, as long as I
have you."

Joseph Knecht seems to have made little use of his
privilege to pay more frequent visits to Waldzell. However, he listened on the radio to one seminar and to a
good many lectures and games. So also, from afar, sitting
in his excellent guest room in the monastery, he took
part in that "solemnity" in the festival hall of the Vicus
Lusorum at which the results of the prize competition
were announced. He had handed in a rather impersonal
and not at all revolutionary, but solid and elegant piece
of work whose value he knew, and he was prepared for
an honorable mention or a third or second prize. To
his surprise he now heard that he had been awarded
first prize, and even before surprise had given way to
delight, the spokesman for the Magister Ludi's office
continued reading in his beautiful low voice and named
Tegularius as winner of the second prize. It was certainly a moving and rapturous experience that the two
of them should emerge from this competition hand in
hand, as the crowned winners. He sprang to his feet with-

out listening to the rest, and ran down the stairs and through the echoing corridors out into the open air.

In a letter to the former Music Master, written at this time, we may read: "I am very happy, revered Master, as you can imagine. First the success of my mission and its commendation by the directorate of the Order, together with the prospect—so important to me—of soon returning home to friends and to the Glass Bead Game, instead of being kept in the diplomatic service; and now this first prize for a Game whose formal aspects I did take pains with, but which for good reasons by no means drained me of everything I had to contribute. And on top of that the joy of sharing this success with my friend—it really was too much all at once. I am happy, yes, but I could not well say that I am merry. Because of the dearth of the preceding period—at any rate what seemed to me a dearth—my real feeling is that these fulfillments are coming rather too suddenly and too abundantly. There is a measure of unease mingled with my gratitude, as if the vessel is so filled to the brim that only another drop is needed to tilt it. But, please, consider that I have not said this; in this situation every word is already too much."

As we shall see, the vessel filled to the brim was destined to have more than just one additional drop added to it. But at the moment Joseph Knecht devoted himself to his happiness, and the concomitant unease, with great intensity, as if he had a premonition of the impending great change. For Father Jacobus, too, these few months were a happy, an exuberant time. He was sorry that he would soon be losing this disciple and associate; and in their hours of work together, still more in their free-ranging conversations, he tried to bequeath to him as much as he could of the understanding he had acquired during a long life of hard work and hard thinking, understanding of the heights and depths in the lives of men and nations. He also had some things to say about the consequences of Knecht's mission, assessing its meaning, and the value of amity and political concord between Rome and Castalia. He recommended that Joseph study the epoch which had seen the founding of the Castalian Order as well as the gradual recovery of Rome

after a humiliating time of tribulation. He also recommended two books on the Reformation and schism of the
sixteenth century, but strongly urged him to make a
principle of studying the primary sources. He advised
Joseph to confine himself to graspable segments of a field
in preference to reading ponderous tomes on world
history. Finally, Father Jacobus made no bones about his
profound mistrust of all philosophies of history.

SIX

MAGISTER LUDI

KNECHT HAD DECIDED to postpone his final return to Wald-zell until the spring, the time of the great public Glass Bead Game, the *Ludus anniversarius* or *sollemnis*. The era when annual Games lasted for weeks and were attended by dignitaries and representatives from all over the world—what we may call the great age in the memorable history of these Games—already belonged forever to the past. But these spring sessions, with the one solemn Game that usually lasted for ten days to two weeks, still remained the great festive event of the year for all of Castalia. It was a festival not without its high religious and moral importance, for it brought together the advocates of all the sometimes disparate tendencies of the Province in an act of symbolic harmony. It established a truce between the egotistic ambitions of the several disciplines, and recalled to mind the unity which embraced their variety. For believers it possessed the sacramental force of true consecration; for unbelievers it was at least a substitute for religion; and for both it was a bath in the pure springs of beauty. The Passions of Johann Sebastian Bach had once upon a time—not so much in the time they were written as in the century following their rediscovery—been in similar fashion a genuine consecratory act for some of the performers and audience, a form of worship and religious substitute for others, and for all together a solemn manifestation of art and of the *Creator spiritus*.

Knecht had had scant difficulty obtaining the consent of both the monks and his home authorities for his decision. He could not quite determine the nature of his position after his reassignment to the little republic of the Vicus Lusorum, but he suspected that he would not long be left unoccupied and would soon be burdened and honored with some new office or mission. For the present he looked forward happily to returning home, to seeing his friends and participating in the approaching festival. He enjoyed his last days with Father Jacobus, and accepted with dignity and good humor the rather demonstrative kindnesses of the Abbot and monks when the time came for farewells. Then he left, feeling some sadness at parting from a place he had grown fond of and from a stage in his life he was now leaving behind, but also in a mood of festive anticipation, for although he lacked guidance and companions, he had, on his own initiative, scrupulously undertaken the whole series of meditation exercises prescribed as preparations for the festival Game. He had not been able to prevail on Father Jacobus to accept the Magister Ludi's formal invitation to attend the annual Game and accompany him, but this had not affected his good spirits; he understood the old anti-Castalian's reserved attitude, and he himself for the moment felt entirely relieved of all duties and restrictions and ready to surrender his whole mind to the impending ceremonies.

Festivities have their own peculiar nature. A genuine festival cannot go entirely wrong, unless it is spoiled by the unfortunate intervention of higher powers. For the devout soul, even in a downpour a procession retains its sacral quality, and a burned feast does not depress him. For the Glass Bead Game player every annual Game is festive and in a sense hallowed. Nevertheless, as every one of us knows, there are some festivals and games in which everything goes right, and every element lifts up, animates, and exalts every other, just as there are theatri-

cal and musical performances which without any clearly
discernible cause seem to ascend miraculously to glorious
climaxes and intensely felt experiences, whereas others,
just as well prepared, remain no more than decent
tries. Insofar as the achievement of intense experiences depends on the emotional state of the spectator, Joseph
Knecht had the best imaginable preparation: he was
troubled by no cares, returning from abroad loaded with
honors, and looking forward with joyous anticipation to
the coming event.

Nevertheless, this time the *Ludus sollemnis* was not
destined to be touched by that aura of the miraculous
and so rise to a special degree of consecration and radiance. It turned out, in fact, a cheerless, distinctly unhappy, and something very close to an unsuccessful
Game. Although many of the participants may have felt
edified and exalted all the same, the real actors and
organizers of the Game, as always in such cases, felt all
the more inexorably that atmosphere of apathy, lack of
grace and failure, of inhibition and bad luck which overshadowed this festival. Knecht, although he of course
sensed it and found his high expectations somewhat
dashed, was by no means among those who felt the fiasco
most keenly. Even though the solemn act failed to reach
the true peak of perfection and blessing, he was able,
because he was not playing and bore no responsibility for
it, to follow the ingeniously constructed Game apprecia-
tively, as a devout spectator, to let the meditations
quiver to a halt undisturbed, and with grateful devotion
to share that experience so familiar to all guests at these
Games: the sense of ceremony and sacrifice, of mystic
union of the congregation at the feet of the divine, which
could be conveyed even by a ceremony that, for the narrow circle of initiates, was regarded as a "failure." Nevertheless, he too was not altogether unaffected by the unlucky star that seemed to preside over this festival. The
Game itself, to be sure, was irreproachable in plan and
construction, like every one of Master Thomas's Games;
in fact it was one of his cleanest, most direct, and impressive achievements. But its performance was specially
ill-starred and has not yet been forgotten in the history
of Waldzell.

When Knecht arrived, a week before the opening of the great Game, he was received not by the Magister Ludi himself, but by his deputy Bertram, who welcomed him courteously but informed him rather curtly and distractedly that the venerable Master had recently fallen ill and that he, Bertram, was not sufficiently informed about Knecht's mission to receive his report. Would he therefore go to Hirsland to report his return to the directorate of the Order and await its commands.

As he took his leave Knecht involuntarily betrayed, by tone or gesture, his surprise at the coolness and shortness of his reception. Bertram apologized. "Do forgive me if I have disappointed you, and please understand my situation," he said. "The Magister is ill, the annual Game is upon us, and everything is up in the air. I don't know whether the Magister will be able to conduct the Game or whether I shall have to leap into the breach." The revered Master's illness could not have come at a more difficult moment, he went on to say. He was ready as always to assume the Magister's official duties, but if in addition he had to prepare himself at such short notice to conduct the great Game, he was afraid it would prove a task beyond his powers.

Knecht felt sorry for the man, who was so obviously depressed and thrown off balance; he was also sorry that the responsibility for the festival might now lie in the deputy's hands. Joseph had been away from Waldzell too long to know how well founded Bertram's anxiety was. The worst thing that can happen to a deputy had already befallen the man: some time past he had forfeited the trust of the elite, so that he was truly in a very difficult position.

With considerable concern, Knecht thought of the Magister Ludi, that great exponent of classical form and irony, the perfect Master and Castalian. He had looked forward eagerly to the Magister's receiving him, listening to his report, and reinstalling him in the small community of players, perhaps in some confidential post. It had been his desire to see the festival Game presided over by Master Thomas, to continue working under him and courting his recognition. Now it was painful and disappointing to find the Magister withdrawn into illness, and to be directed to other authorities. There was, however, some compensation in the respectful good will with which the secretary of the Order and Monsieur Dubois received him and heard him out. They treated him, in fact, as a colleague. During their first talk he discovered that for the present at any rate they had no intention of using him to promote the Roman project. They were going to respect his desire for a permanent return to the Game. For the moment they extended a friendly invitation to him to stay in the guesthouse of the Vicus Lusorum, attend the annual Game, and survey the situation. Together with his friend Tegularius, he devoted the days before the public ceremonies to the exercises in fasting and meditation. That was one of the reasons he was able to witness in so devout and grateful a spirit the strange Game which has left an unpleasant aftertaste in the memories of some.

The position of the deputy Masters, also called "Shadows," is a very peculiar one—especially the deputies to the Music Master and the Glass Bead Game Master. Every Magister has a deputy who is not provided for him by the authorities. Rather, he himself chooses his deputy from the narrow circle of his own candidates. The Master himself bears the full responsibility for all the actions and decisions of his deputy. For a candidate it is therefore a great distinction and a sign of the highest trust when he is appointed deputy by his Magister. He is thereby recognized as the intimate associate and right hand of the all-powerful Magister. Whenever the Magister is prevented from performing his official duties, he sends the deputy in his stead. The deputy, however, is not entitled to act in all capacities. For example, when the Supreme Board votes, he may transmit only a yea or nay in the Master's name and is never permitted to deliver an address or present motions on his own. There are a variety of other precautionary restrictions on the deputies.

While the appointment elevates the deputy to a very high and at times extremely exposed position, it is at a certain price. The deputy is set apart within the official hierarchy, and while he enjoys high honor and frequently may be entrusted with extremely important functions, his position deprives him of certain rights and opportunities which the other aspirants possess. There are two points in particular where this is revealed: the deputy does not bear the responsibility for his official acts, and he can rise no farther within the hierarchy. The law is unwritten, to be sure, but can be read throughout the history of Castalia: At the death or resignation of a Magister, his Shadow, who has represented him so often and whose whole existence seems to predestine him for the succession, has never advanced to fill the Master's place. It is as if custom were determined to show that a seemingly fluid and movable barrier is in fact insuperable. The barrier between Magister and deputy stands like a symbol for the barrier between the office and the individual. Thus, when a Castalian accepts the confidential post of deputy, he renounces the prospect of ever becoming a Magister himself, of ever really possessing the official robes and insignia that he wears so often in his representative role. At the same time he acquires the curiously ambiguous privilege of never incurring any blame for possible mistakes in his conduct of his office. The blame falls upon his Magister, who is answerable for his acts. A Magister sometimes becomes the victim of the deputy he has chosen and is forced to resign his office because of some glaring error committed by the deputy. The word "Shadow" originated in Waldzell to describe the Magister Ludi's deputy. It is splendidly apposite to his special position, his closeness amounting to quasi-identity with the Magister, and the make-believe insubstantiality of his official existence.

For many years Master Thomas von der Trave had employed a Shadow named Bertram who seems to have been more lacking in luck than in talent or good will. He was an excellent Glass Bead Game player, of course. As a teacher he was at least adequate, and he was also a conscientious official, absolutely devoted to his Master. Nevertheless, in the course of the past few years, he had become distinctly unpopular. The "new generation," the younger members of the elite, were particularly hostile to him, and since he did not possess his Master's limpid, chivalric temperament, this antagonism affected his poise. The Magister did not let him go, but had for years shielded him from friction with the elite as much as possible, putting him in the public eye more and more rarely and employing him largely in the chanceries and the Archives.

This blameless but disliked man, plainly not favored by fortune, now suddenly found himself at the head of the Vicus Lusorum due to his Master's illness. If it should turn out that he had to conduct the annual Game, he would occupy for the duration of the festival the most exposed position in the entire Province. He could only have coped with this great task if the majority of the Glass Bead Game players, or at any rate the tutors as a body, had supported him. Regrettably, that did not happen. This was why the *Ludus sollemnis* turned into a severe trial and very nearly a disaster for Waldzell.

Not until the day before the Game was it officially announced that the Magister had fallen seriously ill and would be unable to conduct the Game. We do not know whether this postponement of the announcement had been dictated by the sick Magister, who might have hoped up to the last moment that he would be able to pull himself together and preside. Probably he was already too ill to cherish any such ideas, and his Shadow made the mistake of leaving Castalia in uncertainty about the situation in Waldzell up to the last moment. Granted, it is even disputable whether this delay was actually a mistake. Undoubtedly it was done with good intentions, in order not to discredit the festival from the start and discourage the admirers of Master Thomas from attending. And had everything turned out well, had there been a relation of confidence between the Waldzell community of players and Bertram, the Shadow might actually have become his representative and—this is really quite conceivable—the Magister's absence might have gone almost unnoticed. It is idle to speculate further about the matter; we have mentioned it only because we thought it necessary to suggest that Bertram was not such an absolute failure, let alone unworthy of his office, as public opinion in Waldzell regarded him at that time. He was far more a victim than a culprit.

As happened every year, guests poured into Waldzell to attend the great Game. Many arrived unsuspectingly;

others were deeply anxious about the Magister Ludi's health and had gloomy premonitions about the prospects of the festival. Waldzell and the nearby villages filled with people. Almost every one of the directors of the Order and the members of the Board of Educators were on hand. Travelers in holiday mood arrived from the remoter parts of the country and from abroad, crowding the guest houses.

On the evening before the beginning of the Game, the ceremonies opened with the meditation hour. In response to the ringing of bells the whole of Waldzell, crowded with people as it was, subsided into a profound, reverent silence. Next morning came the first of the musical performances and announcement of the first movement of the Game, together with meditation on the two musical themes of this movement. Bertram, in the Magister Ludi's festival robes, displayed a stately and controlled demeanor, but he was very pale. As day followed day, he looked more and more strained, suffering and resigned, until during the last days he really resembled a shadow. By the second day of the Game the rumor spread that Magister Thomas's condition had worsened, and that his life was in danger. That evening there cropped up here and there, and especially among the initiates, those first contributions to the gradually developing legend about the sick Master and his Shadow. This legend, emanating from the innermost circle of the Vicus Lusorum, the tutors, maintained that the Master had been willing and would have been able to conduct the Game, but that he had sacrificed himself to his Shadow's ambition and assigned the solemn task to Bertram. But now, the legend continued, since Bertram did not seem equal to his lofty role, and since the Game was proving a disappointment, the sick man felt to blame for the failure of the Game and his Shadow's inadequacy, and was doing penance for the mistake. This, it was said, this and nothing else was the reason for the rapid deterioration of his condition and the rise in his fever.

Naturally this was not the sole version of the legend, but it was the elite's version and indicated that the ambitious aspirants thought the situation appalling and were dead set against doing anything to improve it. Their reverence for the Master was balanced by their malice for his Shadow; they wanted Bertram to fail even if the Master himself had to suffer as well.

By and by the story went the rounds that the Magister on his sickbed had begged his deputy and two seniors of the elite to keep the peace and not endanger the festival. The next day it was asserted that he had dictated his will and had named the man he desired for his successor. Moreover, names were whispered. These and other rumors circulated along with news of the Magister's steadily worsening condition, and from day to day spirits sagged in the festival hall as well as in the guest houses, although no one went so far as to abandon the festival and depart. Gloom hung over the entire performance all the while that it proceeded outwardly with formal propriety. Certainly there was little of that delight and uplift that everyone familiar with the annual festival expected; and when on the day before the end of the game Magister Thomas, the author of the festival Game, closed his eyes forever, not even the efforts of the authorities could prevent the news from spreading. Curiously, a good many participants felt relieved and liberated by this outcome. The Game students, and the elite in particular, were not permitted to don mourning before the end of the *Ludus sollemnis*, nor to make any break in the strictly prescribed sequence of the hours, with their alternation of performances and meditation exercises. Nevertheless, they unanimously went through the last act and day of the festival as if it were a funeral service for the revered deceased. They surrounded the exhausted, pale, and sleepless Bertram, who continued officiating with half-closed eyes, with a frigid atmosphere of isolation.

Joseph Knecht had been kept in close contact with the elite by his friend Tegularius. As an old player, moreover, he was fully sensitive to all these currents and moods. But he did not allow them to affect him. From the fourth or fifth day on he actually forbade Fritz to bother him with news about the Magister's illness. He felt, and quite well understood, the tragic cloud that hung over the festival; he thought of the Master with sorrow and deep concern, and of the Shadow Bertram—condemned as it were to sharing the Magister's death—with growing disquiet and compassion. But he sternly resisted being influenced by any authentic or mythical account, practiced the strictest concentration, surrendered gladly to the exercises and the course of the beautifully structured game, and in spite of all the discords and dark clouds his experience of the festival was one of grave exaltation.

At the end of the festival Bertram was spared the additional burden of having to receive congratulants and the Board in his capacity of vice-Magister. The traditional celebration for students of the Glass Bead Game was also cancelled. Immediately after the final musical performance of the festival, the Board announced the Magister's death, and the prescribed days of mourning began in the Vicus Lusorum. Joseph Knecht, still residing in the guest house, participated in the rites. The funeral of this fine man, whose memory is still held in high esteem, was celebrated with Castalia's customary simplicity. His Shadow, Bertram, who had summoned up his last reserves of strength in order to play his part to the end during the festival, understood his situation. He asked for a leave and went on a walking trip in the mountains.

There was mourning throughout the Game village, and indeed everywhere in Waldzell. Possibly no one had enjoyed intimate, strikingly friendly relations with the deceased Magister; but the superiority and flawlessness of his aristocratic nature, together with his intelligence and his finely developed feeling for form, had made of him a regent and representative such as Castalia with its fundamentally democratic temper did not often produce. The Castalians had been proud of him. If he had seemed to hold himself aloof from the realms of passion, love, and friendship, that made him all the more the object for youth's craving to venerate. This dignity and sovereign gracefulness—which incidentally had earned him the half-affectionate nickname "His Excellency"—had in the course of years, despite strong opposition, won him a special position in the Supreme Council of the Order and in the sessions and work of the Board of Educators.

Naturally, the question of his successor was hotly discussed, and nowhere so intensely as among the elite of the Glass Bead Game players. After the departure of the Shadow, whose overthrow these players had sought and achieved, the functions of the Magister's office were temporarily distributed by vote of the elite itself among three temporary deputies—only the internal functions in the Vicus Lusorum, of course, not the official work in the Board of Educators. In keeping with tradition, the Board would not permit the Magistracy to remain vacant more than three weeks. In cases in which a dying or departing Magister left a clear, uncontested successor, the office was in fact filled immediately, after only a single plenary session of the Board. This time the process would probably take rather longer.

During the period of mourning, Joseph Knecht occasionally talked with his friend about the festival game and its singularly troubled course.

"This deputy, Bertram," Knecht said, "not only played his part tolerably well right up to the end—that is, tried to fill the role of a real Magister—but in my opinion did far more than that. He sacrificed himself to this *Ludus sollemnis* as his last and most solemn official act. You all were harsh—no, the word is cruel—to him. You could have saved the festival and saved Bertram, and you did not do so. I don't care to express an opinion about that conduct; I suppose you had your reasons. But now that poor Bertram has been eliminated and you have had your way, you should be generous. When he comes back you must meet him halfway and show that you have understood his sacrifice."

Tegularius shook his head. "We did understand it," he said, "and have accepted it. You were fortunate in being able to participate in the Game as a guest; as such you probably did not follow the course of events so very closely. No, Joseph, we will not have any opportunity to act on whatever feelings for Bertram we may have. He knows that his sacrifice was necessary and will not attempt to undo it."

Only now did Knecht fully understand him. He fell into a troubled silence. Now he realized that he had not experienced these festival days as a real Waldzeller and a comrade of the others, but in truth much more like a guest; and only now did he grasp the nature of Bertram's sacrifice. Hitherto Bertram had seemed to him an ambi-

tious man who had been undone by a task beyond his
powers and who henceforth must renounce further ambitious goals and try to forget that he had once been a
Master's Shadow and the leader of an annual Game.
Only now, hearing his friend's last words, had he understood—with shock—that Bertram had been fully condemned by his judges and would not return. They had
allowed him to conduct the festival Game to its conclusion, and had co-operated just enough so that it would go
off without a public scandal; but they had done so only
to spare Waldzell, not Bertram.

The fact was that the position of Shadow demanded
more than the Magister's full confidence—Bertram had
not lacked that. It depended to an equal degree on the
confidence of the elite, and the unfortunate man had
been unable to retain it. If he blundered, the hierarchy
did not stand behind him to protect him, as it did behind his Master and model. And without the backing of
such authority, he was at the mercy of his former comrades, the tutors. If they did not respect him, they became his judges. If they were unyielding, the Shadow
was finished. Sure enough, Bertram did not return from
his outing in the mountains, and after a while the story
went round that he had fallen to his death from a cliff.
The matter was discussed no further.

Meanwhile, day after day high officials and directors
of the Order and of the Board of Educators appeared in
the Game village. Members of the elite and of the civil
service were summoned for questioning. Now and then
some of the matters discussed leaked out, but only
within the elite itself. Joseph Knecht, too, was summoned and queried, once by two directors of the Order,
once by the philological Magister, then by Monsieur
Dubois, and again by two Magisters. Tegularius, who was
also called in for several such consultations, was pleasantly excited and joked about this conclave atmosphere,
as he called it. Joseph had already noticed during the
festival how little of his former intimacy with the elite
had remained, and during the period of the conclave he
was made more painfully aware of it. It was not only
that he lived in the guest house like a visitor, and that
the superiors seemed to deal with him as an equal. The

members of the elite themselves, the tutors as a body, no longer received him in a comradely fashion. They displayed a mocking politeness toward him, or at best a temporizing coolness. They had already begun to drift away from him when he received his appointment to Mariafels, and that was only right and natural. Once a man had taken the step from freedom to service, from the life of student or tutor to member of the hierarchy, he was no longer a comrade, but on the way to becoming a superior or boss. He no longer belonged to the elite, and he had to realize that for the time being they would assume a critical attitude toward him. That happened to everyone in his position. The difference was that he felt the aloofness and coolness with particular intensity at this time, partly because the elite, orphaned as it now was and about to receive a new Magister, defensively closed its ranks; partly because it had just so harshly demonstrated its ruthlessness in the case of the Shadow, Bertram.

One evening Tegularius came running to the guest house in a state of extreme excitement. He found Joseph, drew him into an empty room, closed the door behind him, and burst out: "Joseph, Joseph! My God, I should have guessed it, I ought to have known, it was likely enough. . . . Oh, I'm altogether beside myself and truly don't know whether I ought to be glad." And he, who was privy to all the sources of information in the Game village, babbled on: it was more than probable, already virtually certain, that Joseph Knecht would be elected Master of the Glass Bead Game. The director of the Archives, whom many had regarded as Master Thomas's predestined successor, had obviously been eliminated from the sifted group of prospects the day before yesterday. Of the three candidates from the elite whose names had hitherto headed the lists during the inquiries, none, apparently, enjoyed the special favor and recommendation of a Magister or of the directors of the Order. On the other hand, two directors of the Order as well as Monsieur Dubois were supporting Knecht. In addition to that, there was the weighty vote of the former Music Master, who to the certain knowledge of several persons had been consulted by several Masters.

"Joseph, they're going to make you Magister!" Fritz exclaimed once more. Whereupon his friend placed his hand over his mouth. For a moment Joseph had been no less surprised and stirred by the possibility than Fritz, and it had seemed to him altogether impossible. But even while Tegularius was reporting the various opinions circulating in the Game village about the status and course of the "conclave," Knecht began to realize that his friend's guess was not likely to be wrong. Rather, in his heart he felt something akin to assent, a sense that he had known and expected this all along, that it was right and natural. And so he placed his hand on his excited friend's mouth, gave him an aloof, reproving look, as if he had suddenly been removed to a great distance, and said: "Don't talk so much, *amice;* I don't want to hear this gossip. Go to your comrades."

Tegularius, though he had meant to say a great deal more, fell silent at once. He turned pale under the gaze of this utter stranger, and went out. Later he remarked that at first he had felt Knecht's remarkable calm and iciness at this moment as if it were a blow and an insult, a slap in the face and a betrayal of their old friendship and intimacy, an almost incomprehensible overstressing and anticipation of his impending position as supreme head of the Glass Bead Game. Only as he was leaving— and he actually went out like a man who had been slapped—did the meaning of that unforgettable look dawn on him, that remote, royal, but likewise suffering look, and he realized that his friend was not proud of what had fallen to his lot, but that he was accepting it in humility. He had been reminded, he said, of Joseph Knecht's thoughtful expression and the note of deep compassion in his voice when, recently, he had inquired about Bertram and his sacrifice. It was as if he himself were now on the point of sacrificing and extinguishing himself like the Shadow. His expression had been at once proud and humble, exalted and submissive, lonely and resigned; it was as if Joseph Knecht's face had become an effigy of all the Masters of Castalia who had ever been. "Go to your comrades," he had said. Thus, in the very second he first heard of his new dignity, this incomprehensible man had fitted himself into it and saw the world from a new center, was no longer a comrade, would never be one again.

Knecht might easily have guessed that this last and highest of his calls, the appointment as Magister Ludi, was coming, or at least he might have seen it as possible, or even probable. But this time, too, his promotion startled him. He might have guessed it, he afterward told himself, and he smiled at his zealous friend Tegularius, who to be sure had not expected the appointment from the start, but all the same had calculated and predicted it several days before the decision and announcement. There were in fact no objections to Joseph's election to the highest Board except perhaps his youth; most of his predecessors had entered on their high office at the age of forty-five to fifty, whereas Joseph was still barely forty. But there was no law against any such early appointment.

Now, when Fritz surprised his friend with the results of his surmises and observations, the observations of an experienced elite player who knew down to its smallest detail the complex apparatus of the small Waldzell community, Knecht had immediately realized that Fritz was right; he had instantly grasped the fact of his election and accepted his fate. But his first reaction to the news had been that rejection of his friend, the refusal to "hear this gossip." As soon as Fritz had left, stunned and very nearly insulted, Joseph went to a meditation room to order his thoughts. His meditation started from a memory that had assailed him with unusual force. In his vision he saw a bare room and a piano. Through the room fell the cool, blithe light of forenoon, and at the door of the room appeared a handsome, friendly man, an elderly man with graying hair and a lucid face full of kindness and dignity. Joseph himself was a small Latin school pupil who had waited in the room for the Music Master, partly frightened, partly overjoyed, and who now saw the venerated figure for the first time, the Master from the legendary Province of elite schools, and the Magister who had come to show him what music was, who then led him step by step into his Province, his realm, into the elite and the Order, and whose colleague and brother he had now become, while the old man had laid aside

his magic wand, or his scepter, and had been transformed
into an amiably taciturn, still kindly, still revered, but
still mysterious elder whose look and example hovered
over Joseph's life and who would always be a generation
and several stages of life ahead of him, as well as im-
measurably greater in dignity and also modesty, in mastership and in mystery, but would always remain his
patron and model, gently compelling him to walk in his
steps, as a rising and setting planet draws its brothers
after it.

As long as Knecht permitted the flow of inner images to
come without direction, as they do, like dreams, in the
initial stage of relaxation, there were two principal scenes
which emerged from the stream and lingered, two pictures
or symbols, two parables. In the first Knecht, as a boy,
followed the Master along a variety of ways. The Music
Master strode before him as his guide, and each time he
turned around and showed his face he looked older, more
tranquil and venerable, visibly approaching an ideal of
timeless wisdom and dignity, while he, Joseph Knecht,
devotedly and obediently walked along after his exemplar, but all the time remaining the selfsame boy, at which
he alternately felt at one moment shame, at another a
certain rejoicing, if not something close to defiant satisfaction. And the second picture was this: the scene in
the piano room, the old man's entering where the boy
waited, was repeated again and again, an infinite number of times; the Master and the boy followed each other
as if drawn along the wires of some mechanism, until
soon it could no longer be discerned which was coming
and which going, which following and which leading,
the old or the young man. Now it seemed to be the young
man who showed honor and obedience to the old man,
to authority and dignity; now again it was apparently
the old man who was required to follow, serve, worship
the figure of youth, of beginning, of mirth. And as he
watched this at once senseless and significant dream
circle, the dreamer felt alternately identical with the old
man and the boy, now revering and now revered, now
leading, now obeying; and in the course of these pendu-
lum shifts there came a moment in which he was both,
was simultaneously Master and small pupil; or rather he

stood above both, was the instigator, conceiver, operator, and onlooker of the cycle, this futile spinning race between age and youth. With shifting sensations he alternately slowed the pace and speeded it to a frantic rush. Out of this process there evolved a new conception, more akin to a symbol than a dream, more insight than image: the conception or rather the insight that this meaningful and meaningless cycle of master and pupil, this courtship of wisdom by youth, of youth by wisdom, this endless, oscillating game was the symbol of Castalia. In fact it was the game of life in general, divided into old and young, day and night, yang and yin, and pouring on without end. Having arrived at this in his meditation, Joseph Knecht found his way from a world of images to tranquility, and after long absorption returned strengthened and serenely cheerful.

When a few days later the directors of the Order summoned him, he went confidently. He received the fraternal greeting of the superiors, a brief clasping of hands and suggestion of an embrace, with composure and grave serenity. He was informed of his appointment as Magister Ludi, and commanded to appear at the festival hall on the day after the morrow for the investiture and swearing-in. This was the same hall in which, so short a while ago, the deceased Master's deputy had completed the dismal ceremonies as if he were a sacrificial beast decked out with gold. The day before the investiture was to be devoted to a careful study, accompanied by ritual meditations, of the formula of the oath and the "breviary for the Magister" under the guidance and supervision of two superiors. This time they were the Chancellor of the Order and the Magister Mathematicae, and during the noon rest of this very strenuous day Joseph vividly recalled his admission to the Order and how the Music Master had talked with him beforehand. This time, to be sure, the rite of admission did not lead him, as it yearly did hundreds of others, through a wide gate into a large community. Rather, he was passing through the eye of the needle into the highest and narrowest circle, that of the Masters. Later he confessed to the former Music Master that on that day of intensive self-examination one thought had given him trouble, one altogether ridiculous notion. He had, he said, feared the moment in which one of the Masters would point out to him how unusually young he was to be receiving the highest dignity. He had seriously had to fight this fear, this childishly vain thought, and to fight as well the impulse to answer, if there should be some allusion to his age: "Why not then wait until I am older? I have never aspired to this elevation, you know." But further self-examination showed him that unconsciously the thought of his appointment, and the desire for it, could not after all have been so far from his mind. And, he went on to tell the Music Master, he had admitted this to himself, had recognized the vanity of his thought and rejected it; moreover, neither on that day nor at any other time did any of his colleagues remind him of his age.

The election of the new Master was, however, all the more animatedly discussed and criticized among those who had hitherto been Knecht's fellow aspirants. He had no downright adversaries, but he had had rivals, among them some who were of riper years than he. The members of this circle were not at all minded to approve the choice without a trial of strength, or at least without subjecting the new Master to extremely exacting and critical scrutiny. Almost in every case a new Magister's inauguration and early period in office is a kind of purgatory.

The investiture of a Master is not a public ceremony. Aside from the Board of Educators and the directorate of the Order, the only participants are the senior pupils, the candidates, and the officials of the faculty which is receiving a new Magister. At the ceremony in the festival hall, the Master of the Glass Bead Game had to take the oath of office, to receive from the authorities the insignia of his office, consisting of certain keys and seals, and to be clad by the Speaker of the Order in the festive robe which the Magister wears at all the major ceremonies, especially while celebrating the annual Game. Such an act lacks the splash and mild intoxication of public festivities; it is by nature ceremonious and rather sober. On the other hand, the mere presence of all the members of the two highest authorities confers an uncommon dignity upon it. The small republic of Glass Bead

Game players is receiving a new lord and master, who
will preside over it and speak for its interests within the
Board. That is a rare and important event, and although
the younger students may not fully grasp its significance
and be conscious only of the ritual, all the other participants are fully aware of just how important it is.
They are sufficiently integrated with their community, so
substantially akin to it, that they experience the event
as if it were part and parcel of themselves.

This time the festive rejoicing was overshadowed by
mourning for the previous Master, by the unhappy temper of the annual Game, and by the tragedy of the
deputy, Bertram. The investiture was performed by the
Speaker of the Order and the Chief Archivist of the
Game. Together, they held the robe high and then
placed it over the shoulders of the new Glass Bead Game
Master. The brief festival oration was spoken by the
Magister Grammaticae, the Master of classical philology
in Keuperheim. A representative of the elite of Waldzell handed over the keys and seal, and the aged former
Music Master in person stood near the organ. He had
come to see his protégé invested, and to give him a glad
surprise by his unexpected presence, perhaps also to offer
a helpful bit of advice. The old man would have liked
to provide the music for the ceremony with his own
hands, but he could no longer risk such exertions and
therefore left the playing to the organist of the Game
Village, but stood behind him turning the pages. He
looked at Joseph with a beatific smile, saw him receive
the robes and keys, and heard him first repeat the oath
and then deliver his extemporaneous inaugural address
to his future associates, officials, and students. Never before had this boy Joseph seemed to him as dear and
pleasing as he was today, when he had almost ceased
to be Joseph and was beginning to be no more than
the wearer of robes and the keeper of an office, a jewel
in a crown, a pillar in the structure of the hierarchy.
But he was able to speak with his boy Joseph alone for
only a few minutes. He conferred his serenely cheerful
smile upon him, and admonished: "Make sure you manage the next three or four weeks well; a great deal will
be asked of you. Always think of the Whole, and always

remember that missing out on some detail does not count
for much now. You must devote your entire attention to
the elite; don't think of anything else. Two men will be
sent to help initiate you. One of them is the yoga specialist Alexander. I have instructed him myself. Pay close attention to him; he knows his business. What you need
is an unshakable confidence that the superiors were right
in making you one of their own. Trust them, trust the
people who have been sent to help you, and blindly
trust your own strength. But be on your guard against
the elite; that is what they expect. You will win out,
Joseph, I know."

The new Magister was familiar with most of the functions of his office, for he had already assisted in the performance of them on various occasions, both in lowly
and responsible capacities. The most important were
the Game courses, stretching from courses for schoolboys
and beginners, holidayers and guests, to the practice sessions, lectures, and seminars for the elite. Every newly
appointed Magister could feel himself equal to all but the
last of these tasks, whereas the new functions which had
previously lain outside his scope caused him far more
concern and effort. Such was the case with Joseph also.
He would have liked to turn first of all, with undivided
zeal, to these new duties, the properly magisterial duties:
sitting on the Supreme Council of Education, working
with the Council of Magisters and the directorate of the
Order, representing the Vicus Lusorum in dealings with
all the authorities. He was all afire to familiarize himself
with these new tasks and to strip them of the menace of
the unknown. He wished that he could initially set aside
several weeks for a careful study of the constitution, the
formalities, the minutes of previous sessions of the Board,
and so on. He knew, of course, that information and
instruction on these matters were readily available to
him. He need only turn to Monsieur Dubois and to the
specialist on magisterial forms and traditions, the Speaker
of the Order. Although not a Magister himself, and therefore ranked below the Masters, the Speaker held the
chair in all sessions of the Board and took care that the
traditional rules of order were observed. In this he

somewhat resembled the master of ceremonies at a sovereign's court.

Joseph would only too gladly have asked this prudent, experienced, inscrutably courteous man, whose hands had just solemnly decked him with the robes of office, for a few private lessons, if only the Speaker had lived in Waldzell instead of Hirsland, half a day's journey away. How gladly, too, Joseph would have fled to Monteport for a while to be instructed in these matters by the former Music Master. But such recourses were out of the question; it was not for a Magister to harbor any such private desires, as if he were still a student. Instead, he had to start off by attending to those very functions which he fancied would give him little trouble, and to concentrate his whole mind on them.

During Bertram's festival Game he had observed a Magister forsaken by his own community, the elite, fighting and as it were suffocating in airless space. He had sensed something then, and his presentiment had been confirmed by the old Music Master's words on the day of his investiture. Now he faced it every minute of his official day, and every moment he could spare for reflection on his situation: that he must above all concern himself with the elite and the tutorship, with the highest stages of the Glass Bead Game studies, with the seminar practice sessions, and with personal intercourse with the tutors. He could leave the Archives to the archivists, the beginners' courses to the present set of teachers, the mail to his secretaries, and would not be neglecting any serious matters. But he did not dare leave the elite to themselves for a moment. He had to keep after them, impose himself on them, and make himself indispensable to them. He had to convince them of the merit of his abilities and the purity of his will; he had to conquer them, court them, win them, match wits with every candidate among them who showed a disposition to challenge him—and there was no lack of such candidates.

In this struggle he was aided by a number of factors which he had earlier considered drawbacks, in particular his long absence from Waldzell and the elite, who therefore looked upon him as something of a *homo novus*. Even his friendship with Tegularius proved useful. For

Tegularius, that brilliant, sickly outsider, obviously did not have to be considered a rival for office, and seemed so little career-minded himself that any preference shown him by the new Magister would not be seen as an affront to other candidates. Nevertheless it was something of a task for Knecht to probe and penetrate this highest, most vital, restive, and sensitive stratum in the world of the Glass Bead Game, and master it as a rider masters a thoroughbred horse. For in every Castalian institute, not only that of the Glass Bead Game, the elite group of candidates, also called tutors—men who have completed their formal education but are still engaged in free studies and have not yet been appointed to serve on the Board of Educators or the Order—constitute the most precious stock in Castalian society, the true reserve and promise for the future. Everywhere, not only in the Game Village, this dashing select band of the younger generation tends to resist and criticize new teachers and superiors, accords a new head the bare minimum of politeness and subordination, and must be convinced, overpowered, and won over on a purely personal basis. The superior must devote his whole being to courting them before they will acknowledge him and submit to his leadership.

Knecht took up his task without timidity, but he was nevertheless astonished at its difficulties; and while he solved them and gradually won the arduous, consuming battle, those other duties which he had been inclined to worry about receded of their own accord and seemed to demand less of his attention. He confessed to a colleague that he had participated in the first plenary session of the Board—to which he traveled by the fastest express and returned in the same way—almost in a dream and afterward had no time to give another thought to it, so completely did his current task claim all his energies. In fact, even during the conference itself, although the subject interested him and although he had looked forward to it with some uneasiness, since this was his first appearance as a member of the Board, he several times caught himself thinking not of his colleagues here and the deliberations in progress, but of Waldzell. He saw himself rather in that blue room in the Archives where he was currently giving a seminar in dialectics every third day, with only five participants. Every hour of *that* bred far greater tension and demanded a greater output of energy than all the rest of his official duties, which were also not easy and which he could not evade or postpone. For as the former Music Master had informed him, the Board provided him with a timekeeper and coach who supervised the course of his day hour by hour, advising him about his schedule and guarding him against too much concentration on any one thing, as well as against total overstrain. Knecht was grateful to him, and even more grateful to Alexander, the man deputized by the directorate of the Order, who enjoyed a great reputation as master of the art of meditation. Alexander saw to it that Joseph, even though he was working to the utmost limit of his strength, practiced the "little" or "brief" meditation exercise three times daily, and that he abided strictly by the prescribed course and number of minutes for each such exercise.

Before his evening meditation he and his aides, the coach and the meditation master, were supposed to review each official day, noting what had been well done or ill done, feeling his own pulse, as meditation teachers call this practice, that is, recognizing and measuring one's own momentary situation, state of health, the distribution of one's energies, one's hopes and cares—in a word, seeing oneself and one's daily work objectively and carrying nothing unresolved on into the night and the next day.

While the tutors observed the prodigious labors of their Magister with an interest partly sympathetic, partly aggressive, missing no opportunity to set him new tests of strength, patience, and quick-wittedness, trying one moment to inspire, the next to block his work, an uncomfortable void had come into being around Tegularius. He understood, of course, that Knecht could not spare any attention, any time, any thought or sympathy for him right now. But he could not harden himself sufficiently, could not resign himself to being so neglected. It was all the more painful to him because he not only seemed to have lost his friend from one day to the next, but also found himself the object of some suspicion on the part of his associates, and was scarcely spoken to. That was hardly surprising. For although Tegularius could not seriously stand in the way of the ambitious climbers, he was known as one of the new Magister's partisans and favorites.

Knecht could easily have grasped all this. To be sure, the responsibilities of the moment involved his laying aside all private, personal affairs for a while, including this friendship. But, as he later admitted to his friend, he did not actually do this wittingly and willingly, but quite simply because he had forgotten Fritz. He had so thoroughly converted himself into an instrument that such personal matters as friendship vanished into the realm of the impossible. If on occasion, as for example in that seminar he held for the five foremost Glass Bead Game players, Fritz's face and figure appeared before him, he did not see Tegularius as a friend or personality, but as a member of the elite, a student, candidate, and tutor, a part of his work, a soldier in the regiment whom he had to train so that he could march on to victory with it. A shudder had gone through Fritz when the Magister for the first time addressed him in that way. From Knecht's look, it was clear that this remoteness and objectivity were not pretense, but uncannily genuine, and that the man before him who treated him with this matter-of-fact courtesy, accompanied by intense intellectual alertness, was no longer his friend Joseph, was entirely a teacher and examiner, entirely Master of the Glass Bead Game, enveloped and isolated by the gravity and austerity of his office as if by a shining glaze which had been poured over him in the heat of the fire, and had cooled and hardened.

During these hectic weeks a minor incident connected with Tegularius occurred. Sleepless and under severe psychological strain, he was guilty during the seminar of a discourtesy, a minor outburst, not toward the Magister but toward a colleague whose mocking tone had grated on his nerves. Knecht noticed, noticed also the delinquent's overwrought state. He reproved him wordlessly, merely by a gesture of his finger, but afterward sent his meditation master to him to calm the troubled soul. Tegularius, after weeks of deprivation, took this concern as a first sign of reviving friendship, for he assumed that it was an attention directed toward himself as a person, and willingly submitted to the cure. In reality Knecht had scarcely been aware of the object of his solicitude. He had acted solely as the Magister, had observed irritability and a lack of self-control in one of his tutors, and had reacted to it as an educator, without for a moment regarding this tutor as a person or relating him to himself. When, months later, his friend reminded him of this scene and testified how overjoyed and comforted he had been by this sign of good will, Joseph Knecht said nothing. He had completely forgotten the affair, but did not disabuse his friend.

At last he attained his goal. The battle was won. It had been a great labor to subdue this elite, to drill them until they were weary, to tame the ambitious, win over the undecided, impress the arrogant. But now the work was done; the candidates at the Game Village had acknowledged him their Master and submitted to him. Suddenly everything went smoothly, as if only a drop of oil had been needed. The coach drew up a last agenda with Knecht, expressed the Board's appreciation, and vanished. Alexander, the meditation master, likewise departed. Instead of a morning massage, Knecht resumed his customary walks. As yet he could not even begin to think of anything like studying or even reading; but now he was able to play a little music some days, in the evening before going to sleep.

The next time he attended a meeting of the Board, Knecht distinctly sensed, although the matter was never so much as mentioned, that he was now regarded by his colleagues as tested and proved. He was their equal. After the intensity of the struggle to prove himself, he was now overcome once more by a sense of awakening, of cooling and sobering. He saw himself in the innermost heart of Castalia, sat in the highest rank of the hierarchy, and discovered with strange sobriety and almost with disappointment that even this very thin air was breathable, but that he who now breathed it as though he had never known anything different was altogether changed. That was the consequence of this harsh period of trial. It had burned him out as no other service, no other effort, had previously done.

The elite's acknowledgment of him as their sovereign was marked this time by a special gesture. When Knecht sensed the end of their resistance, the confidence and consent of the tutors, and knew that he had successfully put the hardest task behind him, he realized that the moment had come for him to choose a "Shadow." In point of fact he would never more sorely need someone to relieve him of burdens than right now, after the victory was won, when he found himself suddenly released into relative freedom after an almost superhuman trial of strength. Many a Magister in the past had collapsed just at this point in his path. Knecht now renounced his right to choose among the candidates and asked the tutors as a body to select a Shadow for him. Still under the impact of Bertram's fate, the elite took this conciliatory gesture very seriously, and after several meetings and secret polls, made their choice, providing the Magister with one of their best men, a deputy who until Knecht's appointment had been regarded as one of the most promising candidates for the office of Magister.

He had survived the worst. Now there was time for walks and music again. After a while he could once more think of reading. Friendship with Tegularius, occasional correspondence with Ferromonte, would be possible. Now and then he would be able to take half a day off, perhaps sometimes permit himself to go away for a short vacation. But all these amenities would benefit another man, not the previous Joseph who had thought himself a keen Glass Bead Game player and a tolerably good Castalian, but who had nevertheless had no inkling of the innermost nature of the Castalian system. Hitherto he had lived in so innocuously selfish, so puerilely playful, so inconceivably private and irresponsible a way. Once he recalled the tart reproof he had incurred from Master Thomas after he had expressed the desire to go on studying freely for a while longer: "You say a while, but how long is that? You are still speaking the language of students, Joseph Knecht." That had been only a few years ago. He had listened with admiration, with profound reverence, along with a mild horror of this man's impersonal perfection and discipline, and he had felt Castalia reaching out for himself as well, seeking to draw him close in order, perhaps, to make of him just such a Thomas some day, a Master, a sovereign and servant, a perfect instrument. And now he stood on the spot where Master Thomas had stood, and when he spoke with one of his tutors, one of those clever, sophisticated players and scholars, one of those diligent and arrogant princes, he looked across to him into a different world of alien beauty, a strange world that had once been his, exactly as Magister Thomas had gazed into his own strange student world.

SEVEN

IN OFFICE

AT FIRST, ASSUMPTION of the Magister's office seemed to have brought more loss than gain. It had almost devoured his strength and his personal life, had crushed all his habits and hobbies, had left a cool stillness in his heart, and in his head something resembling the giddiness after overexertion. But the period that now followed brought recovery, reflection, and habituation. It also yielded new observations and experiences.

The greatest of these, now that the battle was won, was his collaboration with the elite on the basis of mutual trust and friendliness. He conferred with his Shadow. He worked with Fritz Tegularius, whom he tried out as an assistant on his correspondence. He gradually studied, checked over, and supplemented the reports and other notes on students and associates which his predecessor had left. And in the course of this work Knecht familiarized himself, with increasing affection, with this elite whom he had imagined he knew so well. Now its true nature, and the whole special quality of the Game Village as well as its role in Castalian life, were revealed to him in their full reality for the first time.

Of course he had belonged to this artistic and ambitious

elite and to the Players' Village in Waldzell for many years. He had felt completely a part of it. But now he was no longer just a part. Not only did he intimately share the life of this community, but he also felt himself to be something like its brain, its consciousness, and its conscience as well, not only participating in its impulses and destinies, but guiding them and being responsible for them.

In an exalted moment, at the end of a training course for teachers of beginners in the Game, he once declared: "Castalia is a small state in itself, and our Vicus Lusorum a miniature state within the state, a small, but ancient and proud republic, equal in rights and dignities to its sisters, but with its sense of mission lifted and strengthened by the special artistic and virtually sacramental function it performs. For our distinction is to cherish the true sanctuary of Castalia, its unique mystery and symbol, the Glass Bead Game. Castalia rears pre-eminent musicians and art historians, philologists, mathematicians, and other scholars. Every Castalian institute and every Castalian should hold to only two goals and ideals: to attain to the utmost command of his subject, and to keep himself and his subject vital and flexible by forever recognizing its ties with all other disciplines and by maintaining amicable relations with all. This second ideal, the conception of the inner unity of all man's cultural efforts, the idea of universality, has found perfect expression in our illustrious Game. It may be that the physicist, the musicologist, or other scholar will at times have to steep himself entirely in his own discipline, that renouncing the idea of universal culture will further some momentary maximum performance in a special field. But we, at any rate, we Glass Bead Game players, must never allow ourselves such specialization. We must neither approve nor practice it, for our own special mission, as you know, is the idea of the *Universitas Litterarum*. Ours to foster its supreme expression, the noble Game, and repeatedly to save the various disciplines from their tendency to self-sufficiency. But how can we save anything that does not have the desire to be saved? And how can we make the archaeologists, the pedagogues, the astronomers, and so forth, eschew self-sufficient specialization

and throw open their windows to all the other disciplines?
We cannot do it by compulsory means, say by making the
Glass Bead Game an official subject in the lower schools,
nor can we do it by invoking what our predecessors meant
this Game to be. We can prove only that our Game and
we ourselves are indispensable by keeping the Game ever
at the summit of our entire cultural life, by incorporating
into it each new achievement, each new approach, and
each new complex of problems from the scholarly disciplines. We must shape and cultivate our universality,
our noble and perilous sport with the idea of unity, en-
dowing it with such perennial freshness and loveliness,
such persuasiveness and charm, that even the soberest
researcher and most diligent specialist will ever and
again feel its message, its temptation and allure.

"Let us imagine for the moment that we players were
to slacken in our zeal for a time, that the Game courses for
beginners became dull and superficial, that in the Games
for advanced players specialists of other disciplines looked
in vain for vital, pulsating life, for intellectual contem-
poraneity and interest. Suppose that two or three times in
a row our great annual Game were to strike the guests
as an empty ceremony, a lifeless, old-fashioned, formalistic
relic of the past. How quickly, then, the Game and we
ourselves would be done for. Already we are no longer
on those shining heights where the Glass Bead Game
stood a generation ago, when the annual Game lasted
not one or two but three or four weeks, and was the
climax of the year not only for Castalia but for the entire
country. Today a representative of the government still
attends this annual Game, but all too often as a somewhat
bored guest, and a few cities and professions still send
envoys. Toward the end of the Game days these representatives of the secular powers occasionally deign to
suggest that the length of the festival deters many other
cities from sending envoys, and that perhaps it would be
more in keeping with the contemporary world either to
shorten the festival considerably or else to hold it only
every other year, or every third year.

"Well now, we cannot check this development, or if
you will, decadence. It may well be that before long our
Game will meet with no understanding at all out in the

world. Perhaps we shall no longer be able to celebrate it. But what we must and can prevent is the discrediting and devaluation of the Game in its own home, in our Province. Here our struggle is hopeful, and has repeatedly led to victory. Every day we witness the phenomenon: young elite pupils who have signed up for their Game course without any special ardor, and who have completed it dutifully, but without enthusiasm, are suddenly seized by the spirit of the Game, by its intellectual potentialities, its venerable tradition, its soul-stirring forces, and become our passionate adherents and partisans. And every year at the *Ludus sollemnis* we can see scholars of distinction who rather looked down on us Glass Bead Game players during their work-filled year, and who have not always wished our institution well. In the course of the great Game we see them falling more and more under the spell of our art; we see them growing eased and exalted, rejuvenated and fired, until at last, their hearts strengthened and deeply stirred, they bid good-by with words of almost abashed gratitude.

"Let us consider for a moment the means at our command for carrying out our mission. We see a rich, fine, well-ordered apparatus whose heart and core is the Game Archive, which we gratefully make use of every hour of the day and which all of us serve, from Magister and Archivist down to the humblest errand boy. The best and the most vital aspect of our institution is the old Castalian principle of selection of the best, the elite. The schools of Castalia collect the best pupils from the entire country and educate them. Similarly, we in the Players' Village try to select the best among those endowed by nature with a love for the Game. We train them to an ever-higher standard of perfection. Our courses and seminars take in hundreds, who then go their ways again; but we go on training the best until they become genuine players, artists of the Game. You all know that in ours as in every art there is no end to development, that each of us, once he belongs to the elite, will work away all his life at the further development, refinement, and deepening of himself and our art, whether or not he belongs to our corps of officials.

"The existence of our elite has sometimes been denounced as a luxury. It has been argued that we ought to train no more elite players than are required to fill the ranks of our officialdom. But in the first place, our corps of officials is not an institution sufficient unto itself, and in the second place not everyone is suited for an official post, any more than every good philologist is suited for teaching. We officials, at any rate, feel certain that the tutors are more than a reservoir of talented and experienced players from which we fill our vacancies and draw our successors. I am almost tempted to say that this is only a subsidiary function of the players' elite, even though we greatly stress it to the uninitiated as soon as the meaning and justification of our institute is brought up.

"No, the tutors are not primarily future Masters, course directors, Archive officials. They are an end in themselves; their little band is the real home and future of the Glass Bead Game. Here, in these few dozen hearts and heads the developments, modifications, advances, and confrontations of our Game with the spirit of the age and with the various disciplines take place. Only here is our Game played properly and correctly, to its hilt, and with full commitment. Only within our elite is it an end in itself and a sacred mission, shorn of all dilettantism, cultural vanity, self-importance, or superstition. The future of the Game lies with you, the Waldzell tutors. And since it is the heart and soul of Castalia, and you are the soul and vital spark of Waldzell, you are truly the salt of the Province, its spirit, its dynamism. There is no danger that your numbers could grow too large, your zeal too hot, your passion for the glorious Game too great. Increase it, increase it! For you, as for all Castalians, there is at bottom only a single peril, which we all must guard against every single day. The spirit of our Province and our Order is founded on two principles: on objectivity and love of truth in study, and on the cultivation of meditative wisdom and harmony. Keeping these two principles in balance means for us being wise and worthy of our Order. We love the sciences and scholarly disciplines, each his own, and yet we know that devotion to a discipline does not necessarily preserve a man from selfishness, vice, and absurdity. History is full of examples of that, and folklore has given us the figure of Doctor Faust to represent this danger.

"Other centuries sought safety in the union of reason and religion, research and asceticism. In their *Universitas Litterarum,* theology ruled. Among us we use meditation, the fine gradations of yoga technique, in our efforts to exorcise the beast within us and the *diabolus* dwelling in every branch of knowledge. Now you know as well as I that the Glass Bead Game also has its hidden *diabolus,* that it can lead to empty virtuosity, to artistic vanity, to self-advancement, to the seeking of power over others and then to the abuse of that power. This is why we need another kind of education beside the intellectual and submit ourselves to the morality of the Order, not in order to reshape our mentally active life into a psychically vegetative dream-life, but on the contrary to make ourselves fit for the summit of intellectual achievement. We do not intend to flee from the *vita activa* to the *vita contemplativa,* nor vice versa, but to keep moving forward while alternating between the two, being at home in both, partaking of both."

We have cited Knecht's words—and many similar statements recorded by his students have been preserved —because they throw so clear a light upon his conception of his office, at least during the first few years of his magistracy. He was an excellent teacher; the profusion of copies of his lectures which have come down to us would alone provide evidence for that. Among the surprises that his high office brought him right at the start was his discovery that teaching gave him so much pleasure, and that he did so well at it. He would not have expected that, for hitherto he had never really felt a desire for teaching. Of course, like every member of the elite, he had occasionally been given teaching assignments for short periods even while he was merely an advanced student. He had substituted for other teachers in Glass Bead Game courses at various levels, even more frequently had helped the participants in such with reviews and drill; but in those days his freedom to study and his solitary concentration had been so dear and important to him that he had regarded these assignments as nuisances, despite the fact that he was even then skillful and popular as a teacher. He had, after all, also given courses in the Benedictine abbey, but they had been of minor importance in themselves, and equally minor for him. There, his studies and association with Father Jacobus had made all other work secondary. At the time, his greatest ambition had been to be a good pupil, to learn, receive, form himself. Now the pupil had become a teacher, and as such he had mastered the major task of his first period in office: the struggle to win authority and forge an identity of person and office. In the course of this he made two discoveries. The first was the pleasure it gives to transplant the achievements of the mind into other minds and see them being transformed into entirely new shapes and emanations—in other words, the joy of teaching. The second was grappling with the personalities of the students, the attainment and practice of authority and leadership—in other words, the joy of educating. He never separated the two, and during his magistracy he not only trained a large number of good and some superb Glass Bead Game players, but also by example, by admonition, by his austere sort of patience, and by the force of his personality and character, elicited from a great many of his students the very best they were capable of.

In the course of this work he had made a characteristic discovery—if we may be permitted to anticipate our story. At the beginning of his magistracy he dealt exclusively with the elite, with the most advanced students and the tutors. Many of the latter were his own age, and every one was already a thoroughly trained player. But gradually, once he was sure of the elite, he slowly and cautiously, from year to year, began withdrawing from it an ever-larger portion of his time and energy, until at the end he sometimes could leave it almost entirely to his close associates and assistants. This process took years, and each succeeding year Knecht, in the lectures, courses, and exercises he conducted, reached further and further back to ever-younger students. In the end he went so far that he several times personally conducted beginners' courses for youngsters—something rarely done by a Magister Ludi. He found, moreover, that the younger and more ignorant his pupils were, the more pleasure he took in teaching. Sometimes in the course of these years it actually made him uneasy, and cost him tangible effort, to return from these groups of boys to the advanced students, let alone to the elite. Occasionally, in fact, he felt the desire to reach even further back and to attempt to deal with even younger pupils, those who had never yet had courses of any kind and knew nothing of the Glass Bead Game. He found himself sometimes wishing to spend a while in Eschholz or one of the other preparatory schools instructing small boys in Latin, singing, or algebra, where the atmosphere was far less intellectual than it was even in the most elementary course in the Glass Bead Game, but where he would be dealing with still more receptive, plastic, educable pupils, where teaching and educating were more, and more deeply, a unity. In the last two years of his magistracy he twice referred to himself in letters as "Schoolmaster," reminding his correspondent that the expression Magister Ludi—which for generations had meant only "Master of the Game" in Castalia—had originally been simply the name for the schoolmaster.

There could, of course, be no question of his realizing such schoolmasterly wishes. They were arrant dreams, as a man may dream of a midsummer sky on a gray, cold winter day. For Knecht there were no longer a multitude of paths open. His duties were determined by his office; but since the manner in which he wished to fulfill these duties was left largely to his own discretion, he had in the course of the years, no doubt quite unconsciously at first, gradually concerned himself more and more with educating, and with the earliest age-groups within his reach. The older he became, the more youth attracted him. At least so we can observe from our vantage point. At the time a critic would have had difficulty finding any trace of vagary in his conduct of his office. Moreover, the position itself compelled him again and again to turn his attention back to the elite. Even during periods in which he left the seminars and Archives almost entirely to his assistants and his Shadow, long-term projects such as the annual Game competitions or the preparations for the grand public Game of the year kept him in vital and daily contact with the elite. To his friend Fritz he once jokingly remarked: "There have been sovereigns who suffered all their lives from an unrequited love for their subjects. Their hearts drew them to the peasants, the shepherds, the artisans, the schoolmasters, and schoolchildren; but they seldom had a chance to see anything of these, for they were always surrounded by their ministers and soldiers who stood like a wall between them and the people. A Magister's fate is the same. He would like to reach people and sees only colleagues; he would like to reach the schoolboys and children and sees only advanced students and members of the elite."

But we have run far ahead of our story, and now return to the period of Knecht's first years in office. After gaining the desired relationship with the elite, he had next to turn his attention to the bureaucracy of the Archives and show it that he intended to be a friendly but alert master. Then came the problem of studying the structure and procedures of the chancery, and learning how to run it. A constant flow of correspondence, and repeated meetings or circular letters of the Boards, summoned him to duties and tasks which were not altogether easy for a newcomer to grasp and classify properly. Quite often questions arose in which the various Faculties of the Province were mutually interested and inclined toward jealousy—questions of jurisdiction, for instance. Slowly, but with growing admiration, he became aware of the powerful secret functions of the Order, the living soul of the Castalian state, and the watchful guardian of its constitution.

Thus strenuous and overcrowded months had passed during which there had been no room in Joseph Knecht's thoughts for Tegularius. However, and this was done half instinctively, he did assign his friend a variety of jobs to protect him from excessive leisure. Fritz had lost his friend, who had overnight become his highest-ranking superior and whom he had to address formally as "Reverend sir." But he took the orders the Magister issued to him as a sign of solicitude and personal concern. Moody loner though he was, Fritz found himself excited partly by his friend's elevation and the excitable mood of the entire elite, partly by the tasks assigned to him, which were activating him in a way compatible with his personality. In any case, he bore the totally changed situation better than he himself would have thought since that moment in which Knecht had responded to the news that he was destined to be the Glass Bead Game Master by sending him away. He was, moreover, both intelligent and sympathetic enough to see something of the enormous strain his friend was undergoing at this time, and to sense the nature of that great trial of strength. He saw how Joseph was annealed by the fire, and insofar as sentimental emotions were involved, he probably felt them more keenly than the man who was undergoing the ordeal. Tegularius took the greatest pains with the assignments he received from the Magister, and if he ever seriously regretted his own weakness and his unfitness for office and responsibility, he did so then, when he intensely wished to stand by the man he so warmly admired and give him what help he could as an assistant, an official, a "Shadow."

The beech forests above Waldzell were already browning when Knecht one day took a little book with him into the Magister's garden adjoining his residence, that pretty little garden which the late Master Thomas had so prized and often tended himself with Horatian fondness. Knecht, like all the students, had once imagined it as an awesome and sanctified spot, a Tusculum and magical island of the Muses where the Master came for recuperation and meditation. Since he himself had become Magister and the garden his, he had scarcely entered it and hardly ever enjoyed it at leisure. Even now he was coming only for fifteen minutes after dinner, and he allowed himself merely a brief carefree stroll among the high bushes and shrubs beneath which his predecessor had planted a good many evergreens from southern climes. Then, since it was already cool in the shade, he carried a light cane chair to a sunlit spot, sat down, and opened the book he had brought with him. It was the *Pocket Calendar for the Magister Ludi*, written seventy or eighty years before by Ludwig Wassermaler, the Glass Bead Game Master of the day. Ever since, each of his successors had made in it a few corrections, deletions, or additions, as changing times indicated. The calendar was intended as a vade mecum for still inexperienced Masters in their first years in office, and led the Magister through his entire working and official year, from week to week, reminding him of his duties sometimes in mere cue phrases, sometimes with detailed descriptions and personal recommendations. Knecht found the page for the current week and read it through attentively. He came upon nothing surprising or especially urgent, but at the end of the section stood the following lines:

"Gradually begin to turn your thoughts to the coming annual Game. It seems early, and in fact might seem to you premature. Nevertheless I advise you: Unless you already have a plan for the Game in your head, from now on let not a week pass, certainly not a month, without turning your thoughts to the future Game. Make a note of your ideas; take the pattern of a classical Game with you now and then, even on official journeys, and look it over whenever you have a free half-hour. Prepare yourself not by trying to force good ideas to come, but by recalling frequently from now on that in the coming months a fine and festive task awaits you, for which you must constantly strengthen, compose, and attune yourself."

These words had been written some three generations before by a wise old man and master of his art, at a time incidentally in which the Glass Bead Game had probably reached its supreme refinement in the formal sense. In those days the Games had attained a delicacy and wealth of ornamentation in their execution comparable to the arts of architecture and decoration in the late Gothic or rococo periods. For some two decades it had been a Game so fragile that it seemed as if it were really being played with glass beads, a seemingly glassy game almost empty of content, a seemingly coquettish and wanton pastime full of frail embellishments, an airy dance, sometimes a tightrope dance, with the subtlest rhythmic structure. There were players who spoke of the style of those days as if it were a lost talisman, and others who condemned it as superficial, cluttered with ornamentation, decadent, and unmanly. It had been one of the masters and co-creators of that style who had composed the sagacious advice and admonishments in the Magister's calendar, and as Joseph Knecht searchingly read his words a second and third time he felt a gay, blissful stirring in his heart, a mood

such as he had experienced only once before, it seemed to
him. When he reflected, he realized that it had been in
that meditation before his investiture; it was the mood
that had swept him as he imagined that strange round-
dance, the round between the Music Master and Joseph,
Master and beginner, age and youth. It had been a very
old man who had thought and set down these words:
"Let no week pass . . ." and ". . . not by trying to force
good ideas." It had been a man who had held the high
office of Master of the Game for at least twenty years,
perhaps much longer. And in that sportively rococo age
he must undoubtedly have dealt with an extremely spoiled
and arrogant elite. He had devised and celebrated more
than twenty of those brilliant annual Games which in
those days lasted for a month—an old man for whom
the annually recurring task of composing a grand, solemn
Game must long since have ceased to be merely a high
honor and joy, must have become far more a burden
demanding great effort, a chore to which he had to attune
himself, persuade himself, and somewhat stimulate himself.

At this moment Knecht felt something more than
grateful reverence toward this wise old man and experienced adviser—for the calendar had already served him
frequently as a valuable guide. He also felt a joyous, a
gay and high-spirited superiority, the superiority of youth.
For among the many cares of a Magister Ludi, with
which he had already become acquainted, this particular
care did not occur. He really did not have to force himself to think about the annual Game in good time, or
worry about not encountering this task in a sufficiently
joyful and composed spirit. He need not fear any lack of
enterprise, let alone ideas, for such a Game. On the contrary, Knecht, who had at times during these few
months given an impression of being aged beyond his
years, felt at the moment young and strong.

He was unable to yield to this fine feeling for long. He
could not savor it to the full, for his brief period of rest
was almost over. But the inspiriting joyful emotion remained in him; he took it with him when he left; and so
the brief rest in the Magister's garden, and his reading of
the calendar, had after all borne fruit. It had given him

relaxation and a moment of happily heightened vitality, but it had also produced two inspired thoughts, both of which at once assumed the character of decisions. First, whenever he too became old and weary he would lay down his office the moment the composition of the annual Game became a troublesome duty and he found himself at a loss for ideas. Secondly, he would in fact start work on his first annual Game soon, and he would call in Tegularius to be his foremost assistant in this work. That would gratify and gladden his friend, and for himself it would be a good trial step toward a new *modus vivendi* for their temporarily arrested friendship. For the initiative could not come from Fritz; it had to come from the Magister himself.

The task would certainly give his friend plenty to do. Ever since his stay in Mariafels, Knecht had been nurturing an idea for a Glass Bead Game which he now decided to use for his first ceremonial Game as Magister. The pretty idea was to base the structure and dimensions of the Game on the ancient ritual Confucian pattern for the building of a Chinese house: orientation by the points of the compass, the gates, the spirit wall, the relationships and functions of buildings and courtyards, their co-ordination with the constellations, the calendar and family life, and the symbolism and stylistic principles of the garden. Long ago, in studying a commentary on the *I Ching*, he had thought the mythic order and significance of these rules made an unusually appealing and charming symbol of the cosmos and of man's place in the universe. The age-old mythic spirit of the people in this tradition of domestic architecture had also seemed to him wonderfully and intimately fused with the mandarin and magisterial spirit of speculative scholarliness. He had lovingly dwelt on the plan for this Game, though without so far setting down any of it, often enough for the Game to have really been formulated as a whole in his mind; but since taking office he had not had a chance to apply himself to it. Now he resolved to construct his festival Game on this Chinese idea; and if Fritz proved receptive to the spirit of the plan, he would ask him to begin at once on the necessary background studies and the procedure for translating it into the Game language.

There was one difficulty: Tegularius knew no Chinese. It was far too late for him to learn it now. But with some briefing from Knecht himself and from the Far Eastern College, and some reading up on the subject, there was no reason why Tegularius could not become sufficiently acquainted with the magical symbolism of Chinese architecture. After all, no philological questions were involved. Still, that would take time, especially for a pampered person like his friend who did not feel up to working every day, and so it was well to start the business going at once. In this respect, then, he realized with a smile and pleasant feelings of surprise, the cautious old author of the Pocket Calendar had been perfectly right.

The very next day, since his office hours happened to end early, he sent for Tegularius. He came, made his bow with that rather markedly submissive and humble expression he had assumed in his dealings with Knecht, and was quite astonished not to be addressed in the laconic manner his friend had recently adopted. Instead, Joseph nodded to him with a certain roguishness and asked: "Do you recall that in our student years we once had something like a quarrel in which I failed to convert you to my view? It was about the value and importance of Far Eastern studies, particularly Chinese subjects, and I tried to persuade you to spend a while in the college learning Chinese? You do remember? Well, I am thinking again what a pity that I could not persuade you at that time. It would be so fortunate now if you knew Chinese. There's a marvelous project on which we could collaborate."

He teased his friend a while longer, holding him in suspense, and finally came out with his proposal: that he wanted to begin working out the annual Game and would like Fritz, if it were agreeable to him, to take over a large part of this work, just as he had helped with the preparations for the prize Game in the elite competition while Knecht was living among the Benedictines. Fritz looked at him almost incredulously, profoundly surprised and delightfully upset by the merry tone and smiling face of his friend, who had been comporting himself solely as superior and Magister toward him. Joyfully stirred, he was conscious not only of the honor and confidence expressed by this proposal, but also grasped the significance of this handsome gesture. He realized that it was an attempt at healing the breach, at reopening the newly closed door between his friend and himself. He brushed aside the factor of his ignorance of Chinese, and promptly declared his willingness to be wholly at the Reverend Magister's disposal and to devote his full time to developing the Game.

"Good," the Magister said, "I accept your offer. So we shall once again be sharing periods of work and studies, as we used to in those days that seem strangely far away, when we worked through and fought through so many a Game. I am glad, Tegularius. And now the main thing is for you to inform yourself concerning the underlying idea of the Game. You must come to understand what a Chinese house is and the meaning of the rules for its construction. I shall give you a recommendation to the Far Eastern College; they will help you there. Or—something else occurs to me—a prettier notion. Perhaps we can try Elder Brother, the man in the Bamboo Grove, whom I used to tell you so much about. He may feel it beneath his dignity, or too much trouble to bother with someone who knows no Chinese, but we might try it at any rate. If he cares to, this man can make a Chinese of you."

A message was sent to Elder Brother, cordially inviting him to come to Waldzell for a while as the Glass Bead Game Master's guest, since the cares of office did not permit the Magister Ludi to call on him and explain what help he wanted of him. Elder Brother, however, did not leave his Bamboo Grove. The messenger returned with a note in Chinese ink and script. It read: "It would be honorable to behold the great man. But movement leads to obstacles. Let two small bowls be used for the sacrifice. The younger one greets the exalted one."

Knecht thereupon persuaded his friend, not without difficulty, to make the trip to the Bamboo Grove and ask to be received and instructed. But the journey proved fruitless. The hermit in the grove received Tegularius almost deferentially, but answered every one of his questions with amiable aphorisms in the Chinese language and did not invite him to stay, despite the fine letter of recommendation from the hand of the Magister Ludi, drawn elegantly on handsome paper. Rather out of sorts, having accomplished nothing, Fritz returned to Waldzell. He brought back a gift for the Magister: a sheet of paper on which was carefully brushed an ancient verse about a goldfish.

Tegularius now had to try his luck in the College of Far Eastern Studies. There Knecht's recommendations proved more effective. As a Magister's emissary, the petitioner was given a friendly reception and all the help he needed. Before long he had learned as much about his subject as could possibly be acquired without knowledge of Chinese, and in the course of his work he became so intrigued with Knecht's idea of using house symbolism for the underpinning of the Game that his failure in the Bamboo Grove ceased rankling, and was forgotten.

While he listened to Fritz's report on his visit to Elder Brother, and afterward, by himself, while he read the lines about the goldfish, Knecht felt surrounded by the hermit's atmosphere. Vivid memories arose of his long-ago stay in the hut, with the rustling bamboos and yarrow stalks outside, along with other memories of freedom, leisure, student days, and the colorful paradise of youthful dreams. How this brave, crotchety hermit had contrived to withdraw and keep his freedom; how his tranquil Bamboo Grove sheltered him from the world; how deeply and strongly he lived in his neat, pedantic and wise Sinicism; in how beautifully concentrated and inviolable a way the magic spell of his life's dream enclosed him year after year and decade after decade, making a China of his garden, a temple of his hut, divinities of his fish, and a sage of himself! With a sigh, Knecht shook off this notion. He himself had gone another way, or rather been led, and what counted was to pursue his assigned way straightforwardly and faithfully, not to compare it with the ways of others.

Together with Tegularius, he sketched out and composed his Game, using whatever leisure hours he could find. He left the entire task of selection in the Archives, as well as the first and second drafts, to his friend. Given this new content, their friendship acquired life and form once more, though the form differed from that of

the past. Fritz's eccentricities and imaginative subtlety
colored and enriched the pattern of their Game. He
was one of those eternally dissatisfied and yet self-sufficient individuals who can linger for hours over a bouquet
of flowers or a set table that anyone else would regard as
complete, rearranging the details with restive pleasure
and nervous loving manipulations, turning the littlest
task into an absorbing day's work.

In future years the association persisted: the ceremonial
Game represented a joint accomplishment each time
thereafter. For Tegularius it was a double satisfaction to
prove that he was more than useful, indispensable, to
his friend and Master in so important a matter, and to
witness the public performance of the Game as the unnamed collaborator whose part was nevertheless well
known to the members of the elite.

One day in the late autumn of Knecht's first year in
office, while his friend was still deep in his initial studies
of China, the Magister paused as he was skimming
through the entries in his secretariat's daily calendar.
He had come upon a note that caught his interest: "Student Petrus, arrived from Monteport, recommended by
Magister Musicae, brings special greetings from former
Music Master, requests lodgings and admission to Archives. Has been put up in student guesthouse." Knecht
could be easy in his mind about leaving the student and
his request to the Archive staff; that was routine. But
"special greetings from the former Music Master" was
directed only to himself. He sent for the student—who
turned out to be a quiet young man, at once contemplative and intense. Evidently he belonged to the Monteport
elite; at any rate he seemed accustomed to audiences with
a Magister. Knecht asked what message the former Music
Master had given him.

"Greetings," the student said, "very cordial and respectful greetings for you, reverend sir, along with an invitation."

Knecht asked him to sit down. Carefully choosing his
words, the young man continued: "As I have said, the
venerable former Magister requested me to give you his
warmest regards. He also hinted that he hoped to see you
in the near future, in fact as soon as possible. He invites

you, or urges you, to visit him before too long a time has passed, assuming, of course, that the visit can be fitted into an official journey and will not excessively discommode you. That is the burden of the message."

Knecht studied the young man, convinced that he was one of the old Master's protégés. Cautiously, he queried: "How long do you linger in our Archives, *studiose?*"

"Until I see that you are setting out for Monteport, reverend sir," was the reply.

Knecht considered a moment. "Very well," he said. "And why have you not repeated the exact wording of the ex-Master's message, as you should have done?"

Petrus unflinchingly met Knecht's eyes, and answered slowly, still circumspectly choosing his words, as if he were speaking a foreign language. "There is no message, reverend sir," he said, "and there is no exact wording. You know my reverend Master and know that he has always been an extraordinarily modest man. In Monteport it is said that in his youth, while he was still a tutor but already recognized by the entire elite as predestined to be the Music Master, they nicknamed him 'the great would-be-small.' Well, this modesty, and his piety no less, his helpfulness, thoughtfulness, and tolerance have actually increased ever since he grew old, and more so since he resigned his office. Undoubtedly you know that better than I. This modesty of his would forbid him to do anything like asking your Reverence for a visit, no matter how much he desired it. That is why, *Domine*, I have not been honored with any such message and nevertheless have acted as if I received one. If that was a mistake, you are free to regard the nonexistent message as actually nonexistent."

Knecht smiled faintly. "And what about your work in the Game Archives, my good fellow? Was that mere pretext?"

"Oh no. I have to obtain the ciphers for a number of clefs, so that I would in any case have had to cast myself upon your hospitality in the near future. But I thought it advisable to speed this little journey somewhat."

"Very good," the Magister said, nodding, his expression once again grave. "Is it permissible to ask into the reason for this haste?"

The young man closed his eyes for a moment. His forehead was deeply furrowed, as though the question pained him. Then he looked once more into the Magister's face with his searching, youthfully incisive gaze.

"The question cannot be answered unless you would be so good as to frame it more precisely."

"Very well then," Knecht said. "Is the former Master's health bad? Does it give reason for anxiety?"

Although the Magister had spoken with the greatest calm, the student perceived his affectionate concern for the old man. For the first time since the beginning of their conversation a gleam of good will appeared in his rather fierce eyes, and as he at last prepared to state candidly the real object of his visit, his voice sounded a trace friendlier and less distant.

"Reverend Magister," he said, "rest assured that my honored Master's condition is by no means bad. He has always enjoyed excellent health and does so still, although his advanced age has naturally greatly weakened him. It is not that his appearance has so much changed or that his strength had suddenly begun to diminish rapidly. He takes little walks, plays a little music every day, and until recently even continued to give two pupils organ lessons, beginners moreover, for he has always preferred to be surrounded by the youngest pupils. But the fact that he dismissed these pupils a few weeks ago is a symptom that caught my attention all the same, and since then I have watched the venerable Master rather more closely, and drawn my conclusions about him. That is the reason I have come. If anything justifies my conclusions, and my taking such a step, it is the fact that I myself was formerly one of the former Music Master's pupils, more or less one of his favorites, if I may say so; moreover, for the past year I have served him as a kind of secretary and companion, the present Music Master having named me to look after him. It was a very welcome assignment; there is no one in the world for whom I feel such veneration and attachment as I do for my old teacher and patron. It was he who opened up the mystery of music for me, and made me capable of serving it; and everything I may have acquired since in the way of ideas, respect for the Order, maturity, and inner concord has all come from him and is his doing. This past year I have been living at his side, and although I am occupied with a few studies and courses of my own, I am always at his disposal, his companion at table and on walks, making music with him, and sleeping in an adjoining room. Being so close to him all the time, I have been able to keep close watch over the stages of—I suppose I must say, of his aging, his physical aging. A few of my associates comment pityingly or scornfully now and then about its being a peculiar assignment that so young a person as myself should be the servant and companion of a very old man. But they do not know, and aside from myself I suspect no one really knows, what kind of aging the Master is privileged to undergo. They do not see him gradually growing weaker and frailer in the body, taking less and less nourishment, returning from his short walks more fatigued every time, without ever being really sick, and at the same time becoming, in the tranquility of age, more and more spiritual, devout, dignified, and simple in heart. If my office of secretary and attendant has any difficulties at all, they arise solely from the fact that his Reverence does not want to be waited on and tended at all. He still wants only to give and never to take."

"Thank you," Knecht said. "I am happy to know that his Reverence has so devoted and grateful a pupil at his side. And now, since you are not speaking on his orders, tell me plainly why you feel that I should visit Monteport."

"You asked with concern about the reverend former Music Master's health," the young man answered, "evidently because my request suggested to you that he might be ill and it could be high time to pay him one last visit. To be frank, I do think it is high time. He certainly does not seem to me to be close to his end, but his way of taking leave of the world is quite unique. For the past several months, for example, he has almost entirely lost the habit of speaking; and although he always preferred brevity to loquacity, he has now reached a degree of brevity and silence that frightens me somewhat. At first, when he did not answer a remark or question of mine, I thought that his hearing was beginning to weaken. But he hears almost as well as ever; I have made many tests

of that. I therefore had to assume that he was distracted
and could no longer focus his attention. But this, too, is
not an adequate explanation. Rather, it is as if he has
been on his way elsewhere for some time, and no longer
lives entirely among us, but more and more in his own
world. He rarely visits anyone or sends for anyone;
aside from me he no longer sees another person for days.
Ever since this started, this absentness, this detachment,
I have tried to urge the few friends whom I know he
loved most to see him. If you were to visit him, *Domine*,
you would make your old friend happy, I am sure of that,
and you would still find relatively the same man whom
you have revered and loved. In a few months, perhaps
only in a few weeks, his pleasure in seeing you and his
interest in you will probably be much less; it is even possible that he would no longer recognize you, or at any
rate pay attention to you."

Knecht stood up, went to the window, and stood there
for a while looking out and breathing deeply. When he
turned back to Petrus he saw that the student was also
standing, as though he thought the audience over. The
Magister extended his hand.

"I thank you once more, Petrus," he said. "As you
surely know, a Magister has all sorts of duties. I cannot
put on my hat and leave at once; schedules have to be
rearranged. I hope that I shall be able to leave by day
after tomorrow. Would that be time enough, and would
you be able to finish your work in the Archives by then?
Yes? Then I shall send for you when I am ready."

A few days later Knecht left for Monteport, accompanied by Petrus. When they reached the pavilion in the
gardens where the former Music Master now lived—it
was a lovely and beautifully tranquil monastic cell—
they heard music from the back room, delicate, thin, but
rhythmically firm and deliciously serene music. There the
old man sat playing a two-part melody with two fingers—
Knecht guessed at once that it must be from one of the
many books of duets written at the end of the sixteenth
century. They remained outside until the music ended;
then Petrus called out to his master that he was back
and had brought a visitor. The old man appeared in the
doorway and gave them a welcoming look. The Music

Master's welcoming smile, which everyone loved, had always had an open, childlike cordiality, a radiant friendliness; Joseph Knecht had seen it for the first time nearly thirty years before, and his heart had opened and surrendered to this friendly man during that tense but blissful morning hour in the music room. Since then he had seen this smile often, each time with deep rejoicing and a strange stirring of his heart; and while the Master's gray-shot hair had gradually turned completely gray and then white, while his voice had grown softer, his handshake fainter, his movements less supple, the smile had lost none of its brightness and grace, its purity and depth. And this time Joseph, the old man's friend and former pupil, saw the change beyond a doubt. The radiant, welcoming message of that smiling old man's face, whose blue eyes and delicately flushed cheeks had grown paler with the passing years, was both the same and not the same. It had grown deeper, more mysterious, and intense. Only now, as he was exchanging greetings, did Knecht really begin to understand what the student Petrus had been concerned about, and how greatly he himself, while thinking he was making a sacrifice for the sake of this concern, was in fact receiving a benefaction.

His friend Carlo Ferromonte was the first person to whom he spoke about this. Ferromonte was at this time librarian at the famous Monteport music library, and Knecht called on him a few hours later. Their conversation has been preserved in a letter of Ferromonte's.

"Our former Music Master was your teacher, of course," Knecht said, "and you were very fond of him. Do you see him often nowadays?"

"No," Carlo replied. "That is, I see him fairly often, of course, when he is taking his walk, say, and I happen to be coming out of the library. But I haven't talked with him for months. He is more and more withdrawing and no longer seems able to bear sociability. In the past he used to set aside an evening for people like me, those among his former subordinates who are officials in Monteport now; but that stopped about a year ago. It amazed us all that he went to Waldzell for your investiture."

"Ah yes," Knecht said. "But when you do see him oc-

casionally, haven't you been struck by any change in
him?"

"Oh yes. You mean his fine appearance, his cheerfulness, his curious radiance? Of course we have noticed
that. While his strength is diminishing, that serene cheerfulness is constantly increasing. We have grown accustomed to it. But I suppose it would strike you."

"His secretary Petrus sees far more of him than you
do," Knecht exclaimed, "but he hasn't grown accustomed to it, as you say. He came specially to Waldzell, on
a plausible excuse, of course, to urge me to make this
visit. What do you think of him?"

"Of Petrus? He has a first-rate knowledge of music,
though he's more on the pedantic than the brilliant side
—a rather slow-moving if not slow-witted person. He's
totally devoted to the former Music Master and would
give his life for him. I imagine his serving the master he
idolizes is the whole content of his life; he's obsessed by
him. Didn't you have that impression too?"

"Obsessed? Yes, but I don't think this young man is obsessed simply by a fondness and passion; he's not just infatuated with his old teacher and making an idol out of
him, but obsessed and enchanted by an actual and genuine phenomenon which he sees better, or has better
understood emotionally, than the rest of you. I want to
tell you how it struck me. When I went to the former
Master today, after not having seen him for six months, I
expected little or nothing from this visit, after the hints
his secretary had dropped. I had simply been alarmed to
think that the revered old man might suddenly depart
from us in the near future, and had hastened here in
order to see him at least once more. When he recognized
and greeted me, his face glowed, but he said no more
than my name and shook hands with me. That gesture,
too, and his hand, seemed to me also to glow; the whole
man, or at least his eyes, his white hair, and his rosy skin,
seemed to emit a cool, gentle radiance. I sat down with
him. He sent the student away, just with a look, and
there began the oddest conversation I have ever had. At
the beginning, I admit, it was very disturbing and depressing for me, and shaming also, for I kept addressing
the old man, or asking questions, and his only answer

to anything was a look. I could not make out whether my questions and the things I told him were anything but an annoying noise to him. He confused, disappointed, and tired me; I felt altogether superfluous and importunate. Whatever I said to the Master, the only response was a smile and a brief glance. If those glances had not been so full of good will and cordiality, I would have been forced to think that he was frankly making fun of me, of my stories and questions, of the whole useless trouble I had taken to come and visit him. As a matter of fact, his silence and his smile did indeed contain something of the sort. They were actually a form of fending me off and reproving me, except that they were so in a different way, on a differing plane of meaning from, say, mocking words. I had first to wear myself out and suffer total shipwreck with what had seemed to me my patient efforts to start a conversation, before I began to realize that the old man could easily have manifested a patience, persistence, and politeness a hundred times greater than mine. Perhaps the episode lasted only fifteen minutes or half an hour; it seemed to me like half a day. I began to feel sad, tired, and angry, and to repent my journey. My mouth felt dry. There sat the man I revered, my patron, my friend, whom I had loved and trusted ever since I could think, who had always responded to whatever I might say—there he sat and listened to me talk, or perhaps did not listen to me, and had barricaded himself completely behind his radiance and smile, behind his golden mask, unreachable, belonging to a different world with different laws; and everything I tried to bring by speech from our world to his ran off him like rain from a stone. At last—I had already given up hope—he broke through the magic wall; at last he helped me; at last he said a few words. Those were the only words I heard him speak today.

"'You are tiring yourself, Joseph,' he said softly, his voice full of that touching friendliness and solicitude you know so well. That was all. 'You are tiring yourself, Joseph.' As if he had long been watching me engaged in a too-strenuous task and wanted to admonish me to stop. He spoke the words with some effort, as though he had not used his lips for speaking for a long time. And at that

moment he laid his hand on my arm—it was light as a
butterfly—looked penetratingly into my eyes, and
smiled. At that moment I was conquered. Something of
his cheerful silence, something of his patience and calm,
passed into me; and suddenly I understood the old man
and the direction his nature had taken, away from
people and toward silence, away from words and toward
music, away from ideas and toward unity. I understood
what I was privileged to see here, and now for the first
time grasped the meaning of this smile, this radiance. A
saint, one who had attained perfection, had permitted
me to dwell in his radiance for an hour; and blunderer
that I am, I had tried to entertain him, to question him,
to seduce him into a conversation. Thank God the light
had not dawned on me too late. He might have sent me
away and thus rejected me forever. And I would have
been deprived of the most remarkable and wonderful
experience I have ever had."

"I see," Ferromonte said thoughtfully, "that you have
discovered something akin to a saint in our former Music
Master. A good thing that you and none other has told
me about this. I confess that I would have received such
a story with the greatest distrust from anyone else. I am,
taken all in all, not fond of mysticism; as a musician
and historian I am pedantically given to neat classification. Since we Castalians are neither a Christian congregation nor a Hindu or Taoist monastery, I do not see that
any of us qualify for sainthood—that is, for a purely
religious category. Coming from anyone but you, Joseph
—excuse me, I mean *Domine*—I would regard any such
ascription as going off the deep end. But I imagine you
do not mean to initiate canonization proceedings for
our former Master; you would scarcely find a competent
consistory for them in our Order. No, don't interrupt
me, I am speaking seriously; I don't mean that as a
joke at all. You have told me about an experience, and I
must admit that I feel somewhat ashamed, because neither
I nor any of my colleagues here at Monteport has entirely overlooked the phenomenon you describe. No, we
have merely noticed it and paid it little heed. I am reflecting on the reason for my failure and my indifference. One
explanation of course is the fact that you encountered the

Master's transformation as a finished product, whereas I
witnessed its slow evolution. The former Magister you
saw months ago and the one you saw today differed
sharply from each other, whereas we, his neighbors, meeting him every so often, observed almost imperceptible
changes. But I admit that this explanation doesn't satisfy
me. If something like a miracle is taking place before
our eyes, however quietly and slowly, we ought to have
been more stirred by it than we have been, and would
have been if we had been unbiased. Here, I think, I've
hit on the reason for my obtuseness: I was not in the least
unbiased. I failed to observe the phenomenon because I
did not want to observe it. Like everyone else, I noticed
our Master's increasing withdrawal and taciturnity, and
the concurrent increase in his friendliness, the ever-
brighter and more ethereal radiance of his face when we
met and he responded mutely to my greeting. I noticed
that, of course, and so did everyone else. But I fought
against seeing anything more in it, and I fought against
it not from lack of reverence for the old Magister, but in
part out of distaste for the cult of personality and enthusiasm in general, in part out of distaste for such enthusiasm in this special case, for the kind of cult the student
Petrus practices with his idolization of the Master. I've
only fully realized all this as you were telling your story."

Knecht laughed. "That was quite a roundabout way
for you to discover your own dislike for poor Petrus," he
said. "But what now? Am I also a mystic and enthusiast?
Am I too indulging in the forbidden cult of personality
and hagiolatry? Or are you admitting to me what you
won't admit to the student, that we have seen and experienced something real, objective, not mere dreams and
fancies?"

"Of course I admit it to you," Carlo replied slowly and
thoughtfully. "No one is going to deny your experience
or doubt the beauty and serenity of the Magister who can
smile at us in that incredible way. The question is only:
Where do we classify this phenomenon? What do we call
it, how explain it? That sounds like the pedantic schoolmaster, but we Castalians are schoolmasters, after all; and
if I want to classify and find a term for your and our experience, it is not because I wish to destroy its beauty by

generalizing it, but because I want to describe and preserve it as distinctly as possible. If on a journey I hear a peasant or child humming a melody I have never heard before, that is likewise an important experience for me, and if I immediately try to transcribe this melody as precisely as I can, I am not dismissing and filing it away, but paying due honor to my experience, and taking care that it is not lost."

Knecht gave him a friendly nod. "Carlo," he said, "it is a great pity we can so rarely see each other any more. Not all friendships of youth survive reunions. I came to you with my story about the old Magister because you are the only person here whose knowing and sharing it matters to me. Now I must leave it to you to do with my story whatever you like, and to assign whatever term you will to our Master's transfigured state. It would make me happy if you would call on him and stay in his aura for a little while. His state of grace, perfection, wisdom of age, bliss, or whatever we want to call it, may belong to religious life. But although we Castalians have neither denominations nor churches, piety is not altogether unknown to us. And our former Music Master in particular was always a thoroughly pious person. Since there are accounts of blessed, perfected, radiant, transfigured souls in many religions, why should not our Castalian piety occasionally have this kind of blossoming? . . . It is late by now—I ought to go to sleep—I must leave early tomorrow morning. But I hope to come back soon. Let me just briefly tell you the end of my story. After he had said to me, 'You are tiring yourself,' I was at last able to stop straining at conversation; I managed not only to be still, but to turn my will away from the foolish goal of using words in the effort to probe this man of silence and draw profit from him. And the moment I gave up that effort and left everything to him, it all went of its own accord. You may want to substitute terms of your own for mine, but please listen to me, even if I seem vague or confound categories. I stayed about an hour or an hour and a half with the old man, and I cannot communicate to you what went on between us or what was exchanged; certainly no words were spoken. I felt, after my resistance was broken, only that he received me into his peace and his brightness; cheerful serenity and a wonderful peace enclosed the two of us. Without my having deliberately and consciously meditated, it somewhat resembled an unusually successful and gladdening meditation whose subject might have been the Magister's life. I saw or felt him and the course of his growth from the time he first entered my life, when I was a boy, up to this present moment. His was a life of devotion and work, but free of obstructions, free of ambition, and full of music. It was as if by becoming a musician and Music Master he had chosen music as one of the ways toward man's highest goal, inner freedom, purity, perfection, and as though ever since making that choice he had done nothing but let himself be more and more permeated, transformed, purified by music—his entire self from his nimble, clever pianist's hands and his vast, well-stocked musician's memory to all the parts and organs of body and soul, to his pulses and breathing, to his sleep and dreaming—so that he was now only a symbol, or rather a manifestation, a personification of music. At any rate, I experienced what radiated from him, or what surged back and forth between him and me like rhythmic breathing, entirely as music, as an altogether immaterial esoteric music which absorbs everyone who enters its magic circle as a song for many voices absorbs an entering voice. Perhaps a nonmusician would have perceived this grace in different images: an astronomer might have seen it as a moon circling around a planet, or a philologist heard it as some magical primal language containing all meanings. But enough for now, I must be going. It's been a great pleasure, Carlo."

We have reported this episode in some detail, since the Music Master held so important a place in Knecht's life and heart. We have also been drawn into prolixity by the chance circumstance that Knecht's talk with Ferromonte has come down to us in the latter's own record of it in a letter. This is certainly the earliest and most reliable account of the Music Master's "transfiguration"; later, of course, there was a swarm of legends and embroideries.

EIGHT

THE TWO POLES

THE ANNUAL GAME, remembered to this day as the Chinese House Game, and often quoted, was for Knecht and his friend Tegularius a happy outcome to their labors, and for Castalia and the Boards proof that they had done well to summon Knecht to the highest office. Once more Waldzell, the Players' Village, and the elite had the satisfaction of a splendid and exultant festival. Not for many years had the annual Game been such an event as it was this time, with the youngest and most-discussed Magister in Castalian history making his first public appearance and showing what he could do. Moreover, Waldzell was determined to make up for the failure and disgrace of the previous year. This time no one lay ill, no cowed deputy awaited the great ceremony with apprehension, coldly ringed by the malevolent distrust of the elite, faithfully but listlessly supported by nervous officials. Quiet, inaccessible, entirely the high priest, white-and-gold-clad major piece on the solemn chessboard of symbols, the Magister celebrated his and his friend's work. Radiating calm, strength, and dignity, beyond the reach of any profane summons, he appeared in the festival hall in the midst of his many acolytes,

conducting step after step of his Game with the ritual
gestures. With a luminous golden stylus he delicately inscribed character after character on the small tablet
before him, and the same characters promptly appeared
in the script of the Game, enlarged a hundredfold, upon
the gigantic board on the rear wall of the hall, to be
spelled out by a thousand whispering voices, called out
by the Speakers, broadcast to the country and the world.
And when at the end of the first act he wrote the summary formula for that act upon his tablet, with graceful
and impressive poise gave instructions for the meditation, laid down the stylus and, taking his seat, assumed
the perfect meditation posture, in the hall, in the Players' Village, throughout Castalia and beyond, in many
countries of the globe, the faithful devotees of the Glass
Bead Game reverently sat down for the selfsame meditation and sustained it until the moment the Magister in
the hall rose to his feet once again. It was all as it had
been many times before, and yet it was all stirring and
new. The abstract and seemingly timeless world of the
Game was flexible enough to respond, in a hundred
nuances, to the mind, voice, temperament, and handwriting of a given personality, and the personality in this
case was great and cultivated enough to subordinate his
own inspirations to the inviolable inner laws of the Game
itself. The assistants and fellow players, the elite,
obeyed like well-drilled soldiers, yet each one of them,
even though he might be executing only the bows or
helping to draw the curtain around the meditating Master, seemed to be performing his own Game, inspired
by his own ideas. But it was the crowd, the great congregation filling the hall and all of Waldzell, the thousands
of souls who followed the Master down the hieratic and
labyrinthine ways through the endless, multidimensional
imagery of the Game, who furnished the fundamental
chord for the ceremony, the low, throbbing base bell-
note, which for the more simple-hearted members of the
community is the best and almost the only experience the
festival yields, but which also awakens awe in the subtle
virtuosi and critics of the elite, in the acolytes and officials
all the way up to the leader and Master.

It was an exalted festival. Even the envoys from the

outside world sensed this, and proclaimed it; and in the course of those days a good many new converts were won over to the Glass Bead Game forever. In the light of this triumph, however, Joseph Knecht, at the end of the ten-day festival, made some highly curious remarks in summing up the experience to his friend Tegularius. "We may be content," he said. "Yes, Castalia and the Glass Bead Game are wonderful things; they come close to being perfect. Only perhaps they are too much so, too beautiful. They are so beautiful that one can scarcely contemplate them without fearing for them. It is not pleasant to think that some day they are bound to pass away as everything else does. And yet one must think of that."

With this historic statement, the biographer is forced to approach the most delicate and mysterious part of his task. Indeed, he would have preferred to postpone it for a while longer and continue—with that placidity which clear and unambiguous conditions afford to the narrator of them—to depict Knecht's successes, his exemplary conduct of his office, the brilliant peak of his life. But it would seem to us misleading, and out of keeping with our subject, if we failed to take account of the duality, or call it polarity, in the revered Master's life and character, even though it was so far known to no one but Tegularius. From now on our task, in fact, will be to accept this dichotomy in Knecht's soul, or rather this ever-alternating polarity, as the central feature of his nature, and to affirm it as such. As a matter of fact, a biographer who thought it proper to deal with the life of a Castalian Magister entirely in the spirit of hagiography, *ad maiorem gloriam Castaliae,* would not find it at all difficult to describe Joseph Knecht's years as Magister, with the sole exception of the last moments, entirely as a glorious list of achievements, duties performed, and successes. To the eye of the historian who holds solely to the documented facts, Magister Knecht's conduct in office appears as blameless and praiseworthy as that of any Glass Bead Game Master in history, not even excepting that of Magister Ludwig Wassermaler who reigned during the era of Waldzell's most exuberant passion for the Game. Nevertheless, Knecht's period in office came to a most unusual, sensational, and to the minds of many judges scandalous end, and this end was not mere chance or misfortune but a wholly logical outcome of what went before. It is part of our task to show that it by no means contradicts the reverend Master's brilliant and laudable achievements. Knecht was a great, an exemplary administrator, an honor to his high office, an irreproachable Glass Bead Game Master. But he saw and felt the glory of Castalia, even as he devoted himself to it, as an imperiled greatness that was on the wane. He did not participate in its life thoughtlessly and unsuspectingly, as did the great majority of his fellow Castalians, for he knew about its origins and history, was conscious of it as a historical entity, subject to time, washed and undermined by time's pitiless surges. This sensitivity to the pulse of historical process and this feeling for his own self and activities as a cell carried along in the stream of growth and transformation, had ripened within him in the course of his historical studies. Much was due to the influence of the great Benedictine Father Jacobus, but the germs of such consciousness had been present within him long before. Anyone who honestly tries to explore the meaning of that life, to analyze its idiosyncrasy, will easily discover these germs.

The man who could say, on one of the finest days of his life, at the end of his first festival Game and after a singularly successful and impressive demonstration of the Castalian spirit, "It is not pleasant to think that some day Castalia and the Glass Bead Game are bound to pass away—and yet one must think of that"—this man had early on, long before he had acquired insight into history, borne within himself a metaphysical sense of the transitoriness of all that has evolved and the problematical nature of everything created by the human mind. If we go back to his boyhood we will remember his depression and uneasiness whenever a fellow pupil disappeared from Eschholz because he had disappointed his teachers and been demoted from the elite to the ordinary schools. There is no record that a single one of those expelled had been a close friend of young Joseph; what disturbed him was not personal loss, not the absence of this or that individual. Rather, his grief was

caused by the mild shock to his child's faith in the
permanence of Castalian order and Castalian perfection.
He himself took his vocation so seriously as something
sacred, and yet there were boys and youths who had
been granted the happiness of acceptance into the elite
schools of the Province and had squandered this boon,
thrown it away. This was shocking, and a sign of the
power of the world outside Castalia. Perhaps also—
though here we can only speculate—such incidents
aroused the boy's first doubts of the Board of Educators' infallibility, since this Board now and then brought
to Castalia pupils whom it subsequently had to dismiss
again. There is no saying whether these earliest stirrings
of criticism of authority also affected his thinking.

In any case, the boy felt every dismissal of an elite
pupil not only as a misfortune, but also as an impro-
priety, an ugly glaring stain, whose presence was in itself a reproach involving all of Castalia. This, we think,
is the basis for that feeling of shock and distraction
which Knecht as a schoolboy experienced on such occasions. Outside, beyond the boundaries of the Province,
was a way of life which ran counter to Castalia and its
laws, which did not abide by the Castalian system and
could not be tamed and sublimated by it. And of course
he was aware of the presence of this world in his own
heart also. He too had impulses, fantasies, and desires
which ran counter to the laws that governed him, impulses which he had only gradually managed to subdue
by hard effort.

These impulses, he concluded, could be so strong in a
good many pupils that they erupted despite all restraints
and led those who yielded to them away from the elite
world of Castalia and into that other world which was
dominated not by discipline and cultivation of the mind,
but by instincts. To one striving for Castalian virtue that
world seemed sometimes a wicked underworld, sometimes a tempting playground and arena. For generations
many young consciences have experienced the concept of
sin in this Castalian form. And many years later, as an
adult student of history, Knecht was to perceive more
distinctly that history cannot come into being without the
substance and the dynamism of this sinful world of ego-

ism and instinctuality, and that even such sublime creations as the Order were born in this cloudy torrent and
sooner or later will be swallowed up by it again. This is
what underlay all the powerful movements, aspirations,
and upheavals in Knecht's life. Nor was this ever merely
an intellectual problem for him. Rather, it engaged his
innermost self more than any other problem, and he felt it
as partly his responsibility. His was one of those natures
which can sicken, languish, and die when they see an
ideal they have believed in, or the country and community they love, afflicted with ills.

Tracing this same thread further, we come to Knecht's
first period in Waldzell, his final years as a schoolboy,
and his significant meeting with the guest pupil Designori, which we have described in detail in its proper
place. This encounter between the ardent adherent of
the Castalian ideals and the worldling Plinio was not only
intense and long-lasting in its effects, but also had a
deeply symbolic significance for young Knecht. For the
strenuous and important role imposed upon him at that
time, seemingly sent his way by sheer chance, in fact so
closely corresponded with his whole nature that we are
tempted to say his later life was nothing but a reiteration
of this role, an ever more perfect adaptation to it. The
role, of course, was that of champion and representer of
Castalia. He had to play it once more some ten years
later against Father Jacobus, and as Master of the Glass
Bead Game he played it to the end: champion and representative of the Order and its laws, but one who was
constantly endeavoring to learn from his antagonist and
to promote not the rigid isolation of Castalia, but its
vital collaboration and confrontation with the outside
world. The oratorical contest with Designori had been
partly a game. With his far more substantial friendly antagonist, Father Jacobus, it was altogether serious. He
had proved himself against both opponents, had matured
in his encounter with them, had learned from them, had
given as much as he had taken in the course of their
disputes and exchanges of views. In neither case had he
defeated his antagonist; from the start that had not,
after all, been the goal of the disputations. But he had
succeeded in making each of them respect him as a per-

son, and the principles and ideal he advocated. Even if the disputation with the learned Benedictine had not led directly to its practical result, the establishment of a semiofficial Castalian envoy at the Holy See, it would have been of greater value than the majority of Castalians could have guessed.

These embattled friendships with Plinio Designori and with the wise old Benedictine had provided Knecht, who otherwise had had little to do with the world outside Castalia, with some knowledge, or at any rate some intuitions, about that world. Few persons in Castalia could say the same for themselves. Except for his stay in Mariafels, which could scarcely give him any acquaintance with the real life of the outside world, he had neither seen nor experienced this worldly life since his early childhood. But through Designori, through Jacobus, and through his historical studies he had acquired a lively sense of its reality. His intimations, though they were mostly intuitive and accompanied by very meager experience, had made him more knowledgeable and more receptive to the world than the majority of his Castalian fellow citizens, including the higher authorities. He had always been a loyal and authentic Castalian, but he never forgot that Castalia was only a small part of the world, though for him the most valuable and beloved part.

What was the character of his friendship with Fritz Tegularius, that difficult and problematical character, that sublime acrobat of the Glass Bead Game, that pampered and high-strung pure Castalian whose brief visit among the coarse Benedictines in Mariafels had made him so wretched that he declared he could not have stayed there a week, and enormously admired his friend for enduring the life there quite well for two years? We have entertained a wide variety of thoughts about this friendship, have had to reject some of them, while others seemed to stand up to examination. All these thoughts centered around the question of what the root and the significance of this lasting friendship must have been. Above all we should not forget that in all of Knecht's friendships, with the possible exception of that with the Benedictine Father, he was not the seeking, courting, and needy partner. He attracted, he was admired, envied, and loved simply for his noble nature; and from a certain stage of his "awakening" on he was even conscious of this gift. Thus he had already been admired and courted by Tegularius in his early student years, but had always kept him at a certain distance.

Nevertheless, there are many tokens that he was really fond of his friend. As we see it, it was not just the latter's outstanding talent, his nervous brilliance and receptivity, particularly to all the problems of the Glass Bead Game, that drew Knecht to him. Rather, Knecht took so strong an interest not only in his friend's great gifts, but also in his faults, in his sickliness, in precisely those qualities that other Waldzellers found disturbing and frequently intolerable in Tegularius. This eccentric was utterly Castalian. His whole mode of existence, inconceivable outside the Province, was so entirely consonant with its atmosphere and level of culture that if he had not been so eccentric and hard to get along with he might have deserved the epithet arch-Castalian. And yet this arch-Castalian hardly fitted in with his fellows; he was no more popular with them than with his superiors, the officials. He constantly disturbed people, repeatedly offended them, and but for the stout protection and guidance of his prudent friend he would probably have been destroyed very early. For what was called his illness was primarily a vice, a character defect, a form of rebelliousness. He was profoundly unhierarchical, totally individualistic in his attitudes and his conduct. He adjusted to the system only enough to pass muster within the Order.

He was a good, even a shining light as a Castalian to the extent that he had a many-sided mind, tirelessly active in scholarship as well as in the art of the Glass Bead Game, and enormously hard-working; but in character, in his attitude toward the hierarchy and the morality of the Order he was a very mediocre, not to say bad Castalian. The greatest of his vices was a persistent neglect of meditation, which he refused to take seriously. The purpose of meditation, after all, is adaptation of the individual to the hierarchy, and application in it might very well have cured him of his neurasthenia. For it infallibly helped him whenever, after a period of bad conduct, excessive excitement, or melancholia, his superiors disciplined him by prescribing strict meditation exercises under supervision. Even Knecht, kindly disposed and forgiving though he was, frequently had to resort to this measure.

There was no question about it: Tegularius was a willful, moody person who refused to fit into his society. Every so often he would display the liveliness of his intellect. When highly stimulated he could be entrancing; his mordant wit sparkled and he overwhelmed everyone with the audacity and richness of his sometimes somber inspirations. But basically he was incurable, for he did not want to be cured; he cared nothing for co-ordination and a place in the scheme of things. He loved nothing but his freedom, his perpetual student status, and preferred spending his whole life as the unpredictable and obstinate loner, the gifted fool and nihilist, to following the path of subordination to the hierarchy and thus attaining peace. He cared nothing for peace, had no regard for the hierarchy, hardly minded reproof and isolation. Certainly he was a most inconvenient and indigestible component in a community whose idea was harmony and orderliness. But because of this very troublesomeness and indigestibility he was, in the midst of such a limpid and prearranged little world, a constant source of vital unrest, a reproach, an admonition and warning, a spur to new, bold, forbidden, intrepid ideas, an unruly, stubborn sheep in the herd. And, to our mind, this was the very reason his friend cherished him.

Certainly there was always a measure of pity in Knecht's relationship to Tegularius. His imperiled and usually unhappy state appealed to all his friend's chivalric feelings. But this would not have sufficed to sustain this friendship after Knecht's elevation to an official life overburdened with work, duties, and responsibilities. We take the view that Tegularius was no less necessary and important in Knecht's life than Designori and Father Jacobus had been. Moreover, exactly like the other two, he was a dynamic element, a small open window that looked out upon new prospects. In this peculiar friend Knecht sensed, we think, the features of a type. As time went on he realized that the type was one not yet existent except for Tegularius. For Tegularius was a portent of the Castalian as he might some day become unless the life of Castalia were rejuvenated and revitalized by new encounters, new forces. Like most solitary geniuses, Tegularius was a forerunner. He actually lived in a Castalia that did not yet exist, but might·come into being in the future; in a Castalia still sequestered from the world, but inwardly degenerating from senility and from relaxation of the meditative morality of the Order; a Castalia in which the highest flights of the mind were still possible, as well as totally absorbed devotion to sublime values—but this highly developed, freely roaming intellectual culture no longer had any goals beyond egotistic enjoyment of its own overbred faculties. Knecht saw Tegularius as the two things in one: embodiment of the finest gifts to be found in Castalia, and at the same time a portent of the demoralization and downfall of those abilities. Measures must be taken to keep Castalia from becoming a dream-ridden realm populated entirely by Tegulariuses.

The danger was remote, but it was there. Castalia as Knecht knew it needed only to build its walls of aristocratic isolation slightly higher, needed only to undergo a decline in the discipline of the Order, a lowering of the hierarchical morality, and Tegularius would cease to be an eccentric individual; he would become the prototype of a deteriorating Castalia. Magister Knecht's most important insight, the source of all his concern, was that the potentiality for such decadence existed. The disposition for it was there; in fact it had already begun. Probably he would have realized this much later, perhaps never at all, had not this future Castalian, whom he knew so intimately, lived at his side. To Knecht's keen instincts, Tegularius was a danger signal, as the first victim of a still unknown disease would be for a clever physician. And Fritz was after all no average man; he was an aristocrat, a supremely gifted person. If the still unknown disease just coming to light in this forerunner Tegularius were ever to spread and change the whole image of Castalian man, if the Province and the Order were ever to assume the degenerate, morbid form latent

in them, these future Castalians would not be all Tegulariuses. Not everyone would have his precious gifts, his
melancholy genius, his flickering intensity and acrobatic
artistry. Rather, the majority of them would have only
his unreliability, his tendency to fritter away his talents,
his lack of any discipline or sense of community. In
times of anxiety Knecht seems to have had such gloomy
premonitions; and surely it cost him a great deal of
strength to overcome them, partly by meditation, partly
by intensified activity.

The very case of Tegularius offers an instructive example of the way Knecht attempted to overcome morbidity
and temperamental difficulties by meeting them directly.
But for Knecht's watchfulness and pedagogic guidance,
his imperiled friend would in all likelihood have come
to grief early in his life. What is more, he would undoubtedly have introduced endless disturbances into the
Players' Village. There had in any case been a good deal
of such discord ever since Fritz had become a member
of the elite. With consummate art the Magister kept his
friend tolerably well on course, while at the same time
contriving to employ his gifts in the interests of the Glass
Bead Game and to extract fine achievements from Fritz's
talent. The patience with which he coped with the latter's eccentricities, overcoming them by tirelessly appealing to his virtues, must be called a masterpiece in the
technique of human relations. Incidentally, it would be a
fine project which might yield some surprising insights
(we should like to recommend it strongly to some of our
historians of the Glass Bead Game) to subject the annual
Games of Knecht's magistracy to a close analysis of their
stylistic peculiarities. These Games, so majestic and yet
sparkling with delightful inspirations and formulations,
so scintillating and original in their rhythms, yet such
a far cry from smug virtuosity, owed their underlying
idea, their development, and the slant of their series of
meditations exclusively to Knecht's mind, whereas the
fine polishing and the minor details of Game technique
were mostly the work of his collaborator Tegularius.
Even had these Games been forgotten, Knecht's life and
work would lose none of its attractiveness and pertinence
for posterity. But to our great good fortune they have

been recorded and preserved like all official Games. And they do not merely lie dead in the Archives. They survive in our traditions to this day, are studied by the young, supply cherished examples for many a Game course and many a seminar. And in them the collaborator survives, who otherwise would be forgotten, or would at any rate be no more than a strange, shadowy figure out of the past, haunting a host of anecdotes.

Thus, in managing to assign a place to his refractory friend Fritz, and in providing him with an area in which he could work effectively, Knecht enriched the history and culture of Waldzell, while at the same time assuring his friend's memory a certain permanence. Incidentally, this great educator was well aware of the real basis of his educational influence on his friend. That basis was his friend's love and admiration. As we have seen, the Magister's harmonious personality, his innate sense of mastery, had almost from the first won over so many other fellow aspirants and pupils that he counted on this more than on his high office to sustain his authority, despite his kindly and conciliatory nature. He sensed precisely the effect of a friendly word of greeting or appreciation, or of withdrawal and disregard. Long afterward one of his most ardent disciples related that one time Knecht did not speak a single word to him in class and in his seminar, seemingly did not see him, ignored him completely —and that in all the years of his schooling this had been the bitterest and most effective punishment he had ever known.

We have considered these retrospective observations essential in order that our reader may perceive the two antipodal tendencies in Knecht's personality. Having followed our account to the present peak of Knecht's remarkable life, the reader will then be prepared for its final phases. The two tendencies or antipodes of this life, its Yin and Yang, were the conservative tendency toward loyalty, toward unstinting service of the hierarchy on the one hand, and on the other hand the tendency toward "awakening," toward advancing, toward apprehending reality. For Joseph Knecht in his role of believer and devoted servant, the Order, Castalia, the Glass Bead Game were sacrosanct. To him in his awakened, clairvoyant, pioneering role they were, irrespective of their value, full-grown institutions, their struggles long past, vulnerable to the danger of aging, sterility, and decadence. The idea underlying them always remained sacred to him, but he had recognized the particular forms that idea had assumed as mutable, perishable, in need of criticism. He served a community of the mind whose strength and rationality he admired; but he thought it was running grave risks by tending to see its own existence as the be-all and end-all, by forgetting its duties to the country and the outside world. If it continued along this course, growing increasingly separated from the whole of life, it was doomed to fall into sterility. In those earlier years he had had presentiments of this peril; that was why he had so often hesitated, fearing to devote himself solely to the Glass Bead Game. In discussions with the monks, and especially with Father Jacobus, the problem had come to mind ever more forcibly, even while he was bravely defending Castalia. Ever since he had been back in Waldzell, and holding office as Magister Ludi, he had continually seen tangible symptoms of that danger: in the loyal but unworldly and formalistic methods of work among his own officials and in many of the other departments; in the highly intelligent but arrogant expertise of the Waldzell elite; and last but not least, in the touching but worrisome personality of his friend Tegularius.

With his first difficult year in office behind him, he resumed his historical studies. For the first time he examined the history of Castalia with his eyes open, and soon became convinced that things were not going as well as the inhabitants of the Province thought. Castalia's relationships with the outside world, the reciprocal influences operating between Castalia and the life, politics, and culture of the country, had been on the downgrade for decades. Granted, the Federal Council still consulted the Board of Educators on pedagogical and cultural matters; the Province continued to supply the country with good teachers and to pronounce on all questions of scholarhip. But these matters had assumed a routine and mechanical cast. Young men from the various elites of Castalia nowadays volunteered less eagerly, and less frequently, for teaching assignments *extra muros*. Individuals and authorities in the rest of the country less frequently turned for advice to Castalia, whose opinion had in earlier times been sought and listened to even, for example, on important cases of law. If the cultural level of Castalia were compared with that of the country at large, it became apparent that the two were by no means approaching each other; rather, they were moving apart in a deeply troubling way. The more cultivated, specialized, overbred that Castalian intellectuality became, the more the world inclined to let the Province be and to regard it not as a necessity, as daily bread, but as a foreign body, something to be a little proud of, like a precious antique which for the time being the owners would not like to give up or give away, but which they would happily keep stored in the attic. Without fully grasping the situation, people on the outside attributed to Castalians a mentality, a morality, and a sense of self which was no longer viable in real, active life.

The interest of the country's citizens in the life of the Pedagogic Province, their sympathy with its institutions and especially with the Glass Bead Game, were likewise on the downgrade, as was the sympathy of the Castalians for the life and the fate of the country. Knecht had long ago realized that this lack of interest in each other was a grave fault in both, and it was a grief to him that as Master of the Glass Bead Game in his Players' Village he dealt exclusively with Castalians and specialists. Hence his endeavors to devote himself more and more to beginners' courses, his desire to have the youngest pupils—for the younger they were, the more they were still linked with the whole of life and the outside world, the less tamed, trained, and specialized they were. Often he felt a wild craving for the world, for people, for unreflective life—assuming that such still existed out there in the unknown world. Most of us have now and then been touched by this longing, this sense of emptiness, this feeling of living in far too rarefied an atmosphere. The Board of Educators, too, is familiar with this problem; at least it has from time to time looked for methods to combat it, such as by laying more stress on physical exercises and games, and by experimenting with various crafts and gardening. If our observations are correct, the directorate of the Order had of late shown a tendency to abandon some overrefined specialties in the scholarly disciplines and to emphasize instead the practice of meditation. One need not be a skeptic or prophet of doom, nor a disloyal member of the Order, to concede that Joseph Knecht was right in recognizing, a considerable time before the present day, that the complicated and sensitive apparatus of our republic had become an aging organism, in many respects badly in need of rejuvenation.

As we have mentioned, from his second year in office on we find him engaging in historical studies again. In addition to his investigations of Castalian history, he spent much of his leisure reading all the large and small papers that Father Jacobus had written on the history of the Benedictine Order. He also found opportunities to vent some of his opinions on historical matters, and have his interest kindled anew in conversations with Monsieur Dubois and with one of the Keuperheim philologists, who as secretary of the Board was present at all its sessions. Such talk was always a delight to him, and a welcome refreshment, for among his daily associates he lacked such opportunities. In fact the apathy of these associates toward any dealings with history was embodied in the person of his friend Fritz. Among other materials we have come across a sheet of notes on a conversation in which Tegularius insisted that history was a subject altogether unfit for study by a Castalian.

"Of course it's possible to talk wittily, amusingly, even emotionally, if need be, about interpretations of history, the philosophy of history," he declared. "There's as much sport in that as in discussing other philosophies, and I don't have any objection if someone wants to entertain himself that way. But the thing itself, the subject of this amusement, history, is both banal and diabolic, both horrible and boring. I don't understand how anyone can waste time on it. Its sole content is sheer human egotism and the struggle for power. Those engaged in the struggle forever overestimate it, forever glorify their own enterprises—but it is nothing but brutal, bestial, material power they seek—a thing that doesn't exist in the mind of the Castalian, or if it does has not the slightest value. World history is nothing but an endless, dreary account of the rape of the weak by the strong. To associate real history, the timeless history of Mind, with this age-old, stupid scramble of the ambitious for power and the climbers for a place in the sun—to link the two let alone to try to explain the one by the other—is in itself betrayal of the living spirit. It reminds me of a sect fairly widespread in the nineteenth or the twentieth century whose members seriously believed that the sacrifices, the gods, the temples and myths of ancient peoples, as well as all other pleasant things, were the consequences of a calculable shortage or surplus of food and work, the results of a tension measurable in terms of wages and the price of bread. In other words, the arts and religions were regarded as mere façades, so-called ideologies erected above a human race concerned solely with hunger and feeding."

Knecht, who had listened with good humor to this outburst, asked casually: "Doesn't the history of thought, of culture and the arts, have some kind of connection with the rest of history?"

"Absolutely not," his friend exclaimed. "That is exactly what I am denying. World history is a race with time, a scramble for profit, for power, for treasures. What counts is who has the strength, luck, or vulgarity not to miss his opportunity. The achievements of thought, of culture, of art are just the opposite. They are always an escape from the serfdom of time, man crawling out of the muck of his instincts and out of his sluggishness and climbing to a higher plane, to timelessness, liberation from time, divinity. They are utterly unhistorical and antihistorical."

Knecht went on drawing Tegularius out on this theme for a while longer, smiling at his hyperbole. Then he quietly brought the conversation to a close by commenting: "Your love for culture and the products of the mind does you credit. But it happens that cultural creativity is something we cannot participate in quite so fully as some people think. A dialogue of Plato's or a choral movement by Heinrich Isaac—in fact all the things we call a product of the mind or a work of art or objectified spirit —are the outcomes of a struggle for purification and liberation. They are, to use your phrase, escapes from

time into timelessness, and in most cases the best such
works are those which no longer show any signs of the
anguish and effort that preceded them. It is a great good
fortune that we have these works, and of course we Castalians live almost entirely by them; the only creativity
we have left lies in preserving them. We live permanently
in that realm beyond time and conflict embodied in those
very works and which we would know nothing of, but
for them. And we go even further into the realms of pure
mind, or if you prefer, pure abstraction: in our Glass
Bead Game we analyze those products of the sages and
artists into their components, we derive rules and
patterns of form from them, and we operate with these
abstractions as though they were building blocks. Of
course all this is very fine; no one will contend otherwise.
But not everyone can spend his entire life breathing,
eating, and drinking nothing but abstractions. History
has one great strength over the things a Waldzell tutor
feels to be worthy of his interest: it deals with reality.
Abstractions are fine, but I think people also have to
breathe air and eat bread."

Every so often Knecht found time for a brief visit to
the aged former Music Master. The venerable old man,
whose strength was now visibly ebbing and who had long
since completely lost the habit of speech, persisted in his
state of serene composure to the last. He was not sick,
and his death was not so much a matter of dying as a
form of progressive dematerialization, a dwindling of
bodily substance and the bodily functions, while his life
more and more gathered in his eyes and in the gentle
radiance of his withering old man's face. To most of the
inhabitants of Monteport this was a familiar sight, accepted with due respect. Only a few persons, such as
Knecht, Ferromonte, and young Petrus, were privileged
to share after a fashion in this sunset glow, this fading out
of a pure and selfless life. These few, when they had put
themselves into the proper frame of mind before stepping
into the little room in which the Master sat in his armchair, succeeded in entering into this soft iridescence of
disembodiment, in sharing in the old man's silent movement toward perfection. They stayed for rapt moments

in the crystal sphere of this soul, as if in a realm of invisible radiation, listening to unearthly music, and then returned to their daily lives with hearts cleansed and strengthened, as if descending from a high mountain peak.

One day Knecht received the news of his death. He hastened to Monteport and found the old man, who had passed peacefully away, lying on his bed, the small face shrunken to a silent rune and arabesque, a magical figure no longer readable but nevertheless somehow conveying smiles and perfected happiness. Knecht spoke at the funeral, after the present Music Master and Ferromonte. He did not talk about the enlightened sage of music, nor of the man's greatness as a teacher, nor of his kindness and wisdom as the eldest member of the highest ruling body in Castalia. He spoke only of the grace of such an old age and death, of the immortal beauty of the spirit which had been revealed through him to those who had shared his last days.

We know from several statements of Knecht's that he wanted to write the former Master's biography, but official duties left him no time for such a task. He had learned to curb his own wishes. Once he remarked to one of his tutors: "It is a pity that you students aren't fully aware of the luxury and abundance in which you live. But I was exactly the same when I was still a student. We study and work, don't waste much time, and think we may rightly call ourselves industrious—but we are scarcely conscious of all we could do, all that we might make of our freedom. Then we suddenly receive a call from the hierarchy, we are needed, are given a teaching assignment, a mission, a post, and from then on move up to a higher one, and unexpectedly find ourselves caught in a network of duties that tightens the more we try to move inside it. All the tasks are in themselves small, but each one has to be carried out at its proper hour, and the day has far more tasks than hours. That is well; one would not want it to be different. But if we ever think, between classroom, Archives, secretariat, consulting room, meetings, and official journeys—if we ever think of the freedom we possessed and have lost, the freedom for self-chosen tasks, for unlimited, far-flung studies, we may well feel the greatest yearning for those days, and imagine that if we ever had such freedom again we would fully enjoy its pleasures and potentialities."

Knecht had an extraordinary aptitude for fitting his students and officials into their proper place in the service of the hierarchy. He chose his men for every assignment, for every post, with great care. His reports on them show keen judgment, especially of character. Other officials often sought his advice on the handling of personality problems. There was, for example, the case of the student Petrus, the former Music Master's last favorite pupil. This young man, the typical quiet fanatic, had done remarkably well in his unique role of companion, nurse, and adoring disciple. But when this role came to its natural end with the former Magister's death, he lapsed into melancholia that was understood and tolerated for a while. Soon, however, his symptoms began to cause Music Master Ludwig, the present director of Monteport, serious concern. For Petrus insisted on remaining on in the pavilion where the deceased Master had spent his last days. He guarded the cottage, continued to keep its furnishings and arrangements painstakingly in their former state, and especially regarded the room in which the Master had died, with its armchair, deathbed, and harpsichord, as a sort of shrine. In addition to caring for these relics, his only other activity consisted in tending the grave of his beloved Master. His vocation, he felt, was to devote his life to a permanent cult of the dead man, watching over the places associated with his memory as if he were a temple servant. Perhaps he hoped to see them become places of pilgrimage. During the first few days after the funeral he had taken no food; afterward he limited himself to the tiny and rare meals with which the Master had been content during his last days. It appeared that he intended to go so far in *imitatio* of the Master that he would soon follow him into death. Since he could not sustain this for long, however, he shifted to the mode of conduct which would presumably entitle him to become guardian of house and grave, permanent custodian of this memorial site. From all this it was plain that the young man, naturally obstinate in any case and having enjoyed for some time a distinctive position, was bent on holding on to that position and had not the slightest desire to return to the commonplace duties of life; no doubt he secretly felt that he could no longer cope with them. "By the way, that fellow Petrus who was assigned to the late Master is cracked," Ferromonte reported acidly in a note to Knecht.

Strictly speaking, a Monteport music student was no concern of the Waldzell Magister, who should have felt no call to add to his own responsibilities by interfering in a Monteport affair. But things went from bad to worse. The unfortunate young man had to be removed by force from his pavilion. His agitation did not subside with the passage of time. Distraught, still mourning, he had lapsed into a state of withdrawal in which he could not very well be subjected to the usual punishments for infractions of discipline. And since his superiors were well aware of Knecht's benevolent feelings toward the young man, the Music Master's office applied to him for advice and intervention. In the meantime the refractory student was being kept under observation in a cell in the infirmary.

Knecht had been reluctant to become involved in this troublesome affair. But once he had given some thought to it and had decided to try to help, he took the matter vigorously in hand. He offered to take Petrus under his wing as an experiment, on condition that the young man be treated as if he were well and permitted to travel alone. With his letter to the Music Master's office he enclosed a brief, cordial invitation to Petrus, asking him to pay a short visit if it were convenient, and hinting that he hoped for an account of the former Music Master's last days.

The Monteport doctor hesitantly consented. Knecht's invitation was handed to the student, and as Knecht had rightly guessed, nothing could have been more welcome to the young man, trapped as he was in the deplorable situation he had created for himself, than a swift escape from the scene of his difficulties. Petrus immediately agreed to undertake the journey, accepted a proper meal, was given a travel pass, and set out on foot. He arrived in Waldzell in fair condition. On Knecht's orders, everyone ignored the jitteriness in his manner. He was put up

among the guests of the Archive and found himself
treated neither as a delinquent nor as a patient, nor for
that matter as a person in any way out of the ordinary.
He was after all not so ill as to fail to appreciate this
pleasant atmosphere; and he took the road back into life
thus offered him, although during the several weeks of
his stay he remained a considerable nuisance to the Magister. Knecht assigned him the sham task of recording,
under strict supervision, his Master's last musical exercises and studies, and in addition systematically employed
him for minor routine jobs in the Archives. This on the
pretext that the Archives personnel were overburdened
at the moment, and it would be good of him to lend a
hand whenever he had the time.

In short, the temporary deviant was guided back to
the right road. After he had calmed down and seemed
ready to fit himself into the hierarchy, Knecht began ex-
erting a direct educational influence upon him. In a
series of brief talks the Magister relieved the youth of his
delusion that setting up the deceased Music Master as the
subject of an idolatrous cult was either a religious act or
one tenable in Castalia. Since, however, Petrus was still
terror-stricken at the prospect of returning to Monteport,
although he seemed otherwise cured, a post of assistant
music teacher in one of the lower elite schools was provided for him. In that capacity he henceforth behaved
quite acceptably.

We might cite a good many other examples of Knecht's
psychiatric and educative work. Moreover, there were
many young students who fell under the gentle sway of
his personality and were won over to a life in the genuine
spirit of Castalia much the way Knecht himself had been
won over by the Music Master. All these examples show
us the Magister Ludi as anything but a problematical
character; all are testimonies to his soundness and balance. But his kindly efforts to help unstable and imperiled
personalities such as Petrus or Tegularius do suggest an
unusually alert sensitivity to such maladies or susceptibil-
ities on the part of Castalians. They suggest that since
his first "awakening" he had remained keenly alive to
the problems and the dangers inherent in Castalian life.
No doubt the majority of our fellow citizens thought-

lessly or smugly refuse to see these dangers; but he in his forthright courage could not take such a course. And presumably he could never follow the practice of most of his associates in authority, who were cognizant of these dangers but as a matter of principle treated them as nonexistent. He recognized their existence, and his familiarity with the early history of Castalia led him to regard life in the midst of such dangers as a struggle, and one which he affirmed. He loved these very perils, whereas most Castalians considered their community, and the lives they led within it, as a pure idyll. From Father Jacobus's works on the Benedictine Order he had also absorbed the concept of an order as a militant community, and of piety as a combative attitude. "No noble and exalted life exists," he once said, "without knowledge of devils and demons, and without continual struggle against them."

In our Province explicit friendships among the holders of high office are most rare. We need therefore not be surprised that during his first years in office Knecht entered into no such ties with any of his colleagues. He cordially liked the classical philologist in Keuperheim, and felt profound esteem for the directors of the Order; but in these relationships personal affection is almost entirely excluded, private concerns objectified, so that intimacies beyond the joint work on an official level are scarcely possible. Nevertheless, one such friendship did develop.

The secret archives of the Board of Educators are not at our disposal. What we know about Knecht's demeanor at sessions of the Board, or how he voted, must therefore be deduced from his occasional remarks to friends. During his early days in office he tended to keep silent at such meetings, but although later on he spoke up, he seems to have done so only rarely, unless he himself had launched a motion. Mention is made of how quickly he learned the tone traditional at the summit of our hierarchy, and the gracefulness, ingenuity, and wit with which he used these forms. As is well known, the heads of our hierarchy, the Masters and directors of the Order, treat each other in a carefully sustained ceremonial style. Moreover, it has been their custom, or inclination, or secret ruling—since when, we cannot say—to employ more and more carefully polished and strict courtesies, the greater their differences of opinion and the larger the controversial question under discussion. Presumably this formality handed down from the past serves, along with any other functions it may have, primarily as a safety valve. The extremely courteous tone of the debates protects the persons engaged from yielding to passion and helps them preserve impeccable bearing; but in addition it upholds the dignity of the Order and of the high authorities themselves. It drapes them in the robes of ceremonial and conceals them behind veils of sanctity. Such no doubt is the rationale of this elaborate art of exchanging compliments, which the students often make fun of. Before Knecht's time his predecessor, Magister Thomas von der Trave, had been a particularly admired master of this art. Knecht cannot really be called his successor in it, still less his imitator; rather, he was more a disciple of the Chinese, so that his mode of courtesy was less pointed and peppered with irony. But he too was considered among his colleagues unsurpassed in the art of courtesy.

NINE

A CONVERSATION

WE HAVE COME to that point in our study when we must focus our attention entirely upon the remarkable change of course which occupied the last years of the Master's life and led to his bidding farewell to his office and the Province, his crossing into a different sphere of life, and his death. Although he administered his office with exemplary faithfulness up to the moment of his departure, and to his last day enjoyed the affectionate confidence of his pupils and colleagues, we shall not continue our description of his conduct of the office now that we see him already weary of it in his innermost soul, and turning toward other aims. He had already explored all the possibilities the office provided for the utilization of his energies and had reached the point at which great men must leave the path of tradition and obedient subordination and, trusting to supreme, indefinable powers, strike out on new, trackless courses where experience is no guide.

When he became conscious that this had happened, he dispassionately examined his situation and what might be done to change it. He had arrived, at an unusually early age, upon that summit which was all that a tal-

ented and ambitious Castalian could imagine as worth
striving for. Yet neither ambition nor exertion had
brought him there. He had neither tried for his high
honor nor consciously adapted himself to it. It had come
almost against his will, for an inconspicuous, independent scholar's life free of official duties would have been
much more in keeping with his own desires. He did not
especially prize many of the benefits and powers that
followed from his position. In fact, within a short time
after he assumed office, he seemed already to have tired
of some of these distinctions and privileges. In particular,
he always regarded political and administrative work in
the highest Board as a burden, although he gave himself
to it with unfailing conscientiousness. Even the special,
the characteristic and unique task of his position, the
training of an elite group of perfected Glass Bead Game
players, for all the joy it sometimes brought him, and
despite the fact that this elite took great pride in their
Magister, seems in the long run to have been more of a
burden than a pleasure to him. What delighted him and
truly satisfied him was teaching, and in this he discovered by experience that both his pleasure and his success were the greater, the younger his pupils were. Hence
he felt it as a loss that his post brought to him only youths
and adults instead of children.

There were, however, other considerations, experiences,
and insights which caused him to take a critical view of
his own work, and of a good many of the conditions in
Waldzell; or at the least to consider his office as a great
hindrance to the development of his finest and most
fruitful abilities. Some of these matters are known to all
of us; some we only surmise. Was Magister Knecht right
in seeking freedom from the burden of his office, in his
desire for less majestic but more intensive work? Was he
right in his criticisms of the state of Castalia? Should he
be regarded as a pioneer and bold militant, or as a kind
of rebel, if not a deserter from the cause? We shall not go
into these questions, for they have been discussed to excess. For a time the controversy over them divided the
entire Province into two camps, and it has still not entirely subsided. Although we profess ourselves grateful
admirers of the great Magister, we prefer not to take a

position in this dispute; the necessary synthesis which will ultimately emerge from the conflict of opinions on Joseph Knecht's personality and life has long since begun taking shape. We prefer neither to judge nor to convert, but rather to tell the history of our venerated Master's last days with the greatest possible truthfulness. Properly speaking, however, it is not really history; we prefer to call it a legend, an account compounded of authentic information and mere rumors, exactly as they have flowed from various crystalline and cloudy sources to form a single stream among us, his posterity in the Province.

Joseph Knecht had already begun thinking of how he might find his way into fresher air when he unexpectedly came upon a figure out of his youth, whom he had in the meanwhile half forgotten. It was none other than Plinio Designori, scion of the old family that had served Castalia well in the distant past. The former guest pupil, now a man of influence, member of the Chamber of Deputies as well as a political writer, was paying an official call on the Supreme Board of the Province. Every few years elections were held for the government commission in charge of the Castalian budget, and Designori had become a member of this commission. The first time he appeared in this capacity at a session of the directorate of the Order in Hirsland, the Magister Ludi happened to be present. The encounter made a profound impression on him, and was to have certain consequences.

Some of our information about this meeting comes from Tegularius, some from Designori himself. For during this period in Knecht's life, which is somewhat obscure to us, Designori became his friend again, and even his confidant.

At their first meeting after decades, the Speaker as usual introduced the new members of the budget commission to the Magisters. When Knecht heard Designori's name, he felt somewhat stricken at not having immediately recognized the friend of his youth. But he was quick to rectify this by omitting the official bow and the set formula of greeting, and smilingly holding out his hand. Meanwhile he searched his friend's features, trying to fathom the changes which had foiled recognition. During the session itself his glance frequently rested on the once-familiar face. Designori, incidentally, had addressed him by his title of Magister; Joseph had to ask him twice before he could be persuaded to return to the first-name basis of their boyhood.

Knecht had known Plinio as a high-spirited, communicative, and brilliant young man, a good student and at the same time a young man of the world who felt superior to the unworldly Castalians and often baited them for the fun of it. Perhaps he had been somewhat vain, but he had also been openhearted, without pettiness, and had charmed, interested, and attracted his schoolmates. Some of them, in fact, had been dazzled by his good looks, his self-assurance, and the aura of foreignness that surrounded him, the hospitant from the outside world. Years later, toward the end of his student days, Knecht had seen him again, and had been disappointed; Plinio had then seemed to him shallower, coarsened, wholly lacking his former magic. They had parted coolly, with constraint.

Now Plinio once more seemed a totally different person. Above all he seemed to have wholly laid aside or lost his youthful gaiety, his delight in communication, argument, talk, his active, winning, extroverted character. His diffidence on meeting his former friend, his slowness to greet Knecht, and his qualms at taking up the Magister's request to address him with their oldtime intimacy, were signs of a change evident also in his bearing, his look, his manner of speech and movements. In place of his former boldness, frankness, and exuberance there was now constraint. He was subdued, reticent, withdrawn; perhaps it was stiffness, perhaps only fatigue. His youthful charm had been submerged and extinguished in it, but the traits of superficiality and blatant worldliness had also vanished. The whole man, but especially his face, seemed marked, partly ravaged, partly ennobled by the expression of suffering.

While the Glass Bead Game Master followed the proceedings, he dwelt with part of his mind on this change, wondering what kind of suffering had overwhelmed this lively, handsome, life-loving man, and set such a mark on him. It seemed to Knecht an alien suffering, of a kind he had never known, and the more he pondered and probed, the more he felt sympathetically drawn to this suffering man. Mingled with this sympathy and affection was a faint feeling as if he were somehow to blame for his friend's sorrow, as if he must in some way make amends.

After considering and rejecting a variety of suppositions about Plinio's sadness, it occurred to him that the suffering in the man's face was most uncommon. It was, rather, a noble, perhaps a tragic suffering, and its mode of expression was also of a type unknown in Castalia. Knecht recalled having sometimes seen a similar expression on the faces of people who lived in the world, although he had never seen it in so pronounced and fascinating a form. He realized that he knew it also from portraits of men of the past, portraits of scholars or artists in which a touching, half morbid, half fated sorrow, solitariness, and helplessness could be read. To the Magister, with his artist's fine sensitivity to the secrets of expressions and his educator's perception of the various shades of character, there were certain physiognomic signs which he instinctively went by, without ever having reduced them to a system. So, for example, he could recognize a peculiarly Castalian and a peculiarly worldly way of laughing, smiling, showing merriment, and likewise a peculiarly worldly type of suffering or sadness. He now detected this worldly sadness in Designori's face, expressed there with the greatest purity and intensity, as though this face were meant to be representative of many, to epitomize the secret sufferings and morbidity of a multitude.

He was disturbed and moved by this face. It seemed to him highly significant that the world should have sent his lost friend here, so that Plinio and Joseph might truly and validly represent respectively the world and the Order, just as they had once done in their schoolboy debates. But it struck him as even more important and symbolic that in this lonely countenance, overlaid by sorrow, the world had dispatched to Castalia not its laughter, its joy in living, its pleasure in power, its crudeness, but rather its distress, its suffering. That Designori seemed rather to avoid than to seek him, that he responded so slowly and with such resistance, gave Knecht much food for thought. It also pleased him, for he had no doubt that he would nonetheless be able to win Plinio over. To be sure, his former schoolmate, thanks to his education in Castalia, was not one of those unyielding, sulky, or downright hostile commission members, such as Knecht had dealt with more than once. On the contrary, he was an admirer of the Order and a patron of the Province, which was indebted to him for many a service in the past. He had, however, given up the Glass Bead Game many years before.

We are in no position to report in detail how the Magister gradually regained his friend's trust. Those of us who are familiar with the Master's serenity and affectionate courtesy may imagine the process in our own way. Knecht steadily continued to court Plinio, and who in the long run could have resisted the Magister when he was seriously concerned to win someone's heart?

In the end, several months after that first reunion, Designori accepted the repeated invitation to visit Waldzell. One windy, slightly overcast autumn afternoon, the two men drove through a countryside constantly alternating between light and shade toward the site of their schooldays and early friendship. Knecht was in a blithe frame of mind, while his guest was silent but moody, undergoing abrupt alternations, like the harvested fields between sunlight and shadow, between the joys of return and the sadness of alienation. Near the village, they alighted and tramped on foot along the old paths which they had walked together as schoolboys, remembering schoolmates and teachers and some of their topics of discussion in those long-ago days. Designori stayed a day as Knecht's guest, looking on at all of his official acts and labors, as had been agreed. At the end of the day— the guest was due to leave early next morning—they sat together in Knecht's living room, already on the verge of their old intimacy. The course of the day, during which he had been able to observe the Magister's work hour by hour, had made a great impression upon Designori. That evening the two men had a conversation which Designori recorded immediately after his return home. Although it incorporates a few unimportant matters which some readers may feel disturb the even flow of our account, we think it advisable to set down the complete text.

"I had in mind to show you so many things," the Magister said, "and now I did not get to them after all. For example, my lovely garden—do you still recall the Magister's Garden and Master Thomas's plantings? Yes, and so many other things. I hope there will be future occasions for seeing them. But in any case, you have had the chance to check on a good many of your recollections, and you also have some idea of the nature of my official duties and my routine."

"I am grateful to you for that," Plinio said. "Only today have I begun to divine again what your Province really is, and what remarkable secrets it contains, although over the years I have thought about all of you here far more than you suspect. You have afforded me a glimpse of your office and of your life, Joseph, and I hope this will not be the last time and that we shall have many opportunities to discuss the things I have seen here, which I cannot yet talk about today. On the other hand, I am well aware that I should in some way be requiting your cordiality, and that my reserve must have taken you aback. However, you will visit me too some day, and see my native ground. For the present I can only tell you a little, just enough for you to know something about my situation. Speaking frankly, though it will be embarrassing and something of a penance for me, will probably unburden my heart.

"You know that I come from an old family that has served the country well and also been well disposed toward your Province—a conservative family of landowners and moderately high officials. But you see, even this simple fact brings me sharply up against the gulf that separates the two of us. I say 'family' and imagine I am saying something simple, obvious, and unambiguous. But is it? You people of the Province have your Order and your hierarchy, but you do not have a family, you do not know what family, blood, and descent are, and you have no notion of the powers, the hidden and mighty magic of what is called 'family.' I fear that this is also true for most of the words and concepts which express the meaning of our lives. The things that are important to us are not to you; very many are simply incomprehensible to you, and others have entirely different mean-

ings among you and among us. How can we possibly talk
to each other? You see, when you speak to me, it is as
if a foreigner were addressing me, although a foreigner
whose language I learned and spoke myself in my youth,
so that I understand most of what is said. But the reverse is not the case; when I speak to you, you hear a
language whose very phrases are only half familiar to you,
while you are entirely ignorant of the nuances and overtones. You hear tales about a life, a way of existing, which
is not your own. Most of it, even if it happens to interest
you, remains alien and at best only half understood. You
remember our many debates and talks during our schooldays. On my part they were nothing but an attempt, one
of many, to bring the world and language of your Province into harmony with my own. You were the most
receptive, the most willing and honest among all those
with whom I attempted to communicate in those days;
you stood up bravely for the rights of Castalia without
being against my different world and unsympathetic to
its rights, not to speak of despising it. In those days we
certainly came rather close to each other. But that is a
subject we will return to later."

As he paused to marshal his thoughts, Knecht said cautiously: "This matter of not being able to understand
may not be as drastic as you make it out. Of course two
peoples and two languages will never be able to communicate with each other so intimately as two individuals
who belong to the same nation and speak the same language. But that is no reason to forgo the effort at communication. Within nations there are also barriers which
stand in the way of complete communication and complete mutual understanding, barriers of culture, education, talent, individuality. It might be asserted that every
human being on earth can fundamentally hold a dialogue
with every other human being, and it might also be asserted that there are no two persons in the world between whom genuine, whole, intimate understanding is
possible—the one statement is as true as the other. It is
Yin and Yang, day and night; both are right and at times
we have to be reminded of both. To be sure, I too do not
believe that you and I will ever be able to communicate
fully, and without some residue of misunderstanding,

with each other. But though you may be an Occidental and I a Chinese, though we may speak different languages, if we are men of good will we shall have a great deal to say to each other, and beyond what is precisely communicable we can guess and sense a great deal about each other. At any rate let us try."

Designori nodded and continued: "For the time being I want to tell you the little you must know in order to have some inkling of my situation. Well, then, first of all, the family is the supreme power in a young person's life, whether or not he acknowledges it. I got on well with my family as long as I was a guest student in your elite school. Throughout the year I was well taken care of among you; during the holidays I was pampered at home, for I was the only son. I had a deep and in fact a passionate love for my mother; separation from her was the only grief I felt each time I departed. My relationship to my father was cooler, but friendly, at least during all the years of my boyhood and youth that I spent among you. He was an old admirer of Castalia and proud to see me being educated in the elite schools and initiated into such elevated matters as the Glass Bead Game. My vacations at home were gay and festive; I might almost say that the family and I in a sense knew each other only in party dress. Sometimes, when I set out for vacation, I pitied all of you who were left behind for having nothing of such happiness.

"I need not say much about those days; you knew me better than anyone else, after all. I was almost a Castalian, a little gayer, coarser, and more superficial, perhaps, but happy and enthusiastic, full of high spirits. That was the happiest period in my life, although of course at the time I never suspected that this would be so, for during those years in Waldzell I expected that happiness and the crowning experiences of my life would come after I returned home from your schools and used the superiority I had acquired in them to conquer the outside world. Instead, after my departure from you a conflict began which has lasted to this day, and I have not been the victor in this struggle. For the place I returned to no longer consisted in just my home; and the country had not been simply waiting to embrace me and acknowledge my Waldzell superiority. Even at home I soon encountered disappointments, difficulties, and discords. It took a while before I noticed. I was shielded by my naive confidence, my boyish faith in myself, and my happiness, and shielded also by the morality of the Order which I had brought back with me, by the habit of meditation.

"But what a disappointment and disillusionment I had at the university where I wanted to study political subjects. The general tone among the students, the level of their education and social life, the personalities of so many of the teachers—how all this contrasted with what I had become accustomed to among you. You recall how in defending our world against yours I used to extol the unspoiled, naive life? If that was a piece of foolishness deserving punishment, my friend, I have been harshly punished. Because this naive, innocent, instinctual life, this childlike, untrammeled brilliance of the simple soul, may possibly exist among peasants or artisans, or somewhere, but I never succeeded in finding it, let alone sharing in it. You remember too, don't you, how I would speechify about the arrogance and affectation of Castalians, attacking them for being a conceited and decadent lot with their caste spirit and their elite haughtiness. Now I had to discover that people in the world were no less proud of their bad manners, their meager culture, their coarse, loud humor, the dull-witted shrewdness with which they kept themselves to practical, egotistic goals. They regarded themselves as no less precious, sanctified, and elect in their narrow-minded crudity than the most affected Waldzell show-off could ever have done. They laughed at me or patted me on the back, but a good many of them reacted to the alien, Castalian qualities in me with the outright enmity that the vulgar always have for everything finer. And I was determined to take their dislike as a distinction."

Designori paused briefly, and threw a glance at Knecht to see whether he was tiring him. His eyes met his friend's and found in them an expression of close attention and friendliness which comforted and reassured him. He saw that Knecht was totally absorbed; he was listening not as people listen to casual talk or even to an interesting story, but with fixed attention and devotion, as if concentrating on a subject of meditation. At the same time Knecht's eyes expressed a pure, warmhearted good will—so warm that it seemed to Plinio almost childlike. He was swept with a kind of amazement to see such an expression upon the face of the same man whose many-sided daily labors, whose wisdom and authority in the governance of his office he had admired all through the day. Relieved, he continued:

"I don't know whether my life has been useless and merely a misunderstanding, or whether it has a meaning. If it does have a meaning, I should say it would be this: that one single specific person in our time has recognized plainly and experienced in the most painful way how far Castalia has moved away from its motherland. Or for my part it might be put the other way around: how alien our country has become from her noblest Province and how unfaithful to that Province's spirit; how far body and soul, ideal and reality have moved apart in our country; how little they know about each other, or want to know. If I had any one task and ideal in life, it was to make myself a synthesis of the two principles, to be mediator, interpreter, and arbitrator between the two. I have tried and failed. And since after all I cannot tell you my whole life, and you would not be able to understand it all anyhow, I will describe only one of the situations in which my failure was revealed.

"The difficulty after I began attending the university consisted not so much in my being unable to deal with the teasing or hostility that came my way as a Castalian, a show-off. Those few among my new associates who regarded my coming from the elite schools as a glory gave me more trouble, in fact, and caused me greater embarrassment. No, the hard part, perhaps the impossible task I set myself, was to continue a life in the Castalian sense in the midst of worldliness. At first I scarcely noticed; I abided by the rules I had learned among you, and for some time they seemed to prove their validity in the world. They seemed to strengthen and shield me, seemed to preserve my gaiety and inner soundness and to increase my resolve to pass my student years in the Castalian way as far as possible, following the paths that my

craving for knowledge indicated and not letting anything coerce me into a course of studies designed to prepare the student as thoroughly as possible in the short-
est possible time for a speciality in which he could earn
his livelihood, and to stamp out whatever sense of freedom and universality he may have had.

"But the protection that Castalia had given me proved
dangerous and dubious, for I did not want to be like a
hermit, cultivating my peace of soul and preserving a
calm, meditative state of mind. I wanted to conquer the
world, you see, to understand it, to force it to understand
me. I wanted to affirm it and if possible renew and reform it. In my own person I wanted to bring Castalia
and the world together, to reconcile them. When after
some disappointment, some clash or disturbance, I retired to meditate, I derived great benefit at first; each
time, meditation was like relaxation, deep breathing, a
return to good, friendly powers. But in time I realized
that this very practice of meditation, the cultivation and
exercising of the psyche, was what isolated me, made me
seem so unpleasantly strange to others, and actually rendered me incapable of really understanding them. I saw
that I could really understand those others, those people in the world and of it, if I once again became like
them, if I had no advantages over them, including this
recourse to meditation.

"Of course it may be that I am putting it in a better
light when I describe it in this way. Perhaps it was simply
that without associates trained to the same practices, without supervision by teachers, without the bracing atmosphere of Waldzell, I gradually lost the discipline, that I
grew sluggish and inattentive and succumbed to carelessness, and that in moments of guilty conscience I then excused myself on the ground that carelessness was one of
the attributes of this world, and that by giving way to it
I was coming closer to an understanding of my environment. I'm not trying to make things out better than they
are for your sake, but neither do I want to deny or conceal the fact that I went to considerable lengths, that I
strove and fought, even where I was mistaken. I was
serious about the whole problem. But whether or not my
attempt to find a meaningful place for myself was mere

conceit on my part—in any case, it ended as it was bound to end. The world was stronger than I was; it slowly overwhelmed and devoured me. It was exactly as if life took me at my word and molded me wholly to the world whose rightness, naive strength, and ontological superiority I so highly praised and defended against your logic in our Waldzell disputations. You remember.

"And now I must remind you of something else which you probably forgot long ago, since it meant nothing to you. But it meant a great deal to me; it was important, important and terrible. My student years had come to an end; I had adapted, had been defeated, but not entirely. Inwardly I still thought of myself as your equal and imagined that I had made certain adjustments, shed certain customs, more out of prudence and free choice than as the consequence of defeat. And so I also clung to a good many of the habits and needs of my earlier years. Among them was the Glass Bead Game, which probably had little point, since without constant practice and constant association with equal and especially with better players, it's impossible to learn anything, of course. Playing alone can at best replace such practice the way talking to oneself replaces real, serious dialogue. So without really understanding how I stood, what had happened to my player's skill, my culture, my status as an elite pupil, I struggled to save at least some of these values. In those days, whenever I sketched a Game pattern or analyzed a Game movement for one of my friends who knew something about the Game but had no notion of its spirit, it probably seemed akin to magic to these total ignoramuses. Then, in my third or fourth year at the university, I took part in a Game course in Waldzell. Seeing the countryside and the town again, visiting our old school and the Players' Village, gave me melancholy pleasure; but you were not here; you were studying somewhere in Monteport or Keuperheim at the time, and were considered an ambitious eccentric. My Game course was only a series of summer classes for pitiable worldlings and dilettantes like myself. Nevertheless, I worked hard at it and was proud at the end of the course to receive the usual C, that passing mark which qualifies the holder for future vacation courses of the same sort.

"Well, then, a few years later I once again summoned up the energy and signed up for a vacation course under your predecessor. I tried to prepare myself for Waldzell. I read through my old exercise books, made some stabs at the technique of concentration—in short, within my modest limits I composed myself, gathered my energies, and put myself in the mood for the course rather the way a real Glass Bead Game player readies himself for the great annual Game. And so I arrived in Waldzell, where after this longer interval I found myself a good deal more alienated, but at the same time enchanted, as if I were returning to a lovely land I had lost, in whose language I was no longer very fluent. And this time my fervent wish to see you again was granted. Do you by any chance recall, Joseph?"

Knecht looked earnestly into his eyes, nodded and smiled slightly, but said not a word.

"Good," Designori continued. "So you remember. But just what do you remember? A casual reunion with a schoolmate, a brief encounter and disappointment, after which one goes on and thinks no more about it, unless the other fellow tactlessly reminds one about it decades later. Isn't that it? Was it anything else, was it more than that for you?"

Although he was obviously trying very hard to hold himself in check, it was apparent that emotions accumulated over many years, and never mastered, were on the brink of eruption.

"You are anticipating," Knecht said carefully. "We will speak of my impressions when it is my turn to render an accounting. You have the floor now, Plinio. I see that the meeting was not pleasant for you. It was not for me either, at the time. And now go on and tell me what it was like. Speak bluntly."

"I'll try," Plinio said. "I certainly don't want to blame you for anything. I must concede that you behaved with absolute courtesy toward me—more than that. When I accepted your invitation to come here to Waldzell, where I have not been since that second course, not even since my appointment to the Castalian Commission, I made up my mind to confront you with what I experienced at that time, whether or not this visit turned out pleasantly. And now I mean to continue. I had come to the course and been put up in the guest house. The people in the course were almost all about my age; some were even a good deal older. There were at most twenty of us, the majority Castalians, but either poor, indifferent, or slack Glass Bead Game players, or rank beginners who had tardily decided that they ought to obtain some familiarity with the Game. It was a relief to me that I knew none of them. Although our instructor, one of the Archive assistants, really tried hard and was most friendly toward us, the whole thing had from the start the feeling of being a half-baked, useless affair, a make-up course whose random collection of students no more believes in its importance or chance of success than does the teacher, although no one involved will admit it. Why, you might have wondered, should this handful of people get together to engage in something they had no capacity for nor enough interest in to go at it with perseverance and devotion, and why should a skilled specialist bother to give them instruction and assign them exercises which he himself scarcely thought would come to anything? At the time I didn't know—I found out from more experienced persons later on—that I simply had bad luck with this course, that another group of participants might have made it stimulating and useful, even inspiring. It often suffices, I was later told, to have two members of the class who kindle each other, or who already know each other and are good friends, to give the whole course, for all the participants and the teacher as well, the necessary impetus. But you are the Game Master, after all; you must know all about such matters.

"Well, then, I had rotten luck. The animating spark was missing from our haphazard group; there was no impetus, not even a little warmth. The whole thing remained a feeble extension course for grown-up schoolboys. The days passed, and my disappointment increased with each passing day. Still, besides the Glass Bead Game there was Waldzell, a place of sacred and cherished memories for me. If the Game course were a failure, I still ought to be able to celebrate a homecoming, to chat with former schoolmates, perhaps have a reunion with the friend who more than anyone else represented to me our

Castalia—you, Joseph. If I saw a few of the companions of my schooldays again, if on my walks through this beautiful, beloved region I met again the lares and penates of my youth, and if good fortune would have it that we might come close to each other again and a dialogue should spring up between us as in the old days, less between you and me than between my problem with Castalia and myself—then this vacation would not be wasted; then it would not so much matter about the course and all the rest.

"The first two old schoolfellows who crossed my path were innocuous enough. They were glad to see me, patted me on the back and asked childish questions about my legendary life out in the world. But the next few were not so innocuous; they were members of the Players' Village and the younger elite and did not ask naive questions. On the contrary, when we ran into one another in one of the rooms of your sanctuaries and they could not very well avoid me, they greeted me with a pointed and rather tense politeness, or rather a condescending geniality. They made it clear that they were busy with important matters quite closed to me, that they had no time, no curiosity, no sympathy, no desire to renew old acquaintance. Well, I did not force myself on them; I let them alone in their Olympian, sardonic, Castalian tranquility. I looked across at them and their busy, self-satisfied doings like a prisoner watching through bars, or the way the poor, hungry, and oppressed eye the wealthy and aristocratic, the handsome, cultivated, untroubled, well-bred, well-rested members of an upper class with their clean faces and manicured hands.

"And then you turned up, Joseph, and when I saw you I felt rejoicing and new hope. You were crossing the yard; I recognized you from behind by your walk and at once called you by name. At last a human soul, I thought; at last a friend, or perhaps an opponent, but someone I can talk to, a Castalian to the bone, certainly, but someone in whom the Castalian spirit has not frozen into a mask and a suit of armor. A man, someone who understands. You must have noticed how glad I was and how much I expected from you, and in fact you met me halfway with the greatest courtesy. You still recognized me,

I meant something to you, it gave you pleasure to see my face again. And so we did not leave it at that brief warm greeting in the yard; you invited me and devoted, or rather sacrificed, an evening to me. But what an evening that was! The two of us tormented ourselves trying to seem jocose, civil, and comradely toward each other, and how hard it was for us to drag that lame conversation from one subject to another. Where the others had been indifferent to me, with you it was worse—this strained and profitless effort to revive a lost friendship was much more painful. That evening finally put an end to my illusions. It made me realize with unsparing clarity that I was not one of your comrades, not seeking the same goals, not a Castalian, not a person of importance, but a nuisance, a fool trying to ingratiate himself, an uncultivated foreigner. And the fact that all this was conveyed to me with such politeness and good manners, that the disappointment and impatience were so impeccably masked, actually seemed to me the worst of it. If you had upbraided me: 'What has become of you, my friend, how could you let yourself degenerate this way?' the ice would have been broken and I would have been happy. But nothing of the sort. I saw that my notion of belonging to Castalia had come to nothing, that my love for all of you and my studying the Glass Bead Game and our comradeship were all nothing. Elite Tutor Knecht had taken note of my unfortunate visit to Waldzell; for my sake he had put himself through a whole evening of boredom, and shown me the door with undeviating courtesy."

Designori, struggling with his agitation, broke off and with a tormented expression looked across at the Magister. Knecht sat there, all attention, absorbedly listening, but not in the least upset; he sat looking at his old friend with a smile that was full of friendly sympathy. Since Designori did not continue, Knecht rested his eyes on him, with a look of good will and satisfaction, in fact with a touch of amusement. For a minute or longer Plinio bleakly met that gaze. Then he cried out forcefully, although not angrily: "You're laughing! Laughing? You think it was all fine?"

"I must admit," Knecht said smilingly, "that you have described that episode remarkably well, splendidly. That is exactly how it was, and perhaps the lingering sense of insult and accusation in your voice was needed for you to bring it out as effectively as you did and to recall the scene to my mind with such perfect vividness. Also, although I'm afraid you still see the whole affair in somewhat the same light as you did then, and have not fully come to terms with it, you told your story with objective correctness—the story of two young men in a rather embarrassing situation in which both had to dissemble, and one of whom—that is, you—made the mistake of concealing the painfulness of the whole matter behind a gay exterior, instead of dropping the masquerade. It seems as if you were to this day blaming me more than yourself for the fruitlessness of that encounter, although it was absolutely up to you to have set its terms. Have you really failed to see that? But still you have described it very well, I must say. You've called back the whole sense of oppression and embarrassment over that weird evening. For a while I've felt as if I had to fight for composure again, and I've been ashamed for the two of us. No, your story is exactly right. It's a pleasure to hear a story so well told."

"Well now," Plinio began, rather astonished, and with an offended and mistrustful note lingering in his voice, "it's good that my story has amused at least one of us. If you want to know, it didn't amuse me."

"But you do see," Knecht said, "how merrily we can now regard this story, which isn't exactly to the credit of either of us? We can laugh at it."

"Laugh? Why should we?"

"Because this story about the ex-Castalian Plinio who struggled to master the Glass Bead Game and worked so hard for his former friend's appreciation is now past and over with for good, exactly like the story of the tutor Knecht who in spite of all his training in Castalian manners was a total duffer when it came to dealing with this Plinio who suddenly blew in on him, so that today after so many years that clumsy behavior can be held up to him as in a mirror. Once again, Plinio, you have an excellent memory and you've told the story well—I couldn't have done it justice. It's fortunate that the tale is over and done with and we can laugh at it."

Designori was perplexed. He could not help feeling the warmth and pleasantness of the Magister's good humor. It was obviously far removed from mockery. And he felt also that an intense seriousness lay behind this gaiety. But in telling his story he had too painfully relived the bitterness of that episode, and his narrative had been so much in the nature of a confession that he could not change key so readily.

"Perhaps you forget," he said hesitantly, already half persuaded, "that what I related was not the same for me as it was for you. For you it was at most chagrin; for me it was defeat and collapse, and incidentally also the beginning of important changes in my life. When I left Waldzell that time, just as soon as the course ended, I resolved never to return here, and I was close to hating Castalia and all of you. I had lost my illusions and had realized that I would never again belong among you, perhaps had never belonged as much as I had imagined. It would not have taken much more to make me into a renegade and an outright enemy of everything Castalian."

Knecht fixed him with a look at once cheerful and penetrating.

"Certainly," he said, "and of course you're going to tell me all about that soon, I very much hope. But for the present I see our relationship as this: In our early youth we were friends, were parted and took very different paths. Then we met again—this at the time of your unlucky holiday course. You'd become half or entirely a person of the world; I was a rather conceited Waldzeller, much preoccupied with Castalian forms; and today we have recalled this disappointing and shaming reunion. We have seen ourselves and our awkwardness at that time and we have been able to laugh at it, because today everything is completely different. I freely admit that the impression you made on me at that time did in fact embarrass me greatly; it was an altogether unpleasant, negative impression. I could make nothing of you; to me you unexpectedly, disturbingly, and annoyingly seemed unfinished, coarse, worldly. I was a young Castalian who knew nothing of the world and actually wanted to know nothing of it. And you, well, you were a young foreigner whose reason for visiting us I could not rightly understand. I had no idea why you were taking a Game course, for you seemed to have almost nothing of the elite pupil left in you. You grated on my nerves as I did on yours. Of course I could not help striking you as an arrogant Waldzeller without any basis for his arrogance who was bent on keeping his distance from a non-Castalian and amateur at the Game. And to me you were a kind of barbarian, semicultured, who seemed to be making bothersome and groundless claims upon my interest and my friendship. We fended each other off; we came close to hating each other. There was nothing we could do but part, because neither of us had anything to give the other and neither of us could be fair to the other.

"But today, Plinio, we have been able to revive that shamefully buried memory and we may laugh at that scene and at the pair of us, because today we have come together as different men and with quite different intentions and potentialities—without sentimentality, without repressed feelings of jealousy and hatred, without conceit. Both of us grew up long ago; both of us are men now."

Designori smiled with relief. But still he asked: "Are we so sure of that? After all, we had good will enough even then."

"I should think we had," Knecht said, laughing. "And with all our good will we drove and strained ourselves until we couldn't bear it any longer. At that time we disliked each other instinctively. To each of us the other was unfamiliar, disturbing, alien, and repugnant, and only an imaginary sense of obligation, of belonging together, forced us to play out that tedious farce for a whole evening. I realized that soon after your visit. Neither of us had properly outgrown either our former friendship or our former opposition. Instead of letting that relationship die we thought we had to exhume it and somehow continue it. We felt indebted to it and had no idea how to pay the debt. Isn't that so?"

"I think," Plinio said thoughtfully, "that even today you are still being somewhat overpolite. You say 'we both,' but in fact it was not the two of us who were seeking and unable to find each other. The seeking, the love, was all on my side, and so the disappointment and suffering also. And now I ask you: What has changed in your life since that meeting? Nothing. In my case, on the other hand, it was a deep and painful dividing line, and I cannot accept your laughing way of dismissing it."

"Forgive me," Knecht amiably apologized. "I have probably rushed matters. But I hope that in time you too will be able to laugh at that incident. Of course you were wounded then, though not by me, as you thought and still seem to think. You were wounded by the gulf between yourself and Castalia, by the chasm between your world and mine which we seemed to have bridged in the course of our schoolboy friendship but which suddenly yawned before us so fearfully wide and deep. Insofar as you blame me personally, I beg you to state your accusation frankly."

"Oh, it was never an accusation. But it was a plaint. You didn't hear it at the time, and it seems you don't want to hear it even now. At the time you answered it with a smile and a show of good manners, and you're doing the same thing again."

Although he sensed the friendship and profound good will in the Magister's eyes, he was impelled to stress this point; it was necessary for this burden he had borne for so long to be at last thrown off.

Knecht's expression did not change. After a moment's reflection he said cautiously: "Only now am I beginning to understand you, friend. Perhaps you are right and we must discuss this too. Still, may I remind you that you could legitimately have expected me to enter into what you call your plaint only if you had really expressed it. But the fact was that during that evening's conversation in the guest house you expressed no plaints whatsoever. Instead you put as brisk and brave a face as possible on the whole thing, just as I did. Like me, you acted the fearless warrior who has no grievances. But secretly you expected, as you now tell me, for me to hear the hidden plaint somehow and to recognize your true face behind your mask. Well, I fancy I did notice something of the sort at the time, though far from everything. But how was I to suggest to you that I was worried about you, that I pitied you, without offending your pride? And what would have been the good of my extending my hand, since my hand was empty and I had nothing to give you, no advice, no comfort, no friendship, because our ways had parted so completely? As a matter of fact, at the time the hidden uneasiness and unhappiness that you concealed behind a brash manner annoyed me; to be frank, I found it repugnant. It contained a claim on my sympathy which was contradicted by your manner. I felt there was something importunate and childish about it, and it made my feelings chill toward you all the more. You were making claims on my comradeship. You wanted to be a Castalian, a Glass Bead Game player; and at the same time you seemed so uncontrolled, so odd, so lost in egotistic emotions. That was the tenor of my opinion at the time, for I could see clearly that virtually nothing was left of the Castalian spirit in you. You had apparently forgotten even the elementary rules. Very well, that wasn't my affair. But then why were you coming to Waldzell and wanting to hail us as your fellows? As I've said, I found that annoying and repugnant, and at the time you were absolutely right if you interpreted my assiduous politeness as rejection. I did instinctively reject you, and not because you were a worldly person, but because you were asserting a claim to be regarded as a Castalian. But when you recently reappeared after so many years, there was no longer any trace of that. You looked worldly and talked like a man from outside. I noticed the difference especially in the expression of sadness, grief or unhappiness on your face. But I liked everything about you, your bearing, your words, even your sadness. They were beautiful, suited you, worthy of you. None of that bothered me; I could accept you and affirm it all without the slightest inner resistance. This time no excessive politeness and good manners were necessary, and so I promptly met you as a friend and tried to show you my affection and concern. But this time the situation was reversed; this time it was I who tried to win you while you held back. My only encouragement was that I tacitly understood your appearance in our Province and your interest in our affairs as a sign of attachment and loyalty. So then, finally you responded to my wooing, and we have now come to the point of opening our hearts to each other and in this way, I hope, being able to renew our old friendship.

"You were just saying that our meeting at that time was painful for you, but insignificant for me. We won't argue about that; you might be right. But our present meeting, *amice*, is by no means insignificant for me. It means a great deal more to me than I can possibly tell you, more than you can possibly guess. Just to give you the briefest of hints, it means more to me than the return of a lost friend and the resurrection of times past with new force and in a new light. Above all it represents to me a kind of call, an approach toward me from outside. It opens a way for me into your world; it confronts me once more with the old problem of a synthesis between you and us. And this occurs at the right moment. This time the call does not find me deaf; it finds me more alert than I have ever been, because it does not really surprise me. It does not come to me as something alien, something from outside which I may or may not respond to, as I please. Rather, it comes out of myself; it is the twin to a very powerful and insistent desire, to a need and a longing within myself. But let us talk of this some other time; it is already late and we both need our rest.

"You spoke of my good cheer and your sadness, and you meant, it seems to me, that I was not being fair to what you call your 'plaint,' and that I have not been fair to it today either, since I respond to this plaint with smiles. There is something here I don't quite understand. Why should not a complaint be listened to with cheerfulness; why must one wear a doleful face instead of a smile? From the fact that you came to Castalia again, and to me, with your grief and your burden, I think I may conclude that our cheerful serenity means something to you. But if I do not go along with your sadness, do not let myself be infected by it, that does not mean I don't recognize it or take it seriously. I fully recognize and honor your demeanor, which your life in the world has imprinted upon you. It becomes you and belongs to you; it is dear to me and deserves respect, although I hope to see it change. Of course I can only guess at its source; you will tell me or not tell me about it later, as seems right to you. I can see only that you seem to have a hard life. But why do you think I would not or cannot be fair to you and your burdens?"

Designori's face had clouded over once more. "Sometimes," he said resignedly, "it seems to me that we have not only two different languages and ways of expressing ourselves, each of which can only vaguely be translated into the other, but that we are altogether and fundamentally different creatures who can never understand each other. Which of us is really the authentic and integral human being, you or me? Every so often I doubt that either of us is. There were times when I looked up to you members of the Order and Glass Bead Game players with such reverence, such a sense of inferiority, and such envy that you might have been gods or supermen, forever serene, forever playing, forever enjoying your own existences, forever immune to suffering. At other times you seemed to me either pitiable or contemptible, eunuchs, artificially confined to an eternal childhood, childlike and childish in your cool, tightly fenced, neatly tidied playground and kindergarten, where every nose is carefully wiped and every troublesome emotion is soothed, every dangerous thought repressed, where everyone plays nice, safe, bloodless games for a lifetime and every jagged stirring of life, every strong feeling, every genuine passion, every rapture is promptly checked, deflected, and neutralized by meditation therapy. Isn't it an artificial, sterilized, didactically pruned world, a mere sham world in which you cravenly vegetate, a world without vices, without passions, without hunger, without sap and salt, a world without family, without mothers, without children, almost without women? The instinctual life is tamed by meditation. For generations you have left to others dangerous, daring, and responsible things like economics, law, and politics. Cowardly and well-protected, fed by others, and having few burdensome duties, you lead your drones' lives, and so that they won't be too boring you busy yourselves with all these erudite specialties, count syllables and letters, make music, and play the Glass Bead Game, while outside in the filth of the world poor harried people live real lives and do real work."

Knecht had listened to him with unswervingly friendly attentiveness.

"My dear friend," he said deliberately, "how strongly your words remind me of the spirited battles of our school-days. The difference is that today I no longer need play the same part as I did then. My task today is not defense of the Order and the Province against your assaults, and I am very glad that this troublesome task, which over-taxed me at the time, is mine no longer. You see, it's be-come rather difficult to repel the sort of glorious cavalry charge you've once again mounted. You talk, for example, of people out in the rest of the country who 'live real lives and do real work.' That sounds so fine and absolute—practically axiomatic—and if one wanted to oppose it one would have to rudely remind the speaker that his own 'real work' consists partly in sitting on a committee for the betterment of Castalia. But let us leave joking aside for the moment. It is apparent from your words and your tone that your heart is still full of hatred for us, and at the same time full of despairing love toward us, full of envy and longing. To you we are cowards, drones, or children playing in a kindergarten, but at times you have also seen us as godlike in our serenity. From all this, though, I think I may rightly conclude one thing: Castalia is not to blame for your sadness, your unhappiness, or whatever we choose to call it. That must come from else-where. If we Castalians were to blame, your accusations against us would not be just what they were in the dis-cussions of our boyhood. In later conversations you must tell me more, and I don't doubt that we shall find a way to make you happier and more serene, or at least to change your relationship toward Castalia into a freer and more pleasant one. As far as I can see right now, you have a false, constrained, sentimental attitude toward us. You have divided your own soul into a Castalian and worldly part, and you torment yourself excessively about things for which you bear no responsibility. Possibly you also do not take seriously enough other things for which you do bear responsibility. I suspect that it is some time since you have done any meditation exercises. Isn't that so?"

Designori gave an anguished laugh. "How keen you are, *Domine!* Some time, you say? Many, many years have passed since I gave up the magic of meditation. Now you are suddenly so concerned about me! That time you

met me here in Waldzell during the vacation course and
showed me so much courtesy and contempt, and turned
down my plea for comradeship in so polished a manner, I
left here with the firm resolve to put an end to everything
Castalian about me. From then on I gave up the Glass
Bead Game, ceased meditating; even music was spoiled
for me for a considerable time. Instead I found new
friends who gave me instruction in worldly amusements.
We drank and whored; we tried all available narcotics;
we sneered at decency, reverence, idealism. Of course the
thing didn't go on very long at such a crude level, but
long enough to remove completely the last traces of
Castalian veneer. And then, years later, when I occasionally realized that I had gone too far and badly needed
some of the techniques of meditation, I had become too
proud to start again."

"Too proud?" Knecht murmured.

"Yes, too proud. I had meanwhile plunged into the
world and become a man of the world. I wanted nothing
more than to be one with the others; I wanted no other
life than the world's life—its passionate, childlike, crude,
ungoverned life vacillating forever between happiness
and fear. I disdained the idea of procuring a degree of relief and some transcendence over others by employing
your methods."

The Magister gave him a sharp look. "And you endured that, for many years? Didn't you use any other
methods to cope with it all?"

"Oh yes," Plinio confessed. "I did and still do. At times
I go back to drinking, and usually I need all kinds of
sedatives so that I can sleep."

For a second Knecht closed his eyes, as though suddenly weary; then he fixed his gaze upon his friend once
more. Silently, he looked into his face, earnestly probing
at first, but with his own expression gradually growing
gentler, friendlier, serener. Designori has recorded that
he had never before encountered such a look in anyone's
eyes, a look at once so searching and so loving, so innocent and so critical, radiating such kindness and such
omniscience. He admits that this look disturbed him unpleasantly at first, but gradually reassured and overcame

him by its gentle insistence. But he was still trying to
fight back.

"You said that you know ways to make me happier
and more serene. But you don't ask whether that is what
I really want."

"Well," Joseph Knecht said, laughing, "if we can make
a person happier and more serene, we should do it in
any case, whether or not he asks us to. And how could you
not want that and not be seeking it? That's why you are
here, that's why we are once again sitting face to face,
that's why you returned to us, after all. You hate Castalia,
you despise it, you're far too proud of your worldliness
and your sadness to wish to find relief through the use of
reason and meditation. And yet a secret, unquenchable
longing for us and our serenity remained with you all
through these years, luring you to return, to try us once
more. And I must tell you that you have come at the
right moment, when I too have been longing intensely for
a call from your world, for an opening door. But we'll
talk about that next time. You've confided a great deal to
me, friend, and I thank you for it. You will see that I too
have some things to confess to you. It is late, you're leaving tomorrow, and another day of official routines awaits
me. We must go to bed. But please give me another fifteen minutes."

He stood up, went to the window, and looked up at
the starry, crystalline night sky overlaid by the scudding
clouds. Since he did not return to his chair at once, his
guest also stood up and came over to the window beside
him. The Magister stood there, drinking in the cool,
thin air of the autumnal night with rhythmic inhalations.
He pointed toward the sky.

"Look," he said. "This landscape of clouds and sky. At
first glance you might think that the depths are there
where it is darkest; but then you realize that the darkness
and softness are only the clouds and that the depths of
the universe begin only at the fringes and fjords of this
mountain range of clouds—solemn and supreme symbols
of clarity and orderliness. The depths and the mysteries
of the universe lie not where the clouds and blackness
are; the depths are to be found in the spaces of clarity and
serenity. Please, just before going to sleep look up for a

while at these bays and straits again, with all their stars,
and don't reject the ideas or dreams that come to you
from them."

A strange quiver went through Plinio's heart—he
could not tell whether it was of grief or happiness. An
unimaginably long time ago, he recalled, in the lovely,
serene beginnings of his life as a Waldzell student, he
had been summoned in similar words to his first meditation exercises.

"And let me say one word more," the Glass Bead Game
Master resumed, again in his low voice. "I would like to
say something more to you about cheerful serenity, the
serenity of the stars and of the mind, and about our
Castalian kind of serenity also. You are averse to serenity,
presumably because you have had to walk the ways of sadness, and now all brightness and good cheer, especially
our Castalian kind, strikes you as shallow and childish,
and cowardly to boot, a flight from the terrors and abysses
of reality into a clear, well-ordered world of mere forms
and formulas, mere abstractions and refinements. But, my
dear devotee of sadness, even though for some this may
well be a flight, though there may be no lack of cowardly,
timorous Castalians playing with mere formulas, even if
the majority among us were in fact of this sort—all this
would not lessen the value and splendor of genuine serenity, the serenity of the sky and the mind. Granted
there are those among us who are too easily satisfied,
who enjoy a sham serenity; but in contrast to them we
also have men and generations of men whose serenity is
not playful shallowness, but earnest depth. I knew one
such man—I mean our former Music Master, whom you
used to see in Waldzell now and then. In the last years of
his life this man possessed the virtue of serenity to such a
degree that it radiated from him like the light from a
star; so much that it was transmitted to all in the form
of benevolence, enjoyment of life, good humor, trust, and
confidence. It continued to radiate outward from all who
received it, all who had absorbed its brightness. His light
shone upon me also; he transmitted to me a little of his
radiance, a little of the brightness in his heart, and to our
friend Ferromonte as well, and a good many others. To
achieve this cheerful serenity is to me, and to many others,

the finest and highest of goals. You will also find it among some of the patriarchs in the directorate of the Order. Such cheerfulness is neither frivolity nor complacency; it is supreme insight and love, affirmation of all reality, alertness on the brink of all depths and abysses; it is a virtue of saints and of knights; it is indestructible and only increases with age and nearness to death. It is the secret of beauty and the real substance of all art. The poet who praises the splendors and terrors of life in the dance-measures of his verse, the musician who sounds them in a pure, eternal present—these are bringers of light, increasers of joy and brightness on earth, even if they lead us first through tears and stress. Perhaps the poet whose verses gladden us was a sad solitary, and the musician a melancholic dreamer; but even so their work shares in the cheerful serenity of the gods and the stars. What they give us is no longer their darkness, their suffering or fears, but a drop of pure light, eternal cheerfulness. Even though whole peoples and languages have attempted to fathom the depths of the universe in myths, cosmogonies, and religions, their supreme, their ultimate attainment has been this cheerfulness. You recall the ancient Hindus—our teacher in Waldzell once spoke so beautifully about them. A people of suffering, of brooding, of penance and asceticism; but the great ultimate achievements of their thought were bright and cheerful; the smile of the ascetics and the Buddhas are cheerful; the figures in their profound, enigmatic mythologies are cheerful. The world these myths represent begins divinely, blissfully, radiantly, with a springtime loveliness: the golden age. Then it sickens and degenerates more and more; it grows coarse and subsides into misery; and at the end of four ages, each lower than the others, it is ripe for annihilation. Therefore it is trampled underfoot by a laughing, dancing Siva—but it does not end with that. It begins anew with the smile of dreaming Vishnu whose hands playfully fashion a young, new, beautiful, shining world. It is wonderful—how these Indians, with an insight and capacity for suffering scarcely equalled by any other people, looked with horror and shame upon the cruel game of world history, the eternally revolving wheel of avidity and suffering; they saw and understood the fragility of created being, the avidity and diabolism of man, and at the same time his deep yearning for purity and harmony; and they devised these glorious parables for the beauty and tragedy of the creation: mighty Siva who dances the completed world into ruins, and smiling Vishnu who lies slumbering and playfully makes a new world arise out of his golden dreams of gods.

"But to return to our own, Castalian cheerfulness, it may be only a lateborn, lesser variety of this great universal serenity, but it is a completely legitimate form. Scholarship has not been cheerful always and everywhere, although it ought to be. But with us scholarship, which is the cult of truth, is closely allied to the cult of the beautiful, and allied also with the practice of spiritual refreshment by meditation. Consequently it can never entirely lose its serene cheerfulness. Our Glass Bead Game combines all three principles: learning, veneration of the beautiful, and meditation; and therefore a proper Glass Bead Game player ought to be drenched in cheerfulness as a ripe fruit is drenched in its sweet juices. He ought above all to possess the cheerful serenity of music, for after all music is nothing but an act of courage, a serene, smiling, striding forward and dancing through the terrors and flames of the world, the festive offering of a sacrifice. This kind of cheerful serenity is what I have been concerned with ever since I began dimly to sense its meaning during my student days, and I shall never again relinquish it, not even in unhappiness and suffering.

"We shall go to sleep now, and tomorrow morning you are leaving. Come back soon, tell me more about yourself, and I shall begin to tell you, too. You will hear that even in Waldzell and even in the life of a Magister there are doubts, disappointments, despairs, and dangerous passions. But now I want you to take an ear filled with music to bed with you. A glance into the starry sky and an ear filled with music is a better prelude to sleep than all your sedatives."

He sat down and carefully, very softly, played a movement from the Purcell sonata which was one of Father Jacobus's favorite pieces. The notes fell into the stillness like drops of golden light, so softly that along with them the song of the old fountain in the yard could be heard. Gently, austerely, sparingly, sweetly, the lovely separate voices met and mingled; bravely and gaily they paced their tender rondo through the void of time and transitoriness, for a little while making the room and the night hour vast as the universe. And when the friends bade each other good night, the guest's face had changed and brightened, although his eyes had filled with tears.

TEN

PREPARATIONS

Now that Knecht had managed to break the ice, a vital association, revitalizing to the two of them, began between himself and Designori. The latter, who for long years had lived in resigned melancholia, had to admit that his friend was right: what had drawn him back to the Pedagogic Province was in fact the longing for a cure, for brightness, for Castalian cheerfulness. While Tegularius observed the new development with jealous mistrust, Plinio began visiting frequently, even when he had no commission business. Soon Magister Knecht knew all he needed to know about him. Designori's life had been neither so extraordinary nor so complicated as Knecht had imagined after those initial revelations. In his youth Plinio had suffered certain disappointments and humiliations, the more painful to one of his active, enthusiastic temperament, of which we have already heard. He had failed in his efforts to become a mediator between the world and Castalia; he had not contrived to create a synthesis of the worldly and Castalian components in his background and character, and had instead turned into an isolated and embittered outsider. Nevertheless, he was not simply a failure. In defeat and renunciation he had in spite of everything shaped a selfhood.

In him Castalian education seemed to have miscarried. At least it had so far produced nothing but conflicts and disappointments for him, and a profound loneliness difficult for a man of his sort to bear. It seemed, moreover, that since he had once stumbled into this thorny path of maladjustment, he was driven to commit all kinds of acts that increased his isolation and his difficulties. Thus while still a student he found himself irreconcilably at odds with his family, in particular with his father.

Although not reckoned among actual political leaders, his father like all the Designoris had been a lifelong supporter of the conservative, pro-government party. He was hostile to all innovations, opposed to the claims of the underprivileged to new rights and a fair share in the economy. He was suspicious of men without name or rank, devoted to the old order, and prepared to make sacrifices for everything he regarded as legitimate and sacred. Without having any special religious vein, he was friendly toward the Church. And although he did not lack a sense of justice, benevolence, charity, and helpfulness, he was obstinately and on principle opposed to the efforts of tenant-farmers to better their lot. He was wont to cite the program and slogans of his party as a rationalization for this harshness. In reality, what motivated him was neither conviction nor insight, but blind loyalty to his class and the traditions of his family. This spirit was in keeping with a deep chivalrousness and feeling for chivalric honor, and an outspoken contempt for everything that pretended to be modern, progressive, and contemporary.

It was a bitter blow to a man of this sort when his son Plinio, while still in his student days, joined a distinctly oppositional and modernistic party. In those days a youthful left wing of an old middle-class liberal party had been formed, led by a man named Veraguth, a publicist, deputy, and forceful orator. He was a highly emotional populist and libertarian with a tendency to become intoxicated by his own rhetoric. This man courted the students by giving public lectures in university towns, and met with considerable success. Among other enthusiastic followers, he won over Designori. The young man, disappointed with the university and seeking something to sustain him, some substitute for the Castalian morality which had lost its hold on him, seeking some kind of new idealism and program, was carried away by Veraguth's lectures. He admired the man's passion and fighting spirit, his wit, his hortatory style, his good looks and fine speech. Soon Plinio joined a faction of students who had been converted by Veraguth's lectures and were working for his party and aims.

When Plinio's father learned of this, he set out at once for the university town. In a thundering rage, shouting at his son for the first time in his life, he charged him with conspiracy, betrayal of his father, his family, and the traditions of his house, and ordered him to undo his error at once by severing all ties with Veraguth and his party. This was certainly not the right way to influence the young man, who saw his position turning into a kind of martyrdom. Plinio stood up to his father's thunder. He hadn't attended the elite school for ten years and the university for several, he declared, in order to give up his power of judgment. He was not going to let a clique of selfish landowners prescribe his views on government, economics, and justice. In framing this reply, he profited by the example of Veraguth, who modeled himself on the great tribunes of the people in never speaking of his own or class interests, but only of pure absolute justice and humanity.

Plinio's father burst into bitter laughter and suggested that his son at least finish his studies before he meddled in grown-up affairs and fancied that he knew more about human life and justice than venerable generations of noble families whose degenerate scion he was and whom he was now traitorously stabbing in the back. With every word the quarrel grew more bitter and insulting, until the father suddenly stopped in icy shame, as though a mirror had shown him his own face distorted with rage. In silence, he took his leave.

From then on, Plinio's old pleasant and intimate relationship to his paternal home was never restored. He remained loyal to his faction and its neo-liberalism. What is more, after completing his studies he became Veraguth's disciple, assistant, and intimate associate, and a few years later his son-in-law. Since Designori's psychic equilibrium had been disturbed by his education in the elite schools, or perhaps we should say by his difficulties in readjusting to the world and to life back home, so that he was already beset by problems, these new relationships threw him into an exposed, complex, and delicate situation. He gained something of indubitable value, a kind of faith, political convictions, and membership in a party which satisfied his youthful craving for justice and progressiveness. In Veraguth he acquired a teacher, leader, and older friend whom at first he uncritically admired and loved, and who moreover seemed to need him and appreciate him. He gained a direction and goal, work and a mission in life. That was a good deal, but it had to be dearly bought. To some degree the young man came to terms with the loss of his natural position in his father's family and among his peers; to some degree he managed to meet expulsion from a privileged caste, and its subsequent hostility, with a sort of relish in martyrdom. But there were some things he could never get over, above all the gnawing sense that he had inflicted pain on his beloved mother, had placed her in an uncomfortable position between his father and himself, and by doing so had probably shortened her life. She died soon after his marriage. After her death Plinio scarcely ever visited his home, and when his father died he sold the ancient family seat.

Among those who have made heavy sacrifices for a position in life, a government post, a marriage, a profession, there are some who contrive to love their position and affirm it the more on the strength of these very sacrifices. What they have suffered for constitutes their happiness and their fulfillment. Designori's case was different. Although he remained loyal to his party and its leader, his political beliefs and work, his marriage and his idealism, he began to doubt everything connected with these things. His whole life had become problematical to him. The political and ideological fervor of youth subsided. In the long run, the struggle to prove oneself right no more made for gladness than had the trials undertaken out of defiance. Experience in professional life had its sobering effect. Ultimately he wondered whether he had become a follower of Veraguth out of a sense of truth and justice or whether he had not been at least half seduced by the man's gifts as a speaker and rabble-rouser, his charm and nimble wit in public appearances, the sonority of his voice, his splendid virile laughter, and the intelligence and beauty of his daughter.

More and more he began to doubt whether old Designori with his class loyalty and his obduracy toward the tenant-farmers had really held the baser view. He became uncertain whether good and bad, right and wrong, had any absolute existence at all. Perhaps the voice of one's own conscience was ultimately the only valid judge, and if that were so, then he, Plinio, was in the wrong. For he was not happy, calm, and balanced; he was not confident and secure. On the contrary, he was plagued by uncertainty, doubts, and guilts. His marriage was not unhappy and mistaken in any crude sense, but still it was full of tensions, complications, and resistances. It was perhaps the best thing he possessed, but it did not give him that tranquility, that happiness, that innocence and good conscience he so badly missed. It required a great deal of circumspection and self-control. It cost him much effort. Moreover, his handsome and gifted small son Tito very soon became a focal point of struggle and intrigue, of courting and jealousy, until the boy, pampered and excessively loved by both parents, inclined more and more to his mother's side and became her partisan. That was the latest and, so it seemed, the bitterest sorrow and loss in Designori's life. It had not broken him; he had assimilated it and found an attitude toward it, a dignified, but grave, worn, and melancholy way of bearing it.

While Knecht was gradually learning all this from his friend in the course of frequent visits, he had also told him a great deal about his own experiences and problems. He was careful not to let Plinio fall into the position of the one who has made his confession only to regret it at a later hour or, with a change of mood, to wish to take it all back. On the contrary, he won Plinio's confidence by his own candor and strengthened it by his own revelations. In the course of time he showed his friend what his own life was like—a seemingly simple, upright, regulated life within a clearly structured hierarchic order, a career filled with success and recognition, but nevertheless a hard and completely lonely life of many sacrifices. And although as an outsider there was much that Plinio could not entirely grasp, he did understand the main currents and basic emotions. Certainly he could comprehend Knecht's craving to reach out to the youth, to the younger pupils unspoiled by miseducation, and sympathize with his desire for some modest employment such as that of a Latin or music teacher in a lower school, free of glamor and of the eternal obligation to play a public role. It was wholly in the style of Knecht's methods of teaching and psychotherapy that he not only won over this patient by his frankness, but also planted the thought in Plinio's mind that he could help his friend, and thus spurred him really to do so. For in fact Designori could be highly useful to the Magister, not so much in helping him to solve his main problem, but in satisfying his curiosity and thirst for knowledge about innumerable details of life in the world.

We do not know why Knecht undertook the difficult task of teaching his melancholy boyhood friend to smile and laugh again, or whether any thought of a reciprocal service was involved. Designori, at any rate, who was certainly in a position to know, did not think so. He later said: "Whenever I try to fathom how my friend Knecht managed to do anything with a person as confirmedly unhappy as myself, I see more and more plainly that his power was based on magic and, I must add, on a streak of roguishness. He was an arch-rogue, far more than his own underlings realized, full of playfulness, wit, slyness, delighting in magician's tricks, in guises, in surprising disappearances and appearances. I think that the very moment I first turned up at the Castalian Board meeting he resolved to snare me and exert his special sort of influence on me—that is, to awaken and reform me. At any rate he took pains to win me over from the very first. Why he did it, why he bothered with me, I cannot say. I think men of his sort usually do such things unconsciously, as a kind of reflex. When they encounter someone in distress they feel it as their task to respond to that appeal immediately. He found me distrustful and shy, by no means ready to fall into his arms, let alone ask him for help.

"He found me, his once frank and communicative friend, disillusioned and reticent; yet this very obstacle seemed to stimulate him. He did not give up, prickly though I was, and he finally achieved what he wanted. Among other things he made it seem that our relationship was one of mutual aid, as though my strength were equal to his, my worth to his, my need of help paralleled by an equal need on his part. In our very first long conversation he implied that he had been waiting for something like my appearance, that he had in fact been longing for it, and gradually he admitted me into his plan of resigning his office and leaving the Province. He always made me aware of how much he counted on my advice, my assistance, my secrecy, since aside from me he had not a single friend in the world outside, and no experience at all with that world. I admit that I liked to feel this, and that it contributed a good deal toward my trusting him completely and my putting myself more or less at his mercy. I believed him absolutely. But later, in the course of time, the whole thing began to seem totally dubious and improbable, and I would have been unable to say whether and to what extent he really expected something from me, and whether his way of capturing me was innocent or politic, naive or sly, sincere or contrived and a kind of game. He was so far superior to me, and did me so much good, that I would never have ventured to look deeper into the matter. In any case, nowadays I regard the fiction that his situation was similar to mine, and he just as dependent on my sympathy and aid as I on his, as merely a form of politeness, an engaging and pleasant web of suggestion that he wove around me. Only that to this day I cannot say to what extent his game with me was conscious, preconceived, and deliberate, to what extent it was in spite of everything naive and a pure product of his nature. For Magister Joseph was certainly a great artist. On the one hand his urge to educate, to influence, to heal and help and develop the personalities of others, was so strong that he scarcely scrupled about the means he used; on the other hand it was impossible for him to undertake even the smallest task without devoting himself totally to it. But one thing is certain: that at the time he took me under his wing like a friend and like a great physician and guide. He did not let go of me once he held me, and ultimately he awakened me and cured me as far as that was possible. And the remarkable thing, so utterly typical of him, was that while he pretended to be asking me to help him escape from his office, and while he listened calmly and often with actual approval to my crude and simple-minded jibes at Castalia, and while he himself was struggling to free himself from Castalia, he actually lured and guided me back there. He persuaded me to return to meditation. He schooled and reshaped me by means of Castalian music and contemplation, Castalian serenity, Castalian fortitude. He made me, who in spite of my longing for your way had become so utterly un-Castalian and anti-Castalian, into one of your sort again; he transformed my unrequited love for you into a requited love."

Such were Designori's comments, and no doubt he had reason for his admiring gratitude. It may not be too difficult to teach boys and young men the life-style of the Order, with the aid of our tried and true methods. It was surely a difficult task in the case of a man who was already approaching his fiftieth year, even if this man were himself full of good will. Not that Designori ever became anything like a model Castalian. But Knecht succeeded fully in what he had set out to do: in lifting the bitter weight of unhappiness, in leading Designori's touchy, vulnerable soul back to something like harmony and serenity, and in replacing a number of his bad habits by good ones. Naturally the Magister Ludi could not himself undertake all the detailed work that was involved. He enlisted the apparatus and energies of Waldzell and the Order in behalf of this honored guest. For a while he even dispatched a meditation master from Hirsland, the seat of the Order's directorate, to stay a while with Designori and supervise his exercises. But the whole plan and direction of the cure remained in Knecht's hand.

It was in his eighth year as Magister that he at last yielded to his friend's repeated invitations and visited him at his home in the capital. With permission from the directorate of the Order, with whose President, Alexander, he had close and affectionate relations, he devoted a holiday to his visit. Although he expected a great deal of it, he had been putting it off for a whole year, partly because he first wished to be sure of his friend, partly, no doubt, out of a natural timidity. This was, after all, his first step into that world from which his friend Plinio had brought his stony sadness, the world which held so many important secrets for him.

He found the modern house which his friend had exchanged for the old Designori townhouse presided over by a stately, highly intelligent, and reserved lady. She, however, was dominated by her handsome, cheeky, and rather ill-behaved son who seemed to be the center of everything here and who had apparently taken over from his mother a supercilious and rather insulting attitude toward his father.

Initially rather cool and suspicious of everything Castalian, both mother and son soon came under the spell of the Magister, whose office gave him, in their eyes, an almost mythical aura of mystery and consecration. Nevertheless, the atmosphere during this first visit was stiff and forced. Knecht remained rather quiet, observing and awaiting events. The lady of the house received him with formal politeness and inner distaste, as if he were a high officer of some enemy army being quartered on her. Tito, the son, was the least constrained of the three; probably he had often enough looked on in amusement on similar situations. No doubt he had also profited by them. His father seemed to be only playing the part of master of the house. Between him and his wife the prevailing tone was one of gentle, cautious, rather anxious politeness, as if each of them were walking on tiptoe. This tone was maintained far more easily and naturally by the wife than by her husband. As for the son, Plinio was always making overtures of comradeship to the boy which were at times taken up for selfish reasons, at other times impudently rebuffed.

In short, the three lived together in a sultry atmosphere of effort, guiltiness, and sternly repressed impulses, filled with fear of friction and eruptions, in a state of perpetual tension. The style of behavior and speech, like the style of the whole house, was a little too careful and deliberate, as though a solid wall had to be built against eventual breaches and assaults. Knecht also noted that a great deal of Plinio's regained serenity had vanished from his face again. Though in Waldzell or in the guest house of the Order in Hirsland he was by now almost free of gloom, in his own house he still stood in the shadows, and provoked as much criticism as pity.

The house was a fine one. It bespoke wealth and luxurious tastes. In each room the furnishings were of the right proportions for the space; each was tuned to a pleasant harmony of two or three colors, with here and there a valuable work of art. Knecht looked about him with pleasure; but in the end all these delights to the eye struck him as a shade too handsome, too perfect, and too well thought out. There was no sense of growth, of movement, of renewal. He sensed that this beauty of the house and its belongings was also meant as a kind of spell, a defensive gesture, and that these rooms, pictures, vases, and flowers enclosed and accompanied a life of vain longing for harmony and beauty which could be attained only in the form of tending such well-co-ordinated surroundings.

It was in the period after this visit, with its somewhat unedifying impressions, that Knecht sent a meditation teacher to his friend's home. After having spent a single day in the curiously taut and charged atmosphere of this house, the Magister understood much that he had not wished to know but needed to learn for his friend's sake. Nor was this first visit the last. He came again, several times, and on some of these occasions the talk turned to education and the difficulties with young Tito. In these conversations Tito's mother took a lively part. The Magister gradually won the confidence and liking of this highly intelligent and skeptical woman. Once, when he said half jokingly that it was a pity her boy had not been sent to Castalia early, while there was still time for him to be educated there, she took the remark seriously as if it were a reproof, and came to her own defense. She doubted, she said, whether Tito would have been admitted; he was gifted enough, certainly, but hard to han-

dle, and she would never have wished to impose her own
ideas on the boy. After all, a similar attempt in the case
of his father had not worked out well. Besides, neither
she nor her husband had ever thought to claim the old
Designori family privilege for their son, since they had
broken with Plinio's father and the whole tradition of
the ancient house. Finally, she added, with a painful
smile, that in any case she would not have been able to
part with her child, since he was all that made her life
worth living.

Knecht gave a great deal of thought to this last remark,
which obviously had been made without reflection. So
her house, in which everything was so distinguished, elegant, and harmonious, so her husband, her politics, her
party, the heritage of the father she had once adored—so
all this was not enough to give meaning to her life. Only
her child could make it worth living. And she would
rather allow this child to grow up under the harmful conditions that prevailed in this house than be separated
from him for his own good. For so sensible and seemingly
so cool and intellectual a woman, this was an astonishing
confession. Knecht could not help her as directly as he
had her husband, nor did he have the slightest intention
of trying. But as a result of his rare visits and of the fact
that Plinio was under his influence, some moderation
and a reminder of better ways were introduced into the
warped and wrong-headed family situation. The Magister
himself, however, as he gained increasing influence and
authority in the Designori household with each succeeding visit, found himself more and more puzzled by the
life of these worldly people. Unfortunately we know very
little about his visits in the capital and the things he saw
and experienced there, so that we must content ourselves
with the matters we have already indicated.

Knecht had not hitherto approached the President of
the Order in Hirsland any more closely than his official
functions demanded. He probably saw him only at those
plenary sessions of the Board of Educators which took
place in Hirsland, and even then the President generally
performed only the more formal and ornamental duties,
the reception and congé of his colleagues, with the principal work of conducting the session being left to the

Speaker. The previous President, who at the time of Knecht's assuming office was already an old man, had been highly respected by the Magister Ludi, but had made not a single gesture toward lessening the distance between them. For Knecht he was scarcely a human being, no longer had any personality; he hovered, a high priest, a symbol of dignity and composure, silent summit and crowning glory, above the entire hierarchy. This venerable man had recently died, and the Order had elected Alexander its new President.

Alexander was the same Meditation Master whom the heads of the Order had assigned to our Joseph Knecht years ago, during the early period of his magistracy. Ever since, the Magister had retained an affectionate gratitude for this exemplary representative of the spirit of hierarchy. And Alexander himself, during the time he daily watched over the Magister Ludi and became virtually his father confessor, had seen enough of his personality and conduct to come to love him. Both grew aware of the hitherto latent friendship from the moment that Alexander became Knecht's colleague and President of the Order. Henceforth they saw each other frequently and had work to do together. It was true that this friendship lacked a foundation in everyday, commonplace tasks, just as it lacked shared experiences in youth. It was rather the mutual sympathy of two colleagues at the summit of their respective vocations, who expressed their friendliness by a slightly greater warmth in greetings and leave-takings, by the deftness of their mutual comprehension, at most by a few minutes of chatting during brief breaks at a sitting of the Board.

Constitutionally, the President, who was also called Master of the Order, was in no way superior to his colleagues, the other Magisters. But he had acquired an indefinable superiority due to the tradition that the Master of the Order presided over the meetings of the Supreme Board. And as the Order had grown more meditative and monastic during the last several decades, his authority had increased—although only within the hierarchy and the Province, not outside it. Within the Board of Educators, the President of the Order and the Master of the Glass Bead Game had more and more become the twin exponents and representatives of the Castalian spirit. As against the ancient disciplines handed down from pre-Castalian eras—such as grammar, astronomy, mathematics, or music—the Glass Bead Game and discipline of the mind through meditation had become the truly characteristic values of Castalia. It was therefore of some significance that the two present leaders in these fields stood in a friendly relationship to each other. For each it was a vindication of his own worth, for each an extra dash of warmth and satisfaction in his life; for both it was an additional spur to the fulfillment of their task of embodying in their own persons the deepest values, the sacral energies of the Castalian world.

To Knecht, therefore, this meant one more tie, one more counterpoise to his growing urge to renounce everything and achieve a breakthrough into a new and different sphere of life. Nevertheless, this urge developed inexorably. Ever since he himself had become fully aware of it—that may have been in the sixth or seventh year of his magistracy—it had grown steadily stronger. Subscribing as he did to the idea of "awakening," he had unfalteringly received it into his conscious life and thinking. We believe we may say that from that time on the thought of his coming departure from his office and from the Province was familiar to him. Sometimes it seemed like a prisoner's belief in eventual freedom, sometimes like knowledge of impending death as it must appear to a man gravely ill.

During his first frank conversation with Plinio, he had for the first time expressed the thing in words. Perhaps he had done so only in order to win over his friend and persuade him to open his heart; but perhaps also he had intended, by this initial act of communication, to turn this new awakening of his, this new attitude toward life, in an outward direction. That is, by letting someone into his secret he was taking a first step toward making it a reality. In his further conversations with Designori, Knecht's desire to shed his present mode of life sooner or later, to undertake the leap into a new life, assumed the status of a decision. Meanwhile, he carefully built on his friendship with Plinio, who by now was bound to him not only by his former admiration, but also by the gratitude of a cured patient. In that friendship Knecht now possessed a bridge to the outside world and to its life so laden with enigmas.

It need not surprise us that the Magister waited so long before allowing his friend Tegularius a glimpse of his secret and of his plan for breaking away. Although he had shaped each of his friendships with kindness and with regard for the good of the other, he had always managed to keep a clear, independent view of these relationships, and to direct their course. Now, with the re-entry of Plinio into his life, a rival to Fritz had appeared, a new-old friend with claims upon Knecht's interest and emotions. Knecht could scarcely have been surprised that Tegularius reacted with signs of violent jealousy. For a while, until he had completely won over Designori, the Magister may well have found Fritz's sulky withdrawal a welcome relief. But in the long run another consideration took a larger place in his thoughts. How could he reconcile a person like Tegularius to his desire to slip away from Waldzell and out of his magistracy? Once Knecht left Waldzell, he would be lost to this friend forever. To take Fritz along on the narrow and perilous path that lay before him was unthinkable, even if Fritz should unexpectedly manifest the desire and the courage for the enterprise.

Knecht waited, considered, and hesitated for a very long time before initiating Fritz into his plans. But he finally did so, after his decision to leave had long been settled. It would have been totally unlike him to keep his friend in the dark, and more or less behind his back prepare steps whose consequences would deeply affect him as well. If possible Knecht wanted to make him, like Plinio, not only an initiate, but also a real or imaginary aide, since activity makes every situation more bearable.

Knecht had, of course, long ago made his friend privy to his ideas about the doom threatening the Castalian organization, as far as he cared to communicate these ideas and Tegularius to receive them. After he resolved to tell Fritz of his intentions, the Magister used these ideas as his link. Contrary to his expectations, and to his great relief, Fritz did not take a tragic view of the plan.

Rather, the notion that a Magister might fling his post back at the Board, shake the dust of Castalia from his feet, and seek out a life that suited his tastes, seemed to please Fritz. The idea actually amused him. Individualist and enemy of all standardization that he was, Tegularius invariably sided with the individual against authority. If there were prospect of fighting, taunting, outwitting the powers of officialdom, he was always for it.

His reaction gave Knecht a valuable clue as to how to go on. With an easier conscience, and laughing inwardly, the Magister promptly entered into his friend's attitude. He did not disabuse Fritz of his notion that the whole thing was a kind of *coup de main* against bureaucracy, and assigned him the part of an accomplice, collaborator, and conspirator. It would be necessary to work out a petition from the Magister to the Board, he said—an exposition of all the reasons that prompted him to resign his office. The preparation of this petition was to be chiefly Tegularius's task. Above all he must assimilate Knecht's historical view of the origins, development, and present state of Castalia, then gather historical materials with which Knecht's desires and proposals could be documented. That this would lead him into a field he had hitherto rejected and scorned, the field of history, seemed not to disturb Tegularius at all, and Knecht quickly taught him the necessary procedures. Soon Tegularius had immersed himself in his new assignment with the eagerness and tenacity he always had for odd and solitary enterprises. This obstinate individualist took a fierce delight in these studies which would place him in a position to challenge the bigwigs and the hierarchy in general, and show them their shortcomings.

Joseph Knecht took no such pleasure in these endeavors, nor had he any faith in their outcome. He was determined to free himself from the fetters of his present situation, leaving himself unencumbered for tasks which he felt were awaiting him. But he fully realized that he could not overpower the Board by rational arguments, nor delegate Tegularius any part of the real work that had to be done. Nevertheless, he was very glad to know that Fritz was occupied and diverted for the short while that they would still be living in proximity to each other. The next time he saw Plinio Designori he was able to report: "Friend Tegularius is now busy, and compensated for what he thinks he has lost because of your reappearance on the scene. His jealousy is almost cured, and working on something for me and against my colleagues is doing him good. He is almost happy. But don't imagine, Plinio, that I count on anything concrete coming out of this project, aside from the benefit to himself. It is most unlikely that our highest authority will grant this petition of mine. In fact, it's out of the question. At best they will reply with a mild reprimand. What dooms my request is the nature of our hierarchy itself. A Board that would release its Magister Ludi in response to a petition, no matter how persuasively argued, and would assign him to work outside Castalia, wouldn't be to my liking at all. Besides, there is the character of our present Master of the Order. Master Alexander is a man whom nothing can bend. No, I shall have to fight this battle out alone. But let us allow Tegularius to exercise his mind for the present. All we lose by that is a little time, which I need in any case so as to leave everything here so well arranged that my departure will cause no harm to Waldzell. But meanwhile you must find me some place to live on the outside, and some employment, no matter how modest; if necessary I shall be content with a position as a music teacher, say. It need only be a beginning, a springboard."

Designori said he thought something could be found, and when the time came his house was at his friend's disposal for as long as he liked. But Knecht would not accept that.

"No," he said, "I wouldn't do as a guest; I must have some work. Besides, my staying more than a few days in your house, lovely as it is, would only add to the tensions and troubles there. I have great confidence in you, and your wife, too, nowadays treats me in a friendly way, but all this would look entirely different as soon as I ceased to be a visitor and Magister Ludi, and became a refugee and permanent guest."

"Surely you're being a little too literal-minded about it," Plinio said. "Once you've made your break and are living in the capital, you'll soon be offered a suitable post, at least a professorship at the university—you can count on that as a certainty. But such things take time, as you know, and of course I can only begin working in your behalf after you have won your freedom."

"Of course," the Master said. "Until then my decision must remain secret. I cannot offer myself to your authorities before my own authority here has been informed and has made its decision; that goes without saying. But for the present, you know, I am not at all seeking a public appointment. My wants are few, probably fewer than you can imagine. I need a little room and my daily bread, but above all work to do, some task as a teacher; I need one or a few pupils to whom I can be near and whom I can influence. A university post is the last thing on my mind. I would be just as glad—no, I would by far prefer—to work with a boy as a private tutor, or something of the sort. What I am seeking and what I need is a simple, natural task, a person who needs me. Appointment at a university would from the start mean my fitting into a traditional, sanctified, and mechanized bureaucracy, and what I crave is just the opposite of that."

Hesitantly, Designori brought up the project that had been on his mind for some time.

"I do have something to propose," he said, "and hope you will at least think it over. If you can possibly accept it, you would be doing me a service too. Since that first day I visited you here you have given me a great deal of help. You've also come to know my household and know how things stand there. My situation isn't good, but it is better than it has been for years. The thorniest problem is the relationship between me and my son. He is spoiled and impudent; he's made himself a privileged position in our house—as you know, this was virtually pressed on him while he was still a child and courted by both his mother and myself. Since then he's decidedly gone over to his mother's side, and gradually whatever authority I might have had over him has been adroitly taken out of my hands. I had resigned myself to that, as I have to so much else in my botched life. But now that I have recovered somewhat, thanks to you, I've regained hope. You can see what I am driving at. I would think it a

piece of great good fortune if Tito, who is having difficulties in school anyhow, were to have a tutor who would
take him in hand. It's a selfish request, I know, and I
have no idea whether the task appeals to you at all. But
you've encouraged me to make the suggestion, as least."

Knecht smiled and extended his hand.

"Thank you, Plinio. No proposal could be more welcome to me. The only thing lacking is your wife's consent. Furthermore, the two of you must be prepared to
leave your son entirely to me for the time being. If I am
to do anything with him, the daily influence of his
home must be excluded. You must talk to your wife and
persuade her to accept this condition. Go at it cautiously;
give yourselves time."

"Do you really think you can do something with Tito?"
Designori asked.

"Oh yes, why not? He has good blood and high endow-
ments from both parents. What is missing is the harmony of these forces. My task will be to awaken in him
the desire for this harmony, or rather to strengthen it
and ultimately to make him conscious of it. I shall be
happy to try."

Thus Joseph Knecht had his two friends occupied with
his affair, each in a different way. While Designori in
the capital presented the new plan to his wife and tried
to couch it in terms acceptable to her, Tegularius sat in
a carrel in the library at Waldzell following up Knecht's
leads and gathering material for the petition. The Magister had put out good bait in the reading matter he had
prescribed. Fritz Tegularius, the fierce despiser of history, sank his teeth into the history of the warring
epoch, and became thoroughly infatuated with it. With
his enthusiasm for any pastime, he ferreted out more
and more anecdotes from that epoch in the dark prehistory of the Order. Soon he had collected such copious
notes that when he presented them to his friend, Knecht
could use only a tenth of them.

During this period Knecht made several visits to the
capital. Because a sound, integrated personality often
finds easy access to troubled and difficult people, Designori's wife came to trust him more and more. Soon she
consented to her husband's plan. Tito himself, on one

of these visits, boldly informed the Magister that he no longer wished to be addressed with the familiar pronoun, as if he were a child, since everyone nowadays, including his teacher, used the polite pronoun to him. Knecht thanked him with perfect courtesy and apologized. In his Province, he explained, the teachers used the familiar form to all students, even those who were quite grown up. After dinner he invited the boy to go for a walk with him and show him something of the city.

In the course of the walk Tito guided him down a stately street in the old part of the city, where the centuries-old houses of wealthy patrician families stood in an almost unbroken row. Tito paused in front of one of these substantial, tall, and narrow buildings and pointed to a shield over the doorway. "Do you know what that is?" he asked. When Knecht said he did not, he explained: "Those are the Designori arms, and this is our old house. It belonged to the family for three hundred years. But we are living in our meaningless, commonplace house just because after grandfather's death my father took it into his head to sell this marvelous old mansion and build himself a fashionable place that by now isn't so modern any more. Can you understand anyone's acting like that?"

"Are you very sorry about the old house?" Knecht asked.

"Very sorry," Tito said passionately, and repeated his question: "Can you understand anyone's acting like that?"

"Things become understandable if you look at them in the right light," the Magister said. "An old house is a fine thing, and if the two had stood side by side and your father were choosing between them, he probably would have kept the old one. Certainly, old houses are beautiful and distinguished, especially so handsome a one as this. But it is also a beautiful thing to build one's own house, and when an ambitious young man has the choice of comfortably and submissively settling into a finished nest, or building an entirely new one, one can well see that he may decide to build. As I know your father—and I knew him when he was a spirited fellow just about as old as you are—the sale of the house probably hurt no one more than himself. He had had a painful conflict with his father and his family, and it seems his education in our Castalia was not altogether the right thing for him. At any rate it could not deter him from several impatient acts of passion. Probably the sale of the house was one of those acts. He meant it as a thrust at tradition, a declaration of war upon his family, his father, the whole of his past and his dependency. At least that is one way to see it. But man is a strange creature, and so another idea does not appear altogether improbable to me, the idea that by selling this old house your father wanted primarily to hurt himself rather than the family. To be sure, he was angry at the family; they had sent him to our elite schools, had given him our kind of education, only to confront him on his return with tasks, demands, and claims he could not handle. But I would rather go no further in psychological analysis. In any case the story of this sale shows how telling the conflict between fathers and sons can be—this hatred, this love turned to hate. In forceful and gifted personalities this conflict rarely fails to develop—world history is full of examples. Incidentally, I could very well imagine a later young Designori who would make it his mission in life to regain possession of the house for the family at all costs."

"Well," Tito exclaimed, "wouldn't you think he was right?"

"I would not like to judge him. If a later Designori recalls the greatness of his family and the obligations that such greatness imposes, if he serves the city, the country, the nation, justice, and welfare with all his energies and in the process grows so strong that he can recover the house, then he will be a worthy person and we would want to take our hats off to him. But if he knows no other goal in life besides this house business, then he is merely obsessed, a fanatic, a man surrendering to a passion, and in all probability someone who never grasped the meaning of such youthful conflicts with a father and so went on shouldering their load long after he became a man. We can understand and even pity him, but he will not increase the fame of his lineage. It is fine when an old family remains affectionately attached to its residence, but rejuvenation and new greatness spring solely from sons who serve greater goals than the aims of the family."

Although on this walk Tito listened attentively and quite willingly to his father's guest, on other occasions he exhibited dislike and fresh defiance. In this man, whom his otherwise discordant parents both seemed to hold in high esteem, Tito sensed a power which threatened his own pampered freedom, so that at times he treated Knecht with outright rudeness. Each time, however, he would be sorry and try to make up for such breaches, for it offended his self-esteem to have shown weakness in the face of the serene courtesy that surrounded the Magister like a coat of shining armor. Secretly, too, in his inexperienced and rather unruly heart, he sensed that this was a man he might love and revere.

He felt this particularly one half-hour when he came upon Knecht alone, waiting for his father, who was busy with affairs. As Tito entered the room he saw their guest sitting still, with eyes half closed, in a statuesque pose, radiating such tranquility and peace in his meditation that the boy instinctively checked his stride and began to tiptoe out of the room again. But at that point the Magister opened his eyes, gave him a friendly greeting, rose, indicated the piano in the room, and asked whether he liked music.

Tito said he did, although he had not had music lessons for quite some time and had left off practicing because he was not doing so well in school and those drill-masters who called themselves teachers were always keeping after him. Still and all he'd always enjoyed listening to music. Knecht opened the piano, sat down at it, found it was tuned, and played an andante movement of Scarlatti's which he had recently used as the basis for a Glass Bead Game exercise. Then he stopped, and seeing the boy rapt and attentive, began outlining more or less what took place in such an exercise. He dissected the music, giving examples of some of the analytical methods that could be used and the ways the music could be translated into the hieroglyphs of the Game.

For the first time Tito saw the Magister not as a guest, not as a learned celebrity whom he resented as a danger to his own self-esteem. Rather, he saw him at his work, a man who had acquired a subtle, exacting art and practiced it with a masterly hand. Tito could only dimly sense the meaning of that art, but it seemed to be deserving of full devotion and to call forth all the powers of an integrated personality. That this man thought him grown-up and intelligent enough to be interested in these complicated matters also gave him greater assurance. He grew quiet, and during this half-hour he began to divine the sources of this remarkable man's cheerfulness and unruffled calm.

During this last period Knecht's official activities were almost as strenuous as they had been in the difficult time after his assumption of office. He was determined to leave all the areas under his control in exemplary condition. Moreover, he achieved this aim, although he failed in his further aim of making his own person appear dispensable, or at least easily replaceable. That is almost always the case with the highest offices in our Province. The Magister hovers rather like a supreme ornament, a gleaming insigne, above the complex affairs of his domain. He comes and goes rapidly, flitting amiably by, says a few words, nods an assent, suggests an assignment by a gesture, and is already gone, already talking to the next subordinate. He plays on his official apparatus like a musician on his instrument, seems to expend no force and scarcely any thought, yet everything runs as it should. But every official in this apparatus knows what it means when the Magister is away or ill, what it means to find a substitute for him even for a few hours or a day.

Knecht spent his time rushing once more through the whole principality of the Vicus Lusorum, checking everything and especially taking pains to secretly groom his Shadow for the task the man would soon confront, that of representing him in all earnest. But all the while he could observe that at heart he had already liberated himself from all this, had moved far away from it. The preciosity of this well-arranged little world no longer enraptured him. He saw Waldzell and his magisterial function as something that already virtually lay behind him, a region he had passed through, which had given him a great deal and taught him much, but which could no longer tempt him to new accomplishments, to a fresh outpouring of energy. More and more, during this period of slow breaking loose and bidding farewell, he came to see the real reason for his alienation and desire to escape. It was probably not, he thought, his knowledge of the dangers to Castalia and his anxiety about her future, but simply that a hitherto idle and empty part of his self, of his heart and soul, was now demanding the right to fulfill itself.

At this time he once again carefully studied the Constitution and Statutes of the Order. His escape from the Province would not, he saw, be so hard to accomplish, so nearly impossible as he had initially imagined. He did have the right to resign his office on grounds of conscience, and even to leave the Order. The Order's vow was not a lifetime matter, although members had claimed this freedom seldom, and a member of the highest Board never. What made the step seem so difficult to him was not so much the strictness of the law but the hierarchic spirit itself, the loyalty within his own heart. Of course he was not planning to skip out; he was preparing a circumstantial petition for release, and that dear fellow Tegularius was working day and night at it. But he had no confidence in the success of this petition. He would receive soothing assurances, admonishments, would perhaps be offered a vacation in Mariafels, where Father Jacobus had recently died, or perhaps in Rome. But the authorities would not let him go; that seemed more and more clear. To release him would violate all the traditions of the Order. If the Board were to do so, it would be admitting that his request was justified, admitting that life in Castalia, and what was more in such a high post, might in some circumstances not be satisfying to a man, might mean renunciation and imprisonment.

ELEVEN

THE CIRCULAR LETTER

WE ARE APPROACHING the end of our tale. As we have already indicated, our knowledge of this end is fragmentary, rather more in the nature of a legend than of a historical narrative. We shall have to be content with that. We therefore take all the more pleasure in being able to fill out this next-to-last chapter of Knecht's life with an authentic document, namely with that voluminous memorandum in which the Glass Bead Game Master himself presents the authorities with the reasons for his decision and asks them to release him from his office.

As we have repeatedly stated, Joseph Knecht no longer believed in the success of this memorandum which he had had so conscientiously prepared. We must admit, moreover, that when the time came he wished he had neither written nor handed in this "petition." He suffered the fate of all who exercise a natural and initially unconscious power over other men: this power is not exercised without a certain cost to its possessor. Although the Magister had been glad to win his friend Tegularius's support for his plans, and to have made him a promoter and associate in them, the consequences went far beyond what he had conceived or wished. He had coaxed or misled Fritz into undertaking a task whose value he himself, as its author, no longer believed in; but when his friend at last presented him with the fruits of his labors, he could no longer undo the work. Nor, since the purpose of the assignment had been to make Fritz better able to bear their separation, could he lay the data aside and leave them unused without thoroughly offending and disappointing his friend. At the time, we are convinced, Knecht would much rather have brusquely resigned his office and declared his withdrawal from the Order instead of choosing the roundabout mode of the "petition," which in his eyes had become virtually a farce. But consideration for Tegularius caused him to restrain his impatience for a while longer.

It would no doubt be interesting if we had his industrious friend's manuscript at our disposal. It consisted mainly of historical material meant to serve as proof or illustration; but we may safely assume that it contained a good many sharp and witty epigrams on the hierarchy, as well as on the world and world history. But even if this document, composed as it was in months of tenacious labor, were still in existence—as it quite possibly may be—we would have to forbear from publishing it here, since this book of ours would not be the proper place for it.

Our concern is only with the use the Magister Ludi made of his friend's work. When Tegularius solemnly presented this document to him, he accepted it with cordial words of gratitude and appreciation, and knowing what pleasure this would give, asked Fritz to read it aloud. For several days, therefore, Tegularius spent half an hour in the Magister's garden, for it was summertime, and read with gusto the many pages of his manuscript. Often the reading was interrupted by peals of laughter on the part of both. These were good days for Tegularius. Afterward, however, Knecht went into seclusion in order to compose his letter to the Board. We present here its exact text. No further commentary on it is necessary.

The Magister Ludi's Letter to the Board of Educators

Various considerations have prompted me, the Magister Ludi, to present to the Board a special request in this separate and somewhat more private memorandum, instead of including it in my official report. Although I am appending this memorandum to the official accounting that is now due, and await an official reply, I regard it rather as a circular letter to my colleagues in office.

Every Magister is required to inform the Board of any hindrances or danger to his conducting his office in keeping with the Rule. Although I have endeavored to serve with all my strength, the conduct of my office is (or seems to me to be) threatened by a danger which resides in my own person, although that is probably not its sole origin. At any rate, I see my suitability to serve as Magister Ludi as imperiled, and this by circumstances beyond my control. To put it briefly: I have begun to doubt my ability to officiate satisfactorily because I consider the Glass Bead Game itself in a state of crisis. The purpose of this memorandum is to convince the Board that the crisis exists, and that my awareness of it demands that I seek a position other from the one I now hold.

Permit me to clarify the situation by a metaphor. A man sits in an attic room engaged in a subtle work of scholarship. Suddenly he becomes aware that fire has broken out in the house below. He will not consider whether it is his function to see to it, or whether he had not better finish his tabulations. He will run downstairs and attempt to save the house. Here I am sitting in the top story of our Castalian edifice, occupied with the Glass Bead Game, working with delicate, sensitive instruments, and instinct tells me, my nose tells me, that down below something is burning, our whole structure is imperiled, and that my business now is not to analyze music or define rules of the Game, but to rush to where the smoke is.

Most of us brothers of the Order take Castalia, our Order, our system of scholarship and schooling, together with the Game and everything associated with it, as much for granted as most men take the air they breathe and the ground they stand on. Hardly anyone ever thinks that this air and this ground could sometime not be there, that we might some day lack air or find the ground vanishing from under us. We have the good fortune of living well protected in a small, neat, and cheerful world, and the great majority of us, strange as it may seem, hold to the fiction that this world has always existed and that we were born into it. I myself spent my younger years in this extremely pleasant delusion, although I was perfectly well aware of the reality that I was not born in Castalia, but only sent here by the educational authorities and raised here. I knew also that Castalia, the Order, the Board, the colleges, the Archives, and the Glass Bead Game have not always existed, are by no means a product of nature, but a belated and noble creation of man's will, and transitory like all such things. I knew all this, but it had no reality for me; I simply did not think of it, ignored it, and I knew that more than three-quarters of us will live and die in this strange and pleasant illusion.

But just as there have been centuries and millennia without the Order and without Castalia, there will again be such eras in the future. And if today I remind my colleagues and the honorable Board of this platitude, and call upon them to turn their eyes for once to the dangers that threaten us, if I assume for a moment the unenviable and often ludicrous role of prophet, warner, and sermonizer, I do so fully prepared to accept mocking laughter; but I hope nevertheless that the majority of you will read my memorandum to the end and that some of you may even agree with me on a few of its points. That in itself would be a good deal.

An institution such as our Castalia, a small Province dedicated to the things of the mind, is prone to internal and external perils. The internal perils, or at least a good many of them, are known to us; we keep watch for them and take the necessary measures. Every so often we send individual pupils back, after having admitted them to the elite schools, because we discover in them ineradicable traits and impulses which would make them unfitted

for our community and dangerous to it. Most of them,
we trust, are not lesser human beings on that score, but
merely unsuited to Castalian life, and after their return
to the world are able to find conditions more appropriate to them, and develop into capable men. Our practice
in this respect has proved its value, and on the whole
our community can be said to sustain its dignity and
self-discipline and to fulfill its task of being and constantly recruiting a nobility of the mind. Presumably
we have no more than a normal and tolerable quota of
the unworthy and slothful among us.

The conceit that can be observed among the members
of our Order is rather more objectionable. I am referring
to that class arrogance to which every aristocracy inclines, and with which every privileged group is charged,
with or without justification. The history of societies
shows a constant tendency toward the formation of a
nobility as the apex and crown of any given society. It
would seem that all efforts at socialization have as their
ideal some kind of aristocracy, of rule of the best, even
though this goal may not be admitted. The holders of
power, whether they have been kings or an anonymous
group, have always been willing to further the rise of
a nobility by protection and the granting of privileges.
This has been so no matter what the nature of the
nobility: political, by birth, by selection and education.
The favored nobility has always basked in the sunlight;
but from a certain stage of development on, its place in
the sun, its privileged state, has always constituted a
temptation and led to its corruption. If, now, we regard
our Order as a nobility and try to examine ourselves to
see to what extent we earn our special position by our
conduct toward the whole of the people and toward the
world, to what extent we have already been infected
by the characteristic disease of nobility—*hubris*, conceit, class arrogance, self-righteousness, exploitativeness
—if we conduct such a self-examination, we may be
seized by a good many doubts. The present-day Castalian may not be lacking in obedience to the rules of the
Order, in industry, in cultivated intelligence; but does
he not often suffer from a severe lack of insight into his
place in the structure of the nation, his place in the

world and world history? Is he aware of the foundation of his existence; does he know himself to be a leaf, a blossom, a twig or root of a living organism? Does he have any notion of the sacrifices the nation makes for his sake, by feeding and clothing him, by underwriting his schooling and his manifold studies? And does he care very much about the meaning of our special position? Does he have any real conception of the purpose of our Order and life?

There are exceptions, granted, many and praiseworthy exceptions. Nevertheless I am inclined to answer all these questions with a No. The average Castalian may regard the man of the outside world, the man who is not a scholar, without contempt, envy, or malice, but he does not regard him as a brother, does not see him as his employer, does not in the least feel that he shares responsibility for what is going on outside in the world. The purpose of his life seems to him to be cultivation of the scholarly disciplines for their own sake, or perhaps even to be taking pleasurable strolls in the garden of a culture that pretends to be a universal culture without ever being quite that. In brief, this Castalian culture of ours, sublime and aristocratic though it certainly is, and to which I am profoundly grateful, is for most of those associated with it not an instrument they play on like a great organ, not active and directed toward goals, not consciously serving something greater or profounder than itself. Rather, it tends somewhat toward smugness and self-praise, toward the cultivation and elaboration of intellectual specialism. I know there are a large number of Castalians who are men of integrity and worth, who really desire only to serve. I mean the teachers who are the products of our system, who then go out into the country to engage in unselfish and incalculably important service far from the pleasant climate and the intellectual luxuries of our Province. These fine teachers out there are, strictly speaking, the only ones among us who are really carrying out the purpose of Castalia. Through their work alone we are repaying the nation for the many benefits we receive from it. Granted that every one of us brothers of the Order knows that our supreme and most sacred task consists in preserving the intellectual foundation of our country and our world. That foundation has proved to be a moral element of the highest efficacy, for it is nothing less than the sense of truth—on which justice is based, as well as so much else. But if we examine our real feelings, most of us would have to admit that we don't regard the welfare of the world, the preservation of intellectual honesty and purity outside as well as inside our tidy Province, as the chief thing. In fact, it is not at all important to us. We are only too glad to leave it to those brave teachers out there to pay our debt to the world by their self-sacrificing work, and so more or less justify the privileges we enjoy, we Glass Bead Game players, astronomers, musicians, and mathematicians. It is part of the above-mentioned arrogance and caste spirit that we do not much care whether we earn our privileges by accomplishments. Even though our abstemious way of life is prescribed by the Order, a good many of us plume ourselves on it, as if it were a virtue we were practicing purely for its own sake instead of its being the least that we owe to the country that makes our Castalian existence possible.

I shall content myself with merely referring to these internal defects and dangers. They are not insignificant, although in peaceful times they would not come anywhere near imperiling our existence. But as it happens, we Castalians are dependent not only on our own morality and rationality. We depend vitally on the condition of the country and the will of the people. We eat our bread, use our libraries, expand our schools and archives —but if the nation no longer wants to authorize this, or if it should be struck by impoverishment, war, and so on, then our life and studying would be over in a minute. Some day our country might decide that its Castalia and our culture are a luxury it can no longer afford. Instead of being genially proud of us, it may come round to regarding us as noxious parasites, tricksters, and enemies. Those are the external dangers that threaten us.

To portray these dangers in any graphic form, I would probably have to draw upon examples from history. And if I were talking to the average Castalian, I would surely encounter a measure of passive resistance, an almost childish ignorance and indifference. As you know,

among Castalians interest in world history is extremely
weak. Most of us, in fact, not only lack interest but also
respect for history. We fail to do it justice, I might say.
Over the years I have done considerable searching into
the sources of this feeling—this mixture of indifference
and arrogance toward world history—and I have found
that it derives from two causes. First, the content of history strikes us as rather inferior—I am not speaking of
intellectual and cultural history, which is of course within
our purview. Insofar as we have any notions at all about
world history, we see it as consisting in brutal struggle
for power, goods, lands, raw materials, money—in short,
for those material and quantitative things which we regard as far from the realm of Mind and rather contemptible. For us the seventeenth century is the age of
Descartes, Pascal, Froberger, not of Cromwell or Louis
XIV.

The second reason we fight shy of history is our traditional and I would say valid distrust of a certain kind
of history writing which was very popular in the age of
decadence before the founding of our Order. A priori
we have not the slightest confidence in that so-called philosophy of history of which Hegel is the most brilliant
and also most dangerous representative. In the following
century it led to the most repulsive distortion of history
and destruction of all feeling for truth. To us, a bias for
this sham philosophy of history is one of the principal
features of that era of intellectual debasement and vast
political power struggles which we occasionally call the
Century of Wars, but more often the Age of the Feuilleton. Our present culture, the Order and Castalia, arose
out of the ruins of that age, out of the struggle with and
eventual defeat of its mentality—or insanity.

But it is part of our intellectual arrogance that we
confront world history, especially in modern times, in
much the same spirit that the hermits and ascetics of
early Christianity confronted the *theatrum mundi,* the
great theater of the world. History seems to us an arena
of instincts and fashions, of appetite, avarice, and craving for power, of blood lust, violence, destruction, and
wars, of ambitious ministers, venal generals, bombarded
cities, and we too easily forget that this is only one of

its many aspects. Above all we forget that we ourselves are a part of history, that we are the product of growth and are condemned to perish if we lose the capacity for further growth and change. We are ourselves history and share the responsibility for world history and our position in it. But we gravely lack awareness of this responsibility.

Let us glance at our own history, at the periods in which the present pedagogic provinces arose, in our own country and in so many others. Let us glance at the origins of the various Orders and hierarchies of which our Order is one. We see immediately that our hierarchy and our homeland, our beloved Castalia, was certainly not founded by people who held so proudly detached an attitude toward world history as we do. Our predecessors and founders began their work in a shattered world at the end of the Age of Wars. Our official explanation of that age, which began approximately with the so-called First World War, is all too one-sided. The trouble was, we say, that the things of the mind did not count in those days; that the powerful rulers considered intellect itself merely a weapon of inferior quality, and meant only for occasional use. This attitude, we say, was a consequence of "feuilletonistic" corruption.

Very well—the anti-intellectuality and brutality of that period are all too visible to us. When I call it antiintellectual, I do not mean to deny its imposing achievements in intelligence and methodology. But we in Castalia are taught to consider intellect primarily in terms of striving for truth, and the kind of intellect manifested in those days seems to have had nothing in common with striving for truth. It was the misfortune of that age that there was no firm moral order to counter the restiveness and upheaval engendered by the tremendously rapid increase in the human population. What remnants there were of such a moral order were suppressed by the contemporary sloganizing. And those struggles produced their own strange and terrible conflicts. Much like the era of Church schism introduced by Luther four centuries earlier, the entire world was gripped by an immense unrest. Everywhere lines of battle formed; everywhere bitter enmity sprang up between old and young, between fatherland and humanity, between Red and White. We in our day can no longer reconstruct, let alone comprehend and sympathize with the impetus and power of such labels as Red and White, let alone the real meanings of all those battle cries. Much as in Luther's time, we find all over Europe, and indeed over half the world, believers and heretics, youths and old men, advocates of the past and advocates of the future, desperately flailing at each other. Often the battlefronts cut across frontiers, nations, and families. We may no longer doubt that for the majority of the fighters themselves, or at least for their leaders, all this was highly significant, just as we cannot deny many of the spokesmen in those conflicts a measure of robust good faith, a measure of idealism, as it was called at the time. Fighting, killing, and destroying went on everywhere, and everywhere both sides believed they were fighting for God against the devil.

Among us, that savage age of high enthusiasms, fierce hatreds, and altogether unspeakable sufferings has fallen into a kind of oblivion. That is hard to understand, since it was so closely linked with the origin of all our institutions, was the basis and cause of those institutions. A satirist might compare this loss of memory with the kind of forgetfulness that parvenu adventurers who have at last obtained a patent of nobility have for their birth and parentage.

Let us continue to dwell a little longer on those warlike times. I have read a good many of their documents, taking less interest in the subjugated nations and destroyed cities than in the attitude of the intellectuals of the day. They had a hard time of it, and most of them did not endure. There were martyrs among the scholars as well as among the clergy, and the example of their martyrdom was not entirely without some effect, even in those times so accustomed to atrocities. Still and all, most men of mind did not stand up under the pressures of that violent age. Some capitulated and placed their talents, knowledge, and techniques at the disposal of the rulers—let us recall the well-known statement of a university professor in the Republic of the Massagetes: "Not the faculty but His Excellency the General can properly determine the sum of two and two." Others put up a struggle as long as it was possible to do so in a reasonably safe fashion, and published protests. A world-famous author of the time—so we read in Ziegenhalss—in a single year signed more than two hundred such protests, warnings, appeals to reason, and so on—probably more than he had actually read. But most learned the art of silence; they also learned to go hungry and cold, to beg and hide from the police. They died before their time and were envied for this by the survivors. Countless numbers took their own lives. There was truly no pleasure and no honor in being a scholar or a writer. Those who entered the service of the rulers and devised slogans for them had jobs and livelihoods, but they suffered the contempt of the best among their fellows, and most of them surely suffered pangs of conscience also. Those who refused such service had to go hungry, live as outlaws, and die in misery or exile. A cruel, an incredibly harsh weeding out took place. Scientific research that did not directly serve the needs of power and warfare rapidly sank into decadence. The same was true for the whole educational system. History, which each of the leading nations of any given period referred exclusively to itself, underwent revision and fantastic simplification. Historical philosophy and feuilletonism dominated the field.

So much for details. Those were wild and violent times, chaotic and Babylonian times in which peoples and parties, old and young, Red and White, no longer understood each other. After sufficient bloodletting and debasement, it came to its end; there arose a more and more powerful longing for rationality, for the rediscovery of a common language, for order, morality, valid standards, for an alphabet and multiplication table no longer decreed by power blocs and alterable at any moment. A tremendous craving for truth and justice arose, for reason, for overcoming chaos. This vacuum at the end of a violent era concerned only with superficial things, this sharp universal hunger for a new beginning and the restoration of order, gave rise to our Castalia. The insignificantly small, courageous, half-starved but unbowed band of true thinkers began to be aware of their potentialities.

With heroic asceticism and self-discipline they set about establishing a constitution for themselves. Everywhere, even in the tiniest groups, they began working once more, clearing away the rubble of propaganda. Starting from the very bottom, they reconstructed intellectual life, education, research, culture.

Their labors were fruitful. Out of those intrepid and impoverished beginnings they slowly erected a magnificent edifice. In the course of generations they created the Order, the Board of Educators, the elite schools, the Archives and collections, the technical schools and seminaries, and the Glass Bead Game. Today we live as their heirs in a building almost too splendid. And let it be said once again, we live in it like rather vapid and complacent guests. We no longer want to know anything about the enormous human sacrifices our foundation walls were laid on, nor anything about the ordeals of which we are the beneficiaries, nor anything about history which favored or at least tolerated the building of our mansion, which sustains and tolerates us today and possibly will go on doing so for a good many Castalians and Magisters after our day, but which sooner or later will overthrow and devour our edifice as it overthrows and devours everything it has allowed to grow.

Let me return from history and draw my conclusion. What all this means to us at the present time is this: Our system has already passed its flowering. Some time ago it reached that summit of blessedness which the mysterious game of world history sometimes allows to things beautiful and desirable in themselves. We are on the downward slope. Our course may possibly stretch out for a very long time, but in any case nothing finer, more beautiful, and more desirable than what we have already had can henceforth be expected. The road leads downhill. Historically we are, I believe, ripe for dismantling. And there is no doubt that such will be our fate, not today or tomorrow, but the day after tomorrow. I do not draw this conclusion from any excessively moralistic estimate of our accomplishments and our abilities; I draw it far more from the movements which I see already on the way in the outside world. Critical times are approaching; the omens can be sensed everywhere; the world is once again about to shift its center of gravity. Displacements of power are in the offing. They will not take place without war and violence. From the Far East comes a threat not only to peace, but to life and liberty. Even if our country remains politically neutral, even if our whole nation unanimously abides by tradition (which is not the case) and attempts to remain faithful to Castalian ideals, that will be in vain. Some of our representatives in Parliament are already saying that Castalia is a rather expensive luxury for our country. The country may very soon be forced into serious rearmament—armaments for defensive purposes only, of course—and great economies will be necessary. In spite of the government's benevolent disposition toward us, much of the economizing will strike us directly. We are proud that our Order and the cultural continuity it provides have cost the country as little as they have. In comparison with other ages, especially the early period of the Feuilletonistic Age with its lavishly endowed universities, its innumerable consultants and opulent institutes, this toll is really not large. It is infinitesimal compared with the sums consumed for war and armaments during the century of wars. But before too long this kind of armament may once again be the supreme necessity; the generals will again dominate Parliament; and if the people are confronted with the choice of sacrificing Castalia or exposing themselves to the danger of war and destruction, we know how they will choose. Undoubtedly a bellicose ideology will burgeon. The rash of propaganda will affect youth in particular. Then scholars and scholarship, Latin and mathematics, education and culture, will be considered worth their salt only to the extent that they can serve the ends of war.

The wave is already gathering; one day it will wash us away. Perhaps that will be as it should be. But for the present, my revered colleagues, we still possess that limited freedom of decision and action which is the human prerogative and which makes world history the history of mankind. We may still choose, in proportion to our understanding of events, in proportion to our alertness and our courage. We can, if we will, close our eyes, for the danger is still fairly far away. Probably we who are Magisters today will be able to complete our terms of office in peace and lie down to die in peace before the danger comes so close that it is visible to all. But for me, and no doubt for others like me, such peace could not be had with a clear conscience. I would rather not continue to administer my office in peace and play Glass Bead Games, contented that the coming upheavals will probably find me no longer alive. Rather, it seems to me urgent to recollect that we too, nonpolitical though we are, belong to world history and help to make it. Therefore I said at the beginning of this memorandum that my competence as Magister Ludi is compromised, since I cannot keep my mind from dwelling anxiously upon the future danger. I do not allow myself to imagine what form the disaster might assume for us and for me. But I cannot close my mind to the question: What have we and what have I to do in order to meet the danger? Permit me to say a few words more about this.

I am not inclined to urge Plato's thesis that the scholar, or rather the sage, ought to rule the state. The world was younger in his time. And Plato, although the founder of a sort of Castalia, was by no means a Castalian. He was a born aristocrat, of royal descent. Granted, we too are aristocrats and form a nobility, but one of the mind, not the blood. I do not believe that man will ever succeed in breeding a hereditary nobility that is at the same time an intellectual nobility. That would be the ideal aristocracy, but it remains a dream. We Castalians are not suited for ruling, for all that we are civilized and highly intelligent people. If we had to govern we would not do it with the force and naïveté that the genuine ruler needs. Moreover, our proper field and real concern, cultivation of an exemplary cultural life, would be quickly neglected. Ruling does not require qualities of stupidity and coarseness, as conceited intellectuals sometimes think. But it does require wholehearted delight in extroverted activity, a bent for identifying oneself with outward goals, and of course also a certain swiftness and lack of scruple about the choice of ways to attain success. And these are traits that a scholar—for we do not wish to call ourselves sages —may not have and does not have, because for us contemplation is more important than action, and in the choice of ways to attain our goals we have learned to be as scrupulous and wary as is humanly possible.

Therefore it is not our business to rule and not our business to engage in politics. We are specialists in examining, analyzing, and measuring. We are the guardians and constant verifiers of all alphabets, multiplication tables, and methods. We are the bureaus of standards for cultural weights and measures. Granted we are many other things also. In some circumstances we can also be innovators, discoverers, adventurers, conquerors, and reinterpreters. But our first and most important function, the reason the people need us and keep us, is to preserve the purity of all sources of knowledge. In trade, in politics, and what have you, turning an X into a Y may occasionally prove to be a stroke of genius; but never with us.

In former ages, during the wars and upheavals of so-called periods of "grandeur," intellectuals were sometimes urged to throw themselves into politics. This was particularly the case during the late Feuilletonistic Age. That age went even further in its demands, for it insisted that Mind itself must serve politics or the military. Just as the church bells were being melted down for cannon, as hapless schoolboys were drawn on to fill the ranks of the decimated troops, so Mind itself was to be harnessed and consumed as one of the materials of war.

Naturally we could not accept this demand. In emergencies a scholar might be called from his lectern or his desk and made into a soldier. In some circumstances he might volunteer for such service. In a country exhausted by war the scholar must restrict himself in all material things, even to the point of sheer starvation. Surely all this is taken for granted. The higher a person's cultivation, the greater the privileges he has enjoyed, the greater must be his sacrifices in case of need. We hope that every Castalian would recognize this as a matter of course, if the time should come. But although we are prepared to sacrifice our well-being, our comfort, and our lives to the people, when danger threatens, that does not mean that we are ready to sacrifice Mind itself, the tradition and morality of our spiritual life, to the demands of the hour, of the people, or of the generals. He would be a coward who withdrew from the challenges, sacrifices, and dangers his people had to endure. But he would be no less a coward and traitor who betrayed the principles of the life of the mind to material interests—who, for example, left the decision on the product of two times two to the rulers. It is treason to sacrifice love of truth, intellectual honesty, loyalty to the laws and methods of the mind, to any other interests, including those of one's country. Whenever propaganda and the conflict of interests threatens to devalue, distort, and do violence to truth as it has already done to individuals, to language, to the arts, and to everything else that is organic and highly cultivated, then it is our duty to resist and save the truth, or rather the striving for truth, since that is the supreme article in our creed. The scholar who knowingly speaks, writes, or teaches falsehood, who knowingly supports lies and deceptions, not only violates organic principles. He also, no matter how things may seem at the given moment, does his people a grave disservice. He corrupts its air and soil, its food and drink; he poisons its thinking and its laws, and he gives aid and comfort to all the hostile, evil forces that threaten the nation with annihilation.

The Castalian, therefore, should not become a politician. If need be, he must sacrifice his person, but never his fealty to the life of the mind. The mind of man is beneficent and noble only when it obeys truth. As soon as it betrays truth, as soon as it ceases to revere truth, as soon as it sells out, it becomes intensely diabolical. Then it becomes far worse than instinctual bestiality, which always retains something of the innocence of nature.

I leave it to each of you, my esteemed colleagues, to reflect upon the duties of the Order when the country and the Order itself are imperiled. Certainly there will be a variety of opinions. I have my own, and after much consideration of all the questions I have posed here, I have for my part come to a clear conception of what seems to me desirable, of what my duty is. This leads me to a personal petition to the honorable Board, with which I shall conclude my memorandum.

Of all the Masters composing our Board, I as Magister

Ludi am probably most remote from the outside world, by virtue of my office. The mathematician, the philologist, the physicist, the pedagogue, and all the other Masters labor in fields which they share with the profane world. In the ordinary, non-Castalian schools of our country, mathematics and linguistics are part of the normal curriculum. Astronomy and physics have a place in the secular universities. Even the completely untutored make music. All these disciplines are age-old, much older than our Order; they existed long before it and will outlive it. Only the Glass Bead Game is our own invention, our speciality, our favorite, our toy. It is the ultimate, subtlest expression of our Castalian type of intellectuality. It is both the most precious and the most nonutilitarian, the most beloved and the most fragile jewel in our treasury. It is the first precious stone that will be destroyed if the continuance of Castalia is imperiled, not only because it is the frailest of our possessions, but also because to laymen it is undoubtedly the most dispensable aspect of Castalia. Therefore when the time comes to save the country every needless expenditure, the elite schools will be contracted, the funds for the maintenance and expansion of the libraries and collections will be trimmed and ultimately eliminated, our meals will be cut down, our clothing allowance withdrawn, but all the principal subjects in our *Universitas Litterarum* will be allowed to continue except for the Glass Bead Game. Mathematics is needed, after all, to devise new firearms, but no one will believe—least of all the military—that closing the Vicus Lusorum and abolishing our Game will cause the country and people the slightest loss. The Glass Bead Game is the most outlying and most vulnerable part of our structure. Perhaps this explains why the Magister Ludi, head of our unworldliest discipline, should be the first to sense the coming calamity, or at any rate the first to express this feeling to our Board.

In case of political upheavals, therefore, especially if they involve war, I regard the Glass Bead Game as a lost cause. It will deteriorate rapidly, however many individuals cling to it, and it will never be restored. The atmosphere which will follow a new era of wars will not condone it. It will vanish just as surely as did certain highly cultivated customs in musical history, such as the choruses of professional singers of the period around 1600, or the Sunday concerts of figurate music in churches around 1700. In those days men's ears heard sounds whose angelic purity cannot be conjured up again by any amount of science or magic. In the same way the Glass Bead Game will not be forgotten, but it will be irrecoverable, and those who study its history, its rise, flourishing, and doom, will sigh and envy us for having been allowed to live in so peaceful, cultivated, and harmonious a world of the mind.

Although I am now Magister Ludi, I do not at all consider it my (or our) mission to prevent or postpone the ultimate end of our Game. Beauty, even surpassing beauty, is perishable like all other things, as soon as it has become a historical phenomenon upon this earth. We know that and can grieve that it is so, but cannot seriously try to change it, for it is unalterable law. When the Glass Bead Game is destroyed, Castalia and the world will suffer a loss, but they will scarcely be aware of it at the moment, for at the time of great crisis they will be absorbed in saving whatever can still be saved. A Castalia without the Game is conceivable, but not a Castalia without reverence for truth, without fidelity to the life of the mind. A Board of Educators can function without a Magister Ludi. But although we have almost forgotten it, "Magister Ludi" of course originally meant not the office we have in mind when we use the word, but simply schoolmaster. And the more endangered Castalia is, the more its treasures stale and crumble away, the more our country will need its schoolmasters, its brave and good schoolmasters. Teachers are more essential than anything else, men who can give the young the ability to judge and distinguish, who serve them as examples of the honoring of truth, obedience to the things of the spirit, respect for language. That holds not only for our elite schools, which will be closed down sooner or later, but also and primarily for the secular schools on the outside where burghers and peasants, artisans and soldiers, politicians, military officers, and rulers are educated and shaped while they are still malleable children. That is where the basis for the cultural life of the country is to be found, not in the seminars or in the Glass Bead Game. We have always furnished the country with teachers and educators, and they are, as I have said, the best among us. But we must do far more than we have done hitherto. We must no longer rely on a constant influx of the best from the schools outside to help maintain our Castalia. More and more we must recognize the humble, highly responsible service to the secular schools as the chief and most honorable part of our mission. That is what we must seek to extend.

Which brings me to my personal petition to the esteemed Board. I herewith request the Board to relieve me of my office as Magister Ludi and entrust to me an ordinary school, large or small, outside in the country; to let me staff it with a group of youthful members of our Order. I would recruit as teachers those whom I could confidently expect to help instil our principles into young people out in the world.

I hope that the esteemed Board will deign to examine my petition and its reasoning with due benevolence and let me know its decisions.

THE MASTER OF THE GLASS BEAD GAME.

Postscript:
Permit me to cite a remark of the Reverend Father Jacobus, which I noted down in the course of one of his private lessons:

"Times of terror and deepest misery may be in the offing. But if any happiness at all is to be extracted from that misery, it can be only a spiritual happiness, looking backward toward the conservation of the culture of earlier times, looking forward toward serene and stalwart defense of the things of the spirit in an age which otherwise might succumb wholly to material things."

Tegularius did not know how little of his work was present in this memorandum; he was not shown the final version, although Knecht did let him read two earlier, much more detailed drafts. The Magister Ludi dispatched the memorandum and awaited the Board's answer with far less impatience than his friend. He had come to the decision not to involve Fritz in his further actions. He therefore forbade him to discuss the matter any more, merely indicating that it would surely be a long time before the Board reacted to the memorandum.

When in fact the reply arrived sooner than he had expected, Tegularius heard nothing about it. The letter from Hirsland read:

To His Excellency the Magister Ludi in Waldzell.
Esteemed Colleague:

The Directorate of the Order and the Assembly of Masters have taken note of your warmhearted and perspicacious circular letter with more than ordinary interest. We have found your historical observations no less absorbing than your ominous picture of the future, and some of us will undoubtedly long continue to ponder and to draw profit from your reflections, which surely are not groundless. We have all recognized, with gladness and deep appreciation, the principles that inspire you, the truly Castalian principles of altruism. We see that you are motivated by a profound and by now almost instinctive love for our Province, for its life and its customs, a concerned and at the moment somewhat overanxious love. With equal gladness and appreciation we observe the personal overtones of that love, its spirit of sacrifice, its active impulse, its earnestness and zeal, and its heroic element. In all this we recognize the character of our Glass Bead Game Master as we know it; we see his energy, his ardor, his daring. How characteristic of the famous Benedictine's disciple that he does not study history as a mere scholarly end in itself, an aesthetic game to be regarded without emotion, but rather applies his historical knowledge directly to current needs; that his perceptions impel him to take certain measures. And, revered colleague, how perfectly it corresponds with your character that you should feel drawn not to political missions, not to posts of influence and honor, but to the role of simple Ludi Magister, that of a schoolmaster.

Such are some of the impressions, some of the thoughts that were awakened by the very first reading of your circular letter. Most of your colleagues responded in much the same way. The Board has not, however, been able to

take a stand on your warnings and requests. We have met
and held a lively discussion of your view that our very
existence is threatened. Much was said about the nature,
extent, and possible imminence of the dangers. The
majority of our members obviously took these questions
most seriously indeed, and grew quite heated in discussing them. But we are compelled to inform you that on
none of these questions did a majority favor your view.
The imaginative power and farsightedness of your his-
torico-political observations was acknowledged; but
none of your specific conjectures, or shall we say prophecies, was fully approved. None was accepted as wholly
convincing. Only a few of us agreed with you (and then
with reservations) even on the question of the degree to
which the Order and our Castalian system has shared the
responsibility for the unusually long era of peace, or
whether the Order can even be held a factor in political
history. In the view of the majority, the calm that has
descended upon our Continent must be ascribed partly
to the general prostration following the bloodlettings of
the terrible wars, but far more to the fact that the Occi-
dent has ceased to be the focal point of world history
and the arena in which claims to hegemony are fought
out. Certainly we would not wish to cast doubt upon the
true achievements of our Order. Nevertheless, we cannot
grant that the Castalian ideal, the ideal of high culture
under the aegis of disciplined meditation, has any powers
to shape history, any vital influence upon world political conditions. Urges or ambitions of this sort are totally
alien to the Castalian mentality. Several serious disquisi-
tions on the subject have stressed the point that Castalia
seeks neither political sway nor influence on peace or
war. Indeed, there could be no question of Castalia's
having any such purpose, so the argument has gone,
because everything Castalian is related to reason and
operates within the framework of rationality—which certainly could not be said of world history, or said only by
someone willing to revert to the theological and poetic
sentimentalities of romantic historical philosophy. From
that vantage point, of course, the whole murderous, de-
structive course of political history could be explained
as merely the method of cosmic Reason. Moreover, even

the most casual survey of the history of thought shows that the great ages of culture have never been adequately explained by political conditions. Rather, culture, or mind, or soul, has its own independent history—a second, secret, bloodless, and sanctified history—running parallel to what is generally called world history, by which we mean incessant struggles for material power. Our Order deals only with this sanctified and secret history, not with "real," brutal world history. It can never be our task to be continually taking soundings in political history, let alone to help to shape it.

It therefore does not matter whether or not the political constellation is really as your circular letter suggests. In any case, our Order has no right to do anything about it. Our only position must be one of patient waiting to see what comes. And therefore your argument that this constellation requires us to take an active position was decisively rejected by the majority, with only a few votes in its favor.

Your views of the present world situation and your suggestions regarding the immediate future obviously impressed most of our colleagues. In fact, some of them were thunderstruck. But here too, although most of the speakers manifested respect for your knowledge and acuity, there was no evidence that the majority agreed with you. On the contrary, the consensus was that your comments on this matter were remarkable and extremely interesting, but excessively pessimistic. One colleague raised his voice to ask whether it might not be described as dangerous, if not outrageous—but surely frivolous—for a Magister to alarm his Board by such sinister images of allegedly imminent perils and tribulations. Certainly an occasional reminder of the perishability of all things was permissible; every man, and especially everyone holding a high position of responsibility, must occasionally cry out to himself the *memento mori*. But to announce in such sweeping terms the impending doom of the entire body of Masters, the entire Order, and the entire hierarchy was a tasteless assault upon the tranquility and the imagination of his colleagues, and threatened the efficiency of the Board itself. The work of a Magister surely could not profit by his going to his office every day with the thought that his position itself, his labors, his pupils, his responsibility to the Order, his life for and in Castalia—that all this might be wiped out by tomorrow or the day after. . . . Although the majority did not support the colleague who raised this objection, he received considerable applause.

We shall keep our present communication brief, but are at your disposal for a discussion in person. From our brief summary you can already see that your circular letter has not had the effect you may have hoped for. In large part its failure no doubt is based on objective grounds, the incompatibility of your opinions with those of the majority. But there are also purely formal reasons. At any rate it seems to us that a direct personal discussion between yourself and your colleagues would have taken a significantly more harmonious and positive course. We would moreover suggest that it was not only your couching of the matter in the form of a written memorandum that affected the Board adversely. Far more striking was your combining, in a way highly unusual among us, a professional communication with a personal request, a petition. Most of your colleagues consider this fusion an unfortunate attempt at innovation; some bluntly called it impermissible.

This brings us to the most delicate point of all, your request for release from your office and transfer to some secular school system. The petitioner should have realized from the outset that the Board could not possibly approve so sudden and curiously argued a request. Of course the Board's reply is, "No."

What would become of our hierarchy if the Order no longer assigned each man to his place? What would become of Castalia if everyone wished to assess his own gifts and aptitudes and choose his position for himself? We suggest that the Master of the Glass Bead Game reflect upon this subject for a few minutes, and bid him to continue administering the honorable office he has been entrusted with.

In saying this we have met your request for a reply to your letter. We have been unable to give the answer you may have hoped for. But we should also like to express our appreciation for the stimulating and admonitory value of your document. We trust we will be able to discuss its content with you orally, and in the near future. For although the directorate of the Order believes that it can rely on you, that point in your memorandum in which you speak of an incapacity to conduct the affairs of your office naturally gives us grounds for concern.

Knecht read the letter without any great expectations, but with the closest attention. He had expected that the Board would have "grounds for concern," and moreover had had signs that it was truly worried. A guest from Hirsland had recently come to the Players' Village, provided with a regular pass and a recommendation from the directorate of the Order. He had requested hospitality for a few days, supposedly for work in the Archives and library, and had also asked permission to audit a few of Knecht's lectures. An elderly man, silent and attentive, he had turned up in almost all the departments and buildings of the Village, had inquired after Tegularius, and had several times called on the director of the Waldzell elite school, who lived in the vicinity. There could scarcely be any doubt that the man had been sent as an observer to determine whether there were any traces of negligence in the Players' Village, whether the Magister was in good health and at his post, the officials diligent, the students stimulated. He had stayed for a full week and missed none of Knecht's lectures. Two of the officials had even commented on his quiet ubiquitousness. Evidently the directorate of the Order had waited for the report from this investigation before dispatching its reply to the Magister.

What was he to think of this answer, and who had probably been its author? The style betrayed nothing; it was the conventional, impersonal officialese the occasion demanded. But on subtler analysis the letter revealed more individuality than he had thought at first reading. The basis of the entire document was the hierarchic spirit, a sense of justice and love of order. It was plain to see how unwelcome, inconvenient, not to say troublesome and annoying Knecht's petition had been. Its rejection had undoubtedly been decided at once by the author of this reply, without regard to the opinions of others. On the other hand, the vexation was leavened by another emotion, for there was a clear note of sympathy present in the letter, with its mention of all the more lenient and friendly comments Knecht's petition had received during the meeting of the Board. Knecht had no doubt that Alexander, the President of the Order, was the author of this reply.

We have now reached the end of our journey, and hope that we have reported all the essentials of Joseph Knecht's life. A later biographer will no doubt be in a position to ascertain and impart a good many additional details about that life.

We forbear to present our own account of the Magister's last days, for we know no more about them than every Waldzell student and could not tell the story any better than the *Legend of the Magister Ludi*, many copies of which are in circulation. Presumably it was written by some of the departed Magister's favorite students. With this legend we wish to conclude our book.

TWELVE

THE LEGEND

WHEN WE LISTEN to our fellow students talk about our Master's disappearance, about the reasons for it, the rightness or wrongness of his decisions and acts, the meaning or meaninglessness of his fate, it sounds to us like Diodorus Siculus explaining the supposed causes for the flooding of the Nile. We would think it not only useless but wrong to add to such speculations. Instead, we wish to preserve in our hearts the memory of our Master, who so soon after his mysterious departure into the world passed over into a still more mysterious beyond. His memory is dear to us, and for this reason we wish to set down what we have learned about these events.

After the Master had read the letter in which the Board denied his petition, he felt a faint shiver, a matutinal coolness and sobriety which told him that the hour had come, that from now on there could be no more hesitating or lingering. This peculiar feeling, which he was wont to call "awakening," was familiar to him from other decisive moments of his life. It was both vitalizing and painful, mingling a sense of farewell and of setting out on new adventures, shaking him deep down in his uncon-

scious mind like a spring storm. He looked at the clock.
In an hour he had to face a class. He decided to devote
the next hour to meditation, and went into the quiet
Magister's garden. On his way a line of verse suddenly
sprang into his mind:

In all beginnings is a magic source . . .

He murmured this under his breath, uncertain where he
had read it. The line appealed to him and seemed to suit
the mood of this hour. In the garden, he sat down on a
bench strewn with the first faded leaves, regulated his
breathing, and fought for inner tranquility, until with a
purged heart he sank into contemplation in which the
patterns of this hour in his life arranged themselves in
universal, suprapersonal images. But on the way to the
small lecture room, the line of verse came back to him.
He turned the words over in his mind, and thought that
he did not have them quite right. Suddenly his memory
cleared. Under his breath he recited:

In all beginnings dwells a magic force
For guarding us and helping us to live.

But it was not until nearly evening, long after his lecture was over and he had passed on to all sorts of other
routine matters, that he discovered the origin of the
verses. They were not the work of some old poet; they
came from one of his own poems, which he had written
in his student days. He remembered now that the poem
had ended with the line:

So be it, heart: bid farewell without end!

That very evening he sent for his deputy and informed
him that on the morrow he would have to leave for an
indefinite time. He put him in charge of all current
affairs, with brief instructions, and bade good-by in a
friendly and matter-of-fact way, as he would ordinarily
have done before departing on a brief official journey.

He had realized some time earlier that he would have
to leave without informing his friend Tegularius and
burdening him with farewells. This course was essential,
not only to spare his oversensitive friend, but also in
order not to endanger his whole plan. Presumably Fritz

would make his peace with the accomplished fact, whereas an abrupt disclosure and a farewell scene might lead to a regrettable emotional upheaval. Knecht had for a while even thought of departing without seeing Fritz for the last time. But now he decided that it would seem too much like evading a difficult encounter. However wise it was to spare his friend agitation and an occasion for follies, he had no right to make the thing so easy for himself. A half-hour remained before bedtime; he could still call on Tegularius without disturbing him or anyone else.

Night had already settled in the broad inner courtyard as he crossed to his friend's cell. He knocked with that strange feeling of: this is the last time, and found Tegularius alone. Delighted, Fritz laid aside the book he had been reading and invited Knecht to sit down.

"An old poem came to my mind today," Knecht remarked casually, "or rather a few lines from it. Perhaps you know where the rest can be found." And he quoted: "In all beginnings dwells a magic force . . ."

Tegularius traced it with no great trouble. After a few minutes of reflection he recognized the poem, got up, and produced from a desk drawer the manuscript of Knecht's poems, the original manuscript which Knecht had once presented to him. He looked through it and brought out two sheets of paper containing the first draft of the poem. Smilingly, he held them out to the Magister.

"Here," he said, "your Excellency may examine them himself. This is the first time in many years that you have deigned to remember these poems."

Joseph Knecht studied the two sheets attentively and with some emotion. In his student days, during his stay in the College of Far Eastern Studies, he had covered these two sheets of paper with lines of verse. They spoke to him of a remote past. Everything about them, the faintly yellowed paper, the youthful handwriting, the deletions and corrections in the text, reminded him painfully of almost forgotten times. He thought he could recall not only the year and the season when these verses had been written, but even the day and the hour. There came to him now the very mood, that proud and strong feeling that had gladdened him and found expression in the poem. He had written it on one of those special days on which he had experienced that spiritual shock which he called "awakening."

The title of the poem had obviously been written even before the poem itself, and had seemingly been intended as the first line. It had been set down in a large impetuous script, and read: "Transcend!"

Later, at some other time, in a different mood and situation, this title as well as the exclamation mark had been crossed out, and in smaller, thinner, more modest letters another title had been written in. It read: "Stages."

Knecht now remembered how at the time, filled with the idea of his poem, he had written down the word "Transcend!" as an invocation and imperative, a reminder to himself, a newly formulated but strong resolve to place his actions and his life under the aegis of transcendence, to make of it a serenely resolute moving on, filling and then leaving behind him every place, every stage along the way. Almost whispering, he read some lines to himself:

> Serenely let us move to distant places
> And let no sentiments of home detain us.
> The Cosmic Spirit seeks not to restrain us
> But lifts us stage by stage to wider spaces.

"I had forgotten these lines for many years," he said, "and when they happened to come to my mind today, I no longer knew how I knew them and didn't realize they were mine. How do they strike you today? Do they still mean anything to you?"

Tegularius considered.

"I have always had a rather odd feeling about this particular poem," he said finally. "The poem itself is among the very few you've written that I didn't really like. There was something about it that repelled or disturbed me. At the time I had no idea what it was. Today I think I see it. I never really liked this poem of yours, which you headed 'Transcend!' as if that were a marching order—thank God you later substituted a better title—I never really liked it because it has something didactic, moralizing, or schoolmasterly about it. If this element could be stripped away, or rather if this whitewash could be scrubbed off, it would be one of your finest poems—I've just realized that again. The real meaning is rather well suggested by the title 'Stages,' although you might just as well and perhaps better have called it 'Music' or 'The Nature of Music.' For if we discount the moralizing or preachy attitude, it is really about the nature of music, or if you will a song in praise of music, of its serenity and resolution, its quality of being constantly present, its mobility and unceasing urge to hasten on, to leave the space it has only just entered. If you contented yourself with this contemplation or praise of the spirit of music, if you had not turned it into an admonition and sermon—though obviously you had pedagogic ambitions even then—the poem might have been a perfect jewel. But as it stands it seems to me not only too hortatory but also afflicted by faulty logic. It equates music and life solely for the sake of the moral lesson. But that is highly questionable and disputable, for it transforms the natural and morally neutral impulse which is the mainspring of music into a 'Life' that summons, calls, commands us, and wants to impart good lessons to us. To put it briefly, in this poem a vision, something unique, beautiful, and splendid, has been falsified and exploited for didactic ends, and it is this aspect that always prejudiced me against it."

The Magister had been listening with pleasure as his friend worked himself up into that angry ardor which he so liked in him.

"Let's hope you're right," he said half jokingly. "You certainly are right in what you say about the poem's relationship to music. The idea of serenely moving to distant places and the underlying concept of the lines actually does come from music, without my having been conscious of it. I really don't know whether I corrupted the idea and falsified the vision; you may be right. When I wrote the poem, at any rate, it no longer dealt with music, but with an experience—the very experience that the lovely parable of music had revealed its moral aspect to me and become, within me, an awakening and an admonition to respond to the summons of life. The imperative form of the poem, which so particularly displeases you, is not the expression of any desire to command or teach, because the command is addressed to myself alone. That should have been clear from the last line, my friend, even if you weren't already well aware of it. I experienced an insight, a perception, an inward vision, and was bent on telling the content and the moral of this insight to myself, and impressing it on my mind. That is why the poem remained in my memory, although I was not conscious of it. So whether these lines are good or bad, they've accomplished their purpose; the admonition remained alive inside me and was not forgotten. Today I hear it again as if it were brand new. That's a fine little experience, and your mockery can't spoil it for me. But it's time for me to go. How lovely were those days, my friend, when we were both students and could so often allow ourselves to break the rules and stay together far into the nights, talking. A Magister can no longer allow himself such luxuries—more's the pity."

"Oh," Tegularius said, "he could allow it—it's a question of not having the courage."

Laughing, Knecht placed a hand on his shoulder.

"As far as courage goes, my boy, I might be guilty of worse pranks than that. Good night, old grumbler."

Gaily, he left the cell. But on the way out through the deserted corridors and courtyards of the Vicus Lusorum his seriousness returned, the seriousness of parting. Leave-takings always stir memories. Now, on this nocturnal walk, he remembered that first time he had strolled through Waldzell and the Vicus Lusorum as a boy, a newly arrived Waldzell pupil, filled with misgivings and hopes. Only now, moving through the coolness of the night in the midst of silent trees and buildings, did he realize with painful sharpness that he was seeing all this for the last time, listening for the last time to silence and slumber stealing over the Players' Village, by day so lively; for the last time seeing the little light above the gatekeeper's lodge reflected in the basin of the fountain; for the last time watching the clouds in the night sky sailing over the trees of his Magister's garden. Slowly, he went over all the paths and into all the nooks and corners of the Players' Village. He felt an impulse to open the gate of his garden once more and enter it, but he did not have the key with him, and that fact swiftly sobered him and caused him to collect himself. He returned to his apartment, wrote a few letters, including one to Designori announcing his arrival in the capital, and then spent some time in careful meditation to calm his intense emotions, for he wanted to be strong in the morning for his last task in Castalia, the interview with the Head of the Order.

The following morning the Magister rose at his accustomed hour, ordered his car, and drove off; only a few persons noticed his departure and none gave it any thought. The morning seemed to be drowning in the mists of early autumn as he drove toward Hirsland. He arrived toward noon and asked to be announced to Magister Alexander, the President of the Order. Under his arm he carried, wrapped in a cloth, a handsome metal casket normally kept in a secret compartment in his office. It contained the insignia of his office, the seals and the keys.

He was received with some surprise in the "main" office of the Order. It was almost unprecedented for a Magister to appear there unannounced and uninvited. On instructions from the President of the Order he was given lunch, then shown to a rest cell in the old cloisters and informed that His Excellency hoped to be able to find time for him in two or three hours. He asked for a copy of the rules of the Order, settled down with it and read through the entire booklet, to assure himself once more of the simplicity and legality of his plan. Nevertheless, even at this late hour he could not see how to put into words its meaning and its psychological justification.

There was a paragraph in the rules that had once been assigned to him as a subject for meditation, in the last days of his youthful freedom. That had been shortly before his admission into the Order. Now, reading the paragraph again, he meditated on it once more, and while doing so he became aware of how utterly different a person he was now from the rather anxious young tutor he had then been. "If the High Board summons you to a post," the passage read, "know this: Each upward step on the ladder of officialdom is not a step into freedom, but into constraint. The greater the power of the office, the stricter the servitude. The stronger the personality, the more forbidden is the arbitrary exercise of will." How final and unequivocal all that had once sounded, but how greatly the meaning of so many of the words had changed, especially such insidious words as "constraint," "personality," "will." And yet how beautifully clear, how well-formed and admirably suggestive these sentences were; how absolute, timeless, and incontestably true they could appear to a young mind! Ah yes, and so they would have been, if only Castalia were the world, the whole multifarious but indivisible world, instead of being merely a tiny world within the greater, or a section boldly and violently carved out of it. If the earth were an elite school, if the Order were the community of all men and the Head of the Order God, how perfect these sentences would be, and how flawless the entire Rule. Ah, if only that had been so, how lovely, how fecund and innocently beautiful life would be. And once that had really been so; once he had been able to see it that way: the Order and the Castalian spirit as equivalent to the divine and the absolute, the Province as the world, Castalians as mankind, and the non-Castalian sphere as a kind of children's world, a threshold to the Province, virgin soil still awaiting cultivation and ultimate redemption, a world looking reverently up to Castalia and every so often sending charming visitors such as young Plinio.

How strange was his own situation, how strange the nature of Joseph Knecht's own mind! In former days, and in fact only yesterday, had he not considered his own special kind of perception—that way of experiencing reality which he called "awakening"—as a slow, step-by-step penetration into the heart of the universe, into the core of truth; as something in itself absolute, a continuous path or progression which nevertheless had to be achieved gradually? In his youth he had thought it right and essential to acknowledge the validity of the outside world as Plinio represented it, but at the same time deliberately to hold aloof from it. At that time it had seemed to him progress, awakening, to make himself a Castalian. And again it had been progress, and his own truth, when after years of doubting he had decided in favor of the Glass Bead Game and the life of Waldzell. It had been

the same again when at Master Thomas's command he
entered the service, was inducted into the Order by the
Music Master, and later when he accepted the appointment as Magister. Each time he had taken a larger or
smaller step on a seemingly straight road—and yet he
now stood at the end of this road, by no means at the
heart of the universe and the innermost core of truth.
Rather, his present awakening, too, was no more than a
brief opening of his eyes, a finding himself in a new situation, a fitting into new constellations. The same strict,
clear, unequivocal, straight path that had brought him
to Waldzell, to Mariafels, into the Order, into the office
of Magister Ludi, was now leading him out again. What
had been a consequence of acts of awakening had likewise been a consequence of partings. Castalia, the Game,
the magistracy—each had been a theme which needed to
be developed and dismissed; each had been a space to pass
through, to transcend. Already they lay behind him. And
evidently, even in times past when he had thought and
done the opposite of the things he was thinking and doing today, he had somehow known or at least dimly
divined the dubiousness of it all. Had he not, in that
poem written in his student days and dealing with stages
and partings, placed above it the imperative title "Transcend!"?

Thus his path had been a circle, or an ellipse or spiral
or whatever, but certainly not straight; straight lines
evidently belonged only to geometry, not to nature and
life. Yet he had faithfully obeyed the exhortation and
self-encouragement of his poem, even after he had long
forgotten the poem and the awakening he had then experienced. Granted, he had not obeyed perfectly, not
without falterings, doubts, temptations, and struggles.
But he had courageously passed through stage upon
stage, space upon space, composedly and with reasonable
serenity—not with such radiant cheerfulness as the old
Music Master, but without weariness and dejection,
without disloyalty and defection. And if at this point he
had at last become a defector from the Castalian point of
view, if he were flouting all the morality of the Order,
seemingly serving only the needs of his own individuality
—still, this too would be done in the spirit of courage

and of music. No matter how it turned out, he would do it with serenity and a clean tempo. If only he had been able to clarify to Master Alexander what seemed so clear to him; if only he had been able to prove that the apparent willfulness of his present action was in reality service and obedience, that he was moving not toward freedom, but toward new, strange, and hitherto unknown ties; that he was not a fugitive, but a man responding to a summons; not headstrong, but obedient; not master, but sacrifice!

And what about the virtues of serenity, firm tempo and courage? They dwindled in size perhaps, but remained intact. Even if he might not be advancing on his own, but was only being led, even if what he was undergoing was not independent transcending, but merely a revolving of the space outside him around himself as its center, the virtues persisted and retained their value and their potency. They consisted in affirmation instead of negation, in acceptance instead of evasion. And perhaps there might even be some small virtue in his conducting himself as if he were the master and an active focus, in accepting life and self-deception—with its corollary self-determination and responsibility—without examining these things too closely. Perhaps it was inherently virtuous that for unknown reasons he was by nature more inclined to acting than acquiring knowledge, that he was more instinctual than intellectual. Oh, if only he could have a talk with Father Jacobus about these matters!

Thoughts or reveries of this sort reverberated in him after his meditation. "Awakening," it seemed, was not so much concerned with truth and cognition, but with experiencing and proving oneself in the real world. When you had such an awakening, you did not penetrate any closer to the core of things, to truth; you grasped, accomplished, or endured only the attitude of your own ego to the momentary situation. You did not find laws, but came to decisions; you did not thrust your way into the center of the world, but into the center of your own individuality. That, too, was why the experience of awakening was so difficult to convey, so curiously hard to formulate, so remote from statement. Language did not seem designed to make communications from this realm of life. If, once in a great while, someone were able to understand, that person was in a similar position, was a fellow sufferer or undergoing a similar awakening. Fritz Tegularius had to some degree shared this insight; Plinio's understanding had gone somewhat further. Whom else could he name? No one.

Twilight was already beginning to fall; he had been completely lost in his reflections, was altogether remote from his actual situation, when there came a knock on the door. Since he did not respond at once, the person outside waited a little and then tried once more, knocking softly. This time Knecht answered; he rose and went along with the messenger, who led him into the secretariat and without any further ado into the President's office. Master Alexander came forward to meet him.

"A pity you came without warning, so that we had to keep you waiting," he said. "I am eager to hear what has brought you here so suddenly. Nothing bad, I hope?"

Knecht laughed. "No, nothing bad. But do I really come so unexpectedly and have you no idea why I want to see you?"

Alexander gave him a troubled look. "Well, yes," he said, "I do have some idea. I had, for example, been thinking in the past few days that the subject of your circular letter had certainly not been treated adequately as far as you were concerned. The Board was obliged to answer rather tersely, and perhaps both the tone and the substance of the answer were disappointing to you, *Domine*."

"Not at all," Joseph Knecht replied. "I hardly expected any other answer as far as the substance of the Board's reply went. And as for the tone, that pleased me greatly. I could tell that the reply had cost the author considerable effort, almost sorrow, and that he felt the need to mingle a few drops of honey in an answer that was necessarily unpleasant and rather a snub to me. Certainly he succeeded remarkably well, and I am grateful to him for that."

"Then you have taken the substance of the reply to heart, esteemed Master?"

"Taken note of it, and I should say that at bottom I have also understood it and approved it. I suppose the reply could not have been anything but a rejection of my petition, together with a gentle reprimand. My circular letter was something untoward, and altogether inconvenient to the Board—I never for a moment doubted that. Moreover, insofar as it contained a personal petition, it probably was not couched in a suitable way. I could scarcely expect anything but a negative reply."

"We are pleased," the President of the Order said with a hint of acerbity, "that you regard it in this light and that our letter therefore could not have surprised you in any painful way. We are very pleased by that. But I still do not understand. If in writing your letter you already —I do understand you aright, don't I?—did not believe in its success, did not expect an affirmative answer, and in fact were convinced in advance that it would fail, why did you persist with it and go to the farther trouble —the whole thing must have involved considerable effort —of making a clean copy and sending it out?"

Knecht gave him an amiable look as he replied: "Your Excellency, my letter had two purposes, and I do not think that both were entirely fruitless. It contained a personal request that I be relieved of my post and employed at some other place. I could regard this personal request as relatively subsidiary, for every Magister ought to regard his personal affairs as secondary, insofar as that is possible. The petition was rejected; I had to make the best of that. But my circular letter also contained something quite different from that request, namely a considerable number of facts and ideas which I thought it my duty to call to the attention of the Board and to ask you all to weigh carefully. All the Masters, or at any rate the majority of them, have read my exposition—let us not say my warnings—and although most of them were loath to ingest them and reacted with a good deal of annoyance, they have at any rate read and registered what I believed it essential to say. The fact that they did not applaud the letter is, to my mind, no failure. I was not seeking applause and assent; I intended rather to stir uneasiness, to shake them up. I would greatly regret if I had desisted from sending my letter on the grounds you mention. Whether it has had much or little effect, it was at least a cry of alarm, a summons."

"Certainly," the President said hesitantly. "But that explanation does not solve the riddle for me. If you wished your admonitions, warnings, cries of alarm to reach the Board, why did you weaken or at least diminish the effectiveness of your golden words by linking them with a private request, moreover a request which you yourself did not seriously believe would be or could be granted? For the present I don't understand that. But I suppose the matter will be clarified if we talk it over. In any case, there is the weak point in your circular letter: your connecting the cry of alarm with the petition. I should think that you surely had no need to use the petition as a vehicle for your sermon. You could easily have reached your colleagues orally or in writing if you thought they had to be alerted to certain dangers. And then the petition would have proceeded along its own way through official channels."

Knecht continued to look at him with the utmost friendliness. "Yes," he said lightly, "it may be that you are right. Still—consider the complications of the matter once more. Neither the admonition nor the sermon was anything commonplace, ordinary, or normal. Rather, both belonged together in being unusual and in having arisen out of necessity and a break with convention. It is not usual and normal for anyone, without some urgent provocation from outside, to suddenly implore his colleagues to remember their mortality and the dubiousness of their entire lives. Nor is it usual and commonplace for a Castalian Magister to apply for a post as schoolteacher outside the Province. To that extent the two separate messages of my letter do belong together quite well. As I see it, a reader who had really taken the entire letter seriously would have had to conclude that this was no matter of an eccentric's announcing his premonitions and trying to preach to his colleagues, but rather that this man was in deadly earnest about his ideas and his distress, that he was ready to throw up his office, his dignity, his past, and begin from the beginning in the most modest of places; that he was weary of dignity, peace, honor, and authority and desired to be rid of them, to throw them away. From this conclusion— I am still trying to put myself into the mind of the readers of my letter—two corollaries would have been possible, so it seems to me: the writer of this sermon is unfortunately slightly cracked; or else the writer of this troublesome sermon is obviously not cracked, but normal and sane, which means there must be more than whim and eccentricity behind his pessimistic preachments. And that 'more' must then be a reality, a truth. I had imagined some such process in the minds of my readers, and I must admit that I miscalculated. My petition and my admonition did not support and reinforce each other. Instead, they were both not taken seriously and were laid aside. I am neither greatly saddened nor really surprised by this rejection, for at bottom, I must repeat, I did expect it to turn out that way. And I must also admit that I desired it so. For my petition, which I assumed would fail, was a kind of feint, a gesture, a formula."

Master Alexander's expression had become even graver and overcast with gloom. But he did not interrupt the Magister.

"The case was not," Knecht continued, "that in dispatching my petition I seriously hoped for a favorable reply and looked forward joyfully to receiving it; but it is also not the case that I was prepared to accept obediently a negative answer as an unalterable decision from above."

". . . not prepared to accept obediently a negative answer as an unalterable decision from above—have I heard you aright, Magister?" the President broke in, emphasizing every word. Evidently he had only at this point realized the full gravity of the situation.

Knecht bowed slightly. "Certainly you have heard aright. The fact was that I could scarcely believe my petition had much prospect of success, but I thought I had to make it to satisfy the requirements of decorum. By doing so I was, so to speak, providing the esteemed Board with an opportunity to settle the matter in a relatively harmless way. But if it eschewed such a solution, I was in any case resolved neither to be put off nor soothed, but to act."

"And to act how?" Alexander asked in a low voice.

"As my heart and my reason command. I was determined to resign my office and take on work outside

Castalia even without an assignment or leave from the Board."

The Head of the Order closed his eyes and seemed to be no longer listening. Knecht saw that he was performing that emergency exercise used by members of the Order in moments of sudden danger to regain self-control and inner calm; it consisted in twice emptying the lungs and holding the breath for long moments. As Knecht watched, Alexander's face paled slightly, then regained color as he inhaled slowly, beginning with the muscles of the stomach. Knecht was sorry to be inflicting psychic distress on a man whom he so highly esteemed, indeed loved. He saw Alexander's eyes open with a staring, abstracted look, then focus and grow keener. With a faint sense of alarm he saw those clear, controlled, disciplined eyes, the eyes of a man equally great in obeying and commanding, fixed upon him now, regarding him with cool composure, probing him, judging him. He withstood that gaze in silence for what seemed long minutes.

"I believe I have now understood you," Alexander said at last in a quiet voice. "You have been weary of your office or weary of Castalia for a long time, or tormented by a craving for life in the world. You chose to pay more heed to this mood than to the laws and your duties. You also felt no need to confide in us and ask the Order for advice and assistance. For the sake of form and to relieve your conscience, you then addressed that petition to us, a petition you knew would be unacceptable, but which you could refer to when the matter came up for discussion. Let us assume that you have reasons for such unusual conduct and that your intentions are honorable—I really cannot conceive them to have been otherwise. But how was it possible that with such thoughts, cravings, and decisions in your heart, inwardly already a defector, you could keep silent and remain in your office for so long a time, continuing to conduct it flawlessly, so far as anyone can see?"

"I am here," the Magister Ludi replied with unaltered friendliness, "to discuss all this with you, to answer all your questions. And since I have resolved upon a course of self-will, I have made up my mind not to leave Hirsland and your house until I know that you have gained some understanding of my situation and my action."

Master Alexander considered. "Does that mean you expect me to endorse your conduct and your plans?" he asked hesitantly.

"Oh, I have no thought of winning your endorsement. But I hope that you will understand me and that I shall retain a remnant of your respect when I go. This will be my one and only leave-taking of our Province. Today I left Waldzell and the Vicus Lusorum forever."

Again Alexander closed his eyes for a few seconds. He felt battered by the revelations coming all at once from this incomprehensible man.

"Forever?" he said. "Then you are thinking of not returning to your post at all? I must say, you are a master of surprises. One question, if I may ask it: Do you still regard yourself as Magister Ludi?"

Joseph Knecht picked up the small casket he brought with him.

"I was until yesterday," he said, "and consider myself liberated today by returning to you, as representative of the Board, the seals and keys. The insignia are intact, and when you go to inspect things in the Players' Village you will find everything in order."

Slowly, the President of the Order rose. He looked weary and suddenly aged.

"Let us leave your casket standing here for the present," he said drily. "If by receiving the seals I am supposed to be accepting your resignation, let me remind you that I am not so empowered. At least a third of the Board would have to be present. You used to have so much feeling for the old customs and forms that I cannot adjust so quickly to this new mode of doing things. Perhaps you will be kind enough to give me until tomorrow before we go on with our conversation?"

"I am completely at your disposal, your Reverence. You have known me and known my respect for you for a good many years. Believe me, that has not changed in the slightest. You are the only person I am bidding good-by to before leaving the Province, and I am addressing you now not only in your capacity as President of the Order. Just as I have returned the seals and keys to your hands,

I also hope you will release me from my oath as a member of the Order, once we have discussed everything fully, *Domine*."

Alexander met his eyes with a sorrowful, searching look, and stifled a sigh. "Leave me now. You have given me cares enough for one day and provided material enough for reflection. Let that do for today. Tomorrow we shall speak further; return here about an hour before noon."

He dismissed the Magister with a courteous gesture, and that gesture, full of resignation, full of deliberate politeness of the kind no longer meant for a colleague, but for a total stranger, pained the Glass Bead Game Master more than anything he had said.

The attendant who fetched Knecht for the evening meal a while later led him to a guest table and informed him that Master Alexander had withdrawn for meditation and assumed that the Magister would not wish company tonight, and that a guest room had been prepared for him.

The Magister Ludi's visit and announcement had taken Alexander completely by surprise. Ever since he had edited the Board's reply to the circular letter, he had of course counted on Knecht's turning up sooner or later, and had thought of the ensuing discussion with faint uneasiness. But that Magister Knecht, noted for his exemplary obedience, his cultivated formalities, his modesty and profound tact, could one day descend on him without warning, resign his office on his own initiative and without previously consulting the Board, and throw over all usage and tradition in this startling manner—these were acts he would have considered absolutely impossible. Granted, Knecht's manner, tone, and language, his unobtrusive courtesy, were the same as ever; but how appalling and offensive, how novel and surprising, and above all how totally un-Castalian were the substance and the spirit of everything he said. No one hearing and seeing the Magister Ludi would have suspected him of being ill, overworked, irritated, and not completely master of himself. The scrutiny which the Board had recently ordered in Waldzell had turned up not the slightest vestige of disturbance, disorder, or neglect in the life and work of the Players' Village. And nevertheless this appalling man, until yesterday the dearest of his colleagues, now stood here and deposited the chest with the insignia of office as if it were a suitcase, declaring that he had ceased to be Magister, had ceased to be a member of the Board, a brother of the Order and a Castalian, and had dropped in only to say goodby. This was the most disturbing situation his office as President of the Order had ever involved him in, and he had had great difficulty in preserving his outward composure.

And what now? Should he resort to force—place the Magister Ludi under house arrest, say, and at once, this very evening, send emergency messages to all members of the Board and call a meeting? Was there any objection to his doing so? Was that not the most logical and correct procedure? It was, and yet something within him protested. What would he really achieve by such measures? Nothing but humiliation for Magister Knecht, and nothing at all for Castalia; at most some alleviation for himself who would no longer have to face this ugly and complex situation alone, bearing all the responsibility. If anything could still be saved out of this vexatious affair, if any appeal to Knecht's sense of honor were possible and if it were conceivable that he might change his mind, such an outcome could only be achieved in a private interview. The two of them, Knecht and Alexander, would have to fight out this bitter conflict to the end—no one else. And even as he thought this he had to concede that basically Knecht had acted correctly and honorably by refraining from further contact with the Board, which he no longer recognized, but coming personally to consult him, the President, for the final struggle and leavetaking. This man Joseph Knecht, even when he did something so outrageous and repulsive, nevertheless acted with taste and tact.

Master Alexander decided to trust to his own powers of persuasion and leave the entire official apparatus out of the affair. Only now, after he had come to this decision, did he begin to reflect upon the details of the matter and to ask himself to what extent the Magister's action was right or wrong—for after all, Knecht seemed to have no doubt of the integrity and justness of his incredible step. Now that he tried to classify the Magister Ludi's audacious plan and determine where it stood legally—for no one knew the rules of the Order better than he—he came to the surprising conclusion that Joseph Knecht was not in fact violating the letter of the rules. Granted, for decades no one had ever tested the relevant clauses, but the rules did provide that every member of the Order was at liberty to resign any time he so desired. Of course he would at the same time renounce all his privileges and separate himself from the Castalian community. If Knecht now returned his seals, informed the Order of his resignation, and betook himself into the world, he was to be sure doing something unheard of in living memory, something highly unusual, alarming, and perhaps unseemly, but he was committing no infraction of the rules. Incomprehensible the step might be, but it was not illegal in any formal way. And that he chose not to take it behind the President's back, but was ready to come and announce his decision, was in fact more than punctilious. —But how had this venerated man, one of the pillars of the hierarchy, come to such a decision? After all, what he was planning was nothing short of desertion. How could he invoke the written rules when a hundred unwritten but no less sacred and self-evident ties should have kept him from taking this step?

Alexander heard a clock strike. He wrenched himself away from his profitless thoughts, took his bath, spent ten minutes on careful breathing exercises, and then went to his meditation cell in order to store up strength and tranquility for an hour before going to sleep. He would think no more of this matter until the morrow.

Next morning a young servant of the directorate's guest house led the Magister Ludi to the President, and was thus privy to the way the two men greeted each other. Accustomed as the youth was to the manner prevalent among these masters of meditation and self-discipline, he was nevertheless struck by something in the appearance, the bearing, and the tone of these two notables as they greeted each other. There was something new, an extraordinary degree of composure and clarity. It was, so he told us, not quite the usual salutation between two

of the highest dignitaries of the Order, which might be
either a serene and casual ceremony or an act of formal
but joyful festivity—although occasionally it also turned
into a competition in courtesy, deference, and stressed
humility. It was rather as though a stranger were being
received, say a great master of yoga come from afar to
pay his respects to the President of the Order and cross
swords with him. In word and gesture both men were
exceedingly modest and sparing, but their eyes and their
expressions, though tranquil, collected, and composed,
were charged with a hidden tension, as though both
were luminescent or carrying an electric current. Our in-
formant did not have the opportunity to see or hear any
more of the encounter. The two vanished into the office,
presumably going to Master Alexander's study, and remained there for several hours. No one was permitted to
disturb them. What record we have of their conversations comes from accounts set down on various occasions
by the honorable Delegate Designori, to whom Joseph
Knecht related some details.

"You took me by surprise yesterday," the President
began, "and very nearly disconcerted me. In the meantime I have been able to reflect upon the matter somewhat. My viewpoint has not changed, of course; I am a
member of the Board and the directorate of the Order.
According to the letter of the Rule, you have the right
to announce your withdrawal and resign your post. You
have come to the point of regarding your post as burdensome and of feeling an attempt to live outside the
Order as a necessity. What if I were now to propose
that you make this trial, but not in terms of your cate-
gorical decisions—rather in the form of a prolonged or
even an indeterminate leave? Actually, this is what your
petition sought to accomplish."

"Not entirely," Knecht said. "If my petition had been
approved, I would certainly have remained in the Order,
but not in office. Your kind proposal would be an evasion. Incidentally, Waldzell and the Glass Bead Game
would scarcely be well served by a Magister who was
absent on leave for a long or indeterminate period of
time and who might or might not return. Moreover, if
he did return after a year or two, his skills in the conduct

of his office and in his discipline, the Glass Bead Game, would only have suffered, not advanced."

Alexander: "He might have profited in all sorts of ways. Perhaps he would have learned that the world outside is not what he imagined and needs him no more than he does it. He might come back reassured and glad to remain in old and well-tested paths."

"Your kindness goes very far indeed. I am grateful for it; nevertheless I cannot accept it. What I am seeking is not so much fulfillment of idle curiosity or of a hankering for worldly life, but experience without reservations. I do not want to go out into the world with insurance in my pocket, in case I am disappointed. I don't want to be a prudent traveler taking a bit of a look at the world. On the contrary, I crave risk, difficulty, and danger; I am hungry for reality, for tasks and deeds, and also for deprivations and suffering. May I ask you not to press your kind proposal, and altogether to abandon any attempt to sway me and coax me back? It would lead to nothing. My visit with you would lose its value and its solemnity for me if it now brought me approval of my petition after all, when I no longer desire that. I have not stood still since writing that petition; the way I have embarked on is now my one and all, my law, my home, my service."

With a sigh, Alexander nodded assent. "Let us assume then," he said patiently, "that you in fact cannot be influenced or dissuaded. Let us assume that contrary to all appearances you are deaf to all representations, all reason, all kindness, that you are running amok or going berserk, so that people must simply keep out of your path. For the time being I will not try to change your mind or influence you. But tell me what you came here to tell me. Let me hear the story of your defection. Explain the acts and decisions which are to us so shocking. Whether what you have to offer is a confession, a justification, or an indictment, I want to hear it."

Knecht nodded. "Running amok though I am, I pause to express my gladness. I have no indictments to make. What I wish to say—if only it were not so hard, so incredibly hard to put into words—seems to me a justification; to you it may be a confession."

He leaned back in his chair and looked up, where traces of Hirsland's former days as a monastery showed in the vault of the ceiling, in sparse, dreamlike lines and colors, patterns of flowers and ornamentation.

"The idea that even a Magister could tire of his post and resign it first came to me only a few months after my appointment as Magister Ludi. One day I was sitting reading a little book by my once famous predecessor Ludwig Wassermaler, a journal of the official year, in which he offers guidance to his successors. There I read his admonition to give timely thought to the public Glass Bead Game for the coming year. If you felt no eagerness for it and lacked ideas, he wrote, you should try to put yourself into the right mood by concentration. With my strong awareness of being the youngest Magister, I smiled when I read this. With the brashness of youth I was a bit amused at the anxieties of the old man who had written it. But still I also heard in it a note of gravity and dread, of something menacing and oppressive. Reflecting on this, I decided that if ever the day came when the thought of the next festival game caused me anxiety instead of gladness, fear instead of pride, I would not struggle to work out a new festival game, but would at once resign and return the emblems of my office to the Board. This was the first time that such a thought presented itself to me. At the time I had just come through the great exertions of mastering my office, and had all my sails spread to the wind, so to speak. In my heart I did not really believe in the possibility that I too might some day be an old man, tired of the work and of life, that I might some day be unequal to the task of tossing off ideas for new Glass Bead Games. Nevertheless, I made the decision at that time. You knew me well in those days, your Reverence, better perhaps than I knew myself. You were my adviser and father confessor during that first difficult period in office, and had taken your departure from Waldzell only a short while before."

Alexander gave him a searching look. "I have scarcely ever had a finer assignment," he said, "and was then content, in a way that one rarely is, with you and myself. If it is true that we must pay for everything pleasant in life, then I must now atone for my elation at that time. I was truly proud of you then. I cannot be so today. If you cause the Order disappointment, if you shock all of Castalia, I know that I share the responsibility. Perhaps at that time, when I was your companion and adviser, I should have stayed in your Players' Village a few weeks longer, or handled you somewhat more roughly, subjected you to stricter examination."

Knecht cheerfully returned his look. "You must not have such misgivings, *Domine*, or I should have to remind you of various admonishments you felt called upon to give me at the time when I, as the youngest Magister, took the duties of my office too seriously. At one such moment you told me—I have just remembered this—that if I, the Magister Ludi, were a scoundrel or an incompetent and did everything a Magister is forbidden to do, in fact if I deliberately set out to use my high position to do as much harm as possible, all this would no more disturb our dear Castalia or affect it any more profoundly than a pebble that is thrown into a lake. A few ripples and circles and all trace is gone. That is how firm, how secure our Castalian Order is, how inviolable its spirit, you said. Do you recall? No, you are certainly not to blame for any efforts of mine to be as bad a Castalian as possible and to do the greatest possible harm to the Order. Moreover, you also know that what I do cannot shake your own tranquility. But I want to go on with my story. The fact that I could make such a decision at the very beginning of my magistracy, and that I did not forget it, but am now about to carry it out—that fact is related to a kind of spiritual experience I have from time to time, which I call awakening. But you already know about that; I once spoke to you about it, when you were my mentor and guru. In fact I complained to you at the time that since my accession to office that experience had not come to me, and seemed to be vanishing more and more into the distance."

"I remember," the President agreed. "I was somewhat taken aback at the time by your capacity for this kind of experience; it is rather rare among us, whereas in the world outside it occurs in so many varied forms: sometimes in the genius, especially in statesmen and generals, but also in feeble, semi-pathological, and on the whole rather meagerly gifted persons such as clairvoyants, telepaths, and mediums. You seemed to me to have no kinship at all with these two types, the aggressive heroes or the clairvoyants and diviners. Rather you seemed to me then, and until yesterday, to be a good Castalian, prudent, clearheaded, obedient. I thought it completely out of the question that you should ever be the victim of mysterious voices, whether of divine or diabolic origin, or even voices from within your own self. Therefore I interpreted the states of 'awakening' which you described to me simply as your becoming aware occasionally of personal growth. Given that interpretation, it followed that these spiritual insights would not be coming your way for a considerable time. After all, you had just entered office and had assumed a task which still hung loosely around you like an overcoat too big for you —you would still have to grow into it. But tell me this: have you ever believed that these awakenings are anything like revelations from higher powers, communications or summons from the realm of an objective, eternal, or divine truth?"

"In saying this," Knecht replied, "you bring me to my present difficulty: to express in words something that refuses to be put into words; to make rational what is obviously extrarational. No, I never thought of those awakenings as manifestations of a god or daimon or of some absolute truth. What gives these experiences their weight and persuasiveness is not their truth, their sublime origin, their divinity or anything of the sort, but their reality. They are tremendously real, somewhat the way a violent physical pain or a surprising natural event, a storm or earthquake, seem to us charged with an entirely different sort of reality, presence, inexorability, from ordinary times and conditions. The gust of wind that precedes a thunderstorm, sending us into the house and almost wrenching the front door away from our hand—or a bad toothache which seems to concentrate all the tensions, sufferings, and conflicts of the world in our jaw—these are such realities. Later on we may start to question them or examine their significance, if that is our bent; but at the moment they happen they admit no doubts and

are brimful of reality. My 'awakening' has a similar kind
of intensified reality for me. That is why I have given it
this name; at such times I really feel as if I had lain
asleep or half asleep for a long time, but am now awake
and clearheaded and receptive in a way I never am ordinarily. In history, too, moments of tribulation or great
upheavals have their element of convincing necessity; they
create a sense of irresistible immediacy and tension.
Whatever the consequence of such upheavals, be it
beauty and clarity or savagery and darkness, whatever
happens will bear the semblance of grandeur, necessity,
and importance and will stand out as utterly different
from everyday events."

He paused to catch his breath, then continued: "But
let me try to examine this matter from another angle. Do
you recall the legend of St. Christopher? Yes? Well now,
Christopher was a man of great strength and courage, but
he wanted to serve rather than to be a master and
govern. Service was his strength and his art; he had a
faculty for it. But whom he served was not a matter of
indifference to him. He felt that he had to serve the
greatest, the most powerful master. And when he
heard of a mightier master, he promptly offered his
services. I have always been fond of this great servant,
and I must in some way resemble him. At any rate,
during the one period in my life when I had command
over myself, during my student years, I searched and
vacillated for a long time before deciding what master
to serve. For years I remained mistrustful of the Glass
Bead Game and fended it off, although I had long ago
recognized it as the most precious and characteristic
fruit of our Province. I had tasted the bait and knew that
there was nothing more attractive and more subtle on
earth than the Game. I had also observed fairly early
that this enchanting Game demanded more than naive
amateur players, that it took total possession of the man
who had succumbed to its magic. And an instinct within
me rebelled against my throwing all my energies and
interests into this magic forever. Some naive feeling for
simplicity, for wholeness and soundness, warned me
against the spirit of the Waldzell Vicus Lusorum. I
sensed in it a spirit of specialism and virtuosity, certainly

highly cultivated, certainly richly elaborated, but nevertheless isolated from humanity and the whole of life—a
spirit that had soared too high into haughty solitariness.
For years I doubted and probed, until the decision had
matured within me and in spite of everything I decided
in favor of the Game. I did so because I had within me
that urge to seek the supreme fulfillment and serve only
the greatest master."

"I understand," Master Alexander said. "But no matter
how I regard it and no matter how you try to represent
it, I come up against the same reason for your singulari-
ties. You have an excessive sense of your own person, or
dependence on it, which is far from the same thing as
being a great personality. A man can be a star of the first
magnitude in gifts, will-power, and endurance, but so
well balanced that he turns with the system to which he
belongs without any friction or waste of energy. Another
may have the same great gifts, or even finer ones, but the
axis does not pass precisely through the center and he
squanders half his strength in eccentric movements which
weaken him and disturb his surroundings. You evidently
belong to this type. Only I must admit that you have
contrived to conceal it remarkably. For that very reason
the malady seems to be breaking out now with all the
greater virulence. You spoke of St. Christopher, and I
must say that although there is something grand and
touching about this saint, he is not a model for a servant of our hierarchy. One who wishes to serve should
abide by the master he has sworn to serve for good and
ill, and not with the secret reservation that he will change
as soon as he finds a more magnificent master. In assuming such an attitude the servant makes himself his
master's judge, and this indeed is what you are doing.
You always want to serve the highest master, and are
naive enough to decide for yourself the rank of the
masters among whom you make your choice."

Knecht had listened attentively, although a shadow of
sadness passed across his face. Now he continued: "I
respect your opinion, and could not have imagined that
it would be any different. But let me go on with my
story just a little longer. I became Magister Ludi and
in fact was sure for a good while that I was serving the

highest of all masters. At any rate my friend Designori,
our patron in the Federal Council, once described to me
in extremely vivid terms what an arrogant, conceited,
blasé elitist and virtuoso of the Game I once was. But I
must also tell you the meaning that the word 'transcend'
has had for me since my student years and my 'awakening.' It came to me, I think, while reading a philosopher
of the Enlightenment, and under the influence of Master
Thomas von der Trave, and ever since then it has been
a veritable magic word for me, like 'awakening,' an
impetus, a consolation, and a promise. My life, I resolved, ought to be a perpetual transcending, a progression from stage to stage; I wanted it to pass through
one area after the next, leaving each behind, as music
moves on from theme to theme, from tempo to tempo,
playing each out to the end, completing each and leaving it behind, never tiring, never sleeping, forever wakeful, forever in the present. In connection with the experiences of awakening, I had noticed that such stages
and such areas exist, and that each successive period in
one's life bears within itself, as it is approaching its
end, a note of fading and eagerness for death. That in
turn leads to a shifting to a new area, to awakening and
new beginnings. I am telling you about the significance
to me of transcending in order to provide another clue
which may help you interpret my life. The decision in
favor of the Glass Bead Game was an important stage,
as was the first time I took my place in the hierarchy by
accepting an assignment. I have also experienced such
movements from stage to stage in my office as Magister.
The best thing the office has given me was the discovery
that making music and playing the Glass Bead Game
are not the only happy activities in life, that teaching
and educating can be just as exhilarating. And I gradually discovered, furthermore, that teaching gave me all
the more pleasure, the younger and more unspoiled by
miseducation the pupils were. This too, like many other
things, led me in the course of the years to desire younger
and younger pupils, so that I would have liked most to
have become a teacher in an elementary school. In
short, at times my imagination dwelt on matters which
in themselves lay outside my functions."

He paused for a moment to rest. The President remarked: "You astonish me more and more, Magister. Here you are speaking about your own life, and you mention scarcely anything but subjective experiences, personal wishes, personal developments and decisions. I really had no idea that a Castalian of your rank could see himself and his life in such a light."

His voice had a note between reproach and sorrow. It pained Knecht, but he remained equable and exclaimed merrily: "Esteemed Magister, we are not speaking about Castalia, about the Board and the hierarchy at the moment, but only about me, about the psychology of a man who unfortunately has been forced to cause you great inconvenience. It would be improper for me to speak of my conduct of office, the way I have met my obligations, my value or lack of it as a Castalian and Magister. My conduct of office lies open before you. You can easily look into it, as you can into the entire exterior of my life. You will not find much to censure. But what we are concerned with here is something wholly different. I am trying to show you the path I have trodden as an individual, which has led me out of Waldzell and will lead me out of Castalia tomorrow. Please, be so kind as to listen to me a little while longer.

"My consciousness of a world outside our little Province I owe not to my studies, in which this world occurred only as the remote past, but primarily to my fellow student Designori, who was a guest from outside, and later to my stay among the Benedictines, and to Father Jacobus. What I have seen of the world with my own eyes is very little, but Father Jacobus gave me an inkling of what is called history. And it may be that in acquiring that I was laying the groundwork for the isolation into which I stumbled after my return. I returned from the monastery into a land where history virtually didn't exist, into a Province of scholars and Glass Bead Game players, a highly refined and extremely pleasant society, but one in which I seemed to stand entirely alone with my smattering of the world, my curiosity about that world, and my sympathy for it. To be sure, there was enough to compensate me here. There were several men I revered, so that I felt all at once abashed, delighted, and honored to work with them as their colleague, and there were a large number of well-bred and highly cultivated people. There was also work aplenty and a great many talented and lovable students. The trouble was that during my apprenticeship under Father Jacobus I had made the discovery that I was not only a Castalian, but also a man; that the world, the whole world, concerned me and exerted certain claims upon me. Needs, wishes, demands, and obligations arose out of this discovery, but I was in no position to meet any of them. Life in the world, as the Castalian sees it, is something backward and inferior, a life of disorder and crudity, of passions and distractions, devoid of all that is beautiful or desirable. But the world and its life was in fact infinitely vaster and richer than the notions a Castalian has of it; it was full of change, history, struggles, and eternally new beginnings. It might be chaotic, but it was the home and native soil of all destinies, all exaltations, all arts, all humanity; it had produced languages, peoples, governments, cultures; it had also produced us and our Castalia and would see all these things perish again, and yet survive. My teacher Jacobus had kindled in me a love for this world which was forever growing and seeking nourishment. But in Castalia there was nothing to nourish it. Here we were outside of the world; we ourselves were a small, perfect world, but one no longer changing, no longer growing."

He took a deep breath and fell silent for a while. Since the president made no reply, and only looked expectantly at him, he gave a pensive nod and continued: "For me, this meant bearing two burdens, and I did so for a good many years. I had to administer an important office and meet its responsibilities, and I had to deal with this love for the world. My office, I realized from the outside, must not suffer because of this love. On the contrary, I thought it ought to benefit. I hoped to carry out my duties as thoroughly and irreproachably as a Magister is expected to; but if I should fall short in these, I nevertheless knew that inwardly I was more alert and alive than a good many of my more punctilious colleagues, and that I had something to give to my students and associates. I regarded it as my mission to

expand Castalian life and thought slowly and gently
without breaking with tradition, to add to its warmth,
to infuse it with new blood from the world and from
history. By the happy workings of Providence, at the
same time, outside in our country, a man of the world
had precisely the same thought. He dreamed of a *rapprochement* and interpenetration of Castalia and the
world. That man was Plinio Designori."

Master Alexander's mouth took on a slightly sour expression as he said: "Well yes, I have never hoped for
anything very good from this man's influence upon you,
any more than I have from your spoiled protégé Tegularius. So it is Designori who brought you to the point
of a complete breach with the system?"

"No, *Domine*, but he helped me, in part without being aware of it. He brought fresh air into my quietude.
Through him I came into contact with the outside world
again, and only then was I able to realize and to admit
to myself that I was at the end of my career here, that I
had lost all real joy in my work, and that it was time to
put an end to the ordeal. One more stage had been left
behind; I had passed through another area, another space,
which this time was Castalia."

"How you phrase that!" Alexander remarked, shaking
his head. "As if Castalian space were not large enough
to serve a great many people worthily all their lives!
Do you seriously believe that you have traversed this
space and gone beyond it?"

"Oh no," Knecht replied with strong feeling. "I've
never believed anything of the sort. When I say that I
have reached the border of this space, I mean only that
I have done all that I as an official could do here. In
this sense I have reached my limits. For some time I have
been standing at the frontier where my work as Magister Ludi has become eternal recurrence, an empty exercise and formula. I have been doing it without joy, without enthusiasm, sometimes even without faith. It was
time to stop."

Alexander sighed. "That is your view, but not the view
of the Order and its rules. A brother in our Order has
moods, and at times he wearies of his work—there is
nothing new and remarkable about that. The rules show

him the way to regain harmony, to find his center again. Had you forgotten that?"

"I do not think so, your Reverence. My administration is open to your inspection, and only recently, after you had received my circular letter, you conducted an investigation of the Players' Village and of me personally. You learned that the work was being done, that Secretariat and Archive were in order, that the Magister Ludi showed no signs of illness or vagary. I was able to carry on, and sustain my strength and composure, because of those very rules which you so skillfully taught me. But it cost me great effort. And now, unfortunately, it is costing me almost as much effort to convince you that I am not giving in to moods, whims, or vague yearnings. But whether or not I succeed, I insist at least on your acknowledging that my personality and my work were sound and useful up to the moment you last evaluated them. Is that asking too much of you?"

Master Alexander's eyes twinkled rather sardonically.

"My dear colleague," he said, "you address me as if we were two private individuals holding a casual conversation. But that applies only to yourself; you are now in fact a private individual. I am not, and whatever I think and say, I do not speak for myself, but as President of the Order, and he is responsible to his Board for every word. What you are saying here today will remain without consequences. No matter how earnest your intentions, yours is the speech of a private person urging his own interests. But for me, my office and responsibility continue, and what I say or do today may have consequences. I shall plead your cause before the Board. You want the Board to accept your account of the circumstances, or perhaps even acknowledge that you have made a correct decision. Your case then is that until yesterday, though you may have had all sorts of weird ideas in your head, you were an irreproachable Castalian, an exemplary Magister; that you may have experienced temptations, spells of weariness, but that you consistently fought and overcame them. Let us assume that I accept that; but then how am I to understand that the upright Magister who only yesterday obeyed every rule today suddenly defects? You must admit this is more understandable in terms of a Magister whose mind had in fact been impaired, who was suffering from psychic illness, so that he went on considering himself an excellent Castalian long after he had in reality ceased to be one. I also wonder why you make such a point of your having been a dutiful Magister up to the very end. Since you have after all taken the step, broken your vow of obedience, and committed the act of desertion, why be concerned about establishing such a point?"

Knecht protested. "I beg your pardon, your Reverence, but why should I not be concerned about that? My name and reputation is involved, the memory I shall leave behind here. Also involved is the possibility of my working for Castalia on the outside. I am not here to salvage something for myself, or even to win the Board's approval of my action. I counted on being regarded by my colleagues henceforth as a dubious phenomenon, and am prepared for that. But I don't want to be regarded as a traitor or madman; that is a verdict I cannot accept. I have done something you must disapprove of, but I have done it because I had to, because it was incumbent upon me, because that is my destiny, which I believe in and which I assume with good will. If you cannot concede this much, then I have been defeated and have spoken with you in vain."

"Again and again it comes down to the same thing," Alexander replied. "You want me to concede that in some circumstances an individual has the right to break the laws in which I believe and which it is my task to represent. But I cannot simultaneously believe in our system and in your personal right to violate it—please, don't interrupt me. I can concede that to all appearances you are convinced of the rightness and meaningfulness of your dreadful step, and that you believe you have been called to take such action. You certainly don't expect me to approve the step itself. On the other hand, you have achieved something, for I have given up my initial thought of winning you back and changing your decision. I accept your withdrawal from the Order and shall pass on to the Board the news of your voluntary resignation of your post. I cannot make any further concessions to you, Joseph Knecht."

The Magister Ludi made a gesture of submission. Then he said quietly: "Thank you. I have already given you the casket. I now turn over to you, as representative of the Board, my notes on the state of affairs in Waldzell, especially on the body of tutors and my recommendations on the persons I consider possible successors to my office."

He took a few folded sheets of paper from his pocket and placed them on the table. Then he rose, and the President rose also. Knecht took a step toward him, looked into his eyes for a long moment in sorrowful friendliness, then bowed and said: "I had wanted to ask you to shake hands with me in parting, but I suppose I must forgo this now. You have always been especially dear to me, and today has not changed that in any way. Good-by, dear and revered Master."

Alexander stood still. He was rather pale. For a moment it seemed as though he meant to extend his hand to the departing Magister. He felt his eyes growing moist. Then he inclined his head, responded to Knecht's bow, and let him go.

After Knecht had closed the door behind him, the President stood unmoving, listening to the departing footsteps. When the last one had faded away and there was nothing more to be heard, he walked back and forth across the room for a while, until footsteps again sounded outside and there was a soft knock at the door. The young servant entered and reported that a visitor wished to see him.

"Tell him that I can receive him in an hour and that I request him to be brief; there are urgent matters to attend to. No, wait a moment. Also go to the Secretariat and inform the First Secretary to convoke a meeting of the entire Board for the day after tomorrow. All members must attend; only severe illness will be acceptable as an excuse for absence. Then go to the steward and tell him I must leave for Waldzell early tomorrow morning; have my car ready by seven."

"I beg your pardon," the young man said, "but the Magister Ludi's car is at your disposal."

"How is that?"

"His Reverence came by car yesterday. He has just

left word that he is continuing his journey on foot and leaving the car here at your disposal."

"Very well, I'll take the Waldzell car tomorrow. Repeat, please."

The servant repeated: "The visitor will be received in an hour; he is to be brief. The First Secretary is to convoke the Board for the day after tomorrow, attendance mandatory, absence excused only on grounds of severe illness. Departure for Waldzell at seven o'clock tomorrow morning in the Magister Ludi's car."

Master Alexander took a deep breath once the young man had gone. He went over to the table where he had sat with Knecht. Still echoing in his ears were the footsteps of that incomprehensible man whom he had loved above all others and who had inflicted this great grief upon him. He had loved this man ever since the days he had first helped him; and among other traits it had been Knecht's way of walking that had appealed so strongly to him—a firm, rhythmic step that was also light, almost airy, expressing something between dignity and childlikeness, between priestliness and the dance—a strange, lovable, and elegant walk that accorded with Knecht's face and voice. It accorded equally well with his peculiar way of being a Castalian and Magister, his kind of mastership and serenity, which sometimes reminded Alexander of the aristocratically measured manner of his predecessor, Master Thomas, sometimes of the simple, heartwarming former Music Master. So he had already left, in his haste, and on foot, who could say where, and probably he, Alexander, would never see him again, never again hear his laugh and watch the fine, long and slender fingers of his hand drawing the hieroglyphs of a Glass Bead Game phrase. Alexander reached for the sheets of paper that had been left lying on the table and began reading them. They amounted to a brief testament, extremely terse and matter-of-fact, frequently consisting only of cue words rather than sentences; their purpose was to facilitate the Board's work in the forthcoming investigation of the Vicus Lusorum and the appointment of a new Magister. The laconic, sensible remarks stood there in neat, small letters, the words and handwriting just as uniquely and unmistakably typical of Joseph Knecht as his face, his voice, his gait. The Board would scarcely find a man of his stature for his successor; real masters and real personalities were all too rare, and each one was a matter of good luck and a pure gift, even here in Castalia, the province of the elite.

Joseph Knecht enjoyed walking; it was years since he had last traveled on foot. In fact, when he reviewed the matter it seemed to him that his last real walking tour had been the one that had long ago taken him from Mariafels monastery back to Castalia and to that annual game in Waldzell which had been so overshadowed by the death of Magister Thomas von der Trave and had resulted in his own appointment to succeed the Magister Ludi. Ordinarily, when he thought back upon those days, let alone upon his student years and the Bamboo Grove, it had always been as if he were gazing from a cool, dull room out into broad, brightly sunlit landscapes, into the irrevocable past, the paradise of memory. Such recollections had always been, even when they were free of sadness, a vision of things remote and different, separated from the prosaic present by a mysterious festiveness. But now, on this bright and cheerful September afternoon, with the strong greens and browns all around him and the ethereal, gently misted tones of blue verging into violet in the distance, as he trudged along at an easy pace, with frequent pauses to look about him, that walking tour of so long ago did not seem a distant paradise cut off from a resigned present. Rather his present journey was the same as that of the past, the present Joseph Knecht was close as a brother to the Knecht of those days. Everything was new again, mysterious, promising; all that had been could recur, and many new things as well. It was long, long since he had looked out upon the day and the world and seen them as so unburdened, so beautiful and innocent. The happiness of freedom, of commanding his own destiny, flooded through him like a strong drink. How long it was since he had last had this feeling, last entertained this lovely and rapturous illusion. He pondered that, and recalled the time this precious feeling had first been bruised, then given a fatal blow. It had happened during a conversation with Magister Thomas, under the latter's friendly and ironic glance. He now recalled the strange sensation of that hour in which he had lost his freedom. It had not really been a pang, a burning anguish, but rather an onset of timidity, a faint shiver at the nape of his neck, an organic warning somewhere above his diaphragm, a change in the temperature and especially in the tempo of his consciousness of life. That anxious, constricting sensation, the hidden threat of suffocation of that fateful hour, was being recompensed now, or healed.

The day before, during his drive to Hirsland, Knecht had decided that whatever might happen there, he would not repine. Now he forbade himself to think over the details of his conversations with Alexander, of his struggle with him and his struggle to win him. He left himself entirely open to the feeling of relaxation and freedom that filled him like the approach of evening leisure for a peasant whose day's work lies behind him. He was conscious of being safe and under no obligations. For a moment he was utterly dispensable, exempt from all responsibilities, not required to perform any tasks, to do any thinking. The bright, varicolored day surrounded him with a gentle radiance, wholly visual, wholly present, imposing no demands, having neither yesterday nor tomorrow. Now and then as he walked he contentedly hummed one of the marching songs he and his schoolmates used to sing in three or four parts on outings, when he was an elite pupil at Eschholz, and out of that serene early morning of his life small bright memories and sounds came fluttering to him like the chirping of birds.

Under a cherry tree with leaves already showing glints of purple he stopped to rest and sat down in the grass. He reached into the pocket of his coat and took out a thing that Master Alexander would never have guessed he would be carrying, a small wooden flute, which he contemplated for a moment with tenderness. He had not owned this naive, childish-looking instrument for long, perhaps half a year, and he recalled with pleasure the day he had acquired it. He had ridden to Monteport to discuss some problems of musical theory with Carlo Ferromonte. Their conversation had turned to the wood-winds of certain ages, and he had asked his friend to show him the Monteport instrument collection. After an enjoyable stroll through several halls filled with old organ manuals, harps, lutes, and pianos, they had come to a building where instruments for the schools were stored. There Knecht had seen a whole drawer full of such little flutes; he had examined and tried one, and asked his friend whether he might have one. Laughing, Carlo had invited him to choose; still laughing, he had presented him with a receipt to sign; but then he had seriously explained the structure of the instrument, its fingering, and the technique of playing it. Knecht had taken the pretty little toy with him, and practiced on it occasionally—for he had not played a wind instrument since the recorder of his boyhood in Eschholz, and had often resolved to learn one again. In addition to scales, he had used a book of old melodies which Ferromonte had edited for beginners, and every so often the soft, sweet notes of the flute had sounded from the Magister's garden or from his bedroom. He was far from a master of the instrument, but had learned to play a number of chorales and songs; he knew the music by heart, and also the words of a good many of them. One of these songs now sprang into his mind; it seemed highly suitable to the moment. He sang a few lines under his breath:

> My body and head
> Lay asleep like the dead,
> But now I stand strong,
> Gay as the day is long
> And turn my face to heaven.

He brought the instrument to his lips and blew the melody, looking out into the radiant plain that arched toward the distant mountains, listening to the serenely devout song ringing out in the sweet notes of the flute, and feeling at one and content with the sky, the mountains, the song, and the day. With pleasure, he felt the smooth wand between his fingers and reflected that aside from the clothes on his body this toy flute was the only piece of property he had allowed himself to take from Waldzell. In the course of years he had accumulated a good many things that could be more or less regarded as personal property, above all writings, notebooks, and so on. He had left all these things behind; the Players' Village might use them as it wished. But he had taken the flute, and he was glad to have it with him; it was a modest and lovable traveling companion.

On the second day he arrived in the capital on foot and called at the Designori home. Plinio sped down the steps to meet him and embraced him with emotion.

"We have been longing for you, and anxiously waiting for you!" he exclaimed. "You have taken a great step, friend—may it bring good things to all of us. But to think that they let you go! I never would have believed it."

Knecht laughed. "You see, I am here. But I'll tell you about it by and by. But now I'd like to greet my pupil, and of course your wife, and discuss everything with you—how we are going to arrange my new position. I am eager to start on it."

Plinio called a maid and told her to bring his son at once.

"The young gentleman?" she asked, seemingly astonished, but hurried off while Plinio showed his friend to the guest room. He began eagerly describing what preparations he had made for Knecht's arrival, and how he imagined the tutoring of young Tito would work out. Everything had been arranged as Knecht wished it, he said; Tito's mother, after some initial reluctance, had also grasped the reasons for these wishes and assented to them. The family owned a vacation cottage in the mountains, called Belpunt, pleasantly situated on a lake. There Knecht would live with his pupil for the time being. An elderly servant would keep house for them; she had already left several days ago to put the place in order. Of course they could stay there only for a short time, at most till the onset of winter; but such isolation would certainly be beneficial, especially for the initial period. Fortunately, Tito loved the mountains and Belpunt, so the boy made no difficulties about going there. He was even looking forward to the project. At this point Designori remembered that he had an album of photos of the house and its environs. He drew Knecht along into his study, searched eagerly for the album, and when he had found it began showing his guest the house and describing the big farm kitchen-living room, the tile stove, the arbors, the lake shore, the waterfall.

"Does it seem nice to you?" he asked insistently. "Will you feel comfortable there?"

"Why not?" Knecht said calmly. "But I wonder where Tito is. It's been quite some time since he was sent for."

They chatted for a while longer. Then they heard footsteps outside. The door opened, but neither Tito nor the maid dispatched for him entered. It was Tito's mother, Madame Designori. Knecht rose to greet her. She extended her hand, smiling with a somewhat artificial friendliness; he could see beneath this polite smile an expression of anxiety and vexation. She barely managed a few words of welcome and then turned to her husband and impetuously burst out with what was troubling her.

"It's really so awkward," she exclaimed. "Imagine, the boy has vanished and is nowhere to be found."

"Oh well, I imagine he has gone out," Plinio said soothingly. "He'll be along."

"Unfortunately that isn't likely," his wife said. "He's been gone all day. I noticed his absence early this morning."

"And why am I only now being told about it?"

"Because I naturally expected him back any minute and saw no reason to trouble you needlessly. At first I took it for granted that he had simply gone for a walk. When he didn't return by noon I began to worry. You were not lunching with us today or I would have spoken to you. Even then, I tried to persuade myself that it was simply carelessness on his part to make me wait so long. But it seems it wasn't that."

"Permit me a question," Knecht said. "The young man knew I would be arriving soon, didn't he, and about your plans for him and me?"

"Of course, Magister. And he seemed to be agreeable to those plans—or at least he preferred having you as his teacher to being sent back to some school."

"Oh well," Knecht said, "then there is nothing to worry about. Your son is used to a great deal of freedom, Signora, especially of late. It's understandable that the prospect of a tutor and disciplinarian should be rather dreadful to him. And so he's made off at just the moment he was to be turned over to his new teacher—probably less with the hope of actually escaping his fate than with the thought that he'll lose nothing by postponement. Besides, he probably wanted to play a trick on his parents and the schoolmaster they've found for him, and so show his defiance to the whole world of grown-ups and teachers."

Designori was glad that Knecht took the incident so lightly. He himself was full of anxiety; with his intense love for his son, he imagined all sorts of dangers. Perhaps, he thought, the boy had run away in all earnest; perhaps he even intended to do himself some harm. It seemed as if they were going to pay for all their faults of omission and commission in the boy's upbringing, just when they were hoping to remedy things.

Against Knecht's advice, he insisted that something must be done; he could not take this latest crisis passively, and worked himself up to a pitch of impatience and nervous agitation which his friend found deplorable. It was therefore decided to send messages to the homes of a few of Tito's friends, where he sometimes stayed overnight. Knecht was relieved when Madame Designori left to attend to this, and he had Plinio to himself for a while.

"Plinio," he said, "you look as if your son had just been carried dead into the house. He is no longer a small child and is not likely to have been run over or to have eaten deadly nightshade. So get a grip on yourself, my dear fellow. Since the boy isn't here, permit me for a moment to teach you something in his stead. I have been observing you and find that you're not in the best of form. The moment an athlete receives an unexpected blow or pressure, his muscles react of their own accord by making the necessary movements, stretching or contracting automatically and so helping him master the situation. You too, my pupil Plinio, the moment you received the blow—or what you exaggeratedly thought a blow—should have applied the first defensive measure against psychic assaults and resorted to slow, carefully controlled breathing. Instead you breathed like an actor when he seeks to represent extreme emotion. You are not sufficiently armored; you people in the world seem to be singularly exposed to suffering and cares. There is something helpless and touching about your state; though often, when real suffering is involved and there is meaning to such pangs, it is also magnificent. But for everyday life these protective measures are most valuable and should not be ignored. I will make sure that your son will be better armed when he needs such equipment. And now, Plinio, be so kind as to do a few exercises with me, so that I can see whether you have really forgotten it all."

With the breathing exercises, which he guided by strictly rhythmical commands, he was able to distract Plinio from his self-induced agonies until he was willing to listen to rational arguments and dismantle the structure of alarm and anxiety he had so lavishly built. They went up to Tito's room, where Knecht looked benignly around at the confusion of boyish possessions. He picked up a book lying on the night table, saw a slip of paper jutting from it, and found it was a note from the vanished boy. Laughing, he handed the paper to Designori, whose expression immediately brightened. Tito had written that he was leaving at daybreak and going to the mountains alone, where he would wait at Belpunt for his new teacher. He hoped, the message said, that his parents would not mind his having this last little jaunt before his freedom was once more awfully restricted; his spirits sank when he thought of having to make this pleasant little journey accompanied by his teacher, a prisoner under supervision.

"Quite understandable," Knecht commented. "I'll leave for Belpunt tomorrow and will probably find the boy already there. But now you'd better go to your wife and tell her the news."

For the rest of the day the atmosphere in the house was happy and relaxed. That evening, on Plinio's insistence, Knecht summarized the events of the past several days, and in particular described his two conversations with Master Alexander. On that evening he also scribbled some curious lines of verse on a scrap of paper which is today in the possession of Tito Designori. That came about in the following way.

Before dinner his host had left him alone for an hour.

Knecht saw a bookcase full of old books which aroused his curiosity. Idle reading was another pleasure which he had unlearned and almost forgotten in years of abstinence. This moment now reminded him intensely of his student years: to stand before a shelf of unknown books, reach out at random, and choose one or another volume whose gilt or author's name, format or the color of the binding, appealed to him. With pleasure he glanced over the titles on the spines and saw that the shelf consisted entirely of nineteenth- and twentieth-century belles-lettres. Finally he picked out a faded cloth-bound volume whose title, *Wisdom of the Brahmans,* tempted him. Standing for a while, then seated, he leafed through the book, which contained many hundreds of didactic poems. It was a curious composite of learned loquacity and real wisdom, of philistinism and genuine poetry. This strange and touching book held, it seemed to him, a good deal of important esoteric philosophy, but this was almost lost in the heavyhanded treatment. The best poems were by no means the ones in which the poet tried hard to give form to a theory or a truth, but the ones in which the poet's temperament, his capacity for love, his sincerity, humanitarianism, and deep respectability, found expression. As Knecht delved into the book, with mixed feelings of esteem and amusement, he was struck by a stanza which he absorbed with satisfaction and assent. Reading it, he nodded smilingly, as if it had been specially sent to him for this day in his life. It went:

> Our days are precious but we gladly see them going
> If in their place we find a thing more precious
> growing:
> A rare, exotic plant, our gardener's heart de-
> lighting;
> A child whom we are teaching, a booklet we are
> writing.

He opened the drawer of the desk, found a sheet of paper, and copied out the stanza. Later he showed it to Plinio, and commented: "I liked these lines. There is something special about them; they are so dry and at the same time so deeply felt. And they so well suit me and

my momentary situation and mood. Although I am not a
gardener and don't intend to devote my days to the cultivation of an exotic plant, I am a teacher, and am on the
way to my task, to the child I mean to teach. How I am
looking forward to it! As for the author of these lines, the
poet Rückert, I would suppose he possessed all three of
these noble passions: that of gardener, teacher, and writer.
I suppose the third ranked highest with him; he shapes
the stanza so that it receives the maximum stress, and
dotes so on the object of his passion that he becomes
positively tender and calls it not a book, but a booklet.
How touching that is."

Plinio laughed. "Who knows," he observed, "whether
the diminutive is not just a rhymester's trick because he
needed a two-syllable instead of a one-syllable word
there."

"Let us not underestimate him," Knecht replied. "A
man who wrote tens of thousands of lines of verse in his
lifetime would not be driven into a corner by shabby
metrical necessity. No, just listen to it, how loving it
sounds, and at the same time just a little sheepish: a
booklet we are writing. Perhaps it isn't only his affection
that transforms the book into a booklet. Perhaps he also
meant it apologetically. Probably this poet was so devoted to his writing that now and again he felt his own
passion for making books as a kind of vice. In that case
the word booklet would have not only the sense of an
endearment, but also a propitiating, disarming connota-
tion, as when a gambler invites someone to a 'little
game' or a drinker asks for 'just a drop.' Well, these are
speculations. In any case, I find myself in full agreement
and sympathy with the poet about the child he wishes to
teach and the booklet he wants to write. Because I am
not only familiar with the passion for teaching; I'm also
rather inclined to do a little scribbling too. And now that
I have liberated myself from officialdom, I am much
drawn to the idea of using my leisure and good spirits
one of these days to write a book—or rather, a booklet, a
little thing for friends and those who share my views."

"What about?" Designori asked with curiosity.

"Oh, anything, the subject would not matter. It would
only be a pretext for me to seclude myself and enjoy the

happiness of having a great deal of leisure. The tone would be what mattered to me, a proper mean between the solemn and the intimate, earnestness and jest, a tone not of instruction, but of friendly communication and discourse on various things I think I have learned. I don't suppose the way this poet Friedrich Rückert mixes instruction and thinking, information and casual talk, would be my way, and yet something about it appeals strongly to me; it is personal and yet not arbitrary, playful and yet submits to strict rules of form. I like that. Well, for the present I shall not enter upon the joys and problems of writing little books; I have to keep my mind on other tasks. But some time later, I imagine, I might very well experience the joys of authorship, of the sort I foresee: an easygoing, but careful examination of things not just for my solitary pleasure, but always with a few good friends and readers in mind."

Next morning Knecht set out for Belpunt. Designori had wanted to accompany him, but Knecht had firmly vetoed the idea, and when the father attempted to press it, had almost snapped at him. "The boy will have enough to do coming to terms with this nuisance of a new teacher," he said curtly. "To foist his father on him at the same time would scarcely help things."

As he rode through the brisk September morning in the car Plinio had hired for him, his good humor of yesterday returned. He chatted frequently with the chauffeur, asking him to stop or drive slowly every so often when the landscape looked particularly attractive, and several times he played his little flute. It was a beautiful and exciting ride from the lowlands in which the capital lay toward the foothills and on into the high mountains. The journey also led from fading summer deeper into autumn. About noon the last great climb began, over sweeping serpentines, through thinning evergreen forest, past foaming mountain streams roaring between cliffs, over bridges and by solitary, massive walled farmhouses with tiny windows, into a stony, ever rougher and more austere world of mountains, amid whose bleakness and sobriety the flowering meadows bloomed like tiny paradises with doubled loveliness.

The small cottage they reached at last was tucked away

near a mountain lake, among gray cliffs with which it scarcely contrasted. The traveler was at once aware of the austerity, even the gloom, of this kind of building, which so accorded with the ruggedness of the mountains. But then a cheerful smile lighted his face, for in the open door of the house he saw a figure standing, a young man in a colorful jacket and shorts. It could only be his pupil Tito, and although he had not really been seriously concerned about the fugitive, he nevertheless breathed a grateful sigh of relief. If Tito were here and welcoming his teacher on the threshold, all was well; that disposed of a good many possible complications he had been considering during the ride.

The boy came forward to meet him, smiling, friendly, and a little embarrassed. While helping Knecht out of the car, he said: "I didn't mean to be horrid, letting you travel alone." And before Knecht had a chance to reply, he added trustfully: "I think you understood my feeling. Otherwise you would have brought my father with you. I've already let him know that I arrived safely."

Laughing, Knecht shook hands with the boy. He was guided into the house, where the servant welcomed him and promised that supper would soon be ready. Yielding to an unwonted need, he lay down for a little while before the meal, and only then realized that he was curiously tired, in fact exhausted, from the lovely automobile trip. During the evening, moreover, as he chatted with his pupil and looked at Tito's collections of mountain flowers and butterflies, his fatigue increased. He even felt something akin to giddiness, a kind of emptiness in the head that he had never experienced before, and an annoying weakness and irregularity of his heartbeat. But he continued to sit with Tito until their agreed bedtime, and took pains not to show any sign that he was not feeling well. Tito was somewhat surprised that the Magister said not a word about the beginning of school, schedules, report cards, and similar matters. In fact, when he ventured to capitalize on this good mood and proposed a long walk for the morning, to acquaint his teacher with his new surroundings, the proposal was readily accepted.

"I am looking forward to the walk," Knecht added, "and want to ask you a favor right now. While looking at your plant collection I could see that you know far more about mountain plants than I do. One of the purposes of our being together is, among other things, that we exchange knowledge and reach a balance with each other. Let us begin by your checking over my meager understanding of botany and helping me go further in this field."

By the time they bade each other good night, Tito was in excellent spirits and had made some good resolutions. Once again he had found this Magister Knecht very much to his liking. Without using fancy language and going on about scholarship, virtue, the aristocracy of intellect, and so on, as his schoolteachers were prone to do, this serene, friendly man had something in his manner and his speech that imposed an obligation and brought out your good, chivalric, higher aspirations and forces. It could be fun, and sometimes you felt it as a badge of honor, to deceive and outwit the ordinary schoolmaster, but in the presence of this man such notions never even occurred to you. He was—why, what exactly was he like? Tito reflected on this, trying to determine what it was about this stranger that was so likeable and at the same time so impressive. He decided that it was the man's nobility, his innate aristocratic quality. This was what drew him to Knecht, this above all. He was a nobleman, although no one knew his family and his father might have been a shoemaker. He was nobler and more aristocratic than most of the people Tito knew, more aristocratic than Tito's own father. The boy, who highly prized the patrician instincts and traditions of his house and could not forgive his father for having broken with them, was for the first time encountering intellectual aristocracy, cultivated nobility. Knecht was an example of that power which under favorable conditions can sometimes work miracles, overleaping a long succession of ancestors and within a single human life transforming a plebeian child into a member of the highest nobility. In the proud and fiery boy's heart there stirred an inkling that to belong to this kind of nobility, and to serve it, might be a duty and honor for him; that here perhaps, embodied in this teacher who for all his gentleness and friendliness was a nobleman through and through, the

meaning of his own life was drawing near to him, that
his own goals were being set.

Knecht, after being shown to his room, did not lie
down at once, although he craved rest. The evening had
cost him a great effort. He had found it difficult to comport himself so that nothing in his expression, posture, or
voice would reveal his peculiar fatigue or depression or
illness to the young man, who was undoubtedly observing
him closely. Still, he seemed to have succeeded. But now
he had to meet and master this vacuity, this nausea, this
alarming giddiness, this deathly tiredness which was at
the same time restiveness. He could master it only if he
recognized its cause. This was not hard to find, although
it took him some time. The reason for his indisposition,
he decided, was simply the journey which had taken him
in so short a time from the lowlands to an altitude of
close to seven thousand feet. Except for a few outings in
his early youth, he was unaccustomed to such heights
and had not reacted well to the rapid ascent. Probably
this disability would last another day or two. If it did
not disappear by then, he would have to return home
with Tito and the housekeeper, in which case Plinio's
plan for a stay in lovely Belpunt would come to nothing.
That would be a pity, but no great misfortune.

After these reflections, he went to bed, and since sleep
refused to come, spent the night partly in reviewing his
travels since his departure from Waldzell, partly trying
to quiet his heartbeat and his exacerbated nerves. He
also thought a good deal about his pupil, with pleasure,
but without making any plans. It seemed to him wiser to
tame this noble but refractory colt by kindness and slow
domestication; nothing must be hasty or forced in
this case. He thought that he would gradually bring the
boy to an awareness of his gifts and powers, and at the
same time nourish in him that noble curiosity, that
aristocratic dissatisfaction from which springs love for
the sciences, the humanities, and the arts. The task was a
rewarding one, and his pupil was not just any talented
young man whom he had to awaken and train. As the
only son of a wealthy and influential patrician he was
also a future leader, one of the social and political
shapers of the country and the nation, destined to com-

mand and to be imitated. Castalia had failed the Designori family; it had not educated Tito's father thoroughly enough, had not made him strong enough for his difficult position poised between the world and culture. As a result, gifted and charming young Plinio had become an unhappy man with a life out of balance and ill managed. As a further result, his only son was endangered in his turn and had been drawn into his father's difficulties. Here was something to heal and make good; here was a debt to be paid. It seemed meaningful, and gladdened him, that this task should fall to him of all persons, to him the disobedient and seemingly apostate Castalian.

In the morning, when he sensed the house awakening, he rose. Finding a dressing gown laid ready beside his bed, he put it on, and stepped out through the rear door that Tito had shown him the night before into the arcade that connected the house with the bath hut by the lake.

Before him the little lake lay motionless, gray-green. Further off was a steep cliff, its sharp, jagged crest still in shadow, rearing sheer and cold into the thin, greenish, cool morning sky. But he could sense that the sun had already risen behind this crest; tiny splinters of its light glittered here and there on corners of rock. In a few minutes the sun would appear over the crenellations of the mountain and flood lake and valley below with light. In a mood of earnest attentiveness, Knecht studied the scene, whose stillness, gravity, and beauty he felt as unfamiliar and nevertheless of deep concern and instructiveness to him. Now, even more strongly than during yesterday's ride, he felt the ponderousness, the coolness and dignified strangeness of this mountain world, which does not meet men halfway, does not invite them, scarcely tolerates them. And it seemed to him strange and significant that his first step into the freedom of life in the world should have led him to this very place, to this silent and cold grandeur.

Tito appeared, in bathing trunks. He shook hands with the Magister and pointing to the cliffs opposite said: "You've come at just the right moment; the sun will be rising in a minute. Oh, it's glorious up here."

Knecht gave him a friendly nod. He had learned long

ago that Tito was an early riser, a runner, wrestler, and
hiker, if only from protest against his father's casual, un-
soldierly, comfort-loving ways. For the same reason he
refused to drink wine. These leanings occasionally led
him into a pose of being an anti-intellectual child of
nature—the Designoris seemed to have this bent for
exaggeration. But Knecht welcomed it all, and was
determined to share his interest in sports as a means for
winning over and taming the temperamental young
man. It would be only one means among several, and not
at all the most important; music, for example, would
lead them much further. Of course he had no thought of
matching the young man in physical feats, let alone surpassing him. But harmless participation would suffice to
show the boy that his tutor was neither a coward nor a
mere bookworm.

Tito looked eagerly toward the dark crest of the mountain, behind which the sky pulsed in the morning light.
Now a fragment of the rocky ridge flashed violently like
a glowing metal beginning to melt. The crest blurred
and seemed suddenly lower, as if it were melting down,
and from the fiery gap the dazzling sun appeared.
Simultaneously, the ground, the house, and their shore
of the lake were illuminated, and the two, standing in
the strong radiance, instantly felt the delightful warmth
of this light. The boy, filled with the solemn beauty of
the moment and the glorious sensation of his youth and
strength, stretched his limbs with rhythmic arm movements, which his whole body soon took up, celebrating
the break of day in an enthusiastic dance and expressing his deep oneness with the surging, radiant elements.
His steps flew in joyous homage toward the victorious
sun and reverently retreated from it; his outspread
arms embraced mountain, lake, and sky; kneeling, he
seemed to pay tribute to the earth mother, and extending his hands, to the waters of the lake; he offered himself, his youth, his freedom, his burning sense of his own
life, like a festive sacrifice to the powers. The sunlight
gleamed on his tanned shoulders; his eyes were half-
closed to the dazzle; his young face stared masklike with
an expression of inspired, almost fanatical gravity.

The Magister, too, was overpowered by the solemn

spectacle of dawn breaking in this silent, rocky solitude. But he was even more fascinated by the human spectacle taking place before his eyes, this ceremonial dance performed by his pupil to welcome the morning and the sun. The dance elevated this moody, immature youth, conferring upon him a priestly solemnity, suddenly in a single moment irradiating and revealing to the onlooker his deepest and noblest tendencies, gifts, and destinies just as the appearance of the sun opened and illuminated this cold, gloomy mountain dale. In this moment the young man seemed to him stronger and more impressive than he had hitherto thought, but also harder, more inaccessible, more remote from culture, more pagan. This ceremonial and sacrificial dance under the sign of Pan meant more than young Plinio's speeches and versemaking ever had; it raised the boy several stages higher, but also made him seem more alien, more elusive, less obedient to any summons.

The boy himself was in the grip of his impulse, without knowing what was happening to him. He was not performing a dance he already knew, a dance he had practiced before. This was no familiar rite of celebrating sun and morning that he had long ago invented. Only later would he realize that his dance and his transported state in general were only partly caused by the mountain air, the sun, the dawn, his sense of freedom. They were also a response to the change awaiting him, the new chapter in his young life that had come in the friendly and awe-inspiring form of the Magister. In that morning hour many elements conspired in the soul of young Tito to shape his destiny and distinguish this hour above a thousand others as a high, a festive, a consecrated time. Without knowing what he was doing, asking no questions, he obeyed the command of this ecstatic moment, danced his worship, prayed to the sun, professed with devout movements and gestures his joy, his faith in life, his piety and reverence, both proudly and submissively offered up in the dance his devout soul as a sacrifice to the sun and the gods, and no less to the man he admired and feared, the sage and musician, the Master of the magic Game who had come to him from mysterious realms, his future teacher and friend.

All this, like the torrent of light from the sunrise, lasted only a few minutes. Stirred to the core, Knecht watched the wonderful show, in which his pupil before his eyes changed and revealed himself, presenting himself in a new light, alien and entirely his equal. Both of them stood on the walk between house and hut, bathed in the radiance from the east and deeply shaken by their experience. Tito, having barely completed the last step of his dance, awoke from his ecstasy and stood still, like an animal surprised in solitary play, aware that he was not alone, that not only had he experienced and performed something unusual, but that he had also had a spectator. His first thought was how to extricate himself from the situation, which struck him now as somehow dangerous and shaming. He had to act vigorously, and smash the magic of these strange moments, which had totally absorbed and overwhelmed him.

His face, but a moment before an ageless, stern mask, assumed a childish and rather foolish expression, like that of a person awakened too abruptly from a deep sleep. His knees swayed slightly; he looked into his teacher's face with vapid astonishment, and in sudden haste, as though something very important had just occurred to him, something he had neglected, he stretched out his right arm and pointed toward the opposite shore of the lake, which along with half the lake's waters still lay in the great, rapidly contracting shadow of the cliff whose top had already been conquered by the brilliance of the dawn.

"If we swim very fast," he called out with boyish impetuosity, "we can just reach the other shore before the sun."

The words were barely uttered, the challenge to a swimming race with the sun barely issued, when Tito with a tremendous leap plunged headfirst into the lake, as if in his high spirits or his shyness he could not get away fast enough and obliterate all memory of the preceding ritual by intensified activity. The water splashed up and closed around him. A few moments later his head, shoulders, and arms reappeared and remained visible on the blue-green surface, swiftly moving away.

Knecht had not, when he came out, had in mind to

bathe or swim. Both air and water were much too cool, and after his night of semi-illness, swimming would probably do him little good. But now, in the beautiful sunlight, stirred by the scene he had just witnessed, and with his pupil urging him into the water in this comradely fashion, he found the venture less deterring. Above all he feared that the promise born in this morning hour would be blasted if he disappointed the boy by opposing cool, adult rationality to this invitation to a test of strength. It was true that his feeling of weakness and uncertainty, incurred by the rapid ascent into the mountains, warned him to be careful; but perhaps this indisposition could be soonest routed by forcing matters and meeting it head-on. The summons was stronger than the warning, his will stronger than his instinct. He quickly shed the light dressing gown, took a deep breath, and threw himself into the water at the same spot where his pupil had dived.

The lake, fed by glacial waters so that even in the warmest days of summer one had to be inured to it, received him with an icy cold, slashing in its enmity. He had steeled himself for a thorough chilling, but not for this fierce cold which seemed to surround him with leaping flames and after a moment of fiery burning began to penetrate rapidly into him. After the dive he had risen quickly to the surface, caught sight of Tito swimming far ahead of him, felt bitterly assailed by this icy, wild, hostile element, but still believed he could lessen the distance, that he was engaging in the swimming race, was fighting for the boy's respect and comradeship, for his soul—when he was already fighting with Death, who had thrown him and was now holding him in a wrestler's grip. Fighting with all his strength, Knecht held him off as long as his heart continued to beat.

The young swimmer had looked back frequently and seen with satisfaction that the Magister had followed him into the water. Now he peered once again, no longer saw him, and became uneasy. He looked and called, then turned and swam rapidly back. He could not find him. Swimming and diving, he searched for the lost swimmer until his strength too began to give out in the bitter cold.

Staggering, breathless, he reached land at last, saw the dressing gown lying on the shore, and picking it up began mechanically rubbing his body and limbs until the numbed skin warmed again. Stunned, he sat down in the sunlight and stared into the water, whose cool blue-green now blinked at him strangely empty, alien, and evil. He felt overpowered by perplexity and deep sorrow, for with the waning of his physical weakness, awareness and the terror of what had happened returned to him.

Oh! he thought in grief and horror, now I am guilty of his death. And only now, when there was no longer need to save his pride or offer resistance, he felt, in shock and sorrow, how dear this man had already become to him. And since in spite of all rational objections he felt responsible for the Master's death, there came over him, with a premonitory shudder of awe, a sense that this guilt would utterly change him and his life, and would demand much greater things of him than he had ever before demanded of himself.

JOSEPH
KNECHT'S
POSTHUMOUS
WRITINGS

THE POEMS
OF KNECHT'S
STUDENT YEARS

Lament

No permanence is ours; we are a wave
That flows to fit whatever form it finds:
Through day or night, cathedral or the cave
We pass forever, craving form that binds.

Mold after mold we fill and never rest,
We find no home where joy or grief runs deep.
We move, we are the everlasting guest.
No field nor plow is ours; we do not reap.

What God would make of us remains unknown:
He plays; we are the clay to his desire.
Plastic and mute, we neither laugh nor groan;
He kneads, but never gives us to the fire.

To stiffen into stone, to persevere!
We long forever for the right to stay.
But all that ever stays with us is fear,
And we shall never rest upon our way.

A Compromise

The men of principled simplicity
Will have no traffic with our subtle doubt.
The world is flat, they tell us, and they shout:
The myth of depth is an absurdity!

For if there were additional dimensions
Beside the good old pair we'll always cherish,
How could a man live safely without tensions?
How could he live and not expect to perish?

In order peacefully to coexist
Let us strike one dimension off our list.

If they are right, those men of principle,
And life in depth is so inimical,
The third dimension is dispensable.

But Secretly We Thirst . . .

Graceful as dancer's arabesque and bow,
Our lives appear serene and without stress,
A gentle dance around pure nothingness
To which we sacrifice the here and now.

Our dreams are lovely and our game is bright,
So finely tuned, with many artful turns,
But deep beneath the tranquil surface burns
Longing for blood, barbarity, and night.

Freely our life revolves, and every breath
Is free as air; we live so playfully,
But secretly we crave reality:
Begetting, birth, and suffering, and death.

Alphabets

From time to time we take our pen in hand
And scribble symbols on a blank white sheet.
Their meaning is at everyone's command;
It is a game whose rules are nice and neat.

But if a savage or a moon-man came
And found a page, a furrowed runic field,
And curiously studied lines and frame:
How strange would be the world that they revealed.
A magic gallery of oddities.
He would see A and B as man and beast,
As moving tongues or arms or legs or eyes,
Now slow, now rushing, all constraint released,
Like prints of ravens' feet upon the snow.
He'd hop about with them, fly to and fro,
And see a thousand worlds of might-have-been
Hidden within the black and frozen symbols,
Beneath the ornate strokes, the thick and thin.
He'd see the way love burns and anguish trembles,
He'd wonder, laugh, shake with fear and weep
Because beyond this cipher's cross-barred keep
He'd see the world in all its aimless passion,
Diminished, dwarfed, and spellbound in the symbols,
And rigorously marching prisoner-fashion.
He'd think: each sign all others so resembles
That love of life and death, or lust and anguish,
Are simply twins whom no one can distinguish . . .
Until at last the savage with a sound
Of mortal terror lights and stirs a fire,
Chants and beats his brow against the ground
And consecrates the writing to his pyre.
Perhaps before his consciousness is drowned
In slumber there will come to him some sense
Of how this world of magic fraudulence,
This horror utterly behind endurance,
Has vanished as if it had never been.
He'll sigh, and smile, and feel all right again.

On Reading an Old Philosopher

These noble thoughts beguiled us yesterday;
We savored them like choicest vintage wines.
But now they sour, meanings seep away,
Much like a page of music from whose vines

The clefs and sharps are carelessly erased:
Take from a house the center of gravity,
It sways and falls apart, all sense debased,
Cacophony what had been harmony.

So too a face we saw as old and wise,
Loved and respected, can wrinkle, craze,
As, ripe for death, the mind deserts the eyes,
Leaving a pitiful, empty, shriveled maze.

So too can ecstasy stir every sense
And barely felt can quickly turn to gall,
As if there dwelt within us cognizance
That everything must wither, die, and fall.

Yet still above this vale of endless dying
Man's spirit, struggling incorruptibly,
Painfully raises beacons, death defying,
And wins, by longing, immortality.

The Last Glass Bead Game Player

The colored beads, his playthings, in his hand,
He sits head bent; around him lies a land
Laid waste by war and ravaged by disease.
Growing on rubble, ivy hums with bees;
A weary peace with muted psalmody
Sounds in a world of aged tranquility.
The old man tallies up his colored beads;
He fits a blue one here, a white one there,
Makes sure a large one, or a small, precedes,
And shapes his Game ring with devoted care.
Time was he had won greatness in the Game,
Had mastered many tongues and many arts,
Had known the world, traveled in foreign parts—
From pole to pole, no limits to his fame.
Around him pupils, colleagues always pressed.
Now he is old, worn-out; his life is lees.
Disciples come no longer to be blessed,
Nor masters to invite an argument.
All, all are gone, and the temples, libraries,
And schools of Castalia are no more. At rest
Amid the ruins, the glass beads in his hand,
Those hieroglyphs once so significant
That now are only colored bits of glass,
He lets them roll until their force is spent
And silently they vanish in the sand.

A Toccata by Bach

Frozen silence. . . . Darkness prevails on darkness.
One shaft of light breaks through the jagged clouds
Coming from nothingness to penetrate the depths,
Compound the night with day, build length and
    breadth,
Prefigure peak and ridge, declivities, redoubts,
A loose blue atmosphere, earth's deep dense fullness.

That brilliant shaft dissevers teeming generation
Into both deed and war, and in a frenzy of creation
Ignites a gleaming terrified new world.
All changes where the seeds of light descend,
Order arises, magnificence is heard
In praise of life, of victory to light's great end.

The mighty urge glides on, to move
Its power into all creatures' being,
Recalling far divinity, the spirit of God's doing:
Now joy and pain, words, art, and song,
World towering on world in arching victory throng
With impulse, mind, contention, pleasure, love.

Translated by Alex Page

A Dream

Guest at a monastery in the hills,
I stepped, when all the monks had gone to pray,
Into a book-lined room. Along the walls,
Glittering in the light of fading day,
I saw a multitude of vellum spines
With marvelous inscriptions. Eagerly,
Impelled by rapturous curiosity,
I picked the nearest book, and read the lines:
The Squaring of the Circle—Final Stage.
I thought: I'll take this and read every page!
A quarto volume, leather tooled in gold,
Gave promise of a story still untold:
How Adam also ate of the other tree . . .
The other tree? Which one? The tree of life?
Is Adam then immortal? Now I could see
No chance had brought me to this library.
I spied the back and edges of a folio
Aglow with all the colors of the rainbow,
Its hand-painted title stating a decree:
The interrelationships of hues and sound:
Proof that for every color may be found
In music a proper corresponding key.
Choirs of colors sparkled before my eyes
And now I was beginning to surmise:
Here was the library of Paradise.
To all the questions that had driven me
All answers now could be given me.
Here I could quench my thirst to understand,
For here all knowledge stood at my command.
There was provision here for every need:
A title full of promise on each book
Responded to my every rapid look.
Here there was fruit to satisfy the greed
Of any student's timid aspirations,
Of any master's bold investigations.
Here was the inner meaning, here the key,
To poetry, to wisdom, and to science.
Magic and erudition in alliance
Opened the door to every mystery.

These books provided pledges of all power
To him who came here at this magic hour.

A lectern stood near by; with hands that shook
I placed upon it one enticing book,
Deciphered at a glance the picture writing,
As in a dream we find ourselves reciting
A poem or lesson we have never learned.
At once I soared aloft to starry spaces
Of the soul, and with the zodiac turned,
Where all the revelations of all races,
Whatever intuition has divined,
Millennial experience of all nations,
Harmoniously met in new relations,
Old insights with new symbols recombined,
So that in minutes or in hours as I read
I traced once more the whole path of mankind,
And all that men have ever done and said
Disclosed its inner meaning to my mind.
I read, and saw those hieroglyphic forms
Couple and part, and coalesce in swarms,
Dance for a while together, separate,
Once more in newer patterns integrate,
A kaleidoscope of endless metaphors—
And each some vaster, fresher sense explores.

Bedazzled by these sights, I looked away
From the book to give my eyes a moment's rest,
And saw that I was not the only guest.
An old man stood before that grand array
Of tomes. Perhaps he was the archivist.
I saw that he was earnestly intent
Upon some task, and I could not resist
A strange conviction that I had to know
The manner of his work, and what it meant.
I watched the old man, with frail hand and slow,
Remove a volume and inspect what stood
Written upon its back, then saw him blow
With pallid lips upon the title—could

A title possibly be more alluring
Or offer greater promise of enduring
Delight? But now his finger wiped across
The spine. I saw it silently erase
The name, and watched with fearful sense of loss
As he inscribed another in its place
And then moved on to smilingly efface
One more, but only a newer title to emboss.
For a long while I looked at him bemused,
Then turned, since reason totally refused
To understand the meaning of his actions,
Back to my book—I'd seen but a few lines—
And found I could no longer read the signs
Or even see the rows of images.
The world of symbols I had barely entered
That had stirred me to such transports of bliss,
In which a universe of meaning centered,
Seemed to dissolve and rush away, careen
And reel and shake in feverish contractions,
And fade out, leaving nothing to be seen
But empty parchment with a hoary sheen.
I felt a hand upon me, felt it slide
Over my shoulder. The old man stood beside
My lectern, and I shuddered while
He took my book and with a subtle smile
Brushed his finger lightly to elide
The former title, then began to write
New promises and problems, novel inquiries,
New formulas for ancient mysteries.
Without a word, he plied his magic style.
Then, with my book, he disappeared from sight.

Worship

In the beginning was the rule of sacred kings
Who hallowed field, grain, plow, who handed down
The law of sacrifices, set the bounds
To mortal men forever hungering

For the Invisible Ones' just ordinance
That holds the sun and moon in perfect balance
And whose forms in their eternal radiance
Feel no suffering, nor know death's ambience.

Long ago the sons of the gods, the sacred line,
Passed, and mankind remained alone,
Embroiled in pleasure and pain, cut off from being,
Condemned to change unhallowed, unconfined.

But intimations of the true life never died,
And it is for us, in this time of harm
To keep, in metaphor and symbol and in psalm,
Reminders of that former sacred reverence.

Perhaps some day the darkness will be banned,
Perhaps some day the times will turn about,
The sun will once more rule us as our god
And take the sacrifices from our hands.

Soap Bubbles

From years of study and of contemplation
An old man brews a work of clarity,
A gay and involuted dissertation
Discoursing on sweet wisdom playfully.

An eager student bent on storming heights
Has delved in archives and in libraries,
But adds the touch of genius when he writes
A first book full of deepest subtleties.

A boy, with bowl and straw, sits and blows,
Filling with breath the bubbles from the bowl.
Each praises like a hymn, and each one glows;
Into the filmy beads he blows his soul.

Old man, student, boy, all these three
Out of the Maya-foam of the universe
Create illusions. None is better or worse.
But in each of them the Light of Eternity
Sees its reflection, and burns more joyfully.

After Dipping Into the *Summa*
Contra Gentiles

To truth, it seems to us, life once was nearer,
The world ordered, intelligences clearer,
Wisdom and knowledge were not yet divided.
They lived far more serenely, many-sided,
Those ancients of whom Plato, the Chinese,
Relate their incandescent verities.
Whenever we entered the temple of Aquinas,
The graceful *Summa contra Gentiles*,
A new world greeted us, sweet, mature,
A world of truth clarified and pure.
There all seemed lucid, Nature charged with Mind,
Man moving from God to Him, as He designed.
The Law, in one great formulary bound,
Forming a whole, a still unbroken round.
But we who belong to his posterity
Seem condemned to doubt and irony,
To journeys in the wilderness, to strife,
Obsessions, and longings for a better life.

But if our children's children undergo
Such sufferings as ours, they will bestow
Praise upon us as blessed and as wise.
We will appear transfigured in their eyes,
For out of our lives' harsh cacophonies
They will hear only fading harmonies,
The legends of an anguish often told,
The echoes of contentions long grown cold.
And those of us who trust ourselves the least,
Who doubt and question most, these, it may be,
Will make their mark upon eternity,
And youth will turn to them as to a feast.
The time may come when a man who confessed
His self-doubts will be ranked among the blessed

Who never suffered anguish or knew fear,
Whose times were times of glory and good cheer,
Who lived like children, simple happy lives.

For in us too is part of that Eternal Mind
Which through the aeons calls to brothers of its kind:
Both you and I will pass, but it survives.

Stages

As every flower fades and as all youth
Departs, so life at every stage,
So every virtue, so our grasp of truth,
Blooms in its day and may not last forever.
Since life may summon us at every age
Be ready, heart, for parting, new endeavor,
Be ready bravely and without remorse
To find new light that old ties cannot give.
In all beginnings dwells a magic force
For guarding us and helping us to live.

Serenely let us move to distant places
And let no sentiments of home detain us.
The Cosmic Spirit seeks not to restrain us
But lifts us stage by stage to wider spaces.
If we accept a home of our own making,
Familiar habit makes for indolence.
We must prepare for parting and leave-taking
Or else remain the slaves of permanence.

Even the hour of our death may send
Us speeding on to fresh and newer spaces,
And life may summon us to newer races.
So be it, heart: bid farewell without end.

The Glass Bead Game

We re-enact with reverent attention
The universal chord, the masters' harmony,
Evoking in unsullied communion
Minds and times of highest sanctity.

We draw upon the iconography
Whose mystery is able to contain
The boundlessness, the storm of all existence,
Give chaos form, and hold our lives in rein.

The pattern sings like crystal constellations,
And when we tell our beads, we serve the whole,
And cannot be dislodged or misdirected,
Held in the orbit of the Cosmic Soul.

THE
THREE
LIVES

THE RAINMAKER

IT WAS MANY thousands of years ago, when women ruled. In tribe and family, mothers and grandmothers were revered and obeyed. Much more was made of the birth of a girl than of a boy.

There was an ancestress in the village, a hundred or more years ago, whom everyone revered and feared as if she were a queen, although in the memory of man she had seldom lifted a finger or spoken a word. Many a day she sat by the entrance to her hut, a retinue of ministering kinsfolk around her, and the women of the village came to pay their respects, to tell her their affairs, to show her their children and ask her blessing on them. The pregnant women came to ask her to touch their bellies and name the expected child. Sometimes the tribal mother would give the touch, sometimes she only nodded or

413

shook her head, or else remained motionless. She rarely said anything; she was merely there, sitting and ruling, sitting with her yellowish-white hair falling in thin strands around her leathery, farsighted eagle's face, sitting and receiving veneration, presents, requests, news, reports, accusations, sitting and known to all as the mother of seven daughters, and the grandmother and ancestor of many grandchildren and great-grandchildren, sitting and holding in those wrinkled features and back of that brown forehead the wisdom, the tradition, the law, the morality, and the honor of the village.

It was a spring evening, overcast, the darkness falling early. The ancient herself was not sitting in front of the mud hut. In her stead was her daughter, almost as white-haired and stately and not much younger. She sat and rested. Her seat was the threshold, a flat field stone, covered with a skin in cold weather. At a little distance from her a few children, women, and boys squatted in a semi-circle in the sand or grass. They squatted here every evening that it was not raining or too cold, for they wanted to hear the ancient's daughter tell stories or sing spells. Formerly, the ancient herself had done this, but now that she was too old and no longer communicative, her daughter took her place. Just as she had learned all the stories and spells from the old woman, so she also had her voice, her figure, the quiet dignity of her bearing, her movements, and her language. The younger listeners knew her much better than her mother and by now scarcely realized that she sat here in another's place passing on the tales and wisdom of the tribe. The wellspring of knowledge flowed from her lips on these evenings. She preserved the tribe's treasure under her white hair. Behind her gently furrowed old brow dwelt the memory and the mind of the village. Anyone who knew any spells or stories had learned them from her. Aside from her and the ancient, there was only one other guardian of knowledge in the tribe, but he remained hidden most of the time: a mysterious and extremely silent man: the Rainmaker, or as he was also called, the Weathermaker.

Crouching among the listeners was also the boy Knecht, and beside him a little girl named Ada. He was fond of this girl, often played with her and protected her, not out of love, for he knew nothing of that as yet, was still too much a child, but because she was the Rainmaker's daughter. Knecht adored the Rainmaker; next to the ancient and her daughter he admired no one so strongly as the Rainmaker. But the others were women. You could venerate and fear them, but you could not conceive the thought, could not possibly cherish the wish to become what they were. The Rainmaker was a rather unapproachable man; it was not easy for a boy to stay near him. That had to be managed in roundabout ways, and one of these roundabout ways to the Rainmaker was Knecht's concern for his child. As often as possible he went to the Rainmaker's somewhat isolated hut to fetch her. Then he would sit with her listening to the old woman's tales, and later take her home. He had done this today, and now he was squatting beside her in the dark group, listening.

Today the old woman was telling about the Witches' Village:

"Sometimes there is a wicked woman in a village who wishes harm to everyone. Usually these women conceive no children. Sometimes one of these women is so wicked that the village will no longer let her stay. Then the villagers go to her hut at night, her husband is fettered, and the woman is beaten with switches and driven far out into the woods and swamps. She is cursed with a curse and left there. Soon the husband's fetters are removed and if he is not too old, he can take himself another wife. But if the expelled woman does not die, she wanders about in the woods and swamps, learns the language of animals, and when she has roamed long enough, sooner or later she finds her way to a small village that is called the Witches' Village. There all the wicked women who have been driven from their villages have come together and made a village of their own. There they live, do their wickedness, and make magic. But especially, because they have no children of their own, they like to coax children from the proper villages, and when a child is lost in the woods and never seen again, it may not have drowned in the swamp or been eaten by a wolf, but led astray by a witch and taken to the Witches' Village. In the days when I was still little and my grandmother was the eldest in the village, a girl once went to pick bilberries with the others, and while she was picking she grew tired and fell asleep. She was small, the ferns hid her from sight, and the other children moved on and did not notice until they were back in the village and it was already evening. Then they saw that the girl was no longer with them. The young men were sent out; they searched and called in the woods until night fell, and then they came back and had not found her. But the little girl, after she had slept enough, went on and on in the woods. And the more frightened she became, the faster she ran, but she no longer had any idea where she was and only ran farther away from the village, deeper and deeper into wild country. Around her neck, on a strip of bast, she wore a boar's tooth that her father had given her. He had brought it back from the hunt, and with a stone tool bored a hole through the tooth so that the bast could be drawn through it, and before that he had boiled the tooth three times in boar's blood and sung good spells, and anyone who wore such a tooth was protected against many kinds of magic. Now a woman appeared from among the trees. She was a witch. She put on a kindly face and said: 'Greetings, pretty child, have you lost your way? Come along with me, I'll take you home.' The child went along. But she remembered what her mother and father had told her, that she should never let a stranger see the boar's tooth, and so while she walked she slipped the tooth off the strip of bast and tucked it into her belt without being noticed. The woman walked for hours with the girl; it was already night when they reached the village, but it was not our village, it was the Witches' Village. There the girl was locked up in a dark stable, but the witch went to sleep in her hut. In the morning the witch said: 'Don't you have a boar's tooth with you?' The child said no, she had had one, but she had lost it in the woods, and she showed her necklace with the tooth missing from it. Then the witch took a clay pot filled with earth, and three plants were growing in the earth. The child looked at the plants and asked what they were. The witch pointed

to the first plant and said: 'That is your mother's life.'
Then she pointed to the second and said: 'That is your
father's life.' Then she pointed to the third plant: 'And
that is your own life. As long as the plants are green and
growing, you are all alive and well. If one withers, then
the one whose life it is falls sick. If one is pulled out, as
I am going to pull one out now, then the one whose life
it is will surely die.' She took hold of the plant that
meant the father's life and began tugging at it, and when
she had pulled it out a little so that a piece of the white
root could be seen, the plant gave a deep sigh. . . ."

At these words the little girl beside Knecht sprang to
her feet as if she had been bitten by a snake, screamed,
and ran headlong away. She had been sitting for a long
time fighting back the terror caused by the story, until she
could no longer endure it. One old woman laughed.
Other listeners were almost as frightened as the little
girl, but they controlled themselves and remained seated.
But Knecht, startled out of his trance of fear, also sprang
up and ran after the girl. The old woman went on with
her story.

The Rainmaker had his hut close by the village pond,
and Knecht looked for the runaway in this direction. He
searched and tried to lure her out of hiding with coaxing,
reassuring hums, and singsongs and clucks, using the
voice that women use to call chickens, sweet, long drawn-
out notes, intent on enchantment. "Ada," he called and
sang. "Ada, little Ada, come here, Ada, here I am,
Knecht." He sang again and again, and before he had
heard a sound from her or caught a glimpse of her he
suddenly felt her small soft hand force its way into his.
She had been standing by the path, pressed against the
wall of a hut, and been waiting for him since hearing his
first call. With a sigh of relief she moved close to him; he
seemed to her as tall and strong as a man.

"Were you frightened?" he asked. "You shouldn't be,
no one will hurt you, everyone likes Ada. Come, we'll go
home." She was still trembling and sobbing a little, but
was already calmer, and went gratefully and trustfully
along with him.

Dim red light filtered through the doorway of the hut.

Inside, the Rainmaker sat stooped by the hearth. Yellow and red light gleamed through his flowing hair. The hearth-fire was lit and he was boiling something in two small pots. Before entering with Ada, Knecht watched curiously from outside for a few moments. He could see at once that whatever was being boiled was not food; that was done in different pots, and besides it was already much too late to prepare a meal. But the Rainmaker had already heard him. "Who is standing at the door?" he called out. "Step forward, come in! Is it you, Ada?" He placed lids on his pots, raked glowing embers up against them, and turned around.

Knecht was still peering at the mysterious little pots; he felt curiosity, awe, and a sense of oppression all at once, as he always did whenever he entered this hut. He came here as often as he could, made up all sorts of pretexts for coming, but once he was here he always felt this half-thrilling, half-warning sensation of slight uneasiness, of eager curiosity and pleasure warring with fear. The old man knew that Knecht had long been trailing after him, turning up as he did at odd moments and unlikely places. The boy was pursuing him like a hunter following a spoor, and mutely offering his services and his company.

Turu, the Rainmaker, looked at him with his bright hawk's eyes. "What are you doing here?" he asked coolly. "This is no time of day for visits to strange huts, my boy."

"I've brought Ada home, Master Turu. She was listening to the Mother tell stories about witches and all of a sudden she was so frightened she screamed, so I walked her home."

The Rainmaker turned to his daughter. "You're too timid, Ada. Sensible little girls need not fear witches. You're a sensible little girl, aren't you?"

"Yes, but the witches know all sorts of wicked tricks, and if you don't have a boar's tooth . . ."

"I see, you'd like to have a boar's tooth. All right. But I know something even better, a special root I'll give you. We'll look for it in the autumn. It protects sensible girls from all kinds of magic and even makes them prettier."

Ada smiled happily; she was already reassured, now

that the smell of the hut and the familiar firelight surrounded her. Shyly, Knecht asked: "Couldn't I help look for the root? If you would only describe the plant to me . . ."

Turu's eyes narrowed. "A good many little boys would like to know that," he said, but his voice did not sound angry, only slightly mocking. "There's time for that. Perhaps in the autumn."

Knecht slipped away and went to the youth house where he slept. He had no parents; he was an orphan; for that reason, too, he was entranced by Ada and her hut.

Turu the Rainmaker was not fond of words. He did not like to hear himself or others talking. Many tribesmen thought him peculiar, and some sullen. But he was neither. He knew what was going on around him, or at any rate knew more than anyone would have expected in a man seemingly so solitary, absent-minded and full of learning. Among other things he knew quite well that this somewhat bothersome but handsome and evidently clever boy was running after him and observing him. He had noticed this as soon as it began, for it had been going on a year or longer now. He knew, too, exactly what it meant. It meant a great deal for the boy's future, and also meant a great deal for him, the Rainmaker. It meant that this boy had fallen in love with rainmaking and was longing to learn the art. Every so often there would be such boys in the village, and they would begin to hang about him, much as this boy was doing. Some could easily be discouraged and frightened away, others not; and he had taken on two of them as his disciples and apprentices. Both had married into other villages far away and were the rainmakers or simples gatherers there. Since then, Turu had been alone, and if he ever again took another apprentice, it would be to train him as his own successor. That was how it had always been; that was how it ought to be, and it could be no other way. A gifted boy always had to turn up and attach himself to the man whom he saw as the master of his craft. Knecht was talented; he had what was needed; he also had several signs to commend him: above all the look in his eyes, at once piercing and dreamy; the re-

serve and quiet in his manner; and in the expression of
his face and the carriage of his head something questing,
scenting, and alert, an attentiveness to noises and smells.
There was something of the hawk and something of the
hunter about him. Surely this boy could become a
weathermaker, perhaps a magician also. He could be
taught. But there was no hurry; the boy was still too
young, and there was no reason to show him that he had
been recognized. Apprenticeship must not be made too
easy for him; he must go the whole way himself. If he
could be intimidated, deterred, shaken off, discouraged,
he would be no great loss. Let him wait and serve; let
him creep around and pay court.

Knecht sauntered through the gathering night, under
a cloudy sky with two or three stars. He made his way
into the village, content and happily excited. This village knew nothing of the luxuries, beauties, and refinements which we today take for granted and which even
the poorest among us regard as indispensable. The village
had no culture and no arts. Its only buildings were the
crooked mud huts. It knew nothing of iron and steel
tools. Even wheat and wine were unknown. Inventions such as candles or lamps would have seemed dazzling
wonders to these people. But Knecht's life and the world
of his imagination were no poorer on that account. The
world surrounded him like a picture book full of inex-
haustible mysteries. Every day he conquered another little
piece of it, from the animal and plant life to the starry
sky; and between mute, mysterious nature and the breathing soul in his solitary, nervous boyish frame there
dwelt all the kinship and all the tension, anxiety, curiosity, and craving for understanding of which the human
soul is capable. Although there was no written knowledge
in his world, no history, no books, no alphabets, and although everything that lay more than three or four
hours' walk beyond his village was totally unknown and
unreachable, he nevertheless lived fully and completely
in his village, in the things that were his. The village,
home, the community of the tribe under the guidance
of the mothers gave him everything that nation and state
can give to man: a soil filled with thousands of roots

among whose intricate network he himself was a fiber, sharing in the life of all.

Contentedly, he sauntered along. The night wind whispered in the trees. Branches creaked. There were smells of moist earth, of reeds and mud, of the smoke of wood still partly green, an oily and sweetish smell that meant home more than any other; and finally, as he approached the youth hut, there was its smell, the smell of boys, of young men's bodies. Noiselessly, he ducked under the reed mat, into the warm, breathing darkness. He settled into the straw and thought about the story of the witches, the boar's tooth, Ada, the Rainmaker and his little pots in the fire, until he fell asleep.

Turu only grudgingly yielded to the boy's importunity; he did not make it easy for him. But the youth was always on his trail. Something drew him to the old man, though he himself often did not know what it was. Sometimes, when the Rainmaker was off somewhere in a remote spot in the woods, swamp, or heath, setting a trap, sniffing the spoor of an animal, digging a root, or collecting seeds, he would suddenly feel the boy's eyes upon him. Invisible, making no sound, Knecht had been following him for hours, watching his every move. Sometimes the Rainmaker would pretend not to notice; sometimes he growled and ungraciously ordered the boy to make himself scarce. But sometimes he would beckon him and let him stay for the day, would assign him tasks, show him one thing and another, give him advice, set tests for him, tell him the names of plants, order him to draw water or kindle fires. For each of these procedures he knew special tricks, knacks, secrets, and formulas which must, he impressed this on the boy, be kept strictly secret. And finally, when Knecht was somewhat older, he took him from the youth house into his own hut, thus acknowledging the boy as his apprentice. By that act Knecht was distinguished before all the people. He was no longer one boy among others, he was the Rainmaker's apprentice, and that meant that if he bore up and amounted to something, he would be the next Rainmaker.

From the moment the old man took Knecht into his

hut, the barriers between them dropped—not the barrier
of veneration and obedience, but of distrust and constraint. Turu had submitted; he had allowed Knecht to
conquer him by tenacious courtship. Now he wanted
nothing more than to make a good Rainmaker and successor of the boy. In this course of instruction there were
no concepts, doctrines, methods, script, figures, and only
very few words. The Master trained Knecht's senses far
more than his intellect. A great heritage of tradition
and experience, the sum total of man's knowledge of
nature at that era, had to be administered, employed,
and even more, passed on. A vast and dense system of
experiences, observations, instincts, and habits of investigation was slowly and hazily laid bare to the boy. Scarcely
any of it was put into concepts; virtually all of it had to
be grasped, learned, tested with the senses. The basis and
heart of this science was knowledge of the moon, of its
phases and effects as it waxed and waned, peopled by
the souls of the dead whom it sent forth into new births
in order to make room for the newly dead.

Like that evening when he had escorted the frightened
Ada to her father's hearth, another time was deeply
etched on Knecht's memory. This was a time when the
Master woke him two hours after midnight and went out
with him in deep darkness to show him the last rising of
a vanishing crescent moon. The Master in motionless
silence, the boy somewhat tremulous, shivering from
lack of sleep, they waited a long time on a ledge of rock
in the midst of the forested hills, watching the spot indicated by the Master, until the thin, gently curving line
of the moon appeared in the very position and shape he
had described beforehand. Fearful and fascinated,
Knecht stared at the slowly rising heavenly body. Gently
it floated between dark banks of clouds in an island of
clear sky.

"Soon it will change its shape and wax again; then will
come the time to sow the buckwheat," the Rainmaker
said, counting out the days on his fingers. Then he
lapsed into silence again. Knecht crouched as if he were
alone on the rock gleaming with dew. He trembled with
cold. From the depths of the forest came the long-drawn

call of an owl. The old man pondered for a long while. Then he rose, placed his hand on Knecht's hair, and said softly, as if awakening from a dream: "When I die, my spirit will fly into the moon. By then you will be a man and need a wife. My daughter Ada will be your wife. When she has a son by you, my spirit will return and dwell in your son, and you will call him Turu, as I am called Turu."

The apprentice heard all this in astonishment. He did not dare say a word. The thin silvery sickle rose and was already half devoured by the clouds. A strange tremor passed through the young man, an intimation of many links and associations, repetitions and crosscurrents among things and events. He felt strangely poised both as spectator and participant against this alien night sky where the thin, sharp crescent, precisely predicted by the Master, had appeared above endless woods and hills. How wonderful the Master seemed, and veiled in a thousand secrets—he who could think of his own death, whose spirit would live in the moon and return from the moon back into a person who would be Knecht's son and bear the former Master's name. The future, the fate before him, seemed strangely torn asunder, in places transparent as the cloudy sky; and the fact that anyone could know it, define it, and speak of it seemed to throw open a view into incalculable spaces, full of wonders and yet also full of orderliness. For a moment it seemed to him that the mind could grasp everything, know everything, hear the secrets of everything—the soft, sure course of the planets above, the life of man and animals, their bonds and hostilities, meetings and struggles, everything great and small along with the death locked within each living being. He saw or felt all this as a whole in a first shudder of premonition, and himself fitted into it, included within it as a part of the orderliness, governed by laws accessible to the mind. This first inkling of the great mysteries, their dignity and death as well as their knowability, came to the young man in the coolness of the forest as night moved toward morning and he crouched on the rock above the multitude of whispering treetops. It came to him, touched him like a ghostly hand.

He could not speak of it, not then and never in his whole life, but he could not help thinking of it many times. In all his further learning and experiencing, the intensity of this hour was present in his mind. "Think of it," it reminded him, "think that all this exists, that there are rays and currents between the moon and you and Turu and Ada, that there is death and the land of the souls and a returning therefrom and that in your heart there is an answer to all the things and sights of the world, that everything concerns you, that you ought to know as much about everything as it is possible for man to know."

Something like this was what the voice said. For Knecht, this was the first time he heard the inner voice speaking thus, heard the seductive and imperative bidding of man's spirit. He had seen many a moon wander across the sky and heard many a nocturnal owl shrieking; and laconic though the Master was, he had heard many a word of ancient wisdom or of solitary reflection from his lips, but at this moment something new and different had struck him—presentiment of wholeness, the feeling for connections and relations, for the order that included him and gave him a share in the responsibility for everything. If you had the key to that, you did not need to depend on footprints to recognize an animal, or roots or seeds to know a plant. You would be able to grasp the whole world, stars, spirits, men, animals, medicines, and poisons, to grasp everything in its wholeness and to discern, in every part and sign, every other part. There were good hunters who could read more than others in a track, in fewmets, a patch of fur and remains; they could say from a few tiny hairs not only what kind of animal these came from, but also whether it was old or young, male or female. From the shape of a cloud, a smell in the air, the peculiar behavior of animals or plants, others could foretell the weather for days in advance; his master was unsurpassed in this art, and nearly infallible. Still others had an inborn skill: there were boys who could hit a bird with a stone at thirty paces. They had not learned it; they could simply do it; it did not come by effort, but by magic or grace. The stone in their hand flew off by itself; the stone wanted to hit and the bird wanted to be hit. There were said to be others who knew the future, whether a sick man would live or die, whether a pregnant woman would give birth to a boy or a girl. The tribal mother's daughter was famous for this, and the Rainmaker too was said to possess some of this knowledge. There must, it seemed to Knecht at this moment, be a center in the vast net of associations; if you were at this center you could know everything, could see all that had been and all that was to come. Knowledge must pour in upon one who stood at this center as water ran to the valley and the hare to the cabbage. His word would strike sharply and infallibly as the stone in the sharpshooter's hand. By virtue of the mind's power he would unite all these wonderful gifts and abilities within himself, and use them at will. He would be the perfect, wise, insurpassable man. To become like him, to draw nearer to him, to be on the way to him: that was the way of ways, that was the goal, that gave sacredness and meaning to a life.

Something like this was the way he felt, and our attempts to speak of it in our conceptual language, which he could never know, convey nothing of the awe and the passion of his experience. Rising at night, being led through the dark, still woods full of dangers and mysteries, waiting on the ledge in the chill of night and early morning, the appearance of the thin phantom of a moon, the wise Master's few words, being alone with the Master at so extraordinary an hour—all this was experienced and preserved by Knecht as a solemn mystery, as a solemn initiation, as his admission into a league and a cult, into a humble but honorable relationship to the Unnamable, the cosmic mystery. This and many another similar experience could not be put into thoughts, let alone words. Even more remote from his way of thinking, even more impossible than any other thought, would have been words such as this: "Is it only I alone who have created this experience, or is it objective reality? Does the Master have the same feelings as I, or would mine amuse him? Are my thoughts new, unique, my own, or have the Master and many before him experienced and thought exactly the same?" No, for him there were no such analyses and differentiations. Everything was reality, was steeped in reality, full of it as bread dough is of yeast. The clouds, the moon, and the shifting scenes in the theater of the sky, the cold wet limestone under his bare feet, the damp, trickling cold dew in the pallid night air, the comforting homelike smell of hearth smoke and bed of leaves suffusing the skin the Master had slung around him, the dignity and the faint note of old age and readiness for death in his rough voice—all that was beyond reality and penetrated almost violently into the boy's senses. And sense impressions are a deeper soil for growing memories than the best systems and analytical methods.

Although the Rainmaker was one of the few members of the tribe who had an occupation, who had developed a special art and ability, his everyday life outwardly did not differ greatly from that of the other members of the tribe. He was an important man with considerable prestige; he also received payment from the tribe whenever he had to do some service for the community; but this happened only on special occasions. By far his most important and sacred function came in the spring when he determined the proper day for sowing every kind of fruit and plant. He did this by carefully considering the state of the moon, partly by handed-down rules, partly by his own experience. But the solemn act of opening the season of seeding—the strewing of the first handful of grain and seeds on the community land—was no longer part of his office. That task was too high for any mere man; it was performed every year by the tribal mother herself or by her oldest female relative. The Master became the principal person in the village only when he really had to function as Weathermaker. This happened when a long drought, or a long spell of damp and cold, struck the fields and threatened the tribe with famine. Then Turu had to apply the methods effective against drought and poor crops: sacrifices, exorcisms, processions. According to legend, in cases of obstinate drought or endless rain, when all other means failed and the spirits could not be moved by persuasion, pleas, or threats, there was a last infallible method used in the days of the mothers and grandmothers: sacrifice of the Weathermaker himself by the community. The tribal mother, it was said, had witnessed one such sacrifice.

Aside from looking after the weather, the Master also had a kind of private practice as an exorcist, as a maker of amulets and charms, and in some cases as a doctor, wherever medical matters were not reserved to the tribal mother. But for the rest, Master Turu lived the life of every other tribesman. He helped to till the common land when his turn came, and also had his own small garden near the hut. He gathered and stored fruit, mushrooms, and firewood. He hunted and fished, and kept a goat or two. As a farmer he was like all the others, but as hunter, fisherman, and herb gatherer he was not like anyone else. Rather, he was a solitary genius with a reputation for knowing a great many natural and magical tricks, devices, knacks, and aids. It was said he could weave a willow noose which no animal could escape. He had special recipes for fish bait; he knew how to lure crayfish; and there were some who thought that he understood the language of many a beast. But his real specialty was more arcane: observation of the moon and the stars, knowledge of the weather signs, ability to forecast weather and growth, and a command of many magical effects. Thus he was a great collector of plant and animal materials efficacious for remedies and poisons, for working magic, for conferring blessings, and for fending off dangerous spirits. He knew where to find even the rarest plants; he knew when they blossomed and ripened seed, and the right time to dig their roots. He knew where to find all kinds of snakes and toads, knew how to use horns, hoofs, claws, hair. He knew what to do with growths, deformities, weird and horrible excrescences: knots, tumors, burls, and scales, of wood, of leaves, of grain, of nuts, of horns and hoofs.

Knecht had more to learn with his feet and hands, his eyes, skin, ears, and nose, than with his intellect, and Turu taught far more by example and by dumbshow than by words and prescription. The Master rarely spoke coherently, and even when he did his words were only a supplement to his singularly impressive gestures.

Knecht's apprenticeship differed little from the apprenticeship a young hunter or fisherman undergoes with a
good master, and it gave him great pleasure, for he
learned only the things that were already latent within
him. He learned to lie in wait, to listen, to stalk, to watch,
to be on his guard, to be alert, to spy and sense; but the
game that he and his master stalked was not only fox and
badger, otter and toad, bird and fish, but essence, the
whole, meaning, relationship. They sought to determine,
to recognize, to guess and forecast the fleeting, unstable
weather, to know the death lying hidden in a berry or
snakebite, to eavesdrop on the secret relations between
clouds or storms and the phases of the moon, relations
that affected the growth of crops as they did the haleness
or doom of man and beast. No doubt they were really
seeking the same ends as the science and technology of
later centuries, dominance over nature and a control over
her laws; but they went about it in an entirely different
way. They did not stand off from nature and try to penetrate into her secrets by violence. They were never opposed and hostile to nature, but always part of her and
reverently devoted to her. It is quite likely that they
knew her better and dealt more wisely with her. But one
thing was utterly impossible for them: not even in their
most audacious moments would it have occurred to
them to meet nature and the world of spirits without
fear, let alone to feel superior to them. Such hubris was
unthinkable; they could not have imagined having any
other attitude but fear toward the forces of nature, toward
death and the demons. Fear loomed over the life of man.
It could not be overcome. But it could be pacified, out-
witted, masked, brought within bounds, placed within
the orderly framework of life as a whole. The various systems of sacrifices served this purpose. Fear was the permanent pressure upon the lives of these people, and
without this high pressure their life would have lacked
stress, of course, but also lacked intensity. A man who had
been able to ennoble his fear by transforming part of it
into awe had gained a great deal. People of this sort,
people whose fear had become a form of piety, were the
good men and the progressive men of that age. There

were many sacrifices and many kinds of sacrifice; and a certain portion of these sacrifices, with their accompanying rites, fell within the province of the Weathermaker.

Alongside Knecht in the hut, little Ada grew up—a pretty child, the old man's darling; and when he thought the time had come, he gave her to his disciple for a wife. From this point on Knecht was considered the Rainmaker's assistant. Turu presented him to the village Mother as his son-in-law and successor, and thereafter allowed him to carry out many official acts and functions as his deputy. Gradually, as the seasons and years passed, the old Rainmaker lapsed into the solitary meditativeness of age and left all his duties to Knecht. By the time the old man was found dead, crouched over some small pots of magic brew on the hearth, his white hair singed by the fire—the boy, the disciple Knecht had long been familiar to the village as the Rainmaker. He demanded that the village council provide an impressive funeral for his teacher, and as a sacrifice burned a whole heap of precious medicinal herbs and roots over the grave. That, too, had happened long ago, and several of Knecht's children already crowded Ada's hut, among them a boy named Turu. In him the old man had returned from his death flight to the moon.

Knecht fared much as had his teacher in times past. Part of his fear was transformed into piety and thought. Part of his youthful aspiration and his profound longings remained alive, part faded away and evaporated as he grew older in his work, in his love and solicitude for Ada and the children. His foremost passion was still for the moon and its influence upon the seasons and the weather; to this he devoted persistent study, and in knowledge of these matters he reached and ultimately surpassed his master, Turu. And because the waxing and waning of the moon are so closely bound up with the birth and death of men; because of all the fears in which men live, fear of having to die is the strongest, Knecht acquired from his adoration and knowledge of the moon a devout and purified attitude toward death. In his riper years he was less subject to the fear of death than other men. He could speak reverently with the moon,

or supplicatingly or tenderly; he knew that he was
linked to it by delicate spiritual bonds. He knew the
moon's life with great precision, shared with all the
force of his own soul in the episodes of the moon's
destiny. He experienced its disappearance and rebirth
like a mystery within himself, suffered with it, felt
alarm when the dreaded event occurred and the moon
seemed exposed to illness and dangers, change and
harm, when it lost its brightness, changed color, darkened until it seemed on the verge of extinction. At
such times, it was true, everyone sympathized with
the moon, trembled for it, recognized menace and the
imminence of disaster in its eclipse, and stared anxiously
at its old, ravaged face. But precisely at such times Rainmaker Knecht showed that he was closer to the moon
and knew more about it than others. For although he
shared in its suffering, although his heart constricted with
anxiety, his memory of similar experiences was keener, his
confidence better founded. He had greater faith in eternity and a second coming, in the possibility of revising
and conquering death. Greater, too, was the degree of
his devotion; at such times he felt in himself a readiness
to share the fate of the celestial orb to the point of doom
and rebirth. At times he even felt something akin to
temerity, a kind of rash courage and the resolution to
defy death by the power of mind, to strengthen his own
selfhood by surrender to superhuman destinies. Some
trace of this was apparent in his manner; others sensed it
and regarded him as knowing and devout, a man of great
calm and little fear of death, one who stood well with
the higher powers.

He had to prove these gifts and virtues in many hard
tests. Once he had to withstand a period of poor crops
and adverse weather that extended over two years. It was
the greatest trial of his life. Troubles and bad portents
had begun with the repeatedly postponed sowing, and
then every imaginable misfortune had affected the crops,
until in the end they were virtually destroyed. The village had starved cruelly, and Knecht, the Rainmaker,
with it. It was a considerable achievement in itself to
have survived this bitter year without losing all credence

and standing, so that he could still help the tribe bear the catastrophe with humility and some degree of composure. When the next year, after a hard winter in which many of the tribe perished, all the miseries of the preceding year were repeated, when during the summer the common land parched and cracked in a stubborn drought, the mice multiplied fearfully, and the solitary conjurations and sacrifices of the Rainmaker proved as vain as the public ceremonies, the drum choruses, and the processions of the whole community; when evidence mounted that this time the Rainmaker could not make rain, it was no small matter and more than ordinary strength was needed to bear the responsibility and hold up his head against the frightened and infuriated people. There were two or three weeks in which Knecht stood entirely alone confronting the entire village, confronting hunger and despair, confronting the ancient belief among the people that only sacrifice of the Weathermaker could propitiate the powers. He had won the victory by yielding. He had not opposed the idea, had offered himself as the sacrifice. Moreover, with enormous toil and devotion he had helped to alleviate distress, had repeatedly discovered sources of water, divining a spring here, a trickling stream there. Even in a time of greatest distress he had not allowed the villagers to slaughter all their livestock. Above all he had lent his support to the tribal mother, who had succumbed to fatalism and weakness in these difficult times. By advice, threat, magic, and prayer, by example and intimidation, he saved her from collapsing completely and letting everything drift wildly. In those times of calamity and universal anxiety it became apparent that a man is the more useful, the more his life and thinking is turned toward matters of the spirit, matters that go beyond the personal realm, the more he has learned to venerate, observe, worship, serve, and sacrifice. The two terrible years, which had almost cost him his life, ended with his being more highly regarded and trusted than ever, not by the thoughtless crowd, of course, but by the few who bore responsibility and were able to judge a man of his type.

His life had passed through these and many other trials

by the time he reached the best years of his maturity. He had officiated over the burial of two of the tribal mothers, had lost a charming six-year-old son who had been carried off by a wolf. He had survived a severe illness without outside help, acting as his own physician. He had suffered hunger and cold. All this had marked his face, and his soul no less. He had also made the discovery that, in a certain peculiar manner, men of thought gave offense and aroused the repugnance of their fellows. They might be valued at a distance and called on in emergencies, but others neither love them nor accept them, rather give them a wide berth. He had also learned that the sick and unfortunate are far more receptive to traditional magic spells and exorcisms than to sensible advice; that people more readily accept affliction and outward penances than the task of changing themselves, or even examining themselves; that they believe more easily in magic than reason, in formulas than experience. These are matters which in the several thousand years since his era have probably not changed so much as a good many history books claim. But he had also learned that a seeking, thoughtful man dare not forfeit love; that he must meet the wishes and follies of men halfway, not showing arrogance but also not truckling to them; that it is always only a single step from sage to charlatan, from priest to mountebank, from helpful brother to parasitic drone, and that the people would by far prefer to pay a swindler and be exploited by a quack than accept help given freely and unselfishly. They would much rather pay in money and goods than in trust and love. They cheat one another and expect to be cheated themselves. You had to learn to see man as a weak, selfish, and cowardly creature; you also had to realize how many of these evil traits and impulses you shared yourself; and nevertheless you allowed yourself to believe, and nourished your soul on the faith, that man is also spirit and love, that something dwells in him which is at variance with his instincts and longs to refine them. But all these thoughts are no doubt far too abstract and explicit for Knecht to have been capable of them. Let us say: he was on the way to them; his way would some day lead him to them and past them.

While he went his way, longing for abstract thought but living far more in the senses, in the spell of the moon, in the pungency of an herb, the saltiness of a root, the taste of a piece of bark, in cultivating simples, blending salves, submitting to the whims of weather and atmosphere, he developed many abilities within himself, including some that we of a later generation no longer possess and only half understand. The most important of these abilities was, of course, rainmaking. Although there were a good many special times when the sky stayed obdurate and seemed to mock his efforts, Knecht nevertheless made rain hundreds of times, and almost every time in a slightly different way. He would, of course, never have dared to make the slightest change or omission in the sacrifices and the rite of processions, conjurations, and drumming. But that was only the official, the public part of his work, the priestly side, which was for show; and undoubtedly it was very fine and produced a fine exalted feeling when after a day of sacrifices and processions the sky gave way in the evening, the horizon clouded over, the wind began to smell damp, the first drops of rain splattered down. But it had taken the Weathermaker's art to choose the day well, not to strive blindly when the prospects were poor. You could implore the powers, even besiege them, but you had to do so with feeling and moderation, with submission to their will. Even more than those glorious triumphant experiences of felicitous intercession he preferred certain others that no one but himself knew about, and even he knew about them only timorously, more with his senses than his understanding. There were weather conditions, tensions of the atmosphere and of heat, cloud formations and winds, smells of water and earth and dust, threats and promises, moods and whims of the weather demons, which Knecht detected in advance with his skin, his hair, with all his senses, so that he could not be surprised by anything, could not be disappointed. He concentrated the very vibrations of the weather within himself, holding them within him in such a way that he could command the clouds and the winds—not, to be sure, just as he pleased, but out of the very intimacy and attachment he had with them, which totally erased the difference

between him and the world, between inside and outside.
At such times he could stand rapt, listening, or crouch
rapt, with all his pores open, and not only feel the life
of the winds and clouds within his own self, but also
direct and engender it, somewhat in the way we can
awaken and reproduce within ourselves a phrase of
music that we know by heart. Then he needed only to
hold his breath—and the wind or the thunder stopped;
he needed only to nod or shake his head—and the hail
pelted down or ceased; he needed only to express by a
smile the balance of the conflicting forces within himself
—and the billows of clouds would part, revealing the
thin, bright blueness. There were many times of unusually pure harmony and composure in his soul when
he carried the weather of the next few days within himself with infallible foreknowledge, as if the whole score
were already written in his blood in such a way that the
outside world must play every note exactly as it stood.
Those were his best days, his reward, his delight.

But when this intimate connection with the outside
was broken, when the weather and the world were unfamiliar, incomprehensible, and unpredictable, then currents were interrupted and derangements occurred within him. Then he felt that he was not a real Rainmaker,
that his responsibility for weather and crops was an
error and nuisance. At such times he was domestic, behaved obediently and helpfully toward Ada, sedulously
shared the household tasks with her, made toys and tools
for the children, pottered about preparing medicines,
craved love and wanted nothing better than to differ as
little as possible from other men, to conform wholly to
them in customs and morals, and even to listen to the
otherwise vexatious gossip of his wife and the neighboring women about the life, health, and conduct of others.
But in good times his family saw little of him, for then
he roamed, fished, hunted, searched for roots, lay in the
grass or crouched in trees, sniffed, listened, imitated the
voices of animals, kindled little fires and compared the
shapes of the smoke clouds with the clouds in the sky,
drenched his skin and hair with fog, rain, air, sun, or
moonlight, and incidentally gathered, as his Master and

predecessor Turu had done in his lifetime, objects whose inner character and outward form seemed to belong to different realms, in which the wisdom or whimsicality of nature seemed to reveal some fragment of her rules and secrets of creation, objects which seemed to unite symbolically widely disparate ideas: gnarled branches with the faces of men or animals, water-polished pebbles grained like wood, petrified animals of the primordial world, misshapen or twinned fruit pits, stones shaped like kidneys or hearts. He read the veinings of a leaf, the pattern on a mushroom cap, and divined mysteries, relations, futures, possibilities: the magic of symbols, the foreshadowing of numbers and writing, the reduction of infinitudes and multiplicities to simplicity, to system, to concept. For all these ways of comprehending the world through the mind no doubt lay within him, nameless, unnamed, but not inconceivable, not beyond the bounds of presentiment, still in the germ, but essential to his nature, part of him, growing organically within him. And if we were to go still further back beyond this Rainmaker and his time which to us seems so early and primitive, if we were to go several thousands of years further back into the past, wherever we found man we would still find—this is our firm belief—the mind of man, that Mind which has no beginning and always has contained everything that it later produces.

The Weathermaker was not destined to win immortality by any one of his premonitions, or to come any closer to proving their validity. For him, indeed, they scarcely needed proof. He did not become one of the many inventors of writing, nor of geometry, nor of medicine or astronomy. He remained an unknown link in the chain, but a link as indispensable as any other. He passed on what he had received, and he added what he had newly acquired by his own struggles. For he too had disciples. In the course of the years he trained two apprentices to be Rainmakers, one of whom was later to become his successor.

For long years he had gone about his affairs and practiced his craft alone and unobserved. Then, shortly after a great crop failure and time of famine, a boy started appearing, watching him, spying on him, adoring him, and generally skulking about—one who was drawn to rainmaking and the Master. With a strange, sorrowful tug at his heart he sensed the recurrence and reversal of the great experience of his youth, and at the same time had that austere feeling, at once constricting and stirring, that afternoon had set in, that youth was gone and noon-day passed, that the blossom had become a fruit. And to his own surprise he behaved toward the boy exactly as old Turu had once behaved toward him. The stiff rebuff, the delaying, wait-and-see attitude, came of its own ac-cord; it was neither an imitation of his deceased Master nor did it spring from moralistic and pedagogic con-siderations that a young man must be tested for a long time to see whether he is serious enough, that initiation into mysteries should not be made easy, and similar theories. On the contrary, Knecht simply behaved to-ward his apprentices the way every somewhat aging soli-tary and learned eccentric behaves toward admirers and disciples. He was embarrassed, shy, distant, ready for flight, fearful for his lovely solitude and his freedom to roam in the wilderness, to go hunting and collecting alone, to dream and listen. He was full of a jealous love for all his habits and hobbies, his secrets and meditations. There could be no question of his embracing the timid youth who approached him with worshipful curiosity, no question of helping him overcome this timidity by encouraging him, no question of his rejoicing and having a sense of reward, appreciation, and pleasant success be-cause the world of the others was at last sending him an emissary and a declaration of love, because someone was courting him, someone felt drawn to him, and like himself called to the service of mysteries. On the contrary, at first he felt it merely as a troublesome disturbance, infringement on his rights and habits, loss of his inde-pendence. For the first time he realized how much he prized that independence. He resisted the wooing and became clever at outwitting the boy and hiding himself, at covering his tracks, evading and escaping. But what had happened to Turu now happened to him also: the boy's long, mute courtship slowly softened his heart,

slowly, slowly wore down his resistance, so that the more
the boy gained ground, the more Knecht learned to turn
to him and open his mind to him, approve his longing,
accept his courtship, and eventually come to regard the
new and often vexatious duty of teaching and having a
disciple as inevitable, imposed by fate, one of the requirements of a life of thought. More and more he had to bid
farewell to the dream, the feeling and the pleasure of
infinite potentialities, of a multiplicity of futures. Instead of the dream of unending progress, of the sum of all
wisdom, his pupil stood by, a small, near, demanding
reality, an intruder and nuisance, but no longer to be
rebuffed or evaded. For the boy represented, after all,
the only way into the real future, the one most important
duty, the one narrow path along which the Rainmaker's
life and acts, principles, thoughts, and glimmerings could
be saved from death and continue their life in a small
new bud. Sighing, gnashing his teeth, and smiling, he
accepted the burden.

But even in this important, perhaps most responsible
aspect of his work, the passing on of tradition and the
education of successors, the Weathermaker was not spared
bitter disillusionment. The first apprentice who sued for
his favor was named Maro; and when after long delay
and every form of deterrence he accepted the boy, Maro
disappointed him in a way he could never quite reconcile himself to. The boy was obsequious and wheedling,
and for a long time pretended unconditional obedience,
but he had certain faults. Above all he lacked courage.
He was especially afraid of night and darkness, a fact he
tried to hide. Knecht, when he noticed it at last, continued for a long time to regard it as lingering childishness which would eventually disappear. But it did not
disappear. This disciple also completely lacked the gift
of selfless devotion to observation for its own sake, to
the procedures and processes of the Rainmaker's work,
and to ideas and speculations. He was clever, had a quick,
bright mind, and he learned easily and surely whatever
could be learned without surrender of the self. But it
became more and more apparent that he had self-seeking
aims, and that it was for the sake of these that he wanted

to learn rainmaking. Above all he wanted status; he wanted to count for something and make an impression. He had the vanity of talent but not of vocation. He longed for applause. As soon as he acquired some scraps of knowledge and a few tricks, he showed off to his fellows. This, too, could be considered childish and might be outgrown. But he wanted more than applause; he also strove for power and advantages over others. When the Master first began to notice this, he was alarmed and gradually withdrew his favor from the young man. Maro had been an apprentice for some years when Knecht caught him in serious misdemeanors. One time he was induced, in return for presents, to treat a sick child with medicines without his Master's knowledge and authorization. Another time he undertook on his own to rid a hut of rats by reciting spells. And when, in spite of all his Master's warnings and his own pledges, he was caught again in similar practices, the Master dismissed him, informed the tribal mother of the affair, and tried to banish the ungrateful and useless young man from his memory.

His two later disciples compensated for this disappointment, especially the second, who was his own son Turu. He deeply loved this youngest and last of his apprentices, and believed the boy could become greater than himself. Plainly, his grandfather's spirit had returned in him. Knecht experienced the invigorating satisfaction of having passed on the sum of his knowledge and belief to the future, and of having a person who was his son twice over, to whom he could hand over his duties any time these became too heavy for him. But still that ill-favored first disciple could not be dismissed from his life and thoughts. In the village Maro became a man who while not especially enjoying high honor, was nevertheless extremely popular and wielded considerable influence. He had taken a wife, amused many people by his talents as a kind of mountebank and jester, and had even become chief drummer in the drum corps. He remained a secret enemy of the Rainmaker, consumed by envy and inflicting large and small injuries upon him whenever he could. Knecht had never had a gift for friendship and gregariousness. He needed solitude and freedom; he had never sought out respect or love, except for the time he was a boy seeking to win over Master Turu. But now he learned how it felt to have an enemy, someone who hated him. It spoiled a good many of his days.

Maro had been one of those highly talented pupils who in spite of their talent are always unpleasant and a grief to their teachers because their talent has not grown from below and from within. It is not founded on organic strength, the delicate, ennobling mark of a good endowment, of sound blood and a sound character, but is in a curious way something adventitious, accidental, perhaps even usurped or stolen. A pupil of meager character but high intelligence or sparkling imagination invariably embarrasses the teacher. He is obliged to transmit to this pupil the knowledge and methodology he himself has inherited, and to prepare him for the life of the mind—and yet he cannot help feeling that his real and higher duty should be to protect the arts and sciences against the intrusion of young men who have nothing but talent. For the teacher is not supposed to serve the pupil; rather, both are the servants of their culture. This is the reason teachers feel slightly repelled by certain glittering talents. A pupil of that type falsifies the whole meaning of pedagogy as service. All the help given to a pupil who can shine but cannot serve basically means doing harm to service and is, in a way, a betrayal of culture. We know of periods in the history of many nations in which profound upheavals in cultural processes led to a surge of the merely talented into leading positions in communities, schools, academies, and governments. Highly talented people sat in all sorts of posts, but they were people who wanted to rule without being able to serve. Certainly it is often very difficult to recognize such people in good time, before they have entrenched themselves in the intellectual professions. It is equally difficult to treat them with the necessary ruthlessness and send them back to other occupations. Knecht, too, had made mistakes; he had been patient far too long with his apprentice Maro. He had entrusted esoteric knowledge to a superficial climber. That was a pity, and the consequences for himself were far greater than he could ever have foreseen.

A year came—by then Knecht's beard was already quite gray—in which the orderly relationships between heaven and earth seemed to have been distorted by demons of unusual strength and malevolence. These distortions began in the autumn with events of such fearful majesty that every soul in the village shook with terror. Shortly after the equinox, which the Rainmaker always observed with heightened attentiveness and celebrated with solemnity and reverent worship, there was a display in the heavens that had not occurred within the memory of man. An evening came that was dry, windy, and rather cool. The sky was crystal clear except for a few restless small clouds which floated at a very great height, holding the rosy light of the setting sun for an unusually long time. They looked like loose and foamy bundles of light drifting in cold, pale cosmic space. For several days past Knecht had sensed something that was stronger and more remarkable than the feeling he had every year at this time when the days began growing shorter: a seething of the powers in the sky, a sense of alarm in earth, plants and animals, a nervousness in the air, something inconstant, expectant, frightened, lowering in all of nature. The small clouds with their lingering, quivering flames formed part of the strangeness. Their fluttery movements did not correspond with the direction of the wind on the ground. After a long sad struggle against extinction, their piteous red light grew cold and faded, and suddenly they were invisible.

It was quiet in the village. The circle of children before the tribal mother's hut had long scattered. A few boys were still chasing about and tussling, but all the rest of the tribe were in their huts. Everyone had eaten. Many were already asleep; scarcely anyone but the Rainmaker observed the twilit clouds. Knecht walked back and forth in the small garden behind his hut, pondering the weather, tense and restive. At times he sat down for a brief rest on a stump that stood among the nettles and served him for splitting wood. As soon as the last glimmer of cloud was extinguished the stars suddenly appeared against the greenish glow of the sky, and rapidly grew in number and brightness. Where there had been only two or three visible a moment before, there were now ten, twenty. The Rainmaker was familiar with many of them individually and in their groups and families. He had seen them many hundreds of times; there was always something reassuring about their unvarying reappearance. Stars were comforting. Though they hung so high, remote and cold, radiating no warmth, they were reliable, firmly aligned, proclaiming order, promising duration. Seemingly so aloof and far and opposed to life on earth, seemingly so untouched by the warmth, the writhings, the sufferings and ecstasies in the life of man, so superior in their cold majesty and eternity that they seemed to make mock of human things, the stars nevertheless had a relation to us. They guided and governed us perhaps, and if any human knowledge, any intellectual hold, any sureness and superiority of the mind over transitory things could be attained and retained, it would resemble the stars, shining like them in cool tranquility, comforting with chilly shivers of awe, looking down eternally and somewhat mockingly. That was how they had often seemed to the Rainmaker, and although he felt toward the stars nothing like the close, stimulating, constantly changing and recurring relationship he had toward the moon, the great, near, moist orb, the fat magic fish in the sea of heaven, he nevertheless revered them and attached many beliefs to them. To gaze at them for a long time and allow their influence to work upon him, to expose his intelligence, his warmth, his anxiety to their serenely cold gaze, often laved and assuaged him like a healing draft.

Tonight, too, they looked as they always did, except that they were very bright and seemed highly polished in the taut, thin air; but he could not find within himself the repose to surrender to them. From unknown realms some power was tugging at him; it ached in his pores, sucked at his eyes, quietly and continually affected him. It was a current, a warning quiver. In the hut nearby the warm, dim light of the hearth-fire glimmered.

Life flowed small and warm inside: a cry, a laugh, a yawn, human smells, skin warmth, motherhood, children's sleep. All that innocent presence seemed to deepen the night, to drive the stars still further back into the incomprehensible distances and heights.

And now, while Knecht heard Ada's voice inside the hut crooning and humming a low melody as she quieted a child, there began in the sky the calamity that the village would remember for many years. A flickering and glimmering appeared here and there in the still, glittering network of stars, as if the usually invisible threads of the net were suddenly leaping into flame. Like hurled stones, glowing and guttering, a few stars fell slantwise across the sky, one here, two there, a few more here; and before the eye had turned from the first vanished falling star, before the heart, stilled at the sight, had begun to beat again, the lights falling or hurled at a slant or a slight arc across the sky began to come in swarms of dozens, hundreds. A countless host, borne on a vast, mute storm, they slanted across the silent night, as if a cosmic autumn were tearing all the stars like withered leaves from the tree of heaven and flinging them noiselessly into the void. Like withered leaves, like wafting snowflakes, they rushed away and down, thousands upon thousands, in fearful silence, vanishing beyond the wooded mountains to the southeast where never a star had set since time immemorial.

With frozen heart and swimming eyes, Knecht stood, head tilted back, gazing horrified but insatiably at the transformed and accursed sky, mistrusting his eyes and yet only too certain of the direness of what they beheld. Like all who watched this nocturnal spectacle, he thought the familiar stars themselves were wavering, scattering, and plunging down, and he expected that if the earth itself did not swallow him first, the firmament would soon appear black and emptied. After a while, however, he recognized what others could not know—that the well-known stars were still present, here and there and everywhere; that the frightful dispersion was taking place not among the old, familiar stars, but in the space between earth and sky, and that these new lights, fallen or flung, so swiftly appearing and swiftly vanishing, glowed with a fire of another sort from the old, the proper stars. This was somewhat reassuring and helped him regain his balance. But even if these were new, transitory, different stars scattering through the air, still it meant disaster and disorder. Deep sighs came from Knecht's parched throat. He looked toward the earth; he listened to find out whether this uncanny spectacle were appearing to him alone, or whether others were also seeing it. Soon he heard groans, screams, and cries of terror from other huts. Others had seen it too; their cries had alarmed the sleepers and the unaware; in a moment panic had seized the entire village. With a sigh, Knecht took the burden on himself. This misfortune affected him, the Rainmaker, above all others, for he was in a way responsible for order in the heavens. Always before he had known or sensed great catastrophes in advance: floods, hailstorms, tempests. Always he had warned the mothers and elders to be prepared. He had averted the worst evils. He had interposed himself, his knowledge, his courage, and his confidence in the powers above, between the village and consternation. Why had he foreknown nothing this time, so that he could take no measure? Why had he said not a word to anyone of the obscure foreboding he had, after all, felt?

He lifted the mat hung over the entrance of the hut and softly called his wife's name. She came, her youngest at her breast. He took the baby from her and laid it on the pallet. Holding Ada's hand, he placed a finger to his lips, enjoining silence, and led her out of the hut. He saw her patiently tranquil face grow distorted by terror.

"Let the children sleep; I don't want them to see this, do you hear?" he whispered intensely. "Don't let any of them come out, not even Turu. And you yourself stay inside."

He hesitated, uncertain how much to say, how many of his thoughts he ought to reveal. Finally he added firmly: "Nothing will harm you and the children."

She believed him at once, although her face and her mind had not yet recovered from the fright.

"What is it?" she asked, again staring at the sky. "Is it very bad?"

"It is bad," he said gently. "I think it may be very bad.

But it doesn't concern you and the children. Stay in the hut; keep the mat drawn. I must talk to the people. Go in, Ada."

He pressed her through the opening, drew the mat carefully closed, and stood for the span of a few breaths with his face turned toward the continuing rain of stars. Then he bowed his head, sighed heavily once more, and walked swiftly through the night toward the tribal mother's hut.

Half the village was already assembled there. A muted roar rose from them, a tumult half numbed by terror and choked by despair. There were women and men who surrendered with a kind of voluptuous rage to their sense of horror and impending doom. Some stood stiff, rapt. Others jerked about wildly with uncontrolled movements of their limbs. One woman was foaming at the mouth as she danced, alone, a despairing and obscene dance, at the same time pulling out whole handfuls of her long hair. Knecht realized that the effects were already at work. Almost all had succumbed to the intoxication; they were bewitched or driven mad by the falling stars, and an orgy of madness, fury, and self-destructiveness might follow. It was high time to collect the few brave and sensible members of the tribe, and support their courage.

The ancient tribal mother was calm. She believed that the end of all things had come, and that there was nothing to be done about it. Toward the inevitable she showed a firm, hard face that looked almost mocking in its pinched astringency. He persuaded her to listen to him. He tried to show her that the old stars, the ones that had always been, were still in the sky. But she could not grasp it, either because her eyes no longer had the strength to discern them, or because her conception of the stars was too unlike the Rainmaker's. She shook her head and maintained her courageous grin, but when Knecht implored her not to abandon the people to their terror, she instantly was of his mind. A small group of frightened but not yet maddened villagers still willing to be led formed around her and the Weathermaker.

Up to the moment he reached the group, Knecht had

hoped to be able to check the panic by example, reason, speech, explanations, and encouragement. But his brief conversation with the tribal mother had shown him that it was too late for anything of the sort. He had hoped to let the others share in his own experience, to make them a gift of it. He had hoped to persuade them that the stars themselves were not falling, or not all of them, that no cosmic storm was sweeping them away. He had imagined that by such urging he would be able to move them from helpless dismay to active observation, so that they would be able to bear the shock. But he quickly saw that there were very few villagers who would hearken to him, and by the time he won them over all the others would have utterly given way to madness. No, as was so often the case, reason and sensible speech could accomplish nothing here.

Fortunately there were other means. Although it was impossible to dispel their mortal terror by appeal to reason, this terror could still be guided, organized, given shape, so that the confusion of maddened people could be made into a solid unity, the wild, single voices merged into a chorus. But there was no time to be lost. Knecht stepped before the people, loudly crying the well-known prayers that opened public ceremonies of penance and mourning: the lament for the death of a tribal mother, or the ceremony of sacrifice and atonement in the face of perils such as epidemics and floods. He shouted the words in rhythm and reinforced the rhythm by clapping his hands; and in the same rhythm, shouting and clapping his hands all the while, he stooped almost to the ground, straightened up, stooped again, and straightened up. Almost at once ten or twenty others joined in his movements. The white-haired mother of the village murmured in the same rhythm and with tiny bows sketched the ritual movements. Those who were still flocking to the assemblage from the huts at once joined in the beat and the spirit of the ceremony; the few who had gone off their heads collapsed, and lay motionless, or else were caught up in the murmur of the chorus and the religious genuflections. His method was effective. Instead of a demoralized horde of madmen, there now stood a reverent populace prepared for sacrifice and penance, each one benefiting, each one encouraged by now having to lock his horror and fear of death within himself, or bellow it crazily for himself alone. Each now fitted into his place in the orderly chorus of the multitude, keeping to the rhythm of the exorcistic ceremony. Many mysterious powers are present in such a rite. Its greatest comfort is its uniformity, confirming the sense of community; its infallible medicine meter and order, rhythm and music.

While the whole night sky was still covered by the host of falling stars like a rushing, silent cascade consisting of droplets of light—for another two hours it went on squandering its great red globules of fire—the horror in the village changed to submission and devotion, to prayers to the powers and penitential feelings. In their fear and weakness men met the disorder of the sky with order and religious concord. Even before the rain of stars began to slacken, the miracle had taken place; the inner miracle radiated healing powers; and by the time the sky seemed slowly to be quieting down and recovering, all the dead-tired penitents had the redeeming feeling that their worship had placated the powers and restored order in the heavens.

That night of terror was not forgotten. The village talked about it all through the autumn and winter. But soon this was no longer done in timorous whispers, but in an everyday tone of voice and with that satisfaction that people feel when they look back upon a disaster faced and withstood, a peril successfully overcome. The villagers now battened on details; each had been surprised in his own way by the incredible event; each claimed to have been the first to discover it. Some ventured to make fun of those who had been particularly shaken by it. For a long time a certain amount of excitement persisted in the village. There had been a great event; something extraordinary had happened.

Knecht did not share this mood, or feel the same gradual loss of interest in the phenomenon. For him, the whole uncanny experience remained an unforgettable warning, a thorn that continued to prick him. He could not dismiss it on the grounds that it had passed, that the danger had been averted by processions, prayers, and penances. The further it receded in time, in fact, the greater its importance became for him, because he filled it with meaning. It gave full scope to his tendency to brood and interpret. The event in itself, the whole of that miraculous natural spectacle, had been an enormously difficult problem involving many aspects. A man who had once seen it could probably spend a lifetime pondering it.

Only one other person in the village would have watched the rain of stars from a kindred point of view, and on the basis of similar knowledge. That was his own son and disciple, Turu. Only what this one witness would have said, to bear out or to revise his own observation, would have mattered to Knecht. But he had let this son sleep; and the longer he wondered why he had done so, why he had refrained from sharing the sight of the incredible event with the only eyewitness whose judgment he would have taken seriously, the more convinced he became that he had acted rightly, obeying a wise instinct. He had wanted to spare his family the sight, including his apprentice and associate; had wanted to spare him especially, for he loved no one so much as Turu. For that reason he had concealed the rain of falling stars from him, had defrauded him of the sight. He believed in the good spirits of sleep, especially of the sleep of youth. Moreover, if he remembered rightly, the first sight of the heavenly sign had scarcely seemed to betoken any momentary danger to the lives of the villagers. Rather, he had instantly decided that the event was an omen of future disaster, and one that concerned no one so closely as himself, the Weathermaker. The calamity, when it came, would strike him alone. Something was in the offing, a threat from that realm with which his office linked him. No matter what the form in which it came, he would be the one who would chiefly bear its brunt. To keep himself alert to this danger, to oppose it resolutely when it came, to prepare his soul and accept it but not let it intimidate or dishonor him—such was the resolve he came to, such was the command he thought he had received from the great omen. The danger that loomed would call for a mature and courageous man. For that reason it would not have been well to draw his son into it, to have him as a fellow sufferer, or even as a partner in the knowledge. For although he thought so highly of his son, he did not know whether a young and untested person would be able to cope with the menace.

His son Turu, however, was most unhappy because he had slept through the great spectacle. No matter how it was interpreted, it had been a great thing in any case, and perhaps nothing of the sort would happen all the rest of his life. For quite a while he was resentful toward his father on that account. Knecht overcame the resentment by increased attentiveness and affection. He drew Turu more and more into all the duties of his office. In anticipation of things to come, he took greater pains to complete Turu's training and make him as perfect an initiate and successor as possible. Although he rarely spoke with him about the rain of stars, he admitted him with less and less restraint into his secrets, his practices, his knowledge and researches, and allowed the boy to accompany him on his walks and investigations of nature, and to join him in experiments. All this he had previously shared with no one.

The winter came and passed, a damp and rather mild winter. No more stars fell, no great and unusual things happened. The village was reassured. Diligently, the hunters went out looking for game. On racks beside the huts hung stiffly frozen bundles of hides, clacking against one another in windy weather. Loads of wood were dragged in from the forest on long, smoothed boards that rode lightly over the snow. It happened that just during the brief period of hard frost an old woman died. She could not be buried at once; for some days, until the ground thawed again, the frozen corpse was laid out beside the door of her hut.

The spring partly confirmed the Weathermaker's forebodings. It was a dreary, joyless spring, without ardor and sap, betrayed by the moon. The moon was always tardy; the various signs that determined the day of sowing never coincided. In the forest the flowers blossomed sparsely; buds shriveled on the twigs. Knecht was deeply troubled, but did not show it; only Ada and especially Turu could see how anxious he was. He not only undertook the usual incantations, but also made private sacrifices, boiling savory, aromatic brews and infusions for the demons, as well as cutting his beard short on the night of the new moon and burning it in a mixture of resin and damp bark that produced heavy smoke. He postponed as long as possible the public ceremonies, the village sacrifices, the processions, and the drum choruses. As long as possible he kept the accursed weather of this evil spring as his private concern. But eventually, when the usual time for sowing was already many days past, he had to report to the tribal mother. Sure enough, here too he encountered misfortune and trouble. The old tribal mother, who was his good friend and had rather maternal feelings for him, did not receive him. She was ill, lying in bed, and had handed over all her duties to her sister. This sister, as it happened, was distinctly cool toward the Rainmaker. She did not have the older woman's austere, straightforward character, was rather fond of distractions and frivolities, and hence had taken a liking to Maro, the drummer and mountebank, who knew how to entertain and flatter her. And Maro was Knecht's enemy. Knecht sensed at their first conversation her coolness and dislike, although she in no way questioned his proposals. He urged that they postpone the sowing for a while longer, as well as any sacrifices or processions. She agreed to this, but she had received him icily and treated him like a subordinate. She refused his request to see the sick tribal mother, or at least to be allowed to prepare medicine for her.

Knecht returned from this interview dejected, feeling poorer, and with a bad taste in his mouth. For half a moon he tried in his own way to make weather which would permit sowing. But the weather, which had so often followed the same direction as the currents within him, remained unmanageable. It mocked all his efforts. Neither spells nor sacrifices worked. The Rainmaker had no choice; he had to go to the tribal mother's sister again. This time he was virtually pleading for patience, for postponement; and he realized at once that she must have spoken with that clown Maro about him and his affairs. For in the course of the conversation on the necessity of setting the day for sowing, or else ordering ceremonies of public prayer, the old woman showed off her knowledge and used a few expressions which she could only have learned from Maro, the former Rainmaker's apprentice. Knecht asked for three days' grace and then decided that the constellation was more favorable. He set the sowing for the first day of the third quarter of the moon. The old woman consented, and pronounced the ritual words. The decision was proclaimed to the village, and everyone prepared for the rite of sowing.

But now, when everything seemed to be in hand for a while, the demons again showed their malice. On the very day of the longed-for and carefully prepared sowing, the old tribal mother died. The ritual sowing had to be postponed and her funeral prepared instead. It was celebrated with great solemnity; behind the new village mother, with her sisters and daughters, the Rainmaker took his place in the robes reserved for great processions, wearing his tall, pointed fox-fur headdress. He was assisted by his son Turu, who struck the two-toned hardwood clappers together. Great honors were shown to the deceased and to her sister, the new tribal mother. Maro, leading the drummers, kept in the forefront of the mourners and won much attention and applause. The village wept and celebrated, lamented and feasted, enjoyed the drum music and the sacrifices. It was a fine day for all, but the sowing had again been put off. Knecht stood through it all with dignity and composure, but he was profoundly saddened. It seemed to him that along with the tribal mother he was burying all the good days of his life.

Soon afterward, at the request of the new tribal mother, the sowing was likewise celebrated with special magnificence. Solemnly, the procession marched around the fields; solemnly, the old woman scattered the first handfuls of seed on the common land. To either side of her walked her sisters, each carrying a pouch of grain into which the eldest dipped her hand. Knecht breathed a little easier when this ceremony was finally completed.

But the seed sowed so festively was destined to bring no joy and no harvest. It was a merciless year. Beginning with a relapse into wintry frosts, the weather indulged in every imaginable caprice and spite that spring. In summer, when meager crops at last covered the fields thinly, half as tall as they should have been, the last blow of all came: an incredible drought, the worst anyone could remember. Week after week the sun blazed in a white haze of heat. The smaller brooks dried up. Only a muddy marsh remained of the village pond, a paradise for dragon-flies and a monstrous brood of mosquitoes. Deep cracks gaped in the parched earth. The villagers could see the crops withering. Now and then clouds gathered, but the lightning storms remained dry. If a brief shower fell, it was followed by days of a parching east wind. Lightning often struck tall trees, setting fire to their withered tops.

"Turu," Knecht said to his son one day, "this will not turn out well. We have all the demons against us. It began with the falling stars. I think it is going to cost me my life. Remember this: If I must be sacrificed, assume my office at once and insist that my body be burned and my ashes strewn on the fields. You will suffer great hunger through the winter. But the evil spells will be broken. You must see to it that no one touches the community's seed grain, under penalty of death. Next year will be better, and people will say: 'Good that we have the new young Weathermaker.'"

There was despair in the village. Maro incited the people. Frequently, threats and curses were shouted at the Rainmaker. Ada fell sick and lay shaken by vomiting and fever. The processions, the sacrifices, the long, heart-throbbing drum choruses were useless. Knecht led them, for that was his duty, but when the people scattered again, he stood alone, shunned by all. He knew what was necessary, and he knew also that Maro had already besieged the tribal mother with demands that he be sacrificed. For his own honor and his son's sake, he took the last step himself. He dressed Turu in the ceremonial robes, went to the tribal mother with him, and proposed him as his successor, at the same time offering himself as a sacrifice. She looked at him for a short while with a curious, searching glance. Then she nodded and assented.

The sacrifice was carried out that same day. The whole village would have attended, but many lay sick with dysentery. Ada, too, was gravely ill. Turu, in his robes, with the tall fox-fur headdress, all but collapsed from heatstroke. All the dignitaries and leaders of the village who were not ill joined in the procession, including the tribal mother with two of her oldest sisters, and Maro, the chief of the drum corps. Behind them followed the mass of the villagers. No one insulted the old Rainmaker; the procession was silent and dejected. They marched to the woods and sought out a large circular clearing that Knecht himself had appointed as the site of the sacrifice. Most of the men had their stone axes with them to cut wood for the funeral pyre.

When they reached the clearing, they placed the Rainmaker in the center and the dignitaries of the village formed a small ring around him, with the rest of the crowd in a larger circle on the outside. There was an indecisive, embarrassed silence, until the Rainmaker himself spoke.

"I was your Rainmaker," he said. "I did my work as well as I could for many years. Now the demons are against me; nothing I do succeeds. Therefore I have offered myself for a sacrifice. That will placate the demons. My son Turu will be your new Rainmaker. Now kill me, and when I am dead do exactly as my son says. Farewell! And now who will be my executioner? I recommend the drummer Maro; he is surely the right man for the task."

He fell silent. No one stirred. Turu, flushed deeply under the heavy fur headdress, gave a tormented look around the circle. His father's mouth twisted mockingly. At last the tribal mother stamped her foot furiously, beckoned to Maro and shouted at him: "Go ahead! Take the axe and do it."

Maro, axe clutched in his hands, posted himself before his former teacher. He hated him more than ever; the lines of scorn around those silent old lips irked him bitterly. He raised the axe and swung it over his head. Taking aim, he held it aloft, staring into the victim's face, waiting for him to close his eyes. But Knecht did not; he kept his eyes wide open, fixed steadily on the man with the axe. They were almost expressionless, but what expression there was hovered between pity and scorn.

In fury, Maro flung the axe away. "I won't do it," he murmured, and pressing through the circle of dignitaries he lost himself in the crowd. Several villagers laughed softly. The tribal mother had turned pale with rage, as much at Maro's uselessness and cowardice as at the arrogance of the Rainmaker. She beckoned to one of the oldest men, a quiet, dignified person who stood leaning on his axe and seemed to be ashamed of this whole unseemly scene. He stepped forward and gave the victim a brief, friendly nod. They had known each other since boyhood. And now the victim willingly closed his eyes; Knecht closed them tightly, and bowed his head a little. The old man struck with the axe. Knecht fell. Turu, the new Rainmaker, could not say a word. He gave the necessary orders with gestures alone. Soon the pyre was heaped up and the body laid on it. The solemn ritual of making fire with two consecrated sticks was Turu's first official act.

TWO

THE FATHER CONFESSOR

IN THE DAYS when St. Hilarion was still alive, although far advanced in years, there lived in the city of Gaza a man named Josephus Famulus who until his thirtieth year or longer had led a worldly life and studied the books of the pagans. Then, through a woman whom he was pursuing, he had been instructed in the divine doctrine and the sweetness of the Christian virtues, had submitted to holy baptism, renounced his sins, and sat for several years at the feet of the presbyters of his city. In particular he listened with burning curiosity to the popular tales of the life of pious hermits in the desert, until one day, at the age of thirty-six, he set out on the path already taken by St. Paul and St. Anthony, and which so many devout souls have taken since. He gave his goods to the elders, to be distributed to the poor of the community, bade farewell to his friends at the city gate, and wandered out into the desert, out of this vile world, to take up the life of the penitent.

For many years the sun seared and parched him. He scraped his knees on rock and sand as he prayed. He waited, fasting, for the sun to set before he chewed his few dates. Devils tormented him with temptations, mockery, and trials, but he struck them down with prayer, with penitence, with renunciation of self, in the ways we may find described in the Lives of the blessed Fathers. Through many sleepless nights he gazed at the stars, and even the stars provided temptations and confusions for him. He scanned the constellations, for he had learned to read in them stories of the gods and symbols of human nature. The presbyters held this science in abomination, but he was still engrossed by fantasies and ideas he had entertained in his pagan days.

In those times eremites lived wherever the barren wilderness was broken by a spring, a patch of vegetation, a large or small oasis. Some dwelt entirely alone, some in small brotherhoods, as they are pictured in a painting in the Campo Santo of Pisa, practicing poverty and love of neighbor. They became adepts of a languishing *ars moriendi*, the art of dying: mortification of the ego and dying to the world, passing through death to Him, the Redeemer, to the inalienable reward. They were attended by angels and devils; they wrote hymns, expelled demons, healed and blessed, and seemed to have assumed the duty of making up for the pleasure-seeking, brutality, and sensuality of many past and future ages by engendering a mighty surge of enthusiasm and devotion, an ecstatic excess of renunciation. Many of them probably were acquainted with ancient pagan practices of purification, methods and exercises of spiritualization elaborated in Asia for centuries. But nothing was said of such matters. These methods and yoga exercises were no longer taught; they lay under the ban that Christianity more and more sternly imposed upon everything pagan.

In some of these penitents the fervor of their life developed special gifts, gifts of prayer, of healing by laying on of hands, of prophecy, of exorcism, gifts of judging and punishing, comforting and blessing. In Josephus too a gift slumbered, and with the passing years, as his hair began to gray, it slowly came to flower. It was the gift of listening. Whenever a brother from one of the hermitages, or a child of the world harried and troubled of soul, came to Joseph and told him of his deeds, sufferings, temptations, and missteps, related the story of his life, his struggle for goodness and his failures in the struggle, or spoke of loss, pain, or sorrow, Joseph knew how to listen to him, to open his ears and his heart, to gather the man's sufferings and anxieties into himself and hold them, so that the penitent was sent away emptied and calmed. Slowly, over long years, this function had taken possession of him and made an instrument of him, an ear that people trusted.

His virtues were patience, a receptive passivity, and great discretion. More and more frequently people came to him to pour out their hearts, to relieve their pent-up distress; but many of them, even though they had come a long way to his reed hut, would find they lacked the courage to confess. They would writhe in shame, be coy about their sins, sigh heavily, and remain silent for hours. But he behaved in the same way toward all, whether they spoke freely or reluctantly, fluently or hesitantly, whether they hurled out their secrets in a fury, or basked in self-importance because of them. He regarded every man in the same way, whether he accused God or himself, whether he magnified or minimized his sins and sufferings, whether he confessed a killing or merely an act of lewdness, whether he lamented an unfaithful sweetheart or the loss of his soul's salvation. It did not alarm Josephus when someone told of converse with demons and seemed to be on the friendliest terms with the devil. He did not lose patience when someone talked at great length while obviously concealing the main issue. Nor was he stern when someone charged himself with delusory and invented sins. All the complaints, confessions, charges, and qualms of conscience that were brought to him seemed to pour into his ears like water into the desert sands. He seemed to pass no judgment upon them and to feel neither pity nor contempt for the person confessing. Nevertheless, or perhaps for that very reason, whatever was confessed to him seemed not to be spoken into the void, but to be transformed, alleviated, and redeemed in the telling and being heard. Only rarely did he reply with a warning or admonition, even more rarely did he give advice, let alone any order. Such did not seem to be his function, and his callers apparently sensed that it was not. His function was to arouse confidence and to be receptive, to listen patiently and lovingly, helping the imperfectly formed confession to take shape, inviting all that was dammed up or encrusted within each soul to flow and pour out. When it did, he received it and wrapped it in silence.

His response was always the same. At the end of every confession, the terrible ones and the innocuous ones, the contrite ones and the vain ones, he would tell the penitent to kneel beside him and recite the Lord's Prayer. Then he would dismiss him, kissing him on the brow. Imposing penances and punishments was not his business, nor did he even feel empowered to pronounce a proper priestly absolution. Neither judging nor forgiving sin was his affair. By listening and understanding he seemed to take upon himself a share of the transgression; he seemed to help to bear it. By remaining silent, he seemed to bury what he had heard and consign it to the past. By praying with the penitent after the confession, he seemed to receive him as his brother and acknowledge him as his fellow. By kissing him, he seemed to bless him in a more brotherly than priestly, a more affectionate than ceremonial manner.

His reputation spread through the whole neighborhood of Gaza and beyond. Sometimes he was even mentioned in the same breath as the great hermit and father confessor Dion Pugil. The latter's fame, however, was already some ten years older, and was founded on quite different abilities. For Father Dion was celebrated for being able to read the souls of those who sought him out without recourse to words. He often surprised a faltering penitent by charging him bluntly with his still unconfessed sins. Joseph had heard a hundred amazing stories about his acuity, and would never had ventured to compare himself with him. Father Dion was also a wise counselor of erring souls, a great judge, chastiser, and rectifier. He assigned penances, castigations, and pilgrimages, ordered marriages, compelled enemies to make up, and enjoyed the authority of a bishop. Although he lived in the vicinity of Ascalon, people came to him from as far away as Jerusalem and places even more remote.

Like most eremites and penitents, Josephus Famulus

had lived through long years of passionate and exhausting struggle. Although he had abandoned his life in the world, had given away his house and possessions and left the city with its manifold invitations to the pleasures of the senses, he was still saddled with his old self. Within his body and soul were all those instincts which can lead a man into distress and temptation. At first he had struggled primarily against his body; he had been stern and harsh with it, subjecting it to hunger and thirst, to scars and calluses, until it had gradually withered. But even in its gaunt ascetic's shell the old Adam could shamefully catch him by surprise and vex him with foolish cravings and desires, dreams and hallucinations. We know well that the devil lays special siege to penitents and fugitives from this world. When, therefore, people seeking consolation and confession occasionally visited him, he gratefully acknowledged their coming as a sign of grace, and a consolation to him in his ascetic's life. For he had been given a meaning beyond himself. A task had been conferred upon him. He could serve others, or serve God as an instrument for drawing souls to Him.

That had been a wonderful and elevating feeling. But in the course of time he had learned that even the goods of the soul belong to the earthly realm and can become temptations and snares. For often, when such a traveler arrived, either on foot or riding, stopped at his cave for a drink of water, and asked the hermit to hear his confession, a feeling of satisfaction and pleasure would creep over our Joseph. He felt well pleased with himself. As soon as he recognized this vanity and self-love, he was profoundly alarmed. Often he knelt to beg God's forgiveness and ask that no more penitents be sent him in his unworthiness, neither from the huts of the ascetic brethren in the vicinity nor from the villages and towns of the world. But when for a while no one came to confess, he found himself not much better off, and on the other hand when the stream of penitents resumed, he caught himself sinning once more. After a time, listening to some confessions, he found himself subject to spasms of coldness and lovelessness, even to contempt for the penitents. With a sigh he accepted these struggles too, and there were periods during which he inflicted solitary humiliations and penances upon himself after each confession. Moreover, he made it a rule to treat all penitents not only as brothers, but also with a kind of special deference. The less he liked the person, the more respectfully he behaved toward him, for he regarded each one as a messenger from God, sent to test him. Belatedly, after many years, when he was already approaching old age, he arrived at a certain equanimity. To those who lived in the vicinity he seemed to be a man without faults who had found his peace in God.

But peace, too, is a living thing and like all life it must wax and wane, accommodate, withstand trials, and undergo changes. Such was the case with the peace Josephus Famulus enjoyed. It was unstable, visible one moment, gone the next, sometimes near as a candle carried in the hand, sometimes as remote as a star in the wintry sky. And in time a new and special kind of sin and temptation more and more often made life difficult for him. It was not a strong, passionate emotion such as indignation or a sudden rush of instinctual urges. Rather, it seemed to be the opposite. It was a feeling very easy to bear in its initial stages, for it was scarcely perceptible; a condition without any real pain or deprivation, a slack, lukewarm, tedious state of the soul which could only be described in negative terms as a vanishing, a waning, and finally a complete absence of joy. There are days when the sun does not shine and the rain does not pour, but the sky sinks quietly into itself, wraps itself up, is gray but not black, sultry, but not with the tension of an imminent thunderstorm. Gradually, Joseph's days became like this as he approached old age. Less and less could he distinguish the mornings from the evenings, feast days from ordinary days, hours of rapture from hours of dejection. Everything ran sluggishly along in limp tedium and joylessness. This is old age, he thought sadly. He was sad because he had expected aging and the gradual extinction of his passions to bring a brightening and easing of his life, to take him a step nearer to harmony and mature peace of soul, and now age seemed to be disappointing and cheating him by offering nothing but this weary, gray, joyless emptiness, this feeling of

chronic satiation. Above all he felt sated: by sheer existence, by breathing, by sleep at night, by life in his cave
on the edge of the little oasis, by the eternal round of
evenings and mornings, by the passing of travelers and
pilgrims, camel riders and donkey riders, and most of all
by the people who came to visit him, by those foolish,
anxious, and childishly credulous people who had this
craving to tell him about their lives, their sins and their
fears, their temptations and self-accusations. Sometimes
it all seemed to him like the small spring of water that
collected in its stone basin in the oasis, flowed through
grass for a while, forming a small brook, and then flowed
on out into the desert sands, where after a brief course
it dried up and vanished. Similarly, all these confessions,
these inventories of sins, these lives, these torments of
conscience, big and small, serious and vain, all of them
came pouring into his ear, by the dozens, by the hundreds, more and more of them. But his ear was not
dead like the desert sands. His ear was alive and could
not drink, swallow, and absorb forever. It felt fatigued,
abused, glutted. It longed for the flow and splashing
of words, confessions, anxieties, charges, self-condemna-
tions to cease; it longed for peace, death, and stillness to
take the place of this endless flow.

That was it, he wished for the end. He was tired, had
had enough and more than enough. His life had become
stale and worthless. Things went so far with him that at
times he felt tempted to put an end to it, to punish and
extinguish himself, as the traitor Judas had done when he
hanged himself. Just as the devil had plagued him in the
earlier stages of his ascetic's life by smuggling into his
soul the desires, notions, and dreams of sensual and
worldly pleasures, so the evil one now assailed him with
ideas of self-destruction, so that he found himself considering every tree with the view to its holding a noose,
every cliff in the vicinity with a view to casting himself
from its top. He resisted the temptation. He fought. He did
not yield. But day and night he lived in a fire of self-
hatred and craving for death. Life had become unbearable and hateful.

To such a pass had Joseph come. One day, when he
was again standing on one of the cliffs, he saw in the dis-

tance between earth and sky two or three tiny figures. Obviously they were travelers, perhaps pilgrims, perhaps visitors who intended to call on him for the usual reason. And suddenly he was seized by an irresistible craving to leave as fast as possible, to get away from this place at once, to escape from this life. The craving that seized him was so overpowering, so instinctive, that it swept away all the thoughts, objections, and scruples that naturally came to him—for how could a pious penitent have obeyed an impulse without twinges of conscience? But he was already running. He sped back to the cave where he had dwelt through so many years of struggle, where he had experienced so many exaltations and defeats. In reckless haste he gathered up a few handfuls of dates and a gourd of water, stuffed them into his old traveling pouch, slung it over his shoulder, took up his staff, and left the green peace of his little home, a fugitive and restless roamer, fleeing away from God and man, and most of all fleeing from what he had formerly thought the best he had to offer, his function and his mission.

At first he tore on frantically, as if those figures in the distance whom he had seen from the cliff were enemies who would pursue him. But after an hour of tramping, his anxious haste ebbed away. Movement tired him pleasantly, and he stopped to rest, although he did not allow himself to eat—it had become a sacred habit for him to take no food before sunset. While he rested, his reason, skilled in self-examination, once more asserted itself. It looked into his instinctive action, seeking to form a judgment. And it did not disapprove, wild though the action might seem, but rather viewed it with benevolence. His reason decided that for the first time in a long while he was doing something harmless and innocent. This was flight, a sudden and rash flight, granted, but not a shameful one. He had abandoned a post which he was no longer fit for. By running away he had admitted his failure to himself and to Him who might be observing him. He had given up a daily repeated, useless struggle and confessed himself beaten. There was nothing grand, heroic, and saintly about that, his reason decided, but it was sincere and seemed to have been inescapable.

Now he found himself wondering that he had attempted this flight so late, that he had held on for so long. It now seemed to him that the doggedness with which he had for so long defended a lost position had been a mistake. Or rather that it had been prompted by his egotism, his old Adam. Now he thought he understood why this obstinacy had led to such evil, to such diabolic consequences; to such division and lethargy in his soul, and even to demonic possession, for what else could he call his urge toward death and self-destruction? Certainly a Christian ought to be no enemy of death; certainly a penitent and saint ought to regard his life as an offering; but the thought of suicide was utterly diabolic and could arise only in a soul no longer ruled and guarded by God's angels, but by evil demons.

For a while he sat lost in thought and deeply crestfallen, and finally, shaken and profoundly contrite. For from the perspective that a few miles of tramping had given him, he saw the life he had been living with fuller awareness, the miserable life of an aging man who had gone astray, so much so that he had been haunted by the gruesome temptation of hanging himself from the branch of a tree like the Saviour's betrayer. If the idea of voluntary death so horrified him, there certainly lingered in this horror a remnant of primeval, pre-Christian, ancient pagan knowledge: knowledge of the age-old custom of human sacrifice, whereby the king, the saint, the chosen man of the tribe gave up his life for the general welfare, often by his own hand. But this echo of forbidden heathen practices was only one aspect of the matter that made it so horrifying. Even more terrible was the thought that after all the Redeemer's death on the cross had also been a voluntary human sacrifice. As he thought about it he realized that a germ of this awareness had indeed been present in that longing for suicide: a bold-faced urge to sacrifice himself and thus in an outrageous manner to imitate the Saviour—or outrageously to imply that His work of redemption had not been enough. He was deeply shocked by this thought, but also grateful that he had now escaped that peril.

For a long time he considered the penitent Joseph who now, instead of imitating Judas or Christ, had taken flight and thus once again put himself into God's hand. Shame and dejection grew in him the more plainly he recognized the hell from which he had just escaped. After a while his misery lumped in his throat like a choking morsel. It grew into an unbearable sense of oppression, and suddenly found release in a torrent of tears that miraculously helped him. How long he had been unable to weep! The tears flowed, his eyes were blurred, but the deadly strangulation was eased, and when he became aware of himself again, tasted the salt on his lips, and realized that he had been weeping, he felt for a moment as if he had become a child again and knew nothing of evil. He smiled, slightly ashamed of his weeping. At last he rose and continued his journey. He felt uncertain, for he did not know where his flight was leading him and what would become of him. He was like a child, he thought, but there was no longer any conflict or will within him. He moved on easily, as if he were being led, as if a distant, kind voice were calling and coaxing him, as if his journey were not a flight but a homecoming. Now he was growing tired, and reason too fell still, or rested, or decided that it was dispensable.

Joseph spent the night at a water hole where several camels and a small company of travelers were camped. Since there were two women among them, he contented himself with a gesture of greeting and avoided falling into talk. After he had eaten a few dates at sunset, prayed, and lain down to rest, he overheard the conversation between two men, one old and one somewhat younger, for they were lying close by him. It was only a fragment of their talk that he could hear; the rest was lost in whispers. But even this small passage stirred his interest. It gave him matter for thought through half the night.

"All right," he heard the old man's voice saying. "It's fine that you want to go to a pious man and make your confession. These people understand many things, let me tell you. They know a thing or two, and some of them are skilled in magic. When they just call out a word to a springing lion, the beast crouches, tucks his tail between his legs, and slinks away. They can tame lions, I tell you. One of them was so holy that his tame lions actually dug him his grave when he died, neatly scraped the earth into a mound over him, and for a long time two of them kept watch over the grave day and night. And it isn't only lions they can tame, these people. One of them gave a Roman centurion a piece of his mind. That was a cruel bastard, that soldier, and the worst whoreson in all Ascalon. But the hermit so kneaded his wicked heart that the man stole away frightened as a mouse and looked for a hole to hide in. Afterward he was almost unrecognizable, he'd become so quiet and meek. On the other hand, the man died soon afterward—that's something to think about."

"The holy man?"

"Oh no, the centurion. His name was Varro. After the holy man gave him such a jolt, he went to pieces fast—had the fever twice and was a dead man three months later. Oh well, no great loss. But still, I've often thought the hermit didn't just drive the devil out of him. He probably said a little spell that put the man six feet under."

"Such a pious man? I can't believe that."

"Believe it or not, my friend, but from that day on the man was changed, not to say bewitched, and three months later . . ."

There was silence for a little while. Then the younger man revived the conversation: "There's a holy man who must live somewhere right around here. They say he lives all alone near a small spring on the Gaza road. His name is Josephus, Josephus Famulus. I've heard a lot about him."

"Have you now? Like what?"

"He's supposed to be awfully pious and never to look at a woman. If a few camels happen to come by his place and there's a woman on one of them, no matter how heavily veiled, he just bolts into his cave. Lots of people have gone to confess to him—thousands."

"I guess he can't be so famous or else I would have heard of him. What kind of thing does he do, this Famulus of yours?"

"Oh, you just go to confess to him, and I suppose people wouldn't go if he wasn't good and didn't understand things. The story is he hardly says a word, doesn't scold or bawl anyone out, doesn't order penances or anything like that. He's supposed to be gentle and shy."

"But if he doesn't scold and doesn't punish and doesn't open his mouth, what does he do?"

"They say he just listens and sighs marvelously and makes the sign of the cross."

"Sounds like a quack saint to me. You wouldn't be so foolish as to apply to this silent Joe, would you?"

"Yes, that's what I mean to do. I'll find him. It can't be much farther from here. This evening there was a poor monk standing around the waterhole here, you know. I'm going to ask him tomorrow morning. He looks like a hermit himself."

The old man flared up. "You'd be wasting your time. A man who only listens and sighs and is afraid of women can't do or understand anything. No, I'll tell you the one to go to. It's a bit far from here, beyond Ascalon, but he's the best hermit and confessor there is. Dion is his name, and he's called Dion Pugil—that means 'the boxer,' because he piles right into all the devils, and when somebody confesses his sins, my friend, Pugil doesn't sigh and keep his counsel. He sounds off and gives it to the man straight from the shoulder. They say he actually beats some till they're black and blue. He made one man kneel bare-kneed on the rocks all night long and on top of that ordered him to give forty pennies to the poor. There's a hermit for you, my boy, he'll make you sit up and take notice. When he looks at you, you'll shake; his eyes go right through you. None of this sighing business. That man has the stuff. If a man can't sleep or has bad dreams and visions, Pugil will put him on his feet again, let me tell you. I don't say this on hearsay; I know because I've been to him myself. Yes I have—I may be a poor fool, but I betook myself to the hermit Dion, the man of God, God's boxer. I went there in misery, nothing but filth and shame on my conscience, and I left clean and bright as the morning star, and that's as true as my name is David. Remember what I tell you: the name is Dion, called Pugil. You go see him as soon as you can, and you'll be amazed. Prefects, presbyters, and bishops have gone to him for advice."

"Yes," the younger man said, "next time I'm in that

neighborhood I'll consider it. But today is today and here is here, and since I'm here today and the hermit Josephus is located in these parts and I've heard so much good about him . . ."

"Good? What so commends this Famulus to you?"

"I like the way he doesn't scold and make a fuss. I just like that, I tell you. I'm not a centurion and I'm not a bishop either; I'm just a nobody and I'm sort of timid myself. I couldn't stand a lot of fire and brimstone. God knows, I don't have anything against being treated gently—that's just the way I am."

"Treated gently—I like that! When you've confessed and done penance and taken your punishment and purged yourself, all right, maybe then it's time to treat you gently. But not when you're unclean and stand before your confessor and judge stinking like a jackal."

"All right, all right. Not so loud—the others want to sleep."

Suddenly the younger man chuckled. "By the way, I just remembered a funny story I heard about him."

"About whom?"

"About the hermit Josephus. You see, after somebody's told his story and confessed, the hermit blesses him and before he leaves gives him a kiss on the cheek or the brow."

"Does he now? He certainly has peculiar habits."

"And, you see, he's so shy of women. They say that a harlot from the neighborhood once went to him in man's clothing and he didn't notice and listened to her lies, and when she was finished confessing he bowed to her and solemnly gave her a kiss."

The old man burst into titters; the other hastily shushed him, and thereafter Joseph heard nothing more than half-suppressed laughter that went on for a while.

He looked up at the sky. The crescent moon hung thin and keen beyond the tops of the palm trees. He shivered in the cold of the night. It had been strange, like looking into a distorting mirror, listening to the camel drivers talking about him and the office which he had just abandoned. Strange but instructive. And so a harlot had played this joke on him. Well, that was not the worst, though it was bad enough. He lay for a long time pondering the conversation between the two men. And when, very late, he was at last able to fall asleep, it was because his meditations had not been fruitless. He had come to a conclusion, to a resolve, and with this new resolve fixed firmly in his heart he slept deeply until dawn.

His resolve was the very one that the younger of the two camel drivers had not taken. He had decided to take the older man's advice and pay a visit to Dion, called Pugil, of whom he had heard for so many years and whose praises had been so emphatically sung this very night. That famous confessor, adviser, and judge of souls would surely have advice, judgment, punishment for him, would surely know the proper way for him. Josephus would go to him as a spokesman of God and willingly obey whatever course he prescribed.

He left while the two men were still asleep, and after a tiring tramp reached a spot which he knew was inhabited by pious brethren. From there he hoped he would be able to reach the usual caravan route to Ascalon.

The place he reached toward evening was a small, lovely green oasis. He saw towering trees, heard a goat bleating, and thought he detected the outlines of roofs amid the green shadows. It seemed to him too that he could scent the presence of men. As he hesitantly drew closer, he felt as if he were being watched. He stopped and looked around. Under one of the outermost trees, he saw a figure sitting bolt upright. It was an old man with a hoary beard and a dignified but stern and rigid face, staring at him. The man had evidently been looking at him for some time. His eyes were keen and hard, but without expression, like the eyes of a man who is used to observing but without either curiosity or sympathy, who lets people and things approach him and tries to discern their nature, but neither attracts nor invites them.

"Praise be to Jesus Christ," Joseph said.

The old man answered in a murmur.

"I beg your pardon," Joseph said. "Are you a stranger like myself, or are you an inhabitant of this beautiful oasis?"

"A stranger," the white-bearded man said.

"Perhaps you can tell me, your Reverence, whether it is possible to reach the road to Ascalon from here?"

"It is possible," the old man said. Now he slowly stood up, rather stiffly, a gaunt giant. He stood and gazed out into the empty expanse of desert. Joseph felt that this aged giant had little wish for conversation, but he ventured one more query.

"Permit me just one other question, your Reverence," he said politely, and saw the man's eyes return from his abstraction and focus on him. Coolly, attentively, they looked at him.

"Do you by any chance know where Father Dion, called Dion Pugil, may be found?"

The stranger's brows contracted and his eyes became a trace colder.

"I know him," he said curtly.

"You know him?" Joseph exclaimed. "Oh, then tell me, for it is to Father Dion I am journeying."

From his superior height the old man scrutinized him. He took his time answering. At last he stepped backward to his tree trunk, slowly settled to the ground again, and sat leaning against the trunk in his previous position. With a slight movement of his hand he invited Joseph to sit also. Submissively, Joseph obeyed the gesture, feeling as he sat down the great weariness in his limbs; but he forgot this promptly in order to focus his full attention on the old man, who seemed lost in meditation. A trace of unfriendly sternness appeared upon his dignified countenance. But that was overlaid by another expression, virtually another face that seemed like a transparent mask: an expression of ancient and solitary suffering which pride and dignity would not allow him to express.

A long time passed before the old man's eyes returned to him. Then he again scrutinized Joseph sharply and suddenly asked in a commanding tone: "Who are you?"

"I am a penitent," Joseph said. "I have led a life of withdrawal from the world for many years."

"I can see that. I asked who you are."

"My name is Joseph, Joseph Famulus."

When Joseph gave his name, the old man did not stir, but his eyebrows drew together so sharply that for a while his eyes became almost invisible. He seemed to be stunned, troubled, or disappointed by the information he had received. Or perhaps it was only a tiring of the eyes, a distractedness, some small attack of weakness such as old people are prone to. At any rate he remained utterly motionless, kept his eyes shut for a while, and when he opened them again their gaze seemed changed, seemed to have become still older, still lonelier, still flintier and long-suffering, if that were possible. Slowly, his lips parted and he asked: "I have heard of you. Are you the one to whom the people go to confess?"

Abashed, Joseph said he was. He felt this recognition as an unpleasant exposure. For the second time on his journey he was ashamed to encounter his reputation.

Again the old man asked in his terse way: "And so now you are on your way to Dion Pugil? What do you want of him?"

"I would like to confess to him."

"What do you expect to gain by that?"

"I don't know. I trust him, and in fact it seems to me that a voice from above has sent me to him."

"And after you have confessed to him, what then?"

"Then I shall do what he commands."

"And suppose he advises or commands you wrongly?"

"I shall not ask whether it is right or wrong, but simply obey."

The old man said no more. The sun had moved far down toward the horizon. A bird cried among the leaves of the tree. Since the old man remained silent, Joseph stood up. Shyly, he reverted to his request.

"You said you knew where Father Dion can be found. May I ask you to tell me the place and describe the way to it?"

The old man's lips contracted in a kind of feeble smile. "Do you think you will be welcome to him?" he asked softly.

Strangely disconcerted by the question, Joseph did not reply. He stood there abashed. At last he said: "May I at least hope to see you again?"

The old man nodded. "I shall be sleeping here and stay until shortly after sunrise," he replied. "Go now, you are tired and hungry."

With a respectful bow, Joseph walked on, and as dusk fell arrived at the little settlement. Here, much as in a monastery, lived a group of so-called cenobites, Christians from various towns and villages who had built shelters in this solitary place in order to devote themselves without disturbance to a simple, pure life of quiet contemplation. Joseph was given water, food, and a place to sleep, and since it was apparent how tired he was, his hosts spared him questions and conversation. One cenobite recited a prayer while the others knelt; all pronounced the Amen together.

At any other time the community of these pious men would have been a joy to him, but now he had only one thing in mind, and at dawn he hastened back to the place where he had left the old man. He found him lying asleep on the ground, rolled in a thin mat, and sat down under the trees off to one side, to await the man's awakening. Soon the sleeper became restive. He awoke, unwrapped himself from the mat, and stood up awkwardly, stretching his stiffened limbs. Then he knelt and made his prayer. When he rose again, Joseph approached and bowed silently.

"Have you already eaten?" the stranger asked.

"No. It is my habit to eat only once a day, and only after sunset. Are you hungry, your Reverence?"

"We are on a journey," the man replied, "and we are both no longer young men. It is better for us to eat a bite before we go on."

Joseph opened his pouch and offered some of his dates. He had also received a millet roll from the friendly folk with whom he had spent the night, and he now shared this with the old man.

"We can go," the old man said after they had eaten.

"Oh, are we going together?" Joseph exclaimed with pleasure.

"Certainly. You have asked me to guide you to Dion. Come along."

Joseph looked at him in happy astonishment. "How kind you are, your Reverence!" he exclaimed, and began framing ceremonious thanks. But the stranger silenced him with a curt gesture.

"God alone is kind," he said. "Let us go now. And stop

calling me 'your Reverence.' What is the point of civilities and courtesies between two old hermits?"

The tall man set off with long strides, and Joseph kept pace with him. The sun had risen fully. The guide seemed sure of his direction, and promised that by noon they would reach a shady spot where they could rest during the hours of hottest sun. Thereafter they spoke no more on their way.

When they reached the resting place after several strenuous hours in the baking heat, and lay down in the shade of some vast boulders, Joseph again addressed his guide. He asked how many days' marches they would need to reach Dion Pugil.

"That depends on you alone," the old man said.

"On me?" Joseph exclaimed. "Oh, if it depended on me alone I would be standing before him right now."

The old man did not seem any more inclined to conversation than before.

"We shall see," he said curtly, turning on his side and closing his eyes. Joseph did not like to be in the position of observing him while he slumbered; he moved quietly off to one side, lay down, and unexpectedly fell asleep, for he had lain long awake during the night. His guide roused him when the time for resuming their journey had come.

Late in the afternoon they arrived at a camping place with water, trees, and a bit of grass. Here they drank and washed, and the old man decided to make a halt. Joseph timidly objected.

"You said today," he pointed out, "that it depended on me how soon or late I would reach Father Dion. I would gladly press on for many hours if I could actually reach him today or tomorrow."

"Oh no," the other man replied. "We have gone far enough for the day."

"Forgive me," Joseph said, "but can't you understand my impatience?"

"I understand it. But it will not help you."

"Why did you say it depends on me?"

"It is as I said. As soon as you are sure of your desire to confess and know that you are ready to make the confession, you will be able to make it."

"Even today?"

"Even today."

Astonished, Joseph stared at the quiet old face.

"Is it possible?" he cried, overwhelmed. "Are you yourself Father Dion?"

The old man nodded.

"Rest here under the trees," he said in a kindly voice, "but don't sleep. Compose yourself, and I too will rest and compose myself. Then you may tell me what you crave to tell me."

Thus Joseph suddenly found himself at his goal. Now he could scarcely understand how it was that he had not recognized the venerable man sooner, after having walked beside him for an entire day. He withdrew, knelt and prayed, and rallied his thoughts. After an hour he returned and asked whether Dion was ready.

And now he could confess. Now all that he had lived through for years, all that for a long time seemed to have totally lost meaning, poured from his lips in the form of narrative, lament, query, self-accusation—the whole story of his life as a Christian and ascetic, which he had intended for purification and sanctification and which in the end had become such utter confusion, obscuration, and despair. He spoke also of his most recent experiences, his flight and the feeling of release and hope that this flight had given him, how it was that he had decided to go to Dion, the encounter of the previous evening, his feeling of instant trust and affection for the older man, but also how in the course of this day he had several times condemned him as cold and peculiar, or at any rate moody.

The sun was already low by the time he had finished speaking. Old Dion had listened with unflagging attentiveness, refraining from the slightest interruption or question. And even now, when the confession was over, not a word fell from his lips. He rose clumsily, looked at Joseph with great friendliness, then stooped, kissed him on the brow, and made the sign of the cross over him. Only later did it occur to Joseph that this was the same brotherly gesture of forbearance with which he himself had dismissed so many penitents.

Soon afterward they ate, said their prayers, and lay

down to sleep. Joseph reflected for a while. He had actually counted on a strong upbraiding and a strict sermon. Nevertheless he was neither disappointed nor uneasy. Dion's look and fraternal kiss had comforted him. He felt inwardly tranquil, and soon fell into a beneficial sleep.

Without wasting words, the old man took him along next morning. They covered a good deal of ground that day, and after another four or five days reached Dion's cell. There they dwelt. Joseph helped Dion with his daily chores, became acquainted with his routine and shared it. It was not so very different from the life he himself had led for so many years, except that now he was no longer alone. He lived in the shadow and protection of another man, and for that reason it was after all a totally different life. From the surrounding settlements, from Ascalon and from even further away, came seekers of advice and penitents eager to confess. At first Joseph hastily withdrew each time such visitors came along, and reappeared only after they had left. But more and more often Dion called him back, as one calls a servant, ordered him to bring water or perform some other menial task; and after this had gone on for some time Joseph grew accustomed to attending a confession every so often, and listening unless the penitent himself objected. But most of them were glad not to have to sit or kneel before the dreaded confessor Pugil alone; there was something reassuring about the presence of this quiet, kind-looking, and assiduous helper. In this way Joseph gradually became familiar with Dion's way of listening to confession, offering consolation, intervening and scolding, punishing and advising. Only rarely did Joseph venture to question Dion as he did one day after a scholar or literary man paid a call, since he was passing by.

This man, as became apparent from his stories, had friends among the magi and astrologers. Since he was stopping for a rest, he sat for a while with the two old ascetics, a civil and loquacious guest. He talked long, learnedly, and eloquently about the stars and about the pilgrimage which man as well as all his gods must make through all the signs of the zodiac from the beginning to the end of every aeon. He spoke of Adam, the first man, maintaining that he was one and the same as the crucified Jesus, and he called the Redemption Adam's passage from the Tree of Knowledge to the Tree of Life. The serpent of Paradise, he contended, was the guardian of the Sacred Fount, of the dark depths from whose night-black waters all forms, all men and gods, arose.

Dion listened attentively to this man, whose Syrian was heavily sprinkled with Greek, and Joseph wondered at his patience. It bothered him, in fact, that Dion did not lash out against these heathen errors. On the contrary, the clever monologues seemed to entertain Dion and engage his sympathy, for he not only listened with keen attention, but also smiled and nodded at certain phrases, as though he were highly pleased.

After the man had left, Joseph asked, in a zealot's tone, with something bordering on rebuke: "How could you have listened so calmly to the false doctrines of this unbelieving heathen? It seemed to me that you listened not only with patience, but actually with sympathy and a certain amount of appreciation. How could you fail to oppose him? Why didn't you try to refute this man, to strike down his errors and convert him to faith in our Lord?"

Dion's head swayed on his thin, wrinkled neck. "I did not refute him because it would have been useless, or rather, because I would not have been able to. In eloquence and in making associations, in knowledge of mythology and the stars, this man is far ahead of me. I would not have prevailed against him. And furthermore, my son, it is neither my business nor yours to attack a man's beliefs and tell him these are lies and errors. I admit that I listened to this clever man with a good measure of appreciation. I enjoyed him because he spoke so well and knew a great deal, but above all because he reminded me of my youth. For in my younger days I devoted a great deal of my time to just such studies. Those stories from mythology, which the stranger chatted about so gracefully, are by no means benighted. They are the ideas and parables of a religion which we no longer need because we have acquired faith in Jesus, the sole Redeemer. But for those who have not yet found our faith, perhaps never can find it, their own faith, deriving from the ancient wisdom of their fathers, is rightly deserving of respect. Of course our faith is different, entirely different. But because our faith does not need the doctrine of constellations and aeons, of the primal waters and universal mothers and similar symbols, that does not mean that such doctrines are lies and deception."

"But our faith is superior," Joseph exclaimed. "And Jesus died for all men. Therefore those who know Him must oppose those outmoded doctrines and put the new, right teaching in their place."

"We have done so long ago, you and I and so many others," Dion said calmly. "We are believers because the faith, the power of the Redeemer and His death for the salvation of all men, has overwhelmed us. But those others, those who construct mythologies and theologies of the zodiac and out of ancient doctrines, have not been overwhelmed by that power, not yet, and it is not for us to compel them. Didn't you notice, Joseph, how gracefully and skillfully this mythologist could talk and compose his metaphors, and how comfortable he was in doing so, how serenely he lives in his wisdom of images and symbols? That is a token that this man is not oppressed by suffering, that he is content, that all is well with him. Such as we have nothing to say to men for whom all goes well. Before a man needs redemption and the faith that redeems, before his old faith departs from him and he stakes all he has on the gamble of belief in the miracle of salvation, things must go ill for him, very ill indeed. He must have experienced sorrow and disappointment, bitterness and despair. The waters must rise up to his neck. No, Joseph, let us leave this learned pagan in the happiness of his philosophy, his ideas, and his eloquence. Tomorrow perhaps, or perhaps in a year or in ten years something may happen that will shatter his arts and his philosophy; perhaps the woman he loves will die or his only son will be killed, or he will fall into sickness and poverty. Should that occur and we meet him again, we will try to help him; we will tell him how we have tried to master suffering. And if he then asks us: 'Why didn't you tell me that yesterday or ten years ago?' we will reply: 'You were too fortunate at the time.'"

He subsided into a grave silence for a while. Then, as if rousing himself from reveries of the past, he added: "I myself once amused myself with the philosophies of the fathers, and even after I was already on the way of the Cross, playing with theology often gave me pleasure, though grief enough too. My thoughts dwelt mostly on the Creation of the world, and with the fact that at the end of the work of Creation everything in the world should have been good, for we are told: 'God saw everything that he had made, and behold, it was very good.' But in reality it was good and perfect only for a moment, the moment of Paradise, and by the very next moment guilt and a curse had entered into the perfection, for Adam had eaten of the tree which he was forbidden to eat of. There were teachers who said: the God who made the Creation and along with it Adam and the Tree of Knowledge is not the sole and highest God, but only a part of him, or an inferior god, the Demiurge. Creation was not good, they said, but a failure; and therefore created being was accursed and given over to evil for an aeon until He himself, God the One Spirit, decided to put an end to the accursed aeon by means of his Son. Thereafter, they taught, and I thought as they did, the Demiurge and his Creation began to perish, and the world will continue gradually to fade away until in a new aeon there will be no Creation, no world, no flesh, no lust and sin, no carnal begetting, bearing, and dying, but a perfect, spiritual, and redeemed world will arise, free of the curse of Adam, free of eternal damnation and the urges of cupidity, generation, birth, and death. We blamed the Demiurge more than the first man for the present evils of the world. We thought that if the Demiurge had really been God, he would have made Adam differently or have spared him temptation. And so at the end of our reasoning we had two Gods, the Creator God and God the Father, and we did not blanch at passing judgment on the first. There were even some among us who went a step further and contended that the Creation was not God's work at all, but the devil's. We thought all our clever ideas were going to be helpful to the Redeemer and the coming aeon of the Spirit, and so we reasoned out gods and worlds and cosmic plans. We disputed and theologized, until one day I fell into a fever and became deathly ill. In my deliriums the Demiurge continually filled my mind. I had to wage war and spill blood, and the visions and nightmares grew more and more ghastly, until one night when my fever was raging I thought I had to kill my own mother in order to undo my carnal birth. Yes, in those deliriums the devil harried me with all his hounds. But I recovered, and to the disappointment of my former friends I returned to life a silent, stupid, and dull person who soon regained physical strength but never recovered his pleasure in philosophizing. For during the days and nights of my convalescence, when those horrible fevered visions had vanished and I was sleeping almost all the time, I felt the Redeemer with me in every waking moment. I felt strength pouring in and out of me from Him, and when I was well again I was aware of a deep sadness that I could no longer feel His presence. I then felt a great longing for that presence, and regarded this longing as my most precious possession. But as soon as I began listening to disputations again, I could feel how this longing was in danger of vanishing, of sinking into thoughts and words as water sinks into sand. To make a long story short, my friend, that was the end of my cleverness and theology. Since then I have been one of the simple souls. But I do not despise and do not like to bait those who know how to philosophize and mythologize and play those games I myself once indulged in. Just as I had to rest content with letting the incomprehensible relations and identities of Demiurge and Spirit-God, Creation and Redemption, remain unsolved riddles for me, so I must also rest content with the fact that I cannot convert philosophers into believers. That is not my province."

Once, after a man had confessed to murder and adultery, Dion said to his assistant: "Murder and adultery—it sounds atrocious and grandiose, and certainly it is bad enough, I grant you. But I tell you, Joseph, in reality these people in the world are not real sinners at all. Whenever I attempt to put myself entirely into the minds of any of them, they strike me as absolutely like children. They are not decent, good, and noble; they are selfish, lustful, overbearing, and wrathful, but in reality and at bottom they are innocent, innocent in the same way as children."

"And yet," Joseph said, "you often belabor them mightily and paint them a vivid picture of hell."

"Exactly. They are children, and when they have pangs of conscience and come to confess, they want to be taken seriously and reprimanded seriously. At least that is my view. You went about it differently; you didn't scold and punish and deal out penances, but were friendly and sent the penitents off with a brotherly kiss. I don't mean to criticize you, but that wouldn't be my way."

"No doubt," Joseph said hesitantly. "But then tell me why, after I made my confession, you did not treat me as you would your other penitents, but silently kissed me and said not a word about penances?"

Dion Pugil fixed his piercing eyes upon him. "Was what I did not right?" he asked.

"I am not saying it was not right. It was surely right, for otherwise that confession would not have done me so much good."

"Well then, let it be. In any case, I did impose a long and stern penance on you, without calling it such. I took you with me and treated you as my servant, and led you back to your duty, forcing you to hear confessions when you had tried to escape from that."

He turned away; the conversation had already been too long for his liking. But this time Joseph was pressing.

"You knew in advance that I would follow your orders; I'd pledged that before the confession and even before I knew who you were. No, tell me, was it really for this reason that you treated me so?"

Dion Pugil took a few steps back and forth. Then he stopped in front of Joseph and laid his hand on his shoulder. "Worldly people are children, my son. And saints— well, they do not come to confess to us. But you and I and our kind, we ascetics and seekers and eremites—we are not children and are not innocent and cannot be set straight by moralizing sermons. We are the real sinners, we who know and think, who have eaten of the Tree of Knowledge, and we should not treat one another like children who are given a few blows of the rod and left to go their way again. After a confession and penance we do not run away back to the world where children celebrate feasts and do business and now and then kill one another. We do not experience sin like a brief bad dream which can be thrown off by confession and sacrifice; we dwell in it. We are never innocent; we are always sinners; we dwell in sin and in the fire of conscience, and we know that we can never pay our great debt unless after our departure God looks mercifully upon us and receives us into His grace. That, Joseph, is the reason I cannot deliver sermons and dictate penances to you and me. We are not involved in one or another misstep or crime, but always and forever in original sin itself. This is why each of us can only assure the other that he shares his knowledge and feels brotherly love; neither of us can cure the other by penances. Surely you must have known this?"

Softly, Joseph replied: "It is so. I knew it."

"Then let us not waste our time in talk," the old man said curtly. He turned to the stone in front of his hut, on which he was accustomed to pray.

Several years passed. Every so often Father Dion was subject to spells of weakness, so that Joseph had to help him in the mornings, for otherwise he could not stand up by himself. Then he would go to pray, and after prayer he was again unable to rise without aid. Joseph would help him, and then Father Dion would sit all day long staring into space. This happened on some days; on others the old man would manage to stand up by himself. He also could not hear confessions every day; and sometimes, after Joseph had acted as his substitute, Dion would want a few words with the visitor and would tell him: "My end is nearing, my child, my end is nearing. Tell the people that Joseph here is my successor." And when Joseph demurred at such talk, the old man would fix him with that terrible look of his that penetrated like an icy ray.

One day, when he had been able to stand without

help, and seemed stronger, he called Joseph and led him to a spot at the edge of their small garden.

"Here is where you will bury me," he said. "We will dig the grave together; we have a little time, I think. Bring me the spade."

Thereafter he had Joseph dig a little early in the morning every day. If Dion was feeling stronger, he would himself scoop out a few spadefuls of earth with great difficulty, but also with an air of gaiety, as though he enjoyed the work. All through the day this gaiety would persist. From the time he started the project, he remained in continual good humor.

"You will plant a palm on my grave," he said one day while they were working. "Perhaps you will even live to eat its fruit. If not, another will. Every so often I have planted a tree, but too few, far too few. Some say a man should not die without having planted a tree and left a son behind. Well, I am leaving behind a tree and leaving you also. You are my son."

He was calm and more cheerful than Joseph had ever known him, and he grew more and more so. One evening as it was growing dark—they had already eaten and prayed—he called out to Joseph and asked him to sit beside his pallet for a while.

"I want to tell you something," he said cheerfully. He seemed wakeful and not at all tired. "Do you remember, Joseph, the time you were so miserable in your cell near Gaza and tired of your life? And then you fled, and decided to find old Dion and tell him your story? And in the cenobite settlement you met the old man whom you asked to direct you to Dion Pugil? You remember. And was it not like a miracle that the old man turned out to be Dion himself? I want to tell you now how that happened. Because you see, it was strange and like a miracle for me too.

"You know what it is like when an ascetic and father confessor grows old and has listened to so many confessions from sinners who think him sinless and a saint, and don't know that he is a greater sinner than they are. At such times all his work seems useless and vain to him, and everything that once seemed important and sacred— the fact that God had assigned him to this particular place and honored him with the task of cleansing human souls of their filth—all that seems to him too much of an imposition. He actually feels it as a curse, and by and by he shudders at every poor soul who comes to him with his childish sins. He wants to get rid of the sinner and wants to get rid of himself, even if he has to do it by tying a rope to the branch of a tree. That is how you felt at the time. And now the hour of confession has come for me too, and I am confessing: it happened that way to me also. I too thought I was useless and spiritually dead. I thought I could no longer bear to have people flocking to me so trustfully, bringing me all the filth and stench of human life that they could not cope with, and that I too could no longer cope with.

"I had often heard talk of a hermit named Josephus Famulus. People also flocked to him for confession, I heard, and many preferred him to me, because he was said to be a gentle, merciful fellow who asked nothing of them and did not berate them, but treated them like brothers, merely listened to them and dismissed them with a kiss. That was not my way, as you well know, and the first few times I heard stories about this Josephus, his method seemed to me rather foolish and infantile. But now that I had begun to doubt my own way, it behooved me not to pass judgment on this method of Joseph's, or to set up my own as superior to it. What kind of powers did this man have, I wondered. I knew he was younger than I, but still ripe in years. That reassured me, for I would not have found it easy to trust a young man. But I did feel drawn to this Josephus Famulus. And so I decided to make a pilgrimage to him, to confess my misery to him and ask him for advice or, if he gave no advice, perhaps to receive consolation and strength from him. The very decision did me good, and relieved me.

"I set out on my journey and made my way toward the place where his cell was said to be. But meanwhile Brother Joseph had been having the same experience as myself, and had done exactly what I was doing; he had taken flight in order to seek advice from me. When I ran into him, under to be sure odd circumstances, he was enough like the man I had expected for me to recognize him. But he was a fugitive; things had gone badly with him, as badly as for me, or perhaps worse, and he was not at all inclined to hear confessions. Rather, he was all agog to make a confession of his own, and to place his distress in another's hands. That was a singular disappointment to me, and I was very sad. For if this Joseph, who did not recognize me, had also grown tired of his service and was in despair over the meaning of his life—did that not seem to mean that both of us amounted to nothing, that both of us had lived uselessly, were both failures?

"I am telling you what you already know—let me be brief. I stayed alone that night while you were shown hospitality by the cenobites. I meditated, and put myself into Joseph's mind, and I thought: what will he do if he learns tomorrow that his errand is in vain and he has vainly placed his faith in Pugil; if he learns that Pugil too is a fugitive and subject to temptation? The more I put myself into his place, the sorrier I was for Joseph, and the more it seemed to me that God had sent him to me so that I might understand and cure him, and in doing so cure myself. After coming to this conclusion I was able to sleep; by then half the night was gone. Next day you joined up with me and have become my son.

"I wanted to tell you this story. I hear that you are weeping. Weep on; it will do you good. And since I have fallen into this unseemly talkative vein, do me the kindness to listen a little longer and take what I now say into your heart: Man is strange, can scarcely be relied on, and so it is not impossible that those sufferings and temptations will someday strike you once again and threaten to overcome you. May our Lord then send you as kindly, patient, and consoling a son and disciple as He has given to me in you. But as for the branch on the tree and the death of Judas Iscariot, visions of which the tempter sent you in those days, I can tell you one thing: it is not merely a folly and a sin to inflict such a death on oneself, although our Redeemer can well forgive even such a sin. But it also a terrible pity for a man to die in despair. God sends us despair not to kill us; He sends it to us to awaken new life in us. When on the other hand He sends us death, Joseph, when He frees us from the earth and from the body and summons us to

Himself, that is a great joy. To be permitted to sleep when we are tired, to be allowed to drop a burden we have borne for a long time, is a precious, a wonderful thing. Since we have dug the grave—don't forget the young palm you are to plant on it—ever since we began digging the grave I have been happier and more content than in many years.

"I have babbled on long, my son; you must be tired. Go to sleep; go to your hut. God be with you!"

On the following day Dion did not appear for the morning prayer, nor did he call Joseph. When Joseph grew alarmed and looked into Dion's hut, he found the old man in his last sleep. His face was illumined with a childlike, radiant smile.

Joseph buried him. He planted the tree on the grave and lived to see the year in which the tree bore its first fruit.

THREE

THE INDIAN LIFE

WHEN VISHNU, OR rather Vishnu in his avatar as Rama, fought his savage battles with the prince of demons, one of his parts took on human shape and thus entered the cycle of forms once more. His name was Ravana and he lived as a warlike prince by the Great Ganges. Ravana had a son named Dasa. But the mother of Dasa died young, and the prince took another wife. Soon this beauteous and ambitious lady had a son of her own, and she resented the young Dasa. Although he was the firstborn, she determined to see her own son Nala inherit the rulership when the time came. And so she contrived to estrange Dasa's father from him, and meant to dispose of the boy at the first opportunity. But one of Ravana's court Brahmans, Vasudeva the Sacrificer, became privy to her plan. He was sorry for the boy who, moreover, seemed to him to possess his mother's bent for piety and feeling for justice. So the Brahman kept an eye on Dasa, to see that the boy came to no harm until he could put him out of reach of his stepmother.

Now Rajah Ravana owned a herd of cows dedicated to Brahma. These were regarded as sacred, and frequent offerings of their milk and butter were made to the god.

The best pastures in the country were reserved for these cows.

One day a herdsman of these sacred cows came to the palace to deliver a batch of butter and report that there were signs of drought in the region where the herd had been grazing. Hence the band of herdsmen were going to lead the cows up into the mountains, where water and grass were available even in the driest of times.

The Brahman had known the herdsman for many years as a friendly and reliable man. He took him into his confidence. Next day, when little Prince Dasa could not be found, only Vasudeva and the herdsman knew the secret of his disappearance. The herdsman took the boy Dasa into the hills with him. They caught up with the slowly moving herd, and Dasa gladly joined the band of herdsmen. He helped to guard and drive the cows, learned to milk, played with the calves, and idled about in the mountain meadows, drinking sweet milk, his bare feet smeared with cow-dung. He liked the life of the herdsmen, learned to know the forest and its trees and fruits, loved the mango, the wild fig, and the varinga tree, plucked the sweet lotus root out of green forest pools, on feast days wore a wreath of the red blossoms of the flame-of-the-woods. He became acquainted with the ways of all the animals of the wilderness, learned how to shun the tiger, to make friends with the clever mongoose and the placid hedgehog, and to while away the rainy seasons in the dusky shelter of a makeshift hut where the boys played games, recited verse, or wove baskets and reed mats. Dasa did not completely forget his former home and his former life, but soon these seemed to him like a dream.

One day, when the herd had moved on to another region, Dasa went into the forest to look for honey. Ever since he had come to know the woods he had loved them, and this particular forest seemed to him uncommonly beautiful. The rays of sunlight wound through leaves and branches like golden serpents; the noises of the forest, bird calls, rustle of treetops, jabber of monkeys, twined into a lovely, mildly luminescent network resembling the light amid the branches. Smells, too, similarly joined and parted again, the perfumes of flowers, varieties of wood, leaves, waters, mosses, animals, fruits, earth and mold, pungent and sweet, wild and intimate, stimulating and soothing, gay and sad. In some unseen gorge a stream gurgled; a velvety green butterfly with black and yellow markings danced over white flowers; deep among the blue shadows of the trees a branch broke and leaves dropped heavily into leaves, or a stag bellowed in the darkness, or an irritable she-ape scolded her family.

Dasa forgot about looking for honey. While listening to the singing of several jewel-bright small birds, he noticed a trail running between tall ferns that stood like a dense miniature forest within the great forest. It was the narrowest of footpaths, and he silently and cautiously pressed between the ferns and followed where it led. After a while he came upon a great banyan tree with many trunks. Beneath it stood a small hut, a kind of tent woven of fern leaves. Beside the hut a man sat motionless. His back was straight as a rod and his hands lay between his crossed feet. Under the white hair and broad forehead his eyes, still and sightless, were focused on the ground. They were open, but looking inward. Dasa realized that this was a holy man, a yogi. He had seen others before; they were men favored by the gods. It was good to bring them gifts and pay them respect. But this man here, sitting before his beautifully made and well-concealed fern hut, so perfectly motionless, so lost in meditation, more strongly attracted the boy and seemed to him rarer and more venerable than any of the others he had seen. He seemed to be floating above the ground as he sat there, and it was as if his abstracted gaze saw and knew everything. An aura of holiness surrounded him, a magic circle of dignity, a flame of concentrated intensity and a wave of radiant yoga energies, which the boy could not pass through, which he would not have dared to breach by a word of greeting or a cry. The majesty of his form, the light from within which radiated from his face, the composure and bronze unassailability of his features, emanated waves and rays in the midst of which he sat enthroned like a moon; and the accumulated spiritual force, the calmly concentrated will, wove such a spell around him that Dasa sensed that here was someone who, by a mere wish or thought, without even raising his eyes, could kill and restore to life.

More motionless than a tree, whose leaves and twigs stir in respiration, motionless as the stone image of a god, the yogi sat before his hut; and from the moment he had seen him the boy too remained motionless, fascinated, fettered, magically attracted by the sight. He stood staring at the Master. He saw a spot of sunlight on his shoulder, a spot of sunlight on one of his relaxed hands; he saw the flecks of light move slowly away and new ones come into being, and he began to understand that the streaks of light had nothing to do with this man, nor the songs of birds and the chatter of monkeys from the woods all around, nor the brown wild bee that settled on the sage's face, sniffed at his skin, crawled a short distance along his cheek, and then flew off again, nor all the multifarious life of the forest. All this, Dasa sensed, everything the eyes could see, the ears could hear, everything beautiful or ugly, engaging or frightening—all of it had no connection at all to this holy man. Rain would not chill or incommode him; fire could not burn him. The whole world around him had become meaningless superficiality. There came to the princely cowherd an inkling that the whole world might be no more than a breath of wind playing over the surface, a ripple of waves over unknown depths. He was not conscious of this as a thought, but as a physical quiver and slight giddiness, a feeling of horror and danger, and at the same time of intense yearning. For this yogi, he felt, had plunged through the surface of the world, through the superficial world, into the ground of being, into the secret of all things. He had broken through and thrown off the magical net of the senses, the play of light, sound, color, and sensation, and lived secure in the essential and unchanging. The boy, although once tutored by Brahmans who had cast many a ray of spiritual light upon him, did not understand this with his intellect and would have been unable to say anything about it in words, but he sensed it as in blessed moments one senses the presence of divinity; he sensed it as a shudder of awe and admiration for this man, sensed it as love for him and longing for a life such as this man sitting in meditation seemed to be living. Strangely, the old man had reminded him of his origins, of his royalty. Touched to the quick, he stood there on the edge of the fern thicket, ignoring the flying birds and the whispered conversations of the trees, forgetting the forest and the distant herd, yielding to the spell while he stared at the sage, captivated by the incomprehensible stillness and impassivity of the man, by the bright serenity of his face, by the power and composure of his posture, by the complete dedication of his service.

Afterward he could not have said whether he had spent two or three hours, or days, at the hut. When the spell released him, when he noiselessly crept back between the ferns, found the path out of the woods, and finally reached the open meadows and the herd, he did so without being aware of what he was doing. His soul was still entranced, and he did not really come to until one of the herdsmen called him. The man was angry with him for having been away so long, but when Dasa only stared at him in wide-eyed astonishment, as if he did not understand what was being said to him, the herdsman broke off, disconcerted by the boy's strange look and solemn bearing. "Where have you been, my boy?" he asked. "Have you seen a god by any chance, or run into a demon?"

"I was in the woods," Dasa said. "Something drew me there; I wanted to look for honey. But then I forgot about it because I saw a man there, a hermit, who sat lost in meditation or prayer, and when I saw the way his face glowed I could not help standing still and watching him for a long time. I would like to go again this evening and bring him gifts. He is a holy man."

"Do so," the herdsman said. "Bring him milk and sweet butter. We should honor the holy men and give them what we can."

"But how am I to address him?"

"There is no need to address him, Dasa. Only bow and place the gifts before him. No more is needed."

Dasa did so. It took him a while to find the place again. The clearing in front of the hut was deserted, and he did not dare go into the hut itself. He therefore laid his gifts on the ground at the entrance and left.

As long as the herdsmen remained with the cows in

this vicinity, Dasa brought gifts every evening, and once he went there by day again. He found the holy man deep in meditation, and this time too felt impelled to stand there in a state of bliss, receiving those rays of strength and felicity that emanated from the yogi.

Long after they had left the neighborhood and were driving the herd to new pastures, Dasa remembered his experience in the forest. And as is the way of boys, when he was alone he sometimes daydreamed of himself as a hermit and practitioner of yoga. But with time the memory and the dream faded, all the more so since Dasa was now rapidly growing into a strong young man who threw himself with zest into the sports and brawls of his fellows. But a gleam, a faint inkling remained in his soul, a suggestion that the princely life and the sovereignty he had lost might some day be replaced by the dignity and power of yoga.

One day, when they had come to the vicinity of the capital, they heard that a great festival was in preparation. Old Prince Ravana, bereft of his former strength and grown quite frail, had appointed the day for his son Nala to succeed him.

Dasa wanted to go to the festival. He wished to see the city once more, for he had only the faintest memories of it from his childhood. He wanted to hear the music, to watch the parade and the tournament among the nobles; and he also wanted to have a look at that unknown world of townsfolk and magnates who figured so largely in tales and legends, for he knew, although this was only a tale or legend or something even more insubstantial, that once upon a time, ages ago, their world had been his own.

The herdsmen were supposed to deliver a load of butter to the court for the festival sacrifices, and to his joy Dasa was one of the three young men chosen by the chief herdsman for this task.

They brought their butter to the palace on the eve of the festival. The Brahman Vasudeva received it from them, for it was he who had charge of the sacrifices, but he did not recognize the youth. Then the three herdsmen joined the throngs attending the celebrations. Early in the morning they watched the beginning of the sacrifices under the Brahman's direction. They saw the masses of shining golden butter given to the flames, watched as it was transformed into leaping fire; flickering, its light and fatty smoke soared toward the Infinite, a delight to the thrice-ten gods. They watched the elephants leading the parade, their riders in howdahs with gilded roofs. They beheld the flower-decked royal carriage containing the young Rajah Nala, and heard the mighty reverberations of the drums. It was all very magnificent and glittering and also a little ridiculous, or at least that is how it seemed to young Dasa. He was stunned and enraptured, intoxicated by the noise, by the carriages and caparisoned horses, by all the pomp and extravagance; he was also delighted by the dancing girls who cavorted in front of the royal carriage, their limbs slender and tough as lotus stems. He was astonished at the size and beauty of the city, but still and all he regarded everything, in the midst of his excitement and pleasure, with the sober good sense of the herdsman who basically despises the townsman.

That he himself was really the firstborn, that his stepbrother Nala, whom he had forgotten completely, was being anointed, consecrated, and hailed in his stead, that he himself, Dasa, ought by rights to be riding in the flower-decked carriage—such thoughts did not even occur to him. On the other hand, he took a strong dislike to this Nala; the young man seemed to him stupid and mean in his self-indulgence, unbearably vain and swollen with self-importance. He would rather have liked to play a trick on this youth acting the part of rajah, to teach him a lesson; but there was surely no opportunity for anything of the sort, and in any case he quickly forgot all about it, for there was so much to see, to hear, to laugh at, to enjoy. The townswomen were pretty and had pert, alluring looks, movements, and turns of speech. A good many phrases were flung at the three herdsmen which rang in their ears for a long while afterward. These phrases were called out with overtones of mockery, for townsfolk feel about herdsmen just the way herdsmen do about townsfolk: each despises the other. But still and all those handsome, stalwart young men, nourished on milk and cheese and living under the open sky almost all the year, were much to the liking of the townswomen.

By the time Dasa returned from this festival, he had become a man. He chased girls and had to hold his own in a good many hard boxing and wrestling matches with other young fellows. They were now making their way into a different region, a region of flat meadows and wetlands planted to rushes and bamboo trees. Here he saw a girl by the name of Pravati, and was seized by a mad love for this beautiful young woman. She was a tenant farmer's daughter, and Dasa was so infatuated that he forgot everything else and threw away his freedom in order to win her. When the time came for the herdsmen to move along to fresh pastures, he brushed aside advice and warnings, bade farewell to them and the herdsman's life he had dearly loved, and settled down. He succeeded in winning Pravati as his wife. In return he tilled his father-in-law's millet fields and rice paddies, and helped with the work in mill and woodlot. He built a bamboo and mud hut for his wife, and kept her shut up within it.

It must be a tremendous power that can move a young man to give up his previous joys and friends and habits, to change his existence entirely, and to live among strangers in the unenviable role of son-in-law. But so great was Pravati's beauty, so great and alluring the promise of amorous delights that radiated from her face and figure, that Dasa became blind to everything else and surrendered utterly to this woman. And in fact he found great happiness in her arms. Many stories are told of gods and holy men so enraptured by an enchanting woman that they remain locked in intimate embrace with her for days, moons, and years, wholly absorbed by voluptuousness and forgetting all other matters. Dasa, too, would have wished his lot and his love to be like that. But he was destined for other things, and his happiness did not last long. It lasted about a year, and this period, too, was not filled with pure felicity. There was ample room for much else, for vexatious demands on the part of his father-in-law, for the taunts of his brothers-in-law, and for the whims of his young wife. But whenever he went to lie with her on their pallet, all this was forgotten, vanished into thin air, such was the magic of her smile, so sweet was it to caress her slender limbs, so wonderfully did the garden of delight in her young body bloom with a thousand flowers, fragrances, and lovely shadows.

His happiness was not yet a whole year old when, one day, noise and unrest stirred the neighborhood. Mounted messengers appeared announcing the coming of the young Rajah. Then came troops, horses, the supply train, and finally Rajah Nala himself, to hunt in the countryside. Tents were pitched here and there; horses could be heard neighing and horns blowing.

Dasa paid no attention to all this. He worked in the fields, tended the mill, and kept out of the way of hunters and courtiers. But one day when he returned to his hut he found his wife missing. He had strictly forbidden her to set foot outside during this period, while the court was in the neighborhood, and now he felt at once a stabbing pain in his heart and a premonition of disaster. He hurried to his father-in-law's house. Pravati was not there either, and no one would admit to having seen her. The pang in his heart intensified. He searched the cabbage patch and the fields; he spent a whole day and then another going back and forth between his hut and his father-in-law's; he lurked in the field, climbed down into the well, called her name, coaxed, cursed, hunted for footprints.

At last the youngest of his brothers-in-law, who was still a boy, told him the truth. Pravati was with the Rajah; she was living in his tent and had been seen riding on his horse.

Dasa lurked invisibly about Nala's encampment, carrying the sling he had used during his days as a herdsman. Day or night, whenever the prince's tent seemed to be unguarded for a moment, he would steal closer; but each time guards soon appeared and he had to flee. Hiding in the branches of a tree, he looked down on the camp and saw the Rajah, whose repellent face he remembered from the time of the festival. Dasa watched him mount his horse and ride off. When he returned hours later, dismounted, and threw back the tent flap, Dasa could see into the shadowy interior where a young woman came forward to welcome the prince. He nearly fell from the tree as he recognized his wife Pravati. Now he was certain, and the pressure upon his heart grew unbearable. Great as the happiness of his love for Pravati had been, the anguish, the rage, the sense of loss and insult were greater now. That is how it is when a man fastens all his capacity for love upon a single object. With its loss everything collapses for him, and he stands impoverished amid ruins.

For a day and a night Dasa drifted about the woods in the neighborhood. He was utterly exhausted, but after every brief rest the misery in his heart lashed him on. He had to stir and keep moving; he felt as if he would have to tramp on to the end of the world and to the end of his life, which had lost all its meaning and all its glory. Nevertheless, he did not wander off to distant, unknown regions. He remained in the vicinity of his misfortunes. He circled about his hut, the mill, the fields, the Rajah's hunting tent. Finally he concealed himself again in the trees overlooking the tent. He crouched in his leafy hiding place, bitter and burning as a hungry beast of prey, until the moment came for which he had been saving his last energies—until the Rajah stepped outside the tent. Then he slipped silently down from the branch, raised the sling, and struck his enemy squarely in the forehead with the stone. Nala fell and lay motionless on his back. There seemed to be no one about. For a moment the storm of voluptuous, vengeful delight that roared through Dasa's senses was checked, fearfully and strangely, by a profound silence. Then, before a clamor broke out around the slain man and the space in front of the tent began to swarm with servants, Dasa was in the woods, lost in the bamboo thickets that sloped down toward the valley.

In the delirium of action, as he leaped from the tree and aimed the sling, letting it hurl forth its death, he had felt as if he were extinguishing his own life also, as if he were discharging his last spark of vitality and flinging himself, along with the deadly stone, into the abyss of annihilation, content to die if only his hated foe fell a moment before him. But now that the deed had been followed by that unexpected moment of silence, a craving for life which he had not realized was in him drew him back from the abyss. A primitive instinct took possession of his senses and his limbs, drove him into the depths of the woods and the bamboo thickets, commanded him to flee and hide.

Awareness of what was happening came to him only after he had reached a refuge and was safe from immediate danger. As he collapsed exhausted, struggling for breath, his frenzy giving way to weakness and sobriety, he felt disappointment and revulsion at having escaped. But when his breathing slowed and his dizziness passed, this repugnance yielded to a defiant determination to live, and once more his heart gloried savagely in the deed.

The hunt for the killer began. Soon searchers were swarming through the woods. They beat the thickets throughout the day, and he evaded them only because he kept utterly still in his hiding place in the marsh, which no one dared penetrate too deeply for fear of tigers. He slept a little, lay on the alert for a while, crawled on a bit, rested again, and by the third day had made his way beyond the hills, whence he pushed on toward the higher mountains.

The homeless life he led thereafter took him here and there. It made him harder and more callous, but also wiser and more resigned. Nevertheless, during the nights he repeatedly dreamed of Pravati and his former happiness, or what he had in the past called his happiness. He also dreamed many times of the pursuit and his flight—frightful, heart-stopping dreams such as this: He would be fleeing through woods, the pursuers close behind him with drums and hunting horns. Through forest and swamp and briers, over rotting, collapsing bridges, he would be carrying something, a burden, a bale, something wrapped up, concealed, unknown. All he knew about it was that it was precious and that under no circumstances must he let it out of his hands; it was something valuable and imperiled, a treasure, perhaps something stolen, wrapped in a bright cloth with a russet and blue pattern, such as Pravati's holiday dress had been. Laden with this pack, this treasure, or these stolen goods, he would be fleeing and skulking, amid toil and danger, creeping under low-hanging branches or overhanging rocks, stealing past snakes and crossing rivers full of crocodiles on vertiginous narrow planks, until at last he stopped in exhaustion, fumbled with the knot of the string that tied his pack, slowly unwrapped the cloth and spread it out, and the treasure he took out at last and held in shuddering hands was his own head.

He led the stealthy life of a vagabond, no longer actually fleeing from people, but rather avoiding them. And one day his roaming led him through a hilly region of lush grass which looked lovely and serene and seemed to welcome him, as though he ought to know it. In one place he recognized a meadow with softly swaying grasses in flower, in another a willow grove which reminded him of the serene and innocent days when he had not yet known love and jealousy, hatred and revenge. It was the pastureland where he had once tended the herd with his companions; that had been the most untroubled period of his youth. Now he looked back upon it across vast chasms of irrevocability. A sweet melancholy in his heart answered the voices that welcomed him here, the wind fluttering the silvery willows, the jolly song of the little brooks, the trilling of the birds, and the deep golden buzz of bumblebees. It all sounded and smelled of refuge, home; never before, used as he was to the roaming herdsman's life, had he ever felt that a country-side was so homelike, so much part of him.

Accompanied and guided by these voices in his soul, with feelings like those of a soldier home from the wars, he wandered about this pleasant landscape, for the first time in many terrible months not a stranger, a fugitive, a candidate for death, but with an open heart, thinking of nothing, desiring nothing, surrendering utterly to the tranquil present, grateful and somewhat astonished at himself and at this new, unwonted, rapturous state of mind, this undemanding receptivity, this serenity without tensions, this new mode of taking delight in close observation. He felt drawn to the forest which lay beyond the green meadows. In among the trees, amid the dusk speckled by sunlight, the feeling of returning home intensified, and led him along paths which his feet seemed to find by themselves, until he passed through a fern thicket, a dense little forest of ferns in the midst of the greater woods, and reached a tiny hut. On the ground in front of the hut sat the motionless yogi whom he had once watched, and to whom he had brought milk and butter.

Dasa stopped, as if he had just awakened. Everything here was the same as it had been; here no time had passed, there had been no killing and suffering. Here, it seemed, time and life were hard as crystal, frozen in eternity. He stood looking at the old man, and there returned to his heart that admiration, love, and longing which he had felt upon his first sight of the yogi. He looked at the hut and thought that it probably needed some repairs before the onset of the next rainy season. Then he ventured a few cautious steps forward. He entered the hut and peered around. There was little there, almost nothing: a pallet of leaves, a gourd containing some water, and an empty pouch made of bast. He took the pouch and went into the woods searching for food. He returned with fruit and the sweet pith of certain trees. Then he went off with the gourd and filled it with fresh water.

Now he had done all that could be done here. There was so little a man needed to live. Dasa kneeled on the ground and sank into reveries. He was content with this silent repose and dreaming in the woods, content with himself, with the voice within him that had led him here where as a boy he had once sensed something like peace, happiness, and home.

And so he remained with the silent yogi. He renewed the pallet of leaves, found food for the two of them, repaired the old hut, and began building a second for himself a short distance away. The old man appeared to tolerate him, but Dasa could not quite make out whether he had actually taken notice of him. When he rose from his meditation, it was only in order to go to sleep in the hut, to eat a bite, or to walk a bit in the woods. Dasa lived with him like a servant in the presence of a nobleman, or rather the way a small pet, a tame bird or a mongoose, say, lives along with human beings, useful and scarcely noticed. Since he had been a fugitive for so long, unsure of himself, suffering pangs of conscience, seeking concealment and perpetually fearing pursuit, this

life of repose, the effortless small labors and the presence
of a man who did not seem to notice him, did him a
great deal of good for a while. His sleep was not troubled
by frightful dreams; for half and then whole days at a
time he forgot what had happened. The future did not
enter his mind, and if ever a longing or desire came to
him, it was to remain where he was, to be accepted by
the yogi and initiated into the secret of a hermit's life,
to become a yogi himself and partake of the proud indifference of yoga. He had begun to imitate the venerable
ascetic's posture, to sit motionless like him with crossed
legs, like him to gaze into an unknown and superreal
world, and to cultivate apathy to everything around
him. Whenever he made such attempts, he tired quickly;
he found his limbs stiff and his back aching, was plagued
by mosquitoes or bothered by all sorts of itches and
twitches which compelled him to move, to scratch himself, and finally to stand up again. But several times he
had felt something different, a sense of emptiness, light-
ness, and floating in air, such as sometimes comes in
dreams in which we touch the ground only lightly now
and then, gently pushing off from it to drift like a wisp
of fluff. At such moments he had an inkling of what it
must be like to float about that way all the time, body
and soul divesting themselves of all weight and sharing
the movements of a greater, purer, sunnier life, exalted
and absorbed by a beyond, by timelessness and immut-
ability. But these intimations had lasted only a moment.
And every time he plummeted back into his ordinary self,
disappointed, he thought that he must persuade the
master to become his teacher, to initiate him into his
exercises and secret arts and make a yogi of him also. But
how was he to do that? It did not seem as if the old man
would ever notice him, that there would ever be an exchange of words between them. Just as the yogi seemed
beyond the day and hour, beyond the forest and hut, he
also seemed beyond all words.

Nevertheless, one day he spoke a word. There came a
time during which Dasa again dreamt night after night,
often bewilderingly sweet and often bewilderingly dreadful dreams, either of his wife Pravati or the horrors of life
as a fugitive. And by day he made no progress, could not

long endure sitting and practicing, could not help thinking about women and love. He tramped about the forest a great deal. He blamed the weather for his condition; these were sultry days with sudden gusts of hot wind.

One more such bad day came. The mosquitoes hummed. Dasa had had another of his anguished dreams that left him with a sense of fear and oppression. He no longer remembered it, but upon waking it seemed to him that it had been a wretched, outrageous, and shameful relapse into earlier states and stages of his life. All day long he moved restively about the hut, or squatted gloomily. He dabbed at odd tasks, several times sat down for meditation exercises, but would each time be seized by a feverish unrest. His limbs twitched, he felt as if ants were crawling over his feet, had a burning sensation in the nape of his neck, and was unable to endure stillness for more than a few moments. Now and then he cast shy and ashamed glances at the old man, who sat in the perfect posture, eyes turned inward, face floating above his body in inviolable serenity like the head of a flower.

On this day, when the yogi rose and turned toward the hut, Dasa went up to him. He had waited long for this moment, and now blocked his way and with the courage of fear addressed him.

"Forgive me for disturbing your peace, reverend father," he said. "I am seeking peace, tranquility; I would like to live as you do and become like you. As you see, I am still young, but I have already tasted much suffering. Destiny has played cruelly with me. I was born to be a prince and cast out to become a herdsman. I became a herdsman, grew up, strong and happy as a young bull, innocent in my heart. Then my eyes were opened to women, and when I beheld the most beautiful of them, I put my life at her service. Not to possess her would have killed me. I left my companions, the herdsmen. I sued for Pravati's hand, was granted it, became a son-in-law, and labored hard for her. But Pravati was mine and loved me, or so I thought. Every evening I returned to her arms, lay upon her heart. Then, behold, the Rajah came to the neighborhood, the same on whose account I had been cast out as a child. He came and took Pravati from me; I was condemned to see her in his arms. That was the greatest agony I have ever experienced; it changed me and my whole life. I slew the Rajah. I killed and led the life of a criminal and fugitive. Every man's hand was against me; my life was not safe for an hour until I stumbled upon this place. I am a foolish man, reverend father; I am a killer and perhaps may still be caught and drawn and quartered. I can no longer endure this terrible life; I want to be done with it."

The yogi had listened quietly to this outburst, with downcast eyes. Now he opened them and fixed his gaze upon Dasa's face, a bright, piercing, almost unbearably firm, composed, and lucid gaze. And while he studied Dasa's face, seemingly pondering his tale, his mouth slowly twisted into a smile, then a laugh. Soundlessly laughing, he shook his head, and said: "Maya! Maya!"

Utterly bewildered and shamed, Dasa stood stock still. The yogi, before his evening meal, took a short walk on the narrow path that led into the ferns. With quiet, rhythmic step he paced back and forth. After several hundred paces, he returned and entered his hut. His face was once more as it had always been, turned toward something other than the world of appearances. What had been the meaning of the laugh breaking through that impassive countenance? Had that terrible laughter at Dasa's anguished confession and plea been benevolent or mocking, comforting or condemning, divine or demonic? Had it been merely the cynical bleat of an old man no longer able to take things seriously, or the amusement of a sage at another's folly? Had it been rejection, farewell, dismissal? Or was it meant as advice, an invitation to Dasa to follow his example and join in his laughter? Dasa could not solve the riddle. Late into the night he continued to ponder the meaning of this laughter with which the old man seemed to have summed up his life, his happiness, and his misery. His thoughts chewed on it as if it were a tough root that somehow had a hidden savor. And likewise he chewed upon and pondered and mulled over the word that the old man had called out so loudly, so laughingly and gaily and with such incomprehensible amusement: "Maya! Maya!"

He half knew, half guessed the general meaning of the word, and the intonation the laughing old man had given it seemed also to suggest a meaning. Maya—that was Dasa's life, Dasa's youth, Dasa's sweet felicity and bitter misery. Beautiful Pravati was Maya; love and its delights were Maya; all life was Maya. To the eyes of this yogi Dasa's life, all men's lives, everything was Maya, was a kind of childishness, a spectacle, theater, an illusion, emptiness in bright wrappings, a soap bubble—something one could laugh at and at the same time despise, but by no means take seriously.

But although the yogi might be able to dismiss Dasa's life with laughter and the word Maya, Dasa himself could not. Much as he might wish to become a laughing yogi himself, and to see his own life as nothing but Maya, the whole of that life had been roused in him once more during these restive days and nights. He remembered now all the things he had nearly forgotten when he found refuge here after the stresses of his life as a fugitive. There seemed to him only the slightest hope that he would ever be able to learn the art of yoga, let alone to become as adept at it as the old man himself. But then—what was the sense of his lingering in this forest? It had been an asylum; he had recuperated a bit and gathered strength, had come to his senses somewhat. That was something, was in fact a great deal. And perhaps out in the country the hunt for the Rajah's murderer had ended and he could continue his wanderings without any great danger.

He decided to do so. He would depart next day. The world was vast; he could not remain in this hiding place forever.

This decision gave him a measure of peace.

He had intended to leave at dawn. But when he awoke after a long sleep the sun was already high in the sky. The yogi had begun his meditation, and Dasa did not want to leave without bidding good-by. Moreover, he still had a request to make. And so he waited, hour after hour, until the man rose, stretched his limbs, and began his pacing. Then Dasa once more blocked his way, bowed repeatedly, and obstinately remained until the master directed an inquiring look at him.

"Master," he said humbly, "I am going my way. I shall no longer disturb your tranquility. But permit me a request this one last time, venerable father. When I told you about my life, you laughed and exclaimed, 'Maya!' I implore you, teach me more about Maya."

The yogi turned toward the hut, his eyes commanding Dasa to follow. Picking up the water gourd, the old man held it out to Dasa, signing to him to wash his hands. Obediently, Dasa did so. Then the master poured the remainder of the water into the ferns, held the gourd out to Dasa once again, and asked him to fetch fresh water. Dasa obeyed. He ran, emotions of parting tugging at his heart, for the last time down the little footpath to the spring. For the last time he carried the light husk with its smooth, worn rim to the little pool which so often reflected in scattered flecks of light the muzzles of deer, the arching of treetops, and the sweet blue of the sky. Now, as he stooped over it, it reflected for the last time his own face in the russet dusk. He dipped the gourd slowly and thoughtfully into the water, feeling a weird sense of uncertainty. He could not understand why, or why it had hurt him, since he meant to leave anyhow, that the old man had not asked him to stay a while longer, or perhaps stay forever.

Crouching by the brink of the spring, he took a drink. Then he rose, holding the gourd carefully so as not to spill any of the water. He was about to return along the path when his ear caught a tone that both delighted and horrified him. This was the voice he had heard in so many of his dreams, that he had remembered with such bitter longing in many a waking hour. It coaxed so sweetly, sounded so charming, so childlike and loving in the dusk of the forest, that his heart shivered with fright and pleasure. It was his wife Pravati's voice. "Dasa," she called coaxingly.

Incredulously, he looked around, still holding the gourd; and suddenly she appeared among the tree trunks, slender as a reed on her long legs—Pravati, his unforgettable, faithless beloved. He dropped the gourd and ran toward her. Smiling, somewhat abashed, she stood before him, looking up at him with her big doe's eyes. As he approached he saw that she wore red leather san-

dals and a beautiful, costly dress. There was a gold
bracelet on her arm, and precious stones flashed in her
black hair. He checked his stride. Was she still a rajah's
concubine? Had he not killed Nala? Was she still going
about with his gifts? How could she come before him
adorned with these clasps and gems and dare to call his
name?

But she was lovelier than ever, and before he had
time to demand an explanation he could not resist taking
her into his arms, pressing his forehead against her hair,
raising her face and kissing her mouth; and as he did so
he felt that everything had returned to him, that everything was his once more, all that he had ever possessed,
his happiness, love, lust, joy in life, passion. All his
thoughts had already moved far from the forest and the
old hermit; the woods, the hermitage, meditation, and
yoga had vanished, were forgotten. He gave not another
thought to the old man's gourd, which he was to bring
back filled with water. It remained where he had dropped
it by the spring as he rushed toward Pravati. And she,
for her part, began hastily to tell him how it was she
had come here, and all that had happened in the interval.

Her story was astonishing, astonishing and delightful,
like a fairy tale, and Dasa plunged into his new life as if
it were a fairy tale. Pravati was his again; the odious
Rajah Nala dead. The pursuit of the murderer had
long since ceased. But more than all that, Dasa, the
prince who had become a herdsman, had been proclaimed
the rightful heir and ruler. In the city an old herdsman
and an old Brahman had revived the almost forgotten
story of his expulsion and made it the talk of the country. He who had been hunted high and low to be tor-
tured and executed as Nala's murderer was now being
sought much more ardently throughout the land, so that
he could be brought solemnly to his father's palace and
installed as Rajah.

It was like a dream, and what pleased the amazed
Dasa most was the pretty chance that of all the seekers
sent about the country, it had been Pravati who had
found him and been the first to salute him. On the edge
of the forest he found tents erected. The smell of smoke
and roasting game filled the air. Pravati was joyously

hailed by her retinue, and a great feast began at once when she presented Dasa, her husband. Among the throng was a man who had been Dasa's companion in his days as a herdsman. It was he who had led Pravati and the retinue here, with the thought that Dasa might be found at one of the places dear to him from earlier days. The man laughed with pleasure when he recognized Dasa. He ran up to him, ready to embrace him or give him a friendly pat on the back. But his fellow herdsman had become a rajah, and he stopped as if suddenly numbed, then moved slowly and respectfully forward and bowed low. Dasa raised him, clasped him to his breast, affectionately called him by name, and asked how he could reward him. The herdsman wanted a heifer calf, and three were promptly assigned to him from the Rajah's best stock.

More and more people were introduced to the new prince: officials, huntsmen, court Brahmans. He received their salutations. A meal was served; music of drums, sitars, and nose-flutes sounded; and all the festivity and pomp seemed to Dasa like a dream. He could not fully believe in it. For the present the only reality seemed to him Pravati, his young wife, whom he again held in his arms.

Moving by small daily stages, the procession approached the capital city. Runners had been sent ahead to announce that the young Rajah had been found and was on his way. The city resounded with the boom of gongs and drums as Dasa and his retinue approached. A white-clad parade of Brahmans came forward to meet him, headed by the successor of that Vasudeva who some twenty years before had sent Dasa to the herdsmen. The old man had died only recently. The Brahmans hailed the new Rajah, sang hymns, and led him to the palace, where several great sacrificial fires had been lit. Dasa was shown into his new home. There were more welcomings, homages, benedictions, and speeches. Outside the palace, the city celebrated joyfully until late into the night.

Instructed daily by two Brahmans, Dasa quickly acquired the knowledge necessary to a ruler. He attended sacrifices, pronounced judgments, and practiced the arts of chivalry and war. A Brahman named Gopala taught him politics. He explained the position of his house and its regal privileges, what claims his future sons would have, and who were his enemies. The principal one was Nala's mother who in the past had robbed Prince Dasa of his rights and had sought to take his life, and who now must certainly hate her son's murderer. She had fled to the protection of their neighbor, Prince Govinda, and was living in his palace. This Govinda and his house had been dangerous foes from time immemorial. They had made war upon Dasa's forefathers and claimed certain parts of his territory. On the other hand the Prince of Gaipali, Dasa's neighbor to the south, had been friendly with his father and had always disliked Rajah Nala. Visiting him, lavishing gifts upon him, and inviting him to the next great hunt belonged among Dasa's important duties.

The lady Pravati had rapidly adapted to the ways of the nobility. She had the bearing of a princess, and in her beautiful dresses and jewelry she looked splendid, as if she sprang from as fine a lineage as her husband. Year after year they lived together in harmonious love, and their happiness gave them a certain glow, like those whom the gods favor, so that the people adored them. And when, after long waiting, Pravati at last bore him a beautiful boy to whom he gave his father's name, Ravana, his happiness was complete. All that he possessed, all the land and power, the estates and barns, dairies, cattle, and horses, acquired a fresh importance in his eyes, an added glory and value. His wealth had pleased him because it could be lavished on Pravati, whose loveliness could be enhanced with apparel and jewelry. Now his rich possessions delighted him all the more, and seemed far more important, because he saw in them his son Ravana's inheritance and future happiness.

Pravati's chief pleasures lay in festivals, parades, and pomp, luxury in dress and finery, and a large corps of servants. Dasa preferred the joys of his garden. He had ordered rare and precious trees and flowers planted there, and stocked the grounds with parrots and other brilliantly plumaged birds. Feeding and talking with these pets became one of his daily pleasures. In addition, learning attracted him. He proved a grateful pupil of the Brahmans, learned to read and write, memorized many poems and proverbs, and kept a personal scribe who understood the art of making scrolls out of palm leaves. Under the scribe's skillful hands a modest library grew. The books were kept in a small opulent room with gilded paneling of precious woods, carved with reliefs representing incidents in the lives of the gods. Here he sometimes invited his Brahmans, the foremost scholars and thinkers among the priests, to conduct disputations on sacred subjects: on the creation of the world and on great Vishnu's Maya, on the holy Vedas, the power of sacrifice, and the still greater power of penance, by virtue of which a mortal man can make the very gods tremble with fear of him. Those Brahmans who had spoken best and advanced the most elegant arguments received fine gifts. As the prize for a successful disputation, some departed leading away a fine cow. On occasion there was something both ridiculous and touching when great scholars, who a few moments before had been reciting maxims from the Vedas along with brilliant exegeses of the same, or who had just proved the depth of their knowledge of all the heavens and seas, stalked off swollen with pride in their awards, or fell to bickering with one another over their prizes.

In general, for all his happiness, his wealth, his garden, and his books, Prince Dasa at times could not help regarding everything that pertained to human life and human nature as both strange and dubious, at once touching and ridiculous, like those same sagacious and vain Brahmans, at once bright and dark, desirable and contemptible. When his gaze dwelt on the lotus flowers in the ponds of his garden, on the lovely iridescent plumage of his peacocks, pheasants, and rhinoceros birds, on the gilded carvings of his palace, these things sometimes seemed to him virtually divine, aglow with the fires of eternal life. But other times, and even at the same times, he sensed in them something unreal, unreliable, questionable, a tendency toward perishability and dissolution, a readiness to relapse into formlessness, into chaos. Just as he himself had been a prince, became a herdsman, descended to the nadir of a murderer and outlaw, and ultimately became a prince once more, moved and guided by unknown powers, with all his tomorrows forever uncertain, so life's wayward Maya everywhere contained simultaneously nobility and baseness, eternity and death, grandeur and absurdity. Even his beautiful, beloved Pravati had sometimes, for brief moments, appeared to him in a ludicrous light, stripped of her charm; she wore too many bracelets, had too much of pride and triumph in her eyes, and tried too hard to move majestically.

Even dearer to him than his garden and his books was his son Ravana, the fulfillment of his love and his life, the object of his tenderness and solicitude. He was a true prince, a lovely, delicate child, doe-eyed like his mother and inclined to pensiveness and reverie like his father. Often, when Dasa saw the boy standing for a long time in front of one of the ornamental trees in the garden, or sitting on a rug, absorbed in contemplation of a stone, a carved toy, or a feather, eyebrows slightly raised and eyes staring quietly, somewhat absently, it seemed to him that this son was very like himself. Dasa realized fully how intensely he loved him the first time that he had to leave the boy for an indefinite period.

One day a messenger arrived from the frontier region where his land bordered on that of his neighbor Govinda and reported that Govinda's men had launched a raid, stolen cattle, and even kidnapped a number of Dasa's subjects. Dasa immediately made his preparations. He took with him the colonel of his bodyguard and a few dozen horses and men, and set off in pursuit of the raiders. The moment before he rode off, he took his small son into his arms and kissed him; and love flared in his heart like a fiery pang. The force of that pang surprised him; it affected him like some bidding from the unknown; and during the long ride his reflections on it ripened into understanding. For as he rode he pondered the reason he was sitting in the saddle and galloping so sternly and swiftly over the countryside. What power, he wondered, was causing him to undertake such efforts? Pondering, he realized that at the bottom of his heart it was of small concern to him that cattle and men should have been snatched from him somewhere on his borders. Thievery and the flouting of his authority could not suffice to kindle his rage and spur him to action. It would have been more natural to him to have dismissed the news of the raid with a compassionate smile. But to have done so, he knew, would have been to commit a bitter injustice to the messenger. The poor fellow had run all the way with his news until he was ready to drop with exhaustion. No less would he have wronged the people who had been captured and who were now prisoners, carried away from their homes and their peaceful life into foreign slavery. Moreover, all his other subjects, though they had not been harmed in the least, would also have felt wronged. They would have resented his passivity, not understanding why the prince could not protect his country better. They took it for granted that if violence were done to any of them they could count upon their ruler for aid and vengeance.

He realized that it was his duty to undertake this expedition of reprisal. But what is duty? How many duties there are that we so often neglect without the slightest compunction? What was the reason that this duty of vengeance was no trivial one, that he could not neglect it, and that in fact he was not performing it perfunctorily and halfheartedly, but with zest and passion? As soon as the question arose in his mind, his heart answered it, for once again it quivered with that pang he had felt on parting from little Prince Ravana. If the Rajah, he realized, made no resistance when cattle and people were taken from him, robbery and violence would spread from the borders of his country closer and closer to the center, and ultimately the enemy would stand directly before him and would strike him where he was prone to the bitterest pain: in the person of his son. They would take his son, his successor, from him; they would carry the boy off and kill him, perhaps under torture; and that would be the most extreme suffering he could ever experience, even worse, far worse, than the death of Pravati herself. So that was the reason he was riding off so zealously and was so dutiful a sovereign. Not from concern for the loss of cattle and land, not from kindness for his subjects, not from ambition to match his father's noble name, but out of intense, painful, irrational love for this child, and out of intense, irrational fear of the pain he would feel at the loss of this child.

Thus far he had come in understanding during that ride. He had not, however, managed to apprehend and punish Govinda's men. They escaped with their booty, and in order to show his determination and prove his courage he himself now had to raid across the border, damage one of his neighbor's villages, and carry off some cattle and a few slaves.

He had been away many days. On the homeward ride, a victor, he had again sunk into meditation, and returned home very quietly and rather sorrowful. For in the course of his meditations he had realized how entirely ensnared he was, without any hope of escaping; his whole nature and all his actions were caught and being strangled in a diabolic net. While his leaning toward philosophy, his love for quiet contemplation and a life of innocence and inaction, were constantly growing, there was likewise growing from another source his love for Ravana, his anxiety about his son's life and future, an equally forceful compulsion to action and entanglement. Out of affection grew conflict, out of love war. Already, in the effort to mete out justice, he had seized a herd, terrified a village, and forcibly carried off poor innocent people. Out of that, of course, would grow a new act of vengeance, new violence, and so on and on until his whole life and his whole country were plunged in warfare and violence and the clash of arms. It was this insight, or vision, which made him so silent and sorrowful upon his homecoming.

He had been right, for the hostile neighbor gave him no peace. The incursions and raids were repeated. Dasa had to march out again for reprisals and defense, and when the enemy withdrew, his own soldiers and chasseurs had to be turned upon the neighboring people. Mounted and armed men were more and more a familiar sight in the capital. In a good many frontier villages there were now permanent garrisons of soldiers on guard. Military conferences and preparations troubled Dasa's days. He could not see what purpose this endless guerrilla warfare served; he grieved for the plight of the victims, for the lives of the dead. He grieved because more and more he had to neglect his garden and his books. He grieved for the lost peace of his days and his heart. Often he spoke with Gopala, the Brahman, about these matters, and sometimes with his wife Pravati.

Should they not ask one of the respected neighboring princes to act as mediator? For his part he would gladly help to bring about peace by conciliation and surrendering a few pastures and villages. He was disappointed and somewhat angered when neither the Brahman nor Pravati would hear of anything of the kind.

His difference of opinion with Pravati on this question led to an extremely violent quarrel, and ended with a serious estrangement. Insistently, he pleaded his points with her. But she behaved as if every word were directed not against the war and the useless killing, but solely against herself. In a verbose, furious retort she declared that it was precisely the enemy's aim to take advantage of Dasa's good nature and love of peace (not to say his fear of war); the enemy would persuade him to conclude one peace treaty after another, each paid for in small concessions of territory and population. And in the end he would still not be satisfied, but as soon as Dasa was sufficiently weakened, would return to open war and seize everything that was left to him. She was not concerned about herds and villages, merits and demerits, but with the fate of the whole, their survival or annihilation. And if Dasa did not know what he owed to his dignity, his son, and his wife, she would have to be the one to teach him. Her eyes blazed; her voice shook; it was long since he had seen her so beautiful and so passionate, but he felt only sorrow.

Meanwhile the border raids and breaches of peace continued; they came to a temporary end only with the beginning of the rainy season. By now there were two factions at Dasa's court. One side, the peace party, was very small; aside from Dasa it numbered only a few of the older Brahmans. These were all learned men absorbed in their meditations. But the war party, the party of Pravati and Gopala, had the majority of priests and all the army officers on its side. The country armed feverishly, and it was known that the hostile neighbor was doing the same. The chief huntsman instructed Prince Ravana in the art of the bow, and his mother took him along to every inspection of troops.

During this period Dasa sometimes thought of the forest where he had lived for a while as a poor fugitive, and of the white-haired old hermit who lived there absorbed in contemplation. Sometimes he felt a desire to call upon the yogi, to see him again and ask his advice. But he did not know whether the old man was still living, nor whether he would listen and give counsel. And even if he were alive and would advise, everything would nevertheless take its course. Nothing could be changed. Meditation and wisdom were good, were noble things, but apparently they throve only on the margin of life. If you swam in the stream of life and struggled with its waves, your acts and suffering had nothing to do with wisdom. They came about of their own accord, were fated, and had to be done and suffered. Even the gods did not live in eternal peace and eternal wisdom. They too experienced danger and fear, struggle and battle; that he knew from the many tales of the gods.

And so Dasa yielded. He no longer contended with Pravati. He reviewed the troops, saw the war coming, anticipated it in debilitating dreams, and as his body grew leaner, and his face darker, he saw his happiness fading, his gaiety shriveling. There remained only his love for his son. That increased along with his anxiety, increased along with the arming and the drilling of soldiers. It was the flaming red flower in his parching garden. He wondered at how much emptiness and joylessness a man could endure, at how easy it was to grow accustomed to care and gloom, and he also wondered that so anxious and solicitous a love could so painfully dominate a life that had seemingly lost the capacity for passion. Although his life might be meaningless, it was certainly not without a center; it revolved around his love for his son. It was on Ravana's account that he rose from his bed in the morning and spent his days in occupations and exertions directed solely toward war, and therefore repugnant to him. On Ravana's account he patiently conferred with his generals, and withstood majority opinion only to the extent that he prevailed on them to wait and see, not plunge recklessly into adventures.

Just as his joys, his garden, and his books had gradually deserted him, so he was also deserted by those who for so many years had shaped his happiness and represented his pleasures. It had begun with politics, with Pravati's passionate speech excoriating his fear of sinning and love of peace, almost openly calling all that cowardice. She had spoken with flushed cheeks and in fiery phrases of heroism, a prince's honor, and the prospect of disgrace. At that time, stunned and with a sense of giddiness, he had suddenly realized how far his wife had become estranged from him, or he from her. Ever since, the gulf between them had widened. It was still growing, and neither of them did anything to check its growth. Or rather, it should have fallen to Dasa to do something about it. For only he saw the gulf for what it was. In his imagination it more and more grew into the gulf of gulfs, became a cosmic abyss between man and woman, between yes and no, between soul and body. In retrospect he thought he saw the whole thing with complete clarity. He remembered how Pravati, magically beautiful, had captivated him until he parted with his friends, gave up his carefree life as a herdsman, and for her sake lived as a servant in an alien world, the son-in-law in the house of unkind people who exploited his infatuation to extract labor from him. Then Nala had come along, and his misfortunes had begun. The wealthy, handsome Rajah with his fine clothes and tents, his horses and servants, had seduced his wife. That might have cost him little effort, for poor Pravati had not been accustomed to regal splendor. But would she really have been led astray so easily and quickly if she had been faithful and virtuous at heart? Very well, the Rajah had seduced her, or simply taken her, and thus inflicted upon him the most horrible grief he had ever experienced. But he, Dasa, had taken revenge. He had killed the thief of his happiness, and had felt the killing as a moment of high triumph. But scarcely was the deed done than he had had to flee. For days, weeks, and months he had lived in swamp and forest, an outlaw, trusting no man.

And what had Pravati been doing all that time? The

two of them had never spoken much about that. In any case, she had not fled also. She had sought and found him only after he had been proclaimed Nala's successor, because of his birth, and she needed him in order to enter the palace and ascend the throne. Then she had appeared, had fetched him from the forest and the venerable hermit's purlieus. He had been dressed in fine garments, made Rajah, and since then he had had nothing but glory and felicity—but in reality: what had he abandoned at that time, and what had he gained in exchange? He had gained the splendor and the duties of a sovereign, duties that had been initially easy and had ever since grown harder and harder. He had regained his beautiful wife, the sweet hours of lovemaking with her, and then his son, who had taught his heart a new kind of love and increasing concern for his imperiled life and happiness, so that now the whole country was on the brink of war. This was what Pravati had conferred upon him when she discovered him by the spring in the woods. But what had he left behind, what had he sacrificed? He had left behind the peace of the forest, pious solitude, and the presence and the example of a holy yogi. In addition he had sacrificed the hope of becoming a disciple and successor, of sharing the sage's profound, radiant, unshakable peace of soul, of being liberated from the struggles and passions of life. Seduced by Pravati's beauty, entangled by the woman, and infected by her ambition, he had abandoned the only way that led to liberation and peace.

That was how the story of his life appeared to him now. And in fact it could easily be interpreted thus. Only a few blurrings and omissions were needed to see it that way. He had omitted, among other things, the fact that he had not been the hermit's disciple at all. On the contrary, he had been on the point of leaving him voluntarily. But perspectives often shift in hindsight.

Pravati regarded these matters quite differently, although she was far less inclined to reflection than her husband. She did not think about Nala at all. On the other hand, if she remembered rightly it had been she alone who had founded Dasa's good fortune. She was responsible for his becoming the Rajah. She had given him a son, had lavished love and happiness upon him. But in the end she had found him unable to match her greatness, unworthy of her soaring projects. For it was clear to her that the coming war could have no outcome other than the destruction of the enemy and the doubling of her own power and possessions. But instead of exulting in this prospect and collaborating enthusiastically, Dasa, most unlike a prince, hung back from war and conquest and would have preferred to grow old idling away his time with his flowers, trees, parrots, and books. On the other hand there was Vishwamitra, the commander of the cavalry forces. He was a different sort of man, next to herself the most ardent partisan of the war, repeatedly urging that they strike for victory as soon as possible. In any comparison between the two, Vishwamitra could not help showing to advantage.

Dasa had not failed to notice his wife's growing friendship with Vishwamitra. He saw how much she admired him, and let herself be admired by this brave and cheerful but possibly rather shallow, perhaps somewhat unintelligent army officer with his manly smile, his fine strong teeth and well-tended beard. Dasa observed it all with bitterness and at the same time with contempt. He deceived himself into thinking he felt only scornful indifference. He did not spy on them or try to discover whether their friendship had overstepped the limits of decency. He regarded Pravati's infatuation with the handsome cavalryman, and the looks which showed how she preferred him to her unheroic husband, with the same outwardly indifferent, inwardly embittered calm with which he was wont to view everything that happened. Whether his wife was determined upon infidelity and betrayal, or whether she was merely expressing her contempt for Dasa's principles, it did not matter. The thing had come and was developing, was beginning to confront him like the war and the disaster whose imminence he sensed. There was nothing to be done about it. The only possible attitude toward it was one of acceptance, of stoic endurance. For that, instead of attack and conquest, was Dasa's kind of manliness and heroism.

Whether or not Pravati's admiration for the cavalry captain, and his for her, remained within the bounds of morality, in any case Pravati was less guilty than he, Dasa, himself. That much he understood. To be sure, thinker and doubter that he was, he tended to blame her for the evaporation of his happiness. Or at any rate he considered that she was partly responsible for his having stumbled into the complexities of life, into love, into ambition, into acts of revenge and raids. In his thoughts he even blamed woman, love, and lust for everything on earth, for the whole crazy dance, the whole wild chase of passions and desires, of adultery, of death, of killing, of war. But at the same time he knew quite well that Pravati was not to blame. She was not a cause, but herself a victim. She had not made, and could not be held accountable for, either her beauty or his love for her. She was only a grain of dust in the rays of the sun, a ripple in the stream. It should have been his task, and his alone, to withdraw from woman and love, from ambition and the hunger for happiness. He should have remained either a contented cowherd among herdsmen, or else he should have tried to overcome his own inadequacy by the mysterious path of yoga. He had neglected to do so, had failed; he had no vocation for greatness, or else he had not kept faith with his vocation, so that after all his wife was right to regard him as a coward. On the other hand, she had given him this son, this frail, handsome boy for whom he felt so fearful but whose existence filled his own life with meaning, who was in fact a great joy—a painful and fearful joy, certainly, but still a joy, his true happiness. Now he was paying for this happiness with the sorrow and bitterness in his heart, with his readiness for war and death, with his consciousness of moving toward a dire fate.

Meanwhile Rajah Govinda sat in his own capital, listening to the bidding of the mother of Nala, the slain seducer of evil memory. Govinda's incursions and challenges were growing ever more frequent and brazen. Only an alliance with the powerful Rajah of Gaipali could have made Dasa strong enough to enforce peace and neighborly relations. But this Rajah, although he was well disposed toward Dasa, was Govinda's kinsman and had politely repulsed all efforts to win him over to such an alliance. There was no escape, no hope of sanity or humanity. The fated outcome was drawing nearer and would have to be undergone. Dasa himself almost longed for the war now. If only the accumulated lightnings would strike; if only the calamity would come speedily, since it could no longer be averted.

Once more he paid a visit to the Rajah of Gaipali and exchanged fruitless courtesies with him. In his council he urged moderation and patience, but by now he was doing so without hope. For the rest, he improved his armaments. The council was divided only on the question of whether to respond to the enemy's next raid with invasion of his territory and outright war, or whether to await his major offensive, so that the people and all neutrals would see who was truly guilty of violating the peace.

The enemy, unconcerned with such questions, put an end to reflection, discussion, and hesitation. One day he struck. He staged a major raid which inveigled Dasa, along with the cavalry captain and his best troops, into rushing to the frontier. While they were on the way, Govinda's main force invaded the country, stormed the gates of Dasa's capital, and besieged the palace. As soon as Dasa heard the news he turned back. He knew that his wife and his son were encircled in the palace, and that bloody battles were raging in the streets of the city. His heart pounded with fury and sorrow when he thought of his loved ones and the dangers that faced them. Now he was no longer a reluctant and cautious commander. He burned with anguish and rage, urged his men homeward in wild haste, found the battle surging through the streets, cut his way through to the palace, confronted the enemy and fought like a madman until, at twilight on that bloody day, he collapsed exhausted, bleeding from several wounds.

When he recovered consciousness, he found himself a prisoner. The battle was lost. City and palace were in the hands of his enemies. Bound, he was taken before Govinda, who greeted him disdainfully and led him into one of the other rooms of the palace. It was the room with the carved and gilded walls where Dasa kept his scrolls. Here, sitting bolt upright on one of the rugs, stony-faced, was his wife Pravati. Armed guards stood behind her. Across her knees lay their son. Like a broken flower that frail body lay dead, face gray, his garments soaked with blood. The woman did not turn when her husband was led in. She did not see him; she sat staring expressionlessly at the small corpse. But she seemed to Dasa strangely transformed. It took a while before he realized that her hair, which only a few days before he had seen raven black, was now everywhere shot through with gray. She seemed to have been sitting that way for a long time, the boy on her lap, numbed, her face a mask.

"Rayana!" Dasa exclaimed. "Ravana, my child, my flower!" He knelt. His face fell forward upon the dead boy's head. As if in prayer he knelt before the mute woman and the child, mourning both, paying homage to both. He smelled the odor of blood and death, mingled with the fragrance of the aromatic pomade on the child's hair.

With numbed gaze Pravati stared blankly down at the two of them.

Someone touched his shoulder. It was one of Govinda's captains, who ordered him to stand up. The soldiers led him out. He had not addressed a word to Pravati, or she to him.

Bound, he was placed on a wagon and taken to a dungeon in Govinda's capital. There his fetters were partly loosened. A soldier brought a jug of water and put it on the stone floor. The door was closed and barred, and he was left alone. A wound on his shoulder burned like fire. He groped for the water jug and moistened his hands and face. He wanted to drink, but forbore; this way he would die faster, he thought. How much longer would it take, how much longer! He longed for death as his parched throat longed for water. Only death would still the torture in his heart. Only then would the picture of the mother with their dead son be erased. But in the midst of his agony, merciful weariness and weakness overcame him. He sank down and fell asleep.

When he returned hazily to consciousness after this brief slumber, he tried to rub his eyes, but could not. Both hands were occupied, were holding something tightly. When he took heart and forced his eyes open, he saw that he was no longer surrounded by dungeon walls. Greenish light flowed bright and strong over leaves and moss. He blinked several times. The light struck him like a fierce though noiseless blow. A twitch of horror, a shudder of fear, passed through the nape of his neck and down his spine. Once more he blinked, screwed up his face as if he were weeping, and opened his eyes wide.

He was standing in a forest, holding in both hands a gourd full of water. At his feet the basin of a spring reflected browns and greens. Beyond the fern thicket, he recalled, stood the hut and the waiting yogi who had sent him to fetch water, who had laughed so strangely and whom he had asked to teach him something about Maya.

He had lost neither a battle nor a son. He had been neither a rajah nor a father. Rather, the yogi had granted his wish and taught him about Maya. Palace and garden, library and aviary, the cares of sovereignty and paternal love, war and jealousy, his love for Pravati and his violent suspicion of her—all that had been nothing. No, not nothing. It had been Maya! Dasa stood there shattered. Tears ran down his cheeks. His hands trembled, shaking the gourd he had just filled for the hermit. Water spilled over the rim and onto his feet. He felt as if someone had just amputated one of his limbs, removed something from his head. Suddenly the long years he had lived, the treasures cherished, the delights enjoyed, the pangs suffered, the fears endured, the despair he had tasted to the brink of death—all this had been taken from him, extinguished, reduced to nothingness. And yet not to nothingness! For the memory was there. The images had remained with him. He still saw Pravati sitting, tall and rigid, with her hair so suddenly gray, her son in her lap, as though she herself had killed him. The child lay there like the prey of some beast, his legs dangling limply across her knees.

Oh how swiftly, how swiftly and horribly, how cruelly and thoroughly, had he been taught about Maya! Everything had been deranged; charged years had shrunk to moments. All that crowded reality had been a dream. Perhaps, too, he had dreamed all that had happened previously; the tales of Prince Dasa, of his life as a herds-man, his marriage, his vengeance upon Nala, his taking refuge with the hermit. All that had been pictures such as one might admire on a carved palace frieze where flowers, stars, birds, monkeys, and gods could be seen amid the foliage. And was what he was experiencing this moment, what he saw before his eyes, awakening from rulership and war and imprisonment, standing beside the spring, this gourd from which he had just spilled a little water, together with what he was now thinking about it all—was not all this made of the same stuff? Was it not dream, illusion, Maya? And everything he would still experience in the future, would see with his eyes and feel with his hands, up to the moment of his death—was it any different in substance, any different in kind? It was all a game and a sham, all foam and dream. It was Maya, the whole lovely and frightful, delicious and desperate kaleidoscope of life with its searing delights, its searing griefs.

Dasa still stood numbed. Again the gourd shook in his hands and its water spilled, wetting his toes and running into the ground. What ought he to do? Fill the bowl again, carry it back to the yogi, and be laughed at for all that he had suffered in his dream? That was not alluring. He let the gourd tilt, emptied it, and threw it into the moss. Then he sat down on the green bed and began to reflect seriously. He had had enough and more than enough of this dreaming, of this diabolic texture of experiences, joys, and sufferings that crushed your heart and made your blood stand still, only to be suddenly revealed as Maya, so that you were nothing but a fool. He had had enough of everything. He no longer craved either wife or child, either a throne or victory or revenge, either happiness or cleverness, either power or virtue. He desired nothing but peace, nothing but an end of turmoil. He no longer wanted anything but to check this endlessly turning wheel, to stop this endless spectacle, to extinguish it all. He wanted to find rest for himself and extinguish himself. That was what he had wanted when he hurled himself at the enemy in that last battle, slashing all about and being slashed at in return, giving wounds and receiving them, until he collapsed. But what then? Then there was a brief pause of unconsciousness, or slumber, or death, and immediately afterward you were awake again, had to admit the currents of life into your heart once more and once more let the dreadful, lovely, terrible flood of pictures pour into your eyes, endlessly, inescapably, until the next unconsciousness, until the next death. That was, perhaps, a pause, a moment of rest, a chance to catch your breath. But then it went on, and once again you were one of the thousand figures engaged in the wild, intoxicating, desperate dance of life. Ah, there was no extinction. It went on forever.

Unrest drove him to his feet once more. If there were no rest in this accursed round-dance, if his one most acute desire could not be fulfilled, then he might just as well fill his gourd again and bring it to this old man who had sent him on this errand, although he did not really have any right of command over him. It was a service that had been asked of him. It was an assignment. He might just as well obey and carry it out. That was better than sitting here and pondering methods of self-destruction. Altogether, obeying and serving were better and far easier, seemlier and far more harmless, than commanding and taking responsibility. That much he knew. Very well, Dasa, take the gourd, fill it carefully with water, and bring it to your master!

When he reached the hut, the master received him with a strange look, a slightly questioning, half-compassionate, half-amused look of complicity—such a look as an older boy might have for a younger one whom he sees returning from a strenuous and somewhat shameful adventure, a test of courage that has been assigned to him. This herdsman prince, this poor fellow who had stumbled in here, was only coming back from the spring, where he had been for water, and had been gone no more than fifteen minutes. But still he was also coming from a dungeon, had lost a wife, a son, and a principality, had completed a human life and had caught a glimpse of the revolving wheel. The chances were that this young man had already been wakened once or several times before, and had breathed a mouthful of reality, for otherwise he would not have come here and stayed so long. But now he seemed to have been properly awakened and become ripe for setting out on the long journey. It would take a good many years just to teach this young man the proper posture and breathing.

By this look alone, this look which contained a trace of benevolent sympathy and the hint of a relationship that had come into being between them, the relationship between master and disciple—by this look alone the yogi accepted the disciple. This one look banished the fruitless thoughts from the disciple's head. It bound him in discipline and service. There is no more to be told about Dasa's life, for all the rest took place in a realm beyond pictures and stories. He never again left the forest.

ABOUT THE AUTHOR

Born in 1877 in Calw, on the edge of the Black Forest, HERMANN HESSE was brought up in a missionary household where it was assumed that he would study for the ministry. Hesse's religious crisis (which is often recorded in his novels) led to his fleeing from the Maulbronn seminary in 1892, an unsuccessful cure by a well-known theologian and faith healer, and an attempted suicide. After being expelled from high school, he worked in bookshops for several years—a usual occupation for budding German authors.

His first novel, *Peter Camenzind* (1904), describes the early manhood of a writer who leaves his Swiss mountain village to encounter the world. This was followed by *Beneath the Wheel* (1906), the story of a gifted adolescent crushed by the brutal expectations of his father and teachers, a novel which was Hesse's personal attack on the educational system of his time.

World War I came as a terrific shock, and Hesse joined the pacifist Romain Rolland in antiwar activities—not only writing antiwar tracts and novels, but editing newspapers for German prisoners of war. During this period, Hesse's first marriage broke up (reflected or discussed outright in *Knulp* and *Rosshalde*), he studied the works of Freud, eventually underwent analysis with Jung, and was for a time a patient in a sanatorium.

In 1919 he moved permanently to Switzerland, and brought out *Demian*, which reflects his preoccupation with the workings of the subconscious and with psychoanalysis. The book was an enormous success, and made Hesse famous throughout Europe.

In 1922 he turned his attention to the East, which he had visited several times before the war, and wrote *Siddhartha*, the story of an Indian youth's long spiritual quest for the answer to the enigma of man's role on this earth. In 1927 he wrote *Steppenwolf*, the account of a man torn between his individualism and his attraction to bourgeois respectability, and his conflict between self-affirmation and self-destruction. In 1930 he published *Narcissus and Goldmund*, regarded as "Hesse's greatest novel" (*The New York Times*), dealing with the friendship between two medieval priests, one contented with his religion, the other a wanderer endlessly in search of peace and salvation.

The Journey to the East appeared in 1932, and there was no major work until 1943, when he brought out *Magister Ludi*, which won him the Nobel Prize in 1946. Until his death in 1962 he lived in seclusion in Montagnola, Switzerland.

ABOUT THE TRANSLATORS

As a team, RICHARD and CLARA WINSTON hold the Alexander Gode Medal of the American Translators Association. Among the more than one hundred full-length books they have translated are works by Heimito von Doderer (*The Demons; Every Man a Murderer*), Friedrich Dürrenmatt (*The Pledge; Traps; Once a Greek*), Thomas Mann (*Last Essays; The Story of a Novel; Letters to Paul Amann, 1915–1952*), and Theodor Plievier (*Stalingrad*).